Heidi Rice's ~~...~~ shed in 2007, followed by several international ~~...~~ minated titles

G73/16

~~16~~/5/16.

Heidi Rice

SO NOW YOU'RE BACK

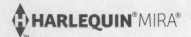

First Published in Great Britain 2016
By Harlequin Mira, an imprint of HarperCollins*Publishers*
1 London Bridge Street, London, SE1 9GF

ISBN: 978-1-848-45464-4

58-0216

Our policy is to use papers that are natural, renewable and recyclable products and made from wood grown in sustainable forests. The logging and manufacturing processes conform to the legal environmental regulations of the country of origin.

Printed and bound by
CPI Group (UK) Ltd, Croydon, CR0 4YY

To Rob, my hero.

Chapter 1

Where r u Mum? Your late. AGAIN!!!

'Bugger.' Halle Best clicked furiously on the iPhone's keypad as she shot out of the car park at St Pancras Station and crossed the loading bay.

There in 2 secs. Honest.

Magnifico-Multitask Mum strikes again, she thought triumphantly as she shoved the phone back in her bag. She kept her head down as the service tunnel at the back of the station led onto the strip of shops and cafés lining the route to the main concourse. Avoiding eye contact with members of the British public had become a habit in the past two years, because she'd discovered they only ever seemed to recognise her and want to waylay her for an autograph— or a chat about their latest baking disaster—when she was in a rush, chronically late or on a collision course with her daughter Lizzie's prodigious temper. As all three defcon positions were currently in countdown mode, she absolutely could not risk it.

Darting past the YO! Sushi on her left and the ticket office on her right, she narrowly avoided a young mum with a pushchair while circumnavigating a group of backpack-toting foreign students going at a pace that would make a geriatric snail look like Usain Bolt.

She sucked in a couple of extra breaths, feeling winded as she hit the main thoroughfare.

Note to self: Get that bloody cross-trainer in the basement out of mothballs.

Raising her head to check her direction, she made eye contact with a sharply dressed office worker who sent her a don't-I-know-you-from-somewhere smile. Halle returned it while shooting past on full steam before the woman figured out the answer.

She hated to be impolite or abrupt with people who recognised her. And up until two years ago, she had always been more than willing to stop and chat about collapsing soufflés or how to make the perfect choux pastry, because she'd gotten a major rush out of any kind of acknowledgement. She was still both humbled and chuffed to bits at any sign that people enjoyed and appreciated her Domestic Diva brand. But in the past twenty-four months, ever since *The Best of Everything* had moved from a morning slot on cable TV to an early evening slot on BBC Two and her third book—*The Best on a Budget*—had hit the bestseller charts, the attention had begun to interfere more and more with even Magnifico-Multitask Mum's ability to keep all the plates in her life spinning.

Hence being a tiny bit tardy to collect her daughter from the Eurostar terminal after Lizzie's four-day trip to Paris to visit her father. The production meeting had overrun, as it always did. But Halle thought she'd programmed in more than enough time to get from Soho to King's Cross. And if it hadn't been for that plonker trying to do a right turn in a no-right-turn zone outside the British Library, she so would have made it here in time. She mentally tucked her frustration away, pasting on what she hoped was her most competent and unflustered smile as she spotted her daughter, slumped glumly on one of the benches by the Eurostar exit, with her boots perched on her suitcase, her iPod earbuds in and her smartphone out as she texted furiously— probably about what an arsewipe her mum was to all her friends on Facebook.

Halle slowed, as love and relief barrelled into her chest and combined with her breathlessness to make her light-headed. Given she was already several crucial nanoseconds late, she might as well take a moment to admire her eighteen-year-old daughter before facing the full force of Lizzie's disgust.

Long-limbed and slim—but not too slim any more, thank goodness—Lizzie had what Halle had always craved, a coltish elegance that was natural and unaffected and didn't require the help of a personal trainer and/or industrial-strength Spanx. The soft tangle of strawberry blonde hair hanging down her back, which had fizzed around her head as a baby and made her look like a cherubic dandelion, was equally arresting. Sometime in the past two years, after what Halle had panicked might be an eating disorder, Lizzie had lost that pudgy tomboyish quality that Halle had always adored and grown into this beautiful if sullen and secretive swan.

Halle shook off the thought to stop the guilt from constricting around her stomach like a freakishly large anaconda. No need to go there, again. Somewhere along the line, Lizzie had stopped being that happy-go-lucky tomboy who had been open and eager about everything and an absolute marvel with her little brother, Aldo, and become a volatile teenager with a quick-fire temper who resented her mother's success and thought the now ten-year-old Aldo was the spawn of Satan.

To be fair, given Aldo's genius for making everyone's life hell, including his own, Halle did secretly sympathise with her daughter on that score. And really the only thing for Halle to remember in the face of her daughter's derision was what the family counsellor had told her.

That teenage rebellion was normal, that it was much better for Halle to have to deal with Lizzie's temper than having her daughter internalise everything and that while Halle's family set-up wasn't completely the norm, very few people's were these days. In fact, the norm these days was pretty much the anti-norm. And, if nothing else, Halle's family—which included a ten-year-old son who didn't have a father, and an eighteen-year-old daughter who saw her father, whose name Halle couldn't say without flinching, only six weeks a year—fitted perfectly into the anti-norm mould.

The truth was, there was nothing Halle could do about Aldo's lack of a father—except hire a wonderful au pair like Trey Carson to take some of the slack. And nothing she needed to do about Lizzie's dickhead of a dad, Luke Best, except remember every time she got the urge to flinch that she only had to deal with Luke's bullshit by proxy these days.

No, all Halle needed to focus on now was one simple truth.

That Lizzie wasn't colourful, durable Tupperware any more, who would bounce if Halle dropped her—as she had so often when her children were small and she'd been juggling two menial jobs, ad hoc childcare and her fledgling party-cake baking business in a Stoke Newington council flat all on her own. Somehow or other, while Halle hadn't been paying the proper attention, because she'd been focused on making her career happen, her daughter had become china. Fragile, delicate, brittle china that had the potential to shatter if Halle let it fall off its perch. But as long as Halle knew that and remained vigilant, ready to handle any potential wobbles, everything would be absolutely fine.

Which meant finding the time to collect Lizzie in person from the Eurostar terminal, especially as she'd just celebrated a milestone birthday in Paris, instead of arranging for a car and driver to do it instead. But the occasional hiccup—like some tosser thinking he could turn right when the sign clearly said he could not—was not Halle's fault, and she must not beat herself up about it. Especially as Lizzie was now perfectly capable of doing that for her.

Pushing the anaconda the rest of the way back down her throat, Halle waved her hand in front of Lizzie's face and smiled as her daughter's head bobbed up and she tugged out her earbuds.

'About time. Where have you been? I've been waiting here forever.'

'Sorry, sweetheart,' Halle said, knowing 'forever' had been a maximum of ten minutes. 'Did the train arrive early?'

'No, you were late. As always.' Lizzie scowled. 'Dad's never late picking me up at the other end, you know.'

Yes, Halle did know, because Lizzie had never missed an opportunity to point out all the things her dad did right and Halle did wrong.

'Well, at least I'm here now,' Halle replied, keeping her beatific smile firmly in place and nobly resisting the urge to list all the things Lizzie's father had done wrong once upon a time. Apart from the fact that would take months, Halle had made a decision sixteen years ago, when she had negotiated Luke's request for visitation rights through the duty solicitor at the Citizens Advice Bureau in Hackney, that never having to talk to Luke again was worth the price of not slagging him off to his daughter.

Her silence on the subject of Luke's betrayal, his selfishness and his numerous character flaws had been agony to maintain when Lizzie was little, and the pain of what he'd done was still fresh, still raw, still all-consuming. But she'd managed it, by keeping three things front and centre in her mind: Lizzie idolised her dad; the less Lizzie knew about her parents' broken relationship, the less likely it was to become a point of conflict between them; and, for all his many faults, which were legion, Luke did love his daughter—unlike Aldo's father, Claudio, who had refused to even acknowledge his son.

Plus, there was a limit to how much Luke could screw up Halle's karma when Lizzie spent only a few weeks of the year with him.

So moments like this, when Lizzie insisted on poking at that old wound, were really only a mild irritation, which Halle could dismiss easily…enough.

'Did you get the bouquet and the gift I sent to your father's place on your birthday?' Halle asked, subtly changing the direction of the conversation away from the minefield of Luke's shortcomings.

'Yeah, thanks. The iPad was cool.'

Halle's smile became strained at Lizzie's surly shrug—and the evidence that she obviously hadn't rated any extra parental brownie points with the lavish gesture. She dismissed the treacherous thought. Easily enough (ish).

You're not in a competition with him. Because if you were, you'd wipe the floor with him.

'Good, I'm glad you liked it. Actually, I booked us a table at the champagne bar here to celebrate your coming of age before we head home.' Halle's smile became genuine at the shock in her daughter's pale blue eyes. 'If you fancy it?'

'You're kidding. You'll let me have a glass of champagne?'

Nice call, Mel. She silently thanked her super-efficient PA, Melanie Blissett, for the suggestion.

'Of course. You're legal now,' Halle said airily, gripping the handle of Lizzie's suitcase and dismissing the pang of something sharp and bittersweet that stabbed into her left ventricle.

No need to go the full wuss.

This would not be the first time her daughter had consumed an alcoholic beverage. It would simply be the first time she'd consumed one with her mother's permission—so really it wasn't a milestone worth getting too emotional about.

'Awesome,' Lizzie replied, finally losing the last remnants of her scowl.

Halle led the way onto the escalator that took them up to the station's impressive upper level and the Grand Terrace, where the champagne bar, which stretched towards a giant sculpture of a couple kissing, was already packed on a Tuesday evening. Halle was grateful that Mel had called ahead and somehow managed to secure them a corner banquette, especially when several of the other patrons gave her penetrating I-know-who-you-are looks as she and Lizzie were led to their seats.

She was careful not to acknowledge them, giving off what she hoped were please-don't-approach-me vibes. Just this once, it would be great not to be recognised. Getting the chance to have a companionable chat with her daughter, without the usual friction, was rare enough, but having quality time with Lizzie without having to ride herd on Aldo, or, worse, settle the arguments between her two children—which was usually more traumatic than trying to negotiate world peace—was virtually unheard of.

She ordered them two glasses of rosé champagne and slid into the bench seat with her back to the rest of the bar—glad when the usual Londoners reserve held true and no one approached them.

'Where's the Antichrist tonight?' Lizzie took the seat opposite. 'With Mr Perfecto, as usual?'

'So you've been missing your brother, have you?' Halle teased, ignoring the jab at Aldo's au pair.

She suspected—even if Lizzie would rather have all her precious Urban Outfitters clothes ceremonially burned than admit it to herself—that her daughter might well have a secret crush on Trey Carson. Which would not surprise Halle in the slightest—she certainly couldn't fault her daughter's taste this time.

Twenty-one going on thirty-five, Trey was kind, gallant, responsible, a lifesaver with Aldo and much better looking than the feckless hipster losers Lizzie had favoured in the past.

When Trey had first started to work for her three months ago, Halle had noticed Lizzie watching him and had panicked. She had instantly recognised the interest in Lizzie's eyes, because it was similar to the puppy-dog eyes Halle herself had once cast at Lizzie's father—when she was a clueless fifteen-year-old desperate to lose her virginity and Luke had been a surly, sexy sixteen-year-old class warrior and sixth-form reject.

Thankfully, for everyone concerned, Trey—unlike Luke—had been far too mature to take advantage of Lizzie's interest. He'd handled the situation perfectly—treating her daughter with the same calm confidence he used to handle her son, while at the same time establishing a professional distance.

And while Lizzie might still have the hots for him, Trey's behaviour had rendered any crush not just harmless but also a surprisingly effective distraction technique. Because as long as Lizzie was busy needling Trey so he would notice her, she'd been steering clear of horrid misogynists like her first boyfriend, Liam—the little bastard who had dumped her a year ago and whose callous treatment Halle was sure had contributed to her daughter's increasingly prickly behaviour.

'I've missed Aldo about as much as I'd miss a septic rash,' Lizzie scoffed as the waiter placed two flutes of sparkling pink champagne in front of them.

'Here's to a long weekend without a septic rash, then.' Halle picked up her glass, ready to humour her daughter for once in the interests of world peace. 'Happy eighteenth birthday, Dizzy Lizzie,' she said, vindicated when her daughter lifted her own glass and didn't make some caustic comment about the childhood nickname.

Lizzie took a cautious sip. 'Wow, that's delicious. Who knew?'

'Do you like it?' Halle tapped her flute to her daughter's, biting off the question she wanted to ask but never would. *Surely you must have tasted the real thing with your father before now?* Seeing as he lived in Paris and had always had the maturity of a housefly, she would have expected Luke to have introduced Lizzie to the joys of champagne years ago.

Lizzie did a discreet burp behind her hand and then giggled. A bright girlish sound that Halle heard so rarely now it always made her grin. 'It's certainly better than the supermarket cider I got pissed on at my seventeenth birthday party.'

Halle stroked the stem of her glass. 'I'm going to pretend I didn't hear that.'

'Don't you start.' Lizzie rolled her eyes, but her tone was

more playful than surly. 'Would you believe, Dad wouldn't let me have a glass when we were out celebrating on Saturday night? Some bollocks about me always being his little girl and him needing more time to adjust.'

The flutter of contentment made Halle's chest swell.

So, Super Dad doesn't do every single thing right.

'I told him I had my first drink when I was fifteen at Guide camp and that him still thinking of me as his little girl was a bit pervy, but he would not give in—even after he told me his news and we had tons more to celebrate.'

'What news?' The contraband enquiry slipped out—probably as a result of the fruity frothy wine and the golden glow of contentment bestowed by her daughter's easy smile.

'Dad's writing his memoirs,' Lizzie replied, the enthusiasm in her voice as effervescent as the champagne. 'He's already been offered a big advance from some publisher in New York.'

'What?' Halle's flute hit the hardwood surface of the banquette table, her bubble of contentment collapsing like a profiterole tower left out in the sun.

'They might even make a film of it. And I'll finally get to go to some decent parties, instead of those boring book launches your publisher arranges.' Lizzie's tone took on a jokey whine. 'Seriously, Mum, why have a party in the kitchen section of John Lewis for fuck sake when you could have it in a West End nightclub?'

'Don't swear,' Halle replied automatically as the taste of pink champagne soured on her tongue. 'What do you mean he's writing his memoirs? What memoirs?'

Luke Best didn't have any memoirs worth publishing. OK, he was an award-winning journalist. She'd give him that. But he wrote about other people's lives, not his own.

Nobody gave a toss about the messenger. They only gave a toss about celebrities. Celebrities like her. Or they would have, if she hadn't worked overtime with the help of her management team and her publicist to keep her private life strictly private and airbrush any mention of Luke Best from her past.

'You know, his life story, that sort of thing,' Lizzie said, the eager excitement making it obvious she was completely oblivious to Halle's collapsing croquembouche. 'And I'm a big part of his life as his only child, so it totally stands to reason I'll be a big part of—'

'But he can't do that…' Halle interrupted, panic and horror combining into a perfect storm in the pit of her stomach— and threatening to rip open the ulcer she'd gotten under control years ago. 'That's a breach of our privacy.'

Did he plan to porn out the most painful part of her life— a life he'd once ripped to shreds with careless abandon— to a bloody New York publisher? Was he mad? Surely this couldn't just be Luke's trademark don't-give-a-shit attitude. What he was planning to do wasn't just thoughtless, or reckless, it was unconscionable, bordering on vindictive. And it would have repercussions, not just for her but for Lizzie and even Aldo—whom Luke had never met but whose childhood he was going to happily destroy for a bloody publishing deal?

All the hurt and anger she'd kept so carefully leashed for so many years, that she had been sure until about ten seconds ago she'd totally let go of, rushed up her torso like a tsunami and threatened to gag her.

* * *

'Mum, chill.' Lizzie lowered her glass and stared at her mum, whose face had gone pinker than the rosé tint of the bubbles in her glass. 'What are you getting so upset about? This isn't about you.'

She and her mum had had some major slanging matches in the past few years. But she'd never seen her mum this shaken. Ever.

'It is about me. Of course it's about me! What else has he got to sell except intimate details of our life together?' The protest surprised Lizzie with its vehemence.

Lizzie had grown to hate her mum's yummy-mummy image, the one she cultivated on her TV show—the TV show that had come to mean so much more in her mum's life than Lizzie or Aldo—because she knew how fake that image was. But she would happily have the serene, relaxed and witty woman who had become a national treasure to millions back right now than the woman visibly trembling in front of her.

'Mum, are you OK? You look weird.'

'Shit.' The expletive burst out of her mum's mouth, disturbing Lizzie even more.

Mum had always been uptight about swearing. Not like her dad, who swore a lot. But her dad always swore in an offhand, colourful way that made Lizzie laugh—especially when he added, 'Pretend you didn't hear that. Don't repeat it, and for fuck sake don't tell your mother.'

'What's the problem with Dad writing a memoir?' she forced herself to ask, even though she wasn't sure she wanted to know the answer.

Because she had a hideous feeling it would involve her mum finally saying something about her dad. Something she wasn't as sure as she'd once been that she wanted to hear.

As a child she'd tried to force her mum to talk about him. And vice versa when she was visiting her dad in Paris. But both of them had always maintained this freaky conspiracy of silence all through her childhood, refusing to be drawn on the subject of their past, how they'd met, married, why they'd ended up apart.

She had friends at school whose parents had divorced and spent their whole time bitching about each other to their kids, so she had eventually stopped asking her own parents to talk about each other—because she'd rather hear nothing than a load of bad stuff. But that hadn't stopped her being ecstatic when her dad had mentioned the book he was writing. Not because they might make a film of it. She wasn't a total loser, she knew that was never going to happen, and if by some miracle it did, they'd get someone else to play her part—someone cool and beautiful and talented, like Scarlett Johansson. Not someone who was stupid and too skinny and had no tits, like her.

No, she'd been excited because she'd wanted desperately to read her dad's book. Not only was he a great writer— she'd read pretty much every article he'd ever written, so she knew that for a fact—but because he'd finally be writing about the one thing she'd always wanted to read. What had happened between him and her mum. In that fluid, focused way that could 'unveil the beating heart of the human condition'. Well, that's what *Time* magazine had said on his profile, when he'd done a story for them about the murder of a socialite in Palm Beach.

Instead of answering the question, her mum locked the whisky-coloured gaze that Lizzie's brother, Aldo, had inherited onto her face, and a concerned frown formed on her brow. The concerned frown that Lizzie knew meant she was about to be lied to. Again.

'It's OK, don't worry, everything will be fine. I just need to call Jamie and get the legal team on this.'

'Why?'

Her mum placed a trembling hand on the table, then lifted her champagne glass and drained the lot, another sure sign she was freaking out, big time.

'Listen, Lizzie, you don't have to worry about any of this.' Her fingers still shook on the glass. 'It's between me and your dad, but it's really not that big a deal.'

Yeah, right. Not a big deal, even though you're swearing and sweating and knocking back champagne like an escapee from Alcoholics Anonymous.

'You're going to stop Dad writing his book. That's it, isn't it?' she said, leading with her frustration so as not to give away how deflated she felt.

Why was her mum such a neurotic control freak? And why did she always have to ruin every single good thing that ever happened in Lizzie's life? Like when she'd first hooked up with Liam, and her mum had worried he was going to turn her into a drug addict because she could smell weed on him the one time she'd met him. Or when Lizzie had finally lost her puppy fat at sixteen—because she'd grown four inches in a year—and her mum had forced them all to go to family therapy because she'd panicked that Lizzie was becoming an anorexic and was on the verge of starving herself to death.

Perhaps if her mum spent more time actually being the Domestic Diva, instead of pretending to be her on TV, she wouldn't freak out all the time about nothing.

'Excuse me, you're Halle Best, aren't you?' An ancient guy of at least fifty hovered next to their table, interrupting Lizzie's thoughts.

No shit, Sherlock.

Lizzie glared at the old git, but, as was always the case with her mum's fans, he didn't even see her sitting there.

'My wife and I love your show.'

'Thank you, that's very generous of you,' her mum replied, all the signs of her previous distress disappearing fast, until all that was left was the serene, polished and totally fake expression she always pasted on when she was doing her Domestic Diva act.

'Do you mind? I hate to be a nuisance, but…' He presented a napkin to her mum, then pulled a pen out of his pocket— obviously not hating being a nuisance enough to not be a total bloody nuisance. 'Could I get your autograph?'

'Yes, yes, of course.' Her mum sent Lizzie a tentative smile—as if to say sorry for the interruption—before taking the pen and signing the napkin. But Lizzie already knew that apologetic smile was as fake as the rest of her mum's act. Her mum was probably rejoicing at being rescued by this jerk.

No way would she get a straight answer out of her now.

Chapter 2

'You are a bastard. *Salaud. Imbécile.*'

Luke Best ducked the jar of cornichon pickles that came flying towards his head and flinched as it shattered against the apartment wall. 'Bloody hell, Chantelle. Calm the fuck down. Why are you so angry?'

'I love you and you lie to me,' she cried.

'No, you don't, and no, I didn't. I told you this wasn't serious from the start. It's not my fault you didn't listen.'

'I hate you now.'

'I get that,' he said as he edged towards the hallway. 'Which is all the more reason for us not to see each other again. We haven't got together in months. You must have seen this coming?'

'You see this coming, *connard*?' Chantelle grabbed an onyx ashtray with an Asterix figurine on it and let it fly.

He ducked again, but the heavy object spun in mid-air, hurtling towards him like an Exocet missile, and smacked into his brow.

Pain exploded.

'Shit!' He touched the developing knot on his forehead and his own temper ignited. 'Right, that's enough.' He marched forward, grabbed hold of one hundred pounds of fuming French womanhood and wedged her against the wall, trapping her throwing arm. 'Quit acting like the Madwoman of Chaillot and get a clue. We've been over since March and you know it.'

He'd tried to do this gently, tried to explain to her that their 'relationship' had never been more than a couple of dirty weekends. But she'd refused to let it go. Refused to get the message. And finally refused to leave him alone while his daughter had been over for her eighteenth birthday.

And that had been the last straw. The nuisance texts and the hung-up phone calls whenever Lizzie answered his phone had been stalkerish enough, but Chantelle's sudden appearance at his place yesterday morning, wearing nothing but a coat, a thong and skyscraper heels, had made him see he had to sort this situation out.

He'd bundled the half-naked woman out of the building before Lizzie woke up, promising to trek over to Chantelle's apartment in the thirteenth arrondissement and 'discuss their relationship' this morning, once Lizzie was safely back in the UK. So here he was, giving it to Chantelle straight, with no sugar-coating and no more avoidance tactics. And what did he get for his straight talking? A bloody head injury, that was what.

'This is over, OK? *C'est fini.*' He gave her a slight shake to get the message across. 'I don't want to see you around my place any more. No calls, no emails, no texts. If I don't answer them, it's because I don't have anything to say to you.' He'd hoped that might be a clue, but apparently Chantelle wasn't good at processing subtle.

'You tell me this now, when we had sex like dogs all weekend?' She meant rabbits, he thought, but he didn't correct her, suddenly weary at the memory of how he'd originally thought the way she mangled all his British expressions was so cute and sexy.

'That was months ago,' he said, his temper dissipating as quickly as it had come.

'Be reasonable, *cherie*,' he said as gently as he could manage while his brow was throbbing from her unprovoked assault. Chantelle was only twenty-five and hopelessly immature from the few actual conversations he could remember them having. 'I told you right from the start I wasn't interested in anything big. This is going nowhere. You need to grow up and figure that out.'

And it was way past time his dick grew up, too, and stopped making stupid decisions that got him into these sorts of fixes.

Ever since Halle, he'd stuck to casual flings, because his life was complicated enough without inviting any more drama into it. But even with casual hook-ups you had to watch your step.

And with Chantelle he'd obviously missed a step.

He'd picked her up in a bar near his apartment in the Marais the night he'd put Lizzie on the plane home to London after their week-long pre-Christmas holiday in St Moritz. And an hour after Chantelle had served him his first drink, they'd been going for it in the bar's stockroom.

Why not admit it? He'd been feeling down, maybe even a little lonely. So he'd jumped on Chantelle and her come-hither looks. And used her for sex.

But he'd already known in that stockroom that Chantelle was needier than the women he usually dated. And while he couldn't have known then she was this unhinged, he still shouldn't have allowed himself to drift into a two-month affair with her.

He soon realised he hadn't picked the best moment to

consider where he'd gone wrong with Chantelle, though, when she sucked in a breath and spat in his face. *'Salaud. Imbécile.'*

He flinched, the spittle dripping off his nose and making the cut above his eye sting. 'Yeah, I know, that's where I came in.'

He wiped his face with his shirtsleeve, ignoring the insults being hurled at him as he headed for the door. Better than getting sticks and stones and Asterix ashtrays lobbed at him.

'You're not the only man in Paris,' Chantelle cried, her voice breaking, her sobbing breaths making a headache bloom under his injured brow. 'I will find another.'

Standing in the doorway, he looked back at her. She was stunning in her fury, her thick dark hair rioting around her head, her eyes a rich caramel, glaring daggers at him like the Angel of Death, and her negligee falling off one shoulder and threatening to expose one full breast.

Thank Christ, she'd finally got the message.

'Bonne chance avec ça.' He sent her a mocking salute, before he slammed the door.

The sound of something crashing against the wood echoed in the stairwell, making him flinch as he jogged down the steps.

The chilly afternoon air in the apartment building's courtyard made the dent in his forehead sting some more. He hunched his shoulders against the pain, writing off the injury as collateral damage.

No more hook-ups with crazy ladies, especially if they have a better throwing arm than Shane Warne.

He headed for the metro station at Les Gobelins, resolving to stay celibate for a while. He had a perfectly good hand that had seen him through his horniest teenage years.

And, if nothing else, he needed to conserve his energy to navigate the perfect storm he had headed his way with Halle. Which he'd set into motion on Saturday night at La Coupole, when he'd told Lizzie about his book deal while they'd been celebrating her eighteenth at the legendary brasserie on Montparnasse.

She'd been excited and enthusiastic about the project, as he'd known she would be—enough to go home and blab all about it to her mother.

He sidestepped a kamikaze scooter as he crossed the busy boulevard and headed into the metro. The train barrelled into the station, its rubber tyres squealing on the rails. He scored a seat for the six-stop journey back to Châtelet before the metro car jostled into motion, the blank stares of the commuters endearing in their indifference.

He'd felt bad for manipulating Lizzie, but how else was he supposed to get Halle's attention? Despite countless overtures in recent years, she was still insisting on communicating every damn thing through their respective legal representatives, which, apart from costing him an arm and a leg, had really begun to piss him off.

No way could she still be mad at him. She'd had a hugely successful career not to mention other relationships. She'd even had another child. So the only motivation for the silent treatment now, that he could see, was stubborn pride and a desire to see him suffer.

Well, sod that, he'd suffered enough.

Halle had limited his access to his child to six weeks a year right up until she'd turned sixteen. And that lack of quality time was still screwing up his relationship with Lizzie now.

Once upon a time it had been a nice little ego boost to have Lizzie dub him Super Dad, because he was the one she did all the fun stuff with. But ever since Lizzie had hit her teens, he'd begun to realise Super Dad was really just a euphemism for Superficial Dad. Then his daughter had let slip she'd been in therapy a year ago—and scared the shit out of him.

Emerging from the underground chaos of concrete and commuters at Châtelet–Les Halles, he crossed through the park situated above the huge interchange towards Rue Rambuteau. Resentment simmered in his gut as he considered all the times he'd got his solicitor to contact Halle's solicitor to set up a meeting with her to talk about their daughter. And all the times he'd been refused, or stonewalled, or rebuffed, or simply ignored.

The mild miasma of sewage, traffic fumes and rotting vegetables from the nearby market blended with tree sap and brick dust from the gravel that surrounded the trees in lieu of grass. Like most Parisian parks, the one at Châtelet was utilitarian, functional and elegant in an entirely prosaic way.

He took a deep breath of the comfortingly familiar scent.

This city had saved him when he'd been stranded here sixteen years ago, broken and bleeding from wounds he'd thought would never heal. The hectic pace of life, the brusqueness and pragmatism of its inhabitants and, best of all, the anonymity had given him space and time to put the shattered pieces back together. He'd built a life here, and a career that, while not as phenomenally successful as Halle's, had given him everything he needed.

Or almost everything.

He touched his thumb to the bruise on his brow, the nagging headache starting to fade. Confrontations were not part of his DNA, he had never been a fan of unnecessary drama— occasional battery by Asterix ashtrays notwithstanding— but he was stronger, wiser and a lot more sorted than he'd been at twenty-one. He had a career he enjoyed, and he had worked hard to be a good dad, but he wanted to be a better one. A more involved one. And he wasn't going to let Halle stand in the way of that any longer.

So he was getting off her naughty step, once and for all.

And the book deal was just his opening salvo.

He was through being treated as if his place in Lizzie's life was as important as a cat flap in an elephant house. Which meant forcing Halle to talk to him about his daughter, at length and at his convenience, where there was no chance of any five-hundred-pound-an-hour dickwads running interference.

* * *

'What do you mean he's refusing to respond through his solicitor? How can he do that?' The knot under Halle's breastbone cinched tighter as she gaped at Jamie Harding, top City solicitor and the head of her legal team. 'Surely if we threaten a court order to stop publication of his book, he has to respond?'

Jamie propped his forearms on his cherrywood desk, brushing the smooth wave of chestnut-brown hair back when it flopped over his brow. 'I didn't say he hasn't responded. I said he's refusing to respond through his solicitor.'

'What's the difference?'

Jamie let out a long-suffering sigh. 'Look, Halle, I know you've always preferred to communicate with Best through us. And that makes sense when it's a legal matter to do with Lizzie's custody. But she's been of age now for two years, and I'm not even sure this book's been written yet. Or if he's actually signed a contract. So if we start throwing our legal weight around, it could be counterproductive.'

'How could it be counterproductive? I want this thing stopped. As quickly and cleanly as possible, before anyone finds out about it.' The hideous thought that people would be able to read about her starry-eyed teenage self, that needy vulnerable girl who'd fallen for Luke Best's dubious charms, made her feel nauseous. She hadn't been able to think about anything else ever since Lizzie had broken the news about Luke's book deal yesterday evening. She'd spent a long night going over all the things Luke could reveal in his memoirs that would humiliate her beyond bearing, and, worse, allow the tabloid press to feast on all the stupid mistakes she'd made where that man was concerned.

The Domestic Diva wasn't just a bakery brand, it was a statement of purpose, a symbol of empowerment, that said to women everywhere, you can come from nothing and still make something of yourself. She didn't want people to know that her whole empire had been built on the pain, the loss, of being ceremonially dumped by an arsehole like Luke Best.

Wasn't it bad enough that the man had screwed her over once, without him wanting to do it again?

'Halle, you need to think with your head here, not your heart,' Jamie said in that patronising tone that reminded her once again why she should never have slept with the guy.

It had been only one night, six years ago, after a party to celebrate her first book deal, and Jamie hadn't even been her solicitor at the time. She'd been horny and tipsy, Jamie had lingered to help clear up, or so he'd said, and they'd ended up in a lip lock over a dishwasher full of dirty champagne flutes.

The sex had been hot—because Jamie had surprising physical stamina for a desk jockey and was as goal-orientated in the bedroom as he later proved to be in the courtroom. But not hot enough to atone for the cripplingly awkward moment the morning after, when a four-year-old Aldo had run into the room to wake her up and accidentally bounced on Jamie's balls. Or all the times since she'd hired Jamie to head her legal team—on the understanding that they would never mention their former indiscretion—when Halle had detected that trace of condescension in Jamie's tone.

Note to self: If you screw a man who later becomes your solicitor, expect him to assume he's your moral and emotional superior.

'I *am* thinking with my head, Jamie,' Halle replied with exactly the same level of condescension. 'Believe me, my heart hasn't been anywhere near Luke Best for a number of years.' Sixteen to be precise.

'OK, well, let me spell it out, then,' Jamie said sharply, obviously miffed that he couldn't out-patronise her. 'We haven't got grounds for an injunction until the book's actually under contract. All that flexing our legal muscles now would achieve—apart from costing you five hundred pounds an hour for my services—is to alert the press to the impending deal and make the advance publishers are willing to offer Best go through the roof. That's what I meant by counterproductive.'

'Ah, I see.'

Bugger, maybe he does have one small, infinitesimal point.

'So what's your advice, then? There must be something I can do?' The knot tangled with the pitch and roll of raw panic. After a sleepless night debating all her options—including sneaking over to Paris and garrotting Luke in his sleep—Halle had convinced herself that Jamie would provide an answer to her predicament this morning. Something quick and relatively painless and fiendishly clever that wouldn't involve the first-degree murder of her child's father.

Jamie leaned forward. His hair flopped over his brow again, but he didn't sweep it back this time. 'My advice would

be…' He hesitated, then sighed, as if he were preparing to say something particularly difficult. 'Go over to Paris and talk to the guy.'

What? 'No.' The jolt of horror didn't do much to settle her roiling stomach. *I'd rather garrotte myself, thanks.* 'I've told you before…' she began, because this wasn't the first time Jamie had suggested the unthinkable. 'That's not an option.' She'd made a decision sixteen years ago that she would never see or speak to Luke Best again, directly or indirectly. Even though they shared a child, she didn't want him to have even the smallest toehold in her life. She'd been so determined about that that she'd never even spent a penny of the money Luke had sent each month towards their daughter's upkeep. Even when she'd really, really needed it. Even when she'd had to work two jobs to survive. She'd set up a trust fund for Lizzie with the money instead, to testify to the fact she would never ever need anything Luke Best had to offer again.

She hadn't been through all that to let Luke back in now. Especially over something this crass.

'Why not?' Jamie continued, being more persistent than usual. 'Why not appeal to his better nature?'

'Luke doesn't have a better nature, it's part of his charm.' *The rat.*

'Yes, but he does care about Lizzie,' Jamie pressed, going the full patronising. 'Surely if you tell him how this will impact on her, he'll back down. The guy's not a complete arsehole.'

'Really, Jamie? And how would you know that?' She struggled to lower her voice. 'Have you ever waited for two weeks for him to come home from a weekend assignment? Texting and emailing, and ringing his mobile and getting no response? Trudging round most of East London

with his two-year-old daughter to speak to all his known friends and associates, begging for news, only to see the pity in their faces or hear the smug sympathy in their tone? And eventually getting a text message saying simply "It's over, I can't come back"? And then spending months more not sleeping, not eating, not knowing how to comfort your child, while racking your brains trying to decipher those six measly words after a four-year relationship—and figure out what you'd done wrong? Because, of course, it had to be your fault he'd left.'

Jamie lifted his hands in a quelling motion. 'OK, Halle, I get it. I know what he did was tough for you and Lizzie.'

'No, you don't know.' She looped her bag over her shoulder. She had to get out of this office. Her voice was getting a bit shrill, a bit shaky, and she didn't plan to make a scene. Not in front of Jamie, and certainly not on Luke's account. What he'd done was a million years ago now and it didn't matter to her any more. 'Offer to pay him off if you have to. But I won't talk to him. And I certainly won't go to Paris to beg him to do the right thing, the decent thing for his daughter.' *Or me.*

Because that would make her feel like that lovelorn teenager again—begging for scraps from a man who had never deserved her.

'Find a way, Jamie, that's what I pay you for. And give me a call when you figure it out.'

Jamie stood as she headed for the door. 'I'm sorry, Halle.'

'Sorry for what?' *Being a patronising twat perhaps?*

'That what he did still hurts so much.'

Halle frowned at the note of sympathy. 'Don't be ridiculous. It doesn't hurt any more. I got over it years ago.' She opened the door, glad to feel in control again. And to have made her feelings clear without losing her cool. Much.

Jamie would do what had to be done. Even if he was a bit of a pain sometimes, he had one of the sharpest legal brains in the country. He'd find a way to make this catastrophe go away without her having to be involved.

'But it's great that you're sorry,' she added. 'Because he never was.'

It took less than a fortnight for Halle to discover she had chronically overestimated the sharpness of Jamie Harding's legal brain—and chronically underestimated the full extent of Luke Best's rat tendencies.

Chapter 3

Halle stepped from the first-class Eurostar carriage into the teeming chaos of the Gare du Nord at nine a.m. on a Monday in early June. She popped another antacid into her mouth, then pursed her lips to ensure the lipstick she'd just applied, again, didn't smudge. After dodging wheel-along suitcases being used as lethal weapons, she paused at the end of the platform to consider the daunting prospect of reaching the station's main exit alive.

Streams of Parisians flowed along the crowded, dimly lit concourse as they rushed towards the RER, TGV and metro interchange at the other end of the station, or stood gathered round the ticket kiosks, a pizza booth and the tables of an ice-cream café—which had been strategically stuffed into the narrow thoroughfare between the Eurostar platform and the exit, to thwart any passengers attempting to get out of the station in one piece.

She'd been to Paris once on a school trip in her teens and had avoided the place ever since. Because she'd felt then, as she did now, that the city's squalid reality didn't live up to the romantic hype.

Her belly did a couple of backflips—the biggest fright

being the one waiting for her at the rendezvous they had arranged in the Marais. Assuming of course Luke bothered to show. Given his abysmal track record, her expectations were fairly low on that score.

She clutched her briefcase and tried not to dwell on what horrors might await her in the café he'd suggested in the Place des Vosges. Or the anger bubbling away like a volcanic pool under her solar plexus and threatening to erupt at any moment despite her copious use of antacids.

How had he managed to engineer things so easily to his own advantage?

Once she'd finally been forced to accept the necessity of meeting him, in person, to 'discuss' his book deal, she'd been absolutely adamant that she would not be discussing anything in Paris. Quite apart from the symbolism of her having to come to him, she hadn't wanted to meet him on his home turf, in an alien city, where she didn't speak the language. But after the limited communications he'd been prepared to make with Jamie, she'd been faced with the stark choice of either getting into a protracted email negotiation with the man himself or caving in quickly so she could get this farce over with before she developed a new ulcer.

In other words, she'd had no choice at all.

That the success of this visit was by no means assured, despite her being forced to give far too much ground already, made the wad of anger and anxiety wedged in her throat only that much harder to swallow.

Nudging and jostling her way through the sea of arrogantly self-possessed Parisians and foolhardy tourists blocking her exit, she finally found what she assumed was the taxi rank. Although it was hard to tell. Unlike the orderly queue you would find at any main-line London station, here there just seemed to be an extension of the melee inside,

with people pushing and shoving as the sound of horns and car engines filled the air in a seething mass of harassed, pissed-off humanity.

Ignoring the rank, she picked her way across the cobble-stoned street in the kitten heels her stylist, Rene, had suggested pairing with a caramel-coloured power suit, after a panicked consultation the night before. As she'd worn the two-thousand-pound designer suit while negotiating her last TV contract, it supplied the dual karma of making her feel both in control and lucky. But Rene had bolstered her confidence still further by pointing out the combo of pencil skirt, loosely tailored jacket and silk blouse made a fashion statement of kick-ass insouciance.

You are a lean, mean kick-ass machine. Not the girl he abandoned.

Repeating the mantra went some way to quelling the rioting lava as she reached the main boulevard. She squeezed her eyes shut and thrust out her hand, hoping none of the vehicles barrelling past lopped off her arm. A squeal of skidding rubber had her prising open an eyelid, to find a cab stopped inches from her toes.

'Bonjour, monsieur,' she addressed the wiry man in the driver's seat.

The cabbie gave a curt nod. *'Bon matin,'* he corrected.

Pulling her iPhone out of her coat pocket, she tapped the calendar app, even though she'd memorised the location during the two-hour train journey from London, and read aloud. *'Le Café Hugo, à la Place des Vosges, s'il vous plaît?'*

The driver grunted, nodded, then flicked his head in a surly gesture, which she took to be the Gallic cabbie's equivalent of 'Hop in, luv.'

As they bounced down the street, then swerved into the

snarl of rush-hour traffic, she rehearsed the speech she'd been working on since yesterday.

She might be famous for her warm, witty, friendly ad-libs to camera on *The Best of Everything*, but she had decided that adhering strictly to the script on this occasion was absolutely imperative.

There was going to be nothing warm, or witty, or friendly about this meeting. She would be businesslike and direct and completely devoid of emotion. She would present Luke with exactly how much she was prepared to offer to make this problem go away, and that would be the end of it. Because she'd come to the conclusion that's exactly what this so-called book deal was really all about.

A barefaced attempt to hold her to ransom.

She'd asked her literary agent to make some discreet enquiries with his contacts in New York and it transpired there had been no deal signed as yet—just as Jamie had suspected.

Halle had forced herself not to overreact about this final betrayal. She was a wealthy woman. Why on earth should she be surprised that an opportunist like Luke would eventually seize the chance to hose her for some cash? As long as Lizzie never found out about her father's mercenary scheme, and the book deal went away, it hardly mattered how she achieved that.

If she had to pay to get Luke Best out of her life forever, she'd do it. She'd already built in a ten per cent increase in the sum she'd discussed with her financial adviser if Luke insisted on negotiating, and Jamie had drawn up the relevant contracts, which she had in her briefcase ready for Luke's signature. As soon as the rat signed on the dotted line, she would be free to make a dignified exit, after making it absolutely clear this meeting marked the end of any and all business between them.

She was a smidgen outside her comfort zone on this. But Luke didn't need to know that. As long as she kept her head and didn't let her anxiety at seeing him again show. And if she could manage to keep her nerves in check while instructing an audience of over a thousand people how to make choux pastry during a live cookery show at London's Olympia, she could bloody well manage it in front of the man who had lobbed her heart into a blender a lifetime ago.

* * *

'Vingt-cinq euros, madame.'

Halle passed a fistful of notes through the grille, pleased when her fingers barely trembled, and waved off the change before stepping out of the cab. She shielded her eyes against the watery sunlight and absorbed the majesty of the palatial garden square that had emerged like an oasis from the rabbit warren of narrow cobblestoned streets they'd bulleted through to get here from the Gare du Nord. As the cab drove away, her gaze landed on the Café Hugo across the road, and the line of tables nestled under the arches of the grand sixteenth-century facade.

She scanned the bunches of customers huddled at the tables away from the spitting rain but saw no sign of the man she had come to meet. She let out a sharp sigh as it occurred to her she might not even recognise him after sixteen years. After all, she never would have expected him to choose somewhere so highbrow and sophisticated for this meeting. The Luke she'd known had been much more at home at the greasy spoon round the corner from their flat—or the local pub—than an elegant pavement café in Paris.

She dismissed the observation. Obviously, she had never known that Luke, either, or he wouldn't have managed to sneak the fact past her that he didn't give a shit about her, and she certainly had no intention of getting to know the

new Luke now. Once this short, sharp shock was over with, she would never have to set eyes on him again. So what did it matter if Luke had become a sophisticated man of the world who could tell the difference between a pint of Stella and a glass of Pouilly-Fuissé?

She crossed the street, skirted the outdoor tables and headed towards the glass doors at the café's entrance, employing the breathing technique she used while they were taping the show, seconds before the green camera light clicked on. The only thing she hoped about the new Luke was that he'd improved his timekeeping—because if he was as fashionably late as he'd once been, the volcano in her stomach was liable to blow.

She entered the darkened café interior, to be greeted by the comforting scent of roasting coffee, sautéed garlic and fresh baking. High-backed leather booths and stained-glass panels coupled with the low lighting from the handblown chandeliers made the bustling inside of the restaurant seem more intimate but no less elegant than the outside.

Her stomach did another uncomfortable flip-flop.

Terrific, intimacy, just the ambience I want for this meeting.

The maître d' stood by a lectern talking to a tall man wearing a long dark blue mac with his back to her.

The spike of recognition at the man's hipshot pose sprinted up her spine just before he looked round and a pair of painfully familiar sky-blue eyes located her standing behind him like a muppet.

'Luke!' The name popped out on a shocked whisper.

How can he have gotten better looking? The sneaky bastard.

She studied the high angles of his cheekbones, the heavy-lidded eyes, which always looked as if he'd just climbed out of bed, the flat place on the bridge of his nose where he'd broken it in a fight and the deadly dimple in his chin,

which had made her the envy of every girl in class 10C when they'd started dating. Then did a quick survey of long legs encased in black jeans, and the navy blue cotton polo neck hugging a chest that looked much broader than she remembered it, too.

Why didn't you give in to your curiosity yesterday and Google him?

If only she had, she would have been much better prepared for her first eyeful of this new, annoyingly even more buff Luke.

'Haley,' he said, murmuring the name she'd had as a girl. The name that had always felt boring and unoriginal until she'd heard him say it. The name she'd changed a year after he'd left.

'It's Halle. I don't answer to that name any more.'

Any more than I intend to answer to you, she thought defiantly, even if hearing that name again on his lips had given her an uncomfortable jolt.

'You mind if I call you Hal?' he replied, the once familiar nickname giving her another unpleasant jolt. 'Halle sounds kind of intimidating,' he said as his gaze drifted up to her hair with a leisurely sense of entitlement.

If that's your intimidated look, I'm not buying it.

She bit down on her frustration.

'Call me whatever you like,' she countered with deliberate nonchalance, knowing when she was being played. If he thought he could get a rise out of her that easily, he'd miscalculated.

Unpleasant jolts be damned.

'Hal it is, then. I'm glad we got that settled.' He swept his hair off his brow. She stared resentfully at the thick, casually styled waves of tawny sun-streaked bronze, long enough now to touch the collar of his mac.

Couldn't he have lost some of that hair? Surely male-pattern baldness is the least he deserves after the shoddy way he treated me?

He planted one hand in his back pocket, as she frowned at his non-receding hairline, and cocked his head to one side. The infuriatingly leisurely gaze dropped down to her kitten heels.

All the muscles in her face and jaw had clenched—in direct counterpoint to his relaxed body language—by the time his eyes finally met hers again.

'You haven't changed.' The rusty tone, rich with appreciation, shimmered over the skin of her nape and made tension scream across her collarbone.

Back off, buster, that's one familiarity too far.

She adjusted the strap of her briefcase to loosen her shoulder blades before she dislocated something.

'If that's supposed to be flattering, it's not.' She laid on as much snark as she could manage while struggling to draw an even breath. 'This happens to be new season Carolina Herrera, not a supermarket own brand.'

His wide lips curved on one side, the half-smile equal parts confidence and rueful amusement—suggesting her attempt at a slap-down had missed its target by a few thousand miles. But then again, she hadn't expected a direct hit so soon. Luke's ego had always been robust. Given how good he looked, she'd hazard a guess it was virtually indestructible now.

'I don't have a fucking clue who Carolina Herrera is,' he said, the casual use of the F-word a prosaic reminder of how she'd once found his genial swearing so sexy.

God, what a clueless muppet I once was.

'But whoever she is,' he added, 'she looks great on you.'

He took a step forward, coming perilously close to her

personal space and forcing her to tilt her head back to meet his gaze.

I do not believe it. Has he actually gotten taller, too?

While he was definitely more muscular than he'd been at twenty-one, how could he have also gained an extra inch in height? At five foot four, she had always felt petite standing next to him, but she certainly didn't remember having to look this far up to see his face.

Sod the kitten heels. I should have worn stilts. It's going to be next to impossible to kick ass as a midget.

He rattled something off in fluent French to the maître d', who laughed and then grabbed a couple of menus, before directing them into the restaurant.

'Jean-François has saved us the best booth,' Luke said.

'Fine.' She refused to worry about what he'd said to put that knowing smile on Jean-François's lips. She had enough crap to process already. 'Let's get this over with,' she added pointedly as she followed the maître d'.

But as she stepped in front of Luke, his palm touched her lower back and sensation rippled across the upper slope of her bum. She stiffened and jerked round.

He held up the offending hand, then tucked it back into his pocket, but the crinkle of humour around his eyes made his easy surrender a decidedly pyrrhic victory.

Swallowing the renewed spike of temper, and the latest unpleasant jolt, she picked up the pace, her kitten heels clicking decisively on the marble tiles. Directed to a booth at the back of the restaurant, she shrugged off her coat and slid onto the well-worn leather seat.

Luke took the seat opposite, nudging her knee as he folded his long legs under the table. She shifted back. Not because she was scared of touching him, but because she did not want him to crowd her.

Lifting her briefcase onto the table, she opened the locks as Luke addressed the maître d' in fluid French.

'Un espresso, un café crème et une sélection de patisseries. Et puis, dire au garçon qu'il devrait nous laisser seul.'

Leaving their menus on the table, Jean-François nodded to Luke, said *'Bon appetite, madame,'* to her, then flashed that knowing smile again and left.

'What did you say to him?' she asked, fervently wishing she hadn't managed to daydream through five whole years of French in school.

'I ordered an espresso for me, a coffee with cream for you and a selection of pastries for the both of us,' he replied drily. 'I assume you still like your coffee milky—and you'll love the pastries here, they're a speciality of the place, they have an amazing pastry chef.'

'I ate on the train,' she lied, just as drily, aggravated that he remembered how she liked her coffee—and suspicious of the pastry order. Was that why he'd suggested this place? Did he think he could charm her into offering him more money? 'And even with my rudimentary French, I know what *café crème* is,' she continued. 'I meant what you said to him after that.'

He rested his forearms on the table, the smug almost-smile finally flatlining.

'I told him to tell the waiter to leave us alone so we could have some privacy for this conversation.' He stretched out his legs, bumping her knee again. She shifted back further, then wished she hadn't when the half-smile returned.

'Relax, Hal, I'm not planning to kidnap you. Yet.'

She pushed out a scoffing laugh. Determined to appear as cool and confident as he did, even if her ulcer burst. 'We won't need too much privacy. This is going to be a very short conversation.'

One dark brow arched. 'I doubt that.'

'Think again.' She plucked the contract out of her brief-case and slapped it on the table, the way she'd rehearsed several times the night before. He didn't even flinch, let alone jump the way she'd hoped. She crushed the prickle of disappointment.

'I'm prepared to offer a generous sum to make this book go away,' she launched into her spiel. 'Even though we both know you haven't actually signed a deal yet.' Her spirits lifted at the crease on his forehead as he studied the wad of papers. 'Lizzie *says* you're a successful journalist, though.' She put the emphasis on 'says' so he would think she doubted Lizzie's conviction, then paused to let the implication also sink in that she had in no way followed his career trajectory. 'She also seems to think you're a competent enough writer to write a book of this nature. And my literary agent concurs that you ought to be able to command an advance given the subject matter. But as I'm not well-known in the US—' *yet* '—because my show's only been syndicated to public service broadcasters over there, she doubts a New York publisher will offer more than a low four-figure advance. Accounting for that, and the dollar exchange rate at the moment, I'm prepared to offer you twenty thousand in pounds sterling, in a lump sum payment, once you sign this contract.' She tapped her nail on the contract for added effect. 'A contract that, once signed, will rescind all your rights now and in the future to write a book that features, alludes to or in any way references me, our past association or either one of my two children in it. Whether in name or via the use of recognisable characterisation and/or pseudonyms.'

She had to rush the last bit of the speech because she was running out of breath. But, otherwise, the swell of pride was

almost as huge as the rush of relief. She'd done it. She'd stuck to the script without wavering or prevaricating and without stumbling, once.

She couldn't assess his reaction because his expression had gone completely blank as he stared at the paperwork, but she congratulated herself again when he brought his hand down to rest on top.

The silence stretched uncomfortably as he thumped his thumb on the pile of papers but didn't pick up the contract to examine it more closely.

The waiter arrived to place their coffees and the pastries in front of them. The buttery scent of freshly baked filou accompanied the artistry of feather-light croissants and eclairs, delicate tarts decorated with exotic fruits and some miniature chocolate and cherry entremets.

'Feel free to read it,' she prompted, to cover the sound of her empty stomach rumbling.

For a split second she thought she saw something brittle flash across his face, but she dismissed the thought when he said lazily, 'What makes you think the book's about you?'

She opened her mouth to tell him she wasn't an imbecile. But shut it again when she realised how neatly he had almost outmanoeuvred her. She would sound vain and self-important if she reiterated the point, even though they both knew she had to be the subject of the book. Because what else did he have to sell but intimate details of their life together? But she didn't plan to get caught out that easily.

Luke as a boy had always had a scathing and vocal dislike of what he called 'pop culture crap' and a huge chip on his shoulder about people with money whom he decreed didn't deserve it—which made her suspect he was likely to be less than impressed by her success as a celebrity chef. With hindsight, she also now realised that Luke's prickly superiority as

a teenager had probably come from the indignity of growing up on a run-down council estate in a 'problem family' while having to rely on benefit cheques, the local food bank and charity-shop clothing to survive. But she didn't plan to give him another opportunity to lecture her on the subject of her 'privileged upbringing' just because her dad had once gone to grammar school.

'I don't care what your book's about as long as myself and Lizzie and Aldo aren't in it,' she said, directing the conversation back where it needed to be. 'In any shape or form. My private life is not for public consumption and neither is theirs.'

He plopped two sugars into his espresso. 'So what you're saying is, *you* want to be able to decide what *I* put into *my* book.'

'Yes.'

He stirred the espresso with maddening patience.

'And I'm prepared to pay a very generous sum for the privilege,' she added.

He took a leisurely sip of his coffee, the dainty cup impossibly tiny cradled in his hand. 'Then I guess my next question's gotta be, what makes you think I want you to pay me for that privilege?'

'What do you mean?'

'I mean, I don't want your money,' he said.

She blinked, the tiny spurt of hope comprehensively drowned out by total astonishment as what he seemed to be implying simply failed to compute. 'So you'd be willing to keep us out of it *without* being paid?'

No way, that couldn't be right. The man was a rat. He'd shown his true colours sixteen years ago. She had not misread this situation that much.

'Not exactly,' he replied.

Bingo. 'I thought not,' she said, pleased she hadn't been wrong. Twenty grand was a small price to pay for the heady satisfaction of finally being right where he was concerned.

'But money's not what I'm after from you.'

'Well, I'm afraid that's all I'm offering.' She had no idea where he was going with this, and she didn't want to know. Luke's cunning plans, his ridiculous schemes, his hidden agendas were not her problem any more. She'd gotten over caring what the heck was going on inside his head years ago.

'All I want is a favour from you,' he continued. 'Then I'll do you one in return and drop the book deal. Autobiography's not really my thing anyway.'

'What favour?' The question spilled out, one split second before she remembered she didn't give a toss about Luke's stupid hidden agenda.

She realised her mistake when his eyes took on the intent gleam that had once excited her to the point of madness, but now looked decidedly feral. 'I'm doing a piece on Jackson Monroe, ever heard of him?'

'Of course I have, he's that American guy who calls himself the Love Doctor and runs some fancy rehab clinic for divorcing celebrities. He was on *The Graham Norton Show* a few weeks ago, pushing his bestselling book.' She searched her memory. 'And talking loads of bollocks about his new method of relationship rehab for the rich and incredibly gullible.'

And what the bloody hell did some jumped-up, smooth-talking twerp who had made a killing pretending to be the answer to the rising divorce rate have to do with the privacy of her and her children?

'He calls himself the Love Surgeon, actually,' Luke said. 'But bollocks is right and I plan to prove it, by going on one of the relationship retreats at his place in Tennessee. But

to do that, I need a plus-one with a profile. Because it's a course for high-profile couples.' He lifted his fingers to do air quotes. 'Who are experiencing a breakdown in their love relationship. And that's where you come in.'

It took a moment for her to process what he was asking. But then realisation hit her square in the face. And the unpleasant jolt hit eight point five on the Richter scale.

'Are you completely fucking insane?' She never used the F-word—not since she'd got over her infatuation with Luke and discovered it wasn't that pleasant coming from your three-year-old daughter. But it shot out without warning as her head started to implode.

He could not be serious. He'd blackmailed her into coming to Paris to give her some bullshit ultimatum for an article he was writing? As if she had nothing better to do? As if her career wasn't far more important and full on than his? As if she were still the wide-eyed, besotted acolyte who had been prepared to do anything for him?

'We don't *have* a love relationship,' she said, just in case he'd missed that salient point. 'We *never* had a love relationship.'

'Gee, that hurts.' He clapped his hand to his chest in a pantomime of wounded feelings. 'I distinctly recall you telling me how madly in love with me you were when we first went all the way.'

'That's funny, because I don't recall any such thing.' Of course she recalled it. And how incredibly crass of him to rub her face in it now.

'Really?' he said, the mocking smile lancing through the last of her composure. 'It was right after I—'

'If I did say something like that…' she interrupted, to stop him going into any more detail. The last thing she needed was to have the humiliating picture stuck in her head of

him lying on top of her with that I've-finally-popped-my-cherry smile on his face while she clung on to him and told him how wonderful he was, because she was desperately trying to romanticise the moment and take her mind off the extreme chafing caused by his enormous cock. 'It was probably because I was suffering from post-traumatic stress disorder.'

'Ouch, another direct hit.'

The teasing comment made her sense-of-humour failure complete.

'OK, I'm off.' She picked up the contract to shove it back in her briefcase and slammed the lid with a satisfying crash. 'I don't have time for this crap.'

'Hey.' He took her wrist. 'I was kidding. No need to get your knickers in a knot.'

'Don't touch me.' She yanked her hand away. Forced herself to breathe, before she smashed her fist into his face and broke his bloody nose a second time.

She wanted to shout at him that their past—and the cruel way he'd treated her—wasn't a joke, could never be a joke, not to her. But that would give him much more importance than he deserved.

'No touching, I promise.' He held his hands up. 'Just hear me out. All I'm asking is two weeks of your time. I know we don't have a relationship any more, but we do have shit we haven't been able to deal with because you have consistently refused to communicate with me directly.'

'I refused to speak to you because I didn't want to speak to you. And it doesn't matter if there's shit we haven't dealt with, because I never plan to speak to you again.'

'What about if the shit has to do with Lizzie?'

The level question stopped her in her tracks. But only for a second. This had nothing to do with Lizzie's shit, and

she had proof. 'Don't try to bring our daughter into this, when you're the one who wants to expose her to the glare of publicity in some grubby tell-all biography just to pocket a few extra quid.'

His jaw tensed, as if he were surprised by the hit. But after a pregnant pause, he spoke again. 'There'll be no book if you give me these two weeks. And once I get the goods on this guy, the piece is going to be huge. *Vanity Fair* is already gagging to publish it...'

'You're not listening to me, Luke.' Some things never changed, it seemed. 'Read my lips. I don't care about your article.' And she certainly didn't want to have to spend two weeks with him—the past twenty minutes had been trying enough. 'Or bloody *Vanity Fair.*'

'That's because you're not looking at the bigger picture here. If this article gets the traction I'm hoping for in the US, it could be great publicity for you. You're trying to break that market, right?'

'How did you know that?' Good God, had he been checking up on her?

'Because it's your obvious next step,' he said, without even breaking stride.

'How could rehashing our disastrous relationship for the purposes of exposing some charlatan possibly be good publicity for me?'

'We won't have to rehash it—what Monroe offers are basically glorified holidays, there's no real counselling involved. But I'll go into the background of our relationship in the piece, that's the angle I'm planning on.'

Her jaw literally dropped at that. She was astonished she couldn't hear it thudding against the floor. 'You are actually insane.'

'It's a great angle. I'm telling you, it might even get you a spot on *Oprah*.'

'*Oprah* went off air years ago.' Which showed how much attention he paid to daytime TV.

He hesitated for a moment. 'Yes, but she still does specials. Like the interview with Lance Armstrong. Your story could qualify.'

'Why the hell would Oprah bother with a story like mine?' she asked, not even sure why she was humouring him. Maybe it was sick fascination. It was almost as if he were dangling over the precipice of an alternative reality.

'Oprah's all about the feel-good feminist angle,' he said, convincing her that he wasn't dangling any longer, he'd dropped right off the cliff. 'That's what her viewers lap up. You fit the bill perfectly. The woman who worked her way back from adversity and stuck it to the guy who did her wrong. That'd be me, by the way,' he added, without even a hint of irony. 'Don't sell yourself short, you're the superhero in this scenario.'

'Uh-huh? And what superhero am I, exactly? The Incredible Dumped Woman?'

Sod humouring him. His mental health issues weren't her concern. 'What the hell makes you think my success has anything at all to do with you?' She stood, determined not to let him see how mad he could still make her.

Bugger the bloody book. She'd just have to get Jamie to issue an injunction or something once it was written. Knowing Luke's inability to finish anything he started, she had probably blown the threat entirely out of proportion anyway. 'And don't worry, I have never sold myself short. You're the one who did that.' She swept out of the booth, ready to make a dramatic exit, when strong fingers clamped on to her wrist, halting her in mid-sweep.

'Sit down.'

She twisted her wrist, but his grip remained firm this time.

'Let go of me right this instant.'

'I'll let go *when* you sit down. We're not finished talking here. You want to cause a scene that'll end up in *Paris Match*, be my guest. This happens to be a popular hangout for the paps.'

Whaaat?

She darted a glance round the restaurant, the blood rushing up her neck. The place was busy but no longer packed. But as she scanned the booths to see if there were any obvious candidates about to draw a telephoto lens on her, she caught sight of the self-satisfied smirk on Luke's lips and realised how ridiculous she was being. She was a celebrity in the UK, not France. She narrowed her eyes at Luke, hoping to eviscerate him with a single glance. 'Paps, my bum.'

'Sit down,' he repeated.

She lifted her wrist, but he still wouldn't let go. She didn't much like the tingles shooting up her arm from the strength in those calloused fingers.

'I'll sit down *when* you let go,' she said.

His fingers released, and she toyed with the idea of striding out despite their bargain. She owed him nothing, certainly not honesty or integrity.

'This isn't a negotiation, Hal. It's a choice. I'll sign your contract and lose the book deal with no money changing hands, but you'll have to come with me for two weeks to Tennessee first and pose as my plus-one.'

'That's Sophie's choice and you know it,' she cried, not caring if every paparazzi in Paris overheard them now. 'What difference is there in having my past idiocy exposed in *Vanity Fair* and probably syndicated round the globe to

getting it rehashed for public consumption in your book? I'll take my chances, thank you, with an injunction once you've actually written the thing. Knowing your bullshit to productivity ratio, you probably won't even finish it.'

'There's no reason why I have to name you in the article. If that's what you're scared of, I can keep your identity secret.'

'Really?' She sat down—which helpfully disguised the renewed tremor in her legs.

'Yes, really,' he said without hesitation, more serious than a heart attack. It was a new look for him. One she was fairly sure she didn't like any more than all his others.

'But what if someone guesses my identity?' Not that she was actually considering his preposterous ultimatum. But theoretically speaking. 'We've got the same last name.'

'Yeah, I know, funny that, seeing as how I don't remember us ever getting married.' Before she could come up with some cutting remark about how eternally grateful she was to have dodged that bullet at least, he continued in the same patient tone. 'Don't worry, no one will guess it's you. Not if I don't want them to.' He watched her, in the focused, intent, all-consuming way that had excited her so much as a teenager, when she'd been desperate for his attention. 'That said, the piece won't be nearly as strong, and you'll lose out on all the great publicity you could get from it. So you can make the final decision about whether you want to remain anonymous once you've read it,' he said. 'Just in case you change your mind.'

She so would not. Did he seriously think the power of his prose would be enough to eradicate the fact that he'd blackmailed her into this?

'I'm willing to bet you do.' His lips curved in an assured

smile. Good God, the man's vanity was as phenomenal as his ego.

'Would you be prepared to put all that in writing?' she clarified. Even though she still wasn't seriously considering his devil's bargain. But where was the harm in exploring all her options?

'You won't accept my word?'

'I wouldn't accept your word if it was tattooed across your arse.'

He chuckled, the sound deep and rich and not remotely insulted. 'I'd rather see it tattooed across *your* arse.' The buzz of something rich and hot in her belly, and the answering hum deep in her abdomen, felt suspiciously familiar. But it wasn't excitement, she decided. Or certainly not sexual excitement. More like the buzz you got from besting a worthy opponent in battle. Not that Luke had ever been remotely worthy of her. But apparently the thought of besting him could still give her a cheap thrill.

'But if you insist,' he added, 'get your solicitor to draw something up and I'll sign it.' He reached across the table, offering his hand. 'Shall we shake on it for now?'

She looked at his outstretched palm, her usual common sense returning. Could she bear two whole weeks stuck in his company? Even if it meant the end of the threat against her and her children?

But as his hand hung there, suspended over the table, the buzz peaked, and a strange calm came over her. And she knew, against all the odds, she actually wanted to take his devil's bargain.

Because she owed it to the girl she'd been.

And because, despite all her protestations to herself, and Jamie, this thirty-minute meeting had proved one galling

fact: she hadn't gotten over Luke's desertion the way she'd wanted to believe.

She'd shut down all those years ago, once all the tears and heartache had drained her dry. And she'd forced herself to rise above the pain and the grief and eventually the anger, because she'd had to, not just to survive and to heal, but so she could handle letting her daughter have the daddy she adored back in her life.

But by never talking to Luke, never seeing him or communicating with him, he'd got off scot-free. He'd never had to explain what he'd done, or why he'd done it. He'd never even had to apologise. And maybe she needed that, to finally get the closure that had alluded her.

She clocked the confident gleam in his gaze, daring her to take him on. The way he'd done so many years ago.

She'd taken the challenge then and lost, catastrophically. But she was older, smarter and a lot richer now. And, best of all, she was totally over him.

Hell yeah, she could survive being stuck with him for two whole weeks. She might even enjoy it. Rubbing his nose in all his shortcomings. In fact, two weeks wouldn't be nearly long enough for that.

'OK, Luke, you've got a deal.'

His fingers trapped hers, the calluses on the ridge of his palm rough to the touch. The memory flash blindsided her: those same calluses caressing the sensitive skin of her inner thigh on the lazy Sunday morning before he'd left for his first proper assignment—the last time they'd made love. When he'd used all the skills they'd learned together to make her come until she screamed, and woke the baby up. The frisson of heat, the shock of memory settled in her breasts, making her nipples tighten against the smooth silk of her bra.

Then his thumb brushed under the red mark on her wrist and, to her horror, the hum in her abdomen pulsed hot.

'What happened here?' he asked. 'It looks nasty.'

Small burns were a hazard of her job; she'd incurred this one a few days ago during a guest spot on BBC One's *Breakfast Kitchen* while whipping a tray of florentines out of the oven. The sore spot tingled as his thumb slid close to the inflamed skin.

She yanked her hand free and rubbed her wrist discreetly on her skirt.

'It'll heal,' she said. *And so, finally, will the wounds you inflicted on me.*

She walked out of the restaurant without another word. But as she hailed a cab to take her back to the station for her noon train, her breasts continued to throb in time with the timpani drum of her pulse.

And it occurred to her there was one key element of their relationship she hadn't factored into her decision to accept his proposal.

And perhaps she should have.

* * *

'Elle est très belle,' Jean-François commented wistfully as the café's door swung shut in Halle's wake.

'Oui, très belle,' Luke replied, not at all wistfully.

And très pissed off with me, still, even after more than a decade and a half.

Enough to piss him right off in return.

She'd offered him money. As if he were some cap-doffing toady whose silence she could buy with a few bob. As if his life story had no import whatsoever compared to hers.

Not that he was actually writing his life story. But that was hardly the point.

Who did she think she was? Did she actually believe

just because she could rustle up the perfect soufflé in ten minutes and mould a working carousel cake topper out of marzipan she was better than him?

'Ça c'est bien?' Jean-François indicated the untouched plate of pastries. *'Votre reunion importante?'*

Not exactly. His important meeting had come close to being a complete bust.

'Yeah, *très bien.'* He stuffed a miniature *chasson aux pommes* into his mouth to sweeten the sarcasm.

So much for his cunning plan. Because what had seemed perfect twenty minutes ago wasn't looking quite so perfect any more.

Perhaps he should have figured out the extent of Halle's hatred. Given that her temper tantrum had lasted sixteen years.

Then again, what he had really underestimated was his own reaction.

He thought he'd come to terms with all the choices he'd made, good and bad, all those years ago. But seeing her again, in the flesh, instead of on TV or in some papped snapshot in a magazine, had proved what a whopper that was. Because despite the gloss and the glamour and the Carolina Whatever-her-name-was designer suit, all he'd been able to see for a moment was the girl he had once fallen arse-over-tit in lust with.

The lush curve of her hips in the fitted skirt, the peaks of her full so-sensitive breasts beneath the silk blouse, the rich honey-blonde hair, which looked soft and tactile despite the ruthless updo, and even the sparkling intelligence behind the brittle contempt in her golden brown eyes.

He'd been reeling from that shock when she'd delivered another sucker punch to the gut. That not only wasn't his infatuation with her as dead as it should be, but he wasn't

as sorted about the rest of it, either. All the stuff he'd had years of therapy to overcome.

Because if he was, how could the misplaced pride and the defensive anger that had screwed him up so royally as a kid have popped out of hiding like a demented jack-in-the-box as soon as she'd slapped him with that insulting offer?

Jean-François left him to finish his lukewarm espresso and full plate of pastries on his own—and reconsider his plan

Getting Halle to come to Tennessee with him had seemed like a no-brainer when he'd thought of the idea a month ago.

Having Halle in tow at Monroe's resort would not only mean he could finally force her to talk to him about Lizzie, but the resulting article—which he planned to be a clever exposé of exactly why Monroe's eccentric methods didn't work—had the potential to be huge.

The guy had come from nowhere to end up with endorsements from a host of Hollywood A-listers within a year. And was causing a storm with his bestseller, *The Extreme Path to Love and Reconciliation*. Getting the goods on the celebrity charlatan could even win him an award, if he pitched it right.

He stirred another sugar into his coffee, topped up the cup from the fresh pot the waiter had deposited on the table and took a fortifying sip. But the sugar-loaded caffeine hit did nothing to disguise the unpleasant taste of apprehension beginning to clog his throat.

Unfortunately, after his first merry meeting with the new, improved ball-busting Halle, he couldn't help wondering about the advisability of getting stuck for two whole weeks in the Tennessee wilderness with a woman who had looked

at him—when she actually bothered to meet his gaze—as if she wanted to stuff his reproductive organs through an industrial-grade mincer.

Chapter 4

'I can't believe it. You got Mr Perfecto to babysit us *both*? That is so humiliating.'

Trey Carson sawed the tuna sandwiches he was making for Aldo's packed lunch in half while attempting to tune out the argument raging in the hall. He wasn't having much success, given that he had become the subject of Lizzie Best's latest spat with her mother—and her shrill angry tone could slice through lead.

He heard the muffled conciliatory tones of her mother's reply, and even though he couldn't make out the words, he had to give his employer points for patience. Halle Best never raised her voice to her children. Especially Lizzie. He often wondered if she had a secret stash of weed in the house to keep her so calm in the face of so much provocation. His own mother would have given him a backhander if he'd dared to speak to her the way Lizzie spoke to her mum. Before she got sick that was...

He cut the sandwiches into quarters.

'Like I care that you're going on some stupid book tour.' Lizzie's lead-slicing tone echoed round the large open-plan basement kitchen again. 'So what else is new?'

Trey reached for the cling film and hastily wrapped the sandwiches, keen to get Aldo out of the line of fire before Lizzie stomped into the kitchen ready to take her frustration out on her little brother. He wasn't in the mood to play referee this morning. Especially now he'd become Public Enemy Number One because his employer had asked him to move in for two weeks while she was away on a book tour in the US.

Keeping his cool around Lizzie for the past three months had been hard enough. Living in the same house with her for a fortnight threatened to up the stakes a lot more. Forget losing his cool, if he wasn't careful he could end up throttling her. And he couldn't do that. Killing his employer's daughter would not look good on his CV. Plus, he'd probably lose his job.

And he needed this job. It paid well, came with good benefits, took his mind off his mum, and he got a kick out of looking after Aldo. The kid was smart and funny and affectionate—and they understood each other. Because Trey knew what it was like to grow up without a dad around and to get labelled a 'problem' by grown-ups who didn't know shit about your life.

The poor kid had been in therapy for his anger management issues when Trey had gotten the job—the eighth au pair Halle had hired in as many months. But all Trey had seen was a confused and scared ten-year-old boy who needed a mate—and a chance to run off all his nervous energy instead of sitting around talking himself into a coma. They'd had a few scary moments when he'd started. Aldo could throw the mother of all tantrums when he set his mind to it. The sort of thing that required an exorcist rather than a time out. But once Trey had discovered the handy trick of

simply ignoring them, Aldo's Damien routine had become less and less frequent.

But while he liked hanging out with Aldo, Aldo's older sister was a whole other matter. She'd been on his case from day one. And this wasn't the first time he'd heard her bad-mouthing him to her mum. And calling him Mr Perfecto.

He'd been unfailingly civil and polite back, or as polite as it was possible to be when someone took great pleasure in needling you, but after three months of watching Lizzie fly off the handle over nothing, not to mention witnessing her never-ending strops and mood swings, the urge to kick back was becoming harder and harder to resist.

'Aren't you going to cut the crusts off?' Aldo said, reminding Trey he didn't have time to consider Lizzie Best's personality disorder. If they didn't get a move on, they were liable to become the target of it.

'You know I hate them,' Aldo added, apparently more concerned about an excess of fibre in his diet than the oestrogen apocalypse going on outside the kitchen door.

'You'll just have to deal.' Trey shoved the cling-filmed sandwiches into Aldo's backpack on top of the crisps and juice box he'd raided from the larder.

'But I'll puke if I have to eat them.' Aldo was nothing if not persistent.

'Don't be so moist. You think John Terry gets his crusts cut off?' The Chelsea deity was Trey's go-to guy whenever Aldo went into serious pester mode. He used the hallowed Terry trump only in cases of emergency. But when Lizzie stomped into the room and climbed onto the stool next to her brother's at the breakfast bar, sporting a face like a thundercloud, that wild puff of sunshine hair falling out of its haphazard ponytail, Trey decided this situation definitely qualified.

'I hate her. This whole set-up is so full of shit.' Lizzie thumped her toe against the counter.

Trey zipped the backpack, knowing better than to pick up the conversational gauntlet.

'What's Mum done?' Aldo piped up, apparently unaware of the feral glint in Lizzie's eyes that said she was likely to gut the next poor bastard who opened their mouth.

'Shut up, you little turd. Like you care.'

'I'm not a turd. You are.'

'Come on, guys, give it a rest.' Trey steeled himself to pull them apart, but instead of thumping Aldo, or having a go at him, Lizzie stared at the countertop.

'I can't believe she still doesn't trust me. At all.'

She didn't sound sulky. She sounded genuinely hurt—as only an eighteen-year-old drama queen could, but her distress arrowed under Trey's usually reliable sense of self-preservation.

'You OK?' he asked.

Her gaze met his and he noticed the sheen of moisture turning the bold blue of her irises a shade darker. The colour matched the Tottenham away strip from last season now, instead of the bluebells he remembered from a rainy camping holiday in Wiltshire with his mum.

Lizzie stared blankly at him, as if she were surprised to see him there. She had amazing eyes. He'd always thought so, even though he pretended not to notice stuff like that. But there was no avoiding noticing this time. Her gaze captivated him, the stormy blue changing shade with her emotions, the lashes long and elegant even with all the gunk she put on them.

She blinked and the spell broke, the sulky irritation returning. 'Excuse me, are you confusing me with someone you actually give a toss about?'

Trey mentally kicked himself. Seemed he was as clueless as Aldo when it came to keeping his mouth shut.

He slung the backpack to Aldo. 'Why don't you give your mum a break?' *And stop acting like a two-year-old.* 'She's a busy woman and she's on her own.'

The intriguing tilt at the corners of Lizzie's round eyes went all squinty.

'I know how busy she is. Or she wouldn't be pissing off on a US book tour. And she's hardly on her own. She has a whole army of minions.' Her gaze raked over him, making it crystal his rank in Halle Best's minion army was no higher than foot soldier.

'Yeah, well...' He shrugged, swallowing the urge to snap back. 'This minion's got work to do.' He rubbed Aldo's crown. The boy giggled, reminding him why he was never going to let the Drama Queen's snooty barbs hit home. Or notice how amazing her eyes were, ever again. 'Let's get you to school, Bcast Boy.'

Aldo clambered off his stool and bid Lizzie a wary goodbye. But as they headed for the back door together, Trey could feel her arresting gaze boring two eye-sized holes into the base of his skull.

And the skin on his neck heated accordingly.

* * *

'Thanks for nada, Mr Perfecto,' Lizzie whispered.

How come he was always right there, watching, and judging, and making her feel like even more of a loser?

Aldo yelled with boyish excitement as Trey Carson challenged him to a race up the outdoor stairs. Trey let her brother have a head start, then sprinted up the stairs after him, his body a blur of graceful, athletic motion as he disappeared from view.

Her knee twitched, her heart beating in heavy thuds.

He made her nervous, that was all it was. She certainly didn't fancy him. He might be fit but he seemed so old and boring. He certainly wasn't cool. He wore straight-legs like her dad, instead of skinny jeans, and battered Nike high-tops, which would have been OK, except they looked as if he actually used them for sports. He was way too serious. He thought her mum was Wonder Woman. And he hadn't updated his Facebook status since last year. Plus, he wasn't even on Instagram, or Snapchat, or WhatsApp, or Twitter, because she'd checked.

But there *was* something about the width of his shoulders beneath his un-hip polo shirts. Something about the way his short hair curled over the top of his ears that should have looked goofy but didn't. Something about the scent of lemon soap and spearmint gum that clung to him, so unlike Liam's scent of eau de stale cigarette butts.

What would it be like to spend time with Trey? To talk to him without resorting to her habitual snark?

Lizzie took her iPhone out of her back pocket and texted Carly. She needed a distraction. The latest argument with her mum must have messed with her sanity if she was actually feeling disappointed she hadn't been able to walk the devil child to school with the moist au pair.

Wozzup? she texted.

Nada. Watching *Friends* reruns... Carly's reply popped up two seconds later, because her best friend was surgically attached to her phone and her texting skills were autistic. U know, The One Where Rach Sucks Joey's dick!!!

Lizzie choked out a laugh, glad her friend couldn't see the insta-blush firing up her neck. You wish.

FYI *Friends* would have been amaze-balls as a porno. Bet Joey's beef is at least 10 inches, Carly replied.

Fancy a trip to Primani 2morrow? Lizzie texted back,

before Carly mortified her even more by teasing her about the size of Trey's beef again.

Thought you were doing something with Superstar-Mum?

She's going on a book tour in the US. No biggie. Means more quality time with my BFF. Lizzie typed the fake reply not wanting to let on to Carly how disappointed she was her mum had bailed on her again.

Carly was not a good ear. Not only did Lizzie have the sneaking suspicion her BFF was more interested in her mum's celebrity than she was in her—ever since *Heat* magazine had published a blurred photo of Lizzie and her mum shopping in Knightsbridge at Christmas, Carly had convinced herself Lizzie's life out-glammed that of the Brangelina clan—Carly had accused her of being a baby if she moaned about her mum's work schedule. So now Lizzie kept her resentment a secret, because she didn't want Carly to know her life was actually about as glamorous as Lisa Simpson's or that Super Nanny, as Carly had nicknamed Trey, thought she was a bigger brat than Bart.

Bullcrap, I'm off to that thing in Clapham 2morrow w/ Kip & the guys. Want 2 cum?

Lizzie stared at Carly's answering text and wanted to hurl her iPhone against the kitchen wall. She stifled the burst of temper, and the hurt beneath, mainly because she knew her mum would refuse to pay for yet another cracked phone screen. But seriously? How could Carly ask that, when she knew Kip and the 'guys' would include Liam? But then, of course she would, because her so-called BFF had told her she was being a baby about Liam, too.

'*Why are you getting so worked up. It was only a BJ, it was only once and it was Amber's eighteenth. And she's fancied Liam for ages.*'

When Lizzie had argued that perhaps Liam should have stumped up some cash for a present for Amber rather than gift-wrapping his cock, she'd got Carly's trademark eye-roll and the one word Lizzie had begun to hate with a passion. Because Liam had used it all the time, too. When he said she was getting too pushy, or too clingy, or doing what he called her 'stalker vibe'.

Whatever.

A word that basically said, *Don't bug me, don't bother me, don't make such a fuss about bugger all. Your opinion, your feelings, your pride don't matter in the big fat scheme of things that do matter.*

You've got a boyfriend who gets caught getting a BJ from one of your friends at her birthday party?

Whatever.

You've got a mum who takes time out from her busy *HELLO!*-style life only because she's having some weird freak-out about you being anorexic?

Whatever.

You've got a dad who still thinks you're his smart, witty, wonderful baby girl. When you know you're not?

Whatever.

You've got a little brother who used to look at you as if you were Hermione Granger and a Powerpuff Girl all rolled into one, but now looks at you as if you're an unexploded bomb?

Whatever.

You're going to be stuck for two weeks with a guy who's weirdly hot but thinks you're a bitch?

Whatever.

Somehow or other that one word had become a curse. And she hated it. But she knew, deep down, there was one thing she hated more than that bastard, buggering, like-I-give-a-shit word...

And that one thing was herself.

She'd dated Liam and given him BJs until her jaw ached because everyone else thought he was cool. She never confided in Carly, even though they were supposed to be BFFs, because she was scared Carly might drop her. She almost wished she did have anorexia because at least then she would feel as if she deserved her mum's attention. Her dad didn't know what she was really like because she didn't have the guts to tell him. Aldo was scared of her because she'd gone postal on him once too often. And Trey thought she was a bitch because most of the time she was. Especially with him. Because...

Because she might be developing a small, inconvenient crush on him. A crush she could never ever let him know about. Because if he found out, he'd be horrified and she'd be mortified.

Her mum and her mum's celebrity had come to symbolise all the things that were wrong with Lizzie's life. But she knew the Domestic Diva was only really responsible for—at most—half of them. The rest of Lizzie's failings were entirely down to Lizzie.

She texted Carly back. Thnx, but I've got to help out with Aldo while my mum's away.

Just pretending her mum would trust her with that responsibility felt good for a moment. But it was another lie, of course. Trey didn't need help with her brother. He was far too efficient for that. And her brother didn't want to spend time with her any more, because Trey was the Aldo Whisperer now.

No wonder her mum had wanted Trey to move in for two weeks. Humiliation sat like a lump of uncooked dough in her stomach. Raw and stodgy and indigestible.

WotevZ. I'll txt u next wk. Enjoy the mini-terminator. And c if you can size up Super Nanny's meat while your at it. Carly's text finished with a grinning devil emoji. And then another one with red cheeks.

The heat flushed all the way to Lizzie's hairline as she texted back a grinning devil as if she was up for the idea, like the fraud she was.

Whatever.

Chapter 5

Halle slotted her new Audi A8 into her dedicated parking space, under the neon sign emblazoned across the brick wall of her cake design studio in Hammersmith.

Best's Bespoke Bakery—Designer Confectionery from the Domestic Diva.

The quiet purr of the car's powerful engine died as she turned off the ignition. The A8 had been a present to herself last Christmas, when her sixth book had topped the *Sunday Times* non-fiction bestseller list. Driving it was usually a great way to lift her mood.

But not today.

She let her gaze linger on the studio's sign while she dialled her assistant, Mel, but the retro swirl of lipstick-red neon wasn't giving her the usual ego boost today, either.

She was still feeling guilty about having to lie to Lizzie this morning—inventing a fictitious US book tour to stave off any unanswerable questions about the two weeks she was about to spend in Tennessee with Lizzie's dad. And Lizzie's predictably pissed-off reaction to the news.

'Hi, Mel,' she said when her PA picked up. 'Just checking

in to find out if the final paperwork came through from Jamie yet.'

Maybe all was not lost.

She didn't have to go anywhere if Luke hadn't signed on the dotted line. Which as of yesterday included her stipulation that he agree not to tell Lizzie about their trip. She didn't want her daughter involved in this fiasco. She was emotionally fragile enough. Why stress her out about something when it meant nothing? If Lizzie figured things out once Luke's article was published, Future Halle could handle it.

'Yup, Jamie emailed it this morning. Apparently, Luke wasn't too happy about the confidentiality clause. But he's signed it.'

'OK, I guess I really am going to Tennessee tomorrow, then.' Halle let out the breath she'd been holding and ticked off the item on the to-do list in her head. The to-do list that would never end. 'I assume everything's booked?'

'Yes, the flight leaves at ten from Heathrow.'

'How long is it?' Where was Tennessee anyway? Hopefully not too far from New York. She'd never been a big fan of hanging suspended in a metal box thirty thousand feet above sea level.

'Nine hours and forty minutes.'

'Nine...' *So nowhere near New York, then. Bollocks.* 'There isn't a shorter flight?'

'I checked. You could get a shorter flight to New York and then transfer for a flight to Atlanta, but there's a four-hour stopover in Newark.'

'Oh...' *Shit.* The take-offs were always the worst part. Two flights would not be better than one. 'Fine.'

She jotted down 'pack Xanax' on the never-say-die to-do list to keep her calm during take-off.

'Are Luke and I travelling together?'

'Yes, he's hiring a car in Atlanta to do the three-hour drive to the resort. It's all in the itinerary I sent through from him a week ago.'

'Right, of course.' That would be the itinerary sitting on her laptop that she had been avoiding. She added 'read itinerary and weep' to the list. Followed by 'pack extra-strength Xanax'. After sixteen years of avoidance, she was going to be spending close to thirteen hours in a confined space with the man. She might need to get comatose.

'The car's booked for six tomorrow to take us to the airport. I spoke to Dave at Crystal PR and he said the publicity junket for the next season of *Best of Everything* won't kick into high gear till you get back, so you're all clear there. Plus, Becky at Random House said there's nothing more to do on the next book till they get the flats from the printers. Is there anything else you need me to do before tomorrow?'

'No, I'm good, thanks, Mel.' Or as good as it was possible to be in her current circumstances. Rearranging her schedule had been easier than expected. And she could certainly do with a break. It would have been nice, though, if this particular break didn't include a travelling companion she had no desire to see again in this lifetime. 'I'm going to spend the next couple of hours getting everything up to speed at the studio. Then I thought I'd do the kids a home-cooked meal tonight.'

She popped 'hit Waitrose' onto the list.

'What a nice idea,' Mel said dutifully. 'What are you cooking?'

'Vegetable lasagne and key lime pie.'

Not exactly a menu worthy of Britain's best-loved baking guru, but Aldo had fixated on key lime pie during their trip to Disney World last summer while Lizzie was with Luke,

and vegetable lasagne had once been Lizzie's favourite dish
of hers. Back when Lizzie had been proud of her mum's career as a master chef.

'They'll love that,' Mel said with a lot more enthusiasm
than Halle felt.

'I hope so,' Halle replied, not holding out much hope. Her
daughter's sulks weren't known for their brevity. So she was
already braced for the silent treatment over the dinner table
after this morning's bust-up.

After saying goodbye to Mel, Halle unplugged her iPhone
from the car's charger and headed into the studio. Once part
of a Victorian wharf used for storing marble imported into
the city—back when the Thames was the main thoroughfare for bringing goods in and out of London—the rehabbed
brick building was now the bedrock of the Domestic Diva
brand.

Halle walked through the tinted glass double doors, waved
to Jonno, their receptionist, then strolled past the luxury
meeting rooms used for client consultations and tastings
and into the cavernous open-plan kitchen at the back. Glass
panelling had been used to replace the old warehouse's loading doors during the refurbishment, flooding the space with
natural light and gifting her dedicated kitchen staff of two
food stylists, one master baker and a couple of assistants
with a spectacular view of the Thames and the grandiose
Harrods Depository on the opposite bank.

Halle loved the way the space made a statement. Of mo-
dernity and ambition.

She breathed in the scent of freshly baked sponge and rose
water. This was where her career had finally taken flight.
Where all those nights spent baking, icing and moulding
decorations in the tiny kitchen of her council flat in Hackney
while the kids were asleep had been validated. But today,

the clean, striking lines of the stainless steel catering ovens and the industrious chatter of her workforce weren't giving her any more of a lift than the sign outside.

Yet more proof—not that she needed it—that she was not looking forward to tomorrow's trip.

The two assistants sent her awed looks from their workbenches. She waved back, in too much of a rush today to stop and have a team-building pep talk about the commission they were working on. From the delicate white and pink sugar flowers they were both moulding out of flower paste, she guessed they were busy on the wedding cake she'd designed for a D-list celebrity a couple of weeks ago.

She raced up the steps to the mezzanine level, which looked down over the baking hub, her sensible heels clicking on the steel risers. Arriving at the glass cubicle she used a couple of days a week as her office, she booted up her computer and collapsed into her chair.

She would also need to fit in a quick, confidential chat with Trey Carson at some point. She added the new item to the to-do list from hell as she opened the document marked 'Consultation Schedule' on her desktop.

Given her daughter's not exactly ecstatic reaction to the news that Trey was going to be sleeping over for the next fourteen days, she ought to give the guy a heads-up on some of her daughter's issues. Figuring out how to do that subtly enough so as not to tread on Lizzie's already fragile ego, or have it lead to World War Three if she found out Halle had spoken to Trey, would have to be another problem for Future Halle, though.

Because Present Halle was too busy mentally kicking Past Halle's arse for agreeing to Luke's stupid stunt in the first place.

Why hadn't she walked away in the Café Hugo three

weeks ago, when Luke had begun talking in tongues about love doctors and *Vanity Fair* articles? Would stopping Luke's memoirs—correction, phantom memoirs—be worth getting stranded for two weeks with him in the Tennessee wilderness however luxurious the resort?

As soon as she'd been back on the Eurostar, in the soulless comfort of first class, without Luke's don't-be-a-chicken smile daring her to lose her grip on reality, the rational, sensible answer to that question had seemed fairly obvious.

Two weeks against phantom-memoir stoppage? Good deal? Um, no.

What she should have done in Paris was tell Luke to take his love-surgeon-article bollocks and shove it right up his superbly toned backside.

But in Café Hugo, the reckless, impulsive, insane streak, which Luke had mined so easily when she was sixteen, had come out of hiding for one last hurrah. And she'd taken him up on the dare.

Once she was back in the UK, and Jamie had fired her an email with the subject line 'Is Your Ex Delusional?' she still could have denied all knowledge of the devil's bargain she'd made with Luke and got Jamie to handle the fallout. But she hadn't. She'd had him draw up a contract for Luke to sign.

Et voilà. She was now having to abide by her side of that contract.

So really the only person to blame for this monumental error of judgement was herself.

Or rather that part of herself—the part she thought had died sixteen years ago while trudging round East London trying to find the father of her child—that refused to back down from a challenge.

Back then, that part of herself had been valiant and stupidly optimistic and determined to prove Luke still loved

her. Now that part of herself was valiant and fatalistic and determined to prove she was totally over him.

But that still gave Present Halle an excellent reason to give Past Halle a really good kicking.

A tap on the door frame helped halt Halle's growing multiple personality disorder from getting any worse. She spotted Carrie, the design studio's general manager and all-round admin superstar, standing on the threshold. Halle winced at the fluorescent pink-and-orange tie-dye mini-dress, which clashed spectacularly with the electric-blue highlights in Carrie's hair.

'Halle, were we expecting you? I didn't have anything in my schedule,' Carrie said, reminding Halle her general manager had a much saner approach to office admin than she did to wardrobe choices.

'Slight change of plans. I'm going to be out of the country for two weeks as of tomorrow.' *In Nowheresville, Tennessee, no doubt whopping Past Halle's arse for the duration.* 'So I thought I'd come in to do a quick run-through of the schedule while I'm away. You'll have to take any client consultations that can't be rearranged.'

'Hold on.' Carrie's brows shot up. 'You're taking a holiday? For two whole weeks?'

The shock on Carrie's face suggested it had been longer than she'd thought since her last two-week break.

'It's not a holiday, exactly. It's more of a personal thing,' she said, sticking to the minimalist story she'd worked out in lieu of the book tour one, which Carrie would see through straight away as she had access to Halle's schedule.

Telling her staff the truth had been quickly discarded. Having to explain to them about Luke and his article would only complicate things. Plus, she didn't want to risk any leaks. This trip was about getting closure for the shockingly bad

life choices she'd made as a teenager. And not about giving the gossip mags a chance to editorialise said shockingly bad life choices for the benefit of their judgemental readers.

'A personal thing?' Carrie looked intrigued, then clapped her hands with glee. 'You found a Mr Best? That's terrific. My work is done.'

Carrie knew about Luke? How the...?

'No wonder you nixed all my blind date suggestions,' Carrie continued with a mock pout. 'You were busy trolling on your own. You could have told me.'

Trolling? Blind date suggestions? Wait a minute. Carrie had said *a* Mr Best.

Oh, thank fuck.

This conversation had nothing to do with Luke and everything to do with her GM's Cupid delusion. Carrie had met Alan the folk guitarist, aka Mr Right On, eighteen months ago and been on a mission to spread the love ever since. Halle was one of the few people at the studio who'd avoided getting stabbed in the arse by Carrie's love dart.

'There is no Mr Best,' Halle said emphatically. *Or not one anyone need know about.* 'And I'm not looking for one. I have a perfectly good vibrator I can date if I need to.'

Not that she'd had many dates with her vibrator lately. In fact, when was the last time she'd gotten Bugs, her Rampant Rabbit, out of the bedside drawer? She did a quick calculation.

Good Lord, had it actually been Christmas Eve? Six whole months?

No wonder Luke's tactile thumb had given her a hot flush. Well, at least it was good to know the anxiety of seeing him again hadn't induced a stress menopause.

She slotted 'get Bugs out of mothballs' onto her to-do list.

'Vibrators can't hug you like a man can,' Carrie stated

with a sanguine look. 'Unless your vibrator's a new model I haven't heard of.'

'Hugs are overrated, as is all the bullshit that goes with them when men supply them.'

'Halle!' Carrie looked scandalised. 'Don't be so cynical. Not all men are bastards.'

'And not all men are like Mr Right On,' Halle countered, cutting the edge out of her voice. Just because she'd learned there was no such thing as a free hug, Carrie didn't need to know that. Yet. 'Now, could we please stop talking about my love life?'

'Dating a vibrator does not count as a love life,' Carrie said emphatically, but she stepped into the cubicle and sat in the spare chair.

Halle shot her a severe look.

Carrie threw back her you're-still-on-my-dating-hit-list look, before saying, 'So where do you want to start? With the client consultation schedule or the fact that the Kane Corporation CEO has come up with yet another brilliant suggestion for the decoration on their sixtieth-anniversary cake?'

'You're joking? But we signed off on that design weeks ago. And isn't the event this Saturday evening?' In two days' time.

The studio took on only about eight hundred cakes a year now. All bespoke designs mostly for celebrity parties or huge corporate events and all handmade by the fabulous team she'd assembled. But even so, each cake had to have the unique Halle Best stamp on it. That's what her clients were paying thousands of pounds per cake for. With her TV and publishing commitments, she no longer had the time to spend hours painstakingly moulding Mexican modelling paste or baking sponges or mixing crumb coating, so her job mostly involved

fronting the studio's PR initiatives, creating the basic designs, instructing the team and schmoozing the clients.

Right from the start, the Kane Corporation's cake had been a hard sell, and an even harder schmooze. Carlton Foster, the CEO, who had insisted on consulting with Halle personally, had been adamant about showcasing the company's product range on the cake because the party would be getting lots of exposure on their social media platforms. Unfortunately, it was next to impossible to make a cake topped with syringes, surgical gloves, catheters and bedpans look edible, let alone appetising. After much negotiation, and some extracurricular schmoozing, Halle had managed to satisfy Foster's marketing zeal while also hopefully preventing his guests' gag reflexes from engaging by suggesting a five-tiered dark chocolate sponge iced with a raspberry and tangerine white chocolate ganache—black, red and orange being the colours of the Kane Corporation logo—decorated with a tasteful montage of 3D illustrations from the company's iconic advertising campaigns of the past sixty years. Foster had signed off on the design two weeks ago. And the party was happening on Saturday at the Kensington Roof Gardens. The sponges would have been baked. The decorations would already be in production. They simply didn't have time for any major rethinks. Or redesigns. But even so…

'What's the suggestion?' *Please don't let it involve the return of the bedpans.*

Halle wanted to be as flexible as possible. When it came to big-occasion cakes, last-minute suggestions or panic attacks were the customers' prerogative. Especially if they were paying ten thousand pounds for the privilege.

'Foster is really keen for us to incorporate something

to illustrate Kane's latest charitable initiative in the Third World.'

'OK.' That didn't sound too disastrous. One new tableau should be doable. If they could persuade one of the stylists to work overtime to get a head start on the new decoration and she could work out a design for it before she left tomorrow morning. 'What's the initiative?'

Carrie smiled, sheepishly. 'A programme to distribute free condoms in sub-Saharan Africa.'

Halle's smile faded as she slapped 'kill Carlton Foster' onto the top of her to-do list.

Chapter 6

What exactly is the point of online check-in?

Luke stood in the queue for the bag-drop desk in Heathrow's Terminal Two, which snaked halfway to Manchester, his boot tapping against the industrial flooring. As a person who'd been born with a serious case of wanderlust, he knew pointless queues were a necessary evil of air travel. But he'd had a six a.m. wake-up call, despite being up till two at his hotel to meet a deadline on a piece for *Time* magazine, to allow for the queue at security—which still loomed large, and no doubt even longer, in his future. So this sodding queue was above and beyond the call of duty.

Halle strode through one of the terminal's revolving doors, followed by a mini entourage that consisted of a woman talking on her smartphone and an older man pushing a trolley with far too many suitcases on it. Luke's boot stopped in mid-tap, as did the dictation in his head of his letter of complaint to the moron who thought two measly bag-drop staff was enough.

From the parade of double takes that followed Halle and her mini entourage through the terminal, it was clear several people recognised her. No one approached her, though. Not

surprising, given those bugger-off vibes she was radiating with every crisp, purposeful stride.

She looked immaculate, and invincible, her hair swept up in a style that left her face bare, but for the few teasing tendrils dangling down her neck. The intimidating light blue power suit and heels were probably some pricey designer brand, a matching set to the outfit she'd worn in Paris. The hum of attraction kicked off in his crotch, annoying him the same way it had when he'd swung round at her gasp in Café Hugo.

Ruthlessly coiffured and expertly styled dominatrix types were not his thing. He preferred a woman who didn't look as if she were about to conquer Poland. But that hadn't stopped him having to stifle all sorts of inappropriate urges while sitting opposite her in Hugo's, mostly involving plucking the pins out of her hairdo and watching the honey-blonde curls bounce off her shoulders.

Funny to think how sunny and unassuming she'd been when they were kids. Young and open and ridiculously naive. Of course, she'd been sixteen going on twenty then, and an exceptionally bad judge of character. Or she wouldn't have attempted to hand him her heart on a platter.

Halle's brows rose as she spotted him, but her gaze remained cool and impersonal.

The composed assessment should have been a welcome relief from the radioactive glare she'd lasered at him three weeks ago over croissants and millefeuille. But it felt more like an anticlimax.

He'd been expecting fireworks. Had prepared for them, ready to offer her a quick apology for what had happened sixteen years ago, thus knocking the hefty chip she still appeared to be carrying around off her shoulder.

The blank look wrong-footed him.

'Hi, Hal.' The tension in his shoulders relaxed despite his disappointment. At least she'd shown up. 'You made it.'

'I made you a promise. And I keep my promises.'

Right. 'Good thing I saved you a place in the queue, then,' he said, deflecting the deliberate dig with a certain amount of gratification.

Maybe not fireworks, then, but definitely a sparkler or two. Sparklers he could work with.

'Aren't we in business class?'

Her proprietary question lit a few sparklers of his own. 'This *is* the business queue. The economy one stretches all the way to Madagascar. I guess they didn't get the memo that business people don't queue.' Or celebrities, apparently.

'Mel, could you go over to the first-class check-in and see if we can arrange an upgrade?' she instructed the woman beside her.

The perky assistant nodded and headed for the empty first-class desk. The old guy followed suit with Halle's bags, leaving them alone—if you didn't count the ten thousand people in the queue.

'You sure you want to waste an extra five grand just to avoid a queue?' he asked, even though he guessed she probably never travelled anything but first now.

The thought lit another sparkler.

'I was up last night until one trying to design a cake decoration inspired by free condoms that didn't actually involve making little foil packets out of modelling paste. So yes, the five grand is well worth it. I need to sleep on this flight.'

They did beds in business. The business class flights he'd paid for out of his own pocket so he could get his apology over and done with. But he refused to let her snotty attitude

or the juvenile reaction in his groin triggered by the word 'condoms' get to him. 'Sounds tasteful, what's the cake for, a stag do?'

'You'd think, but no,' she said cryptically.

The assistant returned looking pleased with herself. 'I've got you an upgrade to first. Derek's loading the bags.'

'Wonderful, thanks, Mel.' Halle turned back to him, her relief palpable for a second, before she covered it with a polite smile. 'I guess I'll see you in Atlanta.'

He frowned after her as she marched off to the first-class check-in.

OK, what was that about? Because the hairs on the back of his neck were going haywire, a sure sign he'd been played.

He did what he always did when his journalistic radar was telling him a source wasn't being entirely truthful. He examined the evidence.

Halle had always been super frugal when they had been together. Pinching every penny—especially the ones they didn't have. And while she had money now, probably more money than she knew what to do with, Lizzie frequently moaned about her mum's penny-pinching ways. So splashing the cash still wasn't her style. Why, then, had she bumped herself up to first, when she could sleep just as easily in business without paying five grand for the privilege?

He watched Halle say goodbye to her crew and head towards the departure gates. She didn't look back at him. His journalistic radar went into meltdown.

Son of a bitch. In business she'd be next to him.

Was that it? She was still trying to stonewall him?

Bugger that. He swung his leather holdall over his shoulder and crossed to the first-class desk. He wasn't into unnecessary expenditure, either, but she'd spent sixteen years

not talking to him. Five grand didn't seem like too much to pay to stop her buying him off for another ten hours.

Here endeth the silent treatment.

* * *

Ushered through the boarding gate, Halle clutched her carry-on luggage, stocked with anti-nausea medication, antacids and the Xanax—which she'd dosed up on in the car on her way to the airport.

She was over Luke. She just wasn't over him enough to spend nine hours and forty minutes in a plane freaking out while he sat beside her being composed and competent and annoyingly buff.

The quest for closure could wait until she was good and ready to deal with it.

And after the hours she'd put in last night finishing off the Kane redesign, the five grand it had cost her for ten extra hours of karma was a totally justifiable expense.

Especially as the Xanax didn't appear to be working yet. Which had to explain why spotting Luke standing in the bag-drop queue in battered jeans and a leather jacket, with his hair dishevelled and his jaw covered in stubble, had made her body hum as if she'd been plugged into an electric socket.

'May I take your bag, Ms Best?' A flight attendant with immaculate make-up and a chignon that could withstand a nuclear holocaust beamed at her as she stepped aboard the plane.

Halle tightened her grip on the bag. 'No, thank you.'

The attendant led her past the galley and the functional luxury of business class and up a spiral staircase into a section way too reminiscent of a vintage *Star Trek* set. Eerie blue-toned lighting illuminated a series of pods, each furnished with a reclining seat, a mirrored wall, a control panel

of knobs that would confuse Lieutenant Uhura and enough leather to fit out an S&M boutique.

Halle tucked her bag into her assigned pod and tried not to think of all the other much more useful and tangible things she could have done with the five grand her flight aboard the Starship *Enterprise* was costing. She was a celebrity. She worked superhard. She had a very healthy bank balance these days. She was entitled to splurge on herself occasionally.

This was not because she'd panicked when she'd seen Luke. She could easily control any and all inappropriate reactions where he was concerned. Simply by remembering how much she despised him. This was because she deserved to pamper herself. And because the take-off alone could cause her acid reflux to go into overdrive—so why add to her stress with an audience?

There were only two other people travelling in first class: a balding, middle-aged executive seated four pods up, who was tapping industriously on his laptop, and an elderly woman three pods across, who was lying back with an eye mask on and was doing a great impression of being already dead.

I should be so lucky.

She quashed the spurt of panic. Once the take-off was over, she could let the pampering begin.

'Would you like a beverage, Ms Best?'

She briefly entertained the idea of deadening her anxiety with champagne. 'Some iced water would be great,' she replied. Getting legless could be her fallback position if the sedative didn't kick in soon.

Settling into her seat, she stared in dismay at the panel of buttons. Sweat collected on her upper lip and the muscles in

her neck began to twitch. If only one of those buttons could whisk her across the Atlantic at warp speed.

'How many knobs does one person need, right?'

Her head swung round so fast at the suggestive comment it was a miracle she didn't get whiplash.

'Luke, what the…?' She searched for the flight attendant. 'You're not supposed to be in here. They'll throw you out.'

'I'll risk it.' The sheepish expression on his too-handsome face instantly threw her back to their schooldays and all those times he'd done something diabolical—like spray-painting an image of Mrs Wendell going down on Mr Truer all over the sixth-form toilets—and she'd been his final line of defence against instant expulsion. Annoyance bunched in her neck muscles, but beneath it was the furtive spike of excitement. A mortifying reminder of how her sixteen-year-old self had once relished his bad behaviour.

'Relax.' He settled into the pod next to her. 'I got an upgrade, too.'

'What?'

He slung his laptop bag under his console while she gaped as if he'd just spoken in Swahili. Either that or she'd gone momentarily deaf and misheard him.

What had happened to Luke Best, class warrior? The guy who thought first-class train carriages were there to be invaded? Even business class had seemed like a stretch.

'I'm a frequent flyer. It only cost a couple of grand extra. And it's tax deductible.' He began to fiddle with the dials on his personal control panel. 'This is actually pretty cool.' Propping his feet on the footrest, he rolled his shoulders and relaxed into the seat. Then sent her a grin that plugged her right back into the electric socket.

'You can't stay here.' The in-flight trauma of taking off was bad enough, she did not need the one man capable of

giving her a nervous breakdown when she had both feet on terra firma as a witness to her humiliation.

'Try me.'

'But doesn't travelling in first go against everything you ever stood for? I distinctly remember you telling me once that the premium seats in Holloway Odeon were an exploitation of the working classes.'

'I've mellowed.'

'You mean you've sold out for a lie-flat bed and some complimentary champagne?' Why did it even surprise her? Luke had never had the courage of his convictions.

'There's complimentary champagne?' He rubbed his hands together. 'Damn, if I'd known that, I would have sold out sooner.'

The flight attendant returned with Halle's iced water.

'Hi there, Debbie,' he said, reading the woman's name badge. 'Is it true you get complimentary champagne in first?'

'Certainly, sir, would you like a glass?'

'You might as well bring the bottle. It's a ten-hour flight and I plan to get my money's worth.'

The attendant hesitated. 'We're only allowed to serve it by the glass I'm afraid, sir.'

'And it's ten o'clock in the morning,' Halle butted in. 'Drinking at altitude will get you pissed. You're supposed to be driving us to the resort when we get off this flying death trap. I refuse to get in a car with you if you're over the limit.' Hadn't the man grown up at all in sixteen years?

'I guess that's me told.' He flashed a sheepish smile at the attendant, whose cheeks shone pink beneath the ten layers of foundation. 'I guess I'll have to pass. I'll have what she's having,' he finished, indicating Halle's glass.

The purser's amplified voice filled the cabin giving them

a rundown of the in-flight services as the stewardess headed off to do Luke's bidding.

Halle gulped down the chilled water, but it did nothing to ease the rawness in her throat.

Shit, shit, shit.

She rolled the icy glass across her forehead, then bent to retrieve her bag.

'Why did you call it a "flying death trap"?'

She ignored Luke's question as she waged war with the child-safety lid on the Xanax bottle. Only to have the bottle whipped out of her hands.

'What are these for?'

'Give me those.' She made a grab for the bottle as he read the label, only to have him hike it out of reach.

'Heavy-duty happy pills. When did you start popping these?'

'It's not Ecstasy. It's a mild drug to help with anxiety. And it's none of your business what pills I pop.'

'Mild, my arse. This stuff can kill you if you take too much of it.'

'You *are* joking?' She skewered him with her best give-me-a-bloody-break look. 'This from the guy who once had so much E he ran down Green Lanes naked declaring to the whole of Hackney he was Sonic the Hedgehog.'

'I was seventeen,' he protested. 'It was Super Mario and I was only half naked, don't exaggerate.'

'Nope, it was definitely Sonic. I remember because I was sober.' Or soberish. 'And all you had on was a baseball cap!'

'Well, then I had all the essential stuff covered, didn't I?' He threw her the challenging grin again, daring her to deny it.

'Essential stuff? What, like your brain, you mean? That

certainly didn't qualify as essential at the time, given it wasn't the organ you did your thinking with.'

His eyes sharpened and she relished the hit. But then the captain's monotone tenor came over the public address system with a rundown of their flying time and their altitude over the Atlantic, and the brief surge of triumph was smothered in panic.

'Give me the bottle.' She stretched out a shaky palm. 'I need another before we take off.'

He lowered the bottle but didn't hand it over. 'How many have you had already?'

She pressed the tip of her tongue to her upper lip and tasted the salty sweat. 'Only one.' Or had it been two? Her mind seemed foggy on the details. But then the flight attendant strolled past to check their bays, and the plane rumbled into motion—and the panic became razor sharp. 'Luke, for Chrissake, hand them over.'

'Look at me.'

She squinted, trying to focus as he held two fingers in front of her face.

'Do you know your pupils are the size of pinpricks?'

'"Prick" being the operative word.' She made a grab for the bottle again and missed by about twenty nautical miles, her coordination skills—along with her dignity—now completely shot.

'Why do you need this stuff anyway?'

Why was he looking at her like that—all stern and concerned? And why couldn't she remember how to speak?

The plane made a lumbering turn onto the runway, then gathered speed. Her stomach lurched up to slam into her larynx. She gripped the armrest hard enough to fracture granite, her nails gouging the leather.

Flying is safe. Remember Rain Man. *You are not going to die.*

'Dammit, Hal, since when have you been scared of flying?'

She would have shot him another give-me-a-bloody-break look but she was far too busy clinging on for dear life.

'Why didn't you say something sooner?' he added.

Because it's stupid and irrational and humiliating and I'd rather lose a limb than admit a weakness to you.

'I'm not scared of flying,' she said, her fingers now fused with the leather. 'I just have issues with the whole concept.'

'What issues, exactly?'

He wanted to have a conversation about this now? When they were both about to die?

Extreme exasperation got the better of her terror for a second. 'Gravitational issues,' she snapped. 'Such as, how does a huge metal box that weighs several tons stay airborne?'

The plane tore away from the runway and her stomach—and the last of her courage—went into free fall.

Please don't let me start whimpering. Or puking.

'Hal, it's called aerodynamics,' he said, all knowledge and reason when she was embarking on a major panic attack.

His pure blue eyes blurred round the edges as she struggled to make sense of the statement. Her stomach rocked against her ribs as the plane banked. She caught a glimpse of chequerboard fields and ribbon roads dotted with toy cars through the window and slammed her eyes shut.

Do. Not. Look. Down. The first rule of upchuck avoidance.

'Excuse me if I'm not convinced by your knowledge of aerodynamics,' she hissed through clenched teeth. 'I happen to know you bunked off every physics lesson you ever had.'

'I did an article on the aerospace industry for a tech website last year.'

A weak scoffing sound was all she could manage, the

rumbling thud of the plane's undercarriage lifting into the fuselage echoing in her stomach.

'And, by the way, this plane is mostly made out of carbon fibre, not metal, if that helps.'

It didn't. She couldn't compute his words any more. Her head tipped back, anchored to the seat, as she ground her teeth hard enough to crack a molar.

'Oh, God.' She panted, hyperventilation the only way to keep breathing as the plane lifted into the cloud bank. Her stomach levitated into her throat. She swallowed convulsively to stop it vomiting out of her mouth. 'I'm not ready to die.'

That would be whimpering.

A warm palm covered the hand she had superglued to the armrest.

'You're not going to die. You're indestructible.' His palm curled over her whitening knuckles and his thumb stroked the small scar on her wrist left by the burn he'd noticed in Paris. 'If we crash, you'll bounce.'

She wanted to tell him he was right, she was indestructible, because she'd had to be. But she didn't feel indestructible. And she had lost the ability to talk, every single muscle and sinew in her jaw and neck having atrophied.

'I need a pill,' she finally managed to squeak. 'Please.' The begging would have embarrassed her, but in the grand apocalyptic scheme of things, having Luke smirk at her while she died didn't seem like such a big deal any more.

'Is everything OK, Ms Best?'

Halle prised open an eyelid to find the stewardess looking down at their joined hands with a benevolent smile.

'I'm fine.' Her whole body shuddered like an alcoholic recovering from an all-night bender. The stewardess didn't look convinced. 'If I could just…'

'For Chrissake, Hal.' Luke's grip on her hand tightened. 'You're freaking out. There's no shame in admitting it. Loads of people don't like flying.'

'I a-a-am not freaking out.' She never freaked out. She happened to be a champion coper—even if her chattering teeth weren't helping to emphasise the point.

'Let go of the chair,' he ordered. 'You're about to break your fingernails.'

'If I let go, I'll fall.' The plaintive plea sounded childish, even to her.

'You're strapped in, Hal. You're not going anywhere.'

'You won't fall, Ms Best. This is an Airbus 380, the newest and best-designed plane in our fleet.' The stewardess's soothing tone managed to be even more annoying than Luke's condescension.

'You don't know that,' she whimpered.

Luke's thumb caressed the web of flesh between her thumb and forefinger. 'I do. Now let go, I've got you.' He massaged into the pressure point. And her fingers released instinctively.

He threaded his fingers through hers and held on to her, just as he'd promised. 'See, you didn't fall.'

She rolled her head towards him, which wasn't easy given that the sinews in her neck had about as much give in them as steel suspension cables. And managed a small nod.

'Now breathe,' he commanded.

Air swelled into her lungs and gushed out as the plane's nose dipped to level off to their cruising altitude.

'That's it, keep doing what you're doing,' he prompted.

She concentrated on taking deep, even breaths, willing her lungs to cooperate. But continued to cling to his hand. The seat-belt sign pinged off and the purser's reassuring voice droned on about their cruising altitude and flight path.

Her gaze drifted to the fluffed cloudscape floating beneath them outside the window. The panic settled to purr under her breastbone, like a sleeping tiger ready to snarl at the first sign of danger, but subdued enough not to bite off her head at the slightest bump.

Luke squeezed her hand. 'You OK?'

'Yes,' she croaked, her throat sore as her neck muscles relaxed.

'You sure? You still look pretty spooked.' He searched her face.

She took another careful breath, sighed when it didn't hurt. 'The take-off's always the worse bit. I'll be OK now.' The Xanax must have finally kicked in, because she was starting to feel pleasantly numb.

Way to go, Xanax, only twenty minutes late to the party.

Luckily, Luke didn't call her on her euphoric state, because she wasn't quite ready to give him back his hand.

'You look terrible,' he said.

Way to go, Luke. You sure know how to make a girl feel good about herself.

'I'll look a lot better once I'm sure we aren't going to get struck by lightning, hit a freak snowstorm, get hijacked or generally encounter anything that might cause us to go down in flames en route.' The burst of verbal diarrhoea came naturally as the extreme panic downgraded to a bog-standard bout of nervous tension.

Nervous tension was doable. She knew how to handle that. She even knew how to use it to her advantage, because she'd had a lot of practice. Her nerves were an old and trusted friend.

The show's first executive producer had once told her that her reaction to stress was the secret of her success, because the sharp, perky motormouthed quips she used to

cope entertained while also making her totally relatable. Embracing the horrendous stage fright before every taping had become a key part of her 'Everywoman appeal'.

'Just so you know, if any of that stuff happens,' she added, on a roll as her body sank into the seat, 'I intend to arm-wrestle you for the Xanax. You have been warned.'

'If any of that stuff happens,' Luke replied drily, 'you're gonna need to be Dwayne Johnson to get to them, because I plan to bolt the lot.'

She laughed, the sound only slightly manic. And released his hand.

He flexed his fingers, probably checking for fractures, and she noticed the dark indents where her nails had dug into his skin.

'I'll keep these just in case.' He flipped the bottle and caught it one-handed. 'No more legal highs for you. Unless the slaphead executive over there turns out to be a hijacker.' He nodded at the bald businessman, who had already resumed typing on his laptop. 'In which case, let the arm-wrestling begin.'

He lifted his bum to shove the bottle of Xanax into the front pocket of his jeans, drawing her fuzzy gaze to his lap. The worn, comfortable denim cupped him, the metal studs of his button fly visible where the placket stretched over his groin. And a question from over twenty years ago popped into her head.

I wonder if he remembered to wear his underwear today?

Her pulse spiked and warmth settled into her lower body as she allowed her mind to drift into the safe, comforting fog of memory.

Chapter 7

She could smell dust and varnish and the faint whiff of boiled cabbage as she stood in the wings of the school hall's stage, waiting to do her piano solo for the Year Ten end-of-term recital.

Her school shoes scraped from side to side on the scuffed floorboards, her lungs sawing in and out. Clammy sweat trickled between her shoulder blades as she undulated the fingers of her right hand, miming the opening movement of the piece she'd practised for hours the previous after-noon. It had to be perfect, or her mum and dad might start questioning the cost of her weekly piano lessons. Then they would surely ring her piano teacher, Ms Havilland, to ask what was going on. And Ms Havilland would tell them their daughter had stopped coming to lessons months ago, and then her mum and dad would know she'd been pocketing the five-pound lesson fee to sneak off and hang out with Luke at the precinct.

And if that happened, her life would be over, because they would ground her forever and she'd never be able to see Luke again.

So, basically, her whole entire life was balancing on the

edge of a precipice, ready to plunge into the abyss at the sound of a single bum note in five minutes' time.

Wiry forearms banded round her waist and a calloused palm captured her gasp as her captor hefted her back into the secretive darkness backstage.

The scent of Lifebuoy soap and the sweet whiff of marijuana had the blast of recognition careering through her and all thoughts of Beethoven, bum notes and imminent disaster shot out of her head on a wild rush of adrenaline and adoration.

It's Luke. Luke's here. Luke will make everything all right.

'Luke, you shouldn't be here. Miss Giddings will have a fit,' she whispered frantically, the thrill pumping through her as she absorbed the determination on his face.

'Let her,' he said, and his lips covered hers.

Molly Tanner's halting rendition of 'Give Peace a Chance' on the pan pipes dimmed, obliterated by the buzz of excitement as Luke's tongue thrust deep, claiming her mouth in hungry furtive strokes. Rough fumbling fingers delved under the skirt her mum had ironed for her less than an hour ago and found the plump, yearning flesh already dampening the gusset of her knickers.

She cupped him in return—the illicit thrill of doing something forbidden streaking from the tips of her breasts to throb against his probing fingers. He hardened and lengthened against her palm, creating a big top in the coarse gaberdine of his uniform trousers.

'That feels ace.' He panted, cooling the sweaty hair stuck to her neck. The thrill turned to white-hot need, tempered by panic, when he ripped open his zipper and wrapped her fingers around the stiff column of naked flesh. Her hand jerked in shock.

'Where are your pants?'

'Forgot them this morning.' His breathing became hoarse and rapid. 'After this, I may never remember them again.'

She'd felt his erection before, prodding against her belly through their clothing when they kissed. She'd even seen it tenting his trousers when they'd done some heavy petting last Thursday, and it had fascinated her. But she'd never realised it would feel this wonderful. Soft and silky, and yet so large and rock hard. It leaped in her hand as she brushed her thumb over the head and made his breathing catch.

This was more than ace. It was totally amazing. To have this power over him, to know he wanted her this much.

His hand folded over hers, directing the speed and strength of her strokes, urging her on with soft grunts of approval.

'That's right, keep going, make me come.' His other hand yanked down her panties. 'I'm going to do you, too,' he hissed, thrilling her even more.

She bucked against his invading fingers as he parted her folds and discovered the burning spot at the top. Excruciating pleasure coiled between her legs.

'Oh!' She sobbed, biting into her lip to muffle the sound.

'Did I hurt you?' He stopped. 'Show me how to do it the way you like it.' His demand sounded feral, intense in the darkness.

'Don't stop, it didn't hurt,' she managed. She grabbed his wrist, directing him the way he had directed her, until he began to press and circle the right spot. 'That's it.'

'You're so wet down there,' he whispered, sounding surprised but pleased. 'It feels wonderful, all soft and slick.'

She grasped his erection again to stroke him, too.

'I know,' she said, as if she did know, but she didn't really.

She'd touched herself before, explored, but it had never made her feel like this. Terrified and desperate and cherished and bad all at once. The tight coil of need twisted

and yanked, ready to shove her off a cliff and make her pee herself at one and the same time.

He groaned as if he were dying, his face pressed into her hair. 'Oh, fuck, yes, yes, I'm coming.'

His thick cock grew even bigger, then jerked in her hand, splattering something warm against her belly where he'd wrenched up her skirt.

His body softened, but those magic fingers never faltered, still rubbing, circling, caressing. She widened her legs, rocked her hips to increase the pressure, and the coil yanked tighter, tighter…

'Hurry up, Hal, go for it.'

'Oh, yes… That's…'

His hand slapped over her mouth, just in time to silence her sobbing cry, as blue ribbons of fire blasted through her torso. White light shot in a glittering arc right out the top of her head, sensation cascading through her body like a Roman candle.

The thunder of applause sounded over the hammering of her pulse, her body's own standing ovation. But as she floated back to earth and saw Luke scrambling to stuff himself and his shirt tails back into his trousers, the enthusiastic clapping became real.

'Oh, bloody buggering hell, Molly's finished,' she whispered, shocked into full consciousness. Of where they were, and what they'd just done. Together.

Luke winked at her and grinned, the slash of white teeth making the slowing pulse in her clitoris spike. 'She's not the only one.'

She wiggled her knickers on, suppressing a snigger, horrified and excited by the funky smell of fresh semen.

Miss Giddings's voice rang out from the stage announcing Haley Dunlop in Form 10C and the piece she was playing.

She scrambled faster. 'I can't go out there.' The chances of her remembering let alone being able to play Beethoven's 'Moonlight Sonata' now was so outside the realm of possibility she might as well have been orbiting Mars. And if she messed this up, everything would be ruined. Her parents would find out about Luke. And stop her from seeing him again. Ever.

''Course you can.' Luke pressed a quick kiss to her nose. 'You can do anything. You're indestructible.'

'But what if they can tell what we've been doing?'

'Who cares?' Spinning her round, he placed a firm hand on her bum and gave her a hefty shove.

She stumbled onto the stage, her cheeks bright with embarrassment, her nerves jangling discordantly, her senses dazed and disorientated. She scanned the hall of bored and encouraging faces, only to spot her mum and dad in the second row, clapping as if she'd won a Nobel Prize.

Startled into movement, she rushed across the never-ending ocean of varnished wood and plopped onto the piano stool, trembling uncontrollably, the feel of semen sticky under her skirt. Could they all see the guilty flush scalding her neck? Or smell Luke's fresh jizz from the stage?

She shot a furtive look over her shoulder and could just about make out Luke's tall figure lurking in the shadows, sending her go-for-it vibes.

Her fingers touched the keyboard, and the complex sequence of carefully rehearsed notes flowed out of the tips on cue. Beethoven's love song—daring and eloquent—reverberated through her as a conspiratorial grin flirted at the edges of her mouth and the feeling of freedom and rebellion sank deep into her soul.

Holy shit. She'd just been treated to her first proper orgasm by the baddest, best-looking boy in the school while

the headmaster, her form tutor, her music teacher and even her parents were less than ten feet away—and it had been amazing. Super amazing.

Being Luke Best's girlfriend was the best thing that had happened to her in her whole entire life. And she would love him forever.

Chapter 8

'Err-hem.'

The sound of throat clearing beckoned Halle back to the present.

'You want to tell me why you've entered a fugue state?' Luke's adult voice, gruffer now and with a cynical edge, hauled her the rest of the way out of memory and into the Airbus 380. 'And why you appear to be fixated on my family jewels?'

She blinked and lifted her head, feeling as if she'd had an out-of-body experience. Out of body except for the hum of heat still throbbing at the memory of his clumsy but devastating caresses. Strange to realise the long fingers now dusted with hair, resting benignly on the armrest, had once sent her soaring into the stratosphere so eagerly.

As a teenager, Luke had been a generous, inquisitive lover. Their sex life hadn't always been good. In fact, it had been bloody awful at times, like the first time they'd had penetrative sex. And the second. And the third. But still he'd tried, always striving to get her off as well as himself. She doubted many teenage boys, now or then, would be that bothered about their girlfriends' satisfaction.

She blinked away the sentimental thought. Luke may have been a generous lover, but why should he get a medal for that? Especially considering he'd had an ulterior motive. He'd been practising his moves on her only so he'd be ready when someone better came along.

The prickle of jealousy made the question in her head spill out of her mouth. 'Do you still forget to wear underwear, like you used to at school?'

It probably wasn't the most diplomatic thing to say, but she suddenly wasn't feeling all that diplomatic. This man had fingered her to her first climax at a fifth-form recital. An erotic moment that was far too vividly imprinted on her brain.

His cheekbones flushed a dull red but it took her several seconds to realise he was blushing. Because she'd only ever seen him blush once before—when she'd come out of the bathroom to show him the pink PREGNANT sign on the pee stick.

'I'm wearing pants now,' he said. 'If that's what you're asking?'

'Why did you?'

'Why did I what?' He looked affronted now as well as embarrassed. A double whammy.

'Forget it. Because now I think about it, that was rather skanky.'

It hadn't seemed at all skanky at the time. It had been hot, but why boost his ego.

'Skanky? Gee, thanks.' The flush spread over his cheekbones.

'Why are you blushing? You used to boast about your commando status at school.'

'No, I didn't.'

'Then how come everyone knew about it?'

'Because I got caught without them once in the locker room by Mr Spurgeon, the gym teacher, and he humiliated me in front of the whole class. I guess word got around after that.'

'All the more reason to try to remember to wear them more regularly, then,' she volleyed back, suppressing the niggle of sympathy.

Luke had forever been in trouble with the teachers. Mostly he shrugged it off, or played up to it. But she had hated the way they treated him back then, making snide remarks and cruel jokes at his expense. Miss Pickles, their perpetually sour home economics teacher, had gleefully referred to him as 'the worst of those Best children'.

No teacher would be allowed to talk to a pupil that way now, especially one who came from a family where free school meals were a way of life. But twenty years ago, the PC revolution hadn't quite found its way to Gallagher Cross Comprehensive.

'I didn't forget to wear them,' he explained. 'I just didn't always have any.'

'Why not?' This was new.

'I had four younger brothers, who I shared a room with, and we didn't have a washing machine, or money for the launderette.' The blush deepened. 'You try keeping clean underpants available when you've only got a couple of decent pairs and every time you wash them and hang them out to dry some little bugger pinches them to wear himself.' He scowled at the memory of his pants-thieving brothers. 'After Spurgeon laid into me, I made clean pants for gym day a priority, but that left the other days pretty hit-and-miss. Mostly miss.'

'Why didn't you ever tell me that?' She'd always thought

he had a choice, and he'd chosen not to wear pants so he could be naked, for her.

'Why would I? I wanted you to think I was cool, not some saddo who only had two decent pairs of pants.'

* * *

Why were they talking about his underwear crisis at school? Seriously? He'd paid an extra five grand for this?

He didn't care if he sounded churlish. He was feeling pretty churlish, so it fit. The way she'd gazed at his crotch had reminded him of how she used to look at him, with that scary combination of lust and adoration and complete and utter trust. Seeing that glazed arousal again had made him feel raw and exposed…and actually kind of hot.

Which was very bad news. He and Halle had always had a strong sexual connection as teenagers, despite a few hiccups in the early days. That connection had cooled off considerably once she'd had Lizzie—because she'd wanted it less and he'd wanted it more. But getting the hots for Halle now was out of the question.

This trip was supposed to open up the lines of communication between them, not turn it into a replay of one of the biggest fuck-ups of his entire life.

'But I wouldn't have told anyone,' she said.

'I know.' Maybe he could stop this canter down memory lane by giving her the answer she wanted.

'Then why didn't you confide in me?'

She wanted to go there? After twenty years? From the earnest expression, it seemed she actually might. *Not gonna happen.* 'Probably for the same reason you didn't want to tell me about your fear of flying. It's humiliating.'

'I do not have a fear of flying,' she said, far too indignantly to be believable.

'Uh-huh, which would explain why I had to prise your hand off the armrest before you broke a finger.'

'Yes, but I'm fine now,' she declared defensively.

From the glazed look when she'd been staring at his lap, and the pink flags in her cheeks, he suspected that was only because she was high as a kite, and still recovering from that freak-out during take-off.

Truth be told, her freak-out had freaked him out a little, too.

By making him remember the girl he once knew. The girl who trusted to luck, believed the best in people and had always been sure that everything would come out right in the end.

Take the day he'd first noticed her. He'd been in the year above, already cultivating a rep for being a waste of good teaching resources. The rest of his class had gone on a history trip to the Tower of London that day, but because he'd failed to bring in the permission slip and the five-pound coach fee—as if he was going to risk a kicking from his dad to pinch a fiver for some dopey school outing—he'd been forced to join Hal's Year Ten drama class.

Sulky and pissed off with himself, because if he'd remembered the stupid trip he would have bunked off, he was not in the mood to do some stupid trust exercise, especially when the teacher had paired him with Hal. Short and cute thanks to a soft layer of puppy fat, she had looked like a studious pixie, her hair sticking up all over the shop. She'd sent him an excited smile and he'd slapped her down, telling her he wasn't going to do the stupid stunt, which involved falling backwards into her arms, because she probably caught like a girl. She'd surprised him, though, with her ballsy comeback: 'Fine, then, you sexist snot-bag, you can catch me.'

He'd stood too far back, ready to let her crash to earth for

calling him a snot-bag, but secretly expecting her to step back, because everyone did when they started to fall, didn't they? But not little Haley Dunlop. She'd spread her arms out like Christ on the cross, straightened her spine and launched herself into thin air. And gone down like a plank. They'd ended up in a heap on the floor, him jumping in to break her fall at the last second before she broke her stupid neck.

But instead of bitching at him, or blabbing to the teacher, she'd laughed, the sunny expression returning as she dusted herself off and said: 'If that's how boys catch, it's a good thing I catch like a girl.'

Reconciling that brave, eager, witty girl with the woman sitting across the aisle from him earlier was impossible. How could that girl, who only three years after their first meeting had screamed her head off through fifteen excruciating hours of labour, but still came out smiling when their newborn daughter was placed in her arms, have been so irrationally terrified of taking off she'd practically given herself lockjaw?

She fronted a live TV show every week. That had to require a lot of guts. She ran her own business empire and had brought up two kids virtually solo. How could she not still be Indestructible Haley?

But as he'd observed her sweating and trembling and trying to hold it together with every last ounce of her strength, he couldn't shake the conviction that the fact she didn't feel lucky any more was down to him.

He'd hurt her. He'd always known that. By bolting like that without a word. But, at the time, he hadn't had a choice. It was either get out or get sectioned. That didn't mean he hadn't felt like shit about what he'd done once he'd pulled himself together. But, until ten minutes ago, he'd had no problems qualifying the guilt.

Especially when Halle had made such a staggering success of her life on the back of his desertion. Because she hadn't just scraped a nil-all draw away to Wigan in the relegation play-offs, she'd scored a bloody hat-trick against Germany and won the World Cup.

But what if her wealth and success were only a mask? What if he'd damaged her in some irrevocable way? What if he'd turned Indestructible Haley into Fallible Afraid of Flying Halle? Did that mean all the ways he'd absolved his own actions were really nothing more than grubby excuses?

The sort of grubby excuses his dad used to reel off, after he'd slapped Mum's head against the table and knocked her front tooth out, or shouted at his youngest brother, Curt, so aggressively he'd made him wet himself. The sort of excuses that meant sod all, because you never learned from them, and they would all be reeled out again the next time you went on a bender and came home tanked up to the eyeballs on self-pity and too many cans of Special Brew.

What did he really know about her life now? The few puff pieces he'd seen in *HELLO!* magazine while waiting in the dentist's didn't count.

It was a sobering thought, guaranteed to make this next fortnight even more complicated than he had anticipated.

'You know what, this was always exactly the problem between us.' Halle interrupted his thoughts. 'You never came clean about anything.'

She shot him her dick-mincing look to reiterate the point. And he had a moment of clarity.

Damn it. He couldn't go back and change what he'd done sixteen years ago, so there was no use getting cut up about it now. And he certainly wasn't the cause of her fear of flying. They'd never flown anywhere when they were together, for the simple reason they couldn't afford it.

'I'd really love to know how my lack of clean underpants became a major problem in our relationship,' he countered.

'I'll tell you how. Because those pants are yet another symbol of your complete failure to communicate about anything.' She pressed her hand to her chest. 'I thought the sun shone out of your arse for four solid years. And yet you never once trusted me with a single one of your secrets.'

She was right, he'd never told her his secrets. But he'd had very good reasons for that. Reasons it had taken him two whole years of therapy to put behind him. And which he had no plans to discuss now, with a woman who had refused to speak to him for sixteen years.

'I thought we just established that my lack of clean underpants wasn't a secret,' he replied. 'The whole school knew about it, remember.'

'Stop being so bloody facetious.'

'*I'm* being facetious? You're the one who's suddenly turned into the underwear police.'

'Fine.' She threw up her hands. 'Make a joke about it, have a good old laugh about how neurotic I am.'

'Does this look like my joking face to you?' He wouldn't be able to crack a smile right now if he had dynamite to hand. 'And when exactly did I accuse you of being neurotic? Because I must have missed that bit of subtext.'

'Oh, shut up.' She clicked off her seat belt and stood, the furrow on her forehead deep enough to rival the Grand Canyon. 'I'm going to the toilet.' She grabbed her purse from under her seat. 'And I'd really appreciate it if you would leave me alone when I return. Getting through this flight without having a breakdown is my main priority and mulling over the crappiest four years of my life is not going to help make that happen.'

She marched off, leaving him to stew in her wake.

Since when had he been the one suggesting they take a stroll down memory lane? Was he the one who had brought up their schooldays? No. And where did she get off saying their four years together had been the crappiest years of her life?

They hadn't all been crap. Had they?

And what, exactly, did any of this have to do with his underpants?

* * *

After slamming the toilet door hard enough to rattle the frame, Halle glared at herself in the mirror above the sink.

Are you on crack? What the hell were you thinking?

Arguing with Luke Best had always been a futile and frustrating task. When they'd been together, she'd spent four long years believing that if she just kept chipping away at that emotional shield, she'd eventually discover the real Luke beneath and be able to fix him. Unfortunately, the real Luke had turned out to be as shallow and thickheaded as the fake Luke. The man had about as much empathy as a slab of reinforced concrete.

So he hadn't had enough clean underwear as a boy? So he'd kept the squalor of his home life a secret? None of that mattered now.

She absolutely refused to feel sorry for that boy. There were no excuses for the callous way he'd treated her. None.

She dumped her purse on the vanity and repinned the few strands of hair that had escaped her chignon during her near-death experience at take-off. She then wet a paper towel and dabbed the back of her neck, which still burned with indignation. After digging out the plastic bag that contained her cosmetics in handy one-hundred-millilitre containers, she set about removing her make-up. And then reapplying it.

Not that it needed repairing. But as the simple ritual unfolded, her nerves settled.

She smoothed on foundation. Obviously, he'd caught her at a weak moment.

She dabbed on powder. A weak moment they could both have avoided if he hadn't insisted on bumping himself up to first, too, just to get in her face.

Her fingers trembled as she rolled out her lipstick, recalling the red indents of her nails on the tanned skin of his hand.

She breathed. He'd held her hand, so what? She would have been fine once the Xanax had kicked in without him there. The tremble faded and she outlined her lips with a fresh layer of pale pink mocha.

Getting fixated on his crotch and the memory of hitting third base at the fifth-form recital had been a major misstep, though. Because the halcyon memory had been distorted by teenage naivety and rioting hormones, making her remember Luke as a troubled boy, reckless and thrilling and eager to please. And sneaking back on the shirt tails of that memory had come all those old futile misguided hopes. That she could change Luke, that she could fix him, by saving him from the demons he refused to talk about.

But it had never happened then, and it wasn't happening now, because there was nothing there to fix, even if she still had the desire to fix it. Which she did not.

Luke is a lost cause. Always was. Always will be.

She packed her make-up back into her purse and took one last look at herself in the mirror.

This was New Halle. This was Truly Indestructible Halle. Not the excitable, easily swayed child who had once been so desperate to make Luke love her, she'd been willing to let him stomp all over her.

This was the woman who had money and class and a career she adored and that had made her a star—on BBC

Two at least—and bought her a house in the most sought-after postcode in London. This was the woman who had two amazing children whom she loved to bits—especially when they weren't trying to kill each other. This was the woman who was happy, no, ecstatic, to live her life on her own terms, and who no longer had to handle hopeless causes like Luke Best.

She swept out of the bathroom, her resolve repaired alongside her make-up.

There would be no more pointless arguments about Luke's inability to share and discuss his fucked-up childhood. There would be no more reminiscing about his magic fingers. And absolutely under no circumstances would there be any more ruminating on whether or not he was wearing underwear.

Because rich, classy, career-orientated supermum Halle didn't care about any of that any more. She was here to make his phantom memoirs go away and to have a two-week break at his expense. And maybe, just maybe, to hear him own up to what a shit he'd been to her back then. But she wasn't going to push, because she didn't need to hear his excuses, or his sob stories, or deal with his drama any more.

She had more than enough of her own.

The plane shuddered as she stepped out of the cubicle. She gripped the door frame, holding on until the judder of air turbulence subsided. Her stomach wobbled, her pulse fluttered, but the nausea didn't return.

How about that? Sitting next to Luke Best had an upside; it had effectively distracted her from her terror of plummeting to her doom from thirty thousand feet.

That or the Xanax.

Chapter 9

Halle held on as the hire car took another tight bend on the solitary two-lane road that had been undulating upwards for over an hour through the lonely, isolated, densely wooded landscape.

Thanks to a surprisingly untroubled sleep—make that virtually comatose sleep—on the plane, and despite her wristwatch telling her it was close to midnight in the UK, she felt alert and well-rested.

The drive from the airport had been a snarl of five-lane freeways edged by nondescript strip malls, which had eventually taken them through Atlanta. The city had been a surprise. After reading *Gone with the Wind* in her teens, she'd expected the quaint peach-tree-lined streets of colonial houses decorated with porches and picket fences, but the mirrored high-rise blocks, not so much. Modern-day Atlanta seemed to be a thriving mix of commerce and Civil War Americana comfortable with, rather than conflicted about, its past.

She'd drifted off to sleep again, Luke silent and apparently lost in his own thoughts beside her, as the road evened out into endless pasturelands lined with orphaned mailboxes,

only to wake up again in the Nantahala National Forest, the mailboxes and most other signs of human habitation now gone.

As the road snaked up through the trees, the landscape had become more primal—and beautiful in its isolation.

This wasn't what America meant to her. Apart from a couple of trips to Disney World with Aldo, she'd only ever been to New York and Los Angeles. During both of those trips, all she'd seen was the inside of corporate offices and a quick tour of the tourist sites—but it had pretty much convinced her that, like in London, where you were supposedly never more than eight feet from a rat (and certainly never more than eight feet from someone who would tell you that), in the US you were never further than eight feet from the nearest Starbucks.

As she scanned the majestic forest of towering oaks and maples and fir trees that edged the road, she guessed they were at least eighty miles from the nearest Starbucks now.

She wished she'd stayed awake long enough on the plane to read Mel's carefully annotated file, loaded on her iBook, that detailed the landscape and the resort and their itinerary for the next two weeks. Because her laptop was currently stuffed in her luggage in the boot of the Lexus and her curiosity had outweighed her desire not to seem incompetent or unprepared about five hairpin bends ago.

'What are we supposed to be doing at this resort?' she asked over the noise of a local radio station playing back-to-back country classics. And steeled herself for a condescending look from Luke.

He thumbed the volume down using the buttons embedded in the steering wheel and flicked his glance from the road. 'You want an answer to that question I'd be happy to oblige, but I've got one for you first.'

She levelled a look at him, noting the testy tone. Did he have the hump about something? Other than her lack of research? 'Ask away, although I can't promise to answer it.'

'Don't worry, I'm not going to ask you for your secret fudge recipe,' he said curtly. 'I was merely going to ask if you've finished sulking. Or is this only another ten-second truce?'

Halle's jaw tensed. Since when had she been sulking? 'I see, so when a woman doesn't have anything to say to you, it must be because she's sulking. And not because you're just not that interesting?' If he thought he was going to hit any bullseyes with a cheap shot like that, he could forget it. She had been in guerrilla training for the past five years with his teenage daughter—who had turned sulking into an art form. 'How very convenient for your ego.'

'You've spoken exactly thirty-two words to me in close to—' he paused to check his watch '—thirteen hours.'

'Thirty-two? That many?'

'Yup, I counted.'

She quelled the spurt of astonishment that he'd been paying enough attention to her to count them. Or that he actually seemed to care enough to be upset about it.

Luckily for him, I'm big enough not to gloat.

'My goodness, you're more interesting than I thought.'

Or not to gloat too much.

If anyone had a right to sulk about this trip, it was her.

'The way I see it,' he said, 'I could be the most boring guy on the planet and that would still get into the *Guinness Book of World-Record Sulks.*'

'Then you'd be wrong. If you'd spent as much time with your teenage daughter as I have, you'd know thirty-three words in thirteen hours wouldn't even be worthy of a mention in the footnotes.'

'Lizzie doesn't sulk.' He looked genuinely surprised. 'Or not much for a teenage girl packed full of rioting hormones.'

Halle's pulse stumbled. Was he serious? Surely he must have some knowledge of their daughter's dark side? How could Luke have escaped all the angst, and the agony, the sullen strops and the cutting remarks that had been her life ever since Lizzie hit puberty?

How was that fair?

'Excuse me, but are you talking about our daughter, Lizzie?' She attempted to clarify. 'The child we conceived nineteen years ago after we got legless at that Oasis gig and had unprotected sex against the back wall of the Clapham Grand? The Lizzie who changed the significance of "Wonderwall" forever?'

He chuckled, even though she hadn't actually intended to be funny. 'It was pretty wonderful, wasn't it, despite the consequences.'

Despite the consequences.

The callow remark hit home. She'd always been suspicious about his reaction to the pregnancy, and all his insincere platitudes at the time, about being willing to respect her choice, live up to his responsibilities and support her and their baby. The fact he'd done a runner to Paris to shack up with another woman a couple of years later when they had needed him the most was a fairly big clue he'd been lying about that, like so much else.

'Don't flatter yourself, Best. The only wonderful thing about that shag was the fact it gave us a daughter.' A daughter he hadn't wanted then, which might explain why he knew so little about her now.

'OK, that does it.' He braked sharply, throwing Halle forward. She slapped her hand down to stop from rearranging her face on the dashboard.

The car shuddered to a stop on the grass verge. She grasped her throat, her heart having slammed into her larynx.

'I know it all went to hell.' He swung round, taking advantage of her inability to talk. 'And I know a lot of that was my fault.'

Her astonishment at the forthright admission of guilt was superseded by shock when he continued, his tone grim. 'But you don't get to rewrite history. We had four years together and not all of them were shit, OK? And it definitely wasn't shit against that wall when we made Lizzie. I still remember how tight and wet you were, and how you gripped me when you came, and how, when I came, it felt as if my balls had exploded. My knees ached because I had to lock them they were shaking so hard when you told me I was your Wonderwall. And even though you were drunk and it was super cheesy, and I made a joke about it, it meant something. To me at least.'

'I think I've swallowed my tongue,' she croaked, her heart now embedded in her diaphragm.

How could he remember that so clearly, so vividly? She didn't want to remember the girl she'd been, or the idiotic things she'd said—and done. But she especially didn't want to know he'd remembered them, too.

He swore softly, lifting a bottle of water out of the cupholder. 'Here.' He unscrewed the cap and offered it to her.

She took a hasty gulp. The cool liquid hit her raw throat and she coughed.

'Sorry, I braked too hard. You OK?' His hand settled between her shoulder blades and rubbed. The coughing subsided and she shifted back. His hand fell away, but the tingles radiating up her spine didn't. Annoyingly.

She studied his face, the harsh expression, the day-old

stubble, the lines that creased the skin around those brilliant blue eyes and the dark smudge of fatigue beneath.

'You look exhausted,' she managed at last. That had to explain the uncharacteristic burst of emotion. One thing Luke had never been was volatile. If anything, he'd always been too laid-back. She'd originally found that reckless devil-may-care charm unbearably sexy, until it became apparent it was merely a symptom of Luke's complete inability to give a shit about anything that mattered.

From the frown on his face now, though, it seemed he might actually give a shit about this. The low murmur of someone singing about their achy-breaky heart on the radio became deafening.

But then the line of his lips quirked and her heart rate eased back out of the danger zone. This Luke she recognised. The one who had tempted her to do inappropriate things, in inappropriate places, while pretending to care, when he never had.

* * *

Shut up and breathe. Breathing is good. It might even stop you making an even bigger tit of yourself.

The heady flow of oxygen cleared the fog of exhaustion that had settled into Luke's brain when they'd crossed the state line about fifty miles back.

'I guess I didn't sleep much on the plane.' Or at all. Because he'd been busy reading through all the research he'd downloaded about Monroe before the trip. And ignoring Halle, curled up in her pod two feet away, her hands tucked under her head in the foetal position she'd favoured when they'd shared a bed.

'Sounds like all that money you spent on your lie-flat bed was wasted,' she said. 'Bummer.'

The air released from Luke's lungs at the snarky comment. Snark was good, too.

Because it was the opposite of sentiment. And sentiment was bad, because it had a bad habit of dredging up all those damn what-ifs. The what-ifs that had hounded him—and hampered his recovery—in the early years, after he'd run away.

He scrubbed his hands down his face to erase the old guilt.

Insane outbursts about that epic shag against the back wall of the Clapham Grand were out. As was rehashing the long-forgotten mistakes he'd once made with Lizzie's mother.

'I can drive,' she said, clearly just as keen to avoid talking about his major loss of cool. 'I actually slept on the plane. And I would rather not end up in a heap of charred metal at the bottom of a ravine.'

'It's not too far now. I can sleep when we get there.' Like the dead. He needed the full ten hours a night if he was going to cope with being this close to Halle without shoving his foot down his throat again.

No doubt about it, she got to him, still.

Those light brown eyes, the colour of aged sherry with the tempting flecks of gold. The ripple of sensation in his crotch when the clasp of her bra had dug into his palm through her silk blouse. For a moment, as she'd coughed her lungs up, she'd seemed like soft, sweet, adoring and permanently optimistic Halle again. The girl who had mesmerised him once.

But that was an illusion. An illusion he wasn't about to get caught out by again.

He shifted in his seat to ease the pressure on his fly before she noticed. Not to worry, he'd be able to control his

sex drive when he wasn't so exhausted his bones had melted into the upholstery.

He shifted the transmission into drive and pulled out onto the empty road while conceding that the decision to remain celibate for the past four months might not have been such a stellar plan. Nothing like adding the pressure cooker of a sex-starved libido to an already charged situation.

'You never answered my question,' Halle said. 'What is there to do at this resort for the next two weeks? I hope there's a pool.'

He eased his foot off the gas to take the next bend in the road, determined not to let the whiney tone rankle. 'I sent your PA my brief for the article with all those details a week ago. Didn't she pass it on?'

'Of course she did, but I have a full-on career, not to mention a commitment to running a household with two children in it on my own. Arranging my schedule to accommodate this trip took up enough of my time.'

Meaning she hadn't bothered to read it. He pressed his foot back on the gas pedal, dragging up his last reserves of patience.

Getting her here had been his priority. Her hostility had been expected. He was an expert at dealing with hostile subjects. When he wasn't on the verge of going into a coma or in the middle of a four-month dry spell.

'All right, well, let me give you a rundown. The resort's facilities are basically luxury log cabins arranged in secluded settings throughout the two-hundred-acre property, which borders the Great Smoky Mountains National Park.' He reeled off the information he'd been reviewing on the plane while she slept. There was no pool, but she didn't need to know that just yet. 'Monroe guarantees privacy and high-end spec for his mostly celebrity and/or super-rich and

gullible clientele.' *Nope, not gonna rise to the pissy tone. At all.* 'His method of therapy, such as it is, seems to be based on a standard cognitive behavioural approach.'

'Hang on a minute. Therapy? What do you mean therapy? You said this was just a glorified holiday.' She sounded horrified. So horrified he almost smiled.

Did she think he was a masochist? As if he would have suggested spending two weeks in couples' therapy with a woman he hadn't spoken to in sixteen years? As tempting as it was to string her along for a few minutes, though, and watch her freak out entirely, he was way too knackered to handle another hissy fit.

'I said his *method* of therapy. There's no actual therapy involved. Which is convenient given that from my research I can't find any evidence of couples' resolution training on his part. What he calls therapy is basically just active participation in "bonding exercises".'

She sighed, her relief palpable as she muttered something under her breath that sounded very religious for a woman who had never gone to church to his knowledge.

'So how exactly am I supposed to fit into all this?' The pissy tone had downgraded to tense, which Luke took as a good sign. 'We don't want to repair our relationship. In fact, we don't even have a relationship to repair,' she continued in an incredulous tone. 'And if you brought me here to pretend we do, then you can forget it, because Oscar-worthy acting was not part of the agreement I signed.'

OK, maybe not completely un-pissy.

'No acting required. Because we do have a relationship that could use some work.' He let the assertion echo in the car above the twang of Hank Williams Sr's guitar.

The Lexus slipped round another bend before she finally

spoke. 'And what relationship would that be?' Scepticism dripped from every word.

'Our relationship as Lizzie's parents.'

Hank Sr wailed melodically about cheating hearts and crying all night over the purr of the car's engine. To her credit, when Halle finally replied, she didn't sound pissy, she sounded astonished.

'Lizzie's eighteen. You walked out when she was two and a half. Why on earth would Monroe believe after all these years we would suddenly want to repair our relationship as her parents?'

Good question. When they could have sorted it out years ago if she had been prepared to stop sulking and actually communicate with him about their daughter.

Unfortunately, having that showdown would have to wait until his brain didn't feel as if it were turning to mush.

'If Monroe asks, I'll do the talking,' he said, stowing his resentment for the time being. He'd waited sixteen years to set Halle straight about his role as Lizzie's dad. He could wait a couple more days. 'But I doubt he will,' he added, feeling suitably magnanimous.

He'd dragged Halle out here to do the right thing for Lizzie. And possibly win a Pulitzer. Not to rehash their past.

'If I'm right about this guy, all he's interested in is the bottom line,' he continued. 'Which in this case is the chance of some great publicity.'

'He knows you're a journalist?'

'Of course he does. He thinks I'm writing a puff piece. The best cover stories are the ones that don't deviate too far from the truth.'

'So he knows who I am, too?'

'Don't worry, he offers his clients complete confidentiality. I checked,' he said, heading off the latest hissy fit at the pass.

'All right, but what happens to your article if he does fix it?'

'Fix our relationship, you mean?' He risked a look away from the road, feeling light-headed. And not just from exhaustion. Was she actually going to admit how counterproductive her sixteen-year sulk had been so soon? 'So we can finally start to communicate amicably with each other about what's best for our daughter?' he added.

'I certainly hope that's not what you asked him to do.' She slanted a look that didn't exactly scream contrite—or amicable. 'Because then you really aren't going to have much of an article on your hands.'

'How do you figure that?' he said, confused now.

'Well, it's hardly a rigorous test of his methods or abilities now, is it?'

'Why not? You've refused to talk to me for sixteen years except through your solicitor, despite repeated requests from me.' *Forget nudging.* 'If you're still pissed off about what I did, I don't see how we're supposed to get past that if you won't speak to me.' *And sod magnanimous, too.* 'If Monroe can put a stop to your epic sulk, I'd not only be impressed, I'd be totally bloody gobsmacked.' Which was exactly why he wasn't about to leave it to Monroe.

'I don't doubt you would be, because it would involve *him* getting *me* to do what *you* want, without you having to get your hands dirty,' Halle replied. 'Which has always been your preferred rule of engagement.'

'What the hell's that supposed to mean?' he shouted, sixteen years of resentment finally blasting through the last of his composure—and his good intentions.

He *was* getting his bloody hands dirty. In fact, they were good and filthy. The shit he'd had thrown at him already included the sad truth he wasn't as immune to Halle as he

should be—not to mention their pointless return trip to the humiliations of his youth on the plane. And they weren't even at the bloody resort yet.

'Didn't it ever occur to you, Luke, the reason I never wanted to talk to you again was simply because I never wanted to be lied to again?'

* * *

Halle watched Luke's brows arrow down.

That'd be a no, then.

'I got over being pissed off with you a long time ago,' she added. Which if she kept saying it often enough must surely make it true. 'My refusal to communicate with you wasn't because I was sulking. It was because I didn't trust you. Because, guess what? Trust has to be earned. I can't imagine what Monroe's going to be able to do about the sad fact you never did a single thing to earn mine.'

He was quiet for a long time, the purr of the engine the only sound. That and Dolly Parton crooning about always loving someone while walking away from them.

Trust Dolly to add the perfect note of irony.

The car slowed as an elaborate sign appeared, looking out of place on the lonely road, proclaiming it was only three miles to The Monroe Couples' Resolution Retreat. They continued on in silence for ten pregnant minutes as the Lexus turned off the highway and took the narrow one-track road.

It wasn't until Luke had given their details to the guard at the manned security booth and driven through the gate to the resort that he spoke again. 'Then I guess it's a good thing Monroe's "bonding exercises" to re-establish trust are so extreme.'

Wait a minute. Extreme. Extreme how?

'Exactly how extreme are they?' Why hadn't she read that bloody itinerary?

She didn't do extreme, not when primeval wildernesses were concerned. She'd never even been tempted to appear on *I'm a Celebrity... Get Me Out of Here!* despite numerous overtures to her agent. And they paid you for that.

'You know, as in Xtreme sports, extreme. Hiking, white-water rafting, wilderness camping, that sort of thing.'

'You are not serious?' she said, unable to quell the tremble of horror.

She didn't do camping. She didn't even do glamping. Sleeping outdoors with only a flimsy layer of nylon between her and the untamed primal wilderness that currently surrounded them might actually be more traumatic than having to sit through two weeks of real couples' counselling with Luke.

And white-water rafting? When I can get seasick in a pedalo? I'll die.

He parked the car in front of a wood-framed reception building that looked like a quaint country farmhouse complete with white picket fence and rocking chairs on the porch.

'Actually, I'm dead serious.' His lopsided smile suggested her horrified reaction wasn't going to cause him any sleepless nights. 'Trust me.'

Chapter 10

Three a.m. and all's crap, frankly.

Halle stared at the digital clock on her iPhone.

Because I'm lying in bed contemplating two solid weeks of extreme sports torture in the company of a man who can infuriate me just by breathing. Oh, yeah, and it's three o'clock in the fricking morning and I'm wide awake.

Of course, it also didn't help that last night she'd discovered the deluxe hillside cabin, overlooking the glorious untamed wilderness of the Great Smoky Mountains National Park, not only didn't have a pool, but it also didn't have a TV, a phone signal or any Wi-Fi.

Obviously, 'rebuilding love relationships' in Jackson Monroe's world involved making sure that those relationships were rebuilt on the bedrock of lots and lots of enforced intimacy. After the thirteen hours she'd spent in Luke's company already, she suspected spending two weeks with him constantly in her face was liable to send her screaming into the woods. Literally.

Suddenly the possibility of closure, the reason she'd agreed to this stupid trip in the first place, didn't look anywhere near as attractive as it had in Paris. What if being this

close to Luke triggered more of those hormonal flashbacks like the one she'd had on the plane? Or, worse, gave him the opportunity to undermine her confidence as a mother?

It had taken years for her to arrive at a good place as a parent, or a good enough place. Lizzie still had issues, issues that Luke was completely oblivious to, but they were normal teenage issues. Their daughter wasn't anorexic or a drug addict and Halle had survived four months of family therapy to prove it. And she wasn't about to let Luke—the part-time parent par excellence—make her feel inadequate.

She should have complained to Luke about their sleeping arrangements the night before but there hadn't been an opportune moment. After signing about a billion release forms and filling out an ominous questionnaire about their physical fitness levels, they'd been shown to their accommodation to find a lavish supper of cold cuts and salads laid out in the cabin's main living area. Luke's head had been lolling over the dishes as soon as he'd sat down and she'd ended up taking pity on him and telling him to go crash out before he face-planted in the potato salad.

She'd decided to tackle the thorny issue of getting a new, separate cabin tomorrow.

But as she'd cleaned up their dinner dishes, she'd rationalised away her qualms. He had a separate room on the cabin's mezzanine level with a separate bathroom. And she didn't even like him. And he didn't like her.

It wasn't as if she actually fancied him. Even the new, more buff Luke wasn't sexy enough to make her forget what a bastard he was, or the underhanded tactics he'd used to get her here. And the 'extreme bonding experiences' detailed in Monroe's brochure—which she'd read last night from cover to cover—should do the rest of the job. If there was anything guaranteed to put inappropriate

thoughts about her ex out of her mind, it was the prospect of white-water rafting.

But now it was 3.15 a.m. She was hideously alert thanks to the jet lag. And she didn't have a thing to do, or a to-do list to start arranging to do it with, for the first time in, well, forever. Which meant she had rather more time than she wanted to consider all the cons of her situation.

She lay in the bed, breathing in the scent of air freshener and lavender polish, listening to the clip-clip-clip of the ceiling fan above her head, and struggled to focus on the pros instead. And not picture the man lying in the bed above her. And the odd and completely arbitrary notion that he might be sleeping in the raw, the way he always used to.

Do not go there. For that way lies more unwanted hormone bumps.

She scanned the pseudo rustic antique furnishings, the sturdy maple-wood dresser, the gleaming oil lamp on top that looked like a forgotten prop from *Little House on the Prairie*, and realised that apart from the potential hazards of sharing a cabin with Luke, it felt good, liberating even, to have the luxury of lying in bed. With not a thing to do.

She really should have thought of taking a week for herself sooner.

Clearly, she had been in serious need of a de-stress. A bit of genuine me time.

With the forest outside still dark, though, she decided she needed something more tangible than no to-do list appreciation to make the most of her first morning of me time.

She padded to the kitchen and took a moment to appreciate the polished surfaces and top-of-the-range appliances and the glorious view of the forest, the dawn light just beginning to set the leaves on fire.

The glass-fronted cabinets were stocked with staples

as well as some local delicacies, assuming that's what a funnel cake was. But before she could read the ingredients, she shoved the package mix back onto the shelf and slammed the door.

She needed a break from the kitchen, and best not cook anything while Luke was in residence, or she might be tempted to poison him. She headed off in search of caffeine.

It took twenty minutes to figure out the coffee machine, which had enough bells and whistles and unexplained buttons to quite possibly perform brain surgery as well as make an espresso. One watery cup of lukewarm coffee later, she returned to her bedroom delighted to see the dawn angling through the line of fir trees that sloped away down the mountainside.

A heavy fog rolled over the cabin's wraparound porch, swirling around the rocking chairs outside and then gradually dispersing as the morning light arrowed through the dense foliage in picturesque shards that reminded her of the eerie setting in a vintage horror movie. She became absorbed in the beauty of the view through the bedroom's glass double doors. And took a moment to absorb the novelty again of having nothing to do. And nowhere to go.

Snuggling back under the intricate patchwork quilt—another of Ma Ingalls's heirlooms, no doubt—she began reading one of the novels she'd downloaded onto her iPad months before and never found the time to read.

It was a good book, just the sort she enjoyed reading in her downtime, downtime that had been virtually absent in far too long. Frivolous and pulpy and romantic, with a fabulously sassy female lead. But then the fabulously sassy female lead met some hot guy in a bar in chapter two, took him home to her apartment and started getting fabulously pornographic with him on her kitchen counter.

Crossing her legs under the quilt, Halle squeezed her melting thigh muscles and flung down the iPad.

Nope, still not going there.

Putting on a sweater over her PJs, she stepped onto the wraparound porch, breathed in the scent of tree resin and musty earth, and congratulated herself on keeping any more of those unwanted hormonal bumps at bay.

Then she spotted a hot tub, lurking at the bottom of the screened porch, steam rising in wisps from under the heavy plastic covering. And a picture of Luke stark naked and fully aroused blasted into her unprotected jet-lagged brain without warning.

Figment-of-her-imagination Luke sat on the edge of the hot tub. His chest muscles glistening as if he'd been oiled like a Chippendale, droplets of water sparkling in the dawn light as they ran down his rock-hewn abdomen, begging her to lick them off. Worst of all, his penis stood thick and magnificently erect, the circumcised head flushed with blood and shiny with the sheen of pre-cum.

Heat blossomed in her sex and her clitoris ached, slick and swollen between her thighs. She swung round and charged back to her room.

Time for action. Tangible action. Right now.

This delusion had nothing to do with Luke, and everything to do with her sadly neglected libido. A blind date with Bugs was all she needed. Clearly, being in Luke's company for more than twenty-four hours, after six months without an orgasm, had been stressful enough to give her pornographic delusions of epic proportions.

Stop thinking in penis euphemisms. It's not helping.

She rushed over to her suitcase, then stumbled to a halt as she recalled the one item—the one single solitary item on the bloody to-do list from hell that had gotten lost in her

scramble to finish the Kane Corp redesign, have a quiet chat with Trey about Lizzie and get a home-cooked meal down her children on Thursday evening.

Seriously? You forgot to pack Bugs!

* * *

'So, folks, it's great to meet y'all. How are y'all enjoying our little resort so far?' Jackson Monroe beamed bonhomie from across the ornate walnut desk.

He was older and rounder in person, Halle decided, than he'd seemed on Graham Norton's sofa a couple of months ago. Bushy eyebrows and the wisps of hair peeking out of his nose and ears, plus the leathery skin, put him in his mid-sixties at Halle's best estimate. But his grey eyes, despite the grandfatherly smile, were sharp and shrewd.

'The cabin's great, thanks, Mr Monroe. The view's astonishing,' Luke replied, the buttering-up routine, which he'd begun two minutes ago when they'd been introduced to Monroe in the reception area, still in full flow.

'Call me Jake, Luke.' Monroe laughed heartily. 'We're all friends here.' His eyes literally twinkled. Halle wondered if he had special eye drops. 'But I do love your proper English manners,' he added, putting on a torturously pompous approximation of a British accent.

Not to mention every cliché in the book *How to Schmooze the Paying Customer for Dummies*, Halle thought. Surely the man had to be a charlatan, because he was oozing enough oily charm to rival the Deepwater Horizon slick.

'And how are you doing, ma'am? I've got to say I'm thrilled to meet the great Halle Best. Nora and I love your show. We catch it every chance we get on our local PBS channel.'

'How wonderful.' She smiled graciously, trying not to

let her irritation show. 'I'm equally thrilled to discover my little ole recipes are bringing in new fans across the pond.'

Monroe chortled amiably while placing his meaty forearms on the desk. 'I hope you're as happy as Luke is with our amenities,' he added, boldly fishing for more compliments.

It was the cue she'd been waiting for. For four hours.

While feeling increasingly annoyed with herself, and Luke.

She'd had a cold shower after her vision on the porch, only to walk into the kitchen to find Luke scoffing down one of the hot buttered blueberry muffins that had been delivered to the cabin for their breakfast. Her gaze had become riveted to the strong column of his throat, his Adam's apple bobbing every time he swallowed.

She'd mentioned the sleeping arrangements and told him, as nonchalantly as possible, that she had assumed she'd have her own private, individual cabin.

He'd laughed and said, 'The cover won't work if we don't bunk together. So I'm afraid you're stuck with me. Don't worry, I'll do my best to keep my hands off you.' Clearly thinking he was being amusing and ironic.

So she'd been forced to drop the subject.

But she still wasn't comfortable with the situation. At all. Spending two weeks waking up to Luke in her kitchen was bad enough, but she definitely didn't want any more pornographic visions of the man screwing with her me time.

'Actually, there is a slight problem with the accommodation,' she began, launching into the strategy she'd hit on to distance herself from Luke, without technically reneging on their agreement. 'For me at least.'

Monroe's smile stretched across his ruddy face, revealing a hint of startlingly white teeth for a man in his sixties.

'I'm real sorry to hear that, Halle. Let me know what it is and we'll get it fixed.'

'I'm afraid I need a cabin with Wi-Fi and phone cover-age. So I can keep in touch with my children. And I've got work commitments. Luke's obviously comfortable where he is. But if I could move, that would be great.'

The jovial smile crinkled at the edges, as if Monroe was having trouble processing the information. 'Well, now. That would be possible if we had Wi-Fi and phone coverage at the resort. But we don't. We don't want our clients distracted during their time here.'

'But... That's... Really?'

Who the hell stays at this resort? The Flintstones?

'You see, Halle, you're here to mend your relationship with Luke.' He linked his fingers together on the desk, the condescension almost as aggravating as the faux sympathy in those shrewd grey eyes. 'We've got a schedule of activi-ties for y'all that will get you rebuilding that all-important trust between you. But your downtime between activities is your quality time, when you're gonna be reconnecting in the comfort and intimacy of your cabin.' His eyes became rheumy, as if he were having a religious experience. 'And that's the unique bedrock of the experience we offer here. So there's no cable, no TV, no internet and no cell phones. Now, you're more than welcome to come over to the lobby area to call your children.' He settled into his chair, his con-siderable bulk spilling over the arms like Jabba the Hutt. 'But we ask our clients to put aside their work commitments while they're here. So they can concentrate on the much more important work of repairing their marriages. And I'm sure you wouldn't want to get distracted from that.'

Actually, I really would.

'But I'm not married to Luke,' she protested. If the truth didn't work with Luke's cover story, tough.

And she never actually had been married to him, but she decided not to mention that and get drawn into a lengthy debate about why she had decided to use Luke's last name. Because she had the sneaking suspicion Grandpa Walton here would be less than receptive to the argument that the Best name had become an important part of her brand.

'We're not even a couple. So we don't actually have a relationship to repair, now do we?' she finished.

He placed his hands on the desk with an audible thump. 'I know that, honey,' he said, smothering her objections with another huge helping of condescension. 'Luke here has apprised me of your situation. And while he may not be your husband any more, he surely is the father of your child.'

'He's only the father of one of my children,' Halle cut in, getting desperate.

'That's as may be,' Monroe continued, the tone still gratingly patriarchal. 'But Luke has told me all about how your daughter, Elizabeth, is struggling to find her place in the world during her difficult teenage years, and how she needs both her parents working together to help her do that.'

Halle shot Luke a stunned glare, irritation morphing into horrified shock.

What had he said to this patronising twat about Lizzie? Was he planning to use their daughter to sell his article?

Luke glared back, sending her a what-the-hell-are-you-playing-at look.

'Isn't that right, Luke?' Monroe interrupted their glare-off.

'Yes, Jake, it is,' Luke agreed, slathering butter as he went like a greased slug. 'Lizzie needs us to work together now. Which is why Halle and I are both here.' The muscles

in his jaw clenched as he shot her another cautionary glare. 'And I'm sure it's going to make a terrific human interest story when we're through.'

'I sure hope so,' Monroe agreed, dismissing Halle as he booted up his computer and printed out a ream of papers.

His voice droned on detailing all the 'Xtreme Trust-Building' exercises that had been arranged for them over the next two weeks while Luke jotted down notes in his reporter's notebook. Halle couldn't hear a word of it over the angry buzzing of a thousand killer bees in her skull.

She'd come all the way to Tennessee to stop Luke writing a book that would expose her and her children to the glare of publicity. And she'd got him to agree not to name her in his article. But what if, by protecting herself, she'd exposed Lizzie instead?

She wanted to whack Luke over the head with a large, blunt object. A six-inch vibrator would have done the job nicely. Unfortunately, hers was back in London sitting in her bedroom drawer, gathering dust.

* * *

'What the hell was that about?' Luke slammed the cabin door, happy to see Halle stiffen before she swung to face him. 'We had an agreement. And you don't get to circumvent it by blabbing to Monroe.'

He'd held on to his temper while she sulked through Monroe's outline. He'd even let her waltz off as soon as they'd left the guy's office, but now they were back in the safety of the cabin, well away from prying eyes, he was getting a few things straight. No way was he letting her stay in another cabin. He didn't care if she needed Wi-Fi. She wasn't in charge any more.

She stormed forward, her face furious. Well, at least he'd got past the epic sulk.

'How dare you think you can use Lizzie in your article, you unscrupulous hack. Well, I'm telling you now it's not going to happen. Because I will sue your bloody socks off if you try.'

'What?' The single word barrelled out on a shocked gasp. Her accusation had come from so far out of left field he hadn't been able to brace before it had smacked into him. 'Exactly how much of an arsehole do you think I am? I'm her father, dammit, her welfare and well-being are just as important to me as they are to you.' *If not more so*, he thought, trying to repel the sharp slither of guilt stabbing under his breastbone.

Maybe that hadn't always been the case. Maybe he *had* been crippled by doubt once, reacting out of fear and self-loathing to Halle's pregnancy and the prospect of fatherhood. But he'd made peace with himself about that years ago.

She'd made him sign a secrecy clause, made him agree not to tell Lizzie where they were. The stipulation had rankled when her solicitor had sprung it on him a week ago. He didn't like being put in a situation that might force him to lie to his daughter if she asked.

But he was livid about it now. Did she seriously believe he would use his daughter to sell a damn article?

He'd been a good dad. Maybe not a perfect dad, because he'd been learning on the job. But he'd been through hell and back to get himself straight, to heal those parts of himself that had destroyed his relationship with Halle and nearly destroyed his relationship with his child. And he'd proved himself in all the years since, proved that he loved his daughter.

He was here now because he wanted an equal place in Lizzie's life. And he was through being sidelined by Halle.

And made to feel as if he didn't deserve to be Lizzie's dad because he'd run once when he was a terrified kid with issues he couldn't control.

He refused to be put on the defensive about that again. By someone who didn't know the first thing about his parenting skills.

He grasped her arm, tugged her forward until they were nose to nose, the fury and hurt at her accusation making his fingers shake.

'The article's going to be about Monroe, his resort and his crackpot methods,' he sneered, determined to get at least one thing straight. 'I agreed not to name you in it, but no way in hell would I name Lizzie, or expose her in any way. I love my daughter. I would never intentionally hurt her. And I happen to be a well-respected journalist.' His voice rose as outraged pride came to the fore. 'I don't need to exploit my daughter to sell my work. My byline is more than enough. And I didn't need a bloody confidentiality clause to keep me in line.'

'OK.' She stepped back, her pale skin livid with colour. 'Let go of me.' She tugged on her arm, and he released her, suddenly brutally aware of the warmth of her skin beneath his thumb.

'OK? That's all you've got to say?' he asked, as stunned by her sudden capitulation as he was by the colour darkening her face now to a rich rosé.

'I'm sorry,' she murmured, stunning him even more. *She was?* 'I'm tired and jet-lagged and I lost my temper. And I guess I overreacted...' She paused, obviously struggling to find the words. 'That's not why I asked you to sign the confidentiality clause.'

'Then why did you?'

'Don't pretend you don't know.' Her cheeks were shining

like beacons now, setting off the gold flecks in her irises and disconcerting him. The short hairs on his nape stood to attention. Because there was something fizzing in the air that didn't feel like fraying tempers any more. Something that felt a lot more dangerous.

Then his gaze got stuck on the full bottom lip she'd trapped between her teeth. And the danger level increased.

'I'm not pretending I don't know. I'm *telling* you I don't,' he said, forcing his gaze away from her mouth, only to get it trapped in her eyes. Drawn in by those tempting gold shards, shining in the hazy amber. 'Why didn't you want me to talk to Lizzie about the article?'

'I just…' She paused. 'I didn't want Lizzie knowing we were coming here together and getting any ideas.'

'Ideas? What ideas?'

Her breath shuddered out and he felt the echo of her sigh. Pretty much everywhere.

'She used to draw pictures, lots of pictures in her free time at primary school.' *Pictures? What pictures?* 'After Aldo was born, she stopped doing them. I guess she got distracted, wrapped up in her new baby brother. But before… Every Friday she would run out of the school gates and hand me another one.'

'I still don't know what you're talking about.' What did Lizzie's artwork as a kid have to do with anything?

'Didn't she ever draw you pictures? She must have.'

Was this some kind of test? That he was being set up to fail? But it didn't feel like a test. For once, she sounded more dismayed than belligerent.

'Of course she did. She used to draw a lot of stuff. She's a talented artist. Always has been. I never tried to discourage that,' he said, annoyed that he sounded defensive. But he still had no clue where she was going with this.

Instead of giving him an answer, she walked past him into the kitchen.

'Hey, you can't just leave me hanging like that.' He followed her into the sunny space, to find her filling the coffee pot at the sink. Her shoulders were rigid beneath the loose linen shirt she wore. 'What's the deal with Lizzie's pictures?'

She put the pot down on the countertop and turned to face him, bracing her arms behind her. 'She always used to draw you and me and her together. As a family,' she replied tightly. 'She never spoke about us getting back together. But I know it took her years to accept we were never going to be a family. Because of those pictures. Now do you understand?'

The tension in her shoulders eased as she fussed with the coffee maker.

He felt the tension she'd released tighten across his own shoulder blades. The guilt he thought he'd overcome back with a vengeance.

What did he say to that? When he'd never noticed, never realised Lizzie had harboured any such hopes? 'I guess I missed that,' he conceded. 'Is that why you didn't want her to know we were here together?'

She nodded.

He took the coffee canister out of the fridge and handed it to her. 'You know, you could have asked me not to tell her and told me why, instead of getting your solicitor involved,' he added, vindicated despite his guilt. Surely this was yet more proof they needed to be talking about Lizzie?

'Really? You would have respected my wishes?' She flicked her hand between the two of them, looking doubtful. 'And kept quiet about us being here? If all I'd done was ask?'

'Yes.'

Her gaze remained steady, the scepticism still very much in evidence.

'If you'd told me you were worried about how Lizzie would react to the news and you'd told me why, of course I would have respected your decision. You're her mother. You know her best.'

And you've spent a lot more time with her than I have. So thanks for that.

He swallowed past the ball of resentment stuck in his throat and waited for her to respond. He wasn't going to blow this by losing his temper again.

'I see.' She spooned the coffee into the espresso cup, clipped it into the contraption, then flicked the switch. Finally, she leaned against the counter and sighed. 'Then I guess I owe you another apology. I didn't know I could trust you to be that mature about it.'

And the reason she didn't know was because she had never given him the chance to prove he wasn't the same bollocksed-up kid he'd been at twenty.

But he didn't plan to blow their fragile truce by pointing that out. He would be reasonable now, even if it gave him an aneurysm. 'Hal, I could bore your arse off with how mature I am now. Especially when it comes to my daughter's well-being.'

Her cheeks flared pink, before she swung round to concentrate on the coffee again.

OK, that might have sounded more mature if you hadn't mentioned her arse.

'I'm glad we got that straight,' he said, making sure he didn't notice how her arse looked in her sunshine-yellow shorts.

Really should not have mentioned that arse.

He forced his gaze back up. 'So now, how about you

explain to me why you were trying to weasel out of our deal in Monroe's office?'

'I wasn't trying to weasel out of our deal,' she said, but the blush bloomed across her collarbone. A sure sign of a guilty conscience.

'Then why were you challenging what I'd told Monroe about us?' Interrogation was usually a good way to get to the truth and it gave him something to concentrate on instead of the skimpiness of the vest top she wore under her loose-fitting shirt. 'We agreed I was going to do the talking. You came close to blowing our whole cover story.'

She crossed her arms over her chest. 'Fine, if you must know, I'm not comfortable sharing a cabin with you.'

'Tough,' he said, determined not to let the evidence of how much she still disliked him bother him. He didn't need her to like him. He just needed her to cooperate with him. And she'd already agreed to do that, in writing. 'The cover story's not going to work if you stay somewhere else. So we're stuck with each other. But you don't have to worry. I'll try to refrain from cutting my toenails in the kitchen sink, or burping after every meal, and I promise to do my fair share of the chores, just like I managed to do when we shared a place in Hackney. Which if you recall was missing a lot more than just Wi-Fi.'

* * *

Halle noted the tone—irritated and apparently clueless. She wasn't buying it. Surely he couldn't still be completely impervious to the undertone? The way his gaze had strayed to her mouth and then her cleavage a moment ago was a dead giveaway.

He must have figured out by now that their mutual animosity wasn't the only reason their sharing a cabin together could get ugly.

Either that or he was a surprisingly crap investigative journalist—contrary to all the boasts about his bestselling byline.

His gaze dipped yet again, this time meandering all the way down to the front of her camisole. Her nipples tightened on cue. And the blast of heat napalmed her cheeks.

'All right, if you absolutely insist, I'll stay put.'

If he isn't going to break cover, then neither am I. After all, I'm not the one who has a problem with impulse-control.

'I insist.' He smiled, like a certain wolf in granny's clothing.

'Fine, then I insist we establish some ground rules,' she added firmly.

She'd already let jet lag and frustration get the better of her temper in Monroe's office, causing her to hit out at Luke and accuse him of stuff that, for once, he might not actually be guilty of.

She didn't think he was a bad father, particularly. The truth was, she didn't really know what kind of a father he was. On Lizzie's initial visits to Paris, she'd quizzed her daughter about Luke to check that he was being a responsible dad. But after those first few glowing reports, she'd stopped encouraging Lizzie to talk about him, because she didn't want to think about him or hear about him, if she didn't have to.

'What rules?' Luke's jaw hardened to granite. 'Because if it includes getting any more third parties involved so you don't have to have a conversation with me, you can forget it.'

It was another dig at her decision to communicate through Jamie. She ignored it. She wasn't apologising for that, even if she had underestimated how much her no-contact rule had pissed him off in recent years.

'Don't worry, no solicitor fees need apply.' She dug a couple of mugs out of the cabinet. 'All I'm suggesting is

that we aim to stay out of each other's way.' She tipped the newly made espresso into one of the mugs, then set up another shot. 'I've got some customer briefs I have to work on.' Not entirely true, but she did have several books to read, preferably the ones that didn't involve feisty copulation on kitchen counters. *Moving swiftly on.* 'And I was looking forward to some genuine downtime while I'm here. But I don't find your company particularly relaxing.'

About as relaxing as making a baked Alaska in the Sahara Desert, if you must know.

He picked up the mug of coffee she'd poured and took a sip, watching her intently over the rim. The careful consideration unsettled her.

As a girl, she'd never been able to figure out what Luke was thinking. It had frightened her then, eventually making her hideously insecure. Unfortunately, that inscrutable expression didn't have a completely negligible effect on her nerves now, either, if the rabbit punches of her pulse were anything to go by.

'I agreed to come all the way to Tennessee,' she continued, 'and to be your plus-one for this stupid article. Apparently, I also agreed to do a load of extreme sports activities that will probably kill me. And to share a cabin with you.' *Stop babbling and get to the point. He doesn't make you that nervous.* 'And while I could dispute that, I won't.' She emptied the second espresso shot into her mug.

'That's big of you.'

'Yes, I thought so,' she replied, matching his sarcasm and raising it. 'But I did not agree to spend two weeks playing house.' She'd done that once for three years. She did not need a reminder. 'So while we're here, alone...' She took a gulp of the coffee, then winced at the bitter aftertaste. 'I

will stay out of your way, and I'd appreciate it if you would stay out of mine.

I.e.: no shared hot-tub time.

He drained his mug and leaned past her to place it in the sink. She shifted to the side to make space for him, the fine hairs on her forearm prickling alarmingly as his elbow skimmed the skin. His gaze caught hers as he stepped back.

And she knew. If he had been unaware of those inappropriate hormone bumps before, he certainly wasn't now. Because she could see the knowledge reflected in his eyes.

'I'll stay out of your way on one condition,' he said.

'What condition?' Deal or no deal, Present Halle wasn't going to be suckered into agreeing to any more impossible bargains Future Halle would be forced to fulfil.

'Once you're back in London, I can email you directly about Lizzie, without getting your damn solicitor involved.'

'Done.' She capitulated quickly, relieved by the harmlessness of the request. And a little surprised how easy it was to agree to.

Maybe she'd been wrong to keep him out of the loop for so long. As Lizzie's dad, he was the only other person who cared about Lizzie as much as she did. Talking with him about their daughter didn't have to be bad.

As long as he was safely on the end of an email. In another country.

Face-to-face, in a luxury mountain cabin in the Tennessee mountains, with no Wi-Fi? Not so much.

'You want to shake on that?' He held out his hand, the way he had in Paris.

She stared at the long blunt fingers, the sun-browned skin, the curved scar by the base of his thumb. And, for one breathless moment, recalled exactly what those calloused fingers had once been capable of.

'No, that's OK.' She wrapped sweaty palms round her mug, the hormone bumps coming out to party as if it were 1999 again. 'I'm good.'

Or as good as I'm gonna get, under the circumstances.

Chapter 11

Sunday mornings suck.

Lizzie grabbed some freshly squeezed OJ from the over-stocked fridge to combat the worst case of dry mouth ever.

Especially Sunday mornings when you get woken up by a vodka hangover that would make Vladimir Putin weep.

The zing of citrus cut through some of the fuzz in her throat but not much. Her mouth still felt like Aldo's hamster had been bedding down by her tonsils. The ache in her head concentrated in her temples as she poured herself a mug of coffee from the pot already percolating. She controlled the whimper of self-pity. Her symptoms were all totally self-inflicted. Unfortunately, they hadn't been self-inflicted in a good cause, like an all-night rave, but rather were the result of one—or maybe five—too many vodka shots while watching back-to-back episodes of *Come Dine with Me* on her new iPad last night.

Was there anything more tragic than getting pissed alone while watching some loud-mouthed bank clerk with a comb-over cook pigs' trotters for three people who couldn't stand him?

No wonder her mum's show was such a hit. At least there was proper cooking in it.

Coffee slopped over the lid of the pot as she dumped it back on the hotplate.

Mr Perfecto must be up already. Probably sneaking around being useful. Making coffee and avoiding her. Resentment edged out the self-pity. She wouldn't have had to barricade herself in her room last night and find her own amusement in the bottom of a vodka bottle if Trey and Aldo hadn't commandeered the games room to watch the Chelsea match and then finish constructing Stamford Bridge on Minecraft.

Not that she was enough of a loser yet to play with fake digital Lego, but it was the principle of the thing. They'd totally left her out. Trey especially. She might as well have been invisible. He'd spoken to her exactly twice during the match. She'd counted. And only after she'd asked him a direct question.

He'd moved into the room across from Aldo's on Friday afternoon and after a day and a half of non-stop activities to which she hadn't been invited she was starting to feel as if she had the Black Death.

She sipped the coffee black, the acrid chicory taste going some way to unstick her tongue from the roof of her mouth, and began riffling the drawers for her mum's emergency supply of ibuprofen. What she needed now was drugs and lots of them.

She prised the round pink pills out of their casing and popped three in her mouth. Mr Perfecto himself strolled into the kitchen and then stopped on the threshold. She almost choked on the last pill, then gulped it down with some coffee.

He must have just had his shower. She'd never seen him

like this before, fresh and damp and rumpled. His cropped
hair flattened against his head in grooves where he'd finger-
dried it with a few impatient swipes. The smooth olive skin
on his jaw was reddened where he'd shaved.

After pausing on the threshold, he walked into the room,
his loose-limbed stride casual but not entirely relaxed. Pronounced pecs stretched the light blue weave of his polo
shirt. Clean but worn Levi's clung to the long muscles of his
thighs and hung loose at his lean waist. Those scuffed Nike
high-tops padded on the floor in time to the thump of her
heartbeat. How could he look good even in that lame shirt?

'You're up?' He didn't disguise his surprise as he reached
for a mug from the cabinet behind her left shoulder. She got
a fleeting glimpse of a flat, lightly furred belly when his
lame polo shirt rose up. And stored away the knowledge
that he had an outie belly button. He lifted the coffee pot
and the citrus scent of his shower gel surrounded her. She
inhaled before she could stop herself. He smelled delicious,
clean and fresh—unlike her.

'Couldn't sleep,' she said, sidestepping away from him
to perch on one of the stools that rimmed the breakfast bar.
And avoid asphyxiating him with the sour smell that probably clung to her. She crossed her arms under her breasts,
embarrassed by the shapeless T-shirt and old boxer shorts
she had on—and her complete lack of a bra. Not that she
had much to hold up, but her breasts felt heavier than usual
all of a sudden.

*New rule: No more coming down to breakfast in your
rattiest night gear while Mr Perfecto, now also known as
Mr Lame-But-Hot, is in residence.*

'Have you got another outing planned for today?' she
asked.

'The Serpentine. I thought we'd go swimming. My weather app says it's going to hit the thirties.'

She nodded. 'Sounds like a plan.'

Why did the fact he had a weather app suddenly seem cute instead of moist, too? She imagined him in swimming trunks and suntan lotion and got light-headed. She had to get an invite—she wasn't spending another day pondering her crappy life while even her little brother saw more action. And a swim would be one way to blitz her hangover. That or kill her, which, either way you looked at it, would cure the problem. Plus, the one good thing about all the weight she'd lost when she'd dumped Liam a year ago was her bum looked virtually non-existent in a bikini. 'Could I come?'

'Do you want to?'

'Why not? I haven't got anything better to do.' It wasn't exactly gracious, but then he'd smell a rat the size of Japan if she were too eager.

'I guess you can. But I'll check with Aldo that he's on-board first, before we make a final decision.'

Aldo will do as I tell him. He's not the boss of me.

'Don't worry, Aldo will be on-board if you suggest it. You're the Aldo Whisperer now,' she said drily, to cover the spike of anticipation. No need to get too excited. It was only a stupid trip to the Serpentine.

'The what?'

'Don't tell me you haven't noticed Aldo hero-worships you.' As he used to do with her. Back when he was a toddler and she wasn't a bitch.

'Yeah, right.' Trey heaped a bowl with Cheerios. 'I wish.'

'He doesn't…?' Was that the tiniest hint of snark? And why did it please her so much? It hardly mattered to her whether Aldo genuflected whenever Mr Lame-But-Hot appeared.

He glanced up and she could see him deliberating for a moment. 'I just happen to know the top-secret formula to handling ten-year-old boys.'

'Which is?' she asked, stupidly pleased by the hint of confidentiality in his tone.

He splashed half a pint of milk into the Cheerios, shovelled a spoonful in his mouth. Chewed and swallowed. 'If I told you that, I'd have to kill you.'

The joke was so cute and so unexpected, she grinned. 'Only if I rat to the au pair police, and I won't.'

'All right, then, here it is…' He propped his elbow on the breakfast bar and leaned towards her, bringing his face close enough for her to pick out the compelling hints of hazelnut in the chocolate brown. And see the small abrasion on his chin where he'd nicked himself shaving. 'Feed them, water them and exhaust them,' he murmured. 'Not necessarily in that order.'

'But that's…way too easy.' Aldo had been a complete nightmare until her mum had hired Trey. Lizzie had been jealous while also a little awed by his ability to solve all her brother's problems, when a team of child psychologists, behavioural therapists and remedial teaching staff had failed.

'Easy?' he scoffed, cradling the bowl in his hand to take another gigantic spoonful. 'Try exhausting a ten-year-old boy. It's not easy. It's bloody hard work. They have more energy than Mo Farah on speed.'

'How did you figure it out?' she asked, the awe showing through.

'Simple. I was a ten-year-old boy myself once with more energy than I knew what to do with. I know what it's like having it all bubbling away inside you. Unless you work it off regularly, you feel like you're going to explode right out of your skin.'

She couldn't imagine him as a ten-year-old boy, he seemed so confident and mature. She could, however, imagine him having enough energy to explode out of his skin. The way his biceps bulged and flexed as he focused on scooping the last of the cereal into his mouth looked powerful, and ridiculously erotic.

She wondered what he did to work all that energy off now?

'And did you?' she asked, not too bothered by the husky timbre of her voice. Even if it was a dead giveaway to the filthy direction of her thoughts. 'Explode, I mean.'

He was far too square to jack off on a regular basis. And far too polite to guess her ratty pyjama shorts were getting a damp spot while she speculated on the possibility.

He finished demolishing the Cheerios and placed the bowl in the dishwasher. But when his eyes met hers, colour crept into her cheeks at the long, considering look. The damp spot grew as she wondered if she'd overestimated his squareness. Or underestimated his mind-reading abilities. She crossed her legs to ease the growing ache between her thighs. And recrossed her arms under her breasts, which now felt as if they had swollen to twice their normal size: i.e., almost big enough to fill a B-cup.

'Not quite.' He broke eye contact to wipe the coffee spill off the countertop with a paper towel. 'Although the school authorities would probably have disagreed.'

She should have apologised for leaving the spill, but she was too rapt by the conversation and the insight into his past. 'Why?'

'Perhaps because I spent more time on exclusion than I did at school.' He pitched the towel into the kitchen bin. All nonchalance. 'Detentions, time outs didn't work on me, so they went large. And that didn't work, either.'

'You got excluded from school? I don't believe it.' *Mr Perfecto, a problem child? Get outta here.*

His eyebrow hiked up. Then his crooked smile sent a jolt of pleasure through her. She'd never seen him smile like that before. Not polite and distant, but warm and a bit wicked. Or at least not at her.

'Why not? Because I'm supposed to be Mr Perfecto?'

'You know about that?'

His lips quirked. 'You don't have a lot of volume control when you're mad.'

She felt instantly contrite. It was a novel feeling. 'I'm sorry. That stuff...' She hesitated, not wanting to explain. 'It's not really about you.' Although she had included him in her war of attrition with her mother. Because she'd been jealous of his success with Aldo, and how much her mum raved about him. And not her. When she hadn't given her mum much reason to rave about her of late. It all felt rather small and petty and juvenile now.

'That's OK.' The smile didn't falter as he shrugged. 'Better to be Mr Perfecto than Mr Arsehole.'

The comment made her feel insecure. Was he sharing the joke with her or taking the piss? He probably didn't like her much. Why would he?

'Why don't I make brownies to take with us to the Serps?' It was a peace offering, pure and simple. She studied his expression to gauge his reaction, keeping watch for any signs of the contempt she'd seen so often from Liam when she'd tried too hard to please him.

'Cool. I'll make the sandwiches.' He seemed relaxed, making it impossible to be sure one way or the other.

Bummer. He was much harder to read than Liam.

* * *

They worked together in silence, the sun streaming through the basement window and lightening Lizzie's mood. After gathering all the ingredients she needed from her mum's larder, she started melting the chocolate. She sensed Trey behind her, slicing the bread and raiding the larder for tins of sweetcorn and tuna to make the sandwich filling Aldo adored. Normally, she would have moaned on principle. Why did Aldo always get the filling he wanted? Just because he refused to eat anything else. The calories in her mum's home-made mayo were catastrophic. But she was too busy catching glimpses of Trey as he worked. At one point, he leaned over her to grab a bowl from the cabinet above her head and she got another heady whiff of that woodsy shower gel. She caught sight of his biceps, round and sturdy beneath the short sleeve of his polo shirt. Did he do weights? Have a gym membership? Liam had always been super skinny. But what had seemed edgy and cool a year ago seemed weedy now next to Trey's solid strength.

Awareness pulsed in places she didn't want it to as his long fingers gripped the sweetcorn tin, his wide wrist flexing as he worked the can opener.

He caught her looking and she averted her eyes, suddenly absorbed in folding beaten eggs and flour in with the melted chocolate and butter mixture. She greased the baking tin and hoped he couldn't see the blotchy blush working its way up the back of her neck like a Virginia creeper.

Slopping the gloopy mixture into the greased tin, she chopped up some salted peanuts and sprinkled them on top. She refused to look his way again while she listened to the sounds of him cling-filming the sandwiches.

'You didn't weigh anything?'

She glanced over her shoulder at the enquiry. 'No need. It's a simple recipe. I've made it with my mum a billion times.' Back in the days when her mum had let her help out with all the baking chores on a Saturday morning.

'You and your mum used to bake together?' The question was tinged with astonishment. As if he couldn't imagine her being helpful.

'Yes, she always had tons to do at the weekend—party food mostly. Kids party catering was how she made her money in the early days, before the cake designing took off.'

'Did you enjoy it?' If he wasn't so hard to read, she might almost have thought he sounded wistful.

She pushed the tray into the oven and slammed the door on the memories. 'It was OK.' She shook off the moment of melancholy. No point in getting cheesy about the good old days. Her mum certainly never did. And why would she? Her mum didn't need her help any more because she had a whole army of helpers who could do the job better than Lizzie ever had.

* * *

It was a glorious day for a visit to Hyde Park, the weather having thrown London for a loop by deciding it was mid-August in the south of France instead of early July in the UK. The sun warmed the still verdant grass, which hadn't had a chance to be beaten down by a thousand tourist loafers yet. The cool spots under the horse chestnut trees, as they walked across Kensington Gardens, smelled of wet earth and tree sap rather than dust and dog shit. After they'd paid the nine pounds for a family ticket to enter the Lido enclosure, Aldo raced ahead to find 'the best spot'. Lizzie hung back with Trey, darting glances past the few other groups already there to make sure none of her friends had decided to come for a morning swim. The last thing she wanted was to get

spotted on something as shudderingly uncool as a 'family outing'. She relaxed, though, after scanning the crowd and seeing no one between the ages of sixteen and thirty, except her and Trey. She relaxed more when it occurred to her it was only ten o'clock. None of her friends would even be out of bed yet and she wasn't sure any of them could swim. And, even if they could, they probably wouldn't be caught dead swimming in the Serpentine with its dark water and squidgy lake bottom—which sunk through your bare toes and made you wonder how much of it was really just duck poo.

Trey strode ahead to join Aldo on the brow of the bank that faced the lake, where her brother stood staking out their 'best spot'. Trey pulled a blanket out of the picnic backpack and lifted it up by two corners to spread it out. All thoughts of duck poo disappeared as Lizzie became momentarily transfixed by the play of muscles in his arms, and the fleeting glimpse of his trim belly and outie belly button again, before his polo shirt settled back to cover his midriff—and the blanket floated onto the grass in perfect symmetry. The shorts and camisole ensemble she'd chosen for the day became uncomfortably tight. And the blotchy blush from this morning crept back up her neck.

There was absolutely no denying it, Trey Carson, lame clothes and all, was supremely, undeniably, super hot. Not just his model-ific features and buff body, but the quiet competence with which he did everything. So hot, in fact, she almost didn't care if Carly and Liam and every one of her friends caught them having a picnic together.

In his own uncool way, Trey was cooler than any of them. Because he didn't seem to care what people thought. Or maybe he just didn't know what was cool and what was uncool, which made him even cooler really. What would it be like to be above all that bullshit? Not to care about saying

the wrong thing, liking the wrong band, secretly being into *Hannah Montana* reruns when everyone was raving about *Game of Thrones* or *Orange is the New Black*... Or getting a rep for being a beg-friend or a frigid bitch.

Just imagining having that freedom made her feel lighter and bigger and more important.

She flicked off her sandals and carried them up the hill while Trey took out the assortment of sandwiches and brownies and crisps and dip they'd packed together for the trip. Funny how domesticity didn't seem totally boring when you were doing it with someone who exuded enough raw energy to fire a nuclear power station.

Aldo whipped off his T-shirt, revealing his sturdy boy's chest already tanned in July because of the olive skin Lizzie suspected he had inherited from that smarmy Italian dipshit her mum had dated for about a nanosecond. As Aldo dropped onto the blanket to kick off his trainers and tug off his socks, Lizzie noticed the roll of puppy fat spilling over the waistband of his shorts, which hadn't been there last summer. She felt a momentary dart of satisfaction at the thought that he would be hitting puberty in the next year or two.

Welcome to purgatory, kiddo.

But the satisfaction was swiftly followed by guilt. *Poor bugger, he has all that crap still to come.* And then a jolt of realisation. She had no idea when it had happened, probably sometime in the past year, but she wasn't crippled by jealousy any more. Why had it never occurred to her until now that his body was a ticking time bomb, just like hers had been at ten or eleven? And, just like her, he didn't even know it. Because no amount of dopey cartoons of naked people with pubic hair or tampon demonstrations in those

furtive, giggly Year Six sex-ed classes could prepare you for how horrendous adolescence was going to be.

It seemed astonishing to her now that when she'd started her periods at thirteen she'd been hopelessly envious of Aldo's simple, sturdy five-year-old boy's body. In the three or four years that followed, she'd been so angry with all the mean tricks her body had started playing on her— bleeding and cramping and gaining hair and pus-y spots where there had once been only smooth, clear skin—that she'd taken it out on Aldo and her mother. Because they didn't have any of this shit to deal with.

Sitting down cross-legged on the blanket, she tilted her head back to absorb the sun's warmth on her cheeks. Her mostly zit-free cheeks, which had required only a minimal dose of concealer this morning.

'Trey, can we go swimming now?' Aldo's urgent shout, pitched to piercing right next to her ear, jolted Lizzie out of her state of grace.

She opened her eyes, ready to launch into a rant, but cut it off, noticing the tiny love handles above the waistband of Aldo's swimming trunks still visible even as he stood up. Energy pulsed through his body as he shifted his weight from foot to foot, waiting not at all patiently for Trey's answer.

How glad was she that she wasn't a ten-year-old boy? It must be a nightmare being on the brink of explosion all the time.

'Sure, probably better to swim before we eat.' Trey hadn't even finished the sentence before Aldo gave a wild whoop and sped off. He charged straight into the lake, the whoop turning to a shriek as he hit the shallows, skidded over and bellyflopped into the water.

'Eww!' Lizzie shuddered. 'What's the betting he got a mouthful of duck poo and feathers with that manoeuvre?'

Trey laughed, warming her cheeks even more. 'I better head in before he drowns himself. You OK to stay by the stuff?'

She shielded her eyes to look up at him. Way, way up. A trickle of anticipation worked its way down her spinal column, releasing refreshing bursts of sensation en route. Was Mr Perfecto going to disrobe right in front of her? Would she be able to stand the suspense? 'Yes, fine. You go ahead.'

And feel free to strip down to your trunks and make me even more grateful I'm not a ten-year-old boy.

She propped herself on her elbows, smiling when Trey turned his back on her, probably to keep an eye on Aldo and—joy of joys—give her the opportunity to appreciate his striptease unobserved. He toed off the Nike high-tops, balanced steadily on each leg to pull off his socks and then tuck them into the trainers. After unhooking his jeans, he bent over to take them off.

Black stretchy Lycra trunks. Thank you, God.

Lizzie almost whooped like Aldo at Trey's excellent choice of swimwear: simple, functional, not budgie-smuggler gross but clingy enough to reveal the awesome contours of his bum, bunching and flexing splendidly as he lifted each leg to strip off his jeans. Crossing his arms, he grasped the hem of his polo shirt and pulled it over his head, then folded it and dropped it on top of the rest of his clothes.

Lizzie swallowed, drool collecting under her tongue at an alarming rate. His back was beautiful, as smoothly muscled as his arse, the wide shoulder blades tapering to the indentation of his ribs and bisected by the perfect line of his spine. Her gaze skated over his delicious bum to examine long legs dusted with curls of dark hair. He had the same olive-toned skin as Aldo. Maybe his dad had been Italian, too. Although his body was nothing like Aldo's—Trey was

a man, not a boy. She breathed through her nose. The whole of his body was beautiful. A work of art. Like that famous statue in Florence with the minuscule willy.

The blush burned her nape as she remembered Carly's constant teasing about the size of Trey's meat. Did she want him to turn around so she could make a considered assessment? Would her lungs continue to function if he did? Dying of asphyxiation would probably not be cool. Although she was beginning to see the appeal now for those people who liked to strangle themselves during sex, because just the sight of Trey's awesomeness was making her light-headed enough to feel euphoric.

The breath she'd been holding burst out when, instead of turning, he ran his thumbs round the waistband of his trunks and dropped his head to concentrate on retying the strings at the front. And she spotted the tattoo.

The red and black ink was faded, but the shape suggested some kind of mythic bird, its wingspan spread across the width of his back, hovering above his coccyx and the slope of his backside, nestled in the demarcation line of white flesh that would usually be covered by his pants.

Lizzie blinked a couple of times, gobsmacked. Mr Perfecto had inked his arse. He'd hinted at his misspent youth earlier, but seriously? What the fuck?

Then again, tattoos were hardly bad-boy insignia these days. She folded her lolling tongue back into her mouth. In fact, tattoos were more like fashion statements; every one of her friends had one, ranging from elaborate cartoon characters and geometric designs to sage Sanskrit sayings that no doubt translated as 'Confucius says I'm a pretentious twat'. She even had a tattoo, despite her near-phobia of needles. A constellation of tiny stars that ran along the line of her instep and then curled round her ankle—and had

looked cheesy and crap almost as soon as she'd survived the horror of having it etched into her foot two summers ago.

But Trey wasn't a follower of fashion, if his wardrobe was anything to go by. And surely that would include body art trends. So why had he laid himself out in a tattoo parlour with his pants off and gotten his arse inked? There had to be a story there. A story she was suddenly very curious to hear.

'I'll see you in a bit.'

She glanced up, past Trey's fascinating arse, to find him watching her from over his shoulder.

'You OK?' he said. 'Your face is kind of red.'

You don't know the half of it. 'I'll put some sunscreen on.'

'You sure you don't want to come in for a swim? Might help you to cool off,' he said, turning to face her.

She kept her eyes firmly on his upper body so as not to overheat completely. Checking out his other assets would have to wait for another day. 'What about our picnic stuff?'

'I can keep an eye on it from the water,' he added, ever practical and helpful.

She debated joining him. Warmed by the offer. And the thought of getting the chance to see all those muscles in sinuous motion, up close and dripping wet. But was forced to discard the idea.

Aldo would be there to play gooseberry like an eager puppy. And there was no point in risking death by drowning in duck-poo-infested water when she had to start working on a strategy to discover all Trey's secrets in under two weeks.

But it wasn't until he strolled away and then executed a perfect dive from the end of the dock—fearlessly arrowing that long body under the murky surface of the lake— that she realised this was the first time she'd been curious about another human being and their backstory for, well, like, forever.

And that the rush of enthusiasm and expectation felt more fabulous than a spot-free T-zone.

* * *

'Trey, did you see me do a somersault?'

Trey peeled his attention from the bank, where Lizzie Best lay on their picnic blanket, the bikini she had stripped down to a lurid red against her pale skin. 'Sorry, buddy, I missed it.' *Because I was far too busy checking out your sister.* The guilty thought had him focusing on Aldo, or trying to.

He still hadn't quite figured out why Lizzie had mellowed so much this morning. But he'd decided to stop asking the question when he'd spotted the stunned expression on her face after he'd stripped down to his trunks.

He'd seen that expression before from women, especially when he was without a shirt. He knew it meant they liked what they saw. Ever since he'd joined the local rugby club at sixteen, in an attempt to handle the loneliness and work off the frustration of being his mum's sole carer, he'd gotten those flattering appraisals from women with increasing frequency. Because a handy by-product of the training was the muscle bulk he'd acquired in all the right places. Usually he appreciated that look. Even if he wasn't able to act on it. But seeing that dazed, unfocused look in Lizzie's cornflower blue eyes had made him instantly wary and yet uncomfortably warm.

Which was totally wrong.

Lizzie was three years younger than him, he wasn't sure she even liked him much and Lizzie's mum had told him all about how vulnerable her daughter was on Thursday night before she'd left. Lizzie having any kind of crush on him would be extremely bad. So how did he account for the tightening in his crotch her look had triggered?

'Why don't you do another one, and I'll watch now?' he said, keeping his gaze off the girl on the bank and trying harder to refocus it on her little brother. The kid he was actually being paid to watch over.

'But I already did it.' Aldo's face fell into a pout. 'I'm not sure I can do another one so good.'

'If you did it once, you can do it again.' Lifting himself up onto the dock, he sat with his legs dangling into the chilly water and swiped his fingers through his hair. Warmth seeped from the weathered boards through his buttocks to tug at his stomach muscles.

If Lizzie was still watching him, it didn't mean anything. So what if he'd noticed her doing that a lot in the past half hour while he and Aldo mucked about in the water? He didn't want her to watch him. Any more than he wanted to watch her.

He folded his arms over his chest, squeezed his biceps and shuddered theatrically. 'But get a move on, because I'm freezing and I want to get dressed.'

And he'd probably be a lot better able to process this situation if he had his clothes on.

Aldo paddled furiously, treading water, the pout disappearing as quickly as it had come. 'OK... I have to take a swim up, though. So don't look away.'

'Don't worry, I won't,' he said on autopilot, used to reassuring Aldo—whom he'd noticed as soon as he'd come to work for Halle was starved for any kind of male attention.

Maybe that was all this was, Trey reasoned, keeping his gaze locked on the lake and Aldo splashing over to one of the buoys and away from Lizzie on the bank. He knew Aldo didn't have a dad, and although Lizzie did, he knew she didn't see him much. Because he lived in Paris. Maybe Lizzie saw him as some kind of surrogate dad figure. Like

Aldo. While her mum was away. The thought made him shudder for real, despite the warmth of the sun on his shoulder blades.

Bloody hell. Terrific. Now the instant awareness he'd felt as her gaze had raked over his chest and her eyes had gone all dreamy felt sort of creepy and incestuous. As well as just really bad news.

Aldo's arms pinwheeled as his bum lifted into the air and his legs flipped over in the water, executing a lopsided underwater somersault that wouldn't win any synchronised swimming awards but still looked pretty accomplished.

He came up for air, spluttering water, his hair slicked to his head like a seal, and Trey gave him a round of applause, forcing his mind firmly back into au pair zone and further away from Lizzie Best danger zone.

The good news was that Aldo was a needy kid, who would help to keep him focused for the next twelve days. Until Lizzie's mum got back. If Lizzie was at all interested in him, he very much doubted her interest would last longer than a week. Especially given that she'd seemed to despise him until about four hours ago. Surely this was just a passing fad. And although he didn't relish the return of the frosty drama queen, he had to concede she was easier to handle than friendly bikini babe.

'That was ace, buddy.' He reached out his arm to lift Aldo out of the water. 'Come on, let's get some lunch.'

Aldo shook his head, the droplets spraying across the surface of the lake and hitting Trey's knees. 'Can't I stay in a bit longer on my own? I want to practise it some more.'

'You're shivering. I think it's time to get out now.'

Aldo gritted his teeth to stop them chattering. 'Ten minutes? Please?' He sent Trey a winning grin. Trey knew he was sunk. Aldo so rarely showed signs of wanting to be

independent, he didn't feel right discouraging him. He nodded, resigned. 'Fine, but no more than ten. Tops.' So much for Aldo, the dependably needy decoy. 'You sure you're OK on your own while I go and get dressed?'

Aldo bobbed his head with undisguised enthusiasm. 'Yes, tell Lizzie to watch, will you? I want her to see my somersault, too.' Aldo's gaze flicked to their spot on the bank that Trey had been avoiding. 'Who's that guy she's talking to?'

Standing, Trey shielded his eyes against the glare of the sun. And felt the inappropriate warmth in the pit of his stomach chill. A lanky kid, about Lizzie's age, stood over her, and although he seemed relaxed, his stance loose, Lizzie definitely didn't. No longer lounging on her elbows, she was sitting bolt upright, her knees hugged to her chest. He couldn't hear what the kid was saying to her, but the way she had her face turned away from him made it clear whatever he was saying, she didn't want to hear it.

'Wait there, Aldo, I'll be back to get you in ten.' He threw the words over his shoulder, not even sure Aldo had heard him, as he headed down the dock at a jog, his eyes trained on the guy with Lizzie.

Then he saw the guy bring his hand from behind his back. It disappeared in front at crotch level.

Lizzie's distressed shout rang out across the park all the way to the water. 'Fuck off and die, Jenkin.'

The families sitting nearby sent her censorious looks for the language. Trey's jog accelerated into a run when he spotted the hot colour scorching her cheeks. As he got closer, he could see what the kid was doing. He was miming jacking off, right in front of Lizzie's face.

The blast of disgust was quickly followed by an explosion of righteous anger. The dirty little pervert. Whoever

he was, he wasn't going to get the chance to fuck off and die, because Trey planned to murder him first.

* * *

'What's the matter, Queen Lizzie? Liam said you're a sure bet for a good blow job.' Jenkin Sawyer's feral laugh added disgust to the liquid fire in Lizzie's belly.

'I told you to fuck off. Do you not understand English?' she hissed, mindful of their audience of shocked yummy mummies.

Resentment washed over her, adding a bitter taste to the bile in her stomach.

Who were they to look at her like that? As if she was in the wrong? As if it was her fault her ex-boyfriend was a sexist dickhead and his friend was a perv?

All these yummy mummies with their yummy kids who had cute, comfortable, polite lives and had probably never had to deal with an arsewipe like Jenkin in their entire life.

She hated Jenkin, always had, the way he stared at her— oozing sleaze and speculation—when she was hanging out with Liam. That look alone had felt like cockroaches were crawling over her flesh whenever she was within ten feet of him, like now. But somehow the judgemental stares of all the clean, comfortable, polite people made the harassment a thousand times worse.

'Stop playing hard to get. You know you love to suck dick.' He cupped his pathetic package again to emphasise the point and she thought she might gag. But as she raised her head to tell him again where he could stick his dick, a shadow fell over her face. And Jenkin's shoulder jerked. His arms flayed and he made a weird squeaking sound before crashing backwards with an audible thump.

Then Trey's big body was blocking her view. His hair-dusted legs akimbo, the wings of his tattoo rising above the

damp fabric of his swimsuit. She could see Jenkin's face, red and sweating and speechless, through Trey's spread legs, gaping up at the man in front of her from his new position on the ground.

'Who the fuck are you?' Jenkin asked, still squeaking.

Trey reached down, grasped the front of Jenkin's Superdry shirt and yanked him up, until they were nose to nose. Jenkin's feet wiggled, his toes barely touching the ground. Lizzie couldn't see his face, his upper body obscured by Trey's back, but she could hear the choking sound in Jenkin's throat as Trey said, low and ridiculously calm, 'I'm a friend of Lizzie's. You come anywhere near her again and you're going to be eating that dick you're so proud of. Got it?'

Jenkin hit the ground, hard, as Trey threw him down again. The double thump as his back and then his head connected with the earth was followed by the whoosh of air expelling from his lungs. He groaned, rolled, holding his ribs and swearing.

'Get up and piss off,' Trey demanded.

Jenkin scrambled to obey, a grimace of pain twisting his face, and raised his hands in supplication. He edged away, the look on his face a picture of shocked panic. 'OK, OK, you can have her.'

Lizzie jumped up from her sitting position, finally able to get her limbs moving round her own shock. She lifted on tiptoes to peer past Trey as Jenkin limped off, like the cowardly perv he was. The grass stain on the back of his shirt waved like a badge of dishonour as he darted through the sea of gaping picnickers and disappeared round the side of the gatehouse—probably to escape the Lido before he ended up having dick sandwich for lunch.

'Are you OK?' Trey asked, his face grave.

She had the strangest urge to laugh, which she recognised

as one part shock and two parts relief. But underneath the inappropriate giggle was a huge wave of gratitude.

Not because he had pounded on Jenkin and got rid of him—she could have got rid of him herself, eventually. Jenkin might be creepy, but he was too weedy and full of himself to be scary. And she was used to dealing with nasty remarks from men. Ever since she'd hit puberty, she'd got depressingly used to everything from wolf whistles to lewd suggestions hurled at her every time she walked past a building site or made eye contact with some arsewipe in a white van. It had scared her at fourteen, it just made her mad now, but beneath the anger was the bubbling cauldron of humiliation.

And that's where the gratitude came in. It felt impossibly gallant of Trey, especially considering she'd always been pretty mean to him, to put himself out on her account. That he would be genuinely outraged by remarks that hadn't surprised her. All her friends had been down on her when she'd broken up with Liam—everyone had sided with him instead of her, even Carly—which had always made her feel as if the taunts were sort of her fault. For being stupid enough to latch on to him. And give him head whenever he wanted it. Those taunts had hurt not because they frightened her, or even outraged her, but because they made her feel diminished and insignificant. Right this minute, she didn't feel small or insignificant for once. She felt important. Because Trey had stood up for her.

Which probably meant she was in serious need of loads more therapy. But still, it felt good. 'Yes, I'm fine. He's just a nuisance, like a bad smell. But he's harmless.'

'Those things he was saying didn't sound harmless to me.' The tight tone sounded a bit judgemental—almost as

if he were blaming her for not being more outraged. The warmth in her belly cooled. 'Liam's your ex, right?'

'How do you know about Liam?' Heat spread across her chest, the way it hadn't when Jenkin had tried to shove his dick in her face.

She'd split up with Liam nearly a year ago, long before Trey had started working for her mum. She couldn't imagine Aldo saying anything about him. He'd hardly even met her ex the whole time they were going out. Liam wasn't the sort of guy you brought home to meet your family.

Instead of replying, Trey bent to pick up the towel and rubbed it over his face and neck, then glanced over to check on Aldo.

She waited for his gaze to connect with hers again, as her chest reached boiling point.

'Your mum mentioned you'd had a bad break-up with him,' he said finally. He threw down the towel and picked up his polo shirt.

Whaaaat?

Horror gripped her insides. 'And why exactly was my mum talking to you about me?'

And how much had she said?

Bloody hell, had her mum told him about the therapy she'd forced her to go to? No wonder he'd been so nice to her this morning. He probably thought she was some kind of fruit loop. The humiliation of having Jenkin think he could get her to give him a BJ in a public park was nothing compared to having the lame but hot au pair think she was a nutjob.

He'd ridden to her rescue not because he thought she was important, but because her mum was probably paying him danger money to babysit her as well as Aldo.

He shrugged, his big shoulder stiff, as he concentrated on

running his thumbs along the bottom of his shirt. Good, she was glad he felt uncomfortable, because she was mortified.

'She worries about you,' he murmured. 'She wanted me to look out for you while she was away,' he added, still engrossed with the stitching on the hem of his shirt.

'Don't kid yourself. She doesn't give a shit about me.' Resentment flared anew to add to the tangle of emotions making her guts feel like a pit of vipers. 'She was probably just worried you'd walk off the job if I said something to upset you. Then she'd have to cut her stupid book tour short.'

'Why are you so angry with your mum?' The question and the incredulous tone punctured her outrage long enough to make her realise how childish she must sound to him.

'I'm not angry with her all the time,' she qualified. *Not every single second anyway.* 'I just want her to stop butting into my life. I'm an adult now and she treats me like a child. I bet she's even paying you extra to watch out for me, too, isn't she?' Like a five-year-old.

Way to go, Mum, why not make me feel like even more of a total loser?

A puzzled frown appeared on his brow. 'I get an hourly rate for looking after Aldo. That's it.'

'Then why did you decide to help me out with Jenkin?' she asked.

'Because the guy was a total arsehole.'

The terse explanation should have mollified her, but it didn't. Especially when he lifted his polo shirt over his head. The sight of his eight-pack stretching enticingly round his outie belly button made all the oxygen suck out of her lungs.

Why does he have to be so freaking hot?

He rubbed his hands through his hair, making the short strands stand up in patches—the haphazard style made him

look even sexier, like a model who'd been professionally rumpled for a Hugo Boss ad.

'Well, just so you know, you didn't have to intervene. I don't need a babysitter.'

'I believe you said that already.' He had the cheek to sound snotty. 'To your mum at top volume before she left.'

So he'd heard that, too, had he? The snakes took a greasy turn in her belly. 'You shouldn't eavesdrop on conversations that have sod all to do with you.'

'I was the subject of that conversation. And it's not like I could fail to hear it the way you were shouting.'

She decided to ignore that and the prickle of shame at the accusation. He knew nothing about her relationship with her mum, so he didn't get to judge her. Even if he did have bionic hearing.

'Just for the record, I was handling Jenkin fine on my own.' Which wasn't entirely true, but she'd be damned if she'd let him feel any more superior than he already did.

'Handling that turd was my pleasure. No guy should ever speak to you like that. And if that's the way your ex treated you—or let his friends treat you—I'm hoping you dumped him from a great height.'

The vote of confidence was so unequivocal and so unexpected, and so unlike the way any of her friends had reacted, her neck got hot. 'Actually, I did.'

The snakes in her belly slithered smoothly away at his nod of approval. Until all that was left was a slight breathlessness.

'I don't suppose you managed to castrate him while you were at it?' His terse tone was only half joking.

A smile flitted across her lips. 'I wish.'

'Me, too.'

'Trey, why didn't you come get me?'

Lizzie turned to find Aldo, dripping wet and shuddering, his hands clasped round his shoulders. The accusatory glare he was sending Trey was only slightly weakened by the way his teeth were chattering like castanets.

'Hey, buddy, I'm really sorry.' Trey grabbed a towel from the pile on the blanket, but as he dropped it over Aldo's shoulders, her brother shrugged it off, the glare intensifying.

'Get off me. You didn't even tell Lizzie about my somersault, did you?'

Lizzie could see the storm clouds hovering, the prickly shrug a sure sign one of Aldo's tantrums was fast approaching. The towel dangled from Trey's fingertips and he let out a heavy sigh, as if bracing himself for the impact.

Lizzie rested her hand on Aldo's rigid shoulder. 'Of course he did. I watched you do it. It was great.' She had less than a moment to contemplate the fact she had actually tried to avert disaster for once, instead of fuelling it, before Aldo turned his glare on her.

'You're lying. I know you are. You never watched, because I waited and you never even looked.'

He had her there, but before she could think of a way out of the white lie, Trey knelt, dropping to Aldo's level. 'I'm sorry, Aldo. I should have been keeping an eye on you, but that guy was saying mean things to your sister and I wanted to make him stop.'

'Who cares if he said mean things to her? She always says mean things to me and you never do anything.'

Trey's chin dropped and he seemed unsure how to react. What could he say? When it was true?

Shame stabbed into Lizzie's chest. How hard had she made Aldo's life in the past few years, and Trey's in the past few months, with the endless sniping and needling?

'I hate you,' Aldo shouted at Trey. 'You don't like me. You only pretend to. Nobody likes me.' Tears mingled with the water on Aldo's face, his body shuddering with more than the cold. He didn't look explosive any more. He looked devastated.

'I do like you, Aldo. You know that's true,' Trey said, but he sounded weary and tense. And not all that convincing.

Hug him, Trey, that's all you have to do to convince him.

She tried to transmit the suggestion telepathically while controlling her own urge to hug her brother. She wasn't the Aldo Whisperer any more. So she'd have to wait for Trey to figure out the obvious.

But Trey didn't budge, or say anything, clearly at a loss as he watched Aldo shiver.

So she knelt down herself and whispered, 'We both like you, Aldo. How about I give you a hug to prove it?'

Her brother looked up, his wobbly chin a dead giveaway. But she could see the suspicion. She braced herself for the rejection she deserved.

She'd made fun of his 'baby ways' so many times in the past few years he probably didn't trust her. The guilt over each one of those throwaway barbs jabbed into her as her brother's gaze rose to Trey, his chin still quivering alarmingly.

The knowledge it was Trey whom he wanted a hug from hurt. Trey, who in the space of three months had made an effort to become Aldo's friend, his confidant, the guy Aldo looked up to like a big brother. Instead of his real big sister.

But Trey stood up and then remained standing, stiff and distant by her side.

Eventually, Aldo's gaze slid back to her. And he dipped his chin. It wasn't a proper nod. She guessed he didn't want

to risk one, in case she was only joking and used this moment to mock him.

The urge to apologise for all the mean things she'd said to her brother over the past few years was swift and fairly agonising. But she didn't give in to it. Because for once she realised this wasn't actually about her.

Standing, too, she took the towel from Trey, swept it round her brother's shoulders and tugged him into her arms. He stood stiffly. His head was nearly to her chin now. He'd gotten so much bigger than the last time she'd done this. But still his body felt achingly familiar. The smell of kid sweat and the brackish scent of the Serpentine fresh on his skin triggered the phantom hint of the baby smell she had once adored. She remembered the weight of him on her tummy in their old flat in Hackney, the squelching sound as he chewed on his bottle and tugged on her hair, totally absorbed while she read *Harry Potter*—even though he was way too little to tell the difference between a Horcrux and a Muggle.

'I like you, Aldo. I like you a lot,' she whispered into his wet hair.

She wasn't sure he'd heard her, until his body softened and his shoulders dropped. The guilt slammed into her, like a gigantic wave knocking her off her feet. But then Aldo's hands settled on the small of her back, chilly despite the warm day. And the wave receded, tugging her back onto dry land. She tightened her arms round her brother's shoulders, silently thanking him for being brave enough to risk ridicule. And hug her back.

Trey cleared his throat. He was staring at them both, his face clouded by an emotion she couldn't read. But one thing was definite, he didn't look anywhere near as confident as usual.

He mouthed the word 'thanks'.

She nodded, wondering what the no-hugging thing was all about, then jotted it down on her ever-growing list of Trey enigmas to investigate at a later date.

Chapter 12

'Why not admit it, we're hopelessly lost.'

'We are not lost, oh voice of doom.' Luke pointed vaguely across the stream that ran alongside the dusty former logging track and adjusted the map. 'I think it's this way.'

'*I think* isn't specific enough.' Halle trudged on, ignoring her companion's latest stupid suggestion. She slapped at her neck, not sure whether the sting was another trickle of sweat or the carnivorous insect that had already feasted on her and was now coming back for dessert.

The jet lag had slammed into her like an eighteen-wheeler yesterday afternoon at approximately three p.m.—for the third day running. So she'd left Luke typing away industriously on his laptop and crashed out. Only to wake up at precisely 4.10 a.m. this morning. It was now eleven. And she was ready to face-plant again. Unfortunately, that was impossible because she appeared to be on a ten-hour scenic hike to nowhere. With a man who didn't know how to read a map.

So far their 'extreme bonding experiences' had been fairly harmless, but just strenuous enough to get her sleeping like the dead—until she woke up before dawn. But she should have asked their perky 'personal concierge', Bill, a

lot more questions when he had said the word 'hike' this morning. Unfortunately, she'd gotten completely fixated on the word 'bears' instead in his opening spiel.

He'd led them to a brand-new SUV and then spent the next half hour droning on about the fascinating culture of the Appalachians and the wide variety of flora and fauna in the Smoky Mountains National Park while driving them thirty miles up Old State Highway 73. During the journey, she'd simply assumed 'hike' in the US vernacular probably translated as a long drive and a very short walk. Turned out it meant a longish drive and an even longer walk. In baking-hot weather, with only a backpack full of supplies and an idiot for company.

'Wait for me, dammit,' she shouted as Luke disappeared into the overgrown trail ahead. 'What makes you think it's this way?' she demanded as he stopped ahead of her.

Time to be proactive. Clearly, slavishly following Luke isn't working.

'Because I am the keeper of the map.' The dappled sunlight cast his face into harsh relief as she drew level, breathing heavily. 'Why didn't you tell them you were so unfit?' he murmured. 'They would have organised something less strenuous.'

His T-shirt stuck to his chest in damp patches, emphasising the sculpted contours of muscle and bone.

Well, that's distracting.

'I am fit.' *Kind of.* 'I'm just not into walking around in circles for no good reason. In five-hundred-degree heat in the middle of the day.'

'Then let's go cool off.' He flung out his arm to indicate the ominous trail ahead. 'According to the map, there's a waterfall this way.'

'The map you can't read?'

'Yup, that's the one.' He waved the map in front of her face, in a gesture just guaranteed to piss her off. 'I have it right here.'

She didn't need to cool off. She just needed to get this over with so she could go back to the privacy of her bedroom, where the firmness of his pectoral muscles would be a lot less distracting and the word 'bears' would not have the same significance. 'Having the map and reading the map correctly are not the same thing.'

'I know how to read a map. I've hiked in the goddamn Hindu Kush for five days embedded with US Special Forces.'

'I don't care if you're a paid-up member of the Taliban, I'm not going into the woods. It's dangerous. There are bears and rattlesnakes and God knows what else out there,' she huffed, scoping out the mile-high forest of mostly coniferous trees that stretched away up the mountainside, the dense vegetation broken up only by the occasional rock escarpment—which probably housed a multitude of bear caves.

'It's not dangerous. It's a marked hiking trail. And, anyway, the snakes and bears will be staying the hell out of our way with the amount of noise you're making.' Luke dragged a bandana out of his back pocket to mop his brow. 'Now stop moaning and look around you.' He spread his arms. 'This place is amazing. Let's go and explore.'

She unlocked her jaw. 'We're not exploring. We're lost. There's a difference.'

He tucked the bandana back into the pocket of his hiking shorts. 'I told you, we're not lost. And, even if you don't trust me—' the thin smile was caustic '—Bill gave me a two-way radio.' He patted his backpack. 'So you can trust that.'

Her weeping thigh muscles disagreed. 'What if we're trespassing?'

'We're in a national park.'

'So what? Everyone in this country has a gun. Some of them even have automatic weapons, ready to shoot down anyone who strays into their path. Especially unsuspecting English people on extreme rambling expeditions,' she added, thinking of the bumper stickers in the convenience store they'd stopped at on their way to the resort four days ago. And the unpleasant illustration of the large, deadly-looking firearm accompanied by the slogan 'come and take it'.

'Most Americans do not own an AK-47,' Luke said. 'Round here they probably only own the odd hunting rifle. We're not in the hood.'

'Personally I don't care if I get accidentally shot by a deer hunter or a gang-banger. I'd still be dead. I think we should stay on the bigger track. Just in case.'

* * *

Luke counted down his straining temper.

Humour her. You've handled NATO generals with secrets to hide and Washington socialites with dementia. You can handle one knackered celebrity chef from Notting Hill.

He attemped to analyse Halle's pinched expression. It was hard to tell whether she was generally concerned about rogue gun nuts combing the woods or just trying to avoid exerting herself more. But they needed to get out of the sun. The red patch on the bridge of her nose was evidence of that.

Only one way to find out. Go on the offensive.

'When did you become such a wimp?'

Her eyes narrowed to slits. 'You really don't want me to answer that when I'm boiling hot, jet-lagged and being eaten alive by mosquitos.'

'Actually, I really do.' He was so over the hands-off approach. After three days of giving her space, he felt as if

he'd been tap-dancing on eggshells for days. She scuttled out of the kitchen every time he entered it. Spent most of the time in the cabin in her bedroom and had barely spoken to him during any of their bonding exercises so far. Remembering her panic attack on the plane, he decided to up the stakes. 'You had a lot more guts as a teenager.'

The blood flowed into her cheeks, pinkening the burned patch on her nose even more. He'd seen Halle lose it before. Not heeding those burning cheeks and furious scowl would be the equivalent of pulling the pin on a grenade. He'd once been prepared to do anything to avoid the explosion. Including lying through his teeth about how excited he was to become an accidental dad at nineteen. But he wasn't that cowardly kid any more. Because he yanked the pin out anyway. 'I guess having Lizzie made you lose your nerve. But I never noticed that before now.'

The blood surged up to her hairline and her hand whacked across his cheek with a resounding crack. Pain exploded in his face, the force of the blow snapping his head back, and popping the muscles in his neck.

He swore and cupped his cheek to contain the fiery heat, vaguely wondering if she'd given him whiplash.

Who knew a celebrity chef could pack a bigger punch than Mike Tyson?

'You unbelievable shit.' The shout ricocheted off the surrounding landscape, echoing like a thunder crack. 'It wasn't Lizzie. It was you.'

The sheen of unshed tears added a golden sparkle to her whisky-brown eyes. Tendrils of sweat-damp hair clung to her forehead, the pale skin above the round neck of her T-shirt had gone blotchy with temper and her chest heaved as if she had just run the London Marathon.

Maybe it was a cliché, but she was even more of a stunner when she was mad.

'I trusted you. I relied on you. And you buggered off and left me when I needed you the most, you bastard.' Her breath huffed out and he saw her exhaustion, not just from the plane journey, or the hike, or the jet lag.

This was bone-weary emotional exhaustion.

The realisation brought with it the memory of their squalid eighth-floor council flat in Hackney. The unreliable lift that stank of piss and the half-hearted use of cheap disinfectant. The gang of teenage boys who hung around the stairwell and sucked their teeth when he struggled up the stairs with Lizzie's buggy. The broken fluorescent light in the bathroom he'd never gotten round to fixing. Lizzie squalling as if she'd been scalded at two in the morning, in the cot from the charity shop they'd jammed up against the dresser in the corner of their bedroom.

Remorse flowed through him, radiating out from the stinging pain in his jaw.

He opened his mouth, but the apology died on his tongue. There was nothing he could say to take that exhaustion away. Nothing he could do to make it better now. And nothing he would have done not to escape then, so giving in to the urge to say sorry sixteen years too late would just be so much self-serving bullshit.

So he said nothing and waited for her to say her piece, each word scoring his conscience.

'I had to pick up and carry on and build something from absolutely nothing, because I had a child who needed me.' She thrust a thumb into her sternum, punctuating the hot air with the rasping breaths of her outrage. 'And I learned not to trust every snake oil salesman who came along, because

I had to. Don't talk to me about guts when you didn't even have the guts to stick around.'

* * *

Halle clenched her fingers into a fist to ease the blazing pain in her palm. She wasn't sure where the sudden burst of emotion had come from. But his smug words had been the trigger. That and the fact she'd been on a knife-edge of spiralling tension for days now.

Something that's also his fault, because he's the one who insisted on us sharing a bloody cabin.

She shook her hand trying to ease the sting. Who knew slapping someone in the face made your palm feel as if it had been branded? Maybe she should have taken into account his rock-solid jaw, and that day-old stubble that had the consistency of sandpaper. But for once there had been no forethought. Only reaction. The volcano, which had been bubbling under her breastbone, had erupted, spewing out her emnity towards him like molten lava detonating through a rock fissure.

He manipulated his jaw, as if checking she hadn't dislocated it. 'I guess I had that one coming,' he said. As always, a master of understatement.

The red stain where her hand had connected with his cheek bloomed under the skin.

The lava turned to ash in her mouth, and her knees trembled, the rawness in her throat making it hard to swallow. 'Ya think?'

She scrubbed her upper arm across her face, brushing away the salty sweat making her eyes sting.

'I didn't stick around because I couldn't,' he said, his tone soft in the still air. 'You have no idea how monumentally screwed up I was back then,' he added. 'All thanks to stuff in my life that had nothing to do with you.'

She guessed he was talking about his family. The dys-
functional, screwed-up family, full of underwear thieves,
whom he had always refused to talk about and had avoided
introducing her to. She'd accepted his explanation then—
that she wouldn't understand, that she was better off not
knowing them because 'they're all arseholes'—but now she
wondered. Why had she always let him decide what she was
strong enough to know about, what she had the maturity to
understand—and all the things she didn't?

But did she really want to go there? Now, after all these
years? The slap had been a simple knee-jerk reaction to his
dumb comment—and the frustration of the past few days.
Why would she want to open up old wounds that had taken
such a long time to heal?

He brushed his thumb across the hollow under her eye
and let it linger for a second too long, before digging his
hand into the pocket of his hiking shorts.

Once upon a time—maybe even yesterday—she would
have apologised for hitting him so hard. Physical violence
had never been her style. But he didn't look as if he was expecting an apology. And if she was being entirely honest,
she didn't really think he deserved one.

He repositioned the backpack on his shoulders. 'Let's go
find that waterfall. Looks like we could both do with some
cooling off.'

'Only if you're absolutely sure it's safe.'

His lips quirked, the grin impossibly sexy. The bastard.
'Don't worry, I'll keep an eye out for Uzi-toting grizzlies.'

* * *

Woods in rural England, on the rare occasions when Halle
had been called upon to walk through them, were comforting ancient places, scattered with wild flowers, the tree bark
musty with moss, the wildlife never much bigger than a bee.

Woods in Tennessee weren't woods at all, but wild untamed forests, both predatory and provocative—with a spectacular and arresting other-worldly beauty she hadn't expected. And which she hadn't taken the chance to appreciate until now.

As they ventured off the sun-brightened logging trail, Luke pointed out a sign, looking like a Disneyland prop, which directed them the 3.2 miles to Cherokee Creek Falls, but had the good grace not to gloat.

Despite the sign, Halle remained vigilant for the first ten minutes, scanning the dense forest of firs and oaks and pine trees, in case a black bear should pop out, eager to bite their heads off. Gradually, though, she relaxed and began to marvel at her surroundings.

The delicious quiet—punctuated only by the intermittent sounds of buzzing insects or distant water—beat with the rhythm of her own footfalls and the patient plod of Luke's hiking boots ahead. Her palm stopped stinging where she'd sandpapered it on Luke's jawline, and her heartbeat finally tracked back to the familiar thump-thump of her normal pulse rate.

The disconnected feeling lingered, as if she existed in a fog—her body clock out of sync with the time of day—but it became a warm, comforting fog instead of the hot, blistering, bone-melting fog of earlier.

She scanned the trees, only occasionally distracted by the sight of Luke's tall athletic form striding down the trail ahead of her. The forest's shadowy depths provided some much-needed shade from the mid-morning sun while holding secret caches of natural wonders, most of which she couldn't identify with any degree of certainty. The oak and maple trees, the azalea blooms and ferns weren't hard to name, even the gnarled thorny branches of the odd hawthorn bush, but easily the most prolific and spectacular plant—a

branched shrub festooned with lime evergreen leaves and dying clusters of spiky white and pink flowers—was unrecognisable but incongruous in its profusion. Bushes of the stuff appeared in every break in the trees as the trail climbed slowly upwards, framing some awe-inspiring glimpses of the Smoky Mountain range, which spread out in a panorama of rolling peaks and misty dips.

After twenty minutes of patient plodding, the trail opened into a wild meadow, which stood like an oasis of vibrant variant green, edged by an array of showy dark pink blooms on its far side. The rambling bushes reminded Halle rather bizarrely of the gardens of a stately home she'd once visited in Wiltshire.

'Are those rhododendron bushes?' she asked, incredulous.

Luke paused to observe the flowering scrubs. 'Yeah. Catawba rhododendrons. They grow wild all over the Appalachians.' Obviously, he'd done his homework, unlike her.

'Do you know what those other plants are, the ones with the white and pink flowers?' she asked, pointing out the other shrubs she'd been unable to identify.

He patted the damp skin of his neck with his bandana. 'I'm pretty sure that's mountain laurel, although I'm no expert. We'll have to ask Bill when he picks us up.'

'It smells incredible.' She drew in a breath of the perfumed air. 'I really didn't expect to see so many flowers.'

'Amazing, isn't it?' Luke tied the bandana round his forehead and Halle's pulse spiked. Apparently, the Smoky Mountain scenery wasn't the only arresting sight on offer.

'Yes, it is.'

Luke's wide shoulders tilted as he let the backpack slide down to drop at his feet. Tucking his hands into his back pockets, he lifted his chin to absorb the sunshine, the quiet moment of contemplation like a benediction. His sun-burnished skin

glowed, stretched tight over the high planes of his cheekbones, and she pictured him as a fallen angel haloed by a nimbus of hallowed light.

She blinked away the romantic thought. Luke Best had never been anyone's idea of an angel. Fallen or otherwise. But the realisation didn't stop the saliva drying in her mouth when a trickle of sweat skated down the corded sinews of his neck to disappear in the hollow of his clavicle. Her pulse fluttered as response tingled over her skin.

'How much further to the falls?' she asked.

Was he really planning to go for a dip in this waterfall? How did she feel about seeing him with less clothes on?

The flutter turned into a punch as her pulse thudded against her neck.

Don't be ridiculous. What's there to be nervous about?

He was just a man. And his body had once been such familiar terrain. She'd known every secret nook and cranny. The slopes of muscle and bone, the ridges of tendon and sinew, the sensitive hollows, the ticklish places, all his erogenous zones. She'd known exactly where and how to touch him, to kiss him and caress him, to make him groan and grunt and sometimes even shout with pleasure.

OK, stop right there.

She shook her head to shake off the sensual fog.

But as he knelt to retrieve the trail map from the backpack and then stood to study it, she took the opportunity to study him. And it occurred to her that the once familiar terrain wasn't as familiar any more.

His body looked much more substantial now, having been wiry to the point of scrawny when he was a young man.

She noted the generous thicket of sun-bleached hair on his shins and how it thinned out above his knees. His forearms were fuzzy with hair, too, while sweaty darker wisps

clung to his chest where his collarbone peeked from the V-neck of his T-shirt.

Apparently, Luke had gained quite a lot of body hair in the past sixteen years, too.

She tucked the thought away, dismissing the pleasantly floaty feeling engulfing her as a by-product of tiredness and the emotional exhaustion from her outburst.

He shoved the map into his pack and swung the bag onto his shoulders. 'Can't be much more than a mile.' He nudged his forehead against the short sleeve of his T-shirt, giving her a glimpse of the dark thicket of hair beneath his armpit. 'Let's get moving. I can't wait to get wet.'

She fell into step behind him, too tired to argue.

But it wasn't until the burble of water cascading over rocks beckoned through the trees that it occurred to her she hadn't packed a swimsuit. And if she'd forgotten her swimwear, what were the chances Mr Spontaneous had remembered his?

I don't care how much I need to cool off, skinny-dipping is out.

* * *

Cherokee Creek poured over the shelves of lichen-covered rock, tumbling into a deep pool of mossy water, which looked cool and inviting and just what Luke had been praying for. Because the sweat soaking his shirt wasn't the only heat he had to worry about.

Halle sat on the shallow pebbled beach in between the rocks, prising off her dusty trainers and peeling off her socks.

'It looks very inviting.' She swept her hair back to retie her ponytail.

'Doesn't it just,' he agreed, because she didn't sound entirely sure.

She'd calmed down since that whiplash-inducing slap. Enough for them to have a conversation about something other than whether or not they were lost. Which was all good. Not so good was the low hum that struck his abdomen every time their eyes met.

Despite her avoidance tactics over the past few days, his awareness of her seemed to be getting more acute. Even after she'd slumped off to bed yesterday halfway through the afternoon, he'd been hard-pressed to concentrate on the notes for his article. His head had been filled to bursting with images of her: shooting him the gimlet eye while they got smarmed to within an inch of their lives in Monroe's office; chomping down on her breakfast muffin this morning; and, just a few minutes ago, pursing her lips into that little moue of surprise as she was blown away by the wild flowers.

Given that she seemed to be waging quite a battle to even be able to stand the sight of him, not one of those images should have been remotely hot. But somehow that didn't stop the heavy weight in his belly lowering to tighten his ball sac as she wiggled her toes.

'I doubt it's safe to swim in it, though.' She tucked her socks into her trainers. 'I can't see the bottom. Dipping our feet in should be enough to cool us off.'

'Suit yourself, but I'm going in.' Because nothing short of a freezing-cold dunking would cool him off enough. He crouched to unlace his boots—and hoped she couldn't hear the roughness in his voice. 'The park authorities don't much like people swimming, but I reckon it's fine as long as you're careful.'

Their gazes connected and he could see his own awareness reflected in the glassy sheen of her eyes.

Dream on, Best, she's not interested unless you can time-travel back to 1998.

'You're mad,' she said, lowering her big toe into the water. 'You do know it's freezing.'

'Spoken like a true girl.' He tugged his T-shirt and shorts off, keen to get into the water before the heat swelling in his gut hit critical mass.

From what his now completely one-track mind could recall of the research he'd done into the region, Cherokee Creek flowed down from the snowmelt on the highest peaks of the Blue Ridge in North Carolina—which should ensure the water was sufficiently cold enough to get his wayward dick under control.

He climbed up to the shelf of granite overlooking the pond. Clamping his teeth together, he cupped protective hands over the Eiffel Tower growing in his pants and leaped into the water, yodelling like a Comanche on the warpath.

He hit with a magnificent splash and heard Halle's yelp of protest, above his own startled hiss, before he plunged under, gulping for breath a split second too late. The cold stung his skin, freezing the heat in his nuts. The shock to his system, though, made getting another stiffy before Christmas unlikely.

Mission accomplished.

Kicking off the rocks at the bottom, he broke the surface spluttering and coughing to expel the ice water he'd inhaled into his lungs.

'You drenched me, you idiot.' Halle stood over the pool wiping the droplets off her face.

'Oops.' He smiled. For once, she sounded amused instead of pissed off.

Mission impossible accomplished.

'How cold is it?' she asked.

'Absolutely bloody freezing.' He shuddered, treading water, his groin now blessedly numb, like the rest of him. 'But it feels great. You coming in?'

She plucked at the soaked cotton of her top, which had moulded to her breasts as if she were modelling a wet T-shirt competition. 'Sod it. All right, then.'

He grinned.

Then she whipped her T-shirt over her head, revealing a plain white sports bra that flattened her breasts against her torso, and the smile died. Her choice of underwear couldn't have been less erotic, but it did more than enough to remind him of the full, firm weight of Halle's breasts, the dusky pink shadow of her supersensitive nipples... The Holy Grail of his teenage years.

Fantasising about Halle's boobs had caused him several mortifying moments as he sat cross-legged in the assembly hall and watched her file in with her class while he imagined the treasures that lay beneath the shapeless pinstriped blouse of her uniform.

Despite the thick fabric of the bra she wore now, which disguised the shape into a flat ridge, he could imagine the plump swell of soft succulent flesh, the large, ripe nipples through the spandex. And the soft sobs of her breathing as he captured them between his lips and tongued them into hard peaks. Damn, he could still remember the night they'd found out a guaranteed way to make her come with penetration was if he licked and nipped all around the areola and then sucked the tip to the roof of his mouth while establishing a deep, even rhythm of strokes. It had required every ounce of his control not to climax before she got there, but despite the occasional mishap, he'd learned to do it the way she liked with some degree of finesse.

He could perform with much more finesse now.

Was that still the only way she could hit the jackpot if he wasn't manipulating her clitoris? Or had she discovered other sure-fire ways to achieve orgasm in the years since?

Blood pumped into his crotch while simultaneously blazing a trail up his neck.

He dived under the water, horrified at how quickly his thoughts had gotten out of control. But as he came up for air, there she was standing on the bank, wiggling out of her hiking shorts. And the torture continued.

She folded the garment and bent to add it to the neat pile she'd assembled, affording him a tantalising glimpse of her lush bottom covered in snug white cotton.

'I'll have you know I'm not a complete pussy,' she declared as she marched towards the water.

Terrific choice of words, Ms Best.

He gave a tight smile. At least she seemed to have forgiven him for that ill-advised comment about her lack of guts.

But as she sat on one of the rocks to dangle one cautious toe into the water, something glittered in the fold of pale flesh above the waistline of her panties. No way! She still wore a stud in the belly piercing she'd gotten at seventeen. So some remnants of the rebellious girl did still remain beneath the sophisticated veneer of the successful career woman.

The startling thought brought with it a renewed surge of excitement, followed by the unsettling feeling of connection.

Ignore it. She's not that girl and you don't want her to be.

She sucked in a breath as she eased herself off the rock. 'Good God, it's a miracle you didn't stroke out jumping into water this cold at your age,' she said.

'Give over, I'm only thirty-seven,' he countered, the teasing a welcome change from the razor-sharp snark. 'And, anyway, I'm a guy. Risking death for no good reason goes with the territory.'

'Tell me about it,' she scoffed. 'I've got a ten-year-old son who thinks he's immortal.'

On a startled gasp, she dropped the rest of the way into the pool with a gentle plop. Shivering while she adjusted to the frigid temperature, she did a smooth breaststroke towards him. Her pale limbs glowed like lightsabres against the dark silted green of the water. 'Wow, it feels glorious.'

She flipped onto her back to paddle away across the swimming hole, and his gaze snagged on the contours of her nipples, poking against the wet and pliant fabric of her sports bra like high-calibre bullets.

He did a shallow dive to duck back under the water's surface, swimming down to explore the cold bottom of the pool, but it was already too late. Arousal sizzled through his system again like a firework ready to explode.

Mission accomplished, my arse.

* * *

'I'm definitely going to get the recipe for this fried chicken from the resort's chef.' Halle bit into her drumstick, humming as she chewed, the sensual combination of spicy coating and chicken juices exploding on her tongue. 'It tastes phenomenal.'

'You do that.' Luke grabbed another wing from the array of picnic food she'd laid out on their drying towels. 'I just plan to eat it.' He set about devouring it in huge mouthfuls.

'I can see that.' She frowned, her skin still zinging from the refreshing chill of their swim.

His hair had started to curl as it dried in the afternoon sun, the bronze strands highlighting the golden brown and adding to the ruggedly sexy combo of dusty hiking shorts, damp T-shirt and two-o'clock shadow.

His wet boxer briefs hung on a branch of mountain laurel, alongside her damp bra and knickers, making her even

more aware of what they both didn't have on beneath their clothing. Not that she needed reminding with her hyper-sensitive nipples rubbing the stretchy cotton of her T-shirt every time she moved.

Maybe she shouldn't have taken him up on his dare. But she refused to regret it.

So what if he looked even better damp and her body acknowledged that? Surely any woman's would after a ten-mile hike followed by the intense stimulation of a freezing-cold dip in her underwear. It was a purely chemical reaction. The result of millions of years of human evolutionary biology. It didn't have any more significance than that. Luckily, she wasn't a Neanderthal woman or a female ape, so she would never be compelled to act on the attraction.

'Problem?' He dumped the skinned bones into the hefty pile of debris he'd accumulated and wiped his hands on a napkin.

'No,' she lied. Her gaze flitted down to his feet, only to encounter the intimate curls of hair on his bare toes.

Get a grip, Queen Kong.

'It's just depressing to realise the man-sized appetite never goes away.' She poured herself another glass from the canister of home-made lemonade Luke had chilled under the waterfall, ready to make small talk as if her life depended on it. 'Aldo already manages to polish off a week's worth of grocery shopping in three days. I may have to buy a pickup truck by the time he hits puberty.'

'He's ten, right?'

'Um-hum.' She nodded, grateful for the neutral topic. Using the empty backpack as a pillow, she stretched out on the sun-heated rock. Not looking at Luke was probably the smartest way to avoid noticing his Neanderthal attractions.

The warmth seeped through her clothing and she yawned.

The quiet hum of the local insect life, the burble of the falls and the scent of mountain laurel mixed with tree resin lulled her towards sleep. Maybe she wasn't the outdoor type, but as wilderness experiences went, the past few hours had been surprisingly relaxing. Give or take the odd blast of Stone Age conditioning.

'So do you know who Aldo's dad is?' It sounded so odd to hear Luke say her son's name, it took a moment for his question to register. When it did, her mellow mood faded. Considerably.

She sat up, her unfettered breasts bouncing uncomfortably. His tone had been conversational rather than accusatory, but even so... 'Of course I know who he is. Not that it's any of your business.'

'So why haven't you told Aldo, then?' he said, apparently untroubled by her indignation.

'How do you know I haven't told him?' she gasped, as the indignation turned to outrage.

'Because Lizzie talks about her kid brother to me. How do you think?' He sent her a level stare that dared her to lie about it. And suddenly she knew exactly what it must be like to be interviewed by him.

'You mean, she bitches about him to you,' she said, redirecting the conversation. She wasn't about to talk to Luke about Claudio.

And she could just imagine what Lizzie had to say to her father about Aldo. The thought made her feel instantly protective of her son.

'You know, it would be really helpful if you didn't humour her on that score,' she continued. 'Aldo's had a few problems with his behaviour and he hasn't found it easy to make friends since we moved to Notting Hill, but...' She wheeled her hand, only too aware she was Aldo's only

cheerleader. 'But he responded well to anger management CBT, he's got a terrific au pair now and he's doing OK.'

The guilt, which was never far away, tightened around her ribs like a vice. If she'd let Lizzie down by giving her a father who had once abandoned her, she'd let Aldo down more by giving him a father who couldn't care less about him.

'He's just a child and he only has me to fight his corner—'

'Lizzie doesn't bitch about him to me,' Luke cut into her passionate defence of her son. 'Or not more than she bitches about everyone. She is a teenage girl, after all.'

'I don't believe you.' How could that be true? When her daughter never missed an opportunity to bitch about her brother to his face, and hers?

'You should,' he said simply. 'When she talks about Aldo, it's usually because she's worried about him, or mad with someone on his behalf. She loves him.'

Halle gulped her lemonade and let the tart sweetness ease her dry throat, caught halfway between the happy glow his revelation created and dismay at the implication that Luke might know more about Lizzie's feelings towards Aldo than she did.

She ran her thumb through the beads of perspiration on the lemonade tumbler. 'Perhaps I should give my daughter more credit.'

And maybe I should have given you more credit, too.

'*Our* daughter,' Luke said, his lips lifting in a gentle smile. 'Don't beat yourself up about it. You're doing the best you can. And however much bitching she does about you, or to you, Lizzie knows that.'

'Does she? Sometimes I think she hates me.' The confession tumbled out before she could prevent it.

'She's giving you grief because she can,' he said, as if

it were the simplest thing in the world. 'All kids do it. It's called growing up.'

The family counsellor had told her something similar, but she'd never been able to believe it. And she didn't now. Easy for Luke to say, when he had been spared their daughter's taunts and tantrums.

'If that's true, why doesn't she give you the same grief?' she said, as all the insecurities she'd worked so hard to suppress crept out of the shadows.

'Because she doesn't trust me the way she trusts you, Hal.'

'I doubt that. You're Super Dad, remember.'

He gave a hollow half laugh. 'Yeah, I know. Which used to be great. But it's not any more.'

'Why not? I'd rather be Super Dad than Crap Mum.'

'Would you?' He glanced at her, the wistful expression for once unguarded. 'I don't even know what she was in therapy for a year ago.'

'She didn't talk to you about it?' How could that be possible, when she'd always assumed Lizzie confided in her father all the things she refused to speak about to her?

He shook his head. 'She let slip that she'd been in counselling. And that was as much as I could get out of her.' He fiddled with one of the chicken bones, the sun casting his face into shadow. 'I've been crapping myself about it ever since.'

'Oh.' He sounded genuinely worried. And even more insecure than her.

'But unfortunately I'm Super Dad, which basically means I'm Superficial-Can't-Be-Trusted-With-Lizzie's-Secrets Dad, too.'

The vehemence of his statement surprised her even more.

Part of her wanted to seize on the irony and point out to

Luke that Lizzie's secrets were not nearly as legion as his own. But the hopelessness on his face stopped her. Was it possible that Luke had struggled, too? That all the pernicious envy, which she had never really acknowledged, about his role as Super Dad in Lizzie's life had been misplaced?

'I got her into therapy because I thought she might be anorexic or bulimic or something.'

He shot upright, his face going bloodless. 'She's anorexic? Why the hell didn't you contact me?'

'It's OK, Luke. Don't panic. She's not and she never was. I completely overreacted about a perfectly normal weight loss a year or so ago.'

'What made you think she had an eating disorder? There must have been a reason.'

Warmth swelled in her chest. She'd never seen Luke with his concerned parent hat on before. It was remarkably cute. Maybe not as cute as watching his toned body cannonball into a mountain pond in his boxers, but close.

More surprising, though, was how comforting it was to realise she wasn't the only one who had performance anxiety issues where their daughter was concerned.

'Honestly?' she said. 'I totally panicked. She got so skinny when she grew. The GP didn't think it was anything to be too concerned about, but I refused to be convinced.' Especially after Lizzie had hooked up with the hideous Liam, and Halle's relationship with her daughter had gone into meltdown... 'She refused point-blank to discuss it with me. So I paid for a very expensive therapist.' Because her working-mother guilt had insisted on hiring the best. 'And it took him four months to tell me the same thing.'

'She's no skinnier than I was at her age,' he pointed out.

'Well, yes, I suppose now you mention it, that's true. Her build's always been more like yours than mine.'

Perhaps if she hadn't been determined to erase all thoughts of Luke from her consciousness, she might have figured that out a bit sooner. And saved herself a few thousand pounds in therapist's fees—not to mention several hundred sleepless nights.

'I'm sorry, Luke.' Apologies had never come easily to her, but she supposed she owed him this much at least. 'I should have got Jamie to tell you what was going on. I just assumed you knew. That Lizzie spoke to you about that sort of stuff.'

'No need to apologise. At least you're speaking to me now.' He stretched his legs in front of him and turned his face into the sun. 'It's hard to know what the best thing is sometimes, when you're stuck doing this all alone.'

His gaze caught hers and, seeing the complete sincerity there, she was suddenly struck by an even more disturbing thought than the last one. A thought that once let loose would not be ignored. Was this the real reason he'd blackmailed her into coming to Tennessee?

'Please tell me you didn't set this whole thing up with Monroe just to get me to talk to you about Lizzie? Because, if you did, I may have to self-harm.'

But as she looked up at the brilliant blue sky, it felt entirely like a trap of her own making. If she had met him halfway, if she had communicated with him, he never would have been forced to pull a stunt like this.

The rueful tilt of his lips turned into a grin. 'Don't be daft, I'm not that cute. Or altruistic.'

'So there is actually an article on Monroe?'

'Of course.' The grin became sly, triggering the dimple in his cheek. 'I've already sold the pitch to *Vanity Fair*, so it'll be well worth my while dragging you out here whatever happens.'

'Good to know.' She smiled, no longer angry with his

tactics. And oddly grateful that there was, and had always been, an article. An altruistic Luke would only be more of a threat to her peace of mind. She didn't want the warm spot under her breastbone getting any bigger.

Plus, she was actually sort of charmed by Luke's unshakeable confidence in his work.

She had a similar pride in her own career achievements. But, more than that, she'd always known how bright he was, and how desperate he had been to get away from where he'd started. For once, she didn't feel bitter that he'd gotten there in the end, even though he'd refused to take her with him.

'So, who is Aldo's dad?'

She eased onto her back, slung her arm across her face to protect herself from the sun's glare—not to mention Luke's curiosity. 'Still none of your business.'

'True, but that doesn't mean I'm not going to keep asking you till you tell me. And I should warn you, I can be very persistent.'

'Really?' She lifted her arm, not feeling quite so charmed by his journalistic confidence. 'I never would have guessed.'

'Come on.' He nudged her with his foot. 'You might as well give it up before I get out the thumbscrews.'

She huffed, wanting to be annoyed, because it was a question she'd resolutely refused to answer from pretty much everyone else. But why not confide in Luke? She didn't have to be specific. And talking about her ill-fated affair with Claudio should help put this arbitrary warm spot back into perspective. 'If you must know, Aldo's dad was a complete tosser.'

'More of a tosser than you think I am?'

She chuckled at the sanguine tone. 'Incredibly, yes.' Even though she'd always been so much angrier with Luke than Claudio. Probably because she'd never kidded herself she

was in love with Aldo's father. 'Not only was he a tosser as a boyfriend, he turned out to be an even bigger tosser as a father.'

That at least was something it seemed Luke had never been.

'How so?'

She swivelled her head to look at him, but his expression was masked by the lengthening shadows of the afternoon. 'Are you really interested in all this?'

'Yeah, I love a good story,' he said, sounding surprisingly earnest. 'Start from the beginning. How did you two meet?'

She listened to the muffled splatter of the water falling onto lichen-covered rocks, felt the dry wind lift the soft hairs on her arm and let herself recount the story she'd never told anyone else, because it had made her feel like such an abject failure as a mother.

'Claudio and I met at a Christmas party I was catering for one of my celebrity clients. His family is a big deal in Italy. They own land in and around Sorrento. He was dabbling in Formula Two at the time and fancied himself a racing driver—which in his case basically entailed being a globetrotting playboy who drove fast cars. He was charming, debonair, and he knew his way round a clitoris. After three dates, I was smitten.'

She'd worked so diligently to drag herself out of the pit where Luke had left her, to make a success of the cake designing, to bring up her baby girl solo, to schmooze as many celebrity contacts as she could and earn a regular spot on Living's morning show as their baking expert. Claudio had been her reward. A chance to finally enjoy at least some of the fruits of being an independent, semi-successful career woman, who hadn't had anything resembling a sex life in close to six years. She'd still been so young, only

twenty-five—unfortunately, she'd also still been stupidly optimistic and incredibly naive, despite the lessons Luke had taught her.

'We'd only been dating a few months when I got pregnant. Which was the result of a drunken bonk in a nightclub toilet.' She gave a pained laugh. 'I seem to have a knack for hitting the jackpot during drunken bonks in and around music venues, don't I?'

'You're not the only one,' he replied wryly.

'Anyway, I planned to have an abortion. It was a hard decision, but I didn't feel I had much of a choice. I had Lizzie to think about. And my career and it had been a mistake.'

And after what had happened with Luke, she didn't want to ever be in that situation again, but she couldn't tell Luke that, it would be far too revealing.

'But Claudio…' She paused, the conflicting emotions always there when she thought about Aldo's father. He *had* been a tosser, but he had at least done one thing right, even if it had been for all the wrong reasons. 'Claudio argued me out of it. He was Catholic, he said, it was a sin and he would be a good father. I suspect now his desire to keep the baby had more to do with his ego than any religious convictions, because he quickly became less keen on the idea as the pregnancy progressed. Dating someone with swollen ankles and ballooning breasts who wanted to hibernate instead of hang on his arm at celebrity parties hadn't been part of the plan, apparently.'

'He didn't like the ballooning breasts? You're kidding,' Luke interrupted. 'I thought that was the best bit.'

She laughed, as she suspected he had intended. The sickening tension in her gut eased, until the ripple of memory brought with it an uncomfortable blast of heat. Luke had

certainly never been turned off by her pregnant body the way Claudio had.

She chucked one of the chewed chicken bones at him, determined to stop the stupid warm spot sinking south. 'Shut up, do you want to hear the rest of this or not?'

He caught the bone one-handed and smiled. 'Absolutely.'

She settled back on the rock. 'So, as the months wore on, we saw each other less and less. By the end of the pregnancy I wasn't into sex, and without that there really wasn't anything else to keep us together. But even so, I thought...' She hesitated, suddenly feeling like a fraud.

Had she really hoped Aldo, once he arrived, would bring Claudio back to her? When she was fairly sure she hadn't wanted Claudio in her life by then?

'Anyway, Claudio finally showed up at the maternity hospital the day after I'd given birth. He held Aldo, for about ten seconds, then handed him back to me and explained, very politely, that he had made a terrible mistake. He said he really wasn't ready to be a father. That he had found someone else more suited to his lifestyle, and that he would be happy to make a financial contribution to Aldo's upkeep, whatever I thought was fair, but he didn't feel there was any point in forming a relationship with the child.' She sighed. '"The child", that's what he called my beautiful baby boy.'

'I hope you took him to the cleaners.'

The bite of anger in Luke's tone felt comforting.

'Actually, no, I told him to shove his offer of financial support somewhere anatomically impossible.' She released a shaky breath. 'The last thing I wanted was his money.'

Because it would have given her a connection to Claudio she didn't want.

Which begged the question why she had never told Luke

the same thing? When she'd always refused to spend any
of the money he'd sent without fail every month for Lizzie?

'He doesn't sound like a tosser. He sounds like a total
arsehole,' Luke said, rescuing her from stressing over that
glaring inconsistency.

'Yes, he was, but…' She forced herself to breathe round
the granite boulder now sitting on her chest. 'I know the
pregnancy wasn't only my fault.'

*Even if two accidental pregnancies in one lifetime makes
me the poster girl for dumb blondes.*

'And it definitely wasn't my fault Claudio turned out to
be such an immature, selfish git.' The pressure on her lungs
became painful.

Bloody hell, why is it still so hard to admit, even now?

'But I wish I could have given Aldo a better dad. Or any
kind of dad really.'

*It might also be nice to know how I've managed to plan
my career so successfully but made such a monumental
cock-up of my private life.*

'So that's why you never told Aldo the guy's name?'

She glanced over at Luke, a bit disorientated to realise he
was still sitting there, listening patiently to her confession.
Luke had never seemed all that priestly. But he'd always had
that knack of letting her do all the talking. After their split,
she'd come to the conclusion that was because he'd never
actually been listening. All he'd really been doing was allowing her to fill the void, so he could avoid talking back.
But now she wasn't so sure. Could that interested crease on
his forehead be so easily faked?

The warm spot grew.

She turned away. *Enough already.* Luke's ability to be
such a patient and attentive listener was simply because he
was a good journalist.

'Once Aldo started asking questions, it was easier to avoid giving him a straight answer than make the effort to contact Claudio again.' She lifted her chin. 'I didn't want to see Aldo hurt.'

Or at least that's what she'd always told herself.

'Fair enough,' Luke said evenly. 'Why set him up to be smacked down?'

'Except that…' She appreciated Luke's vote of confidence, more than he would ever realise. But now she wondered, had Claudio really been the only selfish one involved? 'The truth is I didn't want to contact Claudio.' Yes, she'd been frightened of having her child rejected again, but had she ever really wanted Claudio to be a part of Aldo's life?

'I have no idea how Claudio feels about his son now. It's been ten years. He might have had a change of heart. What if he wants a relationship with Aldo and I'm the one who's stopping it from happening?'

She'd been wrong about Luke, about how deeply he cared for his daughter, because she'd stubbornly refused to talk to him. What if she'd made the same mistake with Claudio and denied Aldo a father just to protect herself?

'If that were the case, what's stopping the guy from contacting you? Or Aldo?' Luke said, reasonably, neatly cutting the guilt down to size. 'He won't, though, because the guy's definitely still an arsehole,' he continued. 'I interviewed Claudio Benedetti last year for a piece I was doing on the Delanyo Scandal and he came across as a selfish, self-aggrandising twat.'

Halle bolted upright at the offhand comment, her heart racing. 'How do you know who he is? I never said his surname.'

What the hell had she done? Luke was a bloody journalist. What if he published the information? Then Aldo would know that…

'Hal, chill the hell out,' he said evenly. 'How many times do I have to tell you? I'm not a celebrity hack, or that much of an arsehole, frankly.'

'But how did you figure out Claudio's identity?'

'Not from your comment about him knowing his way round a clitoris, if that helps,' he countered, a slight edge to his voice. 'I'm a journalist. You gave me enough clues to make an educated guess. I do this stuff for a living, remember. But that doesn't mean I'm going to exploit a ten-year-old boy. I do have a few scruples, you know.' He began packing up the debris from their picnic. 'Although, just for the record, I'm not sure *you* do. What made you fall for that wanker? Are clit skills really that high on your list of attributes?'

Interesting, he certainly seems to have gotten fairly hung up on that nugget of information.

She choked out a laugh, determined not to remember Luke was the one who had introduced her to the gold standard of clit skills.

'I didn't fall for him. I wasn't in love with him.' *Not the way I thought I was with you.* 'I was lonely, I suppose, and he filled a need. Not getting any for six years can make you overlook a heck of a lot of personality flaws.'

He paused while packing the last of their lunch debris into the backpack. 'Hang on a minute. He was your first? After me?'

'Not all of us bounced back as quickly as you did,' she declared, annoyed by the echo of bitterness.

Amelie Brouchard doesn't matter to you any more. She's just a French tart who probably can't even make a decent tarte Tatin.

'And I didn't have a lot of spare time,' she added. 'I had a child to look after.'

Unlike you and Amelie the tart.

'Well, shit.' He relaxed back on his heels. 'I never figured the three years it took me to get back in the game was particularly quick. I stand corrected.'

'Don't bullshit me, Luke.' Annoyance flared, stirring the residual hurt. 'I happen to know you shacked up with your photographer on that assignment, Amelie Brouchard, the day after you walked out on me and Lizzie.'

How could saying the woman's name out loud still bring with it the sting of remembered pain?

'Who told you that?' he asked.

'Your helpful friend Ned.'

'Ned told you Amelie and I were an item?'

'Stop pretending you weren't.' *Really? We're going to play this game?*

Maybe she had misjudged his reliability as a father, but she knew exactly how fickle he had been as a life partner. And she certainly wasn't the gullible nitwit any more who believed everything he told her.

'Amelie and I were never lovers. And Ned knows we weren't,' Luke said. 'I always knew he had the hots for you. That son of a bitch.' He sounded furious.

'Bugger off, Luke. What were you doing living in her apartment for six months if you weren't banging her? I happen to have first-hand knowledge of exactly how much sex you need.'

Because I'm fairly sure the fact I stopped supplying it whenever you wanted it was the real reason you left me.

The accusation echoed off the rocks and sharpened the pain in her chest.

Why was the pain still so raw? At the thought of all the times he'd come on to her and all the times she'd turned him down because she was exhausted after Lizzie's birth?

And all the times she'd been forced to regret that after he'd left. God, it was lowering to realise she could still be angry at how much she'd berated herself for not being more accommodating, more considerate of his sexual needs… And how long it had taken her to finally realise Luke was the one who had been insensitive to her needs. Not the other way round.

'If you must know,' he said, 'I was sleeping in Amelie's spare room while she and her girlfriend went at it every night in the room next door. And while that was certainly an education in sexual frustration, because the walls in that apartment were paper-thin and the two of them were both screamers, I didn't get any, either, for three years. And I never got any with Amelie.'

'You're kidding. Amelie was a lesbian?' The outrage blossomed anew. Spurred on by indignation. Had she been angry at Amelie the French tart for sixteen years, for no good reason?

'She wasn't a lesbian, exactly,' he clarified. 'She had a girlfriend, but she was into guys, too. And they did offer to have a threesome a couple of times.'

That bitch. 'How accommodating of her.'

He shrugged, and the tinge of colour hit his cheeks. 'But I turned them down.'

'How very noble of you,' she said waspishly, not sure now whether she was more annoyed with Luke or Amelie. Or his shit-stirring friend Ned. 'I never would have expected you of all people to be such a prude.'

Am I actually hoping he had a threesome with her now?

'It wasn't that.' The pink tinge touched the top of his ears. 'I mean, it wasn't that I wouldn't have been up for it, so to speak. It's just I couldn't do it.'

'Why on earth not?'

'I don't know, I guess because it felt like cheating, on you.'

She sat perfectly still, listening to the quiet hum of a passing insect. With no clue what to say to that. Or how to deal with the squeezing pain in her ribs.

'Luke, you left me,' she said at last, settling on pointing out the glaringly obvious. 'You didn't even contact me for two weeks. And when you did, I got exactly six torturous words that explained exactly nothing. I had to find out from your wanky friend Ned where you were living over a month later. How on earth could you have felt like you were cheating on me? For three years? Can't you see how ridiculous that is?'

And not all that believable.

But somehow she did believe him. Which made his confession only all the more ridiculous. But not as ridiculous as the feeling of something warm and fluid in her abdomen.

Apparently, I'm glad he didn't have that threesome.

How could the fact he hadn't left her for another woman be important now?

'It's not ridiculous at all.' He stretched his neck, looking more uncomfortable by the second. 'I didn't walk out on you because of our sex life. I know it changed a lot after Lizzie, and it took me a while to adjust to that…but I'm not that much of a shallow jerk.'

'Then why did you leave?'

'I told you, it had nothing to do with you. It was me.'

Well, hooray, that tells me precisely sod all.

'We should get going.' He got up and marched over to the laurel bush to whip his dry boxers off the branch. 'I've gotta figure out how to use the two-way and tell Bill where to pick us up.' Then he strode into the undergrowth, obviously to put his boxers back on.

Subject comprehensively closed.

She lifted her own underwear off the bush, contemplating her next move as she put her bra on under her T-shirt and stuffed her knickers into the pocket of her shorts.

His explanation wasn't just cheesy, it was half-arsed. And if he thought that was all he was going to say on the subject, he had another think coming.

But she needed to be careful and protect herself before she had that discussion.

As they trudged back along the trail towards their pick-up point, she comforted herself with how much better able she was to hear the truth now than she had been sixteen years ago.

She wasn't that reckless girl any more, increasingly scared and anxious, beaten down by the responsibility of a child and terrified of losing the man she loved. Whatever Luke had to say on the subject, if she could shochorn it out of him, she certainly wasn't scared of hearing it any more. Her need to know now was mere curiosity.

Maybe it was time to get in his face, instead of staying out of his way. Why shouldn't this communication thing, the communication thing he'd started by getting her here, work two ways?

Obviously, she'd be a fool not to acknowledge the sexual tension. But she could handle it. She was a mature woman who didn't have sex for the sake of it any more. Especially not with men whom she already knew weren't good for her.

Holding back a branch of laurel that hung across the path, Luke beckoned her to precede him. As she stepped close to him, she inhaled his scent. Lake water and laundry soap and fresh sweat, overlaid with the cinnamon smell of the gum he was chewing. The sinew in his forearm stretched, making the muscles in his shoulder bunch. She caught his gaze on her before it flicked away. The look in his eyes was both wary and intense.

Moisture collected as her naked and unprotected vulva rubbed against the rough linen seam of her hiking shorts.

Awareness snapped in the humid air between them, until his gaze connected with hers again. His jaw moved, working the gum.

'Take out the gum.'

He looked puzzled, but he obeyed, licking his fingers to extract the wad. 'Why?'

She placed her hands on either side of his face, letting the rough stubble abrade her palms.

His jaw tensed. 'Hal, what are you doing?'

He sounded concerned. No wonder. With one arm occupied stopping the branch from whacking them both in the face and the other hand busy holding the gum, he was entirely at her mercy. She took a moment to appreciate the rush of power and to consider her purpose.

Because she had something vitally important to prove.

She might be a smidgeon sex-starved. And far too aware of those intoxicating pheromones that had always hovered around Luke in a cloud, prompting women to do stupid things. But she wasn't afraid of the siren call of her own senses any more. She'd already come a cropper on those rocks once. She wasn't about to go sailing that way again. She was in command of her libido now, and she was immune to Luke's charms. Or immune enough. And here was her chance to prove it.

Then she stopped thinking and let instinct take over. Rising on tiptoes, her chest brushing his, she heard his sharp intake of breath before her lips settled over his.

His mouth pursed into a tight line as she pressed against it. So she licked along the seam of his lips. They opened at last on a tremulous sigh, which brought with it the taste of cinnamon and need. Their tongues tangled briefly. Tip

to tip. Cautious, gentle, coaxing, at first. But then the need turned to exploration, and exploitation, their tongues duelling as he delved deeper. Demanded more.

And a part of her wanted to give in to the demand. To lose herself forever in the kiss.

The part of her that had been romantic and foolish at sixteen, and stupid enough not to have an ounce of forethought or self-preservation. The same part of her that in moments of extreme stress even now wanted to devour Luke because he was a man, a man she desired and had always desired. And who had always tasted so good.

OK, stop tasting him. You're going under.

She wrenched herself away, stepped back and released his cheeks—the tiny tremors racking her body like a heroin addict going cold turkey.

'What was that about?' he asked, the pale blue of his irises vanished behind the dilated pupils.

That was to prove a very important point.

'That was an apology,' she said, grabbing hold of the first viable excuse. 'For slapping you so hard.' She patted his cheek, which appeared to be thankfully unbruised.

He scowled. 'Then thanks, I guess... Although I thought we agreed I deserved that slap.'

'You deserved it sixteen years ago,' she corrected. 'I'm not so sure you deserve it now.'

She shot off down the trail ahead of him, running the tip of her tongue over her lips and gathering the lingering taste of cinnamon.

Hearing his footfalls behind her, matching time with her thundering pulse, she increased her pace. She needed to walk off all the excess energy powering through her system, and hopefully stop her clit from humming as if a thousand

bees had set up an extremely industrious hive in her pants. At least she'd found a cure for her jet lag.

But what was my point again, exactly?

Chapter 13

What was the point of having a crush on the live-in au pair if he was never where he was supposed to be?

Lizzie jogged across the low bridge in the Kyoto Garden in Holland Park. The Japanese waterfall glimmered in the sunshine while Rihanna's 'Rude Boy' got it on in her headphones.

Piss off, peace and tranquility.

She marked time as a mum with a double buggy pushed past her on the brick path, then headed into the cool forested section of the park. Puffing now—a hangover from last night's pizza blowout—she accelerated on the secluded track leading through the untamed grove of elms and weeping willows the half mile to the exit. The park had been quiet this morning, except for the odd nanny-and-toddler combo. School wasn't out yet for the summer, but luckily she had no more college classes, having handed in her final assessment yesterday.

Any excitement at the prospect of having Trey all to herself during the daytime had been quashed in the past few days, though. The man had made himself noticeably scarce, disappearing after the school drop-off each day, only to reappear

at four p.m. with Aldo in tow like the ultimate gooseberry. The burning curiosity to ask him where he'd gone was nothing compared to her irritation that he'd managed to avoid her. For three whole days.

She ran on the spot, waiting for the lights to change at Holland Park Avenue. Jogging across the road, she darted into Ladbroke Mews, running past the exclusive pastel-coloured cottages, her trainers hitting the cobblestones to the rhythm of Beyoncé's 'Single Ladies'. An oldie but a goodie when it came to girl-power mission statements.

Bolting out of the mews, her laboured breath sawing in her lungs, she ran past the palatial houses that stood in a row of Georgian grandeur around Ladbroke Square. She slowed as she approached their four-storey house, its grand portico matching the others in the terrace, as a tall, easily identifiable figure came down the street from the opposite direction. Her heartbeat galloped into her throat, and not just from the exertion of her morning jog.

Trey was back. She slowed to a walk, sucking in air so she wouldn't be huffing and puffing like a hippopotamus when he spotted her.

It was four days now since their day out at the Serps, and either she was becoming paranoid or Trey had been avoiding her every day since. She hadn't pushed it at first; he obviously had a job to do with Aldo—and as much as she might want to hang out with Trey, she hadn't sunk so low as to want to play football in the park.

Unfortunately, she'd managed to miss him and Aldo before they left for school each morning. So she'd set her alarm last night, determined to catch him for morning coffee if it killed her. Pressing the snooze button had been a mistake, though, because she'd managed to snooze until nine o'clock.

But the jog had revitalised her and given her time to

think. Either she was paranoid or Trey had been avoiding her. She tugged out her earbuds and turned off her iPod as she drew closer.

He had his head down as he opened the gate leading to the house's basement entrance.

'Hi, you get Aldo to school OK?' she asked, wincing at the inane question.

His head popped up, and she tried to deduce whether his expression said surprise or irritation, before it became carefully masked.

His gaze flicked down and she winced some more at the thought of what a state she must look, in her oldest sweat-pants and jogging bra. Sweat dripped down the side of her face, and she brushed it off with the sweatband on her wrist.

'Not quite.' He held the gate open for her, preoccupied. 'Aldo went into a tailspin when he realised it was his class's bake sale this afternoon.' He followed her down the cellar stairs into the kitchen.

'Mum usually does something amazing with him for that,' she replied, trying not to let the bubble of resentment surface.

Her mum had always found time to bake with Aldo on the Wednesday evening each term before his class had their sale to raise funds for their end-of-year trip. But she never had time to bake with Lizzie any more. Then again, Lizzie realised, she had never asked. But it was the thought, or rather the lack of it, that counted. Right?

'He told me that.' Trey sounded suitably daunted. 'He's going to have to downgrade his expectations for what I can rustle up to bring in this afternoon.'

She took a moment to appreciate the width of Trey's shoulders as he closed the kitchen door behind them both.

'I could give you a hand.' The opportunity presented itself

like manna from heaven. 'I am my mother's daughter, after all.' Even if they hadn't baked together in years.

He lifted the plastic bag in his hand. 'I've got it covered. I picked something up at the corner shop.'

The comment sounded neutral, friendly even. But Lizzie knew a cold shoulder when she saw one—and she refused to be put off by it—however broad it might be.

This was not paranoia. Trey Carson was definitely avoiding being alone with her. He'd been distant ever since Sunday—distant and unfailingly polite. In other words, he was back to business as usual—humour Lizzie and ignore her. As if the Serps had never happened. As if she hadn't had that tantalising glimpse of the hot enigmatic guy beneath the dodgy polo shirt. Or the tattoo he had inked on his butt.

Well, he could forget that. She planned to seize this opportunity—and get all up in his face now—because passive wasn't working.

He dumped the bag on the kitchen counter and unloaded the contents, obviously expecting her to toddle off to the bathroom without bothering him. Wrong. She wasn't playing that game any more.

She hoisted the ready-to-bake Spider-Man cupcake mix he'd placed on the counter. 'You're not seriously planning to darken my mum's kitchen with this crap, are you? If she finds out, she'll have us both shot at dawn.'

His brow crinkled in a fetchingly puzzled frown. 'I wasn't planning to tell her.'

'Do you have any idea how many E-numbers are in this stuff?' She started reading from the ingredients panel. 'And not just E-numbers. We also have edible gum, non-milk solids, artificial colouring...' She tapped her fingernail on the box. 'Oh, and, the pièce de résistance, guaranteed to give

all ten-year-olds a sugar rush that will blow their heads off, fructose syrup and glucose emulsifiers. Yummy.'

He grabbed the box and placed it back on the counter. 'Apologies to your mum, but this'll have to do.' He lifted one of her mum's stainless steel mixing bowls from the cabinet. 'I need to get these done in an hour. I don't have time for fancy.'

'Why have you only got an hour?' Was he deserting her again for the day? Because it was starting to give her a complex.

He tore off the box's lid. 'I've got somewhere I've got to be.'

Lizzie frowned. *So far, so completely uncommunicative.*

There were about a billion questions she wanted to ask him, but she recognised the stubborn expression on his face. Aldo had worn the exact same one when she'd quizzed him about the full pack of Jammie Dodgers that had been in the biscuit tin last week and had mysteriously vanished without trace a day later.

Boys, or men, with that expression on their face fessed up only if you got sneaky.

He ripped open the package holding the cupcake mix. But as he headed for the fridge to pull out some eggs, she picked the packet up and dumped it head first into the trash.

'Hey, what the hell did you do that for?' Well, at least she'd managed to bypass unfailingly polite.

'I told you.' She slapped her hands together, ignoring the horrified look. 'We're not going to Aldo's bake sale with plastic cupcakes. That much is non-negotiable. This family has a baking reputation to protect.'

'But I don't have time to figure out an alternative.' He trailed off, clearly speechless, the crinkle on his forehead becoming a furrow. 'I didn't want to buy ready-made cakes. And Aldo will flip if I show up with nothing at all.'

'Not a problem. Bring the eggs over here and then get the self-rising flour, the caster sugar and the vanilla essence from the larder.' She swung round the counter and pulled one of the wooden spoons out of the huge earthenware jug her mum kept by the eight-ring hob.

He hesitated, his frown dipping, in two minds about whether to obey her order.

'Get a move on, Trey, we only have fifty minutes now.'

He cursed under his breath and stalked off to the larder. She took the moment alone to wash her hands and repair her ponytail. Catching her reflection in the window glass above the sink, she withheld a shudder.

She just hoped Trey appreciated his women au naturel, because she was sporting full no-make-up selfie chic. She fetched the butter, scooped half of the tub into the bowl and began softening it up with the spoon.

The items she'd requested were unceremoniously dumped at her elbow. 'What are we making?'

'Spider-Man cupcakes, of course.' She sprinkled a generous amount of caster sugar onto the butter.

'Oh, yeah, of course,' he said, still pissed off. 'Because that makes perfect sense now you've chucked the mixture into the bin.'

'They probably have some themed casings in the box,' she said, ignoring the sarcasm. 'Arrange them on a baking tray, then turn the oven on to gas mark five.'

He huffed with indignation but followed her instructions. She took surreptitious glances at him as he fiddled with the casings, hurrying to arrange them in straight rows on the baking tray.

Wherever he was going, he did not want to be late.

The wooden spoon faltered. Did he have a girlfriend? A guy as fit as him with the work ethic of a Trojan would be a

catch, no question, even if he couldn't make cupcakes from scratch. And wore straight-leg jeans.

'Ready,' he said. 'What next?'

She cracked two eggs into the bowl one-handed, comfortable with the familiar routine. 'Grab the flour sieve.' She battered the cake mixture into a smooth consistency while imagining it was his imaginary girlfriend's head.

'Where is it?'

'Up there.' She nodded at the utensils that her mum had hanging from bars over the counter for easy access. He reached up to grab the sieve, and the hem of his T-shirt lifted over the waistband of his jeans. The faded red and black of his tattoo hovered over the well of his spine, inching past the black cotton of his boxers. The T-shirt dropped back into place, and she found herself staring at the faded denim cupping his tight, perfectly defined buns.

Her lips dried to parchment as she imagined running her fingertip over the delicate lines of the drawing—and then dipping it beneath the waistband of his pants.

'What do I do with it?' he asked, wielding the sieve.

'Sift some flour over this mixture.'

He lifted the flour tin and stepped closer. His forearm brushed hers, weighing down the hot brick in her stomach. 'How much?'

She could smell him, the hints of his lemony shower gel above the scent of sugar and vanilla. 'About five hundred grams. I'll tell you when to stop.'

She could hear the steady murmur of his breathing, feel the tension in his arm, above the phlop-phlop-phlop of the spoon, and her own racketing heartbeat. He held the sieve over her bowl and sprinkled the flour with the care and precision of a bomb-disposal expert handling nitroglycerine.

'What's your tattoo supposed to be?'

Flour puffed over the edge of the sieve as the tin jerked and tapped the edge of the bowl.

She carried on mixing, the phlop-phlop-phlop the only sound as the silence stretched. 'Keep sifting,' she prompted, because he seemed to be frozen in place. 'We're not at five hundred grams yet.'

He tipped the tin too steeply and a wedge of flour flopped into the sieve, sending a mushroom cloud of dust into the air.

'That's probably enough now.'

He drew the sieve away. 'Sorry.'

'Is it a bird?' she continued to probe, all innocence. 'The tattoo, I mean.'

'It's supposed to be a phoenix. The artist was pretty low-rent.' He placed the tin of flour onto the counter, resealed the lid, still handling nitro. She'd definitely struck a nerve—which was all the more reason to keep on swinging.

She folded the flour into the mixture. 'Get a spoon out and we can put this in the casings now.'

'How much?'

'About that much.' She ladled a dollop into the bottom of one casing. 'Don't go mad or the sponge will spill over when it rises in the oven.'

'OK.'

They began filling the casings together, side by side. 'When did you get the tattoo?'

His spoon paused in mid-air, before he resumed filling his casing. 'Couple of years back.'

'Why?'

He scraped some more batter out of the bowl, used his finger to plop it into the casings. 'Why are you so interested in it?'

Yup. She had definitely hit a nerve. She liked it. Getting a reaction out of him was better than not getting a reaction.

Especially when those chocolate-brown eyes narrowed on her face. His expression intent. He was seeing her now. No doubt about that. She ignored the pleasant sensations fluttering under her breastbone. Being the focus of Trey Carson's attention was addictive. But she mustn't get distracted.

'It just seems totally out of character for you.'

'Why, because I'm Mr Perfecto?' He sounded prickly, and much more irritated about the nickname than when he'd first told her he knew about it. 'You don't know anything about me. Or my life.'

The pleasant fluttering became discordant and jarring. It was a familiar sensation. One she'd felt often when Carly accused her of being a drama queen, or her mum gave her that weary, harassed look that seemed to say: *Why can't you be the sweet child you once were?* But, this time, she refused to take it personally, to let the implied criticism deflect her from her goal.

He was feeling threatened. He was hitting back. That wasn't necessarily a bad thing. Especially as it was exactly the reaction she'd wanted. Less hostility would be nice, but it was still better than polite and distant.

'I know I don't,' she said, watching him carefully for any reaction. 'But maybe I'd like to?' She placed her spoon into the bowl, wiped her sticky fingers on the tea towel she'd tucked into her sweatpants. 'I enjoyed myself on Sunday at the Serps. I had a good time with you and Aldo. It made me realise I've been pretty shitty to you since you came to work for my mum. And I'd like to turn that around.' She didn't plan to ask him to be her friend, because apart from being totally lame, it would also be pretty transparent. The urge to flirt with him was too enormous. And she'd never been very good at flirting. So she needed to build up to it slowly, organically, if she didn't want to die of mortification in the

process. 'I'm curious about the tattoo because I'm curious about you,' she said, hoping he'd give her points for honesty.

He continued to fill the cupcake casings, but his jaw lost the hard line.

She worked next to him, the silence comforting in its simplicity.

'I got a tattoo because my mum hated them.'

She hadn't really expected an answer. Especially not one that made her feel that rare burst of kinship. 'You did it to annoy your mum? That's hilarious. That's exactly why I got mine.'

'It's not quite the same. I didn't get it to annoy her. I got it to make her feel better.'

'I don't get it,' she said, the bubble of excitement bursting to be replaced by something richer and more compelling than curiosity.

'She was ill,' he murmured, the words flat. 'We both knew it was terminal. I had to care for her. And she felt bad that I couldn't be a normal teenager. So I got a tattoo, to show her I was.'

His eyes met hers, the fathomless brown opaque and unreadable. She supposed the correct thing to do now would be to say sorry. But the word hung in the air, feeling inadequate and dismissive.

She touched his arm, felt the pull of the muscles as they bunched beneath her fingers. 'When did your mother die?' Sympathy wasn't hard to find now, the thought horrifying her.

What would she do if anything ever happened to her own mum? It felt so remote, so unlikely, not something she'd ever considered before, but, now she did, she knew the first thing she'd feel—other than loss—was guilt. At all the things she

had said and done over the past few years to annoy or upset her. Deliberately.

She hadn't even said goodbye to her mum properly before she'd left to go on her book tour. And every time her mum had phoned since, she'd been really stroppy with her.

But what if that was the last time she ever got to speak to her? Or the last time she ever got to see her again?

She couldn't even remember now why she had been so mad with her.

* * *

Trey could see shock and horror in Lizzie's face; what he couldn't see was pity.

He should correct her. And tell her the truth. His mum wasn't dead. She was just sick. Much sicker than she had been four years ago when he'd got that dopey tattoo.

The nurse at the hospice had told him yesterday they didn't think she had much longer. He didn't think so, either. As he held her hand, the papery skin so thin it was translucent, her breathing had sounded tortured, each new breath a titanic struggle to defeat the inevitable.

The nurse had told him the last of the senses to go was hearing, so all he could do now was read her the girly novels she loved. He'd been embarrassed to read them when her sight had first started to go, especially all the sexy bits. He wasn't embarrassed by them any more. The stories took him to foreign lands in times past, with lots of action and adventure and all the sexy bits in between, in the company of characters who were young and fit and able-bodied and didn't need a catheter or a drip. Transporting him out of the sunny cubicle, where the scent of bleach and bodily fluids could always be detected beneath the masking scent of air freshener; away from the sound of rasping breaths and the sight of the thin

grey hair spread out on the pillow, which belonged to a frail husk of a human being who looked nothing like his mum.

Maybe he could have shared all that with Lizzie, the reality of his life outside his job. And the truth about his mum.

She's had multiple sclerosis since I was thirteen. But she's not dead. Not yet.

But he didn't want to tell Lizzie the truth. Because the reality had isolated him so often as a kid. When he was his mum's primary carer. The truth had made him weird, a freak, and different from everyone he knew.

His responsibilities as her carer had never bothered him—cleaning her teeth, washing her hair, helping her with the bedpan, feeding her when she got too weak to eat. It had all just been a growing part of his daily routine. But as the responsibilities grew, other people became aware of them, and that was what had made him uncomfortable: the social workers who were forever encouraging him to join some stupid club; the kids at school who thought he was a loser because he could never hang out after class; the teachers who didn't give him a detention when he didn't do his homework, even though they gave everyone else one.

He didn't want Lizzie to look at him like that, as if he were different, or, worse, pitiful. He wasn't sure she would, because she had always seemed pretty direct—not to mention self-absorbed—but he wasn't going to chance it. Better to take the easy route and tell Lizzie half the truth.

'She died a few years ago.'

'That sucks.'

He smiled at the pithy comment. The honest anger on his behalf so much better than the apology he usually got.

Why did people even say sorry to you when someone died, or got so sick they might as well be dead? Did they think it was their fault? And what was he supposed to say

back? 'Don't worry, it's OK' or 'It's not that bad', as if you were comforting them? Or just 'Thanks'? As if them saying sorry was actually going to help.

'Yeah, it does suck,' he replied.

'Do you have any brothers or sisters?' she asked, slipping the tray of cupcakes into the oven.

'No, it was just me and my mum.'

She threw the oven mitt down. 'That's even suckier, then.'

'I suppose. Although I would have expected you to figure I was better off,' he pointed out. 'Seeing what a hard time you give Aldo.'

Her face flushed a dull red.

He liked that she had no make-up on. She usually wore a lot of gunk around her eyes. She looked better without it. Not that he usually had an opinion on what women wore on their faces. He liked lipstick as much as the next guy. But without the gunk she seemed less remote, more real. And he could see her eyes more, that cornflower blue bold and expressive—as if he were getting a precious glimpse of the real Lizzie behind the hipster mask.

Emotion flittered across her face, easy to read. First embarrassment, then guilt, then the hint of defensiveness. He found all three captivating in their own way. Especially when she held back the snarky comment she probably wanted to say and smiled instead.

Lizzie had a very cute smile when it wasn't ironic.

'Sorry, but those who don't have annoying little brothers,' she said lightly, 'don't get to pass judgement on those who do.'

He chuckled. All the melancholy thoughts of his mother, and the upcoming duty visit to the hospice, neatly dispelled.

'What about those who always wanted a little brother,' he countered, 'and think those who have one ought to appreciate them more?'

'Excuse me, but wanting one and having one are two very different conditions.' She propped one hand on her hip and placed the other on the countertop, her stance combative, and flirtatious. Sweat had gathered in her cleavage, making the skin glisten, spotlighting the small, firm breasts beneath her jogging bra. He dragged his gaze back to her face, with an effort.

'But I give you major points for wanting a little brother like Aldo,' she said. 'After seeing his dark side.'

'His dark side's not so bad. Yours, on the other hand...'

He let the playful insinuation hang in the air. Knowing he shouldn't flirt back with her. He'd been avoiding her all week for this very reason. Flirtation wasn't cool. She was eighteen and fragile beneath all the bravado and bitchiness, according to her mum. And he was twenty-one and in her mum's employ. He'd been careful to keep his distance from day one in this job, but after what had happened at the Serps, he'd been extra careful, realising that friendly Lizzie could be a lot more dangerous than arsey Lizzie.

But today, after all the stress of what was going on with his mum, the chance to think about something else and enjoy some, OK, mild flirting didn't seem like such a major crime. And while Lizzie's mum thought she was fragile, she didn't seem particularly fragile to him. She certainly wasn't naive, or romantic. If her arsehole boyfriend had taught her one thing, it was to be smart around guys, and not get too invested. And it was a lesson she'd obviously learned with interest if the ballsy way she'd handled that prick in the park was anything to go by.

Luckily, he'd learned the exact same thing when he was seventeen and lost his virginity with one of the neighbours. Jenny had been a nice lady, divorced with a young kid and lonely. And the sex had been amazing, at least for him.

He wasn't so sure it had been that great for her in retro-spect, because he'd had the staying power of a tsetse fly and couldn't locate a clitoris without a lot of fumbling. But she'd been sweet enough not to complain.

His mum had totally freaked when she'd found out, so Jenny had moved away. And he'd been crushed. The lone-liness enveloping him. He figured out eventually that he hadn't been in love with Jenny. He'd just needed the chance to escape every Saturday afternoon while her little boy was with his dad. But it had taken him months to get over the misery whenever he'd walked into the house and saw the new people living next door. If there was one thing a kid whose mum had primary progressive MS should have known, it was that nothing stayed the same, and you couldn't rely on anyone.

But for a while he'd relied on Jenny. And he shouldn't have.

Ever since, he'd steered clear of romantic relationships. He already had enough shit to deal with, without asking for more. Once his mum was gone, he'd think about dating, but until then, he didn't need the hassle.

So there was no way he would ever go too far with Lizzie. Which meant it was daft to get paranoid about enjoying her company. Or some extracurricular flirting. If it made them both feel good, and he was well aware of the limitations, where was the harm?

'How can you possibly judge how dark my dark side is,' she replied, her breasts doing that perky thing again as she leaned into his personal space, 'when you've never had an older sister? I can tell you categorically it's perfectly nor-mal to bitch at your little brother. Even my therapist said so.' The colour in her cheeks bloomed like a mushroom cloud. She opened the oven door.

He found it endearing that she was embarrassed about the therapy. He knew that feeling, too. 'Therapists are mostly all talk, though, right?'

She pressed her finger into a cupcake to test it. Then slammed the door, shooting him an uncertain look. 'You've had a therapist, too?'

'I've had several, when my mum was sick. They weren't all bad, but it seemed to me just talking about stuff wasn't going to make my mum better. So what exactly were they being paid for?'

She propped her bottom on the counter, the smile that flitted over her features instant and genuine. 'Same.'

His pulse gave a funny lurch. Not a big deal.

'Aldo isn't any different from other boys his age,' he continued, the blip of panic unsettling enough for him to divert the conversation onto safer ground. Aldo was his area of expertise, after all.

'Except that he doesn't have a dad,' Lizzie pointed out. 'He doesn't even know who his dad is.'

'So what? Neither did I. It didn't do me any harm,' he said easily enough to make himself almost believe it. Until he saw curiosity sharpening her gaze and realised the conversation was right back where he didn't want it again. On him.

* * *

Lizzie knew a lot of people who didn't have dads, not just Aldo. She also knew people who had dads who were dickheads. But still she felt bad for Trey. Which was silly really. Even if Trey had needed a dad once, as she often thought Aldo needed one now, he didn't need one any more. He was strong and competent and confident. Except...

'Why didn't you want to hug Aldo, at the Serps?' She'd been wanting to quiz him about that for days. 'It was so

obvious that's what he needed, and he wanted it from you, not me.'

He looked taken aback by the non sequitur, but then he straightened away from the counter and she knew this wasn't just surprise at the sudden change of topic. Because he looked a lot less relaxed.

'I can't hug him. I shouldn't even touch him really. It's a child protection thing.'

It was her turn to be surprised. 'You mean you've *never* given him a hug?'

'It would be crossing a line I'm not allowed to cross.'

Bullshit was her first thought. And her second. 'Who said you're not allowed to give him a hug? I can't believe my mum told you that.' Her mum thought Trey was God's gift to childcare, and from what she'd observed while he was looking after Aldo—when she wasn't allowing her judgement to be coloured by jealousy—her mum had got that right. 'You're important in Aldo's life, you must know that.'

His jaw went rigid, and she saw the glint of annoyance, so unlike him. 'I'm not his dad, or his big brother. I'm a paid employee.'

He had to know he was more than that. Especially to Aldo. But then she remembered a line from her GCSE English, something about protesting too much. Was it Shakespeare? She couldn't be sure because she'd barely scraped a D in English Literature. But even so, it applied. Trey was definitely protesting too much. The question was why? Then she thought of him standing beside her at the park, that blank look on his face, his fingers curled into a fist, and she had her answer.

'You weren't protecting him, were you? You were protecting yourself.'

The bell on the oven timer chose that precise moment to

ping. He grabbed the mitt and slid the cupcakes out of the oven. But she already had her answer, his rigid expression a dead giveaway.

Trey had no parents and no siblings. He had no family at all by the sounds of it. Was he lonely? Wouldn't it be terribly isolating to work with a family, to become important to them, the way he'd become to Aldo, and not be able to become too invested? Was he scared to get too involved?

'These smell delicious,' he said as buttery steam filled the kitchen and made her stomach rumble. 'Thanks for helping out. I owe you one.'

He didn't understand the dynamics of sibling relationships, that much was obvious. But did he even understand the dynamics of a family relationship? How long had his mum been sick before she died? Had he been the one caring for her? Was that why he was so adept at looking after Aldo?

'I guess we should wait for them to cool down before icing them,' he said, clearly trying to fill the void with inane conversation.

'I need to go have a shower,' she said, feeling indescribably grimy all of a sudden. Certainly some eyeliner wouldn't go amiss. Especially now she had a plan.

She liked Trey; he was a nice guy. And, for the first time ever, despite his lame taste in polo shirts, 'nice' didn't feel like a euphemism for 'boring'. Could this be a sign of her own maturity? Had she finally grown out of wanting to hook up with bad boys who thought they were cool but were really just creepy and sex-obsessed?

Having Trey's warm brown gaze stray involuntarily to her tits had made her feel excited, not dirty, the way Liam had when he'd told her he wanted to come on her boobs.

Trey was hot, and totally cool in his own way. Even if

he didn't know it. But he was also way too reserved and serious.

An intervention was called for. He needed someone to shove him off the sidelines and into the action. And she was the perfect person for that job. She'd spent so much of her life shoving herself into the action.

If that meant passing her flirting proficiency test, so be it.

'I'll be back in ten, and then we can ice them.'

'Cool,' he said, deliberately nonchalant. But she was sure she could feel his chocolate gaze warming her arse as she dashed out of the room.

Score one to Lizzie Best's Play Trey Initiative.

Chapter 14

'OK, folks, you're all set.' Chad, Wilderness Kayaks owner and apparently sole operator, placed the cooler packed with freeze-dried rations, beverages and 'other essentials' into the hatch in the kayak's bow and sealed it. 'Step in and I'll give you a boost.'

'Cheers, mate.' Luke stepped into the fibreglass boat's front cockpit, sat down to extend his legs under the hull and then leaned back to catch the paddle Chad chucked him. All in one fluid movement, with barely a wobble.

The man could have been born in a bloody kayak. Even in the chunky life vest—or personal flotation device, as Chad had called it—Luke looked cool and competent and mouth-wateringly sexy.

Whose stupid idea was that kiss again?

Nine days into their 'extreme bonding activities' and Halle had come to regret that errant lip lock more and more, the odd hormone bump having morphed into an increasingly severe case of can't-take-my-eyes-off-you syndrome.

Their companionable chat at the waterfall hadn't helped. There was only so much distraction smutty novels, work commitments and scenic walks to the reception to phone

or email her children could provide when she was sharing a cabin with a man she was actually conversing with again.

But much more frustrating was the wealth of stuff that remained unsaid. Stuff she had become increasingly aware Luke was determined would remain unsaid. His lightning-fast reflexes to deflect the conversation elsewhere every time they strayed anywhere near the topic of their past were something to behold.

If she hadn't had complete faith in his journalist abilitics, she certainly did now.

Unfortunately, her growing sexual awareness of him was not helping her to handle the gargantuan task of trying to circumvent his avoidance techniques. Which appeared to be even more well honed than they had been twenty years ago.

The only good news so far was that the hot tub remained out of bounds for both of them.

Not so good was the fact that Monroe's programme kept them bonded together like superglue during the day. They'd gone on two more hikes, luckily not to secluded waterfalls, done a two-hour horse ride—which her bottom had only just recovered from—and a geocaching trip the day before, during which they'd resolutely failed to find a single geocache.

But she'd discovered this morning that the next day of the programme involved a two-day kayak trip. Which meant one night spent at an island campsite on Fontana Lake.

And while part of her was pleased to have Luke secured in one spot with nowhere to hide, another part of her was very apprehensive about inviting any more intimacy into their situation.

That and the indisputable fact that she was not a natural-born kayaker.

Her arms were already chaffing on the PFD and she didn't like the look of the Tuckasegee River, even though Chad had

assured them that this fork of it, leading into Fontana Lake, was only a class two—which was supposed to translate as tame for this time of year. Tame was clearly relative, because the white froth rippling ominously over the rocky riverbed while they'd been driving along the NC288 towards their drop-off site in North Carolina did not look tame to her.

Still, at least her uneasiness over their latest adventure was distracting her from her uneasiness at spending the night with Luke at a wilderness campsite.

Because even more unsettling than the spike in sexual awareness had been the building familiarity. Each new day in the cabin brought with it a new reminder of the days they'd once spent together in their cramped council flat in Hackney.

He still drank his coffee black enough to tar the M4. He still smelled of sandalwood and minty toothpaste after his morning shower. He still only bothered to shave every couple of days, giving him an increasingly rakish look on his off days—the specks of grey in his stubble the only appreciable difference.

And to add to her apprehension about their night alone together was the fact she would have to do it without the trusty shield of make-up.

She'd never been high maintenance as a teenager, but an intricate personal grooming regime had become part of her daily routine in the years since. Not only did she not want to risk going out in London without her concealer and eyeliner and end up in some blurred snapshot in *Heat* magazine looking like a bag lady, the careful application of moisturiser and foundation, expensive powders and gels made her feel secure, protected, like a knight donning her armour ready to do battle with the demons of daytime TV.

Armour she needed now more than ever as a defence against Luke's dark arts of dishabille.

She'd already reduced the half hour she gave herself in London each morning to apply her make-up to a measly ten minutes, because it seemed like a rather daft indulgence to go hiking or geocaching in the middle of the Smoky Mountains. But this morning she'd been forced to go cold turkey, when Luke had taken one look at the bulky make-up case and announced, 'You're not taking that. Perfume scents can attract bears. And, anyway, you don't need it. You look great without it.'

How would he know? Seeing as he hadn't seen her without since she was twenty? But as she could hardly point that out without making it seem as if she was wearing make-up for his benefit, she had been forced to leave the case behind. She hadn't even been able to take some portable concealer or lip gloss on pain of a flipping bear attack.

Then again, a day without make-up and the risk of a bear attack might be the least of her worries. After all, there was no guarantee that she'd even get to this campsite alive.

'How long did you say it would take to get there?' Halle asked as she double-checked the fastenings on her PFD for the tenth time.

'Between five and six hours,' Chad replied with an easy smile. 'It's only twelve miles to the camp island from this location.'

'Six hours to paddle twelve miles! Wouldn't it be quicker to walk?'

Chad seemed confused by the question. 'I guess, but you get a great view of the landscape from the water. And the hiking's—'

'Stop moaning and get in the bloody boat.' Luke interrupted Chad's earnest explanation.

'If you don't mind, I'm trying to ascertain how long this is going to take.'

'It's going to take a heck of a lot longer with you standing on the shore. And if we don't put up our tents before night-fall, you're going to be sleeping in the open with the bears.'

'Stop bullying me,' she said, but she scrambled into the boat, the mention of bears having the desired effect.

She shrieked as she put her second foot into the boat and the kayak dipped on one side, obviously planning to toss her out on her arse.

Chad grasped her arm above the elbow to steady her. 'Don't worry, ma'am. It's real hard to roll a kayak,' he re-assured her, as if he'd read her mind. 'They have a much lower centre of gravity than a canoe.'

'Thanks for that.'

Stop calling me 'ma'am'. I'm not your grandmother.

She held on to another shriek as she gripped the sides of the boat and settled into her cockpit behind Luke.

'Your paddle, ma'am.'

She sent Chad a caustic smile as she took the short light-weight pole.

'OK, folks, you're all set. Enjoy your trip.'

Chad gave the boat a hefty shove, jogging the kayak off the sandbank and propelling them into the water. Luke wheeled his paddle in a smooth arc that sent them into the current, the corded muscles of his upper arms flexing and stretching with each stroke.

Halle attempted to match her strokes to his rhythm.

Eventually, they settled into an even glide, the bright blue two-man kayak carried along by the current. Halle absorbed the sunlight on her skin, and the slight drift and pull of the river, managing to relax a little now that they hadn't im-mediately capsized.

Riverbanks crowded with shrubs and trees let off a res-inous perfume to go with the cool fresh scent of the water,

any signs of human habitation vanishing as they left Chad and the drop-off location behind. The Tuckasegee River took a smooth sinuous course through the landscape. The swift current more manageable than she had expected as the water rippled over the stony riverbed.

Halle relaxed into their journey, clipping the surface with her paddle, while letting Luke do most of the work—with six hours to go she planned to conserve her energy.

He rotated his torso, rocking his hips to dig the double-ended paddle into the water. His shoulders lifted and tilted with each stroke, the muscles bunching against the arm-holes of his life vest.

She got a tiny bit transfixed.

Apparently, there was only so much scenery you could admire when you had a man of Luke's physique displaying his natural athletic ability two feet from your nose. Especially if you hadn't gotten laid in over a year.

'Hey, look over there.' He pointed towards the bank. Halle spotted the hawklike bird perched on the top of a hawthorn tree, regal and serene as it stared at them.

'What is it?' she asked as it launched off the branch and swooped into the sky.

'An osprey, maybe. I have an e-book on the local wild-life on my iPad. We can check it out later.'

Halle smiled at his response. Luke had always been inquisitive, enthusiastic about discovering new things. 'Since when did you become a twitcher?'

He glanced over his shoulder, one eyebrow cocked. 'I'm not the one who asked what it was.'

'True.'

He nodded at her paddle, which she'd placed on the hull to watch the bird. 'Start paddling, you freeloader. There's no passengers allowed on this boat.'

'Aye aye, Captain.' She began paddling again, maybe exhaustion was the answer to curbing the liquid tug of the muscles in her abdomen.

* * *

Exhaustion was definitely the answer, followed by extreme boredom. For, however magnificent the Smoky Mountain scenery and its raw, primal overwhelming beauty, or Luke's very flexible, very expansive shoulders, there was only so much of either one you could appreciate when your arms were about to drop off.

By hour three of their kayak adventure, the scenery—both natural and man-made—had become completely beside the point.

The only thing that had kept her going this far was that she didn't want to give in first. She'd been on the receiving end of Luke's superior look rather frequently in the past eight days while trying to keep up on various hikes and horse rides, but he showed no signs of tiring whatsoever.

She steeled herself for the familiar raised eyebrow. 'Isn't it about time for lunch?'

He lifted the paddle out of the water, swivelled round. 'You knackered already? We've only been at it for a couple of hours.'

Hello, superior look.

'I'm not knackered.' *Much.* 'I'm starving. It's got to be about four hours since breakfast. If it's all right with you, I'd like to eat before I start gnawing off my own arm. Or get third-degree sunburn.'

He tipped up the peak of her baseball cap. She struggled to match his superior look under the inspection, although it probably wasn't that effective given that she was totally knackered.

'Did you put the sunscreen on? Your nose looks pink.'

She wrinkled the nose in question, making it sting. 'You're not actually the captain of this little expedition, you know. That was just a joke on my part. Which I would never have made if I had realised you were Captain Bligh in a former life.'

He flipped her cap off. 'He who does the lion's share of the work, gets to do the bossing about.'

'Who says? And give me back the cap. It's the only protection I've got.'

'I say so.' After dipping the cap into the river, he plopped it back onto her head. 'There you go.'

Water soaked her hair and splattered onto her nose and face, dribbling into the neck of her T-shirt.

'I thought you wanted to cool off,' he said.

She tilted the peak up to glare at him. 'That's not what I had in mind.'

'Effective, though, right?'

She couldn't deny the lake water felt glorious on her frazzled skin. But she wasn't ready to be grateful. 'You look pretty hot yourself.' *And in more ways than one*, she thought, her pulse skittering at the dimple in his cheek as he smiled.

He whipped off his own cap and presented it to her. 'Be my guest.'

Scooping up enough water to fill the cap to the brim, she slapped it onto his sweaty hair and drenched him.

Wiping his eyes, he smiled at her. 'Cheers. Now let's go get you fed before you start cannibalising yourself.'

Her stomach rumbled on cue, audible above the gurgle of water, and her accelerated breathing. 'Actually, I'm more likely to eat you after that stunt.'

The quick grin turned the twinkle of mischief to something potent and provocative before he turned back to steer the kayak towards the pebbled cove ahead of them.

The muscles in her abdomen knotted into a tight ball of need.

Whose idiotic idea was that bloody kiss again?

* * *

'How much further is it?' There was no biting off the whine this time. Not after five hours and counting of beautiful never-ending Smoky Mountain wilderness.

She was so over this now. Her arms hurt, her fingers had calluses the size of dirigibles, her stomach had begun to cramp from hunger after two energy bars and an apple two hours ago, and even Luke's flexing shoulder muscles held no appeal whatsoever. She wanted to be back in her house in Notting Hill, preferably with her feet up, on her four-seater Heal's sofa with a gargantuan glass of chilled Pouilly-Fuissé in her hand. Not crossing the Smokies by canoe.

The going had been slow and sluggish, the river dragging beneath the kayak's hull like a pool of treacle. She'd happily embrace the danger of some white water now if it would get them moving a bit faster. To their destination. Any worries about sleeping in the same campsite with Luke had been well and truly quashed because nothing short of five well-oiled male strippers dancing naked on the hull was likely to rouse her lust now.

'Stop asking me that. You sound like Lizzie when she was three.' Luke's cranky reply proved what Halle had suspected for several hours. He wasn't enjoying this excursion any more than she was. He was just better at hiding his discomfort. As he'd always been.

'I never made Lizzie kayak until her arms dropped off when she was three.'

'I wish your tongue would drop off.'

'Tough. My tongue's the only thing that still moves without pain.'

'Believe me, I know that.'

'You didn't answer my question.'

'Can you see a fork in the river ahead of us?' Luke replied. Doing that annoying thing he had perfected in his teens when he didn't want to answer a question, of simply asking another one.

Halle leaned to the side to peer past his broad back. The kayak swayed but didn't tilt. At least she was now confident that nothing short of Godzilla would be able to tip this bloody hunk of fibreglass over. 'No, all I see is more trees.'

'And that's exactly what I see. Which means the campsite's probably a ways yet.'

'I feel like I'm paddling through molasses, though.'

'Yeah, well, I feel like I'm paddling through molasses with an annoying little bird on my shoulder trying to peck my ear off. So count yourself lucky.'

'If she had the strength, this annoying little bird would clout you around said ear with said paddle.'

She swung the paddle in an arc for the five-millionth time to plough it into the sluggish river. Luke's paddle dug in ahead of hers. But then he held it in the water, swinging the boat across the current towards the opposite bank.

'What are you doing?' Halle said, alarmed. Maybe they wouldn't capsize, but after five hours, she didn't want to test the theory.

'See those peaks over there?'

She nodded, noticing the frothing whitecaps chopping up the glassy surface of the water. 'What about them?'

'It's a faster current. If we get into it, we can relax for a bit and just steer.'

'Are you sure that's a good idea?' she shouted above the rumble of the approaching rapids as he navigated towards the rocky outcrops. The far bank looked a lot less benign,

made up of sheer slabs of granite that rose out of the water in a jagged wall of death.

'Wait!' she yelled as the kayak got sucked into the stream and jolted over the swell. The scrape of rock on the hull jarred her feet.

'Too late.' Luke's cry got lost in her shriek and the rush of water as she noticed the escarpment ahead. The fork in the river Chad had told them to look out for. The calm sedentary stream they had been in before veered to the right of the island.

Luke shouldered his paddle to steer the boat to the left of the island. The kayak shot forward, fully engaged in the surging waves slapping at the boat.

He whooped as they gathered speed. And Halle yelped, the shot of terror accompanied by the shimmer of exhilaration.

Water sprayed her sun-stung cheeks and lapped into the cockpit, drenching her shorts. Her cap flipped backwards off her head. Wind lifted the ponytail that had stuck to her neck with sweat, shooting tingles of excitement into her stomach.

Terrific, I'm going to die.

Even so, her next shriek sounded suspiciously like a whoop.

They barrelled down the river together whooping and shouting and going at what felt like a hundred miles an hour. She followed Luke's lead, the muscles of her upper arms screaming as she clung to her paddle and dunked it in the water to counteract the flow and keep the boat on course. Her life vest bumped her chin, but the smile split her face. All the pain, the stress, the strain, even the boredom sped away, until all that was left was an intoxicating rush of adrenaline…

The next delighted whoop cut off in her throat, though, as she spotted the fallen tree, its gnarled trunk hanging over the bank, its branches spearing up through the fast-moving water. Ready to capture and devour them in its clutches.

'Luke, watch out.'

'Fuuuck!' His shout reached her ears just before an angry crunch, as the boat slammed into the thicket of grasping wooden fingers and spun round on its tip.

Suddenly, they were racing down the river at a hundred miles an hour, backwards.

Her next shriek sounded nothing like a whoop.

Another crunch as the kayak caught fast in the branches of another felled tree. Water flowed over the bow. Luke swore copiously in front of her. And Halle's life flashed before her in terrifying Technicolor as the unflippable kayak threatened to flip over and drown them both.

'Right,' Luke shouted over his shoulder. 'Paddle on the right.'

She did as he ordered, but her paddle lifted out of the water. Rocks smashed against the bow as they shot free, then lurched into the bank. Dipping branches scratched at her face, tangled in her hair, wrenching it out at the roots. Luke ducked to escape losing an eye. The boat listed and began to tilt, surging sideways against the current. Luke dumped the paddle and grabbed an overhanging branch to yank himself out of the cockpit.

'Where are you going?' Was he planning to jump? And leave her to die on the boat alone? 'You can't leave me here!'

He didn't reply, but he kicked the bow hard, spinning the kayak round into the right direction, then dropped down, straddling the hull behind her. Suddenly, his arms banded around her waist, the kayak's bow lifted out of the water and she had visions of them tipping over backwards. But the weight of their gear in the front compartment counterbalanced Luke's weight on the hull and they skimmed along. Sinking low at the back, but not going over.

Whisking the paddle out of her numbed fingers, his knees

digging into her sides and his feet dragging in the water, he steered them out of the thicket of roots and branches, and back into the main current.

'Climb up front,' he shouted.

She scrambled out of her cockpit and crawled to land knees first in the seat Luke had vacated. Throwing herself into a crouch, she bumped her chin with a loud thud, which zinged into her temples, then flattened herself on the hull, using her hands to paddle.

'There it is. Head to your right,' came Luke's shout.

She lifted her head with an effort to see a clearing on the far bank, across what looked like about ten miles of fast-flowing river.

After five hours of work, they were going to miss the bloody campsite entirely if they didn't get across the current.

She picked up her pace, wheeling her left arm wildly as she scooped water. She could hear frantic splashing as Luke paddled furiously behind her.

The next few seconds felt like hours. Luke's grunts matched her pants as they both expended every last ounce of their strength to hit the bank before the river drew them past to who knew where.

The sound of scraping gravel on the kayak's hull answered all her prayers as they hit the pebbled beach. She heard the deep splash as Luke leaped into the water and grabbed the line at the bow. He dragged the boat the rest of the way onto solid ground.

She sank face down, gripping the edges of the kayak with cold numbed fingers, attached like a limpet to the solid, unmoving hull. The gear hatch dug into her chest, exhaustion flowing over her. But the warm solidity of the fibreglass under her cheek felt too wonderful to relinquish.

A hand gripped her upper arm and lifted her. She pitched

off the hull to find herself straddling Luke's lap. He cradled her head, one arm wrapped around her back. She buried her face in the fresh damp skin of his neck.

He sat cross-legged on the small beach of pebbles and silt, his boots still in the water. The smell of wet man and the salty taste of sweat backed up in her throat.

'Bugger me, that was a close call.' The gruff murmur rumbled against her ear.

'I thought we were going to die.' Fatigue and relief made her a tad melodramatic.

He chuckled, the husky rumble turning into a laugh. 'Great way to go, though. Killed by a dead tree.'

His laughter loosened hers and a chuckle popped out, fuelled by the renewed spurt of adrenaline and relief. They were alive, and undrowned by dead trees. Life was a truly wonderful thing.

'Who knew dead trees could be so dangerous?' she sputtered past rising hysteria.

'We do, now.'

'Well, next time don't bloody steer into one, then.' The stern rebuke wasn't all that convincing accompanied by the spluttering laughs.

His hands cupped her shoulder blades as he dragged her off his chest. The wide smile caused that tempting dimple to wink in his cheek. 'Aye aye, Captain.'

She shoved him over and rolled off his prostrate form to flop down by his side. The laughter slowly subsided, accompanied by the drift of the river and the muffled buzz of an insect. She batted it away and stared up at the empty blue sky. Knobbly pebbles dug into her spine.

She caught Luke watching her, the fierce gaze almost as disturbing as the tight feeling warming her clammy

skin. And even though she knew she was being insane, she grinned, happy to be alive, in this moment, with him.

'I've got some bad news, Hal,' he said.

'What?'

'We lost a paddle.'

'That's OK, Captain. You're only going to need one paddle to get us to the marina tomorrow. I am now officially a passenger.'

Lurching up, he levered himself on top of her, his knees planted on either side of her hips, his arms above her head, caging her in. The raw-boned face, so handsome, so familiar, his wet hair, shaggy across his brow, only inches from hers. Close enough to make out the twists of silver in the pale blue of his eyes, and trigger the traitorous pulse of arousal.

'Who said it was your paddle we lost?' he muttered, his breath tasting of peppermint against her lips.

'I do.'

His body lowered until his weight pressed into her belly. The delicious pressure made her want to stretch and rub against the hard contours. He lowered to his elbows and framed her face between chilled hands. His gaze glided up to the top of her head, the approval in his eyes not daunted by the bird's nest she probably had doubling for hair.

'Near-death experiences agree with you.'

She gasped, acknowledging the growing ridge in his pants.

Then his lips settled on hers, firm and seeking, his tongue taking advantage of her shocked gasp to claim her mouth. She sucked on his invading tongue, drawing it in. Sensation exploded, pinching her frigid nipples into swollen buds of need.

She flattened her hands on his chest, his T-shirt cool and damp despite the heat, and let the sensual haze envelop her.

Then she pressed her palms to the solid wall of his chest to shove him back. 'Stop, Luke. This isn't happening. We're not doing this.'

'Too late.' His lips nipped hers with sly butterfly kisses.

She braced trembling elbows, shoved harder. 'No, it's not.'

He dragged out a tortured breath. 'OK, OK. You're right.' His laboured breathing echoed in her sternum as he searched her face, his eyes glassy with lust. 'Bloody hell, I can't believe it.'

She clenched her fingers, taking fistfuls of wet T-shirt—barely resisting the urge to pull him in for another round. 'What can't you believe?'

That the heat's still there after all this time? That we're making out like a couple of horny teenagers, soaking wet on a riverbank in the middle of Nowheresville, North Carolina?

She needed specifics, because right now there were too many unbelievables to pick just one.

He groaned. 'That I'm supposed to be a grown-up, but right now I'd give my left nut to be able to fuck you again with no repercussions.'

The hot, hazy fog of nostalgia froze as if she'd just done the ice bucket challenge at the North Pole.

'Get off me.' She slammed her palms against his chest. 'You prick.'

He climbed off her and she scrambled up. She was soaked and exhausted. She didn't have a spot of make-up on. Her chin felt tender where she'd bumped it on the hull, and her lips and jaw stung from the ferocity of his kiss—but the anger was flowing through her like molten magma, ready to incinerate everything in its path.

'No repercussions? No fucking repercussions? Excuse me, but what repercussions did *you* ever suffer from? *I'm* the one who ended up having to bring up our child on my own because you got me pregnant at eighteen.'

He got slowly to his feet, looking impossibly sexy even with his shorts covered in sand and wet to the waist, his T-shirt ripped at the neck—the rat. 'I wasn't talking about getting you pregnant again.'

'Then what were you talking about? What repercussions?' The word cracked into the air, crass and irrational and selfish.

How dare he talk about repercussions when he'd sailed off to a new life in Paris without having to suffer a single one.

'I'm sorry, Halle, OK? I'm sorry.' He tried to take her arm, but she yanked it out of his grasp, the tears stinging her eyes making her even madder.

You're over him. Remember.

But she knew however much she tried to tell herself that, it wasn't true. Could never be true, until she knew the truth.

'I'm sorry,' he said again. As if repetition would make it right. 'I'm sorry I left without a word. I'm sorry you had to survive in that stinking crap hole without me. That I ran out on you and Lizzie. And I'm sorry that I didn't tell you that a long time ago. And what I'm sorry for most of all is that you still hate me because of it.'

'I don't hate you.' *I wish I did.* 'And I don't want a bloody apology. What I want—and what I think you owe me—is an explanation.'

He dropped his chin, perched his hands on his hips, and she could almost hear his mind working, trying to find a way to dodge and evade and escape the request again.

'What's the matter, Luke? Can't you admit it, even now?

That the reason you left us was because you didn't want me to have Lizzie?'

She'd always known it. And the reality of that still tortured her.

'You dragged me all the way out here, to the middle of bloody nowhere to talk about her, and put us both in this pressure-cooker situation, and yet you still can't face the truth, can you?'

She wanted to hear him say it. To own up to it.

He'd bonded with Lizzie, had been unable to resist his baby daughter once she was born, but there had always been that unspoken truth between them. That she hadn't given him a choice.

'It's not as simple as that,' he said. 'It's complicated. I told you, it wasn't to do with you or Lizzie. It was me. It was something I had to deal with that you couldn't be a part of.'

'Bullshit, Luke.' *Not that again.* 'Don't talk in bloody platitudes and don't patronise me. I'm thirty-six years old. I've been a single mother for sixteen years. I've weathered destitution, your desertion, that prick Claudio deciding he didn't fancy being a dad, Lizzie's epic sulks, Aldo's anger management issues, God knows how many hours of family therapy feeling like a total failure. I've iced about a billion cupcakes, finger-mixed pastry until my hands cramped and built a career while juggling two menial jobs. And I've even managed to survive horse riding, hiking, near death in a kayak and eight never-ending days stuck in a cabin with the only man to give me a multiple orgasm sleeping upstairs after a year-long dry spell and forgetting to pack my bloody vibrator.'

His head shot up, the muscles in his jaw twitching as the flash of lust leaped towards her. 'You're not putting that on me. I'm not the one who initiated that bloody kiss

at the waterfall. And I'm also not the one who put a stop to what could have been a perfectly good way to let off steam a minute ago.'

'Oh, grow up, Luke. We're not becoming bonk buddies when we still have enough baggage to fill the Millennium Dome.'

'Why not? It's just sex, for Chrissake.'

'Spoken like a man who still thinks with his penis.'

'You kissed me back, Hal.' He shot an accusatory finger at her. 'And I'm not the one who just mentioned her vibrator.'

'Fabulous. How clever of you. You're absolutely right. I still desire you. I always have.' She snapped her fingers in front of his face, the loud click ricocheting off the surrounding trees. 'We could screw like rabbits right now and I'd enjoy it. But I'm not sixteen years old any more. So I can't just screw you and forget about it. Because letting off steam, as you so charmingly put it, is not going to make all the baggage magically disappear.'

'Who cares? Why would you even want to unpack baggage that's over sixteen years past its sell-by date?'

Is he actually that clueless, or has he had a lobotomy?

'I'll tell you what the bloody point is. The point is, I've been lugging that baggage around with me for sixteen years and I want to dump it now. It's always been there, dragging me down, making me think less of myself as a woman and question my abilities as a mother. It's the reason why I can top the *Sunday Times* bestseller list six weeks in a row, and why A-list stars will pay fifteen thousand pounds for a birthday cake from my studio, but why I can't have an honest conversation with my daughter about why she's lost two stone in six months without getting a two-hundred-pound-an-hour therapist involved.'

'What if I don't want to talk about it?' He cut her off,

desperation edging out the temper. He grasped her arms, his fingers digging into her biceps. 'Can't you see? Lizzie's the only thing that's still relevant between us. We don't have to rake through all that shit any more. We're both past it.'

'You may be, but I'm not.' It took every ounce of her courage to admit it. But she was past caring now. And past pussyfooting around and letting her pride and her fear of humiliation get in the way of getting the closure she needed. 'We made love that morning, you know. The morning you left.'

The knowledge flashed in his eyes. 'Yeah, I remember. We woke Lizzie up.'

'Then I made you a sandwich to take on the train,' she continued. 'Your favourite, ham and cheese on my home-made poppy seed bread. You kissed Lizzie on the forehead and called her your Best girl the way you always did. And you told me how excited you were, that this was it. That you were going to ace the interview. And I was so excited, too. And then you walked out the door and I never saw you again.' She gulped air. She mustn't cry. How could the memories of that day still be so vivid? When she thought she'd buried them so deep? 'You didn't even contact me to talk about seeing Lizzie for two whole months.'

'Jesus, Hal. I know. And I'm sorry. I'm so, so sorry. But I wasn't thinking straight. I wasn't really thinking at all. Not for a long time.'

'You made me feel like nothing. For a very long time. Can't you see an apology isn't enough to take that away? I need an explanation. About what happened to you that day.'

The question hung between them.

He turned his head towards the river, the wet hair sticking to his forehead. 'OK, I guess I owe you that.'

Finally!

She held her breath, not entirely convinced he was really going to give up the information.

He didn't look at her, but after a pause of several never-ending seconds, he finally started to speak in a rough monotone.

'Amelie and I went to some seedy club that night in the Pigalle, after the assignment.' He focused on her at last. 'The interview had gone OK. I'd got some good quotes. We drank too much and I got into a fight with one of the bouncers. I woke up the next morning in her spare room, with a black eye and an unexplained bite mark on my shoulder and the worst hangover of my entire life. I'd missed my train.' He dug the toe of his boot into the pebbles, concentrated on it as he continued. 'I got dressed, got to the Gare du Nord to buy another ticket. To come home to you and Lizzie.' He cleared his throat. 'And I just...' The hesitation turned into a weighty silence.

A million questions slammed into her brain, but she refused to voice them. Imagining herself back at their flat, already worried because he hadn't called, but having no way of knowing the horror that was about to unfold, when the communication never came.

'And I just couldn't buy the ticket,' he said. 'My head felt like a wrecking ball had smacked into it and my shoulder stung like a son of a bitch and my hands were shaking as if I had the DTs. And that's when I started to cry.'

His voice cracked on the word. And she wondered if she'd heard him correctly.

Luke crying? But Luke never cried. That couldn't be right.

'It was a really weird feeling at first, probably because I'm pretty sure I'd never cried before in my life.' He planted his fists into the pockets of his wet shorts. 'Afterwards, during

therapy, I figured out those tears were ones I'd been storing up for years. But at the time, it felt like it wasn't me doing it. That I was looking at myself, shouting, "Snap out of it, Best." But even so, once I'd started, I couldn't stop.'

He braced his shoulders, digging his fists further into his pockets as a shiver ran through him.

'Eventually, though, I ran out of tears. So I sat there until a gendarme came and told me to leave the station because it was closing. It was after midnight. I'd lost my bag, with my mobile and my wallet. I suppose it had been pinched. I wandered around in a daze and eventually found my way back to Amelie's around dawn. She let me get back into the spare bed.' Finally, his eyes met hers and she saw the hollow look she'd seen so often in the weeks, the months before he'd left. 'And I didn't get out of it again for two weeks.'

A million questions hung in the air.

Hadn't he thought about her, about Lizzie? Not once? Why didn't he ask for her help? She could have saved him. Because she had loved him.

But all those questions were in the past now. Futile and pointless.

A shudder ran through her, her damp clothes chilly against her skin. The sunlight unable to penetrate the icy haze of shock.

He'd had a breakdown. A catastrophic one by the sounds of it. And she'd had no idea.

Whatever she'd expected him to tell her, this wasn't it. She thought she'd been prepared, but she hadn't been prepared for this. Because it felt like losing him all over again.

She gripped her elbows, pulled her arms into her chest to stop the chill branching out through her whole body, and bringing with it the miserable feelings of inadequacy and futility that had haunted her at the time.

'Let's set up camp and I'll get a fire going,' he said, running his fingers through his hair and sending it into damp furrows. 'I don't know about you, but my balls feel like they've frozen to the size of walnuts.' The light tone was in direct contrast to the strained expression on his face.

'Mine, too.' She sent him a weak smile, grateful not to have to talk about his revelation. There were so many things she wanted to say, so much more she could ask but wasn't sure she wanted to know.

Like a typical guy he'd given her an entirely literal answer. The exact details of why he hadn't made it home that day, why he hadn't contacted her for two weeks. But he hadn't told her why he'd felt so trapped. What he had been so terrified of.

But could she bear to hear the truth? Her chest already hurt at the thought of him, as he had been then, so smart and witty and full of himself, curled up in a ball of misery on the platform at the Gare du Nord, unable to function.

He dragged their gear out of the kayak hatch and they took turns to change into dry clothing. She gathered firewood, placing the broken branches into the firepit. He set about putting up the first of their two-man tents.

She glanced over at his muffled cursing as he wrestled with the guidelines and hammered the tent's pins into the hard-packed earth.

How could he seem so tough, so invulnerable, so confident now? And yet have been so broken then? Surely it must have been her, and Lizzie—what else could it have been? But how could she not have understood how unhappy he was? And if she had, would she have been able to make it better?

He came over, crouching to light the fire, and she forced the confusing, treacherous thoughts to the back of her mind,

keen to encourage the silence. She'd stopped blaming herself years ago and she refused to drop back into that sinkhole of recriminations all over again.

He stood and stretched out his spine. She heard his vertebrae popping, noticed the pebbled skin on muscular forearms, the wisps of sun-bleached hair standing on end. And had the strangest yearning to be close to him tonight. If only to reassure herself he was OK now.

'You want to eat?' he asked as the dry kindling crackled and caught. 'Before I put up the other tent?'

'Sure,' she said, although she'd never felt less hungry in her life.

Had she totally mucked this up? Trying to rewrite the past? Perhaps Luke was right, and all they needed to put all their old demons to rest was a good hard shag.

'Why don't we just share the one tent?' she suggested, her jaw stretching in a huge yawn. 'Save you having to put up the other one and break any more of your fingers.'

He glanced at her. 'You sure? It's going to be pretty snug.'

'Don't take that as an invitation,' she qualified quickly, just in case he'd read her mind. 'Nothing's going to happen.'

While her spirit might be insane enough to risk doing the wild thing with Luke again, and her mind might be exhausted enough to be able to argue her into it, her body certainly wasn't.

Weeping thigh muscles never lie.

'Don't worry, I know that,' he said, his expression as weary as hers.

'So, the much more burning question is…' She rummaged around in the box of supplies and pulled out two sachets of freeze-dried entrées. 'Do you fancy rehydrogenated chilli mac or rehydrogenated chicken gumbo to go with your sides of beef jerky and trail mix?'

* * *

Prepare to be tortured tonight.

Luke glanced in Halle's direction, stuffing their leftovers and the remaining food into a heavy-duty disposal sack. Her bottom stuck out of the tent, jiggling enticingly in fleecy pyjamas as she struggled to get the sleeping bags into the confined space.

He tied the disposal sack to the cable suspended between a couple of trees at the back of the campsite and hiked it up to the required fifteen feet above ground level that Chad had stipulated.

Chad had given him a long lecture about 'responsible camping behaviour' and 'the black bear safety rules'. Although Chad insisted that incidences had been rare in the past couple of years due to 'bear programming', Luke had listened carefully to the instructions, not wanting to get bitten on the arse by a six-foot black bear in his sleep because he'd failed to wash out their cooking gear properly or store the leftover foodstuffs in a secure location.

However, a clandestine visit from Yogi the Man-eating Bear was not his primary concern at present. Bedding down in a confined space with Halle was. And yet he'd elected not to put up the other tent after her suggestion. Even though he should have, because the odd smashed knuckle would be a lot less painful than a night spent with blue balls.

She'd made him tell her about his breakdown. And then looked at him with that combination of disbelief and shock and pity. Shooting his tidy game plan—of repairing their relationship as Lizzie's parents without raking up all the shit from their past—right out of the water.

She hadn't commented on his revelations, hadn't probed further. But rehashing that time in his life, when everything

had basically collapsed into a pit of self-loathing and despair, had left him feeling tense. And exposed.

Unfortunately, that hadn't made him feel any less horny, which surely meant he needed to be sectioned. Everything was way too raw at the moment to even contemplate sex with Halle. She might as well have a neon sign on her forehead saying 'Danger: Drama Ahead'.

He'd spent the past sixteen years carefully separating sex from emotion precisely because it could lead to this sort of situation. And he wasn't about to break his own rules just because he felt a little horny.

He dragged the kayak onto the bank and fastened it securely.

Halle wiggled back out of the tent and unrolled the sleeping bags. Then paused to hold up the two bags. His breathing stopped as he willed her to unzip them and turn them into one bag.

OK, a lot horny.

The bags remained unzipped, and she flung them into the tent. Side by side. The tension in his gut, though, didn't ease.

She stood to brush the sand and bits of leaves off her pyjamas. 'It's getting chilly,' she said, squinting into the dying light.

Without the shield of immaculately applied make-up she usually wore, she looked younger, and more vulnerable, the reddened patch on her chin where she'd hit the deck earlier matched by a scratch across her cheek.

The sunset illuminated the golden strands in her hair for a few seconds. She'd rinsed the blonde mess before cooking supper, making it spring around her head in a mussy halo. Wild and only partially tamed by the loose knot.

She toyed with the bottom button on her pyjama top, which she'd fastened right up to her neck. Decorated with

dancing pink elephants, the cotton pyjamas were cosy and girlish and more than bulky enough to disguise her lush curves.

She shouldn't have looked the least bit hot.

He'd never seen anything so hot in his entire life.

She glanced at the tent. 'Right, we're all set. I'm gonna crash.'

And that was all the encouragement his cock needed— never the smartest part of his anatomy—to get thick and heavy in his shorts. 'Go ahead, I'll be in in a minute.'

'Fine, but don't wake me up, even if a bear decides to come calling.'

'I hate to break it to you, but my bear-wrestling abilities are fairly minimal, so I may have to wake you up if one decides to drop in for a visit.'

Was he actually hoping for a bear attack just so he'd have a reason to wake her up now?

Apparently, with Halle, your libido is still stuck in a nineties time warp.

'I wasn't expecting you to wrestle the bear,' she said. 'I was expecting you to present yourself as bait.'

He laughed, the sound strained. 'Right, I guess I can manage that much.'

'Good.' She jerked her thumb towards the tent. 'See you tomorrow, then.'

'Sleep tight.' *Because I won't be.*

She was curled up like a boiled prawn when he edged into the cramped space twenty minutes later. The blonde fuzz was the only thing visible above the lump of her sleeping bag. He kicked off his boots, pulled off his shirt and shorts and shuffled into his own sleeping bag, shivering in his boxers. He stared at the dancing light of a firefly through the

thin tent fabric, listened to the sibilant sound of her snoring and closed his eyes. Tight.

While on assignment, he'd slept soundly in a bombed-out building in Gaza, in a favela during the Rio Carnival and at a Woodstock revival concert in Upstate New York with a thousand geriatric hippies outside his tent singing 'Blowing in the Wind' at top volume as they got stoned for old times' sake.

He could manage one night sharing a two-man with Halle with a raging hard-on.

If he had to.

Chapter 15

Call me, bleep me, if you wanna reach me.

Lizzie hummed the theme tune from *Kim Possible*, emboldened by the image of the kung-fu-fighting high school secret agent as she slotted in behind an ancient Asian lady on the escalator. Her gaze remained riveted on Trey as he stepped off thirty steps above her. Darting out from behind her cover, Lizzie leaped up the stairs two at a time, racing to catch Trey before he exited the tube station.

Move over, Kim Possible. Lizzie Best is on fire.

No way was she losing track of him now. Not after following him all the way from Aldo's school in Notting Hill Gate through two interchanges on the tube in the middle of the Monday morning rush hour all the way to St John's Wood.

Maybe her super-secret mission was a bit nuts. But after days of full-on flirting with the guy, she needed an answer to the burning question: where the bloody hell was he disappearing to every day?

Because just like a guy, despite her less and less subtle probing, he was not giving up the information. Or even any useful clues.

Given that she couldn't just ask him, because—duh—
she would totally expire from embarrassment, what other
choice did she have but to take affirmative action? And turn
her morning jog into a spot of top-secret surveillance work.

Trey glanced to the right as he stood at the zebra crossing.
Lizzie ducked behind the low wall that edged the shrubbery
in front of the station, her heart kicking her tonsils. A city
worker tripped over her and shot her a stern, disapprov-
ing look. She glared back at the nosy bugger, but her heart
glided back down her throat as she peered over the planter,
to see Trey crossing the road, still oblivious to his tail.

He headed down a side street.

She crossed the main road and headed after him, keeping a safer distance.

If he spotted her, it would be a lot worse than embarrassing. As in completely mortifying. With possibly devastating
consequences. She didn't want him to think she was a stalker
and never talk to her again.

But Trey spotting her was a risk she'd have to take.

Because she needed to know what he was up to. Had a
right to know, in fact, unless she'd totally misinterpreted all
those hot looks he'd been giving her whenever they were
alone now.

Yesterday had been the last straw, when they'd ended
up in the pantry, fetching stuff to make pasta for Sunday
dinner. She'd made a quip about sun-dried tomatoes being
an aphrodisiac—not exactly subtle, and also complete
bollocks—but even so his gaze had hit her mouth, the potent I-want-to-kiss-you vibe alive in those warm brown eyes.
And everything inside her had melted like one of her mum's
dark chocolate soufflés just out of the oven—making even
the air around them feel hot and decadent and sinfully delicious. But he hadn't made a move. So she'd sent him her

best please-stop-pissing-around-then-and-do-it vibe back to encourage him.

And…waited.

And…waited.

And…nothing.

Not even a peck. Just several more never-ending moments of gut-melting tension followed by a meal of sun-dried-tomato-pesto spaghetti that was completely indigestible thanks to the fireball of unrequited lust burning in her belly.

There had to be some kind of impediment he wasn't telling her about. Because sun-dried-tomato-pesto-gate wasn't the first almost-snog they'd had. And they both knew his I'm-your-mum's-employee excuse had become totally redundant about ten almost-snogs ago.

What if he had a girlfriend? Or a wife and child? It wasn't impossible. Her mum and dad had had her when they were younger than Trey.

Who cared if following him for half an hour across most of West London was borderline insane behaviour, worthy of a restraining order if she got caught? It had to be done.

She hung back, realising the tree-lined street he'd entered didn't provide a lot of camouflage because it was empty apart from the two of them, and a couple of Japanese tourists wearing Beatles T-shirts whom she guessed must be planning to snap a picture of themselves on the Abbey Road crossing round the corner.

Her steps faltered. No. Never. Surely Trey couldn't be lame enough to be a Beatles fan? He was old before his time, but he wasn't *that* ancient. Her panic eased, though, when he carried on past the turning.

Wherever Trey was going, he looked absorbed in the destination. His stride was measured and purposeful if unhurried. Frankly, she ought to get a medal for managing to

follow him this far without being spotted. If only she'd been this proactive with bloody Liam, she would have discovered just how skanky he was before she'd caught him with his dick down Amber's throat.

Lizzie's pulse hit maximum velocity when he stopped abruptly twenty yards ahead.

Had he reached his destination? And what exactly was she supposed to do if he just walked into a flat? Or a house? What would Kim Possible do in such a situation? Or, better yet, James Bond?

Damn, if only she'd watched more Bond movies with Aldo.

But there weren't any houses nearby. The red-brick monolith of a hospital built in the Victorian era took up the whole of their side of the street, its historic design ruined by the grey pollution stains running down the elaborate cornices and the clumsy addition of a disabled ramp.

But all his attention appeared to be concentrated on the sleek modern two-storey building on the opposite side of the road. Large windows and a flat white frontage gave it a striking mock-Georgian appearance to match the grandeur of the leafy North-west London suburb's genuine Georgian architecture. Blue block lettering on one side of the entrance declared the building to be part of the same NHS hospital, St John's and St Elizabeth's.

Trey buried his hands into his jacket pockets and crossed the street.

A hospital? Was he sick? Or visiting someone? Is this where he had been going every single day? For hours?

Lizzie suppressed the pulse of panic as the large automatic doors slid open and Trey disappeared inside.

She crossed the road behind him, bewilderment beginning to mute the excitement of the chase. Careful to stay far

enough outside the double doors not to trigger the opening mechanism, she watched as a male nurse in a blue uniform arrived to greet Trey in the lobby. The older man touched Trey's arm, the gesture consoling.

Trey followed the nurse through another set of sliding doors to the right of the reception desk.

The last of Lizzie's exhilaration collapsed as she read the sign above the frosted glass door that slid closed behind him.

St John's Hospice.

* * *

She could have gone home. She could have pretended not to know what she now did. But she sat in the corner café by the tube station instead, nursing one cappuccino for over an hour—and getting increasingly pissed-off looks from the guy behind the counter—while waiting for Trey to reappear.

When he finally did, instead of heading into the tube station he walked past the café and carried on going down the main road. Tuning out the angry shout from the counter guy when he realised she'd left only a ten-pence tip, Lizzie sped out of the café, intending to catch up with Trey—and say…what?

How did you explain you'd followed someone for close to an hour, then hung around waiting for them to come out of a hospice? Without sounding like a psychopath? Somehow she didn't think saying she'd been a massive fan of *Kim Possible* when she was twelve was going to cut it.

She was out of breath, and still hadn't come up with a believable excuse, fifteen minutes later as she followed Trey through Hanover Gate into Regent's Park. The manicured grassland, leafy trees and elegant pathways opened up like an oasis in the midst of the city's traffic-choked streets. Not too busy on a weekday at noon, the boating lake at the

north end of the park had only a few aimless pedaloes on it manned by easily amused tourists.

Trey wound his way through the empty rows of deck chairs that faced the lake. And sat down in one. She watched him pay the required fee to the hovering deck-chair attendant.

She hesitated several rows behind him. Now he was static, there could be no more excuses.

Still, she approached slowly, noticing the defeated stoop of his shoulders. He thrust shaking fingers through his cropped hair and spent a long moment holding his head in his hands.

She stopped, feeling like an interloper. Intruding on his despair, his personal secrets. Who had he been visiting in the hospice?

Whoever they were, they must be really important to him.

The peacefulness of the park made the bump-bump-bump of her pulse seem deafening.

Whatever he was going through, and from the hunched posture, the weary body language, she could see it was a lot. She didn't want to add to it, but she couldn't just walk away, either. Because that would make her a coward, and a liar, as well as a stalker.

'Trey,' she murmured, not wanting to startle him. His head jerked round anyway.

'Lizzie?' He sounded unsure, as if she might be an apparition.

I wish.

'Hi, can I join you?'

'Yes.' He indicated the deck chair next to his, still frowning, but then his lips lifted in a quizzical smile. 'I didn't know you came to Regent's Park to jog.' His eyebrows popped up. 'You didn't jog all the way here, did you?'

She pushed out an unconvincing laugh. 'Not exactly.'

She took the seat next to his, brutally aware of the strain in his expression and the puzzled half-smile. A smile that was about to disappear when he discovered what she'd done.

She perched gingerly on the deck chair's crossbar.

Not all about you, remember.

He glanced past her, as if expecting to find a reason for her sudden appearance. 'Then how come you're...?'

'I followed you here.'

His gaze snapped back, the half-smile disappearing on cue. 'You... I don't get it.'

'If it's any consolation, neither do I.'

'Where did you follow me from?'

The tone was still bemused rather than annoyed. But she didn't kid herself it would stay that way.

'From outside Aldo's school, when you dropped him off. I've been following you all morning.'

He straightened in the chair, his back stiffening. Blank confusion gave way to shock as it dawned on him where he'd been. What she'd seen. 'What the... What the fuck did you do that for?'

The swear word shocked her. She'd never heard him use the F-word before, not once. Even though she used it liberally and often.

Self-disgust clawed at her throat, making it hard to speak. 'If I'd had any idea where you were going, I wouldn't have done it.'

She'd always known she was a screw-up. But it wasn't until right this second, as she watched the emotions cross Trey's face—none of them remotely complimentary—that admitting it wasn't just another invitation to her five-year-long pity party.

'That's not an answer,' he said. 'Why did you follow me all that way?'

'Because I wanted to know where you were going every day,' she said. 'And you wouldn't tell me.'

He swore again, levering himself out of the chair, and paced off in the direction of the lake.

She wondered forlornly if he'd keep on walking. She wouldn't blame him if he did.

But he stopped a few steps from the water.

'Miss, that'll be five pounds for the next hour. Or twelve pounds for the day.'

Her head whipped round to find the gawky deck-chair attendant standing beside her. She wanted to tell him to piss off. But how could he know he'd just interrupted a pivotal moment in her life?

She handed him a tenner. 'I'll pay for an hour.'

'Cool.' He gave her the change, and a ticket on which he jotted the time and thankfully left.

'What the hell gave you the right to do that?' Trey had returned. He stood in front of her, his arms folded over his chest, his stance taut with barely suppressed fury.

She steeled herself, although mortification didn't seem like such a big deal any more. 'I thought you were going to kiss me yesterday.'

His face remained rigid, the expression blank and un-yielding.

'In the pantry,' she hinted. 'Over the sun-dried tomatoes.'

He said nothing.

'And then, when you didn't,' she continued, 'I wondered if there was a reason why you hadn't. I thought maybe you had a girlfriend. And I wanted to know. So I… I didn't mean to…' She stuttered to a halt.

Don't hate me, please don't hate me.

'Didn't it ever occur to you that maybe I didn't tell you where I was going because I didn't want you to know?'

She lifted her hands, beseeching, as guilt assaulted her. 'I'm so sorry...' The plea choked off. What could she say in her own defence? 'I didn't think.'

'No, you never do.' His voice rose, his handsome features grim with disgust. 'You know what you are?'

She shook her head, the tears stinging her eyes, making her throat raw.

Please don't say it. Not you.

'You're a spoilt attention-seeking little girl. Why would I want to start something with you?'

The accusation cut deep, wounding her in ways Liam's goading, Carly's teasing, her mother's silent censure never had.

'You think just because you're beautiful and smart and rich and you live a charmed life that you get to have whatever you want?' he continued, confusing her.

She wasn't beautiful, or smart. Why would he say that?

She sniffed, the tears dripping off her nose into the grass, the sobs trapped in her throat.

'Are you crying now?' he mocked. 'You think that a few tears are going to make this OK? Crying makes no difference. It doesn't bring your mum back the way you remember her. It won't stop the crippling muscle spasms, or her vision becoming so blurry she can't see you any more. Or the fear in her face when she can't swallow unaided. Crying doesn't change a fucking thing. All it does is make it worse.'

She had no idea what he was saying any more. Was he talking about his mother? The one who was dead? She didn't dare look up, not wanting to see the disgust in his face.

'I'm sorry,' she whimpered, wishing she could just die. 'You're right.' She gulped down the sob. Scrubbed the tears off her cheeks with the heel of her palm. She examined the lawn between her running shoes. Newly cut, the offcuts

decayed in rows of brown against the living green, the earthy smell masked by the aroma of dried grass and diesel fumes.

She wrapped her arms around her midriff in a vain attempt to fold in on herself and hold in the shame.

'Liam cheated on me. Aldo hates me. Even my best friend thinks I'm a waste of space.' *And now you do, too.* 'I know, you're right. I totally deserve it, for being such a selfish, immature bitch.'

* * *

Trey stared at Lizzie's neck, the bumps of her vertebrae clearly defined. The delicate curve of her shoulder blades. So fragile, so vulnerable. A few wisps of hair clung to the back of her neck, which shuddered with the silent sobs she was trying so hard to suppress.

Way to go, you bastard. Look what you've done.

He stood in a daze, the crippling fury seeping out of his pores, and leaving nothing but hollow, weary shock.

How was any of this her fault? His mother's illness? The long agonising wait for her to stop struggling and just die? The crippling guilt that hit every time he arrived at the hospice with the hope Barry, the head nurse, would tell him it was over, and she was gone? It wasn't even entirely Lizzie's fault she'd followed him.

He'd enjoyed flirting with her since they'd made the cupcakes for Aldo's bake sale. Adored the bright, sexy banter. Become addicted to the thrill of just being around her.

He'd used her to escape the hopelessness, the futile anger, the smothering grief of watching his mother die. All he wanted to do right now was bury his nose against her hairline and breathe in the delicious scent of her. The summery shampoo, the spicy scent of patchouli.

His legs trembled, his knees going watery, as his pulse

throbbed painfully in his ears, blocking out the sounds around him.

He sat in the deck chair next to her, let the canvas sling cup his body and rested his head on the wooden strut of the chair back. 'Sorry I shouted at you.'

'That's OK.' The murmured response was thick with unshed tears. 'I totally deserved it.'

He placed his palm on the slope of her back, patted her clumsily. 'No, you didn't.'

Good job, Carson. Her mum said she was fragile. She's a lot more fragile now, you wanker.

'You're right, I'm not a nice person and I'm really immature. I can see that now.'

She hadn't looked at him, her head still bent, her bum perched uncomfortably on the edge of the deck chair as she stared at her feet, as if she were counting the blades of grass between her shoes.

He forced himself out of the chair and knelt down in the grass in front of her.

Her chin lifted, the surprise in her eyes tempered by confusion. Her cheeks were red from her tears, the dusting of freckles across her nose even more pronounced without the benefit of make-up.

He clasped her hands between his, rubbed the icy skin. 'Trey, what are you doing?'

As her wary gaze searched his face, it occurred to him, how much he had come to love just looking at her. Those intelligent blue eyes, so expressive, so open. The soft pink flesh of her collarbone pebbled with goosebumps despite the warm day. The wide mouth, so smart and arsey one minute, so guarded and unsure the next.

She made such a vital contrast to his mother, whose thin, blotchy skin was now tinged an unhealthy yellow. Whose

gaunt features had become all but unrecognisable. Whose opaque eyes saw nothing.

But it was much more than that. Lizzie didn't only symbolise life and youth and vitality; she symbolised freedom and challenge and excitement. She was complicated and fascinating and unique. And he'd treated her like shit.

Which put him in league with her crappy friends and that arsehole she'd dated.

'I'm trying to warm you up a bit,' he said, 'Your fingers are freezing. How can you be so cold when it's such a hot day?'

The blush fired across her cheeks and she tugged her hands loose. 'Why are you being nice to me? When I've been such a bitch?'

She sounded genuinely confused. And kind of concerned for his sanity.

Jesus, she had no idea of her worth. Of how much he liked hanging out with her. Maybe it was about time he told her the truth. Because the hot-and-cold routine hadn't worked out so well. For either of them.

'You're not a bitch. And you're not wrong. I lied.' He brushed his thumb under her eye, the puffy skin damp. 'I'm sorry I made you cry. It's been kind of a shit day. I wasn't expecting to see you.'

She wiped her eyes with the sleeve of her sweatshirt, making the loose fabric droop at the neck to reveal the lacy strap of her vest top. Adrenaline shot through him.

'What did you lie about?' she asked.

'I *did* want to kiss you in the pantry yesterday. And it wasn't the first time.'

'Oh, OK.' He couldn't tell if she was pleased. 'Are you sure? You're not just saying that to make me feel better?'

'No, I'm not just saying it. I thought you could tell.'

'I thought maybe I'd made a mistake,' she countered. 'Usually when guys want to, they don't hold back.'

'Guys like your ex, you mean?'

The blush burned hotter. 'I suppose.'

'Did he cheat on you a lot?'

'Probably.' She shrugged, and the baggy sweatshirt slipped further to reveal one slim shoulder. 'He got bored with me. He said I was always whining and I didn't want to do him enough.'

His jaw tightened. The anger real again.

No shit? I wonder why?

'The more I hear about that prick,' he said, 'the more I wish I could give him a good kicking.' The world was full of wankers like Lizzie's ex, who thought getting sex whenever they wanted it was their due. It wasn't Lizzie's fault she'd fallen for one. Those guys always had lots of moves to excuse their shitty behaviour.

'It wouldn't be much of a contest. You're a lot bigger than he is.' She looked away, but he was pleased to see the small smile. Good to know she wasn't still hung up on the little turd.

Leaning onto his knees, he tugged the sweatshirt back up over her shoulder to hide the strappy top. Her gaze shot to his, no longer demure. No longer devastated, either.

OK, then.

He stood, the look in her eyes stirring stuff that shouldn't be stirred. 'Do you mind if I sit next to you for a while?' he said.

'Don't be silly, you don't have to ask.'

He nodded and sat. Closing his eyes, he let the weariness intrude. He absorbed the quiet, disturbed only by the flutter of some nearby pigeons, the ripple of water against the

paved edge of the lake, the distant shout of a mother calling her child—and the watchful presence of the girl beside him.

He came to sit here most days. The park air a welcome break from the sweet cloying scent of the morphine drip, the vague undertones of bleach and decaying flowers in the hospice. And all those feelings he couldn't always control.

Normally, he liked the silence, the emptiness.

But it was nice to have Lizzie beside him now; it made him feel less alone.

'Could I ask you something, Trey?'

Seeing her earnest expression, he knew what she was going to ask. But he nodded anyway. Because he didn't want her to leave. Not yet.

'Who is it you're visiting in the hospice?'

'My mum.'

He saw surprise. Then distress. Then confusion. All plainly revealed on her face. He steeled himself for the obvious next question.

'Why did you tell me she'd died?'

'Habit, I guess. She's been sick for a long time. And sometimes it's easier not to bother telling people. They tend to think you're either a charity case or a martyr. I hate that, because I'm neither.'

She didn't challenge him. 'What's wrong with her?'

'She has primary progressive MS. She's had it for ten years.' He recited the medical details that had been his life for so long, but that he'd never shared with anyone unless he had to. She listened patiently, without interrupting. And, for once, he didn't feel the need to hide the truth.

'I used to be able to look after her at home. But she had to move to the hospice four months ago because she needed round-the-clock care. I thought it would be quick once she was there. That's what the doctors said. But it hasn't been.'

He could hear the resentment in his tone and wondered if she could hear it, too.

'Does my mum know about her?' she asked.

He studied her face, trying to assess her mood. Would she rat on him? He didn't think so. He'd seen a side of her this past week that was nothing like the spoilt drama queen he'd accused her of being. But could he risk it?

'No,' he said at last, deciding he couldn't lie to her. Not again. 'I figured there was no way she'd give me the job if she knew I had all this going on,' he added in his defence. But it still came out sounding dishonest. 'I really wanted the job. I like Aldo. He's a nice kid. And…' He paused. He didn't want to sound weird, or too needy. 'And it was nice being part of a normal family for a change. Even if I was only an employee.'

* * *

Lizzie smiled, impossibly touched by his honesty. 'You think we're a normal family?'

The slow confidential tilt of his lips tugged at her stomach muscles. 'Normal's relative.'

'Well, normal or not, you probably misjudged my mum. She would still have wanted you for the job. You're brilliant with Aldo.' For the first time, she didn't feel remotely bitter about that.

'It's funny to hear you stick up for your mum.' Her sense of achievement faltered. 'You're always so down on her.'

'I know. I feel kind of ashamed of that now.'

How spoilt must she have looked to him over the past few months? When his own mother was dying, and she hadn't been able to stop having a go at hers?

She stifled the thought.

No more pity parties.

'Is that why you didn't kiss me? Because you were

worried my mum would find out? And sack you?' How come she'd dismissed that possibility so easily? Showed how much attention she paid.

Trey was dedicated and conscientious. And mature. And so responsible.

Which was one of the things she found so sexy about him.

'That was one of the reasons,' he said.

'What was the other?'

'I was worried that if I started kissing you, I'd never be able to stop.'

Holy crap. Lizzie felt her eyes widening to saucer size. *Seriously?*

The tingle of awareness became a torrent when his gaze dipped to the drooping neckline of her sweatshirt. The long look made her breasts feel heavy, no mean feat when they were barely a B-cup.

His gaze slid back to hers, and she let out a breath. A necessity if she wanted to stay conscious with the large obstruction growing at an alarming rate in her throat.

She had a choice here. She could go for it. Or she could back off. Because she knew however much he might want to kiss her, Trey was not going to take the next step.

'Restraint', after all, was his middle name. Right after 'Responsible'.

'Do you want to test that theory?' she asked on a husky murmur.

Good thing 'restraint' and 'responsible' weren't even in her vocabulary.

'Is it that obvious?' he said, his voice a little choked.

She grinned, impossibly pleased. 'Yes, I'd say it is.'

Pushing out of her deck chair, she stood over him. 'Just so you know, Trey. If you want to kiss me, I have absolutely no objections.'

'No?' He smiled up at her.

She straddled his thighs, settled onto his lap, a laugh escaping when the deck chair creaked and she had to grasp hold of the strut next to his head to stop from collapsing on top of him. 'I wonder how much they charge if you break the stupid thing.'

His hands grasped her waist to steady her. 'Whatever it costs, I'd say it's worth it.'

His wide chest expanded as he let out a staggered breath. His hands spread out under her sweatshirt, and his solid thighs quivered beneath hers.

He tugged her down to him, and she opened her mouth to meet him halfway. Excitement making her light-headed.

This was actually happening. At last.

She could taste the minty freshness of his breath. For a split second she panicked she might taste of stale cappuccino, but before she could draw back, his tongue thrust deep, claiming her mouth.

The muscles in his shoulders bunched beneath her palms as she clung on, anchoring herself as his hands stroked up her back, sending delicious shivers all over her body. He took without asking, devoured without holding back, but let her set the pace. His tongue coaxing, persuasive one minute, and hungry the next.

It felt so good, tasted so sweet and so hot. The kiss seemed to go on forever, full of power and demand, but ended way too soon, leaving her yearning for more.

Her whole body shook. The urge to grind her hips against his and increase the contact was overwhelming.

Strong fingers massaged her neck, then rested on her shoulders as his head dropped back. 'That was a really stupid thing to do,' he said, his warm brown gaze fixed on her mouth.

She licked her lips, still tortured by the taste of him, the desire for more. 'I liked it, though.'

She threaded her fingers into the short hair above his ears and trailed her thumbs down his neck. His Adam's apple leaped as the delicious shiver of response coursed through him.

'Me, too, but we still shouldn't have done it,' he said. His rueful smile suggested he didn't regret it. Or at least not much. His cheeks had darkened beneath the olive skin.

Obviously, she'd caught him at a weak moment. When his defences were down. And he hadn't been able to resist her.

She was really pleased about that.

'We can't do it again,' he said.

'OK, if you say so.' *We so are doing that again. And again and again and again.*

No need to press him now, though, while he was feeling fragile and she'd disgraced herself with the stalking incident.

But having him forgive her and understand, about Liam, about everything, or understand enough not to think she was a psycho, and now knowing his secret, getting to understand some of his loneliness and being able to comfort him—there was no going back from that.

He was being cautious. Careful. She understood that. He was a practical, sensible, overly responsible guy who worried about all the stuff she'd made a point of never bothering about.

She was bothering about it now. Because she didn't want to be immature, or selfish, or a spoilt cow ever again. But no bloody way was that going to be their only ever kiss. Not when it felt so awesome.

As well as being sober and mature, he needed to cut loose, let off steam, get a fricking life. He'd lost his temper with her because he'd been wound way too tightly.

And if there was one thing she happened to be an expert at, it was how to unwind. And let loose. And do the wild thing. When the wild thing was required.

Squeezing her waist, he boosted her up until she was off his lap.

'I need to go back to the hospice,' he said, sobering her up.

'Would you like me to come with you?'

'No, that's OK. I should go alone.'

'OK.' She tucked her hands under her arms, trying not to feel rejected. She didn't even know his mum. Why would he want her there?

'Don't feel bad,' he said, as if he'd read her thoughts. 'It was nice of you to offer. I'd love to have you there.' He looked as if he meant it, making her feel much better. 'It's just I'm not sure she'd want people to see her like that.'

'I understand.' Her heart pumped harder at the evidence of how thoughtful he was. 'Shall I pick up Aldo, then, and get dinner on the go? So you don't have to hurry back?'

They began walking through the deck chairs, towards the path out of the park.

'You don't mind?' he said.

'No, of course not. It's the least I can do after behaving like a psychopath.'

He chuckled, the light, untroubled sound making her feel euphoric. 'Thanks. I should be back in time. But I'll text you if I'm going to be late.'

She took his hand, clasped it tight, tugging him to a stop. 'Trey, I mean it. If anything happens, you know, with your mum, and you need to stay with her, or go see her suddenly, just let me know. I can step in and cover for you with Aldo. I want to step in.'

He nodded, his face grave. 'OK, cool. And thanks again.'

He walked her to the tube station, before saying goodbye and heading back to the hospice.

He didn't kiss her goodbye. Made a point of it really.

But she took it as a very good sign that the whole way back to St John's Wood station he didn't let go of her hand. Not once.

Chapter 16

'Remind me never to get in a sodding kayak again.' Halle dumped her overnight kit on the leather sofa in the cabin's living area. Every muscle in her body had atrophied hours ago, during the final stretch of their journey to the pick-up point they'd arranged with Chad at the Fontana Lake Marina.

She'd been woken at dawn by the warbling of an unidentifiable bird, her sleeping bag warm and musty, to find herself alone in the tent. Once she'd gotten up enough energy to crawl out, she'd found Luke brewing coffee over the newly lit firepit, the rugged two-day stubble and creased shorts and shirt making her mouth water almost as much as the scent of hot caffeine.

Thank goodness she'd slept like a dead woman and been completely oblivious to that ripped body right next to her.

Nothing would have happened, because she was convinced she and Luke couldn't be bonk buddies without dire consequences.

And the last time I was this sore and exhausted I'd just given birth to a twelve-pound baby boy with an unfeasibly large head.

Even so, the shimmer of regret had been undeniable. And

now they were back at the cabin, alone again, her aching limbs pleasantly numb, with the definite hum of tension sizzling in the air, and in her gut.

'If I ever see you getting in a kayak again, I'll chop off your arms,' Luke murmured, flopping down onto the sofa beside her gear. 'As long as you promise to return the favour.'

'Done.' She stared at his long body arranged over the maroon leather, his lean muscular physique causing more mini explosions to detonate in her lady bits.

'I need a hot shower, followed by cold Chardonnay and warm food,' she said. 'Any chance you could take care of the second and third order of business from room service,' she added, 'while I take care of the first?'

They'd never eaten dinner together in the cabin before, somehow managing to avoid that intimacy. But after a night sharing a tent, with no naughty business occurring, she figured a shared meal was fairly safe.

He toed off his hiking boots, leaving his white sports socks slouching around his ankles. 'Sure. Any preference for your entrée?'

'As long as it doesn't look or taste like hamster kibble, I'm good.'

But as she walked past him, he took hold of her wrist. Her pulse jumped, the slow rub of his thumb making the mini detonations become somewhat major.

'I've got a better idea. Why don't we check out the hot tub?'

'We?'

'It's a big tub. I can keep to my side.'

Really? 'I'm not...'

'I can't think of a better way to work the kinks out.' He rolled his shoulders.

'Well, I guess...' She certainly had kinks to spare.

'Great.' He stood to undo his shorts. 'You mind if I wear my pants? I'm too knackered to go hunt up my trunks.' He ripped open his flies to reveal loose white cotton boxers, which would probably be a lot more revealing once wet than the stretchy black cotton ones he'd been wearing at the waterfall.

'Fine, as long as the essential bits are covered. I'm going to get my swimsuit on.' She sent him a nonchalant wave that didn't feel all that nonchalant once she'd reached the safety of her room and struggled out of her dusty hiking gear.

Maybe sharing a hot tub with Luke wasn't such a great idea, she thought, recalling the pornographic vision she'd had of him on her first morning in the cabin.

No need to panic. You have excellent impulse control.

Plus, they'd just shared a tent for a whole night with no funny business occurring. And she couldn't think of a better way to work out all the aches and pains from their kayaking adventure.

After a quick shower to wash the trail dust off, though, she made the mistake of wiping the steam off the bathroom's mirrored wall, giving herself a full-frontal view of her naked body. And all its tiny imperfections. Imperfections accumulated over the past sixteen years, which in the harsh fluorescent light suddenly didn't look so tiny.

When had the shallow creases around her eyes begun to morph into a road map of Canada? Or the slight thickening at her waist gotten so pronounced? And when had her breasts lost the last vestiges of their twenty-something perkiness—no matter how much she arched her back?

Hello, attack of the fifty-foot cleavage.

She touched her belly, examining the three silvery two-centimetre long marks she had acquired while comfort eating herself into a coma before Aldo's birth. Did the stretch

marks make the diamanté stud she still wore in her belly piercing look more cougar-ish than cool?

She leaned into the mirror. And what about all her newly acquired war wounds? The bruise on her chin, the scratch across her cheek, the tan lines on her arms and thighs, and the patch of reddened skin on the bridge of her nose, which would be peeling by tomorrow.

She reached for her make-up case, then hesitated.

Who cares what he thinks of your perfectly normal, thirty-six-year-old woman's body?

Step away from the concealer.

Bypassing her bikini—*what was I thinking packing that?*—she dug out the plain black one-piece she'd worn on her last trip to Disney World with Aldo a year ago. After brushing her hand through her hair, which had begun to frizz at the edges, she declared herself good to go.

Sucking in her belly as she stepped onto the deck, just a bit, her breath gushed out when she spotted Luke. With his arms stretched out across the cedar lip of the tub, the water frothing under his sternum and his head tipped back, he appeared to be completely oblivious to her grand entrance.

Unlike Dream Luke, who had been smooth and tanned and oiled, Real Luke clearly didn't wax his chest, the curls of dark hair fanning out across his nipples. But the shine of sweat and steam defining the pronounced muscles and the wisps that tapered into a thin line below the water managed to look a lot more earthy and inviting.

Two glasses stood beside a chilled bottle of wine in a wooden bucket next to the tub.

Nectar of the gods... And women on the verge of sharing a hot tub with the sexy ex they absolutely do not want to have sex with.

'They delivered dinner already?' she said.

His head lifted, and she wondered if she'd woken him up. His eyelids were at half mast as he squinted at her, and she remembered he had always been a bit myopic. He must wear contacts now, because she hadn't seen him wearing his glasses.

'Yeah, they brought it about twenty minutes ago. It can be reheated. Where have you been? I'm about to dissolve.'

Really? You look pretty solid to me.

'I was having a shower. After a night sleeping rough, I didn't want to pollute the hot tub with my grunginess.' She noticed the damp curls of hair flattened on one side of his head, but dry at the scalp. 'Something that obviously didn't bother you.'

She padded across the boards of the deck. Luke remained riveted on her progress the whole way, making her feel like a catwalk model at London Fashion Week, except about a foot shorter and with love handles.

Stop stressing. You look great. And you don't want to attract Luke.

'I had a swim this morning in the lake,' he said. 'Before you woke up. I'm not as grungy as you.'

He had? She really had slept like the dead.

She stepped into the tub. The hot bubbles buffered tired calf muscles, and a contented sigh eased out as she settled onto the ledge a few judicious feet from him. The water rose to her breasts, making them jiggle and float despite the restrictive spandex, and lifting her nipples into ruched peaks.

She couldn't make out a thing under the surface of the water thanks to the steam and bubbles, so she'd just have to take his word for it he'd kept the boxers on.

Her gaze lifted to his face, to find him watching her, and she began to feel a bit light-headed. Which had to be

the heat of the water, and the pounding jets massaging sore muscles. Obviously.

'How come you don't weigh five tons when you're surrounded by all those amazing cakes the whole time?' he murmured.

The appreciative look had her heart bobbing up to join her floating boobs. 'I may not weigh five tons, but I'm also nowhere near as trim as I used to be,' she said, then felt annoyed with herself for employing the thirty-something woman's automatic fallback position. Point out your every flaw before others do it for you.

'Neither am I,' he said.

Yeah, right. If he wasn't as trim, that was only because every extra ounce was now pure muscle. He stretched to hoist the wine out of its bucket and pour them a glass and she got fixated on the bunch and flex of his biceps.

Solid definitely works better on a man.

He handed her a glass. 'You look incredible.'

She shifted on the ledge to let the jets of water pummel her thighs and take her mind off the pumping pulse elsewhere.

'Then cheers.' She clinked her glass to his. 'I never say no to a compliment.' She took a long sip of the wine, the chilly oaken taste easing the dryness in her throat. 'I'd like to say it had something to do with the cross-trainer that's been sitting in my basement for over a year. But it's actually the demands of the show.'

'It's a tough schedule?'

'Not too bad. We tape two a day for two weeks. It's not so much the workload. It's the nerves. I get terrible stage fright. But I try to manage it without relying on my happy pills.' She sent him a quelling look—recalling his reaction to her Xanax on the plane. 'So far I haven't acquired a prescription drug habit and the extreme stress means the last

thing I want to do during a taping is eat. So it's all good.' She sipped her wine to interrupt the babble. Momentarily. 'Except for the two grand I splashed out on that cross-trainer, of course.'

'You always look really chilled on screen.'

She sputtered, choking on her wine. 'You watch the show?' she squeaked, so astonished she didn't even mind she was squeaking.

'Sure, I catch it when I can if I'm not on assignment. Try to record the episodes I miss. They broadcast it in Europe on BBC Worldwide.'

'You're joking, right?' Surely that earnest expression was faked? It had to be. He hated pop culture.

'I like watching it. You're exceptionally good at what you do.' A wry smile split his face. 'Smart, funny, sexy. The nerves don't show. And there's all that great bakery porn, too. I did your triple fudge indulgence cake for Lizzie's birthday this year. It turned out OK, even though I had to substitute a few things. It's hard to get exactly the same ingredients in Paris.'

Her jaw sagged. 'I don't believe it. You? Baking?' *And from one of my recipes?*

Why couldn't she get the stupid heart bumps under control? The stupid heart bumps that reminded her of when she was a teenager and she'd basked in even the smallest praise from him. Funny to think that while she really didn't care what he thought of her physical imperfections—or not too much—his opinion of her show mattered enough to cause those heart bumps.

He hooked a finger under her chin. 'Close your mouth, and stop looking so astonished. I cook for myself all the time. It's called being a new man.'

'When exactly did that happen? Because, as I recall, you

Luke's penis had always been magnificent. So magnificent it had terrified her when they'd first started going all the way as teenagers. And for a very good reason. Size really did matter when that much magnificence was at the disposal of a seventeen-year-old boy who had no clue what to do with it. And the recipient of it was a sixteen-year-old girl who was far too eager to please. But now, seeing that magnificence straining against billowing white cotton, the broad circumcised head peeking above the waistband, she was fairly sure she'd never seen anything so erotic.

She hadn't had any idea at sixteen that Luke was phenomenally well endowed, and to be honest, size really didn't matter when it came to the actual act, in her considered opinion. But those kind of porn-star proportions could be a powerful aphrodisiac, especially when their owner was lounging in a hot tub, making no bones—or rather boners—about the fact he was fully armed and extremely dangerous... Particularly to her flagging impulse control.

'So, about your lack of a vibrator...' The tone was rough with arousal and provocation.

Her gaze finally detached itself from his lap and flicked to his face. And, God help her, she laughed at the hopeful smile on his lips.

Heat fanned out across her chest and throbbed into her bobbing boobs. 'What about it?'

The smile took on a wolfish twist. 'I was wondering if you were looking for a substitute.'

She should have told him no. That a substitute was the last thing she wanted. Especially one supplied by him. But as he studied her over the rim of his glass, the flirtatious dare hovering over the steamy water, her brain short-circuited and something entirely different came out of her mouth.

'I'm afraid Bugs is going to be a very hard act to follow. No pun intended.'

He choked on the sip of wine. 'You gave the thing a name?' He sputtered, placing the glass on the side of the hot tub. 'I think my balls just shrank.'

She grinned at his horrified expression. 'Of course I did. I happen to have a close personal relationship with it.' *OK, way too much information.* But she couldn't bring herself to care, the mischievous sparkle in his eyes a heady relief from the physical and emotional stresses of the past week. She glanced back at his lap, the heat rising up her torso more exciting now than scary. 'They don't look as if they've shrunk very much to me.'

'I guess I lied about that.'

She laughed, the hum of arousal all but deafening now. 'Have you had that sitting on the bench the whole time we've been talking?'

'Are you kidding? He's been raring to get on the pitch for days now. Why the hell do you think I had a swim in a lake full of bollock-freezing snowmelt this morning at six a.m.?' He edged closer, until the long muscles of his thigh rubbed against her leg. 'If you tell me you're not raring for kick-off, too, I'll back off and never mention it again. But if you are...'

With his face dewed with steam, the rough stubble of his beard beaded with moisture and those pure blue eyes sparkling with his invitation to sin, he was as good as irresistible. And it was fairly obvious he knew it.

She hadn't felt this light-headed, or reckless, in years. Was she actually going to do this?

She cleared her throat. Determined not to go down in flames too easily. 'While these football analogies may work

wonderfully as pick-up lines in Paris, I'm going to require more finesse.'

He placed his outstretched hand on her nape, his thumb digging into tight muscles.

'I can do finesse.' The easy confidence was echoed in the delicious play of his fingers. 'What sort of finesse did you have in mind?'

'Maybe a conversation about what you envision happening after the final whistle?'

'I'm thinking we reheat the dinner, finish the Chardonnay and then either crash out or see if you're up for a rematch. Because I probably will be. I've always been insatiable where you're concerned.'

She tilted her head, giving his playful thumb better access, and let the ripple of sexual excitement steam through her body.

Could it really be that simple?

He moved closer and brought both his hands to her shoulders to squeeze and caress and drive her closer to the edge. His erection butted her hip, shooting the ripple of excitement right where she needed it to be.

'I didn't want to have the hots for you, either, Hal. But after spending half the night wide awake getting blue balls in that tent, it occurred to me this really doesn't have to be all that complicated,' he said. 'We're both grown-ups. We're both unattached at the moment. And I for one have some very hot memories of our sex life.'

She licked her lips, clinging to sensible by her fingertips— because her impulse control was now officially dead in the water. 'But what about those repercussions you mentioned yesterday? What if they come back to bite us on the butt?'

'Hal, didn't you know that what happens in a hot tub in

Tennessee—' his voice became gruffer, rasping across her nerve endings '—stays in a hot tub in Tennessee.'

Her heartbeat butted her throat, anticipation and need making every one of her pulse points throb in unison with her rabbiting heartbeat.

'What do you say?' he coaxed, his lips virtually on hers now, his fingers lifting into her hair to pull her closer still.

Her shoulders relaxed as she inhaled the salty, musky scent of him and acknowledged the sharp tug of yearning, which had been torturing her for days. And the last of the reasons why they shouldn't be doing this floated away on the hot stream of lust surging through her bloodstream.

Oh, bugger it. It's only sex.

'OK,' she murmured.

His lips covered hers, the kiss new and hot and avid. And yet achingly familiar. She opened for him, flattening her palms against his ribs. His shiver of response echoed in her sex, their tongues tangling in a battle for supremacy. She delved deep, scraping her nails through the rough hair on his cheeks. His hands lowered to cup her breasts through the tight spandex, his thumbs rubbing her straining nipples. With their mouths fused, he slid his fingers under the cup and drew her breast out. He dropped his head and took the swollen nipple into his mouth.

The hot suction had her lifting off the bench, her hands falling from his face. The shock of arousal, the delicious ache in her breast almost pain.

She fisted her fingers in his hair and tugged him away. 'Stop, Luke, give me a minute.' She adjusted the swimsuit to cover her pouting nipple, her insides sparking with desire and panic.

How could the attraction still be so combustible? Because

what had felt light and flirtatious had swiftly become very...
serious.

'Please tell me you haven't changed your mind, or I may
die.'

She laughed, his horrified expression breaking the tension.

*This is about now, not then. It's just sex. You're both adults
in dire need of an endorphin fix. That's why it's intense.*

'I haven't changed my mind,' she said, because nothing
short of a nuclear apocalypse was liable to stop her now.
'But no way am I having sex in a hot tub. Because...' She
shuddered. 'Just eww.'

He let out a harsh laugh. 'Thank Christ for that. I was
worried you might actually be trying to murder me.'

He stood, sending water cascading over the rim of the
tub, and she got an eye-level view of that magnificent erection outlined in clinging wet cotton. He hauled her up and
stepped out of the tub. 'Let's go, before I explode.'

He dragged off his wet boxers and the erection bounced
free, long and wide and bowed up towards his belly button.
He slung a towel round his waist and she laughed, her eyes
meeting his flushed face. The towel stood out at a weird
angle, doing nothing to disguise the tumescence beneath.

'That looks ridiculous,' she said.

'Hey, no mocking the substitute. He might wilt from performance anxiety.'

'Doubtful, I think you could bat for England with that
thing,' she teased, grabbing a towel. But as she went to wrap
it round her shoulders, he whipped it out of her hands.

'Not so fast. Take off the swimsuit. I don't see why I
should be the only one open to ridicule.'

His grin was quick and feral and entirely too pleased
with itself.

She glanced across the screened porch to the dense woodland beyond that hid them from view. The prickle of apprehension not welcome. She wasn't shy or embarrassed. She looked good for her age. But that didn't alter the fact he hadn't seen her naked in sixteen years.

'I'm not stripping off where anyone can see me.' She made a grab for the towel.

He hiked it out of her reach. 'Unless there are bears out there into cross-species kink, what you've got to show off won't interest anyone but me.' Slinging the towel over his shoulder, he stepped closer, the bulge at his waist butting her belly. 'The swimsuit comes off.' He pushed a thumb under her strap, eased it down.

'For goodness' sake, Luke.' She placed a hand on her shoulder, too late—he'd already dragged the cup off her breast. The heavy flesh spilled out, the cool air making the nipple tingle and swell. 'I'd rather do this inside.' In the dark, if possible.

His thumb traced the edge of the areola. Her breathing sharpened, the tug of sensation arrowing down, as he rolled the engorged tip and stretched it out.

'You know, you're very cute when you're shy, Hal.'

'I'm not shy.'

'Uh-huh, then this won't be a problem, will it?' His eyes met hers, the challenge in them searing her to the core, as he pushed aside the other strap and dragged the wet Lycra down to her waist.

His nostrils flared, accompanied by the guttural groan of appreciation. 'You're so bloody gorgeous,' he said. 'And frankly, these tits are a work of art.'

Her breath came out on a staggered laugh as he bent to lave one straining nipple with his tongue. His large hands

spanned her waist, holding her captive, as he captured the tip, nipping and squeezing it with his teeth. At last, he covered the swollen peak with his mouth, the hot suction lancing through her.

Her body trembled as he lifted his head, then she became suddenly weightless as he scooped her into his arms.

'Luke, put me down, what the hell are you doing?' The gesture was so over the top and yet so romantic it was making her heart beat in an unsteady rhythm.

'Isn't it obvious? I want to go worship these on a bed.' He carried her through the porch doors into her bedroom. Laid her down. He grasped her swimsuit and wrenched the sodden fabric past her hips and off her legs.

He dragged his towel off as he joined her on the bed. The powerful erection bobbed against her belly as he climbed on top of her. Her thighs quivered, her whole body alive and throbbing with the tremor of excitement, of sensual adventure, the anticipation almost as irresistible as the cheeky grin spreading across that handsome face.

'I'm not as young as I used to be. And I've been harder than a tent pole for the better part of a week.' His thumb parted the folds of her sex, circling the perfect spot. 'So we may have to do hard and fast first, and slow and detailed later. How do you feel about that?'

'Uh…that works for me.' She reached for his erection, brushing her thumb across the broad tip to spread the moisture around the bulbous head, desperate to wrestle back control. The old Luke had been eager and enthusiastic and generous in bed; the new Luke appeared to be confident and experienced and a bit too good to be true.

Blood pulsed beneath her hand, his erection as firm as she remembered. She stroked the thick shaft and smiled, triumphant, as his breath rasped against her ear. But then he

thrust one thick finger inside her, still caressing the sweet spot at the apex of her thighs with his thumb.

She cried out, undone.

He dragged her hand off his penis and shifted down to lick her belly button, then trailed his tongue along the sensitive seam at the top of her thigh.

Her knees dropped open, her back arching as she surrendered, offering herself up to the delicious torment. He flicked at the needy bud and she bucked off the bed. The battle lost.

'Easy,' he said, holding her thighs apart.

Arrows of sensation shot through her torso as he got back to work, teasing and torturing her with his tongue. Two fingers thrust inside her, feeding the frenzy for release. She sobbed, the spiral of need winding tight, as she struggled to hold on to her orgasm.

Then he fastened his lips on the swollen bud of her clitoris and suckled.

She screamed, the wave cresting and sending her crashing over the white-hot peak. Exquisite pleasure rippled out, making her shudder as he licked her through the final throes of her orgasm.

Her hoarse sobs subsided as he rose to settle between her spread thighs, the broad head of his erection nudging her sex.

'You're still crazy beautiful when you come, Hal.'

She tried to focus, but the wide smile looked more sweet than smug in the daze of afterglow, reminding her of a boy who no longer existed. The sharp dart of stunned emotion pierced her heart.

'And you've learned some crazy new skills.' She pushed the words out on a husk of breath, forcing down the foolish nostalgia.

Just sex. And just mind-blowing sex. It's all good.

'I aim to please.' He chuckled. 'I hope you're ready for round two.'

She nodded, but as the thick erection stretched tender flesh, she slapped unsteady palms on his chest. 'Wait, Luke.' Her arms shook as she held him back, poised on the brink, her dazed mind finally engaging. 'We need a condom.'

It took a moment for understanding to register on his face.

'I'm clean, I swear. I aced all the tests a year ago for my insurance. And I've never done it without.' His lips stretched into a thin smile. 'Except with you.'

'I'm clean, too, but I'm not using any form of birth control. I haven't had a sexual partner for over a year.' She began to tremble. 'Do you have some condoms?'

He cursed and dropped back on the bed, his erection thrusting up, thick and hard. He covered his face with his arm, his breathing ragged. 'What if I told you, you won't get pregnant?'

'Oh, shit. You don't have any?' He'd started this without even thinking about protection? With their history? Was he nuts?

So much for Mr Confident-and-Experienced.

He dropped his arm. 'No, I don't. I wasn't prepared to be consumed with lust on this trip. Sorry.'

'But surely you get into these situations a lot?' she accused. After sixteen years, she felt like a horny teenager again. And, while she might have had a misguided, misty-eyed moment over that lost boy, she so was not up for a return trip to the sexual frustrations of her youth.

'Apparently not,' he snapped.

She looked at his erection, desperate to feel him inside her. But at least she'd had an orgasm. 'I guess we'll have

to settle for doing it without penetration.' She wrapped her fingers round his shaft, felt it leap in her palm.

But, to her astonishment, he dragged her hand away. 'No, we don't. Listen to what I'm saying. If we're both sure we're clean, we don't have a problem. I can't get you pregnant.'

Her eyes nearly crossed with frustration. 'Yes, you could. I'm only thirty-six. I have not gone through menopause yet. Granted, it's less likely than it was when I was eighteen, but there is no way on earth I'm taking that risk. Especially with you.'

He straddled her, grasping both her wrists to push her into the mattress until they were nose to nose. 'There is no risk with me. I'm sterile. Firing blanks. Get it? I had a vasectomy nearly nineteen years ago.'

She stopped struggling, her whole body going slack with shock as understanding dawned. '*How* many years ago?'

'Shit.' He let go and rolled off her.

'You had a vasectomy right after I got pregnant?' She sat up, crossing her arms over her breasts, feeling hideously exposed when he didn't deny it. 'Why?'

He swore under his breath, his expression tight. 'Because I never wanted to get anyone accidentally pregnant again.' The curt revelation felt like a blow. He caught her wrist. 'Please tell me we're not going to talk about this now.'

'Of course we bloody are.' She tugged her wrist out of his grasp.

He slapped a pillow over his lap. 'So much for batting for England. At this rate I may never get another stiffy again.'

She walked over to the dresser, ignoring the pained tone. She pulled out a T-shirt and put it on, her fingers shaking. She knew the black hole opening up in the pit of her stomach was an overreaction. But overreaction or not, she couldn't seem to stop it.

'What do you want me to say, Hal? I panicked, OK? I was terrified of becoming a father. That was who I was then. That's not who I am now. I spent two years in therapy after that breakdown getting myself straight. I made a mistake. I made a lot of mistakes, but I can't go back and undo them now.'

Firm hands settled on her shoulders, and he turned her to face him.

He stood close, the towel tucked back around his waist. 'So what's the point of dredging it up all over again?'

She stared into his eyes. And saw regret and confusion. How was it possible that he really genuinely didn't get it?

'The point is, I still don't know why you left me.' Her voice sounded surprisingly calm, she realised, considering the way her heart was battering her ribs. 'I understand you had a breakdown, but now I know exactly how terrified you were of becoming a father. Enough to go out and do something that would ensure you would never become a father again.' She gulped down a breath, forced to finally voice the fear that had haunted her but she'd never been strong enough to say then. 'Did you think I'd tricked you? That I'd got pregnant deliberately? Is that why you didn't trust me enough to talk about it?'

To know now how much he hadn't wanted to be a dad, though, brought all the old guilt rushing back. Guilt she'd refused to acknowledge for sixteen years but unfortunately had just found out was still there, festering under her breastbone.

She'd adored being a mum. Because loving Lizzie had been so much simpler and more rewarding than loving Luke. If Lizzie cried or fussed, fixing the problem was easy. With a cuddle, or a fresh nappy, or a quick schlurp of breast milk, or a dose of gripe water and a jiggle until she burped. When Luke looked haunted or hunted and eventually became more

and more remote, she couldn't fix it, because she didn't know how. Until eventually she stopped caring enough to try.

'Jesus, Hal, no, of course I didn't. I knew it was an accident. That's not it at all.'

He drew his thumb across her cheek, his hand trembling, and the painful sting of tears lodged in her throat.

She caught his hand, pulled it away from her face, the tightness in her chest refusing to go away. 'Then why did you have to keep so many secrets? Why couldn't you just be honest with me about how you felt? I spent months after you left torturing myself, convinced it was all my fault. That I'd shut you out somehow after Lizzie was born, that I hadn't done enough to keep you, and it nearly destroyed me.'

He placed his hands on her shoulders, ran his thumbs across her collarbones. His face was a mask of so many conflicting emotions—confusion, frustration, pain.

'Then I'm sorry for that, too. It was never your fault. And I swear, it had nothing to do with you. You've got to believe me. It was me. It was what I came from. It just all became too much, OK?'

'No, it's not OK.' She shook her head, folding her arms around her midriff, the black hole still huge in her belly. 'What was so horrific you couldn't tell me about it? I loved you, Luke, and you abandoned me. If it really wasn't me, or Lizzie, or even another woman, then what was it?'

* * *

Panic clawed at Luke's throat. She didn't look angry or bitter or even resentful. That he could have handled. And deflected and ignored. She simply looked devastated.

And that he couldn't ignore. Not any more. Because unlike all the other women whom he'd slept with but had been

so careful never to get too close to, with Halle the sadness mattered.

He thought he'd healed himself. He thought he'd picked up the pieces and remade himself from the ground up. And finally become a man, ready to own up to his responsibilities, instead of a terrified kid.

But how could he have? When he'd never been able to own up to how much pain he'd caused her?

Time to man up, Best. Because you'll never stop running until you do.

He strode away from her to slump down on the bed, his body rigid with tension and shame. He couldn't look at her and say what he had to say.

'I guess the reason why is pretty simple really. My parents were both chronic alcoholics,' he said. 'She mostly drank to escape. But he was a mean drunk who couldn't control his temper any more than he could control his drinking.'

'He hit you?'

'Occasionally.' He shrugged, remembering the back-handed slaps across the face, those nasty little jabs to the belly that would leave you retching, the mean pinches, the vicious kicks. The parade of everyday abuse that he had lived in fear of as a child but had eventually become as accustomed to as breathing. 'Generally, he pounded my youngest brother, Curt, though,' he said. 'Curt was small for his age and weedy, the runt of the litter. Plus, he had a real knack for being in the wrong place at the wrong time. He pretty much used to wet himself every time Brian…' He stopped, amazed that he still couldn't call the guy by anything but his given name. 'Every time my old man was in the same room. Which would probably explain why Curt was forever pinching my clean underwear.'

Bloody hell, how could it still be so tough to talk about?

Even after all these years and the thousands of euros' worth of therapy? Why did the old ghosts still have the power to make his palms sweat and his head hurt?

But then she sat down beside him, the mattress tilting, and placed her hand on his thigh. Warm through the damp towelling. 'Why didn't social services intervene?' she said.

'They didn't know.' He thrust shaking fingers through his hair. 'The therapist said, when you come from that, you learn not to tell. You learn to keep secrets, because that's your normal, your reality. And you convince yourself your thoughts, your feelings, don't matter, because they fucking didn't. The place was always a tip. Soiled nappies everywhere. Rotting food on the plates piled in the sink. The smell of cigarette butts and stale Special Brew still makes me gag to this day. They didn't hug us, or care about us, or look after us. And a part of me always believed it was our fault, not theirs.'

'I had no idea it was as bad as that.'

* * *

His thigh muscles bunched beneath her palm, and guilt rolled through her at the stark, grim picture he was painting. He'd said it wasn't her fault, but maybe it had been. A little bit.

It had been so easy for her to romanticise and exploit the few things she knew about Luke's home life as a teenager. He'd been the quintessential bad boy. Wounded and wanting, someone who could love her just for her. Unlike her parents, who had always set limits and conditions on their affection.

Leaving home at seventeen, shacking up with Luke, having Lizzie a year later had been an easy way to liberate herself from the weight of those expectations. But all the time it had been the opposite of romantic for him.

'Of course you didn't know.' He focused on her, the

haunted look she remembered shadowing his eyes. 'Why would I ever tell you? You were my escape from all that. Being around you was like having this force field that protected me from them.' He covered her hand on his leg, circled the skin with his thumb. 'The first time we made love, you held me afterwards. You said all sorts of cheesy things about being in love with me.' He chuckled. 'You were such a starry-eyed romantic. But it felt so good to have you hug me like that. To have you hold me like you cared. You made it better, at least for a while.'

'And then I got pregnant with Lizzie. And you were trapped again.' Even if she couldn't have made the connection then, she could see it clearly now. She'd been playing at being a grown-up, while he'd been looking for a way out.

How young and naive she'd been. Because as much as she'd wanted to nurture him in their early days, she'd abandoned the quest as soon as she had Lizzie to focus on. Lizzie, her beautiful baby girl, who had been tiny and new and needy, and had none of the frustrating complexities, the unbreachable defences of her father.

And how ironic, that it had been those dark unknowable qualities in Luke—his moods, his secrets, his inability to share and discuss—that she had blamed him for later on, that had made him so wildly attractive to her in the first place.

She blew out a breath.

God, what a mess we made, both of us.

'We should have waited,' she said. 'We were far too young to have a baby.'

'Well, thank God we didn't wait.' He hooked a tendril of hair behind her ear. 'Or we wouldn't have Lizzie now.'

'I know, but even so, you weren't ready for that kind of responsibility.'

The tightness in her chest loosened. The tightness she had refused to acknowledge for years but had always been there, crouching under her heart, ready to pounce out of the shadows if she didn't keep it ruthlessly controlled.

Was that the real reason she'd refused to talk to him for sixteen years? Not anger, not hurt, but guilt? Because she'd made the decision to have Lizzie without a thought to his feelings, his fears, and had always known, however much she later tried to deny it, that she had been partly to blame for his withdrawal?

'Hal, I would never have been ready. Not until I dealt with where I came from.' Shifting round, he placed his hands on either side of her hips.

She drew back. 'But I put so much pressure on you. And after you'd had all that therapy to get yourself straight, I wouldn't let you come back. I wouldn't even talk to you.'

'Has anyone ever told you you've got an overdeveloped sense of responsibility?'

She let out a shaky laugh at his exasperated look. 'Your daughter has called me a control freak, on numerous occasions. Does that count?'

'It's on the spectrum.' The wry smile was ridiculously comforting. 'The thing is, the therapy helped. But you know what really got me straight?'

'What?'

'Lizzie. Even if you wouldn't talk to me, you let me have her for six weeks a year, when you didn't have to.'

She coughed out a laugh. 'I hate to say it, but I'm pretty sure the main reason I let you see her was because I thought you'd cave after one week of looking after a three-year-old on your own.' She played with the hem of her T-shirt, keen to look anywhere but his face.

God, honesty hour is a bitch.

'You have no idea how miffed I was when Lizzie came back from that first trip with a thousand and one stories about how terrific her daddy was and what a great time she'd had.'

'Oh, yeah?' He sent her a wry smile. 'I'm guessing she didn't mention being sick on the Phantom Manor ride at Disneyland, then. Or wetting the bed the first night because I'd forgotten to stock up on night nappies.'

'No, funnily enough she didn't mention any of that.' Halle laughed at the thought of his struggling to look after a three-year-old, but her amusement was bittersweet.

Suddenly, all those glowing reports over the years, of all the amazing, fabulous, astonishingly awesome stuff Lizzie did in Paris while she was with Luke, could be viewed in a very different light. Was it possible they had never been a stick to beat Halle with? Had Lizzie simply been sugar-coating the truth to protect her daddy and the bond she had with him?

And to think Halle had always thought she'd hidden her anger towards him so well. She'd even boasted about it to the family therapist, when the woman had probed. No, she didn't have any communication with Lizzie's father, but she'd never spoken a disparaging word about him in her daughter's presence. She'd congratulated herself on her forbearance, her magnanimity, her ability to be the bigger, better person. But what if Lizzie had known exactly how she felt all along, and had kept that knowledge a secret, because she'd thought she had to, to keep Luke in her life?

Apparently, hindsight is a bitch, too.

'Lizzie always told me what an amazing time she had with you,' she said. 'I hated that you were Super Dad while I could never quite manage to be Super Mum.'

'I can assure you,' Luke said. 'All the therapy in the world

couldn't really make me Super Dad. Most of the time it felt like Lizzie was parenting me. She's so smart and capable. Just like you always were.'

'Not like me,' Halle corrected. 'If I had been as smart and capable as I thought, I might have realised that by trying to be Super Mum I never gave Lizzie the room to be imperfect. To fail and know it was OK.'

'No need to worry, Super Mum.' Luke's hand rested on her knee. 'I had the failure-by-example part of her parenting well and truly covered.'

She smiled. Even though she knew now she'd never even come close to being Super Mum.

'So are we good now?' he asked.

The steady gaze made her feel shaky and far too aware of him. She had the closure she'd needed for sixteen years. That was enough. It had to be enough. 'Yes, we're good.'

He framed her face. 'Then how do you feel about a spot of make-up sex, to seal the deal?'

She laughed, the giddy rush of endorphins going some way to explain the crazy leap of her pulse. 'Make-up sex sounds good.'

'You're sure?' he said, the hesitant smile scarily sweet. 'Because I'm not sure I can pull out like that again without causing myself a serious injury.'

'I'm sure,' she said, grasping his head to tug him closer.

He slanted his lips across hers. The kiss was deep, hungry, leaving her breathless and yearning. She worked his towel loose, to find him hugely erect. She caressed the thick column from root to tip, loving the feel of him, the velvet steel so soft, and yet so hard, as he groaned.

Threading her fingers through his hair, she brought his face to hers.

'I need you inside me,' she said.

He grasped her waist, wrestled off her T-shirt, the tension dissolving as his rough palms stroked her sides. 'I know.'

She stretched out on the bed, pulling his arm until his body covered hers. His thumb circled her clitoris, one thick finger sliding into her. The coil of longing yanked tight inside her.

'Seriously, Luke, this is one of the few times I don't need foreplay.'

He laughed, the sound strained as he held her hips, positioning her underneath him. She spread her thighs, angled her pelvis until his penis nudged her slick sex. Wrapping her legs around his waist, she grasped his buttocks, ready to beg.

But then he sank into her in one solid thrust.

Her breath expelled from her lungs as she adjusted to the fullness. Her muscles clenched round the thick intrusion as he filled up all the spaces inside her that had felt empty for so long.

'How does that feel?' he asked.

'Good.'

'Better than Bugs?'

She slapped his arse. 'Shut up and move, Best.'

'You asked for it, lady.' He hooked his hands under her knees, leaving her fully open to him, unable to resist the punishing depth of his thrusts, as he established a steady rhythm, which quickly became more furious, more frantic.

The fever built in hot waves, her sex clenching and releasing as he worked a spot deep inside. Maybe size mattered, after all.

His eyes met hers, the pupils dilated, and then his hand splayed across her back and he lifted her to clamp his mouth over a straining nipple.

The hard suction, the shock of memory, sent her spinning as he sucked the rigid nipple to the roof of his mouth.

The fireball of need blazed through her, sending her soaring towards the final edge.

The brutal orgasm slammed into her as his hips pistoned, the deep thrusts gathering pace and purpose. Her mind spun free, the cries of fulfilment echoing off the polished wooden walls.

He grunted as she massaged his thick length, then shouted out as he came and collapsed on top of her.

They panted in unison, the heavy weight of him crushing her into the mattress. He nuzzled her neck, sending sensation echoing into her sex.

'That was fast,' he said.

'It's been a while.' Her throat clogged with the new rush of emotion—the poignant moment of shared intimacy. 'You remembered.'

He lifted off her, his still-firm penis sliding out. 'Remembered what, exactly?' he teased, all mock innocence.

She would have laughed if she didn't suddenly feel so scared.

'You know perfectly well what,' she countered.

'I bet Bugs can't do that,' he said, lifting his eyebrows to accompany the naughty grin.

She gave him a playful punch and chuckled. 'Will you please shut up about Bugs?' And forced back the fear.

Don't be a muppet. You're a smart, successful and eminently sensible career woman now. No way would you ever be idiotic enough to confuse sex with love a second time. Even great sex. Even great mind-blowing make-up sex.

As they lay side by side, both staring at the ceiling fan, the silence disturbed only by the regulatory clip of the fan's blades, he grasped her fingers and raised them to his lips.

'Of course I remembered.' He buzzed a kiss across her knuckles. 'You never forget your first, Hal.'

Her heart punched her ribs, because she didn't feel very sensible any more.

Chapter 17

'Lizzie, are you up?'

A low voice beckoned Lizzie out of dreamland, along with the light tap on her bedroom door.

She clicked on her iPhone. Squinted at the luminous digital clock. Seven a.m. 'Just about.'

A nimbus of light from the hall silhouetted Trey in the doorway. 'Sorry, you're still in bed.'

Thrusting the mess of hair off her face, she smiled at the light blush on his cheeks. 'It's OK, I'm not naked.'

He coughed into his hand. And she could have sworn his gaze flicked to her breasts. Her nipples rose accordingly, thrusting against the thin cotton camisole she wore with pyjama bottoms. She'd seen that look quite a few times, ever since their X-rated snog in the park. Intent and wary, and observant enough to make her mouth water and her thighs go all trembly. However much he might want to deny it, Trey was as aware of her now as she was of him and it felt...empowering. In a Beyoncé 'Single Ladies' kind of way. Because she knew however much he wanted her, Trey would never ask. Never cross that line. And never try to shame her into putting out the way Liam had. So it was

entirely up to her to take the initiative. The thought would have crippled her with nerves a week ago. But, after all those secret looks, now it made her feel strong and sexy and, well, empowered.

She flung back the duvet, leaped out of the bed and whipped her robe off the pile of magazines and assorted other crap littered all over the floor. 'Come in, Trey.'

He stood stranded in the doorway, watching her every move as she tied the robe. 'I need to ask you a favour,' he said, taking a cautious step into the room.

She crossed to the door and pushed it shut behind him. He stared down at her mouth for a moment. A long, exhilarating moment.

'What's the favour?' she asked finally, when he didn't continue.

He snapped back to full consciousness. 'Could you take Aldo to school this morning?'

'Yes, of course.' She put her anticipation on lockdown. Noticing the smudged hollows under his eyes for the first time. He'd gone out last night after putting Aldo to bed. And she didn't know when he'd returned. 'Is it your mum?'

He gave a weary nod. 'It's probably a false alarm. I've had a few of those. But the hospice nurse called and said I might want to come in a bit earlier today. She's had a rough night.'

'Stay as long as you need to. I can pick up Aldo, too, if you want.'

'Thanks.'

But as he reached for the doorknob, she slid her hand into his. 'Trey, wait.'

He turned back. Letting go of his hand, she stretched up on tiptoes and placed her hands against his chest. He felt warm and solid, but the ripple of tension wasn't far behind.

'You look like you could use a hug.'

'Better not,' he said, not denying it.

She touched his cheek, inhaled the scent of his citrus shaving soap and peppermint toothpaste. And waited for his gaze to meet hers.

'I'm not fragile, you know.' She certainly didn't feel fragile any more. 'You don't have to protect me.' The rush of tenderness was as potent as the rush of endorphins. Whatever happened between them in the long-term, even if it was nothing, here and now, she knew he needed her. And she wanted to show him she cared. She peered up at him, then cradled his cheeks and pulled his mouth to hers. 'And it's only a kiss.'

She touched her lips to his. His hands bracketed her hips and, for a second, she thought he would push her away, but then he groaned and tugged her closer, opening his mouth to let her in.

She sank her fingers into his hair, massaging his scalp. The kiss was hot, and tempting, the sweetness and need leaving her breathless. He broke away, his breathing ragged, but held her for a few minutes more, his nose buried in her hair.

'Thanks, that was nice,' he said, ridiculously formal and polite, but with the hint of dry humour.

She drew back, enjoying the amused twist on his lips. 'It was entirely my pleasure.' At least she'd managed to take the misery away for a moment. 'I'll be here when you get back. If you need someone to talk to, call.'

'OK.' He pressed the back of his hand to his lips, as if sealing in the sensation.

'And don't worry, I'll cover for you with my mum when she calls.'

'I can't ask you to do that.'

'You're not asking.' Lifting on tiptoes, she kissed him once

more. The chaste peck one of affection, of understanding and reassurance, this time.

'Thanks,' he said again. Then left the room.

She floated back towards the bed, on a cloud of bliss, until she spotted the clock on her iPhone.

Crapola. Ten past seven, she had a measly forty minutes to get Aldo up, clothed, fed and pack-lunch enabled. A tall order for Super Nanny, let alone a girl with the worst bed hair in the history of the world.

Chapter 18

Get a room, people. Extreme PDAs are the last thing I need this morning.

Halle glared at the couple canoodling on the bench at the far end of the reception building's porch. They were the third loved-up pair she'd spotted this morning since slipping away from Luke, whom she'd left snoring softly in her bed, to jog over to the resort's reception for the noon Skype call she'd scheduled with the kids. She pulled her iPhone out and plugged in the earbuds so she wouldn't have to hear the nauseating murmur of sweet nothings being exchanged ten feet away. She wondered vaguely what Luke was going to do about his exposé, if it turned out Monroe's methods actually worked?

The panic that had propelled her out of Luke's arms like a rocket twenty minutes ago whizzed up the back of her neck and set her scalp alight.

Don't be ridiculous. Monroe's method is just a clever con. Last night was an illusion. The perfect storm of hot make-up sex and long-overdue closure. The ultimate stress buster after surviving a ten-day emotional and physical assault course.

You are not falling for Luke again. That much is non-negotiable.

Signing on to the resort's Wi-Fi, she opened up her Skype app, checked the time and then waited for Lizzie to pick up.

Her daughter's face flashed onto the screen, the bright smile a surprise. 'Hi, Mum, how's things in the US?'

Halle shifted round so only the resort building's white-shingled wall was in view and sent up a small prayer of thanks for the grainy image quality. 'Hi, honey, everything's great.' She pushed the prickle of guilt aside, promising herself there would be no more lies. Once she returned home. 'More to the point, how are you guys doing?'

'We're good, but I asked first. And I want details.' Lizzie leaned into the shot as if trying to peer past her. 'What city are you in? And how have the signings been going?'

'I...' Halle's mind blanked as the prickle of guilt became a thorn, stabbing her in the back. 'I'm in Tennessee. And the signings have been good.' The lie sat on her tongue like a wad of cotton wool, making the fire in her scalp flame hotter. 'It's not like you to be interested,' she said, the reflex action purely defensive, until it occurred to her how hostile the comment sounded.

She braced herself for a tirade. A tirade that for once she thoroughly deserved.

'I know,' Lizzie said, the expected corrosive tone noticeably absent. 'I'm sorry, Mum. I've been so shitty about your career the past couple of years. I feel really bad about it now.'

'You do?' Halle yelped, the guilt starting to strangle her, at the look of genuine contrition on her daughter's face.

She'd waited for years for Lizzie to turn this corner and stop sniping at her every time a meeting overran, or they got stopped by a fan wanting an autograph or she had to stay late at the studio. But why did her daughter have to turn

this pivotal corner today? The very morning after Halle had spent a long and energetic night getting up close and far too pornographic with Lizzie's father...while not being on a whistle-stop book tour of the US.

Halle Best's epic timing strikes again.

'I mean it, Mum,' Lizzie replied, her voice thick with an eighteen-year-old's complete sincerity. 'I've been a real baby about it. When you get home, I want a full report about the book tour. OK?'

Shit.

'Of course, that's fabulous, sweetheart. But when did this happen?' *Time to deflect and deny until you can regroup.* 'You seemed so upset when I left.' And they had basically avoided talking about Lizzie's last epic sulk ever since, in a series of rather stilted phone conversations, during which her daughter had used any available excuse to pass the phone to Aldo or Trey. But not today. Of all days.

'I totally overreacted, as usual. So tell me more about the signings.' The request was filled with the open curiosity and enthusiasm Lizzie had been bursting with before she hit puberty and which Halle had mourned the loss of for years. Until this precise moment. 'What cities have you been to so far?' Lizzie added, perkiness personified. 'Anywhere cool? I hope you took photos.'

'Um...no. Nowhere that exciting really.' *Unless you count a camp island on Fontana Lake with your father.* She cringed, hoping the image was as grainy on Lizzie's end. And her daughter couldn't see the blaze of heat firebombing her cheeks.

'Is Aldo there? And Trey?' She rushed to fill the gap in the conversation before Lizzie asked any more awkward questions that would require the ability to lie like Walter Mitty to answer convincingly. 'I need to touch base with

them before the battery on my phone runs out.' She winced, hating herself even more for the lie.

It's official, I am going to Bad Mother Hell when I die. Where I shall be forced to go to Aldo's parent–teacher conferences for all eternity.

'Um, Aldo's busy. And so is Trey.'

'They are? What are they busy doing?' It was nearly seven o'clock at night in the UK. Surely they couldn't be *that* busy. Trey would have ensured Aldo had done all his homework and was winding down by now, ready for bed at nine.

There was a long pause on Lizzie's end. 'Minecraft. They're busy building something on Minecraft.'

'Well, do you think you could ask them to stop building whatever they're building for a minute? I won't keep them long.'

'Fine. All right, then, I'll go get them, since I'm not good enough,' Lizzie replied, slouching off and looking a lot less perky.

It took a good five minutes, while Halle stared at the view of her empty study and ignored the couple at the end of the porch still staring into each other's eyes with goofy expressions on their faces. And shoved the problem of how she was going to invent enough convincing anecdotes of a whole book tour of the US without gagging on her guilt into Future Halle's domain.

The sound of a hissed conversation off-screen neatly sidetracked the guilt as her mum's alarm bells began to buzz. Was that Lizzie and Aldo she could hear? What were they whispering about so furiously? And where was Trey?

Then Aldo popped into view and sat on the chair, followed by Lizzie, who perched on the arm and slung her

arm over Aldo's shoulders. Which was even weirder—their body language hadn't been that friendly since Aldo was six.

'Hey, Mum,' Aldo said. 'Lizzie told me to tell you I'm good.'

Told me to tell you... The alarm bells got louder. 'That's great, honey. Is everything OK?'

'Yes, Mum, but...'

Lizzie nudged his shoulder. Hard. And he stopped talking.

'But what, honey?' Halle prompted.

Aldo stared at his sister, then turned back to her. 'But nothing, Mum. Everything's good.'

'Are you sure?' she said, suddenly feeling like a hostage negotiator. Her mum's alarm bells were going bonkers. 'How about at school?'

Maybe something had happened and they were trying to keep it quiet. She felt an odd burst of pleasure at the thought. While she certainly hoped Aldo hadn't punched anyone, it would be wonderful to see Lizzie and Aldo being co-conspirators again. As they had been when Aldo was little. As Luke had suggested they still might be.

The thought of Luke brought with it the memory of a muscular arm around her waist and the musk of warm sexually satisfied male that had enveloped her when she woke up. Heat blazed into her cheeks. And she nearly dropped the iPhone.

'Yes, Mum.' Aldo rolled his eyes and stretched the syllables with the harassed patience of a bored ten-year-old. 'But Marcus Ellis is still a total dick.'

'Ignore him,' she said on autopilot. 'So what were you building on Minecraft?'

'Huh?'

The alarm bells kicked off again, but before she could question Aldo further, Lizzie leaned across him. 'Listen,

Mum, we've got to go. Happy signing. Don't get any hand cramps. Bye.'

'Wait a...' she began, but she was already staring at a blank screen where her children had been, her mum's alarm bells now sounding off like the cannon fire finale from the 1812 Overture.

She made two more Skype calls, with no answer. Then tried Trey's mobile and got no joy there, either. Finally forced to give up, she left Romeo and Juliet on the porch giggling like besotted teenagers and headed back down the path towards the cabins.

Each step she took, though, brought with it a rising tide of dismay...and apprehension. But her predicament as a mother, whose kids were clearly hiding something from her, paled in comparison to the much bigger problem posed by the man probably still lying sound asleep in her bed back at the cabin.

She had four days left at the resort, in the company of a man who was as irresistible to her now as he had been twenty years ago.

Four days that, according to Monroe's very helpful brochure, would involve spending 'quality time rebuilding the bonds of intimacy'.

I.e.: four days of waking up with Luke's muscular arms around her. Four days of playing house with him. Four days of discovering even more about the fascinating man he had become. Four days of having his crazy new sex skills and magnificent penis entirely at her disposal. And four days of struggling against all the odds to stop from getting struck by lightning a second time.

Because what were the chances of her coming out of the next four days with her sane, perfectly happy, well-ordered

and successful life intact, given the effect he'd already had on her?

On last night's damning evidence, not a lot, frankly.

Turning round on the path, she took out her phone and hurried back towards the reception building, prepared to give free rein to her mum's alarms bells, if they would just drown out the siren call of her still needy, still misguided and still stupidly reckless heart.

* * *

Luke gazed out onto Halle's porch, the forest canopy giving the midday sun a muted glow. Kind of like the persistent glow in his nuts. That had been going most of the night.

Halle had snuck out a good hour ago. He'd been half awake, his dick getting way ahead of itself as he listened to her skulking around the bedroom. But she'd gone before his consciousness had a chance to catch up with the call for action, leaving him to drift back to sleep, only to wake up again hard as an iron spike courtesy of the scorching-hot memories of their night together and the cloud of her scent that clung to the sheets.

Fully awake now, he levered himself up in bed and tried to get his head around exactly what had happened last night.

In the end it hadn't been that hard to tell Halle stuff he'd only ever told his therapist.

Exhausting themselves with sex afterwards had seemed like the obvious way to go.

But something was nagging at him now. Something that had been nagging at him most of the night, each time he'd seen the shocked arousal in her eyes, each time he'd touched her and revelled in her open, instant response. And especially when they'd snuggled up together, her bum nestled in his crotch and his heart attempting to beat right out of his chest.

She was the only woman who had ever come close to touching that lonely, isolated part of himself, which had crippled him as a kid. And which should have been dead and buried, but apparently wasn't any more—because that lonely kid was popping out again now when he thought about how much he was going to miss Halle, when they both went back to their normal lives.

Sure, they'd have Lizzie—and that was some compensation. He'd be able to call on Halle while forging a new and more honest relationship with his daughter. But while he was already looking forward to having those conversations, they weren't the only conversations he wanted to have with Halle. Because the past ten days had made him realise how much he'd missed the fine art of conversation with someone who was his emotional and intellectual equal in the past sixteen years, who was mature and smart and confident enough to challenge him, who was wise to all his bullshit and who didn't have English as a second language.

The real reason he'd screwed up so badly with Chantelle was because she'd been so young and so adoring. She'd stroked his ego, let him get away with murder, and he'd been paying so little attention he hadn't even realised she actually thought they had a future together.

That would never happen with Halle, because she knew all his tricks, all his faults, and she was as cynical about the L-word as he was.

And what about the sexual connection between them? It was as strong and exciting as it had ever been, but with a brand-new wow factor, because they both knew exactly what they wanted now and weren't afraid to demand it.

No doubt about it, it was a crying shame they had only four days left to explore all these new aspects of their relationship.

Not that he was looking for anything permanent. He wasn't cut out for long-term commitment. No amount of therapy would be able to solve that. But that didn't alter the fact that four days felt like far too short a time to explore all the good stuff, now they'd put all the crap stuff behind them.

He threw off the duvet and headed for Halle's bathroom, refusing to let the melancholy envelop him. They'd achieved much more than he could have ever hoped for. It was all good.

Her scent—bold and floral—drifted around him as he stepped into her shower cubicle. He turned the dial to scorching, contemplating the rest of their day together. And the nights to come. Absently soaping his erection. Eager for her to get the hell back to the cabin so they could get started.

He was climbing the spiral staircase to the mezzanine level and his own bedroom when he heard the cabin's front door opening.

Wherever she'd run off to, she was back. The blossom of warmth that hit his belly disturbed him a little. Four days was more than enough, as long as they made the most of it.

He took his time shaving away two days' worth of beard to prove to himself he wasn't *that* desperate to see Halle again. After yanking on jeans and an old T-shirt, he headed down to the kitchen, drawn by the delicious aroma of cinnamon wafting up the stairwell.

She stood at the counter, her back to him, her damp hair tied up in its habitual knot, drying strands hanging down to touch flushed cheeks, as she beat something in a mixing bowl to within an inch of its life. Skintight jeans, bare feet and a summery minidress added to the effect of sexy, relaxed domesticity.

The reaction in his crotch was swift and predictable. The fist that wrapped around his heart and sucker-punched him in the gut...not so much.

Chapter 19

'Luke!' The wooden spoon stopped in mid wallop as a familiar forearm roped with muscles banded around Halle's midriff.

'Morning. What are you cooking?'

His chest butted her back as he lifted her hair out of the way to bury his face in her neck. The nuzzling kiss triggered a riot of sensations—surprise, arousal and panic.

'Blueberry pancakes. I finally took Monroe up on his offer and raided the restaurant kitchen. The blueberries were picked fresh this morning.'

'Mmmm.' His teeth tugged at her earlobe. 'Watching you cook is such a turn-on.' His palm settled on her belly, sending the riot of sensations south. 'Always has been, always will be.'

She put the bowl on the countertop to turn in his arms, her pulse flapping against her neck like the wings of a trapped albatross.

He looked and smelled delicious. All fresh and groomed and damp from his shower. His cheekbones were even more pronounced without the two-day scruff, and the well-worn Festival de Cannes T-shirt was doing not a lot to disguise the

defined pectoral muscles she'd gotten far too well acquainted with during the night.

Always has been, always will.

He cupped her cheeks, his lips lowering to kiss her.

She shifted away, her bum hitting the counter. 'Why don't I get these on the go, then we can eat.'

'Eat?' His lips quirked in a wary smile as his hands dropped. 'Really? I was kind of hoping all my bakery porn fantasies were about to come true.'

She puffed out a strained laugh. 'So now I know why you watched my show.'

The assured smile had her breath backing up in her lungs, as he settled his hands on her hips. 'It's not my fault you look so hot icing cupcakes. What can I say, you inspire me.'

'I can only imagine.' Given how inspired Luke had been last night, she could imagine quite a lot. 'But I think we should eat first, before we deal with your cupcake fantasies.'

His hands dropped away. 'Fine, but I plan to hold you to that. Do you need anything?'

A backbone would be good, she thought miserably. She was doing the right thing. The safe thing, not just for the kids, but for herself as well.

Tell him, no wimping out allowed.

'Could you hunt up a frying pan?' she said, totally wimping out.

'OK, but be aware you're only going to be fuelling my fantasies while you do that.'

Fabulous, just what I needed to know.

A large heavy-based pan plopped onto the stove as she rinsed the blueberries.

'Anything else that needs doing?'

Apart from me, you mean.

'Could you make some coffee?' Maybe if he wasn't

hovering right beside her elbow, exuding those drive-Halle-crazy pheromones, it would help with her focus.

'All right, you're the boss.'

Was she? She didn't think so, as she watched him get the coffee under way. His competence with the coffee machine reminding her of how competent he was with so much else.

The luxurious sizzle of melting butter filled the kitchen as she dropped the first dollop of batter onto the hot pan. She inhaled the aroma and watched the edges crisp—determined to get her mind out of her knickers.

It didn't take long to get in the zone. Cooking had once been her great escape from the chaos of life in a two-room council flat in a Hackney high-rise with a young child and no money. Creating something delicious within the exacting confines of science and her stringent budget had helped her to focus during the biggest challenges of her life. While blueberry pancakes hardly tested her abilities and she had no budget now, the simplicity of the process, and the comforting aroma of fried fruit and batter that filled the kitchen, helped her to focus again now, and get her priorities straight.

This time with Luke had been an adventure. An adventure she never would have expected. It had healed stuff she hadn't even realised was still broken. But it wasn't her real life.

Her real life was with her children. Who needed her now.

Luke worked alongside her, setting the table, frothing some milk for her latte with that infernal machine and digging the maple syrup out of the box of supplies she'd brought back from the restaurant kitchen.

She flipped the last of the pancakes onto the plate she had warming, decorated the stack with the remaining blueberries and carried the plate to the table.

He placed a steaming latte by her elbow and sat opposite

her. Forking one of the pancakes off the stack, he poured a generous dollop of syrup over it.

She watched him take his first bite, the nerves finally settling in the pit of her stomach, when he gave a rumbling hum of approval.

'Incredible. They taste better than the resort's ones. What did you do?'

'I added a splash of vanilla essence, to lift the flavour of the blueberries. And used buttermilk and melted butter in the batter.'

'Genius.' He quartered the rest of the pancake. As he set about demolishing it in a few bites, it occurred to her how much she had always adored feeding him.

'Listen, Luke, I wanted to let you know how glad I am you blackmailed me into this.' She poured syrup over her own pancake. 'Everything that's happened in the past ten days has been a...well, "surprise" is way too mild a word. I've been stubborn and resistant to change and I should never have shut you out for so long, for Lizzie's sake. And I regret that now. I've also discovered I can survive whitewater kayaking, which is pretty phenomenal, too.'

His next forkful of pancake stopped in mid-air. 'Why am I getting a sense there's a "but" coming?'

Luke had always been smart.

'The but is, I'm afraid I'll have to head home sooner than expected. I've booked a cab to take me back to Atlanta tonight.'

He put his fork down slowly, carefully. 'Why?'

'I had a Skype call with Lizzie and Aldo about an hour ago, and something's not right at home.' It was the absolute truth; her mother's intuition was never wrong about this stuff. Well, apart from Lizzie's anorexia that wasn't, but she'd been under a lot of stress then.

Luke's eyebrows rose up his forehead. She'd expected surprise, even irritation; they'd had an agreement, after all. An agreement that she was being forced to break. What she hadn't expected was for him to look so stunned.

A tiny piece of her heart broke off inside her chest. She steeled herself against it. How easy would it be to fall for the man, the way she had once fallen for the boy? This was exactly why she needed to cut and run. Not that she was cutting and running; she had a perfectly good explanation for leaving early.

'What's wrong, exactly?' he asked.

'It's, well…' She scrambled around for a way to make her case convincingly. 'It's nothing specific. I just have a feeling that something's not right. Lizzie was much perkier than usual. She asked me questions about the book tour. Which is not like her at all. She never shows an interest in my career.'

'You told her you were on a book tour?'

Was that accusation she detected in his tone? 'I had to think of something to explain a two-week trip. I told you why I couldn't tell her the truth.' Even if those reasons seemed a tiny bit spurious and self-serving now.

And, obviously, she should have come up with a much better cover story. But she wasn't a fricking journalist. And she hadn't expected Lizzie to suddenly become curious about her career after six long years of sulky apathy and seething resentment.

'OK, what else?' he said.

'What else, what?'

'What else is making you uneasy? Because I'm not seeing Lizzie being inquisitive about your career as a major problem here. Or not one that requires you to go hightailing it back to the UK four days ahead of schedule and break our agreement.'

'Haven't you got enough now for your article?' she countered, struggling to suppress the sharp pain under her breastbone at his pragmatic response.

What had she expected? That he would beg her to stay? Of course the article was his main concern now. He'd got the only other thing he had wanted already—her agreement to let him contact her directly about Lizzie. Everything else—the hot sex, the candid conversations about their past, the growing sense of companionship and intimacy—had probably just been added extras to him, and not something that he obviously considered a top priority.

Luke had never been the hopeless romantic in their relationship. That had always been her... Which was exactly why she wasn't going to be spending another night in his arms and risk losing her grip on reality.

'We had an agreement,' he said, his expression strained. 'You want to duck out of it, that's fine, *if* there's a problem at home. But I'd like a bit more clarity on what exactly the problem is.'

Temper flickered under the hollow feeling of hurt. 'Aldo was behaving weirdly, too. The two of them were suspiciously pally. And I didn't get to speak to Trey.'

'Who's Trey?'

'Aldo's au pair. He's twenty-one. Aldo adores him. And he's very responsible and conscientious. I check in with him every time I ring or Skype them. Just to make sure there's nothing wrong. But Lizzie cut me off before I could speak to him. I don't even know if he was in the house.'

'What did Lizzie say?'

'Nothing, I didn't get a chance to ask her about Trey. And when I rang his mobile, it went straight to voicemail.'

'No, I mean, didn't you ask Lizzie if everything was OK?'

'Of course I did, and she said everything was great and so did Aldo. But that's not the point...'

'Then what is the point?'

'You're making me sound paranoid,' she countered. He was doing that journalist interrogation thing again. Flustering her and making her sound stupid. 'I'm not paranoid. I know when something is off with my kids.'

He covered the fist she had clenched on the table. 'I'm not saying you're paranoid. But is it possible you're over-reacting?' She could almost hear him thinking about the anorexia-that-wasn't-anorexia panic attack. 'Lizzie's eighteen, Hal. She's a bright kid and she's mature and sensible when she wants to be. Why do you think she and Aldo would be lying about everything being fine?'

She tugged her hand out from under his. Feeling badgered. And defensive. And patronised. She knew she'd made mistakes with her kids. Maybe she hadn't always trusted Lizzie enough. And maybe she hadn't always been one hundred per cent as honest with them both as she should have— certain phantom US book tours being a case in point. But she'd spent a lot more time with Luke's daughter than he had. And he'd never even met Aldo.

'You've never seen Lizzie and Aldo together,' she said. 'Lizzie may tell you how much she loves her little brother, but what I've seen in the past six years is a lot closer to *Alien vs Predator* than *The Care Bears Movie*. The two of them suddenly being best buddies would be fabulous if it were true. But I want to go home and check out what's going on for myself.'

Even if I'm starting to sound totally paranoid to myself now, too. Thanks so much, Carl Bernstein.

'And I don't need your permission to do it,' she added. 'So I'm not even sure why we're having this conversation.'

'We're having this conversation because we agreed that we'd start parenting Lizzie together,' he said with aggravating patience. 'If you say there's a problem, I'm not going to argue about that.'

'Thanks a lot,' she said, not hiding the bite of sarcasm.

So what exactly had he been doing for the past five minutes?

'What time's your flight?'

'Ten. I'm getting a connecting flight through Chicago.' She glanced at the clock on the wall, swallowing down the lump of regret at the realisation she had less than an hour left with him before the cab was due to arrive.

They wouldn't even have time to check out Luke's bakery porn fantasies. She dispelled the thought with an effort as her thighs went all quivery.

It was for the best—she already had enough addiction issues where this man was concerned.

'The cab's arriving at three,' she replied.

He stacked their plates, the remains of the pancakes that their conversation had interrupted congealing on the plate. And she suddenly had a silly wistful moment about that, too. Not realising until that precise second how much she'd wanted to cook a meal for him one last time.

'Cancel the cab. I'll drive us to the airport.'

Her heart rate began to trot at the generous offer. God, she really did have it quite bad. She'd got out just in time.

'That's sweet of you, but not necessary. It's a six-hour round trip.'

He glanced up from the dishwasher. 'Don't be daft, Hal. I'm not coming back here. I'm coming with you.'

Her heart rate shot straight to a gallop. 'But you'll have to change your flight. And what about the article?' *And my grand plan to make a clean getaway?*

He dumped the frying pan into the dishwasher and slammed it closed. 'I've got enough for the article. And changing my flight's not a problem. I'll do it when we get to the airport.'

He took her hands in his and her sweaty palms started to tremble.

'I was going to wait until we left on Saturday to have this discussion. But we might as well have it now.'

'What discussion?' She tried to tug her hands loose, but he held on tight.

'We need to do this together.'

'Do what together?'

'Go back to your place together. Speak to Lizzie together. Tell her what's been going on.'

'What?' She yanked her hands free, her pulse ready to jump right out of her wrist. 'But we can't. It'll only confuse her.'

And me. It'll confuse me. Even more than I'm already confused.

'How?' he said, using that eminently sensible tone that was starting to seriously piss her off. And make her panic go through the roof.

She could feel a trap of her own making starting to close around her.

She'd promised Luke a more substantial role in his daughter's life. A role that she'd inadvertently denied him. And she'd been right to do that. But she wasn't ready to let him back in to this extent. Not yet. And especially not after the events of last night. Their lives had to remain separate, or at least separate enough. She didn't want to fall victim to the same unrealistic expectations that had caught her out once before where he was concerned.

'Because she'll know I've lied to her,' she said. 'About the

book tour. If she really has turned a corner in her attitude to my work, I don't want to jeopardise that.'

'Were you seriously planning to go home and invent a whole book tour for her benefit?'

'Well...' *Yes, actually.*

'Listen to me, Hal. Can't you see that's exactly why we need to do this together. She'll have questions and lots of them. And it would be much better if we were both there to answer them. We've both been pretty damn childish about this for sixteen years. And, whether we intended it or not, Lizzie got stuck in the middle. Let's put her feelings first for a change. You're not the only one who's lied to her. She asked me about what happened to us and I never told her the truth, either. Because I was too ashamed to admit that I'd run away. But I'm not running any more. We need to be straight with her, even if it's going to be hard, so she doesn't get stuck in the middle again.'

She blinked, her heart sinking to her toes, hating his passion and determination and the fact that he was making so much sense. His insistence on being a good father to their daughter wasn't going to make him any less irresistible as a man.

A man who always had been, and always would be, far too dangerous to love.

'Come on, Hal. You know it's the right thing to do,' he coaxed.

'All right,' she said, admitting defeat.

How could she argue with him, when it was the right thing to do for Lizzie? Just not the right thing for her.

'You better get packing,' he said. 'You've got about ten times as much stuff as me.' He ran his thumb across her bottom lip, the heat and affection in his gaze crucifying

her. 'I guess we'll have to take a rain check on my bakery porn fantasies.'

Thank God for small mercies.

She left him, the trap clamping shut around her heart.

Chapter 20

'Where's Trey?'

Lizzie bit back the retort as Aldo's anxious gaze darted over the crowd at the school gates, searching for his invisible au pair.

'He's busy,' she replied. 'We had fun yesterday, didn't we?'

She'd taken him to the cinema to see the latest Marvel superhero movie after school—sitting through enough CGI pyrotechnics to make her head explode.

Maybe she wasn't the Aldo Whisperer, but she was doing her best. Especially as she didn't have a clue where Trey had been since yesterday morning.

He hadn't come home last night and his phone had gone to voicemail all day today. She had a hideous feeling his mum had died. And while the thought of that was bad enough, worse was the worry, writhing in her stomach like a bucket of worms all day, about how he might have reacted. Had he gone on a bender? Was he wandering around West London in a daze of grief? It wasn't like him not to call her back and let her know what was going on.

Plus, her mum had been suspicious when she'd Skyped

yesterday evening, and Lizzie had nearly cracked and told her the truth.

She'd never had any problems lying to her mum in the past, about homework, school and Liam... But she was worried about Trey. Worried about what he might be going through. And she had this insane urge to ask her mum what she should do. Should she go round to Trey's flat? Make sure he was all right? Would he want her to?

But she couldn't ask her mum's advice without breaking the promise she'd made to Trey.

'What's he busy doing?' Aldo whined. 'He promised to take me to Laser Quest today because it's the last day of school. I want him here. Not you.'

The ingratitude of the comment stung. Lizzie's temper spiked. As if she didn't have enough on her plate already without getting the Gestapo treatment.

'His mum probably just died. So why don't you stop thinking about yourself for two seconds?'

'His mum died?' Aldo's face collapsed, bringing Lizzie back to her senses, several seconds too late. 'When? Why didn't he tell me? Doesn't Trey want to look after me any more?' The whine in Aldo's voice might have been aggravating, but for the edge of panic. Aldo had always been chronically insecure. She guessed it came from not having a dad, and having no mates at school thanks to his angry Arthur routine of the past few years. 'Is he ever coming back?'

'He is coming back. He wouldn't just leave us,' she said, to reassure herself as much as Aldo.

Trey's mum was dying; of course he couldn't think about them right now.

But she knew how much Aldo missed him. Because she missed him, too. That sure, solid presence that she'd come to depend on in the past week and a half.

What felt weird, though, was knowing she was the grown-up in this situation. Without her mum or Trey there to take the slack, Aldo was counting on her to say and do the right thing.

'How do you know?' Aldo said, still scared.

'Because I know Trey. He's not like that. He likes you.' *And I hope he likes me, too.* 'And he likes his job. He certainly wouldn't leave without telling us.'

'Where is he, then?'

She walked out of the school, towards home, holding on to Aldo's hand. The way he clung to her was surprisingly reassuring.

Perhaps she should just tell him the truth. She hated it when her mum lied to her, and he probably wouldn't even understand half of it.

'I don't know if Trey's mum is dead yet,' she said, 'but I know she's very sick. That's why he had to go and be with her for a bit.'

'Where is his mum?'

'She's in a hospice in St John's Wood.'

'What's a hospice?'

'It's a special hospital where people go to die. When they're very sick.'

'Why don't we go there, then? So if his mum dies, he won't be all alone? If our mum was going to die, I'd want Trey there. Wouldn't you?'

Lizzie stopped and stared at her brother. Apparently, while she'd been panicking about what the best thing to do was, Aldo had come up with the answer.

* * *

'Hi, my name is Lizzie Best and this is my brother, Aldo.' Lizzie held on to Aldo's hand while sending the receptionist

her most reassuring smile. 'We're friends of Trey Carson and we were wondering if he's here today.'

'Yes, he is,' the older woman said. 'Are you here to pay your respects to the deceased?'

'Trey's dead?' Aldo's distressed cry accompanied the massive leap in Lizzie's heartbeat.

'Oh, no.' The receptionist smiled, almost amused. 'I meant Ms Carson. His mother. I just assumed...'

'His mother died, then?' Lizzie clutched Aldo's hand to stop it juddering.

'Yes, about two hours ago.'

Oh, shit, Trey. No wonder you haven't been answering my text messages.

'Who did you say you are again?' the receptionist added.

'Lizzie Best, we're good friends of Trey's. Really good friends,' she reiterated, seeing the look of suspicion beginning to cloud the woman's face. 'Is he still with his mum, then?'

'He's with the funeral director at the moment.'

'Is there anyone else with him?' she asked. 'Like a friend? Or some family?' They would leave if he had someone with him. Maybe she was wrong. Maybe the loneliness she'd sensed was all in her imagination, and he had loads of people to help see him through this. And he didn't need her or Aldo there.

The woman's face softened, and Lizzie could feel her sympathy for Trey stretch towards them across the Formica desk. 'I'm afraid not. He's the only authorised visitor Ms Carson's had since she arrived four months ago.'

'Could we go through? To offer our condolences?' Lizzie asked, desperate to see Trey. No one should have to do something like this all alone.

The woman hesitated. 'I'm afraid only relatives can be authorised to go through. Were you related to Ms Carson?'

'Yes, we're her...' Lizzie racked her brains. 'Her second cousins, once removed.'

'Are we?' Aldo asked.

'Shhh.' She shot her brother a shut-up-you-muppet look. And, for once, Aldo actually shut up without arguing, knowledge dawning in his eyes.

Unfortunately, knowledge had dawned in the receptionist's eyes, too. And a moment passed as Lizzie waited for that knowledge to turn to refusal.

She braced to make a run for it, giving Aldo's hand a warning pump. If they had to, she and Aldo would storm the doors of the hospice.

But the woman simply indicated the clipboard on the desk, her expression kind and sympathetic. 'Sign in, then you can go through.'

Lizzie scribbled their names on the sheet with the time and date. 'Thank you.'

She rushed through the doors, tugging Aldo with her, in case the receptionist changed her mind.

Light shone into the airy corridor from a glass wall on one side, illuminating an open ward on the other. People lay in curtained-off cubicles, the beds wide and comfortable, like normal beds instead of hospital ones. A few patients glanced their way, most didn't. Lizzie searched the faces, then moved on.

The heavy scent of air freshener and chemicals hung in the air. The few sounds of conversation were muffled, as if the silence were held at bay by the most tenuous of threads. Her Converse and Aldo's high-tops slapped against the stripped wood flooring as they rounded a corner.

Lizzie stopped, and Aldo bumped into her from behind.

Trey sat on a bench in a courtyard garden visible through the glass. The sunlight made his short hair gleam, his head bent over the sheet of paper he held loosely.

He looked so alone. And so exhausted. She pushed open the door to step into the paved garden.

No drama. Only support.

'Trey!' Aldo gave a choked cry as he let go of Lizzie's hand and rushed forward.

Trey's head lifted and he blinked slowly. 'Lizzie? Aldo?' He stood, and the paper drifted to the paving. 'What are you...'

Trey harrumphed as Aldo barrelled into him and wrapped his arms round Trey's midriff, burying his face against his friend's chest.

'Your mum died,' Aldo cried, all the tension and anxiety spilling out in a cascade of messy tears. 'That's so crap.'

Trey's hands came to rest gingerly on her brother's shoulders. 'Hey, buddy, don't cry. It's OK.'

'We came to tell you we miss you,' Aldo blurted out, then sniffled and burrowed into the hug, clinging on as if he was scared Trey would vanish. 'We want you to come home. You have to come home.'

Lizzie walked towards them.

So much for no drama.

Emotion closed her own throat, though, when Trey bent to touch his cheek to Aldo's hair. His arms lowering to hug her brother back.

'I'm sorry. He wanted to come and see you,' she said. 'We both did. If you want us to leave, we will. But we wanted to be sure you're OK.'

Trey's eyes met hers and, to her astonishment, he smiled. 'I am now' was all he said.

* * *

After Trey had handled some more paperwork and spoken to the hospice staff, they went to a McDonald's near the tube station for dinner. Aldo managed to put away a Big Mac and a monster helping of French fries while keeping up a running commentary on every single thing he'd been doing while Trey had been absent, in intricate and unflagging detail. Lizzie noticed Trey hardly touched his quarter-pounder. She didn't have much of an appetite for her filet-o-fish, either. But she welcomed Aldo's inane chatter.

The commentary continued all the way back to Holland Park tube station and the short walk to the house. You'd have thought Trey had been gone for six months, not a day and a half. But still he listened attentively, asking a string of pertinent questions, making Lizzie sure he welcomed the distraction, too.

Aldo was so excited at having his idol back in situ that it took them forever to calm him down enough to finally get him into his pyjamas and off to bed.

Lizzie waited in the kitchen while Trey went upstairs with Aldo to tuck him in and read him another chapter from *The Goblet of Fire*. A ritual she knew the two of them had begun when Trey had moved in twelve days ago.

How could it have been less than two weeks since the morning she'd had that massive row with her mum about Trey coming to stay?

Her phone buzzed on the countertop and she picked it up to see a text from Carly.

Crashing epic party 2nite in Muswell Hill. Wanna cum?

She texted back. No thx, busy.

She'd rather gouge her eyes out than leave Trey this evening, especially to spend time with Carly.

WTF? It's going to be epic!! How lame r u!!!

I'M BUSY.

Doing wot? Sucking off Super Nanny?

The crude suggestion was accompanied by a grinning devil emoji.

Lizzie gritted her teeth as anger flared. Carly would never understand what a sweet and genuinely nice guy Trey was. Inked arse, dopey polo shirts and all. Because her BFF thought 'sweet' and 'nice' were for lame, uncool people who didn't matter.

To think she'd once bought into that bullshit, too, and sucked up to bitches like Carly.

But the past week and a half had given her the major kick up the arse she needed. Hating yourself and the way you behaved wasn't enough, you had to make the effort to change. And that meant ditching Carly.

Why don't u grow up? She tapped out the reply and sent it.

The response came back moments later.

FU loser. Your just a begfriend anyway.

Lizzie switched off the phone and dumped it on the counter.

Carly would slag her off to everyone now. A few weeks ago the thought of losing all her cool points would have paralysed her with fear. But she actually wasn't that bothered.

Turned out there were a lot worse things than losing all your cool points to a bunch of wankers.

Hearing Trey's heavy tread coming down the stairs, she busied herself pouring boiling water over the teabags she'd dumped into her mother's treasured Clarice Cliff teapot.

He entered the room and sat down heavily on her mum's new sofa in the window alcove. He ran his fingers through his hair, sending the short strands into haphazard tufts, lines of fatigue bracketing his mouth.

'Did Aldo go to sleep?' she asked.

'Yeah, he's knackered.' Trey sent her a weary half-smile. 'So knackered, in fact, he nodded off during the bit where Cedric Diggory gets killed in the maze.'

'You look pretty knackered yourself.' She placed a couple of mugs on the countertop. 'I've made a pot of tea, if you fancy a cup.'

'Thanks, milk, no sugar.'

She prepared their tea in silence. Realising how strange it was she didn't even know how he took his tea, and yet he had come to mean so much to her.

Sitting down on the sofa next to him, she handed him the cup. His fingers butted hers as he took it. 'Listen, thanks for coming today.' His thumb touched hers.

'You're welcome,' she murmured.

He lifted the cup and took a swallow, then let out a breath. 'I didn't know how much I needed a friend there, until you two arrived.'

She blew on her own tea, sipped it, watching him as he leaned back into the sofa's comfy cushions. And shut his eyes.

'Was it awful?' she asked. Not knowing what else to say.

He opened his eyes and watched her for a moment, the awareness pulsing between them. Then shook his head as

he straightened to place his cup on the floor. 'Actually, no, it wasn't. It was kind of peaceful, but...' He paused, his jaw tensing, as he rubbed open palms down his face. 'It wasn't how I thought it would be, either.'

'Why not?'

She could see guilt, and regret. She wondered what he could possibly have to feel guilty about.

'I've wanted her to die for months now,' he said so softly she almost couldn't hear him. 'Prayed for it to happen, because I can't even remember what she used to be like, before she got sick. It's like she hasn't been my mum for a long time. But I thought I'd be glad when she'd gone. And I'm not. I've been such a selfish bastard.'

She placed her hand on his leg, stroked the rigid muscles, the urge to comfort quick and instinctive. 'It's not selfish to want her suffering to stop.'

He drew absent circles on the back of her hand with his thumb. 'It would be nice if that was the reason. But it's not. I wanted her to die so I could be free of her.'

Lizzie touched his cheek and waited for his gaze to meet hers.

She couldn't take the grief away; she knew that. But she wanted to say something. Something that would comfort him. And make him realise he had nothing to feel guilty about.

'We all say stupid things we don't mean to people we love. I bet I've said a lot more shitty things to my mum than you ever said to yours.'

A crooked smile crossed his lips and lifted some of the sadness. 'I think you're probably right about that.'

'I know I am,' she continued, heartened by his reaction. 'And you don't even want to know how many times I've wanted to kill Aldo.'

'Yes, but it's not as if you actually wanted him to die,' he countered.

'Actually, I did, especially when he got poster paint on my new Herschel backpack,' she continued, glad when his lips twitched. 'So, basically, if you're a selfish bastard, I must be a complete heinous bitch.'

'Don't say that. You're not a bitch. You're smart and incredibly pretty and you're fun to be around.' The words spilled out with such honest conviction, she thought her heart would burst it was beating so hard. 'I love hanging out with you. You make me feel normal.'

Sympathy and tenderness thudded against her ribcage. 'Then you have to believe me when I say, you're all that stuff and a lot more. No way are you a selfish bastard, Trey. Because I used to go out with a real selfish bastard and I'm now an expert at spotting the difference.'

'You think I'm incredibly pretty?' he said.

'I think you're gorgeous, right down to that low-rent tattoo on your arse.'

'It's not on my arse,' he corrected. 'It's on the base of my spine.'

'Did you have to drop your pants to get it done?'

The smile twitched. 'Maybe.'

'Then it's on your arse, mate.'

He chuckled, then tilted his head to rest his forehead against hers. His thumbs caressed her neck. 'I want to kiss you so bad right now.'

'Then do.'

He shook his head. 'I can't. It would be taking advantage of you.'

She framed his face with her hands, drew his mouth to hers. 'Then I guess I'll have to take advantage of you.'

She teased his lips, tasting the sadness, and the desperation,

beneath the heat. His tongue met hers, their mutual hunger driving a connection that felt real and solid and significant as they sank into the kiss.

His breathing had become slow and sluggish when they finally parted.

'I'm shattered,' he said. 'But I don't want to be alone.'

'Then stay here. And I'll stay with you.'

He settled his long body on the sofa, and she tucked one of the throw pillows under his head. But when she tried to rise, he caught her wrist. 'Could I hold you? I won't try anything, I promise.'

She'd have loved him to try something. But that really would be taking advantage of him. So she nodded and lifted his arm, snuggling under it. He shifted onto his side, to give her more space, as they cuddled together. Her head nestled on his collarbone, his arms secure around her back.

She could feel the steady pump of his heart next to her ear as his breathing evened out. She inhaled the teasing scent of soap and laundry detergent, and the slightly sickly scent of flowers and air freshener, the smell of death that still clung to him.

But as she snuggled against him, she knew she'd never felt more safe, or more alive, in her whole life.

Chapter 21

'I'm still not sure about this, Luke. Seeing you and me together is going to be enough of a shock for Lizzie without us turning up two days early.'

Luke hauled their suitcases out of the back of the cab and handed the driver a ten-quid tip. Halle stood on the pavement, chewing her bottom lip.

Even jet-lagged and tired and extremely stressed, she looked adorable. Adorable enough to have him clamping down on his frustration. Again.

'We agreed we needed to come here and tell Lizzie what's been going on together.' He was holding firm on that no matter how many times he had to talk her down off the ledge. 'The good news is at least your house hasn't burned to the ground,' he said, struggling to lighten the mood.

The huge Georgian pile, five storeys of ornate white plaster, looked impressive even for Notting Hill. But he refused to be intimidated by it. After eight hours on the red-eye and having to route through Chicago to get here, he was more than keyed up enough already. The thought of seeing Lizzie and meeting Halle's son, Aldo, for the first time was

nerve-racking enough without him letting Halle's nerves get to him, too.

They'd spent the past thirty-two hours on a nightmare journey from the resort with Halle insisting on discussing every nuance of this meeting in exhaustive detail. All the things he could say, and all the things he couldn't. And he'd tried really hard not to take her doubts personally.

Whatever way you looked at it, this was a huge step, in all their lives. A huge step that he really didn't want to fuck up. Because he'd come to a few momentous decisions himself— ever since she'd sprung her surprise departure plan on him. And the vague feeling of melancholy that had been bothering him ever since he had woken up to find her gone had turned into a gaping wound right in the middle of his chest.

He'd convinced himself a long time ago he wasn't into relationships. That being Lizzie's dad was the only emotional connection he was capable of. But he'd known in that moment it wasn't true, or not true any more, because the thought of Halle leaving that evening without him had sent him into a tailspin of stunned horror.

He'd finally been forced to acknowledge that despite all the challenges, despite all the tough conversations, the rows and recriminations—and even that whiplash-inducing crack on the cheek—being with her had made him feel more alive, more connected than he had since he'd run away.

She'd challenged him and excited him, frustrated him and driven him mad with lust, but most of all she'd made him realise all the things that had been missing in his life since he'd lost her.

Consequently, he'd spent the whole of the damn red-eye wide awake, considering what his life could be like with Halle back in it. Not just as the mother of his child. Not just as a friend or a fuck buddy. But as more than that.

And the more he'd thought about it, the more he'd realised how important it was not to bugger up this next step. His growing realisation that Halle seemed convinced he was going to do exactly that wasn't doing much to bolster his confidence.

'What are you so scared of, Hal?'

She stared at him blankly, and he wondered if she was going to deny it. But then she sighed. 'Listen, Luke, are you sure this is such a good idea? Springing this on Lizzie? She'll still be in bed. Why don't I have a quick chat with her when she wakes up? Just to smooth things over, prepare her. And then, if everything's OK, I can give you a call and we could come and meet you somewhere. Later.'

He bit down on the new surge of frustration. And the spike of fear. Was this really about Lizzie? Or was she just trying to get rid of him?

'I live in Paris, where exactly am I supposed to be while you're preparing her to see me?' he said, not managing to keep the edge out of his voice.

'I could book you a hotel suite,' she said, far too helpfully for her not to have planned the suggestion ahead of time.

'That's not the point and you know it,' he said, his temper snapping. 'We had an agreement. If you want to back out of it, I want to know why.'

'Could you keep your voice down?' She glanced at the house.

OK, that did it.

He grasped her arm, and her gaze shot back to his. 'Halle, what's really going on here?'

Had he been totally kidding himself? He needed to know if he had any chance with her, before he risked letting her see how much this meant to him, because apparently there was

still enough of that screwed-up kid inside him to be scared to death he'd already buggered this up without intending to.

* * *

'What's really going on is...' Halle tugged her arm out of his grasp. 'She's not my only child.'

'Huh?'

'I don't want you to meet Aldo. Not like this.'

'Why the hell not?'

'He wants a father, Luke, desperately.' She struggled to explain. 'Whenever Lizzie was in Paris with you, he would ask about you incessantly. Does Lizzie's daddy play football? What kind of car does Lizzie's daddy drive? He's always wanted to meet you. But he's never had to see you with Lizzie. He's never had to have his face rubbed in the fact that you're her father and not his. It's going to be agonising for him, seeing you two together and knowing he doesn't have what Lizzie has.'

Instead of looking irritated or defensive, as she would have expected, Luke laughed. He grasped her upper arms, the look on his face a picture of relief. 'Seriously, Halle, is that all?'

'What do you mean, *is that all*? It's a huge deal for him, he's only ten and—'

'And I'm not Claudio,' he interrupted. 'Don't you think I want to meet him, too? I know it's not going to be easy. That we'll have to get to know each other first. And you're right, I'm not his dad. But I would never try to make him feel less because he's not my kid. And the very last thing I would want to do is hurt him.'

'I know that, but—'

'You know what your problem is?' Luke interrupted again.

'No, do tell me,' she said, not making any effort to hide

her irritation with his casual attitude. This was not a joke. She'd been agonising over this for hours—ever since she'd been manoeuvred into agreeing to this meeting.

And OK, maybe it wasn't all about Aldo. Maybe she was ever so slightly terrified at the prospect of seeing Luke bonding with Lizzie and Aldo, and letting those unrealistic expectations that had been dogging her all through the journey home sprint right out of control.

'You need to know you can't control everything,' he said.

'I know that,' she snapped. 'I wouldn't have had to spend two weeks in Tennessee with you if I could.'

'And that didn't turn out so bad, now did it?' He gave her a gentle shake, the approval in his eyes, with that flicker of heat that was never far behind, making her insides churn and melt at the same time. Which was not good.

You see, this is exactly why you need to be establishing distance, and not playing happy families.

'What's your point?' she added, feeling her control, the control she'd worked so hard to build after Luke had left, slipping through her fingers.

'That sometimes you have to trust in people,' he said. 'And, more important, you have to trust in yourself. You're a terrific mum, but you can't fix everything. Life is like baking. It's not a precise science. Sometimes you don't prove the dough quite long enough the second time around and your fancy European novelty bread doesn't turn out how you planned. But it could still be edible. In fact, it might even be better that way.'

'Luke, don't try baking analogies with a master baker.'

He laughed. 'I'm right, though, aren't I?'

A tiny bubble of hope penetrated the panic at the calm assurance in his gaze. What if they could make this work?

What if her expectations weren't completely unrealistic, after all?

'You're going to have to trust Aldo and me to figure our relationship out for ourselves,' he said. 'But just to put your fears to rest, I can promise you this much—whatever happens this morning, I'll do my utmost to make sure Aldo doesn't get hurt. Lizzie means everything to me. And you mean quite a lot to me, too.'

Do I? The heart bumps rose into her throat.

'And he's her brother, and your son,' he added. 'So even though I've never met him, he already means something to me.'

'You're sure?' she asked, the bubble expanding uncomfortably. *Please don't say that unless you mean it.*

'I'm sure,' he said. 'Trust me.'

The knot of panic finally let go of her oesophagus. 'OK.'

As tough as it was, she was going to *have* to trust him. And herself. Because he was right about one thing. Ever since he'd left, she'd tried to control every single thing. And if this trip had taught her one thing—apart from the fact that Luke Best's smile could still make her go weak at the knees—it was that being in control didn't necessarily stop bad things from happening. And trying to control this might actually stop something amazing from happening.

He lifted her suitcase, as well as his own. 'Now, can we take this inside? I want to make a good impression and I work better with caffeine. Especially after eight hours on a plane while I'm still on Tennessee time.'

It occurred to her, as she reached into her bag to find the keys, that however nervous she was, he was probably more so.

And that this was the first day of the rest of her life.

So, no pressure, then.

Five minutes earlier

Lizzie's eyelids fluttered and then snapped open. Her mind registered the sonorous hum wasn't just coming from Trey's measured breathing against her ear, but from the sound of a car driving away on the street outside.

She snuggled against Trey to hide from the light penetrating the shutters. And smiled.

They'd spent the whole night together. Fully clothed, cuddling on the sofa. Was there anything more romantic?

He'd jerked awake a couple times, she guessed dreaming about his mum, or her death. Both times she'd lulled him back to sleep. Glad that she could help, and gladder still that he wanted her to.

But as her cheek brushed the solid wall of his chest, she realised she wasn't feeling glad now so much as very, very curious. Because this situation wasn't just romantic any more, it was also kind of hot.

She slid her hand under his T-shirt to rest against his belly. And took a few stolen moments to explore the soft line of hair that trailed under his belly button and had fascinated her for over a week. Getting bolder, she inched her fingertips under the loose waistband of his jeans, the definite bulge beneath fascinating her. And exciting her.

Wouldn't it be wonderful to do something with that morning erection? She wondered how many girlfriends he'd had. He certainly couldn't have had tons if his mum had been sick since he was a kid. She couldn't think of anything more erotic than getting the chance to seduce him. And maybe then he could seduce her back. She'd never even had an orgasm with Liam. It had always been over too fast, because Liam had about as much interest in foreplay as he

did in having root canal treatment. Trey would be much more considerate.

His erection certainly didn't repulse her, or bore her the way Liam's often had.

She was so busy imagining how much she would enjoy exploring it more, that she jumped when his large hand covered hers.

'Morning, Lizzie.'

She lifted her head, to find his chocolate eyes watching her. 'Hi. You're awake. I'm sorry, I didn't mean to...'

'Don't be.' He sent her a shy, sexy smile, his hair flattened on one side, but still gorgeous.

He looked half asleep, his pupils dilated, his lids at half mast. He didn't move her hand, but he let it go to sweep her hair up on either side of her head.

Her pulse pounded in her ears at the tender affection, the sleepy invitation in those heavy-lidded eyes. Easing her exploring fingertips further into his pants, she stretched up to press her lips to his, the thrill rushing through her.

The kiss became fervent, seeking. She flattened her palm against the warm firm flesh of his belly and thrust her hungry tongue into his mouth.

The click of a lock, the muffled buzz of voices and footsteps seemed to be part of a dream, barely registering over the hot rush of blood to her head. And the beautiful strength of Trey's fingers in her hair.

'Lizzie? Trey?' Her mother's shocked voice pierced through the fog of arousal.

'Who the hell is that?' The harsh male shout yanked her the rest of the way out of the erotic dream. And into a nightmare.

Trey's head snapped back as large hands grabbed the front of his shirt.

'Get the fuck off my daughter.'

Lizzie tumbled backwards off the sofa, her back hitting the floor as Trey was yanked out of her arms. Her mind crashed into complete consciousness as she watched her dad, his face tight with fury, haul Trey up by his shirt front.

Lizzie scrambled up. Her limbs clumsy with shock. 'Stop it... Don't...' she cried on a whimper of breath, her lungs paralysed with horror.

Trey shook his head, obviously confused. 'No, wait...' He raised his hands in defence as her dad's arm drew back, his fist bunched.

'Luke, don't!' her mum yelled behind her. Too late.

Her dad's fist connected with Trey's jaw, the sickening thud reverberating through her as Trey's head rocked back and he crashed to the floor.

'Dad!' she screamed.

'You hit Trey. I hate you!' Aldo raced into the room and launched himself at her dad, kicking him and shouting.

Lizzie rushed to kneel next to Trey.

He held his jaw, blood seeping from his mouth, his expression one of shock and pain and guilt. 'I'm sorry, Lizzie. I'm so sorry.'

'It's OK, you didn't do anything wrong,' she said, tears pouring down her cheeks. How could her dad have hit him like that?

What the fuck is Dad even doing here?

'Yes, I did,' Trey said, his voice breaking. 'I shouldn't have touched you.'

She blanked out her dad's grunts and curses as he held Aldo off while her little brother punched and kicked, trying to batter him like a Teenage Mutant Ninja Turtle.

It serves him bloody right.

'But I wanted you to touch me.' She clung to Trey as he stood.

'I should go.' He looked devastated as he dislodged her clutching fingers.

'Don't go,' she pleaded, but her arms hung limp by her sides, unable to stop him.

Her mother touched Trey's arm, delaying him before he reached the door, but whatever she said, it wasn't enough. He pushed past her and left. The door slammed behind him as he raced up the outside steps.

* * *

'Mum!' Lizzie's wail jolted Halle out of her stunned trance. 'Mum, don't let him go.'

'It's OK, we'll get him back.' She enfolded her daughter in her arms as Lizzie's slender body vibrated with wrenching sobs.

'But he won't come back, not now,' Lizzie cried. 'Not after Dad hit him like that. How could he? Trey's mum died yesterday. He's already been through so much.'

'What?' Halle held her daughter at arm's length.

Shock layered on shock. She had no clue what Luke and she had just walked in on between her daughter and Trey, but it had looked very intense.

'His mum died, yesterday,' her daughter repeated between heaving breaths. 'She's been sick for a long time. Trey used to look after her.'

'I didn't know that.' It seemed there were a lot of things she didn't know.

'Stop kicking me, kid!' Luke's shout drew her back to the present.

She jotted the problem of Trey, and Lizzie, and Trey's dead mother down on Future Halle's to-do list, because Present Halle had a much bigger problem. How could she

have been stupid enough to trust Luke? She'd let him in
here. Let him into her home. And he'd turned into the bloody
Terminator.

She grabbed a saucepan and smashed it down on the
countertop. The sound crashed around the room, calling
time on Luke and Aldo's wrestling match.

'Aldo, stop kicking Luke. Luke, put my son down,' she
demanded in her best obey-me-at-your-peril voice.

Their two heads rose together and, for a split second, as
Luke hugged Aldo round the waist, lifting her son off the
ground to prevent Aldo kicking his shins, the illusion she'd
kept at bay during the long flight home, of Luke and Aldo
becoming father and son, became real.

And then shattered as she registered the tears smearing
her son's cheeks and the sharp frown on Luke's face.

Luke dropped Aldo and Halle grabbed her son's shoulder before he could launch another attack on Luke's shins.
'Don't, Aldo, that's enough.'

'I hate him,' her son sobbed, crumpling against her. 'He
hit Trey.'

'I know. He won't do it again.'

Luke looked shell-shocked, what he'd done finally beginning to dawn on him. She glared at him over her child's
head. Not caring.

How could he have reacted like that? In anger and aggression without a thought to the consequences? How could he
have put her children and Trey through this? She'd trusted
him. How could she have been stupid enough to think for
even a second that he would ever put her needs, her children's needs above his own?

'Lizzie.' She turned to her daughter, who stood forlornly
in the corner, sniffing back tears. 'Could you take your

brother upstairs? I'll be up in a moment to talk to you both, but I need to talk to your father first.'

She prayed that Lizzie wouldn't throw a wobbly, but she braced for it anyway. To her astonishment, Lizzie simply sucked up the last of her tears and threw a consoling arm round her brother's shoulders, before giving her a nod. The expression on her face was one of sympathy and solidarity and total faith. 'Don't worry, Aldo. Mum will sort this out.'

Sending her dad a furious glare, she led her brother out of the room, saying, 'You were really brave, you know. Trey would be proud of you.'

'Who the hell is that guy, and what was he doing with my daughter?' Luke went on the offensive as soon as Aldo and Lizzie had left the room.

Halle's temper soared, the sense of betrayal consumed by her fury.

'That guy is Trey, our au pair. And what he was doing with *our* daughter was obvious. The question is what the hell did you think *you* were doing assaulting him like that?'

'What was *I* doing assaulting him?' He thumped his chest, like the Neanderthal he was. 'He was assaulting my daughter. She's just a kid.'

'She's eighteen years old. I was pregnant with her at that age.'

'It's not the same thing. She's innocent. She's a bloody virgin.'

What planet is he living on?

'The guy's in your employ and he's…what?' Luke continued, his own fury gathering pace. 'Five years older than her?'

'First of all, Lizzie is not a bloody virgin. She lost her virginity when she was sixteen to a toerag called Liam.

And if ever anyone deserved a good kicking, he was the one. Not Trey.'

She tried to dismiss the sharp pang of guilt at the look of abject horror on Luke's face. She'd known he was labouring under some delusions about his daughter's true nature. Maybe she should have said something back in Tennessee. But really it had never even occurred to her to clue him in on Lizzie's sex life. And she'd been right not to, she reasoned. What her daughter chose to confide in her father was her own affair.

'But even if she was a virgin,' she said, 'she's more than old enough to make her own choices. And if she chooses to kiss Trey in her own home, she's entitled to do that.'

'You call that a kiss?' he sputtered, most of the wind sucked out of his sails. 'It looked like a lot more than that to me. He had his tongue down her throat.'

'And she had her hand down his pants,' she shot back and saw Luke flinch.

'Don't remind me.' He groaned, collapsing onto the sofa. 'I'm never going to get that picture out of my head.' He clutched his head in his hands as if he were trying to erase the image.

She spotted the abrasion across his knuckles, where they had connected with Trey's jaw, and her temper ignited all over again.

'And I'm never going to get the picture out of my head of you punching him in the face. And neither is our daughter. Or my son. The boy you told me not five minutes ago you would do everything in your power not to hurt. Well, guess what, Luke? You failed on that one at the first hurdle.'

She realised she was literally vibrating with anger now. But beneath the temper was the huge well of hurt. She'd

trusted him. Just as she'd trusted him once before. And he'd failed her, again.

She should have seen this coming. She should never have been foolish enough to think for even a moment that Luke and she could have a future. This was her own fault, for allowing herself to be led astray again by feelings that were twenty years out of date.

'I need you to leave, now,' she said, a part of her heart ripping open when he stared at her through his fingers. All her foolish hopes of considering a future with him were exposed as the stupid pipe dreams they actually were.

His dark scowl had disappeared to be replaced by...what? Regret? Sorrow? She didn't know, and she couldn't let herself care. Luke had always been a lost cause. How many times was she going to be forced to face that fact before she finally believed it?

* * *

'Don't do this, Hal, not again.' Luke stood, his legs shaky, the finality on her face tearing him to pieces.

'Don't do what?' she said, the neutral tone scaring him even more. He could handle her temper, but nothing? He couldn't handle nothing.

'Don't shut me out. We can fix this. We can fix this if we do it together.'

'You must be bloody joking.'

'I shouldn't have hit him. I realise that. It was a stupid, irrational knee-jerk reaction, but it was a major shock to my system. I hadn't expected to walk in here and find my daughter necking with some guy I don't know on the couch.'

'I know that. It was a shock for me, too. But you didn't see me trying to hit anyone.'

'Yeah, but it wasn't as much of a shock for you because

you're a much bigger part of Lizzie's life than you've ever let me be.'

He had tried not to say it, tried not to go there. But suddenly the unfairness of it all made him want to yell. So he'd overreacted. Gone off the deep end. He'd just had one hell of a rude awakening, discovering his little girl wasn't his little girl any more.

But was that really all his fault?

'That's not true,' she said. 'I let you see her.'

'For six measly weeks of the year.' The fury grew to disguise the panic, the self-disgust. He flexed stinging knuckles and gave his resentment free rein. 'Do you know what that's like? To put her back on a train and know you're not going to see her again for months? And when you do, she'll have changed again and you'll have lost another huge chunk of her childhood?'

'But you never asked for more!' Halle gaped at him.

'Of course I asked for more. I asked your goddamn solicitor about reviewing the visitation rights a hundred times. And when he stonewalled me, I tried to contact you. But my emails bounced back. Your mobile always went to voicemail.' He paced to the door. 'The only thing I didn't do was ask Lizzie, because the one thing I couldn't bring myself to do was make her a go-between. So I had to pretend I was OK with the little time you'd give me. Even though I could feel her drifting further and further out of reach as she got older.'

'I didn't know' was all she said.

'Why would you? You wouldn't talk to me, remember.'

'I told you I was sorry about that. What more can I do?'

'Let me stay now.' He pounced on the opening. 'Let's try to make this right together. Don't close me out again. Or what chance do we have for our future?'

'What future? What are you talking about?'

He stared at her. So this was it. The moment when one of them would have to break cover. He could run away now, lick his wounds, as he'd done sixteen years ago, or he could hold his ground and fight—and admit that his feelings had changed and that he wasn't that sad little bastard any more who had never felt worthy of her.

'I want to be with you, Halle. This trip has convinced me that I want to at least try. Don't chuck that chance away because I did something stupid and rash. Something I already regret.'

She bit her lip, her eyes going glassy with shock…and something… For one bright shining moment, he thought she might admit she felt the same way. That the past twelve days hadn't just been about forgiving their past and repairing their relationship as Lizzie's parents, that it had the potential to be so much more.

But his hope died when she said, 'I have to put my children first. You must see that. Maybe if…'

'This can't wait. Either you want to make this work or you don't.' This was it. Her chance to admit she felt the same. She had to give him something here. Otherwise, he would spend the rest of his life on the outside. Being never quite good enough. Always being tested and found wanting. He'd spent his whole miserable childhood feeling like that and it had nearly destroyed him. Either she thought this thing they had was worth fighting for or she didn't.

'Don't make me choose between my children and you,' she said.

Weariness engulfed him, and a futile feeling of despair. The last of the fight, the fury draining away.

It wasn't any good. No matter what he said. If she couldn't

see it had never been a choice, then what chance had they ever had?

He walked to the door, picked up the holdall he'd dropped as soon as they'd come in.

'When you speak to Aldo and the au pair, tell them both I'm sorry.' He turned the door handle, exhaustion overwhelming him. 'I'll contact Lizzie in a couple of days, once she's calmed down, and grovel my arse off with her.'

He stared at her, not bitter or resentful any more, just desperately sad that it had always been too late to repair the damage he'd done. And their time in Tennessee had done nothing but create an illusion of false hope that had always been bound to shatter.

Chapter 22

Suck it up, your children come first, and if he can't see that, then he really doesn't want you—not who you are now anyway.

Halle repeated the words to herself, over and over again, but even so the two flights it took to get to Aldo's bedroom felt like climbing Mount Kilimanjaro.

Lizzie and Aldo sat huddled on the bed together with their arms around each other. It was a sight Halle had never expected to see again, and it helped to calm her racing heartbeat, and fill a little of the huge pit of despair opening up in her stomach.

Luke had blindsided her, but why hadn't he said anything sooner? Why had he waited until the worst possible moment to reveal his feelings? The simple answer was because they weren't real.

Tennessee had been an illusion, brought on by a year-long dry spell, being in such close proximity to Luke's magnificent cock and the euphoria of being able to unpack the last of the baggage from her past.

She had to go forward now and forget about what they

might have been. That her children seemed to have found each other again while she'd been gone was one huge upside.

One she could use now to help clean up the mess Luke had caused downstairs.

'Has Dad gone?' Lizzie asked.

'Yes.'

'What was he even doing here?' She sounded more astonished than accusing, but still Halle felt the shaft of guilt. She had known it wasn't a good idea to spring this on Lizzie.

Why hadn't she used her head, instead of listening to her foolish heart?

'Why did Lizzie's dad hit Trey?' Aldo asked.

Halle held up her hands. 'OK, guys, listen, I've got a lot of explaining to do. But first things first. Lizzie, why don't you go and have a shower, then try calling Trey on his mobile? So we can make sure he's not badly hurt.'

As shocking as Luke's punch had seemed, Trey hadn't looked badly hurt to her, but she needed to get Lizzie out of the room while she talked to Aldo. And vice versa. She had a lot of talking to do, not just about this morning, but about a host of other things.

She'd never been entirely honest with either of her children. Had peppered her parenting with a parade of small and sometimes huge lies, which had always felt justified, but now felt like the worse kind of cop-out. If she had learned one thing from her time with Luke, it was that keeping secrets—for whatever reason—never worked, and could often cause more hurt than they healed.

She needed to come clean with them both. To answer whatever questions they had for her now honestly. But she couldn't do it to them both at the same time because…well, it was going to be hard enough without being outnumbered. After all, she wasn't Super Mum.

Lizzie got off the bed, looking unsure again. 'I don't know if Trey'll want to speak to me now. Not after what Dad did.'

'What your father did wasn't your fault, sweetheart.'

'Actually, it probably was, a little bit.'

Halle sat next to Aldo, let him cling to her. 'How so?' she asked, surprised again by her daughter's new-found maturity. It wasn't like Lizzie to take the blame for anything.

'Dad doesn't know about Liam. I never told him. I think he still thinks I'm—' she shrugged, the movement stiff and uncomfortable '—like, thirteen when it comes to boys. That's probably why he freaked out when he saw Trey and me kissing.'

The explanation was so practical and forthright, it stunned Halle. Had Lizzie already forgiven her father for that punch?

'You were kissing Trey?' Aldo's face screwed up as if he'd just been force-fed a can of lugworms. 'Yuck!'

Both she and Lizzie laughed, Aldo's horrified reaction breaking the tension.

'That's so gross,' he added to reiterate the point.

'No, it's not. Trey's a really good kisser, actually,' Lizzie said, obviously enjoying her brother's discomfort.

Aldo placed his hands over his ears. 'Yuck! Yuck! Yuck!'

Lizzie began making kissy noises, inciting a louder and more vociferous chorus of yucks.

'All right, both of you, stop it,' Halle cut in, assuming her role as peacemaker, oddly moved by the exchange. Neither of her children could be that badly traumatised by this morning's events if they could still start a sibling spat over nothing.

'Fine, I'm leaving,' Lizzie announced, but the look she sent Halle was one of uncertainty. 'If I can't get in touch with Trey, what are we going to do?'

'Don't worry, we'll figure something out,' Halle said, surprised but also gratified to have her daughter look to

her for reassurance. What exactly she was going to say to Trey, and Lizzie, about that clinch on the couch when they did locate Trey would have to be another problem for Future Halle to solve.

Lizzie nodded and left the room, apparently satisfied with Halle's answer.

'Does Lizzie's dad hate me now, too?' Aldo's question threw Halle's emotions straight back into turmoil as soon as the door had closed behind her daughter.

She slung her arm round her son's shoulders, wishing—as she had so often before—that she could simply take all his insecurities away. 'Of course not, honey. He doesn't even know you.' The surge of anger at Luke for his insane behaviour went some way to quelling the ever-present guilt.

'But I kicked him.'

'Yes, I know, but he punched Trey and you were just defending your friend. Now, I'm not saying violence is ever the answer, but...'

Aldo slanted her his get-real-Mum look, forcing her to abandon her standard 'non-violence' message.

'But, in this case, Luke knows he shouldn't have hit Trey.' Sometimes, honesty was more important than platitudes when it came to peace and reconciliation. 'And he asked me to tell you how sorry he is for doing that.'

'He did?' Aldo's eyes popped wide, but beneath his surprise she could see genuine pleasure. 'Then he doesn't hate me?'

'No, he definitely doesn't hate you.'

Aldo smiled, the same boyish, untroubled smile she'd seen on his face only recently when he was hanging out with Trey.

OK, now I'm confused. Has Aldo forgiven Luke already, too?

'I think Luke's more worried that you might hate him,'

she added. And he had good reason to be as far as she could see.

'Why would I hate him?'

'Um, because he punched Trey.'

'Trey's tough. I bet he could take Lizzie's dad in a fight if he wanted to.'

'Well…I'm not sure that's…' She paused, totally nonplussed now. Where was her non-violence speech when she needed it the most? And how could Aldo be so blasé now, after being so distressed downstairs?

'But Trey didn't punch Lizzie's dad back,' Aldo continued, sounding disappointed. 'So it probably didn't even hurt Trey that much.'

'Right,' she said, still struggling to follow Aldo's ten-year-old logic while coping with the growing realisation that it probably wasn't that far removed from Luke's logic. Or Trey's logic, either. Because when she had waylaid her fleeing au pair at the door, his bloody lip already puffing up like bread dough in the proving drawer, and apologised for Luke's punch, all he'd said was 'I'm so sorry, Ms Best', as if he were the guilty party.

Bloody men! Are they born emotionally obtuse, or is it just the inevitable result of having too much testosterone poisoning their bloodstream?

Because it was beginning to look as if she had been much more traumatised by Luke's punch than either her son or the young man Luke had attacked.

'OK, well…' She hesitated, remembering Aldo's original question. 'The thing is, nobody hates you, Aldo. Even Lizzie when you and she argue.'

'I know,' he said with complete conviction. 'Me and her are friends now,' he continued, confirming what she'd noticed when she'd walked into the room. Something had

definitely changed in their relationship. Something for the better. 'She took me to the movies while Trey's mum was sick. And she didn't moan once.'

'That's wonderful,' she said as more of the pieces of the puzzle fell into place. Lizzie must have stepped in to take care of Aldo while Trey's mum had been dying.

Why hadn't she ever considered putting them together more instead of trying to keep them apart? It chimed with what Luke had said, about trusting their daughter more. Maybe if she had trusted Lizzie and started treating her like a young woman instead of a snotty teenager, given her more responsibility instead of less, she and Aldo's relationship wouldn't have been so fractious these past few years.

'Lizzie doesn't hate me, but I know someone who does.' Aldo's matter-of-fact comment cut neatly into Halle's guilt trip.

'Who?'

'My dad.' His whisky-coloured eyes, so like her own, suddenly seemed much older than ten years. 'That's why he never wanted to see me, isn't it?'

Blood slammed into her heart.

Unable to bear the blank acceptance in Aldo's gaze, the answer came to her. Why not tell him Claudio was dead? Then he'd never have to know the truth. Claudio didn't hate him. It was worse than that. Claudio didn't even care he existed. How could you tell a ten-year-old that and not expect them to be devastated? Especially a ten-year-old like Aldo, whose confidence had taken so many knocks in recent years.

The urge to tell her son anything that would make the pain of rejection go away was as strong as it had ever been. He was just a child—the wadded-up piles of dirty socks stuck at the end of his bed, the comics strewn all over the floor, the hamster rattling its cage as it sprinted to nowhere

on its wheel, the piles of Yu-Gi-Oh! cards neatly stacked on his desk, probably in order of greatest hit points or something, the smell of bubblegum that lingered in the room were all testament to that.

But as she opened her mouth, swearing to herself this would be her final white lie, Aldo said, 'Is it because I did all that bad stuff at school? Is that why he doesn't like me? Could you tell him I'm much better now? And I don't do that stuff much any more?'

And the lie died on her tongue.

'Oh, Aldo.' She dragged him into her arms and hugged him hard. The guilt all but destroying her at the eagerness, the hope in his tone.

How could she have gotten things so wrong? By not telling him the truth, by almost lying to him again, she'd made him believe her mistakes and Claudio's character flaws were somehow his fault.

He struggled out of her arms, his expression earnest and confused. 'It's all right, Mum, don't cry. What are you sad about?'

She scrubbed the errant tears away. 'I'm not sad. I'm emotional. Because I've just realised how amazing my son is.'

'Really?' He wrinkled his nose in astonishment, making her realise that while she may have told him that a hundred times, she'd never made him believe it.

'Yes, really. Do you want me to tell you about your dad?'

He nodded, the eagerness still there. She hated that she would have to crush his hope, but there were much worse things than not having a relationship with your father. And one of them was having a father as selfish and self-absorbed as Claudio in your life, or one who was a violent alcoholic, like Brian Best.

The thought brought with it thoughts of Luke, a man who

had been terrified of becoming a father and yet had risen to the challenge despite his fear. She pushed the thought to the back of her mind.

Don't start getting overemotional about Luke again, or you'll start blubbing like your namesake, Halle Berry, on Oscar night and never get this done.

'Your dad, your biological father,' she corrected, because Claudio had never deserved to be anyone's dad, 'is called Claudio Benedetti. He's Italian. And we weren't going out for very long when I discovered I was going to have you.'

'Did he know about me?'

She gulped past the huge lump blocking her throat. 'Yes, he knew I was pregnant. And he did meet you once, when you were a tiny baby.'

She sucked in another breath and soldiered on. She'd had ten years to get ready for this. Why the hell wasn't she much better prepared? Winging it had become her forte on the show, but never in her private life.

Then she remembered what Luke had said. The nerves didn't show on screen.

Come on, Halle, you can do this.

'But he decided he didn't want to be a father. Even though he was one. That was his decision, because he's a selfish immature man, and it's his loss, because you are such a terrific kid. And he'll never know how terrific.'

She braced for more questions, ones that might be impossible to answer. But Aldo sat for a moment without speaking, clearly contemplating everything she'd said, then he shrugged. 'OK.'

'OK?' She'd been terrified of having this conversation for ten years. Could it really be that painless? 'Are you sure?'

'Well, my dad sounds like a dickhead. But Trey said he

never met his dad and he was glad, because he thinks his dad was probably a dickhead.'

Perfectly put, Trey. Why didn't I think of that?

'Trey's right,' she agreed. Apparently, she had even more to thank Aldo's au pair for than she'd realised. Whatever had been going on between Lizzie and him on the couch, she hoped Lizzie had managed to contact him. '"Dickhead" sums up Claudio perfectly,' she added.

'You said "dickhead".' Aldo sniggered, both scandalised and excited.

'I know, but sometimes you just have to call a dickhead, a dickhead.'

He giggled some more, clearly delighted with his mother's newly acquired Tourette's. The uninhibited chuckle reminded Halle of when he was a baby and Lizzie would blow on his tummy to hear that distinctive belly laugh.

Maybe her children hadn't changed nearly as much as she'd thought.

'I love you to bits.' She tousled his hair and planted a smacking kiss on his cheek. 'You do know that, right?'

'Yuck.' He backhanded his face, wiping away her kiss as if he'd just been slimed by a ten-foot slug. Then rolled his eyes dramatically, a picture of ten-year-old mortification.

'Duh, Mum. Of course I know *that*.'

Chapter 23

'Any luck contacting Trey?' Halle asked as she closed Lizzie's bedroom door behind her.

Her daughter shook her head, her expression hopeless, as she threw her phone down on the bed. 'No, his mobile keeps going to voicemail.'

Halle sat down on the bed beside her daughter and patted her knee. 'How about you, Aldo and I go round to see him?'

Lizzie's eyes lit with gratitude and she hugged Halle round the waist. 'Can we? Really?' She paused, then peered up at Halle. 'So you're not mad at us?'

'Why would I be mad?'

'Because we were snogging on the couch.'

Hmm, well, there is that.

'I'm not mad, but…' She pushed Lizzie's hair behind her ear, waited for her daughter to sit up. 'I'd like to know exactly what is going on between you two. Have you been sleeping together?'

The blush fired up Lizzie's neck and she scowled. 'God, Mum!' she whined, sounding more like the teenager Halle remembered.

'Honey, I'm entitled to ask. I just wanted to know if we

have to take another trip down to the family planning clinic.'
And if she had to have some serious words with them both.

Lizzie jumped off the bed, looking horrified now. 'Mum,
stop it. You're embarrassing me.'

'Then you really shouldn't neck on the kitchen couch.'
She smiled at her daughter's mortification, deciding to take
the blazing red cheeks as a no. 'First thing on a Thursday
morning. Where your father and I can find you. Frankly, I
was a little embarrassed, too. What you were doing looked
rather—' she hesitated, deciding to spare Lizzie's blushes,
despite her amusement '—involved.'

'It *was* involved. But that's as far as we've gone.' Lizzie
flopped back down on the bed, sounding distinctly disappointed. So clearly the not-sleeping-together hadn't been
Lizzie's idea. 'I think I probably just caught Trey at a really
weak moment, though. His mother just died yesterday and
he was cut up about it. Plus, he was still half asleep and I
practically jumped him.'

'He didn't look like he was objecting much to me.'

Lizzie's blush flared anew, but she looked more pleased
than mortified at the observation.

'But more to the point,' Halle said, 'when did all this
happen? Because, as I recall, you were rather antagonistic
towards Trey before I left.'

'That's only because I had a massive crush on him.'

'I see.'

'He's such a wonderful guy, Mum. He's so much more
mature and responsible than any of the other guys I know.
He really cares about people, and he doesn't try to be cool,
he just is cool. And…' She grinned at Halle, her flushed
cheeks warming to the subject. 'He *is* super hot.'

The dreamy tone reminded Halle of her own infatuation with Luke at Lizzie's age. She pushed aside yet more

thoughts of Luke. At least Trey was older and clearly not as
screwed up as Luke had been. But even so…

'I thought he told me his mother was dead,' she said, still
struggling to get the events of the past twelve days straight
in her head.

Lizzie looked at her feet. 'He was worried you wouldn't
hire him if you knew. She's been in a hospice for months,
and she's been sick for years.'

'I see.'

'You're not mad at him, are you, Mum?'

Well, he had lied, but she'd done a few of those white lies
herself and she could see now he'd been very vulnerable.
And she'd put him on the spot by asking him to move in
without even realising it. Plus, it sounded as if he'd been
super honourable with Lizzie, despite their couch clinch.
'No, I'm not mad at him. But I do think I need to have a
little talk with him.'

'You're not going to fire him, are you?'

'That would be up to all three of us, and him. I think
Aldo would be devastated if he leaves. But I'm not going
to pretend that it wouldn't be uncomfortable to have him
here looking after Aldo and knowing that the two of you
are an item.'

'But we're not really an item.'

'Are you sure?'

'I'd like us to be an item. I'm not going to lie, but I care
about him, Mum. Much more than I ever did for Liam and I
guess it would be better for him if we cooled it for a bit. You
know, he's dealing with all this stuff with his mum dying,
and I think Dad punching him in the face probably didn't
help much. Trey takes stuff really seriously. He'll probably
think it's all his fault that Dad punched him. I don't want
him to feel bad.'

'It sounds like you've given this a lot of thought.' *And been super mature about it, too,* Halle thought, her admiration for her daughter increasing. Lizzie was putting Trey's needs first, and while this might just be puppy love, it still showed a level of maturity that she had never managed with Luke at Lizzie's age.

There's that bitch hindsight again, come back to bite me.

Lizzie nodded, her face sober. 'I have. I've had a lot of time to think over the past week or so. Getting to know Trey, making things up a bit with Aldo, and I've realised I've been a total bitch for a while now. I don't want to be that person any more.'

'Lizzie, you're not a bitch.'

'If you say so, Mum.' Lizzie sent her a look that said, *Yes, I am, but it's nice of you not to rub it in.* 'Can I ask you a question?'

Halle nodded. 'Of course.'

'What *was* Dad doing here?'

'Ahhh.'

'Don't lie. Please.'

'I won't,' she said, but she didn't defend herself against the accusation. Clearly, Lizzie had known as well as Aldo that she had not been entirely truthful in her dealings with them. How humiliating to get caught out by your kids. 'I may have been a bit, shall we say, economical with the truth about where I've been the past twelve days.'

'You mean you lied.'

You are so busted, lady. 'Yes, I lied.'

'So where were you?'

'Would you believe with your father in a log cabin in Tennessee at an extreme couples' retreat?'

'No way.' Lizzie couldn't have looked more shocked if

Halle had just announced she'd flown to Jupiter to marry an alien.

'There was hiking and kayaking involved.' Halle shuddered. 'So yes, way.'

'Why?'

Because he blackmailed me into it. The easy answer very nearly came out of her mouth. But she knew that wasn't the whole truth any more. Not even half of the truth really. And after sixteen years, Lizzie deserved to finally hear the whole truth.

Luke had been right about that, too.

'Because we had a lot of stuff to sort out between us. Stuff that I've allowed to fester for sixteen years. He wants to be a much bigger part of your life.' Why hadn't she realised that was what this had really been all about all along? The hot-tub sex, the soul-searching, probably even the Monroe article had all been a by-product. 'And he couldn't see a way to do that when I wouldn't talk to him about you.'

She had thought of contacting Jamie to see if what Luke had said was true, that he'd tried to change the terms of the custody agreement in recent years and Jamie hadn't informed her. But, on careful consideration, she knew it was true. She'd been very clear with Jamie that she wanted to have no contact with Luke. That Jamie was supposed to handle everything without involving her, so that was just what he'd done. He was a solicitor, not a marriage guidance counsellor. And, anyway, he'd tried to tell her Luke wasn't such a bad guy in his office, as soon as she found out about the memoirs, and she'd refused to listen.

'But why didn't Dad just ask me?' Lizzie said. 'I've been able to see him whenever I want since I was sixteen.'

'I know, but I think he was worried he'd be putting you in the middle if he asked you without getting me onside first.'

And how could she not have realised that, either. That while she'd been shutting him out, Luke had been putting their daughter's welfare first.

'But, Mum, how could you spend all that time in Tennessee with him when you hate him?'

The matter-of-fact statement had the last of Halle's hope dying, that maybe Lizzie had never been aware of her anger towards Luke.

'I don't hate him.' *And I probably never did.* 'And I'm sorry that I made you think that.' Did she love him? She pushed the thought back.

Not about you. This is about your daughter, and all the lies and half-truths you've told, the secrets you've kept, to protect yourself from hurt while refusing to admit that you were hurting her.

'We actually had a good time while we were in Tennessee. We cleared the air and... There was a lot of stuff that happened years ago, before you were born and when you were little, that we needed to deal with. And we did.' And they had done a lot of other stuff besides, which their eighteen-year-old daughter would never know about.

'What stuff?' Lizzie asked.

Halle felt her cheeks getting warm. 'It's a long story.'

'I'm not going anywhere,' Lizzie prompted. 'Please tell me, Mum.' She played with the quilt cover, clearly torn about asking. 'I've always wanted to know what happened between you and Dad, but neither of you ever wanted to speak about it.'

Because we've been cowards, both of us.

Luke had admitted as much back at the resort. Now it was her turn to do the same.

Slinging her arm round Lizzie's shoulders, she hugged her tight. 'OK, well, I guess I should start at the beginning.

The first time I spoke to your father, he was sixteen, I was fifteen and we were in a drama class together. He told me I caught like a girl and I believe I called him a sexist snot-bag.'

Lizzie choked out a laugh. 'Go on, this sounds like it might be pretty funny.'

'You have no idea,' Halle said wryly.

*   *   *

It took almost an hour, during which Aldo came in twice scavenging for food, and Trey finally sent Lizzie a two-line text, which simply read:

I'm at home, I'm fine & I'm really sorry. Pls tell yr Mum I'm sorry 2.

Even so, Lizzie stayed riveted to the story, at turns inquisitive, sad, surprised and delighted. Some of it she had known, but most of it she hadn't. Halle didn't tell her everything, skating over the truth about how Lizzie had been conceived—she doubted her daughter had ever been an Oasis fan—and the more traumatic details of Luke's childhood or the full scope of his breakdown in the Gare du Nord. That would be Luke's story to tell. But it did occur to her as she was tiptoeing through the details that if Luke had been there as they had originally arranged, those bits would have been much easier.

She'd also avoided any mention of all the make-up sex… Because it wasn't relevant any more. And no eighteen-year-old, no matter how mature, wanted to hear intimate details about her parents' sex life.

By the end of the story, Halle was exhausted. Reliving her history with Luke, with his perspective now added into the mix, had been like going on a roller-coaster ride, those huge peaks and devastating dips both shockingly dramatic

and also painfully inevitable. She'd never been a big fan of roller coasters; they'd always made her nauseous even as a teenager. And, in many ways, this metaphorical one was no different. But as she finished off the story and saw Lizzie's rapt expression, the bone-deep relief she felt went some way to calm the huge swell of emotion rising up in her stomach.

At least she could finally step off the roller coaster and step away from the emotional burdens of her past. Unfortunately, that didn't help much with handling the emotional burdens of her present.

'So you did love him once?' Lizzie said, sounding awestruck.

'Yes, I did. I loved him very much.' She'd questioned that so many times in the years since, even in the past twelve days. Maybe it hadn't been the forever type of love. Neither of them had been ready for that then; they'd been far too young. But still it felt good not to have to hate her romantic, optimistic sixteen-year-old self any more for falling so fast and so thoroughly for that troubled, traumatised seventeen-year-old boy. What disturbed her now, though, was the realization that mature, sensible, pragmatic Halle may well have done the same damn thing all over again.

'So what happens now?' Lizzie asked.

'Well...' Halle brushed her hands down her jeans. 'I'd like to have a shower and change my clothes, and then I think we should head over to Trey's place and make sure he's really OK.' It was something they'd already agreed to do when his text had come through.

Lizzie sent her a sideways look. 'I meant what happens to you and Dad.'

'Nothing happens to me and your dad,' she said nonchalantly, determined to ignore the great gaping hole opening

up in her chest. 'Except that we get to start over as your parents and get on your case as a united front.'

One thing they must not do, she decided, was let their latest bust-up close the lines of communication again. But somehow she didn't think that would be a problem. Luke had seemed resigned, not bitter, when he'd left. Unfortunately, that observation only made the hollow ache more painful.

'Really, Mum? Is that all you want? Because when you were talking about Dad just now, it sounded like there might be more.'

Halle shook her head, determined not to put any of this stuff on her daughter. Lizzie was their child, she was still a teenager, she wasn't Halle's confidante. She couldn't put her in the middle of all this and expect her to understand. But as she opened her mouth to deny it, to stick to her conviction that whatever had been developing with Luke, it would never have worked, the breaker rose up and crashed over inside her.

'Bloody hell.' Her shoulders began to shake, her vision blurred, the swell breaking like a tsunami and sweeping away everything in its path.

Lizzie's arm came round her shoulders. 'Why are you crying, Mum?'

'I think I've done something really idiotic.' She scrubbed the tears away with an impatient hand, but more tears just kept coming, the sadness overwhelming her again as her daughter's arm tightened.

'Which is?' Lizzie asked.

'I've fallen in love with him again.' She sighed, the breath backing up in her lungs.

Good God, don't you dare start sobbing now.

'Ignore that,' she said. 'I'm being ridiculous. It's just the

pressure, that's all. It can't be true. I can't possibly be in love with him. Not after twelve days.'

Any more than he could possibly be in love with me.

'Why are you trying to argue yourself out of it? Being in love's not a bad thing, you know.'

She looked round to find Lizzie smiling at her, the grin on her face so sweet and so pleased and so sure.

Oh, baby, it's so much simpler when you're young.

'I know he can be a total idiot at times,' Lizzie continued. 'But he's a guy, so you've got to make allowances for that,' she added, the hope and encouragement in her expression not doing much to calm the churning waves still buffeting Halle. 'But he's mostly a pretty terrific dad. And I bet he'd make a pretty terrific boyfriend if you gave him half a chance.'

Halle sniffed and coughed out a half laugh, unsure whether to be mortified or just impossibly touched that she was now getting dating advice from her daughter.

And not really having a clue where she was going to go from here.

Well, whatever happens next, one thing's for sure. Luke Best has managed to turn me into a complete basket case again.

Chapter 24

'OK, guys, we're here. According to his CV, Trey lives at number 6A.'

Lizzie's stomach bounced at her mum's overly bright tone as they parked in front of the narrow Victorian terrace. Lizzie noted the peeling paint on the plasterwork, the rusted bike buried in the long grass of the communal front garden and the broken gate that led down to the basement flat, which had burglar bars on the front window.

She'd never given any thought to where Trey might live, but it was hard not to notice the massive gulf between the immaculate grandeur of her family's six-million-pound Georgian house in Notting Hill and this run-down building located in the un-gentrified end of Kensal Rise, which had probably been split into council flats a generation ago, and hadn't seen much work done on it since.

Her guilt over initiating their kiss that morning multiplied a few thousand times.

It had been impulsive and immature and selfish. Trey needed this job. And she'd put him in a tough position, jumping him the way she had.

Aldo hopped out of the car. He skipped from foot to foot,

as if he had a thousand Mexican jumping beans down his pants. 'I'm gonna go ring his bell.'

'Aldo, wait!' Her mum managed to grab his sleeve before he could race off. She peered back across the driver's seat at Lizzie, keeping a firm grip on Aldo's arm.

'Lizzie needs to talk to him first,' her mum said, the look of total faith in her eyes warming Lizzie from the inside.

'But I want to see him, too,' Aldo whined.

'We'll speak to him in a bit,' her mum said. 'But Lizzie has things she needs to say to him first that you might not want to hear.'

'Kissing stuff?' Aldo gagged on the horror of it.

Her mum's lips quirked. 'Possibly.'

Lizzie smiled at Aldo's forceful 'yuck'. Her stomach muscles twisted uncomfortably, though, as she climbed out of the car.

This was likely to be the hardest conversation she'd ever had in her life. And she wasn't sure she could pull it off. Her track record when it came to having mature and sensible conversations pretty much sucked.

Her mum gripped her hand. 'Do you need any advice?'

Lizzie nodded, realising she wanted her mum's advice more than anything.

'Be honest with him. However hard that is.' She squeezed her fingers and then let go. 'Take as long as you need. Aldo and I will wait in the car till you're ready for us.'

'Thanks, Mum.'

Lizzie headed down the basement steps to Trey's front door, tuning out Aldo's cry of protest as their mum loaded him back into the car.

She pressed the bell and heard it buzz loudly inside the flat. The blinds on the bay window were drawn, so she couldn't see in. Maybe he wasn't at home any more.

The thought of a reprieve didn't make her stomach settle, though. Then she heard the sound of footsteps and the click of the latch. And her stomach went into free fall.

Trey appeared in the doorway. His eyebrows leaped up his forehead, his expression not happy or horrified, just stunned. 'Lizzie, what are you doing here?'

'Hi, my mum's waiting in the car.' She jerked her thumb over her shoulder. 'With Aldo, because all three of us wanted to make sure you're really OK, after what happened this morning. And we all wanted you to know that we want you to come back to work. Not today, obviously, just when you're ready.' She was starting to babble, but she didn't care. Babbling was better than being struck dumb. 'But I wanted to talk to you first because…I have some apologising to do.'

The heat in her face had hit boiling point, so she was glad to see that beneath his olive-toned skin, his face had gone a spectacular shade of magenta, too.

'A *lot* of apologising to do really,' she added.

'No, you don't,' he said, the words firm and succinct, as she noticed the reddened swelling at the side of his mouth and the nasty gash in his lip. 'I'm the one who needs to apologise.' He glanced past her. 'To your mum, and Aldo and your dad…' His eyes locked back on hers. 'But most of all to you. What I did was totally inappropriate. Jesus.' He ran an exasperated hand through his hair, sending the short strands into cute tufts. 'I still can't believe I was kissing you like that on your mum's sofa! Your dad should have hit me a lot harder.'

Her heart ticked into her throat. God, keeping her hands off him was going to be even tougher than she thought. He was so stupidly gallant, and totally adorable. But beneath the

surge of love—and lust—was the new and heady feeling of confidence.

Trey being Trey, of course he was taking all the responsibility for the scene this morning. She'd have to set him straight on that score. Because, seriously, did he really think that kiss had been his idea?

But how come she'd never realised before how much power she had? Using that power for good instead of evil was going to make life tough for a while. Not least because she now knew exactly how awesome Trey and his kissing skills were.

But when had anything good, anything worthwhile, ever been easy? And did she really want it to be? She'd recently discovered, not just from Trey, but from what her mum had told her about her and her dad's relationship, that real grown-up relationships were tough to negotiate for a very good reason. They involved two people whose needs and desires, whose hopes and dreams, all had to be met. Dancing through that minefield successfully without blowing your foot off en route was never going to be easy.

But at least she and Trey would be dancing through the minefield together. And if it was going to take much longer than planned to get to the other side, who cared? Because it was how they got there that mattered.

'Trey.' Her heart swelled into her throat at his earnest expression. 'I know we're going to have to cool it when you come back to work. Because it would make my mum super uncomfortable if she caught us kissing like that again. And Aldo would probably have a breakdown.' And the chances of them being able to stop at kissing were iffy at best. And the last thing she wanted to do was make his life harder.

'Yeah, I know,' he said, the magenta on his cheeks darkening.

'But before the no-kissing rule takes effect...' Lifting on tiptoes, she held his cheeks in her palms. 'I want you to know, you're the best kisser I've ever met, and I'm completely bonkers about you.'

She pressed her lips lightly to his, mindful of his swollen mouth, keeping the kiss tender, and chaste, but filling it with all the affection she felt.

His hands settled on her waist, making her feel ridiculously cherished.

'Same,' he murmured as they parted.

Her heart soared.

The shy smile he sent her turned to a wince as he touched his fingers to his split lip. 'Ouch.'

She laughed and took his hand. 'Come on, we better go talk to my mum and Aldo, before Aldo explodes.'

After she had led him up the outside stairs to the car and watched Aldo nearly knock him flat, she shared a secret smile with her mum.

She hadn't messed up. And she would do everything in her power not to mess up in the future. Because she was the Trey Whisperer now.

Chapter 25

'The most important thing is not to over-whip the cream.' Halle scooped the fragrant Baileys-scented cream onto the thin base of chocolate sponge, aware of the camera panning in for a close-up. 'Because as much as we all love butter, cream is always preferable in your chocolate roulade.'

She let the babble effect take over as she scored the sponge at one end and wound the roulade in a perfect pinwheel twirl of chocolate, cream and Christmas indulgence.

After another close-up, the director yelled 'Cut' in her earpiece. The studio silence turned into industrious noise as the crew sprang into action to get ready for the re-set.

Della, the hair and make-up girl, rushed over wielding her powder puff. 'Just a quick dab to get the shine.'

'Is it just me or are the lights especially hot today?' Halle remarked as Della powdered her nose and forehead and then whipped her trusty comb out of the tool belt hung round her waist and began arranging the wayward strands of Halle's updo.

She smiled at Halle. 'That's the problem with doing your Christmas Special at the beginning of August.' She spread her arm, indicating the array of ornately wrapped

presents with nothing inside them dressing the counter of the country kitchen they were using for the shoot. 'It feels so wrong.'

Halle took a steadying breath, trying to tune out the sound of Bill, the floor manager, directing the two cameramen for their next shot. A runner arrived holding a finished and dressed chocolate roulade aloft, which had been made to Halle's specific recipe in the prep kitchen next door. He placed it on the antique table the props people had dressed beside the towering beribboned Christmas tree in the farmhouse's front parlour.

Halle flicked through the script in preparation for her final piece to camera while Della continued fussing with her hair, knowing she'd probably forget the lot as soon as she started speaking and end up winging it as usual.

Christmas in August was a hazard of her job, especially with her new book, *The Best Family Christmas*, due out in October. They needed to get a jump on her Christmas Special so they could access edited clips and release them on YouTube to publicise the book launch.

'Perfect,' Della remarked, assessing her work. 'You're good to go.' The make-up girl clasped Halle's hand. 'It's going to be another hit. You look lush.'

Halle smiled, her nerves a lot steadier than usual despite being in the midst of a take. Because performing for a TV camera had one indisputable advantage. By heaping on pressure in the here and now, the pressure to perform professionally and entertainingly on the director's cue and not curdle her whipped cream, the one thing she didn't have time to do was think about Luke.

It had been two weeks now since their return from Tennessee. Two weeks since he'd walked out of her kitchen door, and although they'd had a few stilted email conversations

about Lizzie—and their daughter's momentous decision to apply to art college in Paris—that had been the sum total of their communication.

And it was killing her.

She missed him. She wanted to see him. To chat and tease and, OK, yes, she might as well admit it, to lick along the line of his happy trail until his belly muscles quivered.

She needed his relaxed, much more pragmatic approach to relationships, and parenthood, his ego-boosting advice, not to mention the chance to gaze at that buff body, in various states of dishabille. And know that it was hers, to do with as she wished.

But every time she'd come close to picking up the phone, on those nights at home after Aldo was in bed and she could hear Lizzie saying goodbye to Trey at the door, their conversation muffled and confidential and full of that unstated sexual tension that hummed in the air between them, she'd stopped herself.

He'd given her an ultimatum, a stupid false ultimatum that had been entirely unnecessary. Between him and her kids. She could see now that she'd blown the whole punch-gate incident out of proportion. Trey had come back to work a week later, the day after they'd all attended his mother's cremation in the imposing surroundings of Kensal Green Cemetery. Despite the hollow exhaustion wrought by grief, Trey appeared unharmed by Luke's unprovoked attack and eager to return to work. Even his lip had healed.

Luke had also contacted Lizzie and invited her to visit him in Paris in a couple of weeks to check out colleges. Lizzie had accepted the invitation enthusiastically and, from what Halle could gather, not a lot of grovelling had been involved. Even Aldo seemed to have forgiven Luke, peppering her with a load more questions about Lizzie's

dad, all of which had been curious and keen rather than resentful.

But even so, Halle couldn't bring herself to make the first move. And she knew, deep down, it had nothing to do with punch-gate, or the ultimatum or her children's reaction to him. Deep down it had to do with trust and accountability and equality in their relationship. And all those boring things she'd ignored the first time she'd fallen so heavily for Luke.

She'd always been the one to make the first move. The one to make the most compromises. Because she'd always loved him more than he had loved her. Or that was how it had felt at the time. She knew now there had been tangible reasons for that. That Luke as he was at seventeen, at twenty even, had been incapable of trusting anyone enough to love them fully and openly with no holding back because of the hideous insecurities of his childhood. But that didn't alter the fact she couldn't be the one to do the chasing again.

If she was, she would feel compromised—maybe not now, maybe not even in a month's time, but the inequality would be a part of their relationship again. She had to be able to trust him fully and completely. She had to know that he cared enough about her to put in the effort to make this work. And she couldn't have that if she was the one who made the first move.

In some ways, it might seem stupid and juvenile, a layover from their past. A tit-for-tat form of one-upmanship. But that was the way she felt. He'd told her he wanted more. But if he had really meant that, if he had really wanted to try, surely he could have contacted her and asked her again, properly.

Unfortunately, the only problem with Halle's Last Stand was that it required Luke to make the first move. And, after two whole weeks of virtually no contact, she was beginning

to believe that she would be waiting around forever. Much as she had done once before.

As they shot the final set-up and Halle waxed lyrical about the magical quality of family Christmases, whatever type of family you had, the melancholy of the past fortnight began to overwhelm her. Would she be wrapping presents alone again this Christmas Eve while her kids were in bed? Why did that make her feel bereft, when it never had before?

The director called it a wrap, and she thanked everyone before slipping away as the sound technician, Jeff, started to chop up the three different roulades they'd had baked for the taping to share among the salivating crew.

Clare, the wardrobe girl, handed her a change of clothes as she headed out to the trailer they'd set up for her round the back of the farmhouse in Cambridgeshire. Sweat gathered under the armpits of the heavy velvet dress she'd worn for the Christmas Special as she walked through the farmhouse's kitchen gardens, the sunshine blazing through the orchard of pear and apple trees.

She closed the trailer door and dropped the summer dress wrapped in dry-cleaner's plastic on the small daybed, then crossed to the dressing table. After firing up the kettle, she clicked on her laptop and checked her emails.

Her heart bobbed into her throat as she scrolled through everything that had come in since yesterday and spotted the subject line 'Monroe Article for Review'.

But the flash of hope, of anticipation, died when she realised the email didn't come from Luke, but from his agent, Stan Chalmers.

She opened the email, scanned the contents. The article Luke had written was attached. The article on their couples' retreat in Tennessee. The one he'd promised her he'd give her a chance to review.

The melancholy, which had been sitting like a lump of unleavened dough in her belly for a fortnight, swelled to epic proportions. She grabbed a couple of tissues from the dispenser and blotted the thick camera-friendly mascara to stop it running down her cheeks in rivulets and making her look like a victim of the Black Death.

Bloody hell. How come he can still turn me into a gibbering wreck with one careless act?

She sniffed. But she knew this act wasn't careless. It was deliberate.

It wasn't an act of betrayal. She'd always known he would write this article. That this had been a job for him, first and foremost, not an excuse to take a soggy, fraught trip down memory lane. And end up having too much make-up sex.

But somewhere along the way she'd hoped, stupidly hoped, that what he'd blurted out two weeks ago meant he had become as invested in their future as she had. But, obviously, all that talk about taking things further, doing more than just bonking each other senseless for old times' sake had been just that. Talk. Said on the spur of the moment so she'd let him stay.

And here was the evidence, sitting in an email attachment. An email attachment that he hadn't even been thoughtful enough to send to her himself.

Slowly and methodically, she used the eye make-up remover and then her cleansing creams to remove the pancake foundation and eye gunk that Della had applied four hours ago. She peeled out of her Christmas dress, stepped into the trailer's tiny shower cubicle and had as long a shower as was possible standing under the feeble, lukewarm spray.

After changing into the muslin dress, she brewed herself a cup of mint tea. Then took the laptop, settled on the

trailer's narrow plaid upholstered couch and pressed the download button on the email attachment.

The blue monitor line filled as the article downloaded.

So this was finally the end? Not just of her and Luke and their chances for a future together, but the end of all those foolish hopes that had once burned so brightly between them and, despite all the mistakes, all the hurt, all the anger and all the misconceptions over the past sixteen years, had come out of hiding in Tennessee.

She felt an odd sense of detachment, the melancholy dulled to the low persistent ache of a loss too huge to really comprehend as she clicked on the attachment.

Then she read the opening lines of Luke's article:

When you trash the one relationship in your life that means everything to you, it's human nature to try to find a way to justify that. To make excuses, to push the blame elsewhere, to persuade yourself this relationship was never as important as you thought. Pride, past mistakes, bad luck and even recreational sex can all be brought into play to keep you from acknowledging the incontrovertible truth: that you were the one who trashed it, and you need to be the one to fix it. This is the story of how, during eleven days in Tennessee this summer—with some extreme help from Jackson Monroe's Couples' Resolution Retreat—I finally figured that out...

Twenty minutes later, Halle snorted dramatically into the last of her tissues as she read the final lines.

Monroe's retreat is based on what appears to be a simplistic, completely unscientific and apparently

entirely intuitive method. And obviously there's no guarantee it will work for everyone. But if it can make someone like myself realise the magnitude of what he's chucked away not once, but quite possibly twice, and bare all in an article in Vanity Fair, *it's got a lot to offer those of us who are dumb as a rock.*

I just hope to hell it didn't work its magic on me too late.

Wiping her eyes with the wadded-up tissue, Halle grabbed blindly for her mobile phone and keyed in a message to her PA.

Mel, I need to get from Cambridge to Paris, TODAY.

Then she texted her daughter.

Lizzie, can u & Troy hold the fort this evening? I'm making a flying visit 2 Paris 2 proposition ur father!!

She laughed delightedly when Lizzie's reply popped onto her phone two seconds later accompanied by a pair of clapping hands surrounded by confetti.

OMG! Way TMI Mum!?! But g4i! xoxo

Chapter 26

Luke scribbled a note on his pad, propped the pen behind his ear, then carried on typing, inhaling the fragrance of freshly baked filou, strong coffee and the acrid echo of a thousand cigarettes that still clung to the wooden booths in Café Hugo despite the smoking ban introduced in 2008.

He came here often to work, the quiet of his apartment somehow much more disturbing than the chattering hum of other people's conversations, the clatter of cutlery and crockery, the light slap of shoe leather on marble tiling as the waiters hurried past with trays of patisseries. Of course, he'd been here even more often than usual in the past two weeks. Ever since returning from London and the Punch-Up at Halle's Kitchen Corral.

Because in the past fourteen days, the silence in his apartment had become unbearable.

He gulped down another shot of the cooling coffee and eased back in the booth. Before clicking away from the document he was working on—an 'Insider's Guide to the Hidden Treasures of the Marais' for *National Geographic* magazine—to check his emails. For about the two millionth time in the past eighteen hours.

He cursed as the two new messages turned out to be a subscription circular and some spam about Russian mail-order brides.

Just what I need—a hook-up with Olga from Omsk—to turn my personal life completely to shit.

He deleted the messages, flagging Olga as spam so his damn filter could stop doubling as the demon matchmaker from hell, then stared at his empty inbox.

Eighteen hours since he'd poured out his heart in a magazine article, in one last desperate attempt to make amends for all his mistakes, both old and new. And no word from Halle.

So that was it, then. She'd finally washed her hands of him. Of them. Who could blame her? He flexed the stiff fingers of his right hand, still feeling the phantom ache in his knuckles that had healed over a week ago.

Unfortunately, there was no way to heal what he'd done. Not just charging into her home and behaving like a lunatic—his fingers curled into a fist, or rather behaving like his old man, and smashing his fist into some poor kid's jaw because of his own shortcomings as a parent. But also issuing that nutjob ultimatum.

He could have waited. He should have waited, for Halle to talk to the kids. But instead of behaving like a grown-up, he'd panicked and tried to put Halle on the spot. All those insecurities from his childhood had risen up to strangle his sense of proportion, not to mention the self-awareness that had been forged in fire after his breakdown, years of therapy and eleven life-changing days in the Smoky Mountains.

He rested the back of his head on the booth and examined the yellowed cornice on the ceiling.

No wonder she no longer wanted to have anything to

do with him. Some soul-searching, lots of extreme sports activities, too much hot-tub sex and a heartfelt article for *Vanity Fair* wasn't going to atone for the never-ending list of fuck-ups he'd subjected her to over the years.

Especially if he kept right on fucking up.

He heard the tap of heels approaching the booth but ignored them to click back on his work document. Probably just one of the waitstaff come to refill his coffee cup.

'Merci,' he murmured, not bothering to look up as the girl stopped by his booth.

But instead of filling the cup, the waitress slid into the booth opposite him. His head came up, and he blinked to try to dispel the apparition sitting across from him.

Halle smiled back at him, her cheeks flushed, her soft blonde hair secured in that habitual knot and her magnificent cleavage displayed temptingly above the bodice of a snug summer dress emblazoned with mutant sunflowers.

'Hello, Luke,' said the apparition.

He groaned. He was having some sort of psychic freak-out brought on by weariness and stress and bone-deep regret. But he had no clue how to stop it.

'Hi, Halle,' he replied, deciding to humour it. And himself. If delusions were the only way he could carry on a conversation with her, then he'd take them.

His gaze tracked down to her cleavage and the plump flesh that he'd explored at his leisure in Tennessee. Blood pulsed into his groin and he wondered vaguely, exactly how psychotic you had to be to get a boner from a hallucination.

As if in slow motion, she lifted a dark leather purse and pulled out an iPad. She placed the tablet on the table, keyed in the code, then turned it the other way up and slid it across to him until he could read the standfirst of his *Vanity Fair* article on it.

Cool, so far, so totally certifiable.

'I thought I should come and tell you in person,' Dream Halle said, sounding super-real now and making him doubt his sanity even more. 'I'm not going to let you publish a word of this.' Damn, he could even smell that delicious floral scent of summer flowers and vanilla essence. As hallucinations went, this one was actually pretty hot.

He nodded, still in a trance. 'You hated it, then?'

He would have been embarrassed by the quiver of vulnerability in his voice. But hell, this was a delusion. And it was his delusion. So what did it matter what it thought of him? Real Halle had already dumped him for the last time, so why not let Dream Halle pick through the pieces?

She shook her head, the movement making a curl of hair escape her updo and bob down to bounce on her shoulder. He resisted the urge to capture it and let the gossamer silk wind itself round his finger. He didn't want to shatter the illusion. Not yet.

'I didn't hate it,' she said, her smile spreading across her full lips and making the heat and the gratitude throb harder in his crotch. 'I loved it. Almost as much as I love you.'

He did a mental fist pump, his heart galloping at the seductive sincerity in her words.

Way. To. Go. Best hallucination EVAH.

But then her smile quirked, the twinkle of ironic amusement in those golden eyes dimming his euphoria.

'But I've been in agony for two weeks,' the illusion said. 'Why the hell didn't you contact me sooner, you stupid snot-bag?'

He frowned, watching the tear slip along her lid and hang in her lashes to sparkle in the corner of her eye like crystal.

Hang on a minute. Why was his dream delusion calling him a snot-bag? Couldn't he even go insane properly?

He reached out to lift the tear off her lashes, deciding it was probably time to make Dream Halle vanish before he got towed off to a mental hospital…and the tip of his forefinger connected with warm, soft, solid flesh.

He shot out of the booth, slamming his knee into the tabletop with a resounding thud. Pain ricocheted up his thigh as he swore viciously and his cup went flying. Coffee sprayed over the tablet, his laptop and his notebook as he gaped at the woman in front of him. The woman who had come to mean everything to him. And who he had always believed, deep down, he had never ever truly deserved— but who was sitting in front of him now in all her three-dimensional glory and telling him she loved him.

And he said the first thing that came into his head.

'What the ever-loving fuck? You're actually real?'

* * *

'Last time I checked.' Halle laughed at the look of utter shock on Luke's face. Luke's gorgeous, handsome, deliciously scruffed and completely astonished face. She grabbed a couple of napkins from the table dispenser and blotted the flow of spilled coffee before it could drip onto the floor. 'You might want to rescue your laptop,' she remarked, hearing the sizzle of firing circuits as she wiped the splatter off her iPad.

He glanced at the expensive MacBook Air, which had taken the brunt of the spillage. 'Sod that.' He grasped her arm and hauled her out of the booth. 'I can replace a laptop. I can't replace you.'

He folded his arms around her, apparently not caring about the coffee-soaked napkin in her fist that dripped down his shirt. Cradling her cheek, his gaze lifted to her chignon, then focused on her lips. 'It's really you? You're really here?' he said, the catch in his voice, the quiver of uncertainty

even more beautiful than the adoration reflected in those pale blue eyes.

'Yes, I'm really here,' she murmured, finding it hard to get the words out round her elation. 'By the way, I wanted to ask you, what happened to the exposé you were going to write on Monroe's retreat?' she teased, knowing that he'd used the article to speak to her directly, in the only way he knew how.

Lizzie had been right. He was an amazing writer. His article had ripped her apart and then put her back together again. Foolishly he'd taken all the blame for their bust-up, done far too much grovelling and generally proved how much he wanted to make this work. And made her realise that they were equals now, that whatever happened next, they would be going into this together. As adults who knew each other's flaws, each other's weaknesses, but loved each other more because of them.

His mouth tipped up in a lopsided grin. 'It's kind of tough to write an exposé on a method that actually worked.'

'Ah, yes, fair point.' She grinned back at him, her heart swelling until it closed off her air supply.

'I guess I'm going to have to write that bloody puff piece I promised him, after all,' he said, the mock regret making her heartbeat race up to warp speed. 'Even though it goes against every one of my journalistic instincts.'

Dropping the sopping tissue, she curled her wet fingers round the back of his neck and drew him closer, until their lips were millimetres apart and she could taste the coffee and the desire on his breath. 'I may know a way to make your journalistic instincts feel better about that.'

'Oh, yeah?'

'Uh-huh. But it may require some additional research.'

She dug her fingers into his hair, caressing his scalp as

his arms wrapped around her hips, dragging her against the hard planes of his body. The *very* hard planes of his body.

And then she opened her mouth and captured his thrusting tongue in a soul-stirring, super-hot piece of very important journalistic research.

Epilogue

'Aldo Best, get your butt down here and clean up this crap now,' Luke shouted up the stairs. 'Or there will be consequences.'

He marched back into Halle's basement kitchen and whipped the tea towel off his shoulder to take the roast out, feeling harassed.

Halle was due back from the studio in fifteen minutes and he wanted the place to look good. He had plans for tonight. Important plans. Which didn't involve the kitchen looking like a bloody tornado had hit it.

The tornado in question poked his head round the door two seconds later, the innocent expression on his face not fooling Luke for a second. 'What consequences?' Aldo said.

'Consequences that have yet to be decided…but will be a lot worse for you than me,' Luke said, doing his best to keep his straining temper in check. Aldo liked to test his boundaries, because he knew exactly how important it was to Luke that the two of them get on. And generally they did

get on. They got on really, really well. Almost like a real father and son.

He and Halle had decided to take things slowly the past five months. He'd kept his place in Paris and still spent the weekdays there. Even though they'd soon started stretching his weekends in London to four days, he hated having to head back every Tuesday morning. So they'd agreed a week ago he would hang out in Notting Hill over the whole three weeks of the Christmas holidays and see how things went.

And everything had been going great. Until this morning, when Halle had rushed off to the production offices to record an interview that was being screened before her Christmas Special tomorrow and Trey and Lizzie had shot off to do a ton of last-minute shopping together—which he had a sneaking suspicion was just an excuse for them to flirt their arses off without an audience. He resisted a shudder as he basted the meat. While he'd been left to do a thousand and one chores, including cooking the dinner, and Aldo had taken it upon himself to turn into the child of Satan.

Originally, Luke had made a fuss of the kid for Halle's sake, and Lizzie's sake, and because it made everyone's life easier when he was staying over, but the truth was, now he flat-out adored the little monster.

But even though he'd fallen for the boy months ago, he'd been careful not to push the whole Dad routine. He didn't want to scare the kid off by getting too heavy-handed. They were both still feeling their way, but he knew when he was being dicked around. And he had a feeling they might have reached their Armageddon and he was finally going to have to start putting his foot down. Because today Aldo had gone out of his way to strain his patience to breaking point and beyond.

Aldo's eyes narrowed and he waltzed over to the pile

of Yu-Gi-Oh! cards and Lego strewn all over the sofa and coffee table that he and Trey had been playing with that morning.

Propping his hands on his hips, Aldo declared, 'Why do *I* have to clean it up, when Trey made the mess, too?'

'Because Trey is out Christmas shopping with your sister and you're not.'

Aldo turned, his eyes stormy with antagonism. 'Well, I'm not doing it and you can't make me, because there aren't any consequences.'

Luke slid the roasting tin back into the oven, still holding on to his temper. Just. 'Oh, yeah, well, how about if I told you the consequences are gonna involve me slinging the lot of it in the bin if you don't start clearing it up in the next ten seconds?'

Armageddon it is, then.

Aldo's eyes narrowed to slits. 'Go on, then. See if I care,' he shouted, then drew his leg back and kicked the Harry Potter castle he'd made earlier with all his might. Hogwarts exploded, firing pieces of Lego across the room like a barrage of ground-to-air missiles.

'OK, that's it.' Luke slammed the oven door with a crash, threw down the tea towel and raced after Aldo as the boy shot out of the room as if his pants were on fire.

They soon will be, you little bugger.

He caught up with Aldo on the stairs, jerked him up under his arm and carried him back into the kitchen as the kid kicked and screamed like a banshee.

'Get off me, get off me. I hate you. I'm not doing it.'

Aldo's flying heels connected with Luke's shin. Luke stumbled, limping, as pain rocketed up his leg.

'Shit, that hurt, you little…' He dumped the boy on the

sofa, sat down and grabbed the kid by his T-shirt before he could leap away again, then hauled him over his lap.

He raised his arm, about to lay his hand across Aldo's backside, when the boy's panicked screams cut through the buzzing in Luke's skull, shocking him into immobility.

'You can't tell me what to do. Because you're not my dad and you don't want to be,' Aldo sobbed.

Luke dragged shaking fingers through his hair as the boy's cries turned to big fat heart-wrenching sobs.

He lifted Aldo off his lap and cradled the kid in his arms. 'It's OK, Aldo. I've got you. Let it out.'

Thank Christ he hadn't actually followed through and smacked the child. But even though he hadn't hurt Aldo, he had humiliated him, and he knew that could be just as bad.

Hugging the boy close, Luke let Aldo cling to him until the heaving sobs had quietened into choking pants of misery and vulnerability.

There was only one way to fix this. By coming clean with the boy and laying his feelings on the line. He'd planned to wait to square things with Aldo, until he had everything squared with Aldo's mother, but that was the coward's way out. He couldn't let Halle do all the heavy lifting, because this decision was between him and Aldo and not Aldo's mum.

'I know I'm not your dad,' he said, raising the boy's chin until their gazes met. He pushed the sweaty hair off Aldo's forehead. 'But I want to be, very much.'

Aldo blinked, staring at him out of Halle's whisky-coloured eyes, his tear-streaked face a picture of astonishment. 'You do?' He hiccoughed. 'Really?'

'Yeah, I really do.'

'But why?' Aldo asked, as if he genuinely couldn't figure out why anyone would want to be his father.

Luke blinked, too, getting misty-eyed himself.

Jesus, the kid is killing me.

He could have said all the obvious things. That he'd come to adore the little boy's tenacity, his tough boyish exterior and the tender heart beneath it, so like his mother's. That he wanted to do everything in his power to make them all—all four of them—a family. That he couldn't think of a child who needed a dad more than Aldo. And he couldn't think of anyone better to do the job than someone who wanted to be Aldo's dad as much as he did. But somehow he didn't think any of that would wash as well as one simple truth.

'Because I need someone to play football with if I'm going to live here full-time,' he said. 'And Lizzie's not into playing football much any more. Plus, she's mostly living in Paris these days.'

And when she wasn't, she was way too busy flirting with Trey, he thought but decided not to add.

'I could do that.' Aldo's face split into an eager grin, his eyes sparkling like the fairy lights they'd strung on the Christmas tree together two days before. 'I *love* playing football and I live here all the time, too.'

'I know. That's why I can't think of anyone better to be my son,' Luke said, emotion careering through him. The way it had when he'd first held Lizzie in his arms, when she was a couple of minutes old. 'So the job's yours if you want it,' he added as nonchalantly as he could manage while his throat was aching.

Aldo might be ten, but he would be Luke's kid now, too. A Best in a lot more than name only. If he said yes.

'Would you get angry with me if you were my dad?' Aldo asked, still sounding eager. And although Luke knew he would do his absolute utmost never to lose his temper with

the boy again, he sensed that wasn't what Aldo wanted to hear right now.

'I might,' he said, trying to look grave. 'If you did something as diabolical as you just did again. And I would have to discipline you. But I promise never to spank you.'

'Why?' Aldo said, sounding curious rather than intimidated, which Luke took as a very good sign.

'Because hitting someone doesn't make you right. It just makes you meaner. Especially if you're bigger than they are.' And Luke refused to become his father, no matter how many buttons Aldo pressed, or Harry Potter castles he kicked over.

'But what *would* you do, then?' Aldo asked, intrigued now. 'If I was really naughty?'

'I'd probably ground you, I guess. Or make you go to your room,' he said, making it up as he went along. This was new territory for him, too. He'd never had to discipline Lizzie as a kid, because he had only ever been Super Dad with her, never Everyday Dad. 'Which would be a hell of a pain in the arse for both of us,' he added. 'Because then neither of us would be able to play football.'

Aldo glanced around him at the mess he'd made. 'If I cleaned this up now, would you play football with me after dinner?'

Luke smiled. Damn, the boy drove a hard bargain— especially as they'd have to play in the frostbitten garden in the pitch-dark. 'I would if you were my son.'

Aldo climbed off his lap and started the arduous task of clearing up Harry Potter's decimated castle with undisguised enthusiasm, then said, very nonchalantly, 'OK, Dad.'

Luke's smile burst into what he figured was probably the cheesiest Christmas grin imaginable, even though he felt pretty idiotic.

To think he'd agonised about getting Aldo on-board for weeks, when all he'd ever really had to do was ask.

* * *

He was carving the roast five minutes later, Aldo still picking bits of Lego out of Halle's window pots, when he spotted Halle and Trey and Lizzie all coming down the basement stairs together.

'Look who I found outside,' Halle said as she walked in the door. She raised her eyebrows at Luke in the silent they-were-kissing-again signal the two of them had been using a lot in the past two days, now that Trey and Lizzie were officially an item.

Trey had stopped being Aldo's au pair five days ago. He was going to be starting an access course in January so he could think about going to college with the money his mother had left him in her will. And with Lizzie just back from Paris, where she had started her art course two months back, the two of them had been spending every spare second together.

Luke wasn't comfortable with the situation, but he was doing his best not to go off at the deep end. And Halle was helping out by running interference.

'Yeah, I can just imagine,' he whispered to Halle as he drew her close for a kiss.

'Mmmm, that smells glorious,' she said, smelling pretty glorious herself, her signature scent and the feel of her chilly cheek against his making his stomach muscles go all tight and tingly. 'Watching you carve is such a turn-on,' she added, the naughty twinkle in her eye making him want to forget all about dinner and sling her over his shoulder.

'Mum, Dad, get a room,' Lizzie said, laughing, as Trey helped her out of her coat.

Ever the gallant young suitor, Luke thought, shooting the

guy a cautionary glare as he picked up the carving knife and fork. Trey sent him a level look back, not cowed in the slightest.

The guy was genuine and hard-working, all right, and he'd gone out of his way to be as honourable as possible with Lizzie. But Luke knew honour and integrity took you only so far when twenty-something hormones were involved. So he intended to keep an eye on them both. He couldn't exactly stop the two of them from getting together, he knew that, but that didn't mean he was letting the boy get up to anything on his watch.

'My God, Aldo,' Halle said, tripping over the fairly major mess Aldo had yet to pick up as she went to hang up her coat. 'What happened here? It looks like a Lego–Yu-Gi-Oh! apocalypse.'

Aldo got off his hands and knees and dumped some more of the Lego into the box. Luke stealed himself for what he might say to Halle about the almost-smacking incident. He would have some explaining to do, but he could handle it, now that Aldo and he had come to an understanding. And if everything went as he hoped later on tonight, once he and Halle were alone, Aldo wouldn't just be his responsibility by virtue of that agreement.

'The Harry Potter castle broke,' Aldo said, being very economical with the truth. 'But Dad said he would play football with me if I picked it all up.'

Love and pride blossomed in Luke's chest as Halle's head whipped round and she mouthed the word 'Dad?' to him, looking stunned but happy.

Lizzie and Trey had heard it, too, because Trey was smiling at him and Lizzie had her hand over her mouth, her eyes sheened with emotion.

Luke lifted his eyebrows at all three of them as Aldo began gathering up the Yu-Gi-Oh! cards.

Yeah, that's right, get over it, folks.

'Aldo's correct. My son and I have an important match planned for later,' he said, just as nonchalantly as Aldo. 'But first things first. Lizzie, Trey, you guys set the table.' He began directing the troops. 'And, Hal, stop standing there and crack open some wine. I've had a really bloody exhausting day.'

* * *

Halle hummed her favourite Sam Smith ballad as the hot water pounded tired muscles, a secret smile flitting over her lips the way it had been all evening. Ever since she'd walked into the house two hours ago, after breaking Trey and Lizzie apart from a very hot-looking clinch on the basement stairs, to find Luke carving a delicious roast dinner in the kitchen, and her son… She paused to rinse her hair… *Their* son actually doing what he was told for once.

She sung the first few lines of the chorus in her off-key voice as the happiness engulfed her, steaming up the shower cubicle.

She couldn't wait for Christmas morning tomorrow. Waking up with Luke wrapped around her, the presents all waiting under the tree in the living room. Including one very important one that she'd made specially this afternoon at the cake studio. A miniature Christmas cake in the shape of a football pitch with 'Marry Me' inscribed in flowing blue letters on the top.

The secret smile split into a grin. Maybe it was forward of her, but she really didn't care. She'd waited for Luke to pop the question, but she suspected that there was still enough of the young rebel inside him to consider marriage unnecessary. Especially as they all had his name anyway.

In her more paranoid moments she'd also wondered if he had avoided the issue because her net income was more than his. Male pride was one of those tricky things you had to tiptoe around occasionally. But she'd done enough tiptoeing. She wanted to start the next phase of their journey, to have him move in permanently, especially after Aldo's little declaration tonight, and for her that meant making it official. So she was putting Luke on the spot tomorrow morning, whether he liked it or not.

She jolted as the shower door opened and cool hands settled on her stomach.

'You're freezing,' she yelped as Luke's long chilly body pressed against her back and cold lips nibbled her neck.

'That's because I've been playing football for the past half hour in below-freezing temperatures with our son,' he murmured, the humour in his voice warming her even more than the press of his erection against her buttocks.

Our son.

She turned in his arms to wrap her arms round his neck. The hot water flowed down his back as steam rose off those magnificent shoulders and dewed his devastating face. 'When did it happen? When did he start calling you "Dad"?'

Luke's sensual lips quirked in a lopsided smile. 'I'll tell you all about it later, but first…' His hands clasped her waist and dragged her against him, until his erection butted her belly. 'I need to get my circulation flowing again before I lose a limb.'

Reaching down, she circled his penis, soapy fingers running up and down the huge shaft as her sex clenched with anticipation. 'This limb feels fairly solid to me,' she teased.

He chuckled then, dragging her hand away, whisked her round, until her hands were braced against the wall, and strong hands bracketed her hips, positioning her.

His fingers parted her folds to circle the aching bud of her clitoris while he pressed into her from behind.

'How about we test that theory?' he murmured against her neck.

And her delighted laugh turned into a soft sob of pleasure.

* * *

'So what's the story?' she asked, half an hour later, as she sat at her dressing table in her robe and watched Luke, his naked body gilded by lamplight, as he dried himself with rough strokes of the towel. 'With you and Aldo?'

Despite an earth-shattering orgasm in the shower, her sex got a little moist and she wriggled on the seat, already anticipating the long night ahead, as he rubbed the towel over his groin.

Good Lord, the man has turned me into a total sex junkie.

He looked up, his hair arranged in haphazard tufts as he hooked the towel around his waist, the easy smile so endearing her heart clenched, right alongside her sex.

And not just a sex junkie. My name is Halle Best and I am a Luke-aholic.

'We made an agreement,' he said as he walked across the room to pick his jeans up off the floor, then pulled something out of the pocket. 'I get to be his dad if I agree to play football with him whenever he wants. Or maybe it was the other way around.'

She grinned at his reflection. 'Sounds like a win-win to me, either way. For everyone concerned.'

He came back to her, one hand hidden behind his back. 'It will be, if everything goes according to plan tonight.'

'There's a plan?'

He nodded. 'The dinner was just the start.'

'And the shower sex?' she asked, teasing him a little more.

'That was a spontaneous addition to the plan,' he said,

but then the cocky grin sobered. 'I have something for you. An early Christmas present that I want you to open now.'

So saying, he produced a black velvet jeweller's box—a ring-sized box—from behind his back.

Her heart stopped beating. Then slammed into her ribs as all the breath squeezed out of her lungs in one gigantic rush.

'Oh!' was all she could manage round the huge boulder lodged in her throat.

She took the box out of the palm of his hand, her fingers trembling uncontrollably. As big dewy tears slipped over her lids.

'Hey.' He captured one on his knuckle, tipped her face up to his. 'Don't cry. You don't have to say yes right away. I just didn't want to give it to you tomorrow in front of everyone, in case...' His shoulder hitched uncomfortably and the tiny flash of vulnerability that still lurked in his eyes even after all these years had her heart swelling to impossible proportions.

I love you so much, Luke Best. You're the very best thing that has ever happened to me.

The words formed in her head, but she couldn't say them, her throat was too thick with happy tears.

'You know, in case,' he continued, 'I put undue pressure on you.'

The dam broke, the happy tears cascading down her cheeks as she leaped up and threw her arms round his neck, the ring box still clasped in her fist. 'Yes, yes, a thousand times yes. You silly bugger.' She stepped back to cradle his beautiful face in one shaking palm. 'As if I was ever going to say no.'

He laughed, the relief on his face almost as pronounced as the bright sheen of adoration in his eyes. 'Perhaps you should check the ring first, before you make a final decision.'

'Don't be daft. I'm afraid you're stuck with me, even if there's a ring pull in here,' she said as she opened the box.

Inside was a delicate platinum ring with a scattering of tiny garnets surrounding a diamond. She wept some more as he placed it carefully on her finger.

'I figured it would match your eyes,' he said.

'Oh, Luke.' She admired the ring; it was absolutely exquisite. But really she would have been perfectly ecstatic with a ring pull. 'This is the best Christmas present ever.' She peered up at him. 'I have a confession to make.'

He dragged her closer. 'Yeah?' He nuzzled her earlobe, sending shivers of sensation down her neck.

'I was going to ask you, too, tomorrow,' she said. 'But in front of everyone, so you would have absolutely no opportunity to say no.'

'You are such a ball-buster.' He chuckled. 'That must be why I love you to fucking bits.'

She thrust her fingers into his hair, loving the silky feel of it, as she drew his face down to hers for a long-overdue kiss. 'I'm so happy, I feel like a teenager again,' she whispered against his lips.

'I know,' he said. 'Except this is better. Because we're both indestructible now.'

And then he set about proving it, for the rest of the night.

* * * * *

Acknowledgements

Writing a book is supposed to be a solitary pursuit, until your publisher asks you to write the acknowledgements, and you suddenly realise how many other people got involved along the way. So here's my chance to send big, shouty thank yous to just a few of those people… My husband Rob for his suggestion that I rip off Shakespeare when I couldn't come up with a plot. My best mate Catri, who insisted we go to the Great Smokey Mountains for one of our US road trips. My best writing mate Abby Green, for telling me I *so* could write a longer book, over and over again until it stuck. My other great writing mates Fiona Harper, Iona Grey and Scarlet Wilson for consulting on everything from covers to sagging middles and dealing with my many, many anxiety attacks. To my editor Bryony Green for giving me revisions that made this story even better than I could make it on my own (the sulking was just for show, honest!). To the wonderful TonyB at Smokey Mountain Kayaking for his willingness to share his in-depth knowledge of kayaking and the Smokies. To culinary superstar Faenia Moore for her willingness to share her in-depth knowledge of baking and TV cookery shows. And finally to Anna Baggaley and everyone at Harlequin Mira for all your support on this, as it turns out, not at all lonely journey.

Loved this book?
Let us know!

Find us on **Twitter @Mira_BooksUK**
where you can share your thoughts, stay up
to date on all the news about our upcoming
releases and even be in with the chance of
winning copies of our wonderful books!

Bringing you the best voices in fiction

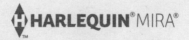

ma Donoghue

D0683193

Also by E

Novels

Stir Fry
Hood
Life Mask
Landing
The Sealed Letter
Slammerkin
Room

Short Story Collections

Kissing the Witch
The Woman Who Gave Birth to Rabbits
Touchy Subjects

touchy subjects

EMMA DONOGHUE

virago

VIRAGO

First published in Great Britain in 2006 by Virago Press
First published in the United States in 2006 by Harcourt, Inc.

First published in paperback in 2011 by Virago Press

A CIP catalogue record for this book
is available from the British Library.

ISBN 978-1-84408-739-6

Typeset in Bembo by M Rules
Printed and bound in Great Britain by
Clays Ltd, St Ives plc

Virago Press
An imprint of
Little, Brown Book Group
100 Victoria Embankment
London EC4Y 0DY

An Hachette UK Company
www.hachette.co.uk

www.virago.co.uk

This book is for Finn Claude Donoghue Roulston,
with a big wet kiss.

contents

babies

touchy subjects

Sarah's eyes were as dry as paper. Jet lag always made her feel ten years older. She stared past the blonde chignon of the receptionist in Finbar's Hotel. Twenty to one, according to the clock on the right. One take away eight was minus seven. No, try again. Thirteen take away eight was five. Twenty to five, Seattle time. Morning or evening? Wednesday or Thursday?

She shut her eyes and told herself not to panic. A day either way would make no difference. *Please let it not make any difference.*

'Ms Lord?' The Germanic receptionist was holding out the key.

Sarah took it and tried to smile. There were four different clocks behind the desk, she realized now. The one she'd been reading was New York, not Dublin. So here the time was a quarter to six, but according to her body clock it was . . .

Forget it.

Bag in hand, she stumbled across the marble floor towards the lifts.

A young assistant porter in Edwardian stripes brought up her double espresso ten minutes later. Sarah felt better as soon as she smelt it. She even flirted with the boy a little. Just a matter of

3

'That was quick,' and a tilt of the eyebrows, just to shake herself awake. He answered very perkily.

Even if, to a boy like that, thirty-eight probably seemed like ninety. *Every little hormone helps.*

Her heart thudded as the caffeine hit home. She dragged the chair over to the window; sunlight was the best cure for jet lag. Not that there was ever much sunlight to catch in Ireland, but at least it was a clear evening. Her eyes rested on the long glitter of the river as she drained her espresso. Time was you couldn't even have got a filter coffee in Dublin; this town had certainly come on. You could probably get anything you needed now if you paid enough. She winced at the thought: too close to home.

Knotted into the starchy robe, she flexed her feet on the pale red-and-black carpet and considered the dress spread out on the bed. She knew it was comical, but she couldn't decide what to wear. This was a big night, most definitely, but not the kind of occasion covered in the book on manners her mother gave her for her eighteenth birthday. (Sarah still kept it on her cookery-book shelf in Seattle; guests found it hilarious.) Whatever she wore tonight had to be comfortable, but with a bit of glamour to keep her spirits up. Back home, this sleeveless dress in cream linen had seemed perfect, but now it was creased in twenty places. Like her face.

Sarah was tempted to keep on the dressing gown, but it might frighten Padraic. She wished she knew him better. Why hadn't she paid him a bit more attention at all those Christmas do's? She was sure there was a chapter on that in her etiquette manual: *Take the trouble to talk to everyone in the room.* Last year her entire corporation had undergone a weekend's training in power networking, which boiled down to the same thing, with motives bared. *Work the party. You never know when someone might turn out to be useful.*

4

Was she using Padraic? Was that what it all amounted to?

No more bloody ethical qualms, Sarah reminded herself. This was the only way to get what she wanted. What she needed. What she deserved, as much as the next woman, anyway.

The dress was impossible; it would make her look like cracked china. She pulled the purple suit she'd travelled in back on; now she was herself again. Cross-legged on the bed, she waited for her heartbeat to slow down. Six twenty. That was OK; Padraic was only five minutes late. All she wanted was to lie down, but a nap would be fatal.

There was that report on internal communications she was meant to be reading, but in this condition she wouldn't make any sense of it. She stretched for the remote and flicked through the channels. How artistic the ads were, compared with back home in Seattle. Sarah paused at some sort of mad chat show hosted by a computer. Was that Irish the children were talking? How very odd.

Please let him not be very late.

The Irish were always bloody late.

Padraic was relieved that Finbar's Hotel was way down on the quays opposite Heuston Station, where he was unlikely to bump into anyone he knew. He stood outside for a minute and gawked up at the glistening balconies. He remembered it when there was only a peeling facade, before that Dutch rock star and his Irish wife had bought it up. What would it cost, a night in one of those tastefully refurbished rooms? It was a shame all the yuppies had to look down on was the Liffey.

The first things he noticed when the doors slid open were the white sofas, lined up like a set of teeth. Ludicrous – they'd be black in a month. Padraic grinned to himself now to relax his jaw. Greg in marketing had this theory about all tension and pain originating in the back teeth.

Padraic was the kind of man who always wore his wedding ring, and it hadn't occurred to him to take it off. But as he stood at the desk and asked the receptionist whether Ms Lord had checked in yet, he thought he saw her eyes flicker to his hand. He almost gave in to a silly impulse to put it behind his back. Instead, he tugged at the neck of the Breton fisherman's jumper he had changed into after work.

The receptionist had the phone pressed to her ear now. She sounded foreign, but he couldn't tell from where. What was keeping Sarah? What possible hitch could there be?

Poor woman, he thought, for the twentieth time. *To have to stoop to this.*

'Padraic?'

He leapt. He felt his whole spine lock into a straight line. Then he turned. 'Máire, how *are* you! You look stunning! I don't think I've seen you since Granny's funeral. Didn't I hear you were in England?' The words were exploding from his mouth like crumbs.

His cousin gave him a Continental-style peck on the cheek. 'I'm only back a month.'

Her badge said MÁIRE DERMOTT, RECEPTION MANAGER. He jabbed a finger at it. 'You're doing well for yourself.' If he kept talking, his cousin couldn't ask him what he was doing here.

'Oh, early days,' she said.

'It all looks fabulous, anyway,' he said, wheeling round and waving at the snowy couches, the bright paintings, the rows of tiny lamps hanging like daggers overhead. He edged away from the desk, where the receptionist had got Sarah on the phone at last.

'So how's Carmel?' asked Máire. 'And the boys?'

Padraic was about to give a full report on his respectable family life when the receptionist leaned over the desk. 'Excuse me, Mr Dermott. If you'd be so good as to go up now, the room is 101. And please tell Ms Lord that the champagne is on its way.'

He offered Máire a ghastly smile. 'Friend of Carmel's.'

His cousin's face had suddenly shut down. She looked as snotty as when they were children doing Christmas panto-mimes and she always made him play the ox.

Padraic gave a merry little wave of the fingers. 'Catch you later,' he said, backing away.

On the way to the lifts Padraic glanced into the establishment designated as the Irish Bar, which looked just like the one he and Carmel had stumbled across in Athens. He pressed repeatedly on the lift button, then put his hand against his hot face. It was god's own truth, what he'd told his cousin about Sarah being a friend of Carmel's. But it was also, under the circumstances, the worst possible thing to say. His father's side of the family were notorious gossips. Once again, Padraic Dermott had dug himself a pit with his own big mouth.

Sarah was standing in the door of room 101, her heart ticking like a clock. When she saw him coming down the long corridor she felt a rush of something like love. 'Hi!' she called, too loudly.

'Hey there!'

They kissed, as if at a cocktail party. Padraic's cheek was a little bristly.

'Come in, come in! I'm thrilled to bits to see you!' She knew she sounded stage-Irish; she was overcompensating. She didn't want him to think she was some transatlantic ice queen who'd forgotten how to travel by bus.

Thank god there were armchairs, so they didn't have to sit on the bed. Padraic hunched over a little, hands on his knees, as if ready for action. She tried to remember if they'd ever been alone in a room together before.

'How was your flight?'

'Oh, you know.' Sarah yawned and shrugged. 'How's business these days?' she asked.

'Not bad,' he said, 'not bad at all.' She could see his shoulders relax a little into the satin-finish chair. 'We're diversifying a good bit. Lots of opportunities.'

'I'll bet,' she assured him.

'And yourself?'

'Well, I got that promotion.' She added a little rueful smile. Not that he would have any idea which promotion she meant.

'Of course you did!'

Did she detect a touch of irony? Surely not. 'And the lads?' she asked.

'Doing great,' he told her. 'Fiachra's in the senior school this year.'

Sarah nodded enthusiastically. 'I brought them some stuff . . .' Her voice trailed off as she nodded at the heap of presents on the sideboard. She didn't mean to play the rich Yank, buying herself a welcome.

'Ah, you're very good.' Padraic was craning over his chair to see the presents.

Then a silence flickered in the air between them.

'D'you ever see anything of Eamonn these days?' His tone was ostentatiously light.

'Not really,' said Sarah. 'He's in Boston.'

'Mmm. I just thought—'

'That's nearly as far from Seattle as from Dublin.'

'Right.'

Padraic was looking as if he wished he hadn't mentioned Eamonn's name. She hadn't sounded touchy, had she? She hadn't meant to, if she had. It was just the general twitchiness of the occasion. Padraic just sat there, looking around at the furnishings. And then, thank Christ and all his saints, a knock on the door.

The boy in stripes brought in the champagne on a tray. Was that a hint of a smirk on his face? Sarah squirmed, but just a little. In her twenty years away from Ireland she had taught herself not to give a shit what anybody thought.

Five minutes later, Padraic's hands were still straining at the wire around the cork. Sarah thought for an awful moment that she'd have to ring down and ask for the boy to be sent back up.

'Excellent!' she said, when the pop came, very loud in the quiet room. The foam dripped onto the table. 'Ooh, doesn't it make a mess!'

And then she realized she sounded just like that nurse in the *Carry On* films, and the laughter started in her throat, deep and uncouth.

Padraic looked at her, owl-eyed, then started laughing, too. His face was red. He filled both glasses to the brim.

'I swear, I didn't mean—' she began.

'I know you didn't.'

'It was just—'

'It was,' he said, knocking back half the glass and wiping one eye.

Sarah felt a bit better after that little icebreaker. She offered to refill his glass.

'Better not,' said Padraic, all business now. 'You know what Shakespeare said.'

She tried to think of all the things Shakespeare ever said.

'"Drink,"' he explained. '"It makes a man and then mars him . . . provokes the desire, but takes away the performance."'

'Really?'

Padraic added, 'It's the only quote I ever remember.'

Sarah nodded. Privately she was sure Shakespeare had never said any such thing; it sounded more like Morecambe and Wise. It was time she took charge of this conversation. 'Listen,' she began in the voice she used at meetings. Was she imagining it, or did Padraic sit up straighter? 'Listen,' she tried again, more gently, 'are you sure you're OK about this?'

'Absolutely,' said Padraic.

'No, but really, you've only to say.' She let the pause stretch. 'It's a lot to ask.'

'No bother.'

Typical bloody Irishmen, can't handle any conversation more intimate than buying a paper. Sarah pressed her fingertips together hard and tried again. Her voice was beginning to shake. 'I hope you know I wouldn't be here if there was any other way.'

'I know that, sure.'

'I can't tell you how grateful I'll be – I mean, I am, already.' She stumbled on. 'The only thing is, I get the feeling Carmel kind of talked you into this?'

'Nonsense,' he said, too heartily. 'I'm more than happy. Glad to be of use.'

She winced at the word.

'Well now.' Padraic got up and straightened the sleeves of the shirt he wore beneath that ridiculous striped jersey. 'I suppose I should get down to business.' From his jacket pocket he produced a small empty jar that said HEINZ PEAS & CARROTS FOR BABY.

Sarah stared at it. 'How suitable.' Her throat was dry.

He peered at the ripped label. 'Would you look at that! I

grabbed the first clean jar I could find that wasn't too big,' he added a little sheepishly.

Compassion swept over her like water. 'It's perfect.'

They stood around as if waiting for divine intervention. Then Sarah took a few light steps towards the bathroom. 'Why don't I wait—'

'Not at all,' he said, walking past her. 'You stay in here and have a bit of a nap.'

She heard the key turn in the bathroom door.

A nap? Did he seriously think she could sleep through what might turn out to be the hinge of her whole life?

Padraic knew he was being paranoid, but just in case. Sarah might think of some further instructions and burst in on him in that scary suit with the pointed lapels. Anyway, he'd never been able to relax in a bathroom without locking the door.

The jar looked harmless, standing beside the miniature elder-flower soap. He tried perching on the edge of the bath, but it was too low; he feared he might fall backwards and damage his back. *Dublin Businessman Found Committing Lewd Act in Luxury Hotel.* All right for the likes of George Michael, maybe, but not recommended for a career in middle management. And his cousin Máire would never forgive him for the publicity.

He tried sitting on the toilet – with the lid down, so it would feel less squalid, more like a chair. He leaned back, a knob poked him between the shoulderblades, and the flush started up like Niagara. He stood up till the sound died down. Sarah would think he was wasting time. Sarah would think him a complete moron, but then, he'd always suspected she thought that anyway.

Now, these weren't the sort of thoughts to be having, were they? Relaxing thoughts were what were needed; warm

11

thoughts, sexy thoughts. Beaches and open fires and hammocks and . . . no, not babies. Would it look like him, he wondered for the first time, this hypothetical West Coast child?

He hadn't been letting himself think that far ahead. All week he'd been determined to do this thing, as a favour to Carmel, really, though Carmel thought he was doing it for her best friend. He'd been rather flattered to be asked, especially by someone as high-powered as Sarah Lord. He couldn't think of any reason to refuse. It wasn't your everyday procedure, and he wasn't planning to mention it to his mother, but really, where was the harm? As Carmel put it the other night, 'It's not like you're short of the stuff, sweetie.'

Still, he preferred not to dwell on the long-term consequences. The thought of his brief pleasure being the direct cause of a baby was still somehow appalling to Padraic, even though he had three sons and loved them so much it made his chest feel tight. He still remembered that day in Third Year when the priest drew a diagram on the blackboard. The Lone Ranger sperm; the engulfing egg. He didn't quite believe it. It sounded like one of those stories adults made up when they couldn't be bothered to explain the complicated truth.

Padraic sat up straighter on the glossy toilet seat. He did ten complete body breaths. It was all he remembered from that stress training his company had shelled out for last year. Three hundred euro a head, and the office was still full of squabbles and cold coffee.

He unzipped his trousers to start getting in the mood. Nothing stirring yet. All Very Quiet on the Western Front. Well, Sarah couldn't expect some sort of McDonald's-style service, could she? *Ready in Five Minutes or Your Money Back.* She wasn't paying for this, Padraic reminded himself. He was doing her a great big favour. At least, he was trying to.

He zipped up his trousers again; he didn't like feeling watched. If he could only relax there would be no problem. There never was any problem. Well, never usually. Hardly ever. No more than the next man. And Carmel had such a knack . . .

He wouldn't think about Carmel. It was too weird. She was his wife, and here he was sitting on a very expensive toilet preparing to hand her best friend a jar of his semen. At the sheer perversity of the thought, he felt a little spark of life. *Good, good, keep it up, man. You're about to have a wank,* he told himself salaciously, *in the all-new, design-award-winning Finbar's Hotel. This is very postmodern altogether. That woman out there has flown halfway round the world for the Holy Grail of your little jarful. Think what the pope would say to that!*

This last taboo was almost too much for Padraic; he felt his confidence begin to drain away at the thought of the pontiff peering in the bathroom window.

Dirty, think honest-to-god dirty thoughts. Suddenly he couldn't remember any. What did he used to think about when he was seventeen? It seemed an aeon ago.

He knew he should have come armed. An hour ago he was standing at the Easons magazine counter, where the cashier had looked about twelve, and he'd lost his nerve and handed her an *Irish Independent* instead. Much good the *Irish Independent* would be to him in this hour of need. He'd flicked through it already and the most titillating thing in it was a picture of the president signing a memorial.

This was ridiculous. *You're not some Neanderthal; you were born in 1961.* Surely he didn't need some airbrushed airhead to slaver over? Surely he could rely on the power of imagination?

The door opened abruptly. Sarah, who had turned her armchair to face the window so as not to seem to be hovering in a predatory way, grinned over her shoulder. 'That was quick!'

Then she cursed herself for speaking too soon because Padraic was shaking his head as if he had something stuck in his ear. 'Actually,' he muttered, 'I'm just going to stretch my legs. Won't be a minute.'

'Sure, sure, take your time.'

His legs? Sarah sat there in the empty room and wondered what his legs had to do with anything. Blood flow to the pelvis? Or was it a euphemism for a panic attack? She peered into the bathroom; the jar was still on the sink, bone-dry.

Five minutes later, it occurred to her that he had run home to Carmel.

The phone rang eight times before her friend picked it up. 'Sarah, my love! What country are you in?'

'This one.'

'Is my worser half with you?'

'Well, he was. But he's gone out.'

'Out where?'

Curled up on the duvet, Sarah shrugged off her heels. 'I don't know. Listen, if he turns up at home—'

'Padraic wouldn't do that to you.'

There was a little silence. In the background, she could hear the *Holby City* theme on the television, and one of the boys chanting something, over and over. 'Listen, Carmel, how did he seem this morning?'

Her friend let out a short laugh. 'How he always seems.'

'No, but was he nervous? I mean, I'm nervous, and it's worse for him.'

'Maybe he was a bit,' said Carmel consideringly. 'But, I mean, how hard can it be?'

14

Who started giggling first? 'Today is just one long double entendre,' said Sarah eventually.

'How long?'

'Long enough!'

And then they were serious again. 'Did you bully him into it, though, Carmel, really?'

'Am I the kind of woman who bullies anyone?'

This wasn't the time for that discussion. 'All I mean is, I know you want to help.'

'We both do. Me and Padraic both.'

'But you most of all, you've been through the whole thing with me, you know what it's been like, with the clinic . . . And I swear I wouldn't have asked if I had anyone else.' Sarah was all at once on the brink of tears. She stopped and tried to open her throat.

'Of course.' After a minute, Carmel went on more professionally. 'How's your mucus?'

'Sticky as maple syrup.'

'Good stuff. It's going to happen, you know.'

'Is it?' Sarah knew she sounded like a child.

'It is.'

All at once she couldn't believe what she was planning. To wake up pregnant one day and somehow find the nerve to go on with it, that was one thing, but to do it deliberately . . . *For cold-blooded and selfish reasons,* as the tabloids always put it. In fantastical hope, as Sarah thought of it. In fear and trembling.

'Are you sure you can't come over for a little visit?' asked Carmel.

'I really can't. I've a meeting in Brussels tomorrow morning, before I head back to the States.'

'Ah well. Next time.'

*

Padraic was leaning on the senior porter's desk, which was more like a lectern. He spoke in a murmur, as if at confession.

'Our library on the third floor has all the papers as well as a range of contemporary Irish literature, sir,' muttered the slightly stooped porter, as if reading from a script.

'No, but magazines,' said Padraic meaningfully.

'We stock *Private Eye, Magill, Time* . . .'

'Not that kind.' Padraic's words sounded sticky. 'Men's magazines.'

The old man screwed up his eyes. 'I think they might have one on cars . . .'

'Oh, for Christ's sake,' he said under his breath.

Then, at his elbow, just the woman he could do without. 'Are you all right there, Padraic?'

'Máire.' He gave her a wild look. She was just trying to catch him out at this stage. Was she following him all over the hotel to examine the state of his trousers? Just as well he didn't have the bloody erection he'd spent the last fifteen minutes trying to achieve. She'd probably photograph it for her files.

'This gentleman—,' began the porter in his wavering voice.

'I'm grand, actually.' And Padraic walked off without another word.

What did it matter if they thought he was rude? Máire had clearly made up her mind that he was cheating on Carmel with his wife's best friend. When the fact was he would never, never, never. He wasn't that type of guy. He had his faults, Padraic admitted to himself as he punched at the lift button, but not that one. He was a very ordinary man who loved his family. There was nothing experimental about him; he didn't even wear coloured shirts.

Then what the fuck am I doing here?

He didn't have a key to room 101; he had to knock. Sarah

let him in, talking all the while on a cordless phone. Her smile didn't quite cover her irritation. 'Cream,' she said into the phone. 'Cream linen. But it didn't travel well.' He gave her a thumbs-up and headed into the bathroom.

Now he was well and truly fucked. Tired out, without so much as a picture of Sharon Stone to rely on. Funny how it seemed so easy to produce the goods when they weren't wanted. He considered the gallons of the stuff he'd wasted as an adolescent when he locked himself into the bathroom on a daily basis. He thought of all the condoms he'd bought since he and Carmel got married. And tonight, when all that was required was a couple of spoonfuls . . .

He sat on the toilet and rested his head on his fists. What on earth had induced him to agree to this mad scheme? It just wasn't him. He knew Irish society was meant to be modernizing at a rate of knots, but this was ridiculous. It was like something off one of those American soaps with their convoluted plots, where no one knows who their father is until they do a blood test.

Sarah was still on the phone; he could hear her muted voice. Who was she talking to? She was probably complaining about him, his lack of jizz, so to speak. Padraic stared round him for inspiration. A less sexy room had never been devised. Sanitary, soothing. The only hint of colour was Sarah's leopard-skin toilet bag.

Reckless now, he unzipped it and rifled through. *Pervert,* he told himself encouragingly. Looking through his wife's friend's private things . . . her spot concealer, her super-plus tampons. He felt something stirring in his trousers. He sat down again and reached in. He clung to this unlikely image of himself as a lecherous burglar, an invader of female privacies. A man who could carry a crowbar, who might disturb a woman who was having her bath, some independent single businesswoman with sultry lips, a woman like Sarah . . .

Oh my god. If she only knew what he was thinking, barely ten feet away—

Never mind that. *Hold on to the fantasy. The crowbar.* No, chuck the crowbar, he couldn't stoop to that. He would simply surprise . . . some beautiful, fearful woman and seize her in his bare hands and—

If Carmel knew he had rape fantasies she'd give him hell.

Never mind. Do what you have to do. Keep at it. Nearly there now. Evil, smutty, wicked thoughts. The gorgeous luscious open-mouthed businesswoman . . . bent over the sink . . . her eyes in the mirror . . .

By now he had forgotten all about the jar. His eye fell on it at the last possible minute.

Now wouldn't that have been ironic, Padraic told himself as he screwed the lid back on with shaking hands.

It didn't look like very much, it occurred to him. He should have brought a smaller jar. A test tube, even.

He gave himself a devilish grin in the mirror. Endorphins rushed through his veins. Now what he'd love was a little snooze, but no, he had a delivery to make.

Sarah was reading some spiral-bound document, but she leapt up when he opened the door, and the pages slid to the floor. 'Wonderful!' she said, all fluttery, as he handed over the warm jar. Her cheeks were pink. She really was quite a good-looking woman.

'Hope it's enough,' he joked.

'It's grand, loads!'

It struck him for the first time that she might need some help with getting it in. *Oh god, please let her not upend herself and expect me to . . .* But he was too much of a gentleman to run

18

away. He hovered. Sarah, acting like she did this every day, produced a syringe.

'Wow,' said Padraic. 'I hope they didn't search your bag at customs.'

'No, but it did show up on the X-ray screen.' She gave a breathless little laugh.

'Wow,' he said again. Then, 'It might have been easier to do it the old-fashioned way!'

It was a very cold look she gave him. Surely she couldn't think he meant it? A touchy subject, clearly. (Weren't they all, these days?) Padraic knew he should never make jokes when he was nervous. He felt heat rise up his throat.

'I'll get out of your way, then, will I? Treat myself to a whiskey. Maybe you'll come down and join me after?'

He couldn't stop talking. Sarah smiled and nodded and opened the door for him.

She tried lying on the bed with her bare legs in the air, but it was hard to keep them up there. *Hurry, hurry,* she told herself; the jar was cooling fast. How long was it they lived? Was it true that boy sperm moved faster but girl sperm lived longer? Or was it vice versa? Not that she gave a damn. She'd take whatever God sent her, if he was willing to use this form of special delivery. *Please just let this work.*

Finally, she ended up lying on the carpet with her feet up on the bed. She felt almost comfortable. It was crucial to feel happy at the moment of conception, someone at work had told her. Awkwardly, leaning up on one elbow, she unscrewed the lid of the jar and began to fill the syringe. It was certainly easier at the clinic, where all she had to do was shut her eyes, but it felt a lot better to be doing this herself without anyone peering or poking. Just her and a little warm jar full of magic from a nice Dublinman with a name. Nothing frozen, nothing anonymous.

There, now, she had got a good grip on the plunger. She would just lay her head back and take a few relaxing breaths . . .

The knock came so loud that her hand clenched.

'No thank you,' she called in the direction of the door.

No answer. She took one huge breath and pressed the plunger.

Afterwards, she could never remember hearing the door opening. All she knew was that the assistant porter was standing there staring, in his ludicrous striped jacket, like something out of Feydeau. And she was on her feet, with her skirt caught up around her hips. 'Get out,' she bawled. She tugged at the cloth and heard a seam rip. There was wetness all down her legs.

The boy started to say something about turning down the sheets.

'Get out of my room!'

The door crashed shut behind him.

Afterwards, when she had mopped herself up, Sarah scrubbed at the carpet with a damp facecloth. The mark was milky, unmistakable against the square of red wool. They'd think she and Padraic had done it right here on the floor.

She wanted to go down the corridor and find that porter. She longed to spit at another human being for the first time in her life. 'Look, boyo,' she would scream in his ear, 'if I can make myself pregnant, I'm sure I can turn down my own sheets.'

But she hadn't, had she? All she'd done was stained the carpet.

The funny thing was, now he'd started, the dirty thoughts wouldn't stop coming. They raced merrily through his head. All the way down in the lift Padraic watched the other passenger in the mirrored wall. She was fifteen years too old for the red dress and black leather, but still, not bad at all. A hooker, or just somebody's bit on the side? This hotel was a stranger place than it looked from the outside; behind all that fresh paint you'd never know what was going on. He shook his head to clear it as the lift glided to a stop. He let the woman get out first.

The Irish Bar was stuffed with people, singing rebel songs Padraic hadn't heard in years; it seemed to be some sort of wake. After two whiskeys he felt superb. Relief and alcohol danced through his body together, while his hormones played 'It Had to Be You'.

Tonight had demanded his all, and his all was what he had given. With a bit of luck, one lonely frustrated woman's life would be transformed, and a little bit of his DNA would grow up next door to the Pacific Ocean. With a light tan and rollerblades . . .

There was his cousin, consulting a clipboard and talking to the barman. He shouldn't have got so het up earlier; she was only taking an interest. He'd been in a bit of a state, he could admit that now. When he'd finished his third whiskey, Padraic gave a little wave, but Máire didn't seem to see. He squeezed his way over and waited for a break in the conversation, then put his hand on her arm.

'Hello again,' she said.

'It's not what you think,' he announced satirically.

'Right.' She seemed to be speaking to her clipboard.

'No, really. I mean, yes, I'm here to meet a woman, obviously, but it's about a hundred and eighty degrees opposite to what you're obviously thinking.'

Máire looked up, and her eyes were hard. 'Listen, Padraic, it's none of my business.'

'But the thing is, Carmel knows I'm here,' he assured her,

tugging at her sleeve. 'Old school friend. Carmel set the whole thing up, in fact.'

His cousin looked slightly revolted, and he was just about to explain, when he remembered that he had promised both Carmel and Sarah never to tell a soul about their little arrangement. So he had to let go of Máire's sleeve. She was out the door like a shot.

Knees against the bar, he idled over his next drink, planning how to describe the evening to his wife. *Oh, we got the business over with in the first ten minutes – nothing to it.* But he mustn't make it sound like too much fun, either. Carmel was being remarkably kind to her friend, when you came to think about it – lending out her husband like a sort of pedigree stud. He savoured the image.

Funny, he thought. That old porter's paging another Mr Dermott. Then two things occurred to Padraic: that it was him who was being paged, and that he was very nearly pissed. He'd only had a few, but then he'd forgotten to have dinner.

'The lady upstairs would like to know when you're coming back, sir,' said the porter. A little too loudly and pointedly, Padraic thought.

He was up in room 101 in three minutes.

'I'm so sorry,' Sarah stuttered. 'I can't believe—'

He acted like a gentleman. He assured her it could happen to anyone. (Anyone, he mentally added, who made a habit of inseminating herself in hotel bedrooms.) He swore the stain would hoover out: 'These people are professionals.' (He could just imagine the chambermaid telling Máire that her cousin had spurted all over the carpet.) He grabbed the empty jar and headed back into the bathroom.

This time, Sarah said to herself, she'd stay calm. This time she'd lock the door. This time she'd get it right. And then tomorrow she'd be on her way back to Seattle, and . . . *Maybe. You never know. Carmel said it would happen.* This was still the right day. Her chances were pretty good.

Padraic popped his head out of the bathroom. Only now did she notice how dark red his face had gone. 'I might be a little while.'

'How many have you had?' She didn't mean it to sound quite so cutting, but she thought she had a right to know.

He leant on the doorjamb. All the softness went out of his voice. 'What's that supposed to mean?'

She shrugged.

'I thought my shift was over, you know,' he went on acidly. 'As far as I knew you'd got what you wanted, you were finished with me, and I had the right to a drink.'

'You've had more than one,' she pointed out neutrally.

'And if you'll give me a minute,' he shouted, 'I can still fucking well get it up.'

They avoided each other's eyes.

'Jesus,' he added, 'no wonder . . .'

He turned to go back into the bathroom, but Sarah was on her feet. There was nothing she hated more than unfinished sentences. 'No wonder what?'

'No wonder you have to resort to this sort of carry-on.'

Her eyes stood out in her face. 'You mean because no man would have me? Is that what you think?'

'I never said that.' Padraic was leaning his head against the doorjamb now. 'It's just, you must admit, you come on a bit strong.'

'That's because this is my last chance,' she bawled at him.

He shifted on the spot. 'Don't say that. Sure, a fine-looking woman—'

'Getting a man is easy,' she spat.

He was taken aback. The pity in his eyes faded.

'It's having children with one that's turned out to be impossible,' she said between her teeth.

'Why didn't you and Eamonn—'

'Because we were divorced by the time we were thirty. Then the guy I was with for six years after that didn't happen to like children. You're welcome to all the details.' Sarah's voice was shaking like a rope. 'I'm thirty-eight years old. I've been paying a clinic thousands of dollars a month for fertility drugs that make me sick and frozen sperm that doesn't work. What else do you suggest I do?'

He considered the carpet. 'I was just . . . I suppose I was wondering why you left it so late.'

'Oh, don't give me that. Just don't you dare.' She felt breathless with rage. 'How was I meant to know what I wanted at twenty-five? Men have no fucking idea. You'll still be able to make a woman pregnant when you're seventy!'

Padraic flinched at the thought.

After a minute, very quietly, he asked, 'But sure . . . why me? Couldn't you just have gone out one night and picked up a stranger?'

Sarah sat on the edge of the bed and wept. Her elbows dug into her thighs.

'I didn't want the child of some pickup,' she said at last, very slowly, the words emerging like pebbles. 'Quite apart from what else I might pick up from him.' She waited till her voice had steadied enough for her to go on. 'I wanted the child of a nice man, and all the nice men were taken.'

After a long minute, she felt the bed bounce as Padraic sat down beside her. 'Not all, surely,' he said after a minute. He sounded like a child who'd just been told the truth about Santa Claus.

Her smile came out a bit twisted. She turned her head. 'Don't worry about it, Padraic,' she drawled. 'I get by just fine without the husband and the SUV and the house in the sub-urbs.'

He didn't know how to take that. She watched him staring at his shoes.

'All I want is a child.' Sarah said it softly. She was never so sure of anything in her life.

'OK,' he said after a minute. 'I'll have another bash.' He stood up. 'You haven't seen me at my best tonight,' he added hoarsely.

She gave a little sniff of amusement and wiped her eyes. 'I suppose not.'

'You try getting an erection in a toilet without so much as a copy of *Playboy*. I'm not seventeen any more, you know.'

Sarah giggled and blew her nose. 'Sorry.' *Go on,* she told herself. *Make the offer.* 'Shall we just call the whole thing off, then?'

She could tell he was tempted. Just for a minute. Until he thought of what Carmel would say.

'Not at all,' said Padraic. He stood up. 'A man's gotta do.'

'Are you sure?'

'I'm going back in there,' he declared, 'and I'm not coming back out empty-handed. You just lie down and think of Ireland.'

'No,' she said, jumping up, 'I'll go in the bathroom. You could do with a change of scenery.'

She handed him out his jar, then locked the door. She looked herself in the eye, then turned on the cold tap and washed the salt off her face.

Padraic stood before the wardrobe mirror and stared down into his trousers. Not an enticing sight. Visibly tired, old before its time. He eyed his face and counted his wrinkles. Salmon couldn't eat after they mated, he remembered; they just shrivelled away. What was there left for him in this life, now he had served his time, genetically speaking?

But tonight's job wasn't quite over yet.

He felt utterly exhausted. Nerves, alcohol, and a fight to round it all off. But he had to rise to the occasion now. *Noblesse oblige.* He thought of Carmel's last birthday. He'd been knackered from work, and half a bottle of champagne hadn't helped, but he knew she wanted to be ravished, he could almost smell it off her. So he had claimed to be full of beans, and though it took an enormous effort, it was all right in the end. He'd known it would work. It always worked in the end, him and Carmel.

Padraic lay down on the bed. He wanted to be home in her arms.

This room had no more resources than the bathroom, really. He flicked through the TV channels (with the sound down, so Sarah wouldn't think he was time wasting). Not a drop of titillation. After five minutes of *Dirty Dancing,* he realized he was finding Patrick Swayze far more appealing than the girl, and that raised such disturbance in the back of his head that he switched off the telly.

He lay down again and scanned the room. The prints were garish abstracts; nothing doing there. There was the phone, of course. If only he had memorized a number for one of those chat lines. He'd rung one once, in a hotel room much nastier than this one, somewhere in the North of England. All he remembered was that the woman on the line had a terribly royal-family accent, and spoke very, very slowly to bump up his bill.

If he rang downstairs and asked for the number of a chat line, he was sure to get Máire. She'd tell her mother. She'd probably tell *his* mother.

Padraic shut his eyes and tried out a couple of trusty old fantasies. Only they weren't working any more. He wondered whether one traumatic evening had rendered him permanently impotent. He felt exhausted. Somehow the idea of having a voluntary sexual impulse seemed like a remnant of his youth. Maybe that was it, his lot.

All at once he knew what number to ring.

'Hello there,' said Carmel, and her voice was so warm he thought he could slip right into it and sleep. 'Are you coming home soon?'

'Any minute now. I just need a bit of help,' he admitted.

'Are you still at it?'

'She spilt the first lot.'

Carmel let out a roar of laughter. 'I should have warned you,' she said. 'When we shared a flat, Sarah was always knocking over cups of tea.'

'Are you comparing my precious seed to a beverage, woman?'

'The comparison is entirely in your favour.' Her voice changed for a minute; her mouth moved away from the phone and he heard her say, 'You go and brush your teeth, love. I'll be up as soon as I've finished talking to Daddy.'

He wanted to tell her to say good night from him, but he wasn't meant to be thinking like a daddy now.

Carmel's voice was all his again now, going low like only she could do. For a respectable wife and mother she could sound like a shocking wee slut. 'Are you ready for round two, big boy?' she asked.

'I don't think I can.'

'Can't means won't,' she said in her best schoolmistress voice.

He laughed into the phone, very softly.

'All right now,' she crooned. 'Enough of this nonsense. Shut your eyes.'

'I just want to come home.'

'You are home.'

'I am?'

'You're home in your bed with me. Nothing fancy.'

'Not a seedy motel?'

'Not Finbar's Hotel, either. We could never afford it. You're home in bed with me and the kids are fast asleep and you're flat on your back, with your hands above your head.'

'Surrendering, like?'

'Exactly.'

Carmel, he thought a few minutes later with the part of his mind that was overseeing the rest, should consider a career move. She could make a mint on one of those chat lines. And to think of all this lewdness being saved up for a big eejit like him. He kept his eyes squeezed shut and pretended his hands were hers. She always knew what to do. She was working him into a lather. She was going to make it all right.

Sarah was leaning against the sink, praying. It had been so long, she hardly remembered what to say. She got the words of the Hail Mary all arseways, she knew that much. *Blessed is the fruit?* Mostly what she said was *please.*

The bathroom door opening made the loudest noise. Padraic's grin split his face like a pumpkin. She seized the jar. Half as much as last time, but still, there must be a few million ambitious little wrigglers in there. She rushed over and lay down on the carpet.

'Will you be all right now?' he asked.

'Yeah, yeah,' she said, 'you go on home.'

He gathered up the pile of presents for his boys. When he was at the door, he turned to give a little finger wave. She had already filled the syringe.

'See you at Christmas, I suppose,' he said. And then, 'Fingers crossed.'

They both crossed their fingers and held them in the air.

Sarah started laughing before the door shut behind him. She was still laughing when she pressed the plunger.

expecting

I thought I saw him last Friday, stooping over the grapefruits in my local supermarket. Without stopping to make sure, I put my half-full basket down beside the carrot shelf and walked out the door marked ENTRANCE ONLY.

It might not have been him, of course. One round silver head is pretty much like another. If I'd seen his face, if the strip of mirror over the fruit counter had been angled the right way, I'd have known for sure: soft as a plum, as my mother would have said, if she'd ever met him. But it was probably someone else, because he never shopped on a Friday, and why would he come all this way across town to a perfectly unremarkable new supermarket? Besides, I never told him where I lived.

We had only ever met on Saturdays, in the windswept shopping centre I had to go to before the supermarket opened down the road. That first time, I was toying with an angora jumper on the second floor of the department store when I caught his eye. I figure they're safe to smile at if they're over sixty. He moved away with something long and green over his arm; I shifted over and browsed through five kinds of silk dresses before realizing I was in the maternity section. Not that it mattered much, of course, since anyone can wear any old shape nowadays.

The elderly gentleman held the heavy swing door open for me to go through first. 'Best to take things easy,' he commented, and I smiled, trying to think of something original to do with pasta for dinner. As we emerged into the shopping centre he asked a question that was half drowned out by the clamour of the crowd. I said 'Mmm,' rather robotic as usual among strangers. Thinking back, later that afternoon, I did remember hearing the word *expecting,* but I presumed he meant rain.

I bumped into him again in the charity furniture shop ten minutes later. Gallant, he insisted on lifting a table for me to look at the price. I only clicked when he said, 'The dress is for my daughter; she's due in July. And yourself?'

I shook my head.

He must have thought I was rebuking his curiosity; his face went pink from the nose out. 'Pardon me.'

'No no, it's all right,' I flustered.

'Early days yet, then,' he said confidentially.

It suddenly seemed like far too much trouble to explain; we could be standing here all day. Besides, this garrulous stranger would think me a fool, or worse, a wistful spinster type given to browsing through maternity dresses. So I said nothing, simply grinned like a bashful mum-to-be, as the magazines would say.

It's not the first mistake, but the first cowardice, that gets us into trouble. Why was it so hard to say that I hadn't heard his original question, as we came out of the department store? If only I'd said, 'I'm afraid I'm not expecting anything!' and made an awkward joke of the old-world euphemism.

And of course when the following Saturday, cup in hand, he edged over to my table in the shopping centre's single faded café, it was impossible to go back to the beginning. He told me

31

all about his daughter's special high-calcium diet. I saw now that clearing up that first misunderstanding would have been child's play compared to this: How could I admit to having lied? I tucked my knees under the table, nodding over the pros and cons of disposable nappies.

He was lonely, that much was clear. I was a Saturday shopper because it was the only day I had free, whereas since his retirement he had developed a taste for the weekend bustle at his local shopping centre. But not a weirdo, I thought, watching him swallow his tea. All he wanted was to chat about this cyclone of excitement that had hit the year his only daughter got pregnant at thirty-three. 'Me too,' I said without thinking. Thirty-three, really? He thought that was a wonderful coincidence. And from amniocentesis we slipped on to living wills and the judicial system, his small mobile face shifting with every turn of conversation.

For a few weeks the office was a bag of cats, and I forgot all about him. Then one Saturday, rushing by with a baguette under my arm, I saw him staring bleakly into the window of what used to be the Christmas Shop. For the first time, it was I who said hello. When, after pleasantries about crocus pots, he began telling me about his daughter, and how the hospital said it was nothing she'd done or not done, she hadn't overstrained or failed to eat, just one of these things that happen in most women's lives, I wished I had followed my first impulse and walked right by. I didn't want to spare the time to sit beside him, making fork marks in an almond slice.

He fell silent at one point, and as some kind of strange compensation I began to rhapsodize about my own phantom pregnancy. I'd never felt better; it was true what they said about the sense of blooming. Instead of wincing, his face lit up. He said he would bring me a cutting from last Sunday's paper about prenatal musical appreciation. I promised him I was drinking lots of milk.

Walking home with a box of groceries on my hip, I began to count weeks. If I had met him just after payday, which was the fifth of the month . . . I realized with a spasm of nausea that I should be beginning to show.

At this point the ludicrousness of the whole charade hit home. Since it was clearly impossible to explain to this nice old man that I had been playing such a bizarre, unintentional, and (in light of his daughter's miscarriage) tasteless joke, I would just have to make sure I never saw him again.

But I didn't manage to make it to the huge supermarket in the town centre after work any day that week. Come Saturday I crawled out of bed late and pulled on baggy trousers. His steel-wool head was before me in the queue at the flower stall; when he looked around, I waved. Yes, his daughter was back at work, these daffs were for her, and wasn't a bit of sunshine wonderful? Only when he had walked away did I realize that I had my hand on the small of my back, my belly slumped over my loose waistband.

The next Saturday I did my hand washing and baked scones with the end of the cheddar, then sat knotted up in an armchair and read some papers I'd brought home from work. My mother dropped by; when I offered her some tea, there wasn't any milk or sugar, so I had to justify the empty shelves by claiming not to have felt well enough to go out.

Afterwards, I lay on the sofa with the blanket she'd put over me, watching the sky drain. I was heavy with a lie I couldn't begin to explain. If I'd made a joke of it to my mother, she'd probably have called him a nosy parker.

My ribs were stiff; I shifted to face the rough woollen back of the sofa. If it were true, would I be throwing up in the mornings? Would I be feeling angry, or doubtful, or (that old pun) fulfilled? I grinned at myself and went to put on my makeup for a night out dancing.

The following Friday I managed to sneak away from work early enough to shop in town. I had packed my briefcase full of papers, then shoved them back in the in-tray.

Saturday I spent hoeing the waking flower beds outside my basement flat. Some friends arrived with *Alien* and popcorn. One of them noticed me holding my stomach after a particularly tense scene and raised a laugh by warning me not to throw up on the sofa.

Truth was, I'd been trying to remember at what point it would start kicking. For a few seconds I'd believed in it.

It was time to call a halt. The next Saturday I trailed up and down the shopping centre for an hour and a half in the spring chill. Every time I went into the library or the pet shop, I was sure he had just left. When the tap on the shoulder did come, as I was reading the list of prices in the window of the hair salon, I jerked so fast he had to apologize. But looking shocked and pinched did suit my story, I supposed.

As we neared the top of the café queue, his bare tray shuffling along behind mine, I rehearsed my opening line: 'I'm afraid I lost the baby.' It sounded absentminded and cruel. I tried it again, moving my lips silently. The beverages lady cocked her ear, thinking she'd missed my order; I cleared my throat and asked for a strong coffee. It was all my fault for having let a tiny lie swell into this monstrosity.

Before I could begin, he placed his shopping bag on the chair between us. 'I'm glad I caught you today,' he said pleasurably. 'I brought it along last week, but I didn't run into you. I was going to return it, but then I thought, who do I know who'd make good use of it?'

Under his bashful eyes, I drew out the folds of green silk. 'Wouldn't your daughter wear it anyway?' I asked.

He shook his head hastily.

'You shouldn't have,' I said. 'It's beautiful.' I slumped in the plastic seat, my stomach bulging.

He folded the dress back in its tissue paper and slipped it into the bag.

Though I didn't even know his surname, I felt like I was saying goodbye to a lifelong friend, one who had no idea that this was goodbye. I insisted he have a third of my lemon tart. We talked of Montessori schools and wipeable bibs, of our best and worst childhood memories, of how much had stayed the same between his generation and mine but would be different for my baby. We decided it was just as well I was due in August as the weather might be mild enough to nurse in the garden. When I looked at my watch it was half two, the coffee cold in the pot.

As I stood up, I had an hysterical impulse to say that if it proved to be a boy I'd name it after him. Instead, I mentioned that I was going off on an early summer holiday, but yes, of course I'd be home for the birth.

The new regime was a manageable nuisance. On Saturdays now I went straight from karate class to a shopping centre twice as far away in the other direction. An old friend of mine, meeting me laden with bags on the bus, mocked me for being so upwardly mobile, to go that far in pursuit of walnut-and-ricotta ravioli. One Saturday in May my mother asked me to come along to the old shopping centre, to help her with a sack of peat moss, and I had to invent a sudden blinding headache.

The dress I wore as often as the weather allowed; it seemed the least I could do. The leaf-green silk billowed round my hips as I carried my box of groceries close to the chest. There was room under there for quintuplets, or a gust of summer air. When August came and went and nothing happened, I felt lighter, flatter, relieved.

That was five years ago, but always I keep one eye out for him, even on the streets of other cities where my new job takes me. I have my story all ready: how I shop on Sundays now when my mother can take the children, two boys and a small girl, yes, quite a handful. He's sure to compliment me on having kept my figure. And his daughter, did she try again?

I felt prepared, but last Friday when I thought I saw him among the grapefruit I backed out in panic. What do you say to a ghost, a visitor from another life?

It occurs to me all of a sudden that he may be dead. Men often don't live very long after they retire. I never thought to ask how old he was.

I find it intolerable not to know what has become of him. Is this how he felt, wondering about me? On Saturday when I woke in my cool white bed, I had to fight off the temptation to drive down to the shopping centre and park there, watching through the windscreen for him to walk by.

the man who wrote
on beaches

As a child he'd never known what to put. He always started
out along the expanse of saturated sand with a yip of excitement, but after scraping the first great arc with the edge of his
sneaker, he'd stand with his leg extended like a dog trying to
piss. Everything took so long on sand, you might as well be
using Morse code. You'd better be sure you still meant what
you were writing by the time it was done. Once he'd put
HELLO, but his brothers laughed and scuffed out the O with
their toes.

Then another time on another beach, some New Year's Day
when he was maybe fourteen and alone, he'd written COCK-
SUCKERS in letters as long as himself. It looked so terrible,
printed so starkly for the clouds and every passing stranger to
read, and he'd thought the first wave would wipe it out, but in
his nervousness he'd dug too deep with the crescent of mussel
shell, so the small frills of water only smoothed his words,
glossed over a mistake he'd made on the K. The letters looked
graven, as if on a headstone, the obscenity emerging from the
beach itself. So after such a long while of standing with his back
to the wind, he'd dragged a line through the whole word with
the toe of his pointed shoe, lurching along on the other foot,

but still it was legible or could be guessed at anyhow, since no other word looked like that one.

The day he was forty-three, he accepted Jesus Christ as his Lord and Personal Saviour. It was quite a shock to his system.

A few weeks before, he had been driving through downtown Tacoma on a sticky afternoon much like any other. Traffic was slow as molasses and he found himself staring at a bus shelter with a poster on it that said in large pink letters, JESUS IS THE WAY.

He might well have seen it before, on other days when he'd been preoccupied with what to make for dinner or whether Margaret had remembered to call the IRS from the office about those tax forms, but the fact was that only on that particular day was there a chink open in his mind as he glanced at that bus shelter, a crack wide enough for those words to drop in. And for a moment he forgot a lifetime's worth of wisecracks about the Born Agains; for a moment he thought, *What if it was true? What if just maybe?*

Wouldn't that explain a lot of things, like what a mess this country had gotten itself into? Wouldn't that make some sense of how his life had turned out after all the promising things his report cards had said, after all his dumb dreams of changing the world?

Not that he was complaining. He'd been to Corsica and Bali and Scotland and the Everglades; he had a home with a view of Puget Sound and a good job and a great collection of German steins and a lot of laughs. Above all, he had Margaret, who was twice what he deserved. But it struck him sometimes that in a couple more decades he would be dead without ever having figured things out. And think of it: All these years he'd been using the word *Jesus* as a colourful form of ouch – if he dropped a wrench on his foot, say – when for all he knew the Born Agains were right, and Jesus just might be the way.

He was still half joking, or at least he thought he was.

Waiting for the lights to change, he tried it out loud. 'Jesus?' so it sounded like he was calling softly over the car door to someone in the street he thought he remembered from high school who probably wouldn't know him any more.

But all at once he was sick to his stomach, felt so bad in fact that when the light changed he pulled right instead of left and parked in front of a fire hydrant. He laid his wet forehead on his hands where they gripped the steering wheel and said, maybe out loud or maybe in his head, he didn't know, 'I'm nothing, I'm scum, Jesus, Jesus, Jesus.'

When he finally got home he watched some drag racing and waited for it to wear off, like a hangover, or heartburn. Margaret came home with antipasti from the deli; she felt his back where his T-shirt was stuck to it. He blamed the heat.

But by the weekend he still felt the same way. So come Sunday morning he walked down the road till he came to the first building with the word *Jesus* on it.

It was the Church of Jesus Our Lord. He thought he'd bolt at the end of the service, but strangers gathered round to welcome him. It turned out it wasn't them who'd paid for the sign at the bus shelter downtown, that was the Church of Christ Crucified, but still, 'No objections,' said the pastor. 'It was Our Lord who led your feet to our door.'

He still felt sick, standing there. These people weren't his sort of people, or so he would have said a week before. Their phrases were foreign to him; there was talk of missions and calls and walks with God. When they used words like *voice,* or *light,* he was never sure if they were to be taken literally. Their clothes were funny and the pastor stood too close to him. He knew he might turn these people into a big joke at the next office party. He felt like James Dean and wished he hadn't worn his leather jacket. He felt like a sinner. And when an old lady who'd introduced herself as Mrs Keilor said, 'See you next week,' part of him was so relieved he thought he might go down on his knees and cry.

Which was exactly what he did a few weeks later, on his forty-third birthday. Pastor Tull said it took a lot of folks that way.

For the first few weeks he hadn't said a word to Margaret about where he was going; he let her think he was stretching his legs. And when he began to mention the church it was all very cool; he tried to sound like an anthropologist on the Nature Channel.

'Do you actually believe any of that stuff?' Margaret asked lightly in the middle of Sunday dinner, and he shrugged and took another slice of salmon.

But on his birthday he walked home and told her he'd accepted Jesus Christ as his Lord and Personal Saviour. He said it all in a rush before he lost his nerve; he could hear how odd the words sounded as they left his mouth, like a very dry sort of joke.

Margaret let out a single whoop of laughter. He didn't take offence; it was a sound she always made when an appliance broke down or she slept through the alarm and missed her car pool. After a minute she came over to give him a hug with stiff arms and say, 'Whatever makes you happy.' As if it was a line she'd found in a magazine.

A couple of months on, he started bringing her to the odd church social. She seemed to come willingly enough, just as years ago she used to accompany him to occasional hockey games, because that was his thing. She recognized a guy from her accounts department, and they talked about the crazy new ventilation system. She admired Pastor Tull's moustache.

Mrs Keilor was in charge of the salad table. She whispered a question about whether his wife was saved, too. 'Not yet,' he said, as if he had great hopes. He was afraid somebody would ask Margaret the same question; he kept one ear out for her sharp laugh.

Margaret had no time for the abstract; that was something he always used to love about her. If she couldn't touch it, smell it, taste it, then it didn't matter. Her favourite exclamation was 'Unreal'. Whenever he started talking hypotheticals, she would reach for her sewing box, so the time wouldn't be completely wasted. Once she got around three sides of a cushion cover while he was wondering aloud about the future of democracy.

He didn't talk about his ideas, these days. He kept his new books on his side of the bed; he left his new cassettes in the car so he could play them on the way to work. He only watched the Bible Channel on the evenings when Margaret was out at the Y. And she quietly worked around this latest and most obscure of his hobbies.

He waited for her to ask, but she didn't. He would have welcomed her questions; he still had a bunch of his own. But Margaret was content not to understand. He couldn't figure that out. How she could bear not to know what was going on in his head. In his heart. In what he was learning, with some embarrassment, to call his soul.

He was dreaming about Jesus these days; that was something he wouldn't have told Margaret even if she'd asked. In the dreams he was generally walking up a mountain behind Jesus, who only looked about twenty-two, thin but surprisingly solid. You could lean your head on his bony shoulder. Jesus could speak without moving his lips.

He never had difficulty getting up these mornings; he just asked Jesus to get him out of bed and next thing his feet were on the rug. And work got done just like that. The things he had expected to be hardest were almost easy. He had thrown away his Zippo the day after his birthday and hadn't had a single drag since. Every time he got the craving he said, 'Jesus, Jesus, Jesus,' in his head till it went away. The same with beer. After Josh Miles at the church, who used to be an alcoholic, took him aside for a word, he saw he was better off without the stuff. Now he didn't miss it, didn't need it. He still dusted his stein collection, but he was thinking of donating it to a charity raffle. After a couple of weeks, Margaret got the hint and stopped asking would he like a cold one from the refrigerator. She teased him a little about what a clean-living guy he'd become – but not in front of friends.

Another thing, he wasn't sure their friends were his friends any more. They were the same people; it was him who'd changed. For the first year ever he put down every cent he'd made on his tax return. He could only talk about things like that to his church friends, those people in cheap shoes he'd have bust a gut laughing at a couple of months back.

What he couldn't tell them, though, was that Margaret wasn't his wife.

At a church picnic he watched her blowing bubbles with a four-year-old. Mrs Oberdorf had her eye on him. 'You and your wife been blessed with any children?' she asked in her cracked voice.

'Not yet.'

She nodded, her mouth twisted with sympathy.

He hoped she'd think it wasn't their fault. He hoped she wouldn't use the word *husband* in front of Margaret.

One evening when she was pinning up new drapes he said it. 'We should get married one of these days.' But it didn't sound romantic enough. It sounded like clearing out the garage.

Margaret took the pins out of her mouth. 'You think so?' She had this way of letting words hover like smoke.

'I know we used to say we didn't need it, but recently I've been reconsidering.'

She pinned up another fold of fabric.

'It might feel good. It might be the thing to do,' he added, as if he were kidding around. He hoped she wouldn't hear the guilt behind his voice.

'OK. What the hell,' said Margaret. He winced, but not so she'd notice. 'We've both done it before and it didn't kill us.'

Then she laughed until he laughed, too, and she came over and kissed him on the ear.

But as he was signing his name in the register – his ballpoint pressing the paper a little too hard – he knew that this time wasn't going to be like those other times. Neither he nor his first wife in DC nor Margaret nor her first husband in LA had had the slightest idea what they were really doing. This time would be the real thing, because now he knew what a promise was. Now he knew what the words meant.

To show she wasn't taking the whole thing too seriously, Margaret was wearing red. He didn't care; it looked good on her. 'You can bring your God buddies if you like,' she'd told him, but he said that was all right, he'd rather keep it small, just the two of them and a pastor (not Pastor Tull, just some Unitarian) and a few friends who drove down from Seattle and Vancouver.

After the ceremony he was high like he hadn't been since that time he tried cocaine at the prom. He was a bank robber who'd made it to Acapulco.

The next Sunday after church he said the word. 'My wife and I are taking a vacation,' he mentioned to Mrs Keilor, and relief stabbed him through the ribs.

For their honeymoon – about ten years too late, according to his mother in San Francisco, but she sent them a cheque anyhow – he and Margaret were going to drive right down the West Coast. That first night in a motel in Mount Saint Helens he lay under the weight of his wife and moved and shut his eyes. It felt like he was running down the right road at last. But later when he was letting the condom slither off him, he wanted to cry.

They hiked up a volcano the next day, cinders crunching like cornflakes under their feet. Later they squatted over tide pools and saw anemones blossom like green doughnuts and purple sea urchins as big as their hands. Margaret tilted her face up to the sun while he took pictures and figured out the distances between towns.

In Eugene, Oregon, he woke up in the middle of the night and had to shake her awake. 'Honey,' he said urgently. Then, apologetically, 'Honey, I just realized, we're meant to have children.'

The words shocked his ears.

At first Margaret didn't answer, and he thought she was still asleep, till he saw the line of her jaw. Then she said, 'For god's sake.'

Exactly, he was tempted to say, but didn't.

In the morning he woke up to find her packing.

He stared at her knotted hands, ramming two pairs of his socks into a corner. 'Who was it,' Margaret asked, 'just remind me who was it who talked me out of it all those other times?'

'You were never sure—,' he began.

'That's right, I wasn't sure, but you sure were.' A little bead of spit on her lip caught the sunlight. She plucked up another pair of socks but didn't put them in the bag. 'Who was it always told me it would be madness to go off the Pill? Who was it said we'd lose all our freedom, tie ourselves down?'

His throat felt like it was full of wadding. He cleared it. 'Guess everybody gets tied down one way or another.'

Margaret's hands were jammed into the pockets of her silky dressing gown; her nails were stretching the seams. 'Who was it kept saying he wasn't ready?'

'I don't know,' he said, nearly whispering. 'I don't know who that guy was.' There was a silence so complete he could hear the chambermaid vacuuming at the other end of the motel. 'But I'm different now.'

'You can say that again.' She stared at him; her eyes were hard as hazelnuts. 'You're on another planet.'

'I'm finally ready,' he pleaded.

'Oh yeah?' Her voice was bigger than the room. 'Well, I'm forty-two, so you and your friend Jesus can go to hell.'

It took them two days to drive home. Awhile before they stopped for a burger on the first day he thought Margaret was crying, but she was looking out the window so he couldn't be sure. At the motel he called his mother and told her there'd been an emergency at work and he'd been called back. She'd always been able to tell when he was lying, but she didn't say so.

When they pulled into their driveway at the end of the second day, Margaret laid her hand on his thigh and said, 'OK.'

He wasn't sure what it meant. Pax? Or, this marriage is over?

'OK,' she said, 'let's give it a shot.'

She got pregnant twice before the end of the year, which he took as a good sign. The first one made it to two months, the second to five. That one was a boy. He made the nurse give him the little body, for burial. Quite a few people from the Church of Jesus Our Lord turned up, though Margaret didn't come back with them for the chicken supper afterwards, which everybody said was understandable.

The strange thing was that he had known the boy wouldn't make it to term. At the funeral it was like there was cotton wool round his heart, keeping the pain at bay. He and Margaret were going to have a girl; he just knew it.

He didn't mind waiting a little while longer so Margaret could build her strength up before trying again. It felt strange to be buying rubbers – in a drugstore in the next town, so no one from the church would see him – but he thought Jesus probably wouldn't have a word to say about it, under the circumstances.

On Christmas Eve he asked Margaret to come to church with him, just for once. On the way home she said, 'One last shot, OK?' as if she were talking about pinball.

That night as he came his legs shook like bowstrings. His mind swam inside her. He could almost see the egg, glowing at the end of the dark tube; he registered the shock when the single chosen sperm, blindly butting, felt the membrane give way and seal him in.

The next day he started making a list of girls' names. He kept the list in the glove compartment so as not to annoy Margaret, who didn't believe in counting chickens.

Nothing happened till March, when Margaret started throwing up her Cheerios and smiling at strangers. 'Third time lucky,' he told her on the way home from the ultrasound. His head was so full of a single image – the tiny curled chipmunk that was going to be their daughter – that he could hardly see the road. The nurse said you couldn't be sure so early, but yes, it did look kind of like a girl.

'Laura?' he suggested, idling at a traffic light. 'Leona? Lucy?'

'We'll see,' said Margaret, smiling. And then, 'The light's changed.'

As the time went by, he bloomed. It was no hardship, he

found, to be patient with a pushy new guy at work. When Margaret's strange uncle who picked his nose came to town, they put him up on the sofa bed for a whole week. Prayer was easy; he'd never had so much to say.

Margaret, on the other hand, was getting more wired by the month. She wouldn't let her forty-third birthday be celebrated in any way, not even dinner out, not so much as a bunch of flowers or a card. The bigger she grew, the more substantial their future seemed to him, and the less she seemed able to believe in it. He wondered if she was frightened about the birth; it did seem to him a terrible prospect, and he cracked a joke about how the human race would soon die out if women were as cowardly as men.

Margaret didn't laugh.

'You'll have to trust God, hon,' he said, a little nervously, as he knew the word made her twitch, but it was the only one he could think of.

She laughed then, and said, 'I've never even met him.'

He had a feeling everything would be better once they were a family. With Laura coming to church with him every week, first in one of those slings on his chest, and then in her little black patent shoes, surely Margaret wouldn't want to be left behind. It made sense that once she saw how good Jesus had been to them, she'd understand all the rest of it.

Meanwhile, she didn't understand the slightest thing he said. She was always taking offence. She thought he was looking for sex when he was just as happy stroking her belly. She said the baby kept kicking her in the ribs. One day he was playing chase-the-foot when Margaret shoved him so hard he fell off the bed.

When he got to his feet, she was laughing in that appalled way of hers. 'Oh, I'm such a bitch these days,' she said between

47

snorts. 'I'm so sorry, honey, I'm so sorry. I'm scared, you know?'

'Of the birth?'

'No, moron,' said Margaret, still laughing. 'Scared it won't happen.'

He could tell she was an inch away from tears so he lay down beside her.

San Francisco should be levelled to the ground, he thought, when his mother called to tell him about her knee. It was only a little fall, but she'd rolled about twenty feet down the sidewalk till she landed against a fire hydrant.

He knew he should be there to take her home from the hospital. If there was ever a time to be a good son, this was it. But he rested his ear on Margaret's drum of a belly and couldn't lift it away.

'Get out of here,' she said, pretty gently. 'Those bastards owe you two weeks of vacation.'

'Not now.'

'Yes, now. Get out of my hair for a while. It'll be a good three months before this baby lifts a finger.'

So here he was, back on the coast. By the time he passed the Oregon state line he was breathing easier, and the farther he drove, the more peaceful he felt. He took his time; he saw all the places he and Margaret had missed on their truncated honeymoon. He could feel the horizon curving around him like a hand.

It was then he started writing again. Just on beaches, at first. There was a little cove beside a lighthouse, washed clean as a slate by the morning tide. There was one small girl picking up shells on the waterline, and her family sunbathing farther up the beach. He stood staring out to sea, and all at once he knew what to write. JESUS IS THE WAY, he put, in letters so big and clear they could probably be seen from a low plane. All the time he was marking them with the toe of his shoe, he was thinking of the surprise people would get when they wandered down the beach that afternoon. That's how you did it: by surprise. Minds were like mussels: You shouldn't try to force them open; it was better to catch them at an idle moment and slip inside.

He was just finishing the Y when he noticed the little girl's mother. She was standing at a distance, reading the words upside down. When his eyes met hers, she grabbed the child's hand and hurried back up the beach.

It gave him an odd feeling, as if she thought he was some kind of pervert or something. But you couldn't expect people to understand if they hadn't gone down their road to Damascus yet. That's all he wanted: to give people a glimpse of it, to throw strangers a split second of the joy that was filling him up these days so he hardly needed to eat except for a bag of grapes in the car.

Whenever he got a surge of happiness, he wanted to ring Margaret, but she'd said the sound of the phone was getting on her nerves these days, and he knew she needed a break from him, so he sent her postcards instead. He told her things he'd never thought to mention before. 'Did you know you are the most beautiful woman in the world?' he wrote on a picture of a glacial lake, and 'I love you more every day,' on a shot of a leaping salmon.

Words were pouring out of him. He was a bit shocked with himself, the day he wrote on a wall outside Portland. He hadn't done a thing like that since he was a kid. But this wall already said DONT MES WITH THE MOFO BOYZ, LOLA SUCKS DICK, and ME N U 4EVER '03, so he felt he could only improve it by adding JESUS SAVES with a little can of white spray paint he got at the corner hardware store.

Then, when he was walking through a grove of old-growth redwoods the next afternoon, his heart started to knock like a rattle. The forest was bigger than the biggest cathedral, but humans had had no share in the building. He felt like an insect. The trees were wider than he was tall, and taller than anything; all he could hear was a lone woodpecker. At one point where a huge tree had fallen across the path, the rangers had cut a section away to let walkers through. On the weathered wood, ridged by the chain saw, someone had cut ANGIE LOVES JEFF. He couldn't resist; he took out his Swiss army knife and carved the words JESUS LOVES US ALL.

These days Laura was so clear in his mind that he could nearly see her, running along beside him. When he rented a gas lantern to go down an old lava tube, clambering down from the glare at the tunnel mouth into the cooling darkness, he promised himself that he'd bring her here someday. Half a mile in, where the floor was slick with ice and the roof of the cave reached its highest point, he'd hold the heavy lantern up to show her the ridges and grooves the lava had left when it flowed away, the tiny kiss shapes of its final drops. Then he'd turn off the lantern for a minute and she'd yelp with fright, but she'd grip his fingers and know that everything was going to be all right.

The next day he saw the best sunset he'd ever seen in his life. There was a phone booth by the side of the road, so he pulled in and rooted around in the glove compartment for his bag of quarters. Margaret would be out at her organic gardening class; he could just leave a message.

But she was home. At first he didn't recognize her voice, it was so muffled. She must have been drinking. When he said, 'Margaret? Honey?' there was a click.

The connection must have broken. So he fed in more quarters and tried again.

When she picked up the phone again, the first thing she said was 'I lost it.'

'What?' he said stupidly.

'You heard me.'

'You lost it?'

'It wasn't my fault.'

He hardly knew what he was saying. 'Was it a girl?'

There was such a long pause he thought the line was broken. Then Margaret said, 'It doesn't matter.'

The phone seemed stuck to his ear; sweat was running down his throat. 'Margaret, honey,' he said, as if that were a sentence.

'It's over.'

It seemed a matter of urgency to say the right thing now. There was a sudden beeping, and he fed in his last quarters. 'Listen,' he said, too loud, as if his voice had to cover the distance by itself. 'Listen, we'll try again in a little while.'

'Like hell we will,' she roared.

His legs were shaking; he leaned back against the glass.

'To think I let you put me through this, you and your fucking Jesus!' Margaret's voice crackled down the line. 'At forty-three, to think I was such a fool.'

There was a silence that seemed impermeable.

'You know, I was happy enough before we went and got married.' Her sobs were as loud as the words they punctuated. 'I had a full life. I was perfectly happy enough with no ring and no children. Weren't you? Weren't you happy enough?'

He was still trying to think of an answer when the line went dead.

The sun was a smear of red at the base of a dark sky. He went down and sat on the beach until his legs stopped shaking.

The last of the light caught blades of shell in the sand. He dug one up with the point of his shoe. He couldn't think of anything to write, so he pushed it back, pressing down till he felt the hard damp sand give way and bury it.

He knew he should call the hospital to leave a message for his mother that he wasn't coming, but all he had in his pockets was small change. So he turned the car around and started the long drive home.

oops

James was overnighting with his oldest friends before a flight to the Yucatán. He'd managed to avoid ever sleeping in Eoin and Neasa's flat before. It was a dingy little fourth-floor on the wrong quay of the Liffey. Back in his twenties, some years before the Dublin boom began, James himself had been far-sighted enough to snap up an elegant little cottage in Ballsbridge, which was now worth nine-and-a-half times what he'd paid for it – a thought that always gave him a frisson of satisfaction. But unfortunately on the day before his trip to photograph the Yucatán for *Luxury* magazine, the workmen were in to install a sauna in his basement, and the dust played havoc with his sinuses, so he had no choice but to accept his friends' offer.

As always, James averted his eyes from the flat itself – cluttered with equipment his friends were storing for the rest of their sax quintet – and he remarked that they'd got an *outrageously* good view of the river. After dinner he insisted on taking them to a new club where you didn't actually have to dance if, like Neasa and Eoin, you loathed what passed for music these days; you could just lie around on yellow velvet couches on the balcony and look down on it all.

Back in the flat, their sofa bed felt to James like a grill, only slightly padded with tinfoil. In the middle of the chilly January night, he staggered along the tiny corridor to the loo. Fumbling around on the shelf for paracetamol to ward off his hangover, his fingers found a curved white oblong of plastic; a futuristic glasses case, maybe, or a makeup holder? Curious, James pressed the little button on top. Suddenly a tiny blue light came on. 'Oops,' he said under his breath, and stepped back, knocking several dusty bottles of essential oils into the bath with a dreadful clatter. He pressed the button again, but the light wouldn't go off.

He thought no more about it till a fortnight later when he got back to Dublin Airport with a Yucatánian glow to his cheekbones. Picking up some melatonin to ward off jet lag in the pharmacy, he noticed a cardboard woman in a red dress, holding the same strange little device in her hand. A speech bubble said TIMERA™: BECAUSE I NEED TO KNOW.

James goggled at the small print. She needed to know what? TIMERA™ IS THE NEW AND UNIQUE FAMILY PLANNING DEVICE THAT WORKS IN HARMONY WITH NATURE'S CYCLES TO GIVE YOU CONTROL OVER YOUR BODY AND YOUR LIFE. What a laugh, thought James, a contraceptive computer! He quite understood that Neasa and Eoin had never wanted to swap their shiny saxophones for smelly babies; it was only natural.

But then he remembered the little blue light that had come on when he'd pressed the button. Oh Jesus, he thought then.

As the taxi inched its way through the gridlocked city, James shut his eyes and thought furiously. He wished he'd paid more attention to that lesson on the rhythm method at the community school that he, Neasa, and Eoin had all left nearly twenty years ago. He regretted his lack of information about women's innards in general. Maybe what his wretched fumbling with the button had done was to reset the thing so the days the machine would now call safe would, in fact, be highly dangerous. Oh Christ, why hadn't the woman just stayed on the Pill like everyone else?

James had his Nokia out and their number half dialled before he thought of what he might say. *Hi, I'm passing through Swords; I just thought you should know that two weeks ago I pressed your little button* . . . Hot mortification swept up his face. He was being paranoid, ridiculous. He put his phone back on his belt and put the matter from his mind.

Till a soft May evening in his little house when he was feeding his old friends crispy duck legs in chile-lime broth, and Eoin burped faintly and said, 'What'cha think, Neasa? Is it time for the news?'

James assumed they wanted to switch on *Newsnight,* but no.

'I'm pregnant,' Neasa told him, with a tight little grin.

He thought he might throw up there and then, on his grandmother's linen tablecloth. But his mind was working at top speed, churning out conclusions: (*A*) It was all his fault. (*B*) The constant anti-abortion propaganda in their teens must have worked, because clearly Neasa and Eoin had decided to go through with having this baby. (*C*) He must never, never, never tell them what he'd done.

'Wow!' he shrieked, his face a mask of delight.

He knew this appalling accident would transform his friends' lives; what he never expected was how much it was going to change his own.

He dropped heavy hints until they asked him to be Angela's godfather, and his christening present was 1,000 euros in a savings account, to start her college fund. (He'd wanted to make it

5,000 euros but knew that would look suspicious.) Then he became the regular Tuesday babysitter, plus any evening Eoin and Neasa were off at a jazz gig. Because, in fact, they didn't give up their music, not at all; that baby could fall asleep only to the sounds of the sax.

When at, say, five years old, Angie stayed the night in her uncle James's cream-linen spare room in Ballsbridge, he always fed her organic vegetables and put Gregorian chant on the mini-disc player. Whenever he went abroad on a shoot – which wasn't as often, now, because of what he wryly called his 'family responsibilities' – he brought home exquisite and educational toys. He would leave his darkroom at a moment's notice to drive her halfway across Ireland to reconstructed folk villages and drama festivals. On Angie's tenth birthday, James started giving her regular fistfuls of banknotes, and once when she was furious with him after he called her T-shirt sluttish, she told her parents about the money and got him into serious, though temporary, trouble.

His other friends thought he was mad. He'd never told any of them about what he thought of as his secret parenthood: the fact that, by one careless mistake, he had made this child happen.

At thirteen, the girl announced her name was now Ang, to rhyme with *bang*. For the next four years she was foul.

'Sometimes I don't like her at all,' Neasa said softly to James, looking out the window of his house to where her daughter sat between the fountain and the Japanese maple, talking on her mobile, her back as convex as a shield.

His friend's confession filled him with panic. He had thought it was working out all right. He had assumed that every child turned into a wanted child, even if she'd been unwanted to begin with, even if her conception had been a bloody awful

56

blunder, never meant to happen. But then, how could he say that Ang had never been meant to happen? – since he loved her, himself, with a guilty fervour of ownership that was unaffected by any of her shifting moods, unaffected by all the nasty things she'd said to him over the years, from her first howl of 'You're poo' to their latest spat, when she'd called him a 'sad old suburban queen'.

The summer she left school, she emerged from adolescence, shakily, like a convalescent. One day James looked at her across the table of a noodle bar and realized that she was an utterly charming young woman, sitting here, telling this middle-aged man her plans to work her way across Australia, her eyes shining at him as if he mattered to her, as if he always would. How did this happen?

At Ang's goodbye party, James gave her a discreetly wrapped bumper pack of extra-strength condoms; she blushed, but said yes, of course, she promised she'd be careful.

Four martinis later, James sat heavily on the arm of Neasa's chair and murmured in her ear, 'I know you never wanted to have her, but isn't she fabulous?'

Neasa stared at him.

'Sorry, what I meant was—,' he backtracked. And then he couldn't help himself: the eighteen-year-old story was spilling out in a passionate hiss – the little plastic machine, the terrible blue light.

Neasa was smiling strangely. 'You daft egg,' she said at last, 'you poor eejit! It was for ovulation, not contraception.'

He could feel his eyes cross.

'We wanted a baby. We'd been trying for a year and a half.' She laughed a little hoarsely.

'So what you're telling me,' he said blankly, 'is that I made no difference.'

'None at all!' She grinned at him

And James, who should have felt relieved, went home early from the party with a stitch between his ribs as if there was something he'd lost.

through the night

What sent Una over the edge was people asking 'Does she sleep through the night?' For some reason it was often the first thing strangers said after 'What a lovely baby.' Una was all right with the lovely baby line, she could smile and nod, her eyes only slightly shiny, and she could even cope with remarks like 'It must be so much fun!' If she just kept nodding and smiling, she found, people assumed that having a two-month-old baby was just like in the diaper ads, or the way they dimly and fondly remembered it. 'Treasure every moment,' the bank manager commanded her, rubbing his beard. All this Una could take. But when someone approached her in the supermarket or queuing at an ATM and tickled whatever bit of Moya was sticking out of the sling and said the fatal words, 'Is she sleeping through the night yet?' . . .

Before the birth, before Moya – BM, as Silas called it – Una had not been a crier. In fact, she'd been known for her ability to sit dry-cheeked through *Titanic* or *It's a Wonderful Life,* while Silas was gulping by her side. Before her periods she'd turn slightly snappish, and when her father died, back in Ireland, she'd gone very quiet for a month or so. But crying wasn't something she did. Even pregnant, she'd maintained her steadiness.

These days – AM, After Moya – Una didn't recognize herself. It was as if there'd been some transformation at the cellular level: a weakening of all the walls. She cried sitting on the toilet – 'Just coming, Moya, just a minute; I promise, Mum needs just a minute more' – she cried when she couldn't get her snowboots laced up one-handed and had to shout for Silas; she cried when he was at the office and it took her four hours to make and eat a peanut butter sandwich. She always let herself cry in the shower because her face was wet anyway so it didn't count. She dissolved every time she had to answer the phone, if not with the first hello then as soon as Moya's name came up; she cried so much when trying to book an electrician to fix the furnace thermostat that she had to put the phone down.

Whenever Una slept – for of course she did get to sleep, at certain periods in each twenty-four-hour cycle when Silas took Moya downstairs between feeds (it was just that these tainted, uneasy mouthfuls of unconsciousness bore no relation to the blissful, unthinking seven-hour nights she'd known BM) – whenever she slept, she didn't have time to dream, and only the cheap digital watch she kept on her wrist at all times convinced her that she'd added, say, another forty-three minutes of sleep to her total. She wept in the night when she slumped over to nurse Moya again and looked down the street where not a single other light was on. She wept hardest in the early morning when she was meant to be catching up on her sleep, when the baby was downstairs with Silas but Una could still hear her shrieks through three wooden doors, could hear them so faintly but persistently that she thought she might be having an aural hallucination.

Delusions of all kinds afflicted her. Again and again in the night she'd hear Moya's whimperings from the cot attached to the bed, and lean over, pick up the baby, put her to her breast . . . but why were the cries continuing, getting more frantic? She'd wake properly then and realize that Moya was still lashing about in the cot, so who was this other baby at her breast? Only the balled-up duvet, which fell apart in her sweaty, shuddering hands. And there was Silas, smooth-faced in sleep at her side, like some absolute stranger.

But even to use the terms *night* and *day* was misleading. Day and night were human inventions, Una realized, and Moya – a startled visitor from another planet – had never heard of them. There no longer was any night for Una, in the old sense, the switch-off, shed-your-troubles, knit-up-the-ravelled-sleeve-of-care sense. Hers was a work shift that never really ended even when she was meant to be relaxing, one long day that spun on sickeningly through dark and light, sound and silence. She didn't hate other people, not even Silas; she lacked the energy, or perhaps it was that she felt entirely cut off from them, marked out by her fated, perpetual punishment.

Una had always got on well with her mother, despite their differences. So when Rose flew in from Cork for a weeklong stay, Una put the baby down on the rug, for once, and fell into her arms.

'Barry's Tea,' said her mother, unpacking her bag, 'and Bewley's Dark Roast, and a couple of boxes of Black Magic, aren't they your favourite?'

'That's lovely, Mum,' said Una regretfully, 'but I'm off caffeine, in case it keeps Moya awake.'

'How many times does she have you up at night now?'

Una gave a little shrug. 'Five or six.'

'How long each time?'

'Forty minutes, an hour.'

'Ah, you poor child! No wonder you look so awful.'

Which, of course, made Una cry.

*

That first night, Rose took her pill and popped in her earplugs, as always when she was in a strange place. Before she swallowed it, she did register a pang of guilt, but it would hardly do any good for her to be lying awake listening all night, would it?

Rose's idea of being a good grandmother was taking the baby for long walks, but the hard-packed, jagged snow of an Ontario January made it impossible to get the buggy round the block. 'Besides, it's too cold to take her out,' said Una, putting the wailing baby back against her chest, tightening the sling and swaying from side to side.

Her daughter wore a glazed look, Rose thought, like someone with Alzheimer's. 'It'll be lovely when the weather warms up,' she said blandly, before remembering that spring here didn't come till May.

Silas dropped them off at a café downtown on his way to work. Two sips into her decaf latte Una unbuttoned her shirt to feed Moya. This startled Rose, but she didn't let it show; times change, and sure, why not? She looked around to see if there was a smoking section, but apparently not; she decided it wasn't worth standing outside in the driving snow.

Una discussed her mental state as if it was a not-particularly-interesting ongoing war in a country she couldn't spell. 'Not *depression,* I wouldn't call it that, Mum; I've only got three of the eight symptoms in the books.'

That was something else Rose found strange: It was all books nowadays; young mothers didn't so much as wipe a bottom without consulting the authorities ('Front to back for girl babies,' Una had corrected her this morning).

'Some women I've talked to at La Leche meetings, they say the baby blues are so normal' – Una broke off to yawn – 'It's probably hormones, or the shock of giving birth. Like, I remember, the day we came home from the hospital, I was convinced Moya would never be safe in the outside world; I had this craving to put her back in.'

Rose had a simpler explanation. 'Wouldn't anyone lose their marbles from this kind of sleep deprivation? Sure that's how they torture prisoners!'

Una smiled faintly.

'If I could just buy you one good night's sleep! I really don't – I've been casting my mind back thirty years,' Rose said, her forehead wrinkled, 'but I really can't remember having such a hard time with you or Donal.' Of course, their father had given them a bottle at three in the morning, that helped, and because they were in their own room she hadn't been roused by every little peep out of them. 'You were both awfully good . . .'

She'd forgotten: That was one of the forbidden terms. 'They're not good or bad, Mum,' Una repeated. 'They're just babies with needs.'

Rose decided to be frank. 'But it's ridiculous for Moya to be carrying on like this, at the two-month mark. She's preying on your feelings, I'm afraid; you cuddle her so constantly in that sling thing, she's spoiled rotten—' *Damn,* that was another of the words.

'There's no such thing as *spoiling* a two-month-old,' her daughter said tightly. 'The current scientific consensus—'

'Oh, I'm not saying there's any badness in her,' Rose interrupted. 'I just mean she's got into dangerous habits.'

Una's stare was cold. 'Babies worn in slings for three hours a day cry less and thrive better, it says so in all the books.'

Moya let out a high-pitched wail; Una switched her to the other breast. Rose bit her lip and suggested they have a couple of those lovely looking muffins. By the time she came back with the plate, Una's cheeks were striped with tears again.

Rose found, over the next few days, that every conversation

with her daughter ran straight into a wall. The present generation seemed hedged in by rules, miserably committed to something known as 'attachment parenting'. (In her day, Rose would have liked to say, they'd just got on with it, watched a lot of telly, and had a laugh when they could.) Everything she suggested had already been judged impossible. No, Una couldn't pump milk for Silas to give the baby at night, because she felt she only barely had enough as it was, and if she skipped a feed she might jeopardize her supply. Sorry, Una wasn't willing to leave Moya with a babysitter so she could have a proper slap-up lunch out with her mother. No, she didn't see how it would help to try to make the baby sleep in her own room.

As for the little bits of folk wisdom Rose couldn't help offering when she saw her sunken-eyed daughter leap up again – 'Give her a bottle of water instead, surely she can't still be hungry,' or 'Why wouldn't you let her grizzle for five minutes, see if she'll drop off back to sleep' – these were received as if she'd proposed sticking the infant's foot in a broken beer bottle. The briefest suggestion of giving Moya some kind of sedative to let Una catch up on some sleep sent Una off on a five-minute rant about adults poisoning babies for their own convenience.

'Sweetheart,' Rose burst out finally, 'I don't mean to play the interfering granny, I really don't, you're doing a marvellous job' – Moya made a choking sound and brought up white curds on Una's sleeve – 'I just can't stand seeing you in this state. Don't you think you're being a bit hard on yourself, playing the martyr?'

Una's eyes were huge. With fury? Or just exhaustion?

'Babies are tougher than they look. I didn't run to pick you up every time you opened your mouth, and you grew up all right, didn't you?' There was a pause. *Didn't you,* she wanted to ask again.

Nobody quite understood, Una thought, and her mother least of all. Hadn't she chosen to have Moya, planned it, wanted it for years? So she just had to do it the best way she could, even if she felt tangled in a nightmare that wouldn't let her wake up. From the sound of it, her mother's generation had ignored all their instincts when it came to looking after tiny, vulnerable human beings. They'd smoked and drank through pregnancy and labour, bottle-fed their babies and left them dangling from doors for hours, dosed them with alcoholic gripe water, jammed plastic pacifiers in their mouths, left them in barred cots to cry it out . . . Of course they needed to believe that they'd done what was right, instead of just what was handy. But who could say how much of the fucked-up state of so many of Una's friends might not be due to buried memories of wailing away alone on those long-gone nights?

'Darling, it's just that you're in such a bad way,' Rose was saying. 'Tonight, why don't I stay up with the baby for an hour or two?'

But could I trust you to bring her in when she's hungry? Una wanted to say. Instead she forced a smile and said it was OK, she was feeling not too bad this evening.

It was quite pleasant to have company while Silas was out, she supposed, but on the other hand, guests always needed looking after. And Rose, with her dry-clean-only cashmere, after-dinner cognac, and shivering smoke breaks on the porch, seemed such an irrelevance. Shouldn't Moya have brought them closer together instead of the opposite? To avoid discussing the contentious subject of the baby, Una would raise some topic of the day – airline security or pensions or the

Atkins diet – but of course all she cared or knew about at the moment was the baby, so all she could contribute was the odd robotic syllable.

Rose, for her part, seemed to be learning to resist the temptation to give advice – which left her with nothing but platitudes. 'Hang on in there,' she'd say, squeezing her daughter's shoulder. 'It'll be different when she's more active; she'll suddenly get the hang of day and night, wait till you see. One of these mornings you'll wake up after a good night's sleep, you'll hardly believe it!'

Una nodded, as if talking to a mad person at a bus stop.

The morning she was to fly back to Dublin, Rose woke early, for her, and pulled out her earplugs. She lay listening to the beautiful silence till she heard Silas pulling the front door closed behind him. She put her dressing gown on and peeped round the other bedroom door. There lay the baby, in the cot attached to her parents' bed, and there was Una, flat on her back, her arms uncurled, as if drifting down a stream. Her face was peaceful, almost young again.

Rose must have stood on a creaky floorboard as she backed out, because suddenly Una was bolt upright, eyes wild. She snatched up the baby, who began to shriek.

'Good morning,' said Rose, like some nervous chambermaid. She rather wished she'd stayed in bed.

'Jesus. Jesus Christ,' Una said into Moya's fuzzy scalp. 'It's light out.'

'It certainly is. Twenty past seven.'

'I thought she'd died in the night.' Una's face was contorted with tears again.

Rose suppressed a sigh. 'She's grand. She's had a lovely long sleep, that's all.'

'I don't believe it. Could she have been crying and I just didn't hear her?'

'There wasn't a peep out of her,' said Rose firmly, not mentioning the earplugs.

Una managed a weak laugh.

'Didn't I promise you things would get better?'

'You did.'

'Now, don't be expecting her to pull off a trick like this every night—'

'I won't,' Una assured her mother. 'I don't care if she doesn't do it again for months. Now I know it's possible—' Faith glittered in her eyes.

'So how do you feel?'

'Fabulous.'

'I'll bring you up a cup of coffee,' said Rose.

'Decaf,' said Una, with a smile, sinking back into the pillows with Moya.

That hadn't gone quite the way she'd planned, Rose thought as she went down the stairs. She'd meant to move from told-you-so to a cheerful confession that she'd given the baby half a teaspoon of her cognac last night. *See,* she'd intended to say, *it did you good, and it didn't do her a bit of harm!* But something in Una's eyes had made her reconsider this morning, and perhaps discretion was the better part of motherhood, after all.

do they know it's
christmas?

Trevor could barely see the traffic light through sheets of rain.

'Quick, before it turns red,' muttered Louise.

'It's amber.'

'Amber means go if you can. Go on!'

It was red now; he hit the brake and felt it judder. The wipers kept up their whine.

A small sigh. 'Sorry I snapped,' she said.

'That's OK.' Leaving Limerick, they'd been snarled up in Christmas-shopping traffic for the best part of an hour.

'I should have rung Mrs Quirk to ask her to look in on the babies,' Louise muttered.

'Mallarmé hates her,' Trevor pointed out.

'I know, but it's better than leaving them alone on such a hideous evening. I'd try her now, but the phone's acting up again. Hey, we could ask your folks for another one for Christmas.'

The mobile phone had been unreliable ever since Proust had ripped the charger out of the wall. 'Proust's always so curious about things,' said Trevor. 'Do you think he's the most intelligent of the three?'

Louise turned on him. 'That's not a fair question.'

'I know, I know, I don't mean it . . . divisively.'

'They're all really bright in their own ways. Light's changing,' she pointed out.

His tires squealed through the puddles. 'You think they're all perfect,' he accused her fondly.

'No I don't. Well, nearly,' she conceded. Nose pressed to the blurred window, her tone sank again. 'I wish we were home.'

'Twenty minutes.'

'Fifteen, if you shift your arse. Gide gets so fractious when it pisses down like this.'

'We're living in the wrong climate,' he observed, not for the first time. 'Not to mention a cultural wasteland.'

'Yeah, well next time Barcelona University has simultaneous openings in classics and sociology we must remember to apply.'

'Ho ho ho,' he chuckled like some grim Santa.

Trevor's favourite moment was always when he put his key in the lock. Eruption, joyous noise, crashes against the other side of the door. Tonight he tried to take his raincoat off, but Gide felled him.

'Sweeties, gorgeous-gorgeousnesses,' Louise was crooning, Proust swinging high in her arms. 'We're home, yes we are, yes we are.'

'Let Daddy get up. No licky face, no licky,' Trevor was telling Gide gruffly.

'How's he meant to know not to lick it when you offer it to him like a big jam doughnut?' Louise bent down to kiss her husband under one eye. 'Mallarmé doesn't lick faces, does she, lovely girl. Who's a lovely quiet girl?'

'Did you miss us, Mallarmé?' Trevor asked, sleeking her yellow fur. 'Were you bored silly? Just another three days till the holidays and then walkies anytime.'

Proust writhed in ecstasy in Louise's arms, and Gide began another round of barking.

'Trevor!'

'I said the *W*-word, didn't I?' Trevor rebuked himself.

As he was putting away the bagfuls of Christmas shopping, he said, 'We've bought no presents for them yet.'

'Oh, I know. Do you think – one big one each, or several smalls?'

'Smalls, definitely. They love tearing off the paper.'

'They always like some new squeakies. But remember last year,' said Louise, 'when we gave Gide that rubber apple that was too small and I had to do the Heimlich manoeuvre?'

'That was the most terrifying moment of my life,' said Trevor. 'Hey, I asked the dean of arts what he's getting his poodle and he said nothing.'

'You mean he didn't answer?'

'No, I mean he said, *"Nothing."* He said, and I quote, *"She doesn't know it's Christmas!"'*

Later on, Trevor was making his weekly call to his parents in Belfast. 'Not much new, Mum. Except that Proust just gave us the fright of our lives by turning the telly on! With the remote.'

'Is she the fat one?' asked his mother.

Trevor felt that familiar wave of irritation. 'Proust is a he; he's tiny,' he reminded her. 'The one you mean is Gide, but actually he's been on diet food for three weeks and if you look at him head-on he's really not—' A rubber Bart Simpson, wet with drool, squeaked at Trevor's feet. 'Not now, Gide, Daddy's on the phone.' Proust was scrabbling against Trevor's leg; they really would have to steel themselves to clip his claws this evening.

His mother was making some remark about the *pack*.

'There's only three of them,' he objected. 'Greta's got three kids, and you never confuse the boys with the girls!'

She let out a short laugh. 'Oh, Trev, it's hardly the same.'

He'd given up on breaking his family of the habit of calling him Trev. He chewed his lip, as he picked up the wet toy to bounce it against the far wall. Proust raced after it, but Gide shoved him out of the way. 'Be nice,' Trevor warned them. 'Share your squeaky.' Then, with false warmth, 'Tell you what, Mum, maybe they'll give you a framed photo for Christmas, with their names on.'

A couple of minutes later he walked into the kitchen, where Louise was frying chicken breasts. 'Save me a crispy bit,' he said, to postpone what he had to say.

'Mallarmé likes the crispy bits. You're getting polenta. So how's life in Belfast?'

He let out his breath with the sound of a fast puncture. 'We were talking about Christmas. I was telling Mum not to worry about bedding for the babies, we'll all sleep together on our blow-up mattress.'

'Uh-huh.'

'And she said actually this year, with Greta and Mick and all the kids being over from Sydney, she and Dad were wondering if we could maybe . . . do something with the dogs.'

'Do something?' repeated Louise. 'What does she mean? Do what?'

Trevor cleared his throat. 'Not bring them.'

Her eyes were little dark buttons.

The last three days of term crawled by; the stack of exam papers deflated. To celebrate the holidays, Louise and Trevor went for a long hike across the Cliffs of Moher. Gide barked fiercely at mountain goats. 'Do you think Proust's coat is looking dull?' she asked.

'Hmm?' Trevor stared down into his half-zipped jacket, where Proust was curled up. 'Maybe a wee bit.'

'The vet says you can put vegetable oil in their food to increase shine. We'll have to take Mallarmé to that grooming place this week; she's all burrs,' added Louise, watching the dog lope silently away towards a group of Japanese tourists.

'Yeah, she must have a bit of collie in her, she gets so snaggled. Mallarmé!' Trevor tried again, more loudly. 'Mallarmé, no! Come back!'

'She won't bite, will she?' said Louise, breathless as she ran.

'She bit Mrs Quirk last week.'

'Only because she messed with Mallarmé's ears.'

'Don't touch her ears,' Trevor bawled at the tour group.

Afterwards, when Mallarmé was back on her leash, Louise burrowed around in the bag for dog biscuits and Mars bars. 'You're brooding about Christmas, aren't you?'

'A bit,' admitted Trevor.

'That was a really good phone message you left your parents.'

'You think so?'

'Nicely balanced, you know, between warmth and firmness.'

'You sound like that trainer.' They'd gone on a night course called Good Dog! but dropped out after three weeks.

Louise giggled reminiscently. 'Well, handling parents isn't so very different, I suppose.'

'Except you know where you are with dogs,' said Trevor. 'They never claim to love you and then stab you in the back.'

'Trevor!' she protested. 'Leave it, Gide,' she said, suddenly turning. 'Drop it, dirty. Gide! Give. Give to Mammy.'

He watched her wrestle a Ballygowan bottle out of the dog's jaws. 'How can my parents have the gall to say leave them at home, when it's hundreds of miles away and we'll be gone for forty-eight hours!'

'I suppose we could hire a sitter,' she volunteered.

'But they'd hate to be away from us at Christmas. I mean,' he said, conscious of having strayed into irrationality, 'they may not know exactly what it is – in the theological sense – but they can sense it's a special occasion.'

'You know,' murmured Louise, 'there may be class issues involved here.'

'Such as?'

'Well, your parents have a fundamentally suspicious attitude towards our lifestyle. Being academics, going to the opera . . . and I suspect they see our dogs as an expensive whim.'

Trevor groaned. 'It's not like we spent thousands of pounds buying pedigree puppies! We rescued them from the pound.'

'Mmm,' said Louise, 'but remember how they made fun of the plaid coats and shoes? And there was this one time – I didn't tell you because I knew you'd be annoyed – but your dad asked me how much we spent a year on their food and vet bills.'

He winced.

'It's understandable; he did grow up on a farm where dogs were just exploited workers,' she added. 'And your mother's from a tiny terrace where there was barely enough food for the kids.'

'That's it,' said Trevor, so sharply that Proust started to whimper and worry the zip of his jacket. 'It's all about kids. They're trying to punish us for not having any! What my mother's saying at a sort of unconscious level is "I won't let your pseudo-children under my roof. Lock them up and throw away the key."'

'Oh, hang on, hon—'

'She is! She's saying, "Have some real children like your sister, Greta, and then maybe I'll love you!"'

'Come on, Trevor, she does love you; they both do.'

'Then what about the proverbial love my dog?'

Louise was scanning the skyline distractedly. 'Did you see which way Gide went?'

Trevor jumped to his feet. '*Gide!*'

They both caught sight of him simultaneously, a hundred feet away, as he raced along the edge of the cliff.

That evening, during dinner, Proust left a long red scrape across Louise's collarbone. 'Put him down on the floor,' Trevor urged her. 'Remember, the trainer said to punish him by withdrawing our attention. *Proust, sit!*'

'He's only acting out, poor baba,' said Louise, setting him down. 'They all are; they always pick up our vibes when we're upset.'

'Make a nasty sound . . . ,' Trevor dropped a fork on the tiles. Proust stared back at him, unmoved. 'Then turn our backs.'

They twisted away from him in their chairs. Trevor looked at his half-eaten risotto and felt his appetite drain away. He stood up and adjusted the framed photo of the dogs carrying the flower baskets on Louise and Trevor's wedding day. 'How's he reacting?'

'Hang on,' breathed Louise, peeking over her shoulder.

'Don't make eye contact,' Trevor warned her.

'He's gone.'

They found Proust in the living room, watching the blank screen.

'Do you think we've hurt his feelings?' asked Louise.

'Dunno. It's a fine line between gentle discipline and crushing his spirit. Proust?' Trevor crouched to stroke the tiny dog behind the ears. 'I don't think he likes the Chopin.'

'OK, I'll switch to Mozart.'

'Proust? Want to turn the telly on again?'

They didn't check their messages till they were going to bed. There was only one, from Belfast. 'Trevor, this is your

mother,' it began, as always. 'Your dad and I have been thinking about it like you asked, and we've decided we really can't
have your dogs this Christmas. Sorry about that, but. There's
your dad's allergy, and Lucy and Caitríona are still awful small,
and the general chaos and peeing on the rugs. Not to mention
the incident last year, I didn't want to have to bring it up,
but—'

The voice changed to a gruffer one. 'Let me talk to him.
Trevor, those creatures are a menace, especially the quiet one.
After it bit your mother, I have to tell you, I thought it should
have been put down. So let's have no more nonsense – stick
them in kennels and let's all of us have a nice peaceful
Christmas together, who knows when we'll get the chance
again.'

At two in the morning Trevor was wide awake in the dark.
'Have they ever even seen a kennel? I still feel guilty about that
time we went to Athens and left the babies in that, that *concen-
tration camp*,' he said, spitting out the words. 'And Dad's always
had a runny nose; he's only called it an allergy since he started
watching *ER*. Animals get blamed for everything. Remember
that part-timer in Spanish who claimed she'd gone to a party
where there was a cat and she was wheezing for six months
afterwards?'

'Calm down, sweetie.' Louise was stroking his arm.

'And as for the so-called incident with Mum—'

'It wasn't a real bite.'

'It was a quick reflex snap, that's all. I *told* her not to touch
Mallarmé's ears.'

'Anyway, no skin was broken.'

'It's as if they said, "Don't bring your Negro friends to our
house,"' Trevor ranted. 'It's a human rights issue. Well, a rights
issue.'

A silence. Then Louise rolled heavily away from him. 'I give up,' she said in a small voice. 'It's not worth the grief.'

'What do you mean?'

'You should go on your own, see your sister and all. And then when you come home on the twenty-seventh, we'll have our own Christmas dinner.'

'Oh, but Louise!' He started to sit up. Did she want him to accept gratefully or to say he wouldn't dream of it? 'You're wonderful. But you shouldn't have to make the sacrifice.'

'Believe me,' she said into the pillow, 'I couldn't swallow a bite of turkey in that atmosphere.'

Christmas Eve in Belfast, and Trevor had escaped into what they used to call the good room to ring Louise. He listened to *Santa's Pop Faves* blaring through the wall from the living room, mingled with the voices of his squabbling nieces, and longed to be back in the house outside Limerick, where Christmas crackers full of doggie treats would be hanging from the tree, and Louise and the babies would probably be curled up watching *Lady and the Tramp*.

Before he'd finished dialling, his father's bald head came round the door. 'You on the phone, Trev?'

'It's OK,' he said, putting it down.

'Carry on, don't mind me,' he said, dropping heavily into an armchair.

'Louise is out, actually,' Trevor lied, 'probably on a walk.' Then he felt awkward for having implicitly brought up the dogs; it wasn't as if he wasn't trying his best to make this a cordial visit.

His father blew his nose like an elephant trumpeting.

'How's your allergy?' asked Trevor neutrally.

'Nah, I'm just getting over a cold.'

His mother came in and set down a large bowl of toffees. 'I've just been mopping up the stairs; poor Lucy got sick.'

'Why don't you take the weight off your feet, love?'

'Just for a sec, then. All right, Trev?' she said as she sat down beside him.

'Aye, Mum.'

'The kids are wee dotes, with their Aussie accents, aren't they? Oh' – turning to her husband – 'you'll have to have a look in the U-bend for me; wee Jasmine dropped my wedding ring down the sink.'

His father let out a small sound of exasperation.

'Oh well, accidents do happen,' she said.

The words burst out of Trevor. 'That wasn't what you said last year about Proust chewing through the Christmas lights!' There was an awful silence. He tried to regain control. 'I just think, Mum, there's rather a double standard operational here. I don't think you're aware how unconsciously biased you are towards Greta.'

His father's eyes narrowed. 'You high-and-mighty tosser.'

'I beg your pardon?'

'You heard me, Professor Pillock, that's if your ears are *operational*!'

His mother flapped her hands. 'Ah, stop it now – Trev's just missing his doggies.'

Trevor nearly punched her.

His father grunted. 'The boy's besotted!'

'Boy?' he repeated. 'I'm forty-three years old.'

'Then act it. Jesus Christ, if I have to hear one more word about those wretched animals—'

'I don't believe this!' Trevor was practically screaming. 'I have to leave my entire family behind, while Greta and Mike jet in with three of the brattiest girls on the face of the planet—'

77

'Trev!' His mother's voice was a gunshot. 'That's enough.'

'At least the girls don't climb on your arm and start humping it,' his father observed.

Trevor thought he might cry. 'This is unfair, it's oppressive, it's humiliating—'

'Sure it's Christmas,' said his mother.

He collected his bag and left. The drive was more than seven hours, but at least he was going the right direction this time. It was two o'clock on Christmas morning when he drew up outside the house. There was one light on, in the bedroom. Trevor let himself in quietly. In the hall he almost stumbled over the small table that they always left out for Santa. Suddenly starving, Trevor ate the mince pie in one bite and rinsed it down with the brandy. Upstairs, a door opened and the dogs hurled themselves down the steps. Trevor squinted into the light and grinned up at his wife. 'I'm home,' he said.

domesticity

lavender's blue

Leroy and Shorelle had always wanted a slate blue house. It had come up on their first date, in fact, driving to the lake: Shorelle said, 'When I get a house I'm going to paint it that exact colour,' indicating with one long manicured nail a three-storey redbrick Colonial with porch and gingerbread the shade of a rain-threatening sky.

'Me too,' said Leroy, unnerved by the coincidence.

'Really? Are you just saying that?'

'No way! That's the colour I've always wanted.'

She gave him a smile so slow, so intricately blooming, that he very nearly drove into the curb.

For the first three years they lived in Shorelle's apartment above a discount shoe outlet, then when the baby was coming they managed with the help of Leroy's stepfather to scrape together a ten per cent down payment on a nice little two-bed in a neighbourhood that was neither too graffitied nor too suburban, neither too noisy nor too white. On the porch, the Realtor told them they wouldn't find the house they were looking for at a better price. 'Is that because of the colour?' Leroy asked.

The Realtor screwed up her forehead. 'What's wrong with the colour? It's a nice sort of faded adobe pink.'

He let out a brief laugh. 'I'd call it Puke Peach.'

Shorelle rolled her eyes at him.

'Well, after closing day you can paint it whatever you like,' the Realtor said a little crisply.

But life intervened, of course. Moving in and getting the place fixed up – curtains, wallpaper, bookshelves, magnets to keep the kitchen cupboards shut – took all their energy, and then Africa came along. (Leroy wasn't a hundred per cent fond of that name, but Shorelle believed she should have the casting vote. 'Twenty-six hours of labour, five stitches,' she reminded him stonily.)

There was something the public health nurse said that stuck in Leroy's head: that the days would be long but the years would be short. That was so true; every day with a small mewling baby seemed like a mountain to climb, but *blink!* and here was Africa at her first birthday party, triumphant fists full of chocolate cake. And the house was still the colour of puke.

Leroy would have liked to paint it himself, but the sad fact was he had no head for heights, and now he was a father he was noticing in himself this strange, almost cheerful refusal to do dumb things: His life wasn't his own to risk. He never even rode pillion on his friend CJ's Honda Magna any more. So he asked around for a painter who wouldn't rip him off. He ended up hiring a quiet white guy called Rod who lived a couple of blocks away.

'You picked your colour yet?' Rod narrowed his eyes at the roofline.

'Not quite, but it'll be some kind of slate blue.'

Rod seemed to have been born with a neutral expression. He handed Leroy a brochure. 'That's the only brand I use,' he said, 'but they can colour-match whatever you want.'

'Great.'

That evening Leroy and Shorelle sat on the porch with Africa stumbling back and forth between them. They flicked through sheaves of paint chips. 'Well, not Niagara,' said Shorelle with some scorn, 'and not Old China, either. Where do they come up with these names?'

Leroy snickered in agreement. 'Who'd paint their house Muddy Creek?'

'Or Yacht Fantasy!' She pulled a strip of glaring royal blue from Africa's mouth and showed it to him. 'Timothy says his clients come in with scraps of cloth, lipsticks, dead leaves, even, going "*This* is it." Half the time he's got to talk them out of it.'

'Why's he got to?' Timothy, owner of a small interior design company, was Shorelle's best friend from school, whom Leroy had always pretended to like. Before the baby, on nights when Leroy was working late, she used to go over there to watch black-and-white movies and eat Timothy's homemade gelato.

'Because they've got no clue what they're doing!'

'Well, I don't think we need to hire anyone to pick a paint for our house; it's not that big a deal,' said Leroy flippantly. He held up three blues against each other; they seemed to melt in and out. 'Is there one actually called Slate Blue?'

'Oh no, that would be too easy. Wait up – here's a Blue Slate, but it's not blue at all,' Shorelle complained, 'it's plain grey.'

'This one's kinda nice – Porch Lullaby.'

'Yeah, it's nice, but it's not slate blue.'

'No.'

'I thought we agreed—'

'We do,' he assured her. 'I just can't tell which is what we agreed on.'

She laughed at his grammar, and Africa joined in, looking from face to face.

Finally, when they'd gone indoors, Shorelle found another

brochure called Historic Tints. 'Look, Leroy, I think we've got it – Evening Sky.'

'What's historic about these ones?'

'Oh, that just means more expensive.'

He groaned.

Over breakfast, they glanced at the Evening Sky chip and it still looked good, so Leroy dropped it off in Rod's mailbox on his way to work.

For three days it rained, and then they were at Shorelle's parents' for the weekend. By the time they got back on Sunday evening, roughly the top third of the house had been painted. Leroy turned off the car and stared up.

'Wow!' said Shorelle.

'Wow is right,' he said in horror.

'Rod's a fast worker. Look, Africa' – as she heaved the drowsy child out of the car seat – 'look at the lovely colour our house's going to be.'

'That,' said Leroy, 'is not slate blue.'

'Oh, Leroy.'

'It's not what we chose.'

'It must be. It just looks different against the peach.'

'It's purple!'

'It's catching the last of the sunset, that's all.'

The argument continued right through Africa's bath and bedtime. 'You think it should be darker, then?'

'Not exactly darker,' said Leroy.

'Lighter?'

'Just less gaudy. Bluer.'

'What, like royal blue?'

'No! I'm just saying, right now it stands out like a neon sign.'

'That's because everybody else on this street paints their houses boring neutrals,' objected Shorelle.

Leroy stalked out on the porch to gather more evidence, but it was too dark to tell what he was looking at.

'It's a lurid shade of lavender,' he told her in bed, in the whisper they always used after Africa had gone to sleep. 'If you look at it with no preconceptions — if you didn't know it was meant to be blue — I'm telling you, purple's what you'd see. People are going to say, "Oh yeah, you're the guys who live in that lavender house."'

'Well, so?'

He stared at her in the dark. 'You're fine with that?'

'Lavender's blue, anyway, like the song says.'

He felt frustration tingling in the roots of his hair. 'That's a nursery rhyme, Shorelle; they're not supposed to make sense. *Lavender's blue, diddle diddle, lavender's green* . . . I guess you're going to tell me it's green now?'

'That's the stalk and stuff,' she informed him. 'The leaves are green; the flowers are blue.'

'They're frigging purple!'

First thing in the morning Leroy was out there again, staring at the freshly painted woodwork. He knew he was going to be late for work, but he hung around till Rod showed up in his van. 'Hey!'

A nod for answer.

'I think we've maybe got a problem,' said Leroy, clearing his throat. 'Is that really the colour I gave you?'

Rod produced the dog-eared chip from his back pocket, set up his ladder, climbed up, and held the chip against the paint-work. Leroy could barely see it, which, he supposed, meant it was the same shade. 'OK,' he said unhappily.

'They colour matched it.'

'Yeah, I'm not calling you a liar. I just — I guess I didn't know it would come out so bright.'

Rod climbed down.

'It's awful, isn't it?'

The painter didn't demur.

'Maybe it's because there's so much of it,' Leroy hazarded. 'And outside, in the sun. Or maybe because it's gloss, that must make it shinier. Or do I mean darker? More intense, I don't know.'

Rod stood with arms folded, looking up at the woodwork.

Leroy shaded his eyes. 'Shorelle likes it, can you believe that? I told her, it'd be great in a scarf or something, but not on a house.'

'Women have different eyeballs,' said Rod at last.

Leroy stared at him.

'I mean, literally. It's the layout of the light-receptor cells. So your wife and you are probably seeing different colours.'

'Really, is that true?'

'Also, blues can be tricky.' Rod seemed to be relaxing into conversation.

'You said it! Seems like they turn green or grey or purple depending what you put them up against.' Leroy could hear a whining tone in his voice, so he deepened it. 'And the names don't help. Evening Sky, it's nothing like an evening sky.' Rod didn't answer, but Leroy became aware how foolish it was to pay any attention to the names some schmuck of a copywriter made up. 'What do you think, Rod?'

A massive shrug. 'You're the customer.'

'I know, but you work with this stuff.'

'You can have your house any colour you like. Take your time.' He looked at his shoes. 'It's up to you.' Another pause. 'It's you folks who've got to live with it.'

What was he hinting? That this colour would be impossible to live with? Leroy tried to reckon up how much they'd already spent on Rod's labour and all those pots of historic lavender paint. 'No, but what would you do?'

'Me personally?' Rod scratched his eyebrow with one stained finger.

'Sure.'

'I kinda liked the peach.'

'No way!' Leroy stared at the old flaking woodwork.

'But if you're looking to increase the resale, go for cream. It's classic.'

Later, Leroy told Shorelle, 'Rod's agreed to get on with sanding and priming the porch floor, so we've got a couple days to make up our minds about the colour.'

'I thought we already had,' said Shorelle, shredding a bit of beef with her fork to put on Africa's tray.

'Honey, don't be like that.'

'I'm not being like anything. We looked at lots of brochures, we discussed it, we agreed—'

'We were in a rush! The light was bad. And those were the wrong colours. Here, look, I picked up some more paint chips at Home World today—'

'What were you doing way over there?'

'I drove by after from work.'

'So that's why you were late picking her up from day care. They called – they left a message.'

Leroy decided to ignore that. He would take a fresh tack. 'Remember our first date? That house we drove past, the perfect slate blue?'

Half a smile.

'Let's go take a look at it again, compare it to these chips.'

'Right now? I don't know. Africa's bath—'

'Oh, she looks clean enough, she can skip it for once.'

The sky was pink and pearl, and the breeze coming in the

sunroof was delicious. Leroy kept one hand on Shorelle's leg as he drove, and in the back Africa was making her birdlike sounds into her plastic cell phone.

'We've been up and down this street four times,' Shorelle pointed out.

'OK, Ms Clever, where do you think it was?'

She pursed her lips. 'One of those side streets past the church?'

He shook his head. 'Why would we have gone down a side street?'

'I don't know; you were driving.'

'Well, exactly. I was taking you straight to the lake, I was all excited about our first date and maybe making out in the dunes, I'd hardly have started combing the side streets.'

Shorelle scanned the houses. 'Well, it's not here. Maybe they repainted it.'

'Why would they have done that? It was perfect as was.'

'Turn here,' she told him, and he did, so suddenly that Africa's cell phone flew across the car.

'It can't be down here,' he said over the child's screams. 'It was a real big house, three storeys at least. Don't you remember?'

Shorelle was twisted round in her seat belt trying to retrieve the toy. 'It was years ago,' she said through her teeth.

When they got home there was still enough light in the sky for the gaudy shine of the top half of the house to make him wince. He was ashamed to think of people driving by, making remarks about it.

While they were brushing their teeth, he passed on Rod's theory about the sex of eyeballs. 'Oh please,' said Shorelle, spitting foam. 'That's just bullshit male bonding.'

'No, you're missing the point, he didn't say we see *better*—'

88

'Well, if it comes to that, far more guys are colour-blind than women are.'

At four in the morning Shorelle took hold of his shoulder. 'OK, I give in,' she said, gravely.

'What?'

'If you stop heaving about and let me get some sleep, OK, you can change the colour.'

Halfway through his morning bagel, Leroy grinned at Shorelle. 'So you agree it's a bit too purple?'

'No, I think it's beautiful, actually.'

'But honey—'

'You win, OK, Leroy? Do it — tell Rod to throw away all that paint and start again, never mind the cost. Whatever makes you happy,' she said, checking her watch.

He pored over the latest brochures. What if the colour he chose came out even worse than the first? Delphinium was pallid; Foggy Dusk looked like dirty water; Deep Shale was depressing. Denim Jeans had the potential to be glaring; Lake Prospect was plain navy. Leisure Time — what the hell kind of name for a colour was that? 'Maybe we should err on the safe side and go for Rocky Creek,' he suggested, sliding over the catalogue.

Shorelle looked at it without much interest. 'That's grey.'

As soon as she'd said it, it was true. 'Bay of Fundy?' he suggested, tapping the card.

'Urgh.'

'You barely looked at it.'

'It only takes a second to hate something,' she told him. 'Imagine living with that for the next however-many years . . .'

Leroy consulted the couple of neighbours he knew to say hi to; they all agreed the current patch of Evening Sky was an eyesore. Several suggested cream; he had to be polite enough to pretend to be considering it. He asked a guy going by with his short-haired poodle, and a woman from FedEx. Shorelle came out with Africa on her hip. 'Timothy's going to drop by Monday morning,' she announced.

'Oh yeah?' he said neutrally.

'I thought, if you're polling every passing dog, it's time to call in an expert.'

'Rod's an expert,' Leroy pointed out.

'No he's not; he's just some guy who happens to paint houses for a living. Décor is Timothy's business.'

'Interiors,' said Leroy, aware he was quibbling. 'He'll probably suggest pistachio or cerise.'

'Oh, for Christ's sake.' She mouthed the swearword, so Africa wouldn't hear it. 'You have got to get over your gay thing.'

'Since when have I had a gay thing?'

'Since forever. You get all sulky like some rapper thug.'

Leroy chewed his lip.

'Timothy's in the business; he knows about colour. We've got so stuck on this, I thought we could do with an objective opinion.'

But there was no such thing as objectivity, Leroy was coming to realize. Colours were private passions and weaselly turncoats, bland-faced losers and enemies in disguise. His head ached from pursuing, through a forest of azures and cornflowers, cyans and midnights, the perfect slate blue.

On Monday he was sitting waiting for Rod on the gritty primed porch. 'Hey,' said the painter, getting out of his van. 'You picked a colour?'

'I think so.' He scanned the strip in his hand nervously, checked that he'd folded it so the right one showed. 'It's not absolutely what we had in mind, but it seems the nearest to it, at least as far as we can tell.' The *we* was a lie; the last time he'd brought out the brochures for a discussion, Shorelle had screamed and said she was going to put them down the Garburator.

The painter adjusted his baseball cap.

'It's called Distant Haze,' said Leroy as he handed it over, immediately wishing he'd used its number instead.

Roy glanced at it and put it in his back pocket.

Was that it? No endorsement, after all this work? Leroy heard a car door open and looked over at the slim guy getting out of a black PT Roadster convertible. 'Timothy!' he called, overdoing the enthusiasm. 'Friend of Shorelle's,' he told the painter in an apologetic undertone. 'This'll only take a second—'

'Rod, my man!' Timothy and Rod were embracing.

Leroy blinked. Well, it was a bear hug, he supposed. 'You know each other.'

'Rod's done a lot of great work for me over the years. Looking good, man,' said Timothy, giving the painter's shoulder something between a whack and a rub. 'Where've you been?'

'Busy,' said Rod, with a brief grin.

Leroy hadn't known the painter was capable of cracking a smile.

'I've got half an hour, you want to grab a coffee?'

'Why not,' said Rod, heading for the convertible.

Leroy's jaw was throbbing. They weren't even going to ask him along. 'Hey, what about the house, Tim?' He knew the guy hated to be called Tim. 'That's the colour Shorelle likes,' he added mockingly, pointing at the upper section of paintwork.

Timothy shook his head. 'Stylish in itself, but not on a west-facing street.'

Leroy should have felt vindicated.

Rod produced the folded chip from his back pocket. 'That's their latest.'

Timothy tilted it to the light. 'Grey?'

Leroy stalked over. 'It's slate blue; it's called Distant Haze. If you put it up against real grey – against the pavement, even – you can see how blue it is.'

'OK,' said Timothy, as if humouring a child. 'Listen, tell Shorelle I'll call her later?' He made that annoying finger-and-thumb-spread gesture that meant a phone.

'So Tim, what would you do?' Leroy was leaning on the hood, aware he was holding them up, trying to sound casual.

'With this house?'

'Yeah.'

'Cream, probably,' said Timothy.

'Can't go wrong,' said Rod.

'Classic.'

Leroy waved them off with a rictus smile. He shut his eyes, saw hot and red.

the cost of things

Cleopatra was exactly the same age as their relationship. They found this very funny and always told the story at dinner parties. Liz would mention the coincidence a little awkwardly, then Sophie, laughing as she scraped back her curls in her hands, would persuade her to spit out the details. Or sometimes it would be the other way round. They prided themselves on not being stuck in patterns. They each had things the other hadn't – Liz's triceps, say, and Sophie's antique rings – but so what? Friends would probably have said that Sophie was the great romantic, who'd do anything for love, whereas Liz was the quiet dependable type, loyal to the end. But then, what did friends know – what could friends imagine of the life that went on in a house after the guests had gone home? Liz and Sophie knew that roles could be shed as easily as clothes; they were sure that none of their differences mattered.

They had met a few months before Cleopatra, but it was like a room before the light is switched on. After the party where they were introduced, Sophie decided Liz looked a bit like a younger Diane Keaton, and Liz knew Sophie reminded her of one of those French actresses but could never remember which. At first, their conversations were like anybody else's.

Then, on one of her days off from the gardening centre, Liz had come round to Sophie's place to help her put up some shelves in the spare bedroom. Sophie insisted she'd pay, of course she would, and Liz said she wouldn't take a dollar, though they both knew she could do with the money. When the drill died down, they thought they heard something. Such a faint sound, Liz thought it was someone using a chain saw, several houses down, but then Sophie pointed out that it was a bit like a baby crying. Anyway, she held the second shelf against the wall for Liz to mark the holes. They were standing so close that Liz could see the different colours in each of Sophie's rings, and Sophie could feel the heat coming off Liz's bare shoulder. Then that sound came again, sharper.

They found the kitten under the porch, after they'd tried everywhere else. Its mother must have left it behind. Black and white, eyes still squeezed shut, it was half the size of Sophie's cupped hand. Now, Liz would probably have made a quick call to the animal shelter and left it at that. She didn't know then how quickly and completely Sophie could fall in love.

It knew it was on to a good thing, this kitten; it clung to Sophie's fingers like a cactus. They said *it* for the first few days, not knowing much about feline anatomy. It was hard to give a kitten away, they found, once the vet told you she was a she, and especially once you knew her name. They hadn't meant to name her, but it was a long hour and a half in the queue at the vet's and it started out as a joke, what a little Cleopatra she was, said Liz, because the walnut-sized face in the corner of the shoe box was so imperious.

Sophie was clearly staggered by the bill of two hundred dollars for the various shots, but soon she was joking that it was less than she spent on shoes, most months. Liz was a little shocked to hear that, but then, Sophie did wear very nice shoes. Sophie plucked out her Visa card and asked the receptionist for a pen, it having been her porch the kitten was left under. Liz, watching her sign with one long flowing stroke, decided the woman was magnificent. Her hand moved to her own wallet and she spent ten minutes forcing a hundred-dollar bill into Sophie's breast pocket, arguing that they had, after all, found the kitten together.

Cleopatra now belonged to both of them, Sophie joked as Liz carried the box to the car, or rather, both of them belonged to her. It was – what was the word? – *serendipitous*.

That first evening they left the kitten beside the stove in her shoe box with a saucer of milk, hoping she wouldn't drown in it, and went upstairs to unbutton each other's clothes. So, give or take a day or two, they and Cleopatra began at the same time.

These days she was a stout, voluptuous five-year-old, her glossy black and white hairs drifting through every room of the ground-floor apartment where Liz now paid half the rent, never having meant to move in exactly but having got in the habit of coming over to see how the kitten was doing so often that before she knew it, this was home. On summer evenings, when Sophie took out the clippers to give Liz a No. 3 cut on the porch, Cleopatra would abuse the fallen tufts as if they were mice. Cleopatra had commandeered a velvet armchair in the lounge that no one else was allowed to sit on, and in the mornings if they delayed bringing her breakfast, the cat would lift the sheet and bite the nearest toe, not hard but as a warning.

They had a fabulous dinner party to celebrate their anniversary, five years being, as Liz announced, approximately ten times as long as she had ever been with anybody else. Three of their guests had brought champagne, which was just as well, considering how hard Liz and Sophie were finding it to keep their heads above water these days. Sophie's hair salon had finally gone out of business, and Liz's health plan didn't stretch to same-sex partners.

Over coffee and liqueurs they were prevailed upon to tell the old story of finding the kitten the very day they got together, and then Sophie showed their guests the marks Cleopatra had left on her hands over the years. Sophie had bought appallingly expensive steel claw clippers at a pet shop downtown, but the cat would never let anyone touch her feet. Her Highness was picky that way, said Liz, scratching her under her milk-white chin.

They knew they shouldn't have let her lick the plates after the smoked salmon linguini, but she looked so wonderfully decadent, tonguing up traces of pink cream. That night when they had gone to bed to celebrate the best way they knew how, the cat threw up on the Iranian carpet Liz's mother had lent them. It was Sophie who cleaned it up the next morning, before she brought Liz her coffee. Cleopatra wasn't touching her food bowl, she reported. 'She must still be stuffed with salmon, the beast,' said Liz, clicking her tongue to invite Cleopatra through the bedroom door.

The next day she still wasn't eating more than a mouthful. Liz said it was just as well, really – Cleopatra could do with losing a few pounds – but Sophie picked up the cat and said that wasn't funny.

They'd been planning to take her to the new cat clinic down the road to have her claws clipped at some point anyway. It took a while to get her into the wicker travel basket; Liz had to pull her paws off the rim one by one while Sophie pressed down the lid an inch at a time, nervous of trapping her tail. The cat turned her mutinous face from the window so all they could see was a square of ruffled black fur.

The clinic was a much more swish place than the other vet's, and Liz thought maybe they should have asked for a list of prices in advance, but the receptionist left them alone in the examining room before she thought of it. Cleopatra could obviously smell the ghost aromas of a thousand other cats. She sank down and tucked everything under her except her thumping tail. The place was too much like a dentist's waiting room, but Liz, who knew that Sophie relied on her to be calm, read the posters aloud and pretended to find them funny. WHY YOUR FURRY FRIEND LOVES YOU, said one poster on the wall. IN SICKNESS AND IN HEALTH, began another. The two of them whispered to each other and gave the cat little tickles, as if this sterile shelf was some kind of playground.

Dr McGraw came in then, spoke to the cat as if he was her best friend but stroked her in the wrong place, above her tail, which flapped like an enemy flag. When he took hold of her face, her paw came round so fast that she left a red line down the inside of his wrist. Liz and Sophie apologized over and over, like the parents of a delinquent child. Dr McGraw, dabbing himself with disinfectant, told them to think nothing of it. Then he called in Rosalita to wrap the cat in a towel.

Swaddled in flannel, Cleopatra stared at the doctor's face as if memorizing it for the purposes of revenge. He put a sort of gun in her ear to take her temperature and bared her gums in an artificial smile to see if they were dehydrated. He squeezed her stomach and kidneys and bladder, and she made a sound they'd never heard before, in a high voice like a five-year-old girl's, but it was hard to tell if she was tender in the areas he was pressing, or just enraged.

Liz had to make out the check for fifty dollars as Sophie was already up to her Visa limit. They carried the basket to the car, Cleopatra's weight lurching from side to side. They joked on the way home that the vet wouldn't try calling her Sweetums next time.

That night on the couch Sophie yawned as she put down her book, let her head drop into Liz's lap, and asked in a lazy murmur what she was thinking. In fact, Liz had been fretting over her overdraft and wondering whether they could cancel cable as they hardly ever watched it anyway, but she knew that was not what Sophie wanted to hear, so she grinned down at her and said, 'Guess.' Which wasn't a lie. Sophie smiled back and pulled Liz down until her shirt covered Sophie's face, then they didn't need to say anything.

Cleopatra still wasn't eating much the next day, but she seemed bright-eyed. Sophie said the clinic had rung, and wasn't that thoughtful?

The following evening when Liz came home the cat wasn't stirring from her chair. Liz began to let herself worry. 'Don't worry,' she told Sophie as she dropped her work clothes in the laundry basket. 'Cats can live off their fat for a good while.'

The two of them were tangled up in the bath, rubbing lavender oil into each other's feet, when the phone rang. It was Rosalita from the clinic. Liz felt guilty for the cheerful way she'd answered the phone and made her voice sadder at once.

Rosalita was concerned about little Cleo, how was she doing?

Liz didn't like people who nicknamed without permission; she'd never let anyone call her Lizzy, except Sophie, sometimes. Not bad, she supposed, she told Rosalita; hard to tell, about the same really.

By the time she could put the phone down, her nipples were stiff with cold. She'd left lavender-scented footprints all the way down the stairs. When she got back to the bathroom, Sophie had let all the water out and was painting her nails purple.

What did she mean, the cat was not bad? Sophie wanted to know. The cat was obviously not well.

Liz said she knew. But they could hardly take her for daily checkups at fifty dollars a go, and surely they could find a cheaper vet in the Yellow Pages.

No way, said Sophie, because Cleopatra had already begun a course of treatment with the clinic and they were being wonderful.

Liz thought it was all a bit suspect, these follow-up calls. The clinic stood to make a lot of money from exaggerating every little symptom, didn't they?

Sophie said one of the things she'd never found remotely attractive about Liz was her cynicism. She went down to make herself a cup of chamomile and didn't even offer to put on the milk for Liz's hot chocolate. When Liz came down, Sophie was curled up on the sofa with the cat on her lap, the two of them doing their telepathy thing.

Sophie was probably premenstrual, Liz thought, but she didn't like to say so, knowing what an irritating thing it was to be told, especially if you were.

She knew she was right about that the next day when Sophie came in from a pointless interview at a salon downtown and started vacuuming at once. In five years Liz had learned to leave Sophie to it, but Liz was only halfway down the front page of the paper when she heard her name being called, so loudly that she thought there must be an emergency.

Sophie, her foot on the vacuum's off switch, had dragged the velvet armchair out from the wall and was pointing. What did Liz call that? she wanted to know.

'Vomit, I guess,' said Liz.

Why hadn't she said something?

'Because I didn't know about it,' said Liz, feeling absurdly like a suspect. Yes, she'd been home all day, but she hadn't heard anything. A cat being sick was not that loud. Yes, she cared, of course she cared, what did Sophie mean didn't she care?

That night Sophie didn't come to bed at all. Liz sat up reading a home improvement magazine and fell asleep with the light on.

The next day Rosalita called at eight in the morning when Liz was opening a fresh batch of bills, before she'd had her coffee. Nerves jangling, Liz was very tempted to tell Rosalita to get lost. She wondered whether the clinic was planning to charge her for phone consultations. 'Hang on,' she said. 'I'll be right back.' She went into the kitchen to look at Cleopatra, who was lying on her side by the fridge like a beached whale and hadn't touched her water, even. Sophie was kneeling beside her on the cold tiles. Liz wanted to touch Sophie, but instead she stroked the cat, just how she usually liked it, one long combing from skull to hips, but there was no response.

Sophie went out to the phone and asked Rosalita for an appointment. 'Please,' Liz heard her say, her voice getting rather high, and then, after a minute, 'Thanks, thank you, thanks a lot.'

Liz took the afternoon off work and brought the car home by two, as promised.

That afternoon the two of them stood in the examining room at the clinic, staring at the neatly printed estimate. Rosalita had left them alone for a few minutes, to talk it all over, she had said with a sympathetic smile. The disinfected walls of the little white room seemed to close in around them. Cleopatra crouched between Sophie's arms. Liz was reading the list for the third time as if it were a difficult poem.

After a minute she said, 'I still don't really get it.'

Sophie, staring into the green ovals of Cleopatra's eyes, said nothing.

'I know she's sick. But surely she can't be as sick as all that,' Liz went on. 'Like, she still purrs.'

Sophie scratched behind the cat's right ear. Cleopatra shook her head vehemently, then subsided again.

'It's not that I'm not worried.' Liz's voice sounded stiff and theatrical in the tiny room. She went on, a little lower, 'But eleven hundred dollars?'

It sounded even worse out loud.

'That's an extraordinary amount of money,' said Liz, 'and number one we haven't got it—'

At last Sophie's head turned. 'I can't believe we're even having this discussion,' she said in a whisper.

'We're not having it,' said Liz heavily. 'It's not a discussion till you say something.'

'Look at her,' pleaded Sophie. 'Look at her eyes.' There was a tiny crust of mucus at the corner of each. 'They've never been dull before, like the light's been switched off.'

'I know, sweetheart,' said Liz. She stared at the crisp print to remember her arguments. 'But eleven hundred dollars—'

'She's our cat,' Sophie cut in. 'This is Cleopatra we're talking about.'

'But we don't even know for sure if there's anything serious wrong with her.'

'Exactly,' said Sophie. 'We don't know. We haven't a clue. That's why I can't sleep at night. That's why we're going to pay them to test her for kidney stones and leukemia and FOP disease and anything else it could possibly be.'

'FIP,' Liz read off the page. 'FIP disease. And it's a vaccine, not a test.'

'Whatever,' growled Sophie. 'Don't pretend to be an expert; all you're looking at is the figures.'

'Hang on, hang on,' said Liz, louder than she meant to. 'Let's look at it item by item. Hospitalization, intravenous catheter insertion . . . Jesus, sixty dollars to put a tube up her ass, that can't be more than thirty seconds' work. IV fluids, OK, fair enough. X-rays . . . why does she need three X-rays? She's less than two feet long.'

Sophie was chewing her lipstick off. 'I can't believe you're mean enough to haggle at a time like this.'

'How can you call me mean?' protested Liz. 'I just get the feeling we're being ripped off. This is emotional blackmail; they think we can't say no.'

There was a dull silence. She tried to hear other voices from other rooms and wondered if Rosalita was standing outside the door, listening.

'Look,' she went on more calmly, 'if we left out these optional blood tests we could trim off maybe three hundred dollars. What the hell is feline AIDS anyway? Cleopatra's a virgin.'

'I don't know what it is, but what if she has it?' asked Sophie. 'What if two months down the road she's dying of it and you were too damn callous to pay for a test?'

'It's probably just crystals in her bladder,' said Liz weakly. 'The doctor said so, didn't he?'

Sophie curled over Cleopatra, whose eyes were half shut as if she was dreaming. Liz stared around her at the cartoon cats on the walls, with their pert ears and manic grins.

After a few minutes silence, she thought they'd probably got past the worst point of the row. Now if she could only think of something soothing to say, they'd be onto the homestretch.

But Sophie stood up straight and folded her arms. 'So what is she worth then?'

'Sorry?'

'A hundred dollars? Two hundred?'

Liz sighed. 'You know I'm mad about her.'

'Yeah?'

'I can't put a figure to it.'

'Really?' spat Sophie. 'But it's definitely under eleven hundred, though; we know that much.'

'We don't have eleven hundred dollars,' said Liz, word by word.

'We could get it.'

Liz was finding it hard to breathe. 'You know I can't take out another loan, not so soon after the car.'

'Then I'll sell my grandmother's fucking rings,' said Sophie, slamming her hand on the counter with a metallic crack. 'Or would it make your life simpler if we just had her put down here and now?'

'Give me the damn form,' said Liz, pulling the estimate towards her and digging in her pocket for her pen.

Sophie watched without a word as Liz signed, her hands shaking.

Dr McGraw carried Cleopatra away to the cages. The cat watched them over his shoulder, unforgivingly.

Out in the car, Sophie sat with the empty basket on her lap. Liz couldn't tell if she was crying without looking at her directly, but she had a feeling she was. Liz thought of their early days when they went to the cinema a lot and Liz always knew just when Sophie needed her to reach over and take her hand.

She drove home, taking corners carefully.

'I'm just curious,' said Sophie at a traffic light. 'What would you pay for me?'

'*What?*' Liz's voice came out like a squeal of brakes.

'If I was rushed into the emergency room and a doctor handed you an estimate. What would I be worth to you?'

Liz told her to shut the fuck up.

Rosalita rang the same evening, her voice bright. Crystals in the bladder, that's all it was. Little Cleo was doing fine, had taken well to the new diet, and they could pick her up the next morning. That would be just ninety-eight dollars.

So the cat came home, and for a while everything seemed like it ever was.

And when six months later Sophie left Liz for a beautician she met at the cosmetic academy and moved into the beautician's condo in a building with a strict no-pets policy, Liz used to hold on to Cleopatra at night, hold her so tight that the cat squirmed, and think about the cost of things.

pluck

On rare occasions, over the years that followed, if he was having a few pints with a mate, Joseph thought of asking, *Would you break up with your girlfriend over a hair on her chin? Don't laugh,* he'd add, *it's not funny.*

But the question sounded impossible when he put it in words, so he never did ask it.

It was most unlike him, the whole thing. He'd always been glad Róisín didn't cover her fuzzy peach face with layers of foundation. He relished her bushy black eyebrows that almost met, like Frida Kahlo's. *Perfection Incarnate,* that was one of his names for her. They were in agreement that Róisín was not only the brains of the relationship but the beauty as well. Joseph was the pancreas, maybe, or the kneecap.

For seven years they'd lived in a skinny terraced house and had no problems. None that Joseph knew of, anyway. Then after a while they hadn't the time for problems, because they had Liam instead. Liam was never a problem; he was the opposite of all problems. So when Joseph was made redundant from a telesales job he'd hated anyway, they decided it was perfect timing: he'd stay home and mind the boy.

One Sunday, Liam was up till two with a tickly cough, so

the next morning there wasn't a peep out of him. Joseph lay among the pillows, relishing the lie-in. He scratched his stubble and watched Róisín run in and out, power-dressing. Tights half up, she dipped into the wardrobe for a pair of heels and stubbed her forehead on the hinge. Then she stumbled over to the bedside table to scoop up her watch and earrings. Joseph leaned out far enough to hold her legs in a rugby tackle.

Róisín told him to get lost, but not as if she meant it.

'Stay home today,' he offered, 'and I'll kiss every inch of your body.' He used to say that a lot in the old days, when they were students and every day was twice as long. She stooped down to kiss him now and he arched up like a turtle to meet her mouth.

It was then he noticed it. One dark bristle, just under her chin, a quarter of an inch long.

He must have let go of her legs, because she said, 'What?'

Joseph shook his head as if he didn't know what she meant.

'You were looking funny.'

He lay back against the pillows and denied it with a laugh.

'Dadda!' In the next room Liam sent up his wail. Róisín made a lunge for her briefcase, and Joseph struggled out of the sheets.

It wasn't like Joseph went round thinking about it all day every day after that; he wasn't some kind of Neanderthal, like his father. He'd been born in 1970, for god's sake. He could ask for Tampax Super Plus in the chemist without lowering his voice more than a notch. He'd never wanted Róisín to be some airbrushed pinup or Stepford Wife. He'd always liked the dark fuzz on her thighs, her crazy-paving bikini line, the scattered hairs that danced their way to her navel. He had a habit of burying his face in the spiral curls under her arms. So why would it bother him, one little hair on her chin?

But somehow he couldn't shed the childhood image of an

old great-aunt with a full set of quivering whiskers, and how once when she'd tried to kiss him he'd run away screaming. And every night now when he read fairy tales to Liam, the book seemed to fall open to the same picture of a toothless, mole-studded, hairy-faced witch.

Joseph was aware he was overreacting; he knew he'd have to snap out of it soon. It wasn't that he brooded, exactly, only that being home all day left a lot of little chinks of time free for thinking.

One evening he was waiting up for Róisín and couldn't find the remote, so he flicked through a magazine she'd left on the coffee table. FREE YOURSELF FROM FACIAL HAIR FOREVER, a headline ordered. His eyes scuttled over the diagrams. The follicles looked like blueprints of mining shafts.

When he heard Róisín's key in the lock, Joseph stuffed the magazine down the side of the sofa.

She was still peeling off her coat in the hall when he rushed out and hugged her. Under cover of a kiss, he stroked her chin. But he couldn't feel a thing.

The next morning the demented chirp of the alarm clock woke Joseph first. Róisín's face was half immersed in the pillow. He bent over, very carefully, to see if the hair had grown at all. Was there really only one? How many could sprout below the line of her jaw before she'd notice?

Her eyes were very blue. He jerked back. She grinned up at him confusedly.

It wasn't a turnoff; it wasn't as simple as that. It was more that Joseph would be sitting beside Róisín on a park bench as she played clap-handies with Liam, say, and suddenly she'd turn her head a fraction and he'd see it. It interrupted the smooth curve of her chin. And a little frisson would go through him, like lust but not quite.

It had become a sort of tic, this habit of peering at his girl-friend's chin. The little hair there wasn't sharp like the ones that pushed out of his own skin overnight. It was so soft he could barely feel it when he found a pretext to stroke her face. It was just a wisp, really. There was no harm in it. So why did he long to take it between his nails and yank it out?

It was like an itch in his fingers, too deep to scratch. It disgusted him.

Another man might have simply asked her to pluck it.

But Joseph couldn't imagine saying those words. Not to Róisín. This sort of thing was a delicate matter; you didn't just tell a woman she was growing a beard. They were sensitive about these things. It would be best if it came up naturally in the course of conversation, but if he tried to lead their dinner-time conversation gradually round to female facial hair he knew he'd make a hash of it. She might be cross that he thought it was any of his business to tell her which bits of her body were acceptable. Or worse, she might be hurt; she might think he didn't fancy her any more, now she wasn't twenty-one, now she had stretch marks and other proofs of a body that had been lived in.

Not that he was God's Gift to Womanhood himself. He never had been. Joseph stood at the bathroom mirror, these mornings, and stared at the hair matted on his brush. Had he always shed that much? His hairline seemed to be in the same place it had always been, but maybe the change was so infinitesimal he wouldn't notice until the day he woke up bald. He tried to laugh at that thought, but only managed the half grin of a stroke victim. He ran his fingers across his head, and another hair came away, wrapped round his thumb.

Maybe there were only a given number of hairs in the world, and they had to be shared out.

Surely Róisín would laugh if she knew what was scurrying through his mind, these days. It could become one of her running gags. 'Be careful of Bearded Ladies, Jo-Jo,' she might say. 'They have a habit of running away with the circus.'

The real question wasn't whether she would be hurt if he asked her to pluck it, Joseph realized. The real question was, What if she said no?

In the library he left Liam slamming Barbie and Ken's heads together and ducked round the corner. He thought it might take some research, but the first encyclopaedia told him all he needed, and more than he wanted to know.

It turned out that a hair was a filament or filamentous outgrowth that grew from the integument of an animal or insect. Joseph had never known he had an integument. He also learned that although in many cultures beards were a symbol of the dignity of manhood, there was nothing intrinsically masculine about facial hair at all. Native American and Chinese men didn't tend to develop much hair on their faces; Mediterranean women did. Even in the British Isles, the incidence of facial hair among women was much higher than was commonly supposed.

Joseph felt slightly breathless, at this point. He had been tricked. To think of all those hairy-chinned women out there on the streets, plucked and waxed and powdered down, going about their business with nobody knowing a thing . . .

He read on distractedly. Both men and women of high birth in ancient Egypt wore metal ceremonial hairpieces on their chins. Then there was Saint Uncumber, who prayed to God to deliver her from men and was delighted when he gave her a beard.

Joseph let the encyclopaedia sag shut. He edged round the corner to Self-Help, where he found a book called *Women Are*

Cats, Men Are Dogs: Making Your Relationship Work. He had to skim through Sexual Positions, Money Worries and In-law Trouble before he found the right section.

Instead of commenting negatively on her appearance, say 'Honey, I'd like to treat you to a top-to-toe makeover. You deserve the best.'

Joseph tried out that line, under his breath, but it sounded like bad karaoke.

Down on his knees on the cork tiles, a few hours later, he tried to unclog the bath; the plunger made a violent gulp. He finally had to use his fingers in a tug-of-war with the long clot of soap and hair; more and more of it unreeled as if it grew down there. From the colour it looked more like his than hers. Queasy, he flicked it into the bin.

He was tidying up the living room after lunch when he noticed that Róisín's magazine was on the coffee table again. She must have found it stuffed down the side of the sofa cushion. She must have wondered. Joseph stared at the crumpled cover, wondering what exactly she'd have wondered. SIZZLING SUMMER SANDALS. PEACE OF MIND IN JUST TEN DAYS. HOW TO TELL IF HE'S CHEATING.

These days he was trying to ensure that sex wouldn't happen. Not that he didn't feel like it. But he knew that sex brought his guard down, and he was afraid that it would ruin some intimate moment if Róisín caught him staring fixedly at her chin.

He was just playing for time. He knew he had to tell her, whether it sounded reasonable or not. He had to say something at least, make a joke of it instead of a sore point. Otherwise he was going to lose his tiny mind.

They used to be able to tell each other anything, the two of them. That's what they'd boasted, in the early days. Everyone went round saying things like that at college. *Tell me. Honestly. I really want to know.*

Later that afternoon Joseph had a better idea. He ran upstairs to the bathroom and ransacked the cupboard like a burglar. He rooted through all Róisín's paraphernalia: eyelash crimpers, toenail sponges, an old diaphragm. Finally he recognized the tweezers. He was holding it up to the light to check its grip when he sensed he was being watched. He turned. Róisín in her stocking feet, arms piled high with files, staring.

'You're home early! Sorry about the mess,' he said as if it was a joke.

'What are you doing with my tweezers?' she asked.

'Got a splinter, down the playground,' Joseph improvised.

Róisín took hold of his hand and tugged him towards the window. She peered at the map of lines: head, heart, fate. 'I don't see anything.'

'It's tiny,' said Joseph, 'but it's driving me mad.'

That evening he was watching some stupid quiz when Róisín came in and sat on the arm of the sofa. 'You're in a funny mood these days,' she said, so softly that he thought at first she was commenting on the programme.

'Am I?' Joseph assured her he didn't know why he seemed that way. No, he didn't miss his old job; what was there to miss? No, Liam wasn't getting on his nerves, no more than usual. It was nothing.

At which point Róisín reached for the remote and muted the TV.

Joseph stared at the flickering images. He wasn't ready to look at her yet. He was choosing his words. 'It's nothing that *matters*,' he said at last, too cheerfully. 'It's—'

'It's me,' interrupted Róisín, 'isn't it?'

And he turned to look at her then, because her voice was stripped down like a wire. Naked. The skin below her eyes was the blue of a bird's egg.

Joseph gathered her into his arms and lied with his whole heart. 'Of course it's not you. Why would it be you? You're grand. You're Perfection Incarnate,' he added, pressing his lips to her neck, trying to shut himself up.

She twisted her head. 'But are you—'

'I'm just tired, love,' he interrupted, so she couldn't finish the question. 'I'm just a bit tired these days.' He faked an enormous, apelike yawn.

It was two in the morning before he could be sure she was in deep sleep. He opened his eyes and sat up, feeling under the pillow for the pen torch and the tweezers.

Hovering over Róisín, he aimed the tiny light at her chin. His thumb pressed hard on the ridged plastic of the switch. Arms shaking, he caught the little hair in his narrow beam. With the other hand he reached out to close the tweezers on it. Please god he wouldn't stab her in the chin.

Just then Róisín stirred and rolled towards him, onto her face. Joseph lurched back and snapped off the torch. He shoved everything under his pillow and lay down flat. His heart was hammering like police at the door.

He lay quite still for a long time. Veils of darkness hung all round him. He was sinking.

Then Róisín spoke. 'Can you not sleep?'

Joseph didn't answer.

In the morning he lay hollow-eyed, watching Róisín put on her lipstick in the bedroom mirror. She grabbed her bag and came over to give him a kiss.

She turned to open the door. He hauled himself upright and put on a casual voice. 'Hey. You know that tiny wee hair under your chin?'

He waited for the world to crack apart.

'Which?' Róisín doubled back to the mirror without

breaking stride. She stuck her jaw out and threw back her head. 'Got it,' she said in a slightly strangled voice. Her finger and thumb closed together and she made a tiny, precise movement. Like a conductor might, to finish a symphony.

She brushed her fingers together and gave Joseph a little wave on her way out.

strangers

good deed

Sam had always thought of himself as a pretty decent guy, and who was to say he wasn't? While he was doing his MBA at the University of Toronto he'd been a volunteer on the Samaritans' phone line. These days he couldn't spare the time, but he made regular tax-free contributions to schemes for eradicating river blindness in sub-Saharan Africa and improving children's sports facilities in the Yukon. He always wore a condom (well, not always, just when he was having sex), and he never pushed past old ladies to get on a streetcar.

The day it happened, he was coming down with a head cold. Funny how such a petty thing could make such a difference. Not that it felt petty at the time; it was a January cold, one of those brutes that makes you screw up your eyes all week and cough wetly for the rest of the month. So Sam – sensibly enough – had left the office before rush hour in order to get home and take care of himself. He had his Windsmoor coat buttoned up to the throat as he hurried towards the subway station. His friends seemed to live in down jackets all winter, but Sam refused to abandon his dress sense so he could look like a walking duvet. Today he did keep his cashmere scarf looped over his nose and mouth, to take the ice out of the air. With a hot whiskey and something mindless like *Nip/Tuck* and an early night, he thought he could probably head this cold off at the pass.

He walked right by the first time, like everyone else. It was a common sight, these last few winters, street persons in sleeping bags lying on the hot-air vents. The first time you saw it you thought: *My god, there's a guy lying in the middle of the sidewalk, and everyone's walking round him like he's invisible. How bizarre. What a sign of the times.* But you got used to it – and, to be fair, it was probably much warmer for the homeless, lying on the air vents, than if they had to tuck themselves away against the wall of a bank or a travel agency.

This particular guy near the intersection of Bloor and Bay seemed pretty much like all his peers: a crumpled bundle with eyes half closed and a not-entirely-unsatisfied expression. *Probably Native,* thought Sam, *but you should never assume.* It was only when Sam had got as far as the crossing, blowing his nose on his handkerchief with awkward leather-gloved hands, that his brain registered what his eyes must have seen. Just as sometimes by the time you ask someone to repeat themselves, you've realized what they've said. Anyway, that's when Sam saw it in his mind's eye, the little trickle of blood. He thought he must have imagined it. *Classic white middle-class guilt hallucinations,* he said to himself. Then he thought: *So the guy's bleeding a little from the lip, not necessarily a big deal, I sometimes chew my lips to shreds when I'm working on a big presentation.*

The lights changed but something wouldn't let Sam cross. Instead, he clenched his jaw and waded back against the tide of commuters. He picked a place to stand, near enough to the street person to get a good look at him, but not so near that anyone would notice. Besides, if he stood too close, the guy might wake up and take offence and bite him or something. A significant percentage of them were mentally ill, Sam had read in the *Street Times,* and no wonder, considering. But there was no sign of this particular guy waking up anytime soon. The blood from his mouth had trickled all the way round and under his chin, now, like some kind of Frankenstein party makeup. He had a dirty white beard.

Sam had no idea what to do, and frankly, all he felt was irritation. Where were human feelings when you wanted them? The timing was so inappropriate. Why couldn't this have happened on another winter afternoon, when Sam wouldn't have had a cold and so would have been able to respond like the person he truly was?

His eyes were dripping; he thought they might freeze shut. He unfolded his handkerchief and mopped at his face. An unworthy thought occurred to him: *Why did I look round at all when I should have kept my head down and run for the subway?*

There was a foul reek of spirits coming off the guy when Sam bent nearer. It occurred to him to touch the guy, but he didn't know where. Or why, now Sam came to think of it. On a theoretical level, he knew that the rigours of life on the street would drive just about anyone to alcoholism, but he still couldn't help finding it gross.

'Excuse me?' he said, sniffing loudly so his nose wouldn't drip on the guy. 'Sir?' How ludicrously genteel. 'Mister? Are you OK?'

No answer. Sam's breath puffed out like white smoke. He made up a reply: *Sure I'm OK, mister; I love to spend my Friday nights lying on the sidewalk, bleeding from the mouth.*

Sam was crouched beside the guy now. Commuters kept streaming past; nothing interrupted the flow on Bloor and Bay. They probably assumed Sam was some kind of weirdo friend of the guy on the ground, despite the Windsmoor coat – which was trailing in the gutter's mound of dirty old snow, he noticed, snatching up the hem. Now he wasn't upright and moving at speed, like the commuters, it was as if he'd left the world of the respectable and squatted in the mud. They'd probably think the coat was stolen. Damn them for a bunch of cold salaried bastards. It wouldn't occur to one of them to take the time to stop and—

And what, exactly? What was Sam going to do?

His nose was streaming now, and his legs were starting to freeze into place. He almost lost his balance as he rooted for his handkerchief. He ripped one leather glove off, reared up, and blew his nose. It made the sound of a lost elephant.

Quick, quick, think. What about first aid? Shit, he should have volunteered to go on that in-house course last year. Shreds of traditional advice swam giddily through Sam's mind. Hot sweet tea was his mother's remedy for everything, but it would be tough to come by; the nearest stall said ESPRESSO EXPRESS. Whiskey? Hardly the thing if the guy was full of alcohol already. Put his feet higher than his head? What the fuck was that about? Sam wondered.

The guy on the ground hadn't moved. The blood didn't seem to be flowing at speed, exactly. It hadn't dripped onto the pavement yet. In films, bleeding from the mouth always meant you were a goner; the trickle only took a few seconds to grow into a terrible red river.

Sam shifted from foot to foot to keep his circulation going, like a hesitant dancer at an eighties disco night. Maybe, it occurred to him with an enormous wave of relief, maybe the blood on this guy's face was an old mark he hadn't washed off. If you didn't have a mirror you probably wouldn't even know you had blood on your chin. Maybe a bit of bleeding was the natural result of drinking methanol or whatever the cocktail of choice was these days. Well, not choice; Sam didn't mean choice, exactly.

But the thing was, how could he be sure? How was a personnel officer with no medical experience to tell if there was something seriously wrong going on here? He shouldn't call 911 on a whim. If they sent an ambulance, it might be kept from some other part of the city where it was really needed. They got these false alarms all the time; hadn't he seen something on City TV about it? And the homeless guy probably wouldn't thank him for getting him dragged into the emergency room, either . . .

And then Sam looked at the guy on the ground, really looked for the first time; he felt a wave of nausea roll from the toes he could no longer feel, all the way to his tightening scalp. The man lay utterly still, not even shivering in the hard air that seemed liable to crystallize round them both any minute now. Sam was not repelled by the guy, exactly; what turned his stomach was the sudden thought that he himself, by some terrible knot of circumstances such as came down on successful people all the time, might someday end up lying on an air vent with people stepping round him and an overeducated ignorant prick in a Windsmoor coat standing round inventing excuses for not making the call that could save his life.

Sam reached for his cell phone, but the pocket of his coat was empty. At first he couldn't believe it; thought he'd been robbed. Then he remembered laying it down beside his computer after lunch. Today of all days! His head was made of mucus.

He dialed 911 from the phone box at the corner. He was afraid they wouldn't believe that it was an emergency – that they would hang up on him – so he sounded inappropriately angry, even when he was giving the address. 'The guy looks seriously ill,' he barked.

It hadn't occurred to Sam to wonder what he would do once he had made the call. He hovered outside the phone box, as if waiting for another turn. In a sense, there was nothing else to do now; the proper authorities had been called in, and Sam was just a passerby again, with every right to head home to his condo and nurse his cold. But in another sense, he thought with self-righteous gloom, he was the only connection. What if the ambulance never turned up? What if the medics couldn't see the guy on the ground because the human traffic was too thick?

A sneeze shook him like a blow from a stranger. With grudging steps he walked back to the guy on the ground, who hadn't stirred. It occurred to Sam for the first time that the guy might be dead. How odd that would be, for such a dramatic thing not to show on a human face, except by this discreet ribbon of blood and a certain blueness about the lips. He thought maybe he should see if there was any sign of life in the guy, but he couldn't decide which bit of dirty raincoat to lay his hand on. If he wasn't dead, Sam should keep him warm; yes, that was definitely to be recommended. Sam stared around to see if there was a department store on the block. He could buy a blanket, or one of those rugged tartan picnic rugs. He would be willing to pay up to, say, $100, considering the seriousness of the occasion; $125, maybe, if that was what it took. But the only stores in view sold lingerie, shoes, and smoked meats. He blew his nose again.

Take off your coat, Sam told himself grimly. He did it, wincing as the cold air slid into his armpits. He was wearing a wool-blend suit, but it wasn't enough. This was probably a crazy idea, considering his own state of health.

He laid the Windsmoor over the man; it was stagey, like a gesture from some Shakespearean drama. No response yet.

What if the warmth made the guy wake up, and Sam had to make conversation? No sign of life, nor death, either. The coat lay too far up the guy's body, so it almost covered his head; it looked like the scene after a murder, Sam thought with a horrified inner giggle. He stooped again, took the coat by its deep hem and dragged it delicately backwards until it revealed the dirty white beard. Sam's keys slid out of a pocket and caught in a grating; he swooped to retrieve them. Jesus, imagine if he'd lost his keys on top of everything! Then he remembered his wallet and had to walk around the guy to reach the other pocket. Passersby might think he was picking the pockets of a dead man, like a scavenger on a battlefield.

He let out a spluttering cough. He could just feel his immune system failing. This cold would probably turn into something serious, like post-viral fatigue or something. He should sit down and try some deep breathing. But where? The heating vent in front of him would be the warmest, but it would look so weird, a guy in an $800 suit squatting on the sidewalk beside a bum. But then, who did he think would be looking at him? he asked himself in miserable exasperation. And why should he care?

Sam let himself down on the curb at last. It was so cold on his buttocks, through the thin wool, it felt like he had wet himself. He stood up and kept moving, jigging on the spot. He couldn't remember the last time he'd been out in January without a winter coat. Like one of those squeegee punks who lived in layers of ragged sweaters. Was that snow, that speck in his eye, or just a cold speck of dust? He rubbed his leather-gloved hands against his cheeks. His sinuses were beginning to pulse.

Twice he heard a siren and began preparing his story – which in his head sounded like a lie – and twice it turned out to be police, zooming by. After a quarter of an hour he no longer believed in the ambulance. His shoulders were going into tremors. For a moment he envied the guy on the vent, who looked almost cozy under the Windsmoor coat. He considered borrowing it back for a few minutes, just to get his core temperature up, but he was afraid of how it would look to passersby and afraid to touch the guy again, besides. *The bum probably brought this on himself,* he thought very fast. *What goes around comes around. These people get what they deserve.*

Sam knew this was madness; he must be running a fever. He blew his nose again, though his handkerchief was a wet rag.

He felt a moment of pure temptation, melting sugar in his veins. All he had to do was pick up his coat, shake it off, put it on, and walk away.

He very nearly cried.

Thirty-two minutes by his Rolex by the time the ambulance showed up. He wanted to be gruff with the paramedics, but his voice came out craven with gratitude, especially when they said no, the guy wasn't dead. He begged them to let him climb into the ambulance after the stretcher. They seemed to think this was a sign of his concern and reluctantly agreed, but the truth of the matter was that Sam was too cold to walk. He would have got into any heated vehicle, even with a psychopathic truck driver. Also there was the matter of his coat.

At the hospital the staff didn't tell him anything. The doors of the ward flapped shut. The last thing Sam saw was his coat, draped over the end of the trolley. It occurred to him to ask for it back, but he couldn't think how to phrase it.

It turned out they really did call people John Doe, like in the movies. The forms were mostly blank, even after Sam and the receptionist had done their best. Sam was staggered by all the things he didn't know about the guy and couldn't begin to guess: *age, nationality, allergies.* He left his own name and address, as well as a little note about his coat, and set off walking to the subway. He was streaming from the eyes, the nose, the mouth, even. The dark night wrapped round him.

He knew he should feel better now. He had been a civic-minded citizen; committed what his Scout Leader had called a Good Deed for the Day; displayed what editorials termed 'core Canadian values'. So why did he feel like shit?

'Bad day?' asked the owner of the corner shop as he sold Sam a carton of eggnog.

Was it written that plain on his face? Sam nodded without a word. Only halfway down the street did it occur to him that, compared with nearly dying on the pavement, his day had been almost a pleasant one.

Sam waited till Monday before calling the hospital. He went down into the park to call, so no one from the office would get curious about his query. No, said the receptionist – a different one – she was not authorized to report on the condition of a patient except to a party named as the next of kin. Sam explained over and over again about John Doe not having any known kin. 'I'm as near to kin as anyone else. You see, I'm . . .' But what was he? 'I called about him, originally. I called 911,' said Sam in a voice that sounded both boastful and ashamed.

The receptionist finally figured out which particular John Doe they were talking about. She relented enough to say that the patient had discharged himself that morning.

'What does that mean?'

'I'm not at liberty to say, sir.'

Sam let the phone drop back into place. Guilt, again, that twinge like whenever he went on the leg-curl machine at the gym. He should have visited the hospital yesterday. What would he have brought, though? Roses? Grapes? A bottle of methanol? And what would he have said? *Here I am, your saviour?*

Maybe in the back of his mind Sam had been thinking it would be like in the movies. An unexpected, heartwarming friendship of opposites; he would teach the street person to read, and in return would learn the wisdom of life in the rough. Who did he think he was kidding?

Sam went back to work with a poppy-seed bagel.

He got over his cold. He took up racquetball. He gave up on ever seeing his coat again, though he did keep one eye out for it on the various homeless guys downtown.

One evening, while watching the news, Sam dimly remembered something from Sunday School about having two coats and giving away one. On a whim, he got up and opened his closet. Twenty-six coats and jackets. He counted them twice and he still couldn't believe it. He thought of giving away twenty-five of them. A dramatic gesture; faintly ludicrous, in fact. Which one would he keep, a coat to clothe and protect him in all seasons? Which one outer garment would say everything that had to be said about him? Which was the real Sam?

He shut the closet.

Always after that he thought of the whole thing as the Coat Episode – as if it had happened on *Seinfeld*. It was like touching a little sore that wouldn't heal up, every time he remembered it. What good had he done? There was no such thing as saving someone's life. You couldn't make it easy for them to live or worth their effort. At most what you did was lengthen it by a day or a year, and hand it back to them to do the living.

At dinner parties, Sam liked to turn the petty happenings of his working day into funny stories. But never this one. Several times he found himself on the point of telling it – when the harshness of the winter came up as a topic, or provincial policy on housing – but he could never decide on the tone. He dreaded sounding pleased with himself, but he didn't want to beat his breast and have his friends console him, either.

What he would really have liked to tell them was his discovery: that it was all a matter of timing. If he'd been in the full of his health, that day, he was sure he'd have risen grandly to the occasion. His courage would have been instant; his gestures, generous and unselfconscious. Then again, if he'd felt a fraction worse – if he'd discovered that he'd lost his handkerchief, say – he knew he'd have scurried on by. What Sam used to think of as his conscience – something solid, a clean pebble in his heart – turned out to depend entirely on the state of his nose.

Five weeks later the hospital sent his Windsmoor coat back in a plastic bag. It smelt harsh, as if it had been bleached. Sam hung it in his closet, but whenever it occurred to him to wear it that winter, his hand skidded on by.

Finally he gave it to the Goodwill and bought a down jacket, like everybody else he knew.

the sanctuary of hands

After a messy ending, the thing to do is to get away. Put several hundred miles between yourself and the scene of the crime. Whether you call yourself victim or villain, the cure's the same: get on a plane.

I flew from Cork to Toulouse and rented an emerald green sports car that cost three times as much as I would have been willing to pay under normal circumstances. I knew that if I sat in some four-door hatchback, my self-pitying panic would well up like heartburn. The thing to do was to pretend I was in a film. French, for preference. I drove out of Toulouse like Catherine Deneuve. I wore very dark shades, a big hat, and an Isadora Duncan gauzy scarf, long enough to strangle me.

My plan was simple. I would spend fourteen days driving through the Pyrenees fast enough to drown out every sound and every thought, and if despite my best efforts there were any tears, the sun and the wind would wipe them off my face. In the afternoons I would find somewhere green and shady to read – at Heathrow Airport I'd picked up a silly novel about Mary Queen of Scots – and then in the evenings I'd round off my four-course table d'hôte with a large cognac and a sleeping pill. I didn't intend to talk to anyone during the next fortnight, so my schoolgirl French wouldn't have to stretch to more than the occasional *merci*.

On the seventh day, driving between one craggy orange hill and another, it came to me that I hadn't touched another human being for a week. I supposed my elbow in its linen sleeve must have brushed past someone else's in one of those painfully narrow hotel corridors, but no skin was involved. And, not knowing anyone, I was exempt from all the kiss-kissing the locals did. I looked down now at my hands on the steering wheel; they were clean and papery.

When I stopped for lunch, I remembered I'd finished my book the night before and left it by the bed. Over my espresso I could feel boredom beginning to nibble. No, not boredom: *ennui,* that was the word, it came back to me now. Much more film-starrish. Ennui was about sunshine like white metal and a huge black straw hat and simply forgetting the name of anyone who'd ever hurt you and anyone you'd ever hurt.

The next sign said CAVERNES TROGLODYTIQUES, over a shaky line drawing of a bear, so that's where I turned off the road. To be honest, I wasn't quite sure what trogloditic caverns were, but they sounded as if they might be cool, or cooler than the road, at least.

But after standing around at the mouth of the cave for a quarter of an hour with a knot of brown-legged Swedes and Canadians, I was just about ready to go back to the car. Then the old woman in the jacket that said GUIDE finally clambered up the rocks towards us, and behind her, a straggling crocodile of what I thought at first were children. None of them seemed more than five feet tall, and they wore little backpacks too high up, like humps. When I saw that they were adults – What's the phrase these days? *People with special needs?* – I looked away, of course, so that none of them would see me staring. That was what my mother always said: *Don't stare!,* hissed like a puncture.

Three or four of the Specials, as I thought of them, had smiles that were too wide. One of them peered into my face as if he knew me. They kept patting and hugging each other, and two men at the back of the group – quite old, with Down's syndrome, I thought, hard to tell how old but definitely not young – were holding hands like kindergarten kids. I looked for the leader of the group – a teacher or nurse or whatever, someone who would be giving them their own little tour of the prehistoric caves – but then I realized that we were all going in together.

At which point I thought, *Fuck it, I don't need this.*

But we were shuffling through the cave mouth already, and to get out I would have had to shove my way back through the Specials, and what if I knocked one of them over? There was one girl, a bit taller than the rest, with a sort of helmet held on with a padded strap across her chin, as if she were going into outer space. Fits, I thought. We're about to descend into a trogloditic cavern with someone who's liable to fits. There was a balding man behind her in an old-fashioned grey suit. He seemed so pale, precarious, with his eyes half shut. I wondered if the same thing that had damaged their brains had stunted their growth, or maybe they hadn't been given enough to eat when they were children. You heard terrible stories.

As we left the sunlight behind us, I realized that my clothes were completely unsuitable for descending into the bowels of the earth. My sandals skidded on the gritty rock; my long silk sundress caught on rough patches of the cave wall, and what the hell had I brought my handbag for? The air was damp, and there were little puddles in depressions on the floor. Beside the little lamps strung up on wires, the stone glowed orange and red.

The guide's accent was so different from that of the nun who taught us French at school that I had to guess at every other word she spoke. She aimed her torch into a high corner of the cave now and pointed out a stalactite and a stalagmite that had been inching towards each other for what I thought I heard her say was eight thousand years. That couldn't be right, surely? In another twelve thousand, she claimed, they would finally touch. And then she launched into a laughably simplistic theory of evolution, for the benefit of the Specials, I supposed. Her words boomed in the cavern, and whenever she stopped to point something out, we all had to freeze and shuffle backwards so as not to collide. I couldn't remember the last time I'd been at such close quarters with a herd of strangers. There was perfume eddying round, far too sweet, and I'd have laid a bet it came from that girl behind me with the Texan accent.

Basically, the guide's story was that we used to be monkeys – 'Non! Non!' protested one or two of the more vocal Specials, and 'Si, si!' the guide cried. We used to be monkeys, she swore – speak for yourself, I wanted to tell her – but then one day we stood up and we wanted to use tools so what did we have to grow?

I peered at her blankly in the half-light. What did we have to *grow*?

'*Les mains!*' she cried, holding up her splayed right hand, and three or four of the Specials held theirs up, too, as if to play Simon Says, or to prove their membership of the species. The guide went on to explain – I could follow her better now that I was getting used to her accent – that everything depended on growing real hands, not paws; hands with thumbs opposite the fingers, for grip. She moved her wrinkled fingers like a spider, and one of the Specials wiggled his right back at her. They seemed irrationally excited to be here, I thought; maybe even a big damp cave was a thrill compared to their usual day.

I shivered where I stood and tucked my hands under my arms to warm them. It occurred to me that it must have been a sad day, that first standing up. I imagined hauling myself to my feet for the first time ever, naked apart from the fur. No more bounding through the jungle; now I'd have to stagger along on two thin legs. All at once my head would feel too heavy to lift, and the whole world would look smaller, shrunken.

One of the Specials giggled like a mynah bird, too close to my ear. I edged away from her, but not so fast that anyone would notice. They didn't know the rules, it occurred to me: how much space to leave between your body and a stranger's, how to keep your voice down and avoid people's eyes. They didn't seem to know about embarrassment.

The guide wasn't at all discomfited, either, not even when the Specials let out echoing whoops or hung off her hands. Now she was saying that the cave dwellers only lived half as long as people do nowadays and had much smaller brains than we do. I stared up at the dripping ceiling so as not to look at any of the Specials. Were they included in her *we*? Then the guide asked why we thought people had lived in these freezing old caves. After a few seconds she answered herself, in the gushing way teachers do: Because it was worse outside! Imagine thousands of years of winter, up there, she said, pointing through the rock; picture the endless snow, ice, leopards, bears . . .

I could feel the cold of the gritty floor coming up through my sandals. I tried to conjure up a time when this would have counted as warm. Jesus! Why they all hadn't cut their throats with the nearest flint scraper, I couldn't imagine. Funny thing, suicide; how rarely people got around to it. We seemed to be born with this urge to cling on. Like last Christmas when I gave my brother's newborn my little finger and she gripped it as if she were drowning.

The guide was leading us down a steep slope now, and the Specials swarmed around her. Except for the pale man with the half-shut eyes, who hung back, then suddenly stopped in his tracks so I bumped into him from behind. I backed off, but he didn't move on. I tried to think what to say that would be politer than '*Allez, allez!*' The guide looked over her shoulder and called out a phrase I didn't understand, something cheerful. But the man in front of me was shaking, I could see that now. His head was bent as if to ward off a blow. It was a big balding head, but not unnaturally big. I might have taken him for a civil servant, if I'd passed him in the street, or maybe a librarian. '*Peur,*' he said faintly, distinctly. '*J'ai peur.*' He was afraid. What was he afraid of?

The guide shouted something. My ears were ringing. I finally understood that she was suggesting mademoiselle might be kind enough to hold – what was his name? – Jean-Luc's hand, just for the steep bit. I looked around to see whom she could mean. Then I felt the blush start on my neck. I was the only mademoiselle in sight, kind or otherwise – the Texans having dropped back to photograph a stalactite – so I held out my hand, a little gingerly, like a birthday present that might not be welcome. I thought of taking him by the sleeve of his jacket, the man she'd called Jean-Luc. But he looked down at my hand, rather than me, and slipped his palm into mine as if he'd known me all our lives.

To be honest, I'd been afraid his fingers might be clammy, like pickled cucumbers, but they were hot and dry. We walked on, very slowly; Jean-Luc took tiny, timid steps, and I had to hunch towards him to keep our hands at the same level. All I could think was, *Thank god it's dark in here.*

In hopes of distracting myself, I was trying to remember the last time I'd held hands with a stranger. A *céilí*, that was it, with my sister's boyfriend's cousin, and our palms were so hot with sweat we kept losing our grip in the twirls and apologizing over and over. I remember thinking at the time that hands were far too private to exchange with strangers. Those Victorians knew what they were doing when they kept their gloves on.

The Texan family was coming up behind now, their shadows huge as beasts on the cave wall. I could hear the girl giggle and mutter to her parents. My cheeks scalded with a sort of shame. I knew we probably looked like something out of Dickens, me with my big hat and Jean-Luc with his shiny head no higher than my shoulder: a monstrously mismatched bride and groom. Though really, why I should have cared what some small-town strangers thought of me, I couldn't say. The Texans didn't even know my name, and I'd certainly never see them again once we got out of this foul cave. Funny to think I'd come on this holiday to distract myself from serious things like tragedy and betrayal, only to find myself sweating with mortification at the thought that a couple of strangers might be laughing at me.

On an impulse I stepped sideways, flattening myself against the cave wall, jerking Jean-Luc with me. His pale eyes looked a little startled, but he came obediently enough. When the Texans had almost reached us I said rather coldly, 'Go ahead,' and let them squeeze past.

That was better. Now there was no one behind us and we could go at our own pace. The passage was getting more precarious, twisting down into the hillside. The roof was low; once or twice it scraped against my absurd straw hat. I had to walk with a stoop, lifting my dress out of my way like some kind of princess. Jean-Luc was saying something, I realized, but so quietly I had to bend nearer to make out the words – nearer, but not too near, in case my face brushed his. My heart rattled like a pebble in a can. I hadn't counted on conversation. What if he was asking me something, and I didn't understand his accent, and he thought it was because I didn't want to speak to him?

'La belle mademoiselle,' that was it. That's all it was. 'La belle mademoiselle m'a donné la main. Elle m'a donné la main.' He wasn't talking to me at all, he was reassuring himself, telling himself the story of the pretty lady who gave him her hand. He had an amazing voice, deep like an actor's. For a moment I was absurdly warmed by the fact that he thought I was *belle,* even if he couldn't have much basis for comparison.

The floor was slick, now, and the passage had narrowed so much I had to walk ahead of Jean-Luc, twisting my arm backwards and waiting for him to catch up with me every couple of steps. I could feel his hand twitch like a rope. He was starting to wheeze, casting anxious glances at the craggy walls closing in on us. The air was dank. I couldn't hear the guide any more, the group had left us so far behind. Damn her to hell, I thought.

The man's breath was coming faster and harsher in his throat. Had he any idea why he was being dragged down into these prehistoric sewers? I wondered. I supposed I should tell him there was nothing to be afraid of. He had a little wart on the edge of one finger, I could feel it, or maybe it was a callus. I gave his hand a small and tentative squeeze. Jean-Luc squeezed back, harder, and didn't let go. I could feel the fine bones shifting under his skin. Well that was all I needed, for this poor bastard to have a heart attack and die on me, twenty thousand leagues below the earth! The thought almost made me laugh. I wished I knew how old he was. Baldness didn't mean anything; I knew a boy who started losing his hair at twenty-two. I cleared my throat now, trying to think of something comforting to say. Every word of French had deserted me. *'Faut pas . . . Faut pas avoir peur,'* I stuttered hoarsely at last, praying I had my verb ending right. How would it translate? One should not be afraid. It is a faux pas to have fear.

I thought Jean-Luc might not have heard me or taken it in; he still stared ahead fixedly, as if anticipating a cave bear or mammoth around every corner. His eyes were enormous; the occasional beam of light showed their whites. But as we ducked under an overhang, I heard it like a mantra, under his breath: *'Faut pas avoir peur. Mademoiselle dit, "Faut pas avoir peur".'*

I grinned, briefly, in the dark. He was doing all right. Mademoiselle had told him not to be afraid. We'd get out of here in one piece.

When we came to a set of deep steps spiralling down in to the rock, I went first, so that at least if he slipped I could break his fall. But Jean-Luc held on to my hand like a limpet, and I didn't want to scare him by tugging it away, so I held on with the tips of my fingers, our arms knotted awkwardly in the air, as if we were dancing a gavotte. His arm was weaving and shaking; it was like wrestling a snake. My silk hem got under my feet, then, and the pair of us nearly crashed down on one of those stubby little stalagmites. Now that would be funny, if we snapped off ten thousand years' worth of growth and got sued by the French state.

The steps began to twist the other way, and I found my arm bent up behind my back as if I was being led to my death. This was ludicrous; I was going to dislocate something. I stopped for a second and switched hands as fast as I could. Jean-Luc stared at me, but held on to the new hand. *'Pas de problème,'* I said foolishly. No problem. Could you say that in French or did it sound American?

We found our rhythm again, and I could hear Jean-Luc

behind me, repeating, '*Pas de problème, pas de problème*,' in a ghost's whisper. Our joined hands were the only spot of heat in this whole desolate mountain.

At last the path levelled out and we found ourselves in a huge cavern where the rest of the group stood watching the guide point out painted animals with her torch. A few faces looked over at us. I relaxed my grip, but Jean-Luc held on tight. For a moment I felt irritated. He wasn't afraid of falling any more; he was just taking advantage. And then I almost laughed at the thought of this peculiar gentleman taking advantage of me. I stood with his warm cushioned hand in mine, the pair of us gazing forward like a bashful couple at the altar. I was cold right through, now, and my nipples were standing up against the silk of my dress; I angled myself a little away from Jean-Luc so he wouldn't see.

I tried to pay attention to the guide. I peered up at the rock walls: orange, greenish grey, and a startling pink. There were scrawl marks that looked as if they'd been done with fingers on a thousand long nights. The paintings were of horses and lions and bears, or so the guide said, and the Specials were laughing and pointing as if they could make them out, but to be honest the rusty overlapping squiggles on the rock all looked alike to me. Whatever the cave dwellers' powers of endurance, it occurred to me, they hadn't been able to draw for shite.

The guide said something I didn't catch, and then let out a surprisingly young laugh and flicked off the light switch. Blackness came down on us like a falling tent. Some of the Specials shrieked with excitement, but Jean-Luc cleaved to my hand as if it were a life belt. I tried to squeeze back, even though he was hurting my fingers. My eyes strained to find any speck of light in the darkness. It suddenly struck me that this was entirely normal behaviour for a trogloditic cavern. When the cold and the dark and the weight of a mountain pressed down on you, what made more sense than to grab the nearest living hand and hold on as tight as you could?

When the lights came back on, I blinked, relieved. A fat boy with a baseball cap on sideways edged back to us, and tried to take hold of Jean-Luc's other hand, but Jean-Luc shook him off, almost viciously. I looked away and bit down on my smile.

What did we think they ate, the cave dwellers? the guide was asking. Most of the Specials grinned back at her as if it were a joke rather than a question. Did they go to a supermarket, she suggested, and buy veal? One or two nodded doubtfully. No, she told us, there were no supermarkets! This claim caused quite a stir among the Specials. Now the guide was shining her torch on a painted animal; I couldn't tell what it was. She announced with grim enthusiasm that the cave dwellers hunted animals with sticks and cooked them in the fire.

'*Non!*'

'*Non!*'

'*Tuer les animaux?*'

A shock wave ran through the group as she nodded to say that yes, they killed the animals. A tiny woman with a squeezed-up face sucked in air. '*Manger les animaux?*' Yes, indeed, they ate the animals. The Specials' reactions were so huge and incredulous that I began to suspect them of irony. Had no one ever told them what sausages were made of?

That's what the cave dwellers did, the guide insisted. And they caught fish, too, she told us, in nets made out of their own hair. And they turned animal skin into leather by soaking it in their own urine, then chewing it till it was soft. At least, I feared that was what she said; the cave was a confusion of voices, now, and all I could think about was how cold I was. I was starting to shake as if I had a palsy. People must always have been cold in those days, it occurred to me. Maybe they knew no different, so they didn't notice it. Or, more likely, maybe they couldn't think about anything else. The minute you woke up, you'd have to start working as if your life depended on it, because it did: build up the fire, eat, keep moving, pile on more clothes, keep eating, never let the fire go out, even in your sleep. They'd all have slept in one big heap, the guide was saying now, putting her head on the shoulder of the girl in the helmet and miming a state of blissful unconscious; if you slept alone, she said, you'd wake up dead. Jean-Luc, by my side, must have heard this, because he let out a single jolt of laughter. I turned my head to smile at him, but he was looking down at his shoes again.

I thought the tour had to be nearly over by now – all I could think of was getting back up into the sunlight – but the guide led us through a little passage so tight we had to go in single file. Jean-Luc and I stayed knotted together like a chain gang. At last the group emerged into a chamber, the smallest so far. The guide mentioned that the man who had discovered these caverns called this one the Sanctuary of Hands.

Then she lifted her torch, and all at once I could see them; they sprang out to meet the light. Handprints in red and black, dozens – no, hundreds of them – daubed on top of each other like graffiti, pressed onto the rock as high as someone on tiptoes could reach. This was how you signed your name, about twenty-seven thousand years ago, said the guide with a casual swing of her torch. The prints glowed in the wide beam as if they were still wet. They were mostly left hands, I saw now, and smallish; perhaps the prints of women or even children. I stepped up to one for a closer look and Jean-Luc crept along behind me.

The handprint nearest us only had three and a half fingers. I recoiled, and the guide must have noticed, because she swung her torch round to where we were standing. I backed out of the blinding light. Yes, she said, many of these hands appeared to be missing a piece or two. This was a great mystery still. Some archaeologists said the cave dwellers must have lost fingers in accidents or because of the cold, but others thought the people must have cut them off themselves. For a gift, she said, almost gaily, did we understand? To give something back to the gods. To say *merci,* thank you.

Jean-Luc stared at the print on the wall a few inches from his head. He let go of my hand, then, and laid his own against the rock, delicately fitting his short pale fingers to the blood-red marks. He turned his head and looked at me then, for the first time, and his mouth formed a half smile as if he were about to tell me a great secret. But '*Touche pas!*' called the guide sternly. '*Faut pas toucher,* Jean-Luc!' Touching was forbidden; I should have told him that. His hand contracted like a snail, and I took it into mine again. It was chilled by the rock.

We followed the group up a long widening tunnel that seemed to have been dug out in modern times, and soon I could smell fresh air. After some very steep steps, we were all panting audibly, even the backpackers, and Jean-Luc's hand was hot in my grip again. He and I were the last to emerge, wincing in the sunlight like aged prisoners set free. The hills were a jumble of rocks on every side, and the half-reaped valley slid away below us. The sun warmed my face, and the air tasted sweet as straw.

Every year for a week or two there would be a sort of summer, the guide was explaining; the snow might shrink away just enough to let the cave dwellers come out and sit on the ground.

And what became of them in the end? someone asked her. Well, she said with a little shrug, one year they must have come out and found the snow gone and the sun shining. Then they walked down into the valley and never came back.

On the way down to the car park, I began to wonder when Jean-Luc was going to let go of my hand. I didn't want to have to wriggle it out of his grasp, but I could see the group leader waiting for them by the little bus. I hoped Jean-Luc didn't think I was coming home with the Specials. All of a sudden I felt appallingly sad. I wished I knew what to say to him, in any language.

But at the edge of the car park he disengaged his sticky fingers from mine and turned to face me, very formally. '*Au revoir, mademoiselle*,' he said, which I supposed could be translated as 'Until we meet again,' and I smiled and nodded and took up his hand again for a second to shake goodbye. He was puzzled by this, I could tell, but he let me shake it, as if it were a rattle.

'*Au revoir*, Jean-Luc,' I repeated, more often than I needed to, and waved until he'd disappeared into the bus. I did look for his profile in the window, but the glass was white in the glare of the sun.

WritOr

Appalled by his credit-card debts, the writer succumbed to a one-year writer-in-residence job at a small college in the mountains. Until he sold the Great Novel for a hefty enough sum to pay the rent on his apartment for a few years, pragmatism seemed to be called for. In the distant past, the writer had tried every joe-job he could think of: he'd picked grapefruit and filed insurance applications, fried pancakes and sold fitness equipment door-to-door. Since then, he'd supplemented his royalties by other means that he was even less proud of: he'd written inane articles for in-flight magazines and lived two years too long with a doctor because it was just so damn handy not to have to worry about the rent. This year, at least, he would be making his living in a job which was, if not literature itself, then at least not unconnected with it.

As jobs went, the writer thought this would probably turn out to be a rather pleasant one. Interesting, even, at the human level as well as the intellectual one. Packing his possessions into the locker room at the self-storage facility, the day before his departure, he tried to visualize the office that awaited him at the college, perhaps with a view of the bluish mountains. He imagined himself mentoring a few bright young poets and diffident, late-blooming novelists whose brief visits to his office – Mondays and Fridays only – would leave him ample time to work on the Great Novel.

Dear Mr Writer-in-Residence (I'm afraid I don't know your Name),

I would greatly like to Introduce Myself. My name is Herb Leland and I call myself a WritOr that is not just someone who Happens to write but who am a Storyteller from the very Depths of my Be-ing. The Truth is that I must WRITE OR DIE so to me the word WritOr which came to me during one long Sleepless Night eighteen months ago expresses this fully. I am sure you Understand being a Multi-Talented Wordsmith Yourself.

I take great Pleasure in enclosure of the following two Book manuscripts The Long and Lonely Road that is a Memoir that follows Me from Ages one to fifty-three (my present age) and Serendipity a Novel about my character Lee Herbert's Journey from Naivete through Confusion to a (eventually) sense of Atuneness with Everything around him. I have been working on them for Ten Years and they are now done.

I look forward to our Appointment on Friday next 6 September at 9:15 am when You will be able to give a full Critique of my Works' strengths and any Possible shortcomings. There are so few Kindred Spirits in this town so I am Most excited at the prospect of being able to Share with you.

Herb Leland's epistle – written in looped, purple letters – made the writer laugh out loud. He was tempted to pin it to the corkboard in his office, but he supposed that wouldn't be nice. Perhaps his year's sojourn among small-town eccentrics would bring out a new humour and warmth in his writing, a sort of Sarah Orne Jewett quality.

His office was narrower than he had expected; the high walls were stubbled with the ubiquitous cream paint. The framed prints he'd shipped from home looked minute. One wall was occupied by a vast set of dark bookshelves; he filled a few inches of one with his complete works – three slimmish volumes – then reconsidered and turned them face out, so they took up half a shelf. Proof that he was a professional, a 'published writer' as Marsha the secretary of English kept calling him.

'I'm curious,' he asked the self-professed WritOr at their first meeting, 'about why you use so many capital letters. Are you trying for a Germanic effect?'

Herb Leland's white, swollen face looked back at him in puzzlement. 'The capitals are for added meaning,' he confided, 'and emphasis.'

'Ah,' said the writer. 'You know, Herb, in my view, it's best to let the emphasis . . . grow out of the choice of words. When you capitalize something, it doesn't really add to its meaning. As such.'

The middle-aged man's face split into a broad smile.

The writer grinned back at him nervously.

'That's exactly what the last three writers-in-residence said,' marvelled Herb.

The writer shrugged, as if to say that life was full of coincidence.

At the end of that first Monday, tired but still amused, he strolled home to the cheapest ground-floor apartment he had been able to find. (He was intending to live simply this year, saving most of his stipend to reduce his debts.) The rooms smelled of something cooked, something he couldn't identify even when he sniffed the air and free-associated, as he'd learned to do many years ago in a workshop on overcoming writer's block.

He sent a flippant e-mail to all his friends. *Currently ensconced in college community in small-town America. Pray for me!*

What should he call them, he wondered, the unknowns

lined up in his day planner? 'My writers' seemed a little optimistic. 'My visitors' sounded like a hospital. 'My students', maybe, except that Marsha had given him to understand that very few of the locals who had made appointments to see him would turn out to be enrolled at the college. 'The student body here are into football,' she told him regretfully. On his corkboard someone – probably Marsha – had pinned an article from the *Campus Calendar* in which the provost was quoted as saying, 'The Writer-in-Residence is our college's ambassador to the wider community – a way for us to reach out the window of our so-called Ivory Tower and truly touch the lives of those we live and work alongside.'

By the second week the writer was seeing ten of them a day.

He worked late into the night on the manuscripts they left in his pigeonhole; he made extensive notes for his own reference. He read Christian magazine columns and chapters of legal thrillers, bits of action screenplays and one twenty-page piece entitled 'Absurdist Collage Poem'. Instead of scribbling anything in the margins – that would be too schoolteacherish, he thought – the writer typed out long lists of tentative suggestions under the headings Micro (spelling, grammar) and Macro (genre, plot, theme).

'Jonas,' he asked, one morning, 'could you read me this sentence here?'

The boy looked at where the writer was pointing. He cleared his throat raspingly. '*It was then immeasurably time for it to be enacted, the action that required to be carried out as aforesaid.*'

The writer let the words hang on the air for a few seconds.

'Do you see what I mean about how your vocabulary in this story tends slightly to the abstract, rather than the concrete? How it could possibly be hard for some readers to tell what's actually going on?'

Jonas scratched a spot on his chin. 'No.'

An hour later the writer was struggling with Mrs Pokowski. 'When you say on page one that "The savages recognized the White Man as lord of their dark and mysterious jungle,"' he quoted neutrally, 'don't you think perhaps some readers might be bothered by that?'

She furrowed her brow. 'You mean the word *savages*?'

'Ah, yes, for one thing . . .'

'Well, I didn't want to put *niggers*,' she said virtuously.

After lunch (a tuna sandwich at his desk) came Pedro Verdi with his genetic-engineering near-future fantasy. 'OK,' said the writer, taking a peek at his notes to refresh his memory, 'so the opening scene takes place in a hospital?'

A shrug from the bank teller. 'Well, you think it's hospital.'

'Yes,' said the writer, not wanting to seem stupid. But after a minute, he couldn't help asking, 'Isn't it?'

'Yeah, yeah, it's hospital,' Pedro conceded, 'but I no want my readers to be too sure, you know?'

'Don't worry, they won't be,' said the writer heavily. 'Now' – trying to read his own handwriting – 'there's some ambiguity about the newborn daughter.'

'Aha. Yes. There has been mix-up,' articulated Pedro, leaning forward with his elbows on his knees. 'Only it's no really mix-up, but you don't find it out till after.'

'Mr Verdi.' The writer meant to sound stern, rather than petulant. 'By my count there are three newborn babies in this book.'

'Pedro, please.' The bank teller loosened his Bart Simpson tie.

'Fine. Pedro. Now, which baby is the genetically modified telepath?'

'Me, I prefer to leave that open. Tell you the truth, I no

146

decided yet,' said Pedro, lying back and gazing out the window.

Three hours later the tiny office was feeling full. Maybelline Norris had brought her mother, a weighty woman introduced only as 'my mom, she's my best friend', who sat with her chair several feet behind Maybelline's.

'Who's your favourite poet?' the writer asked, to put off discussion of Maybelline's own work.

'Dunno. Jewel, I guess,' the girl said. 'If I like stuff, I don't pay much attention to who actually wrote it, you know?'

The writer couldn't think of any other general questions. His eyes flickered between the two Norris women.

'So hey, do you like my poems?' Maybelline asked brightly.

'They're very interesting,' he lied. 'I like some . . . more than others.'

The girl's mother squinted at him disapprovingly.

His eyes fell to the manuscript on his lap, and he silently reread a verse at random.

> *Hurts hurts*
> *like   crazy*
> *My emotionality*
> *crushingly hemmed in*
> *like   cactus flowers*
> *Utterly longing   for the monsoon*

'Have you ever tried . . . redrafting any of your poems?' he suggested.

'Oh no,' Maybelline reassured him. 'I wouldn't want to mess with the magic. I don't know where they come from; I just shut my eyes and it flows. I call up my mom and I say, "Mom, I've just written another poem," and she says, "Wow, that's so wonderful! You're so talented!"'

The writer's eyes veered to the mother, just for politeness, but she only nodded.

'I showed a bunch of them to my teacher back in eleventh grade and she said, "Wow, you can write. You can really write!"'

It astonished the writer, how tiring it was, this listening business.

'I've got about maybe a thousand of them at home! But these ones are like the crème de la crème,' said Maybelline, her eyes resting fondly on the manuscript. 'I showed them to my swim coach and she said, "Wow, this stuff deserves to be published."'

The writer allowed his eyebrows to soar up, as if in encouragement rather than disbelief.

The girl's mother leaned forward then. 'But then there's copyright, ain't there?' she said darkly.

This took him aback.

'Yeah,' said Maybelline regretfully. 'My mom thinks, what if I send my poems to like a magazine or something, and they get stolen?'

'Stolen?' the writer repeated.

'Yeah, you know, published under another name. Like the editor's, maybe.'

His throat was dry; he suddenly longed for a martini. 'No one would ever do that,' he said faintly.

'Really?' said Maybelline, smiling.

'Trust me. It's never going to happen.'

Even on the days when he didn't have office hours, he found it hard to get much of his own work done; this job was so distracting, somehow. But when he did manage a page, at least he approved of what he wrote. It might not be Faulkner, but it was a damn sight better than Herb Leland.

His office collected sounds, he found. Chain saws outside where the dead trees were coming down; gurgles in the ducts as the heating revved up at the start of October; high-pitched giggling in the corridors. Sometimes he imagined that students were pausing to read the résumé pasted to his office door, and laughing at it. He wished he'd left out the line about the *New York Times Book Review* calling his work 'profoundly promising'; it would mean something only if he were still twenty-four.

He stared at his shelf, the few inches his slim hardbacks took up. His name in three different typefaces, repeated, as if it were a phrase that meant something. So sweet to his eyes; so insubstantial.

He rather wished he hadn't pinned a head shot on his door, either. Now people recognized him in the corridors and took him by the elbow to ask one of the four FAQs of the trade:

'Did you always want to be a writer?'

'Where do you get your ideas?'

'How many hours a day do you write?'

'How can I get published?'

But when the writer did a lunchtime reading from his poetry collection, only eleven people showed up. To think that on the plane, flying down here, he had worried about his privacy, how to keep people from prying into every detail of his life! As if they gave a damn. Nobody was remotely curious about him as a person except for Herb Leland, who seemed to have formed an unconscious crush. And Herb's questions were hardly probing, either; they were more along the lines of 'Do you realize how Honoured we feel to have You Living here among us?'

Most nights the writer read detective novels and ate microwaved macaroni.

'I guess I'm a would-be writer,' one housewife introduced herself coyly.

After that, in his head he called them all 'my would-be's', meaning that they perhaps would have been writers if they'd been born with a tittle of talent. It never occurred to them to supplement their high school education by consulting a dictionary. They seemed to feel – like Humpty Dumpty but without his powers – that words should mean what they wanted them to mean: that *un-usual* was a brand-new coinage, that it was possible to *riposte* someone, that drunks fell down *unconscientious* in the street.

By mid-October the writer realized that he shouldn't waste his energy trying to teach the would-be's about literature or anything else. His job was to listen. And it was not just casual nodding along that was required, either, but an intense, full-frontal, eyes-locked kind of attention.

The would-be's claimed they longed for honest criticism. 'Be brutally honest with me, man,' said BJ, a trainee electrician and spare-time rapper who was writing a novel about his recent adolescence and owned seventeen how-to-get-published books. 'Hit me with it!' But BJ didn't really mean it; none of them did, the writer discovered.

'Should I chuck the thing in the stove?' one grandmother asked, her eyes watery and fearful, but it was obviously a rhetorical question.

To be honest was to hurt. Even a mild remark like 'I'm not a big fan of limericks' could make a would-be's face implode.

But to be kind was to lie. The days he said things like 'It's wonderful you've written a whole novel,' he went home feeling greasy with deceit.

This had to be how therapists felt, he realized one long Monday afternoon, when Doug McGee – fifty-something, with eczema — began yet again to unravel the story of how his parents, teachers, and so-called friends had crushed his self-esteem from an early age. The writer crossed and recrossed his legs.

His next visitor, Meredith Lopez Jones, was in love with her writer's block — or *blockage,* as she called it, as if it were in her colon. 'I still don't have anything to show you,' she murmured proudly. 'I suffer from SAD, did I tell you? I withdraw from the world right after the equinox. I just curl up like a seed in the earth all winter, that's all I do.'

Apart from coming in to bore the pants off me twice a week, the writer added mentally.

'Last summer I stayed up all night and tried to get it all down on paper, everything, the whole universe, you know? But my head was so full of images I thought it might burst! I burnt it all the next day, of course.'

The writer pursed his lips as if regretting this.

Meredith pressed her cheekbones so hard she left white fin-gerprints. 'I'm so afraid of writing something mediocre! That's always been my problem. Probably because I was raised as a woman in this society. The scars run deep. No matter how many people have told me I'm an amazingly talented person, I can't quite believe it.'

The writer nodded, unable to quite believe it, either.

Clearly, writing was not an ordinary hobby like wine making or kung fu. It attracted the most vulnerable people; the strange, the antisocial, the sad. Some were struggling with addictions or mysterious debilitating illnesses; others wrote endless versions of their childhood traumas. One quite young, balding man called Jack had been divorced five times already; 'Got no knack for picking 'em, I guess.' His memoir-disguised-as-a-short-story was full of phrases like 'there going to blame me' and 'their's no way out'. The writer stared at the page exhaustedly, wondering if it was worth correcting the spelling.

He had come to dread his office hours. He relied on certain basic survival techniques. He kept an enormous bag of gourmet brownie bites in his filing drawer. After each visit he'd gobble one to lift his spirits, or at least his blood-sugar level. A visit from Stinking Steve – who had a bloated, sun-browned face and always wore the same Disney World sweatshirt – merited two brownie bites. When the writer's aunt sent him a home-made pomander for his office – a beribboned orange studded with cloves – he didn't laugh at it. He hung it on his desk lamp and pressed his nose to it between sessions. It made him feel like a medieval troubadour in a world of serfs.

It occurred to him to ask Marsha to tell the would-be's that his appointment diary was all filled in for a fortnight, but some-how he couldn't bring himself to do it. Besides, she seemed like a woman of integrity, and she might report him to the dean of arts.

He was not doing much with the Great Novel these days. He feared the terrible writing of the would-be's might be con-tagious. Whenever he wrote a sentence, he had to stop and check it for mixed metaphors. All the fatuous rules he'd been spouting this term looped through his head. *Write what you know*, he thought. *Show, don't tell. Verbs and nouns are stronger than adjectives and adverbs.* This was painting by numbers; it felt like a uniquely pointless way to spend the rest of his life. *Avoid the passive voice.* He tried to remember, when was the last time he'd written anything in the white heat of inspiration?

There was just one café in town that roasted its own beans. The writer tried going there with his laptop to have a go at chapter three over a latte, but people stared, and he got a crois-sant crumb lodged between Q and W.

He went back the next day with paper and pen and ordered a bracing shot of wheatgrass. He'd composed just half a sentence when two blonde girls whose names he couldn't remember came over to say how awesome it was to find him here, and would he mind looking at their essay plans? The topic was Believing in Ourselves.

He e-mailed his friends: *Making whoopee in the mountains. My office gets the best sunsets. Oh, the life of a state-subsidized sybarite! Great Novel coming along nicely. Miss you all, naturally, but not enough to come home.*

He knew this was a stupid policy – he could hardly keep up this pretense forever – but right now he couldn't bear to tell anyone what a mistake he had made.

As an experiment, he started working to rule. He no longer read any of the manuscripts jammed into his pigeonhole. The would-be's never seemed to notice.

'Why don't you tell me the overall story in your own words,' he murmured, eyes shut, to Tzu Ping.

Off she went: 'Well, it starts when I'm – I mean when my character – is in second grade . . . ,' and soon her time was up.

Later the same day, Mrs Pokowski frowned at the pristine manuscript he handed back to her. 'Did you like chapter three?'

'Very much,' said the writer. 'But' – here he flicked through the pages and picked out a line at random – 'I'm a little confused by the metaphors in this sentence: *"A fragile essence of deep buried undigested resentments were locked away behind a veil of stone."'*

'What's to confuse?' asked Mrs. Pokowski coldly.

With Linda Shange, he only ever had to glance at the first paragraph. 'Linda,' he said, 'you see the way you keep telling us how nice your protagonist is? Here, for instance: *"She was a sweet and kind person who never killed mice."'*

'Yes, she really was, in real life,' said Linda beatifically.

'The danger is,' he told her, 'you might actually put some readers off.'

She looked shocked.

'We don't need to like your protagonist all the time,' he told her, yet again, 'we just need to care what happens to her.'

One week, every story presented to him seemed to contain some reference to child abuse. He was irritated by this craven following of literary fashion. 'Lenny,' he said to the golden-haired boy majoring in English, 'couldn't you pick a more original angle? The hard-drinking, big-fisted Daddy is kind of a stereotype. And isn't it rather implausible that it would be the *eldest* boy he'd rape?'

'But that's what happened,' said Lenny.

The writer stared at him.

The boy gave an awkward little grimace and pushed his blond fringe out of his eyes. 'If I slept in the bed nearest the door, you know . . . he'd come in and do it to me and leave the younger ones alone.'

The writer covered his mouth with his hand. He found himself unable to give the standard speech about the distinction between fiction and autobiography. In an unsteady voice, for the last five minutes of the session he talked about Lenny's excellent use of nature imagery.

So he cultivated compassion. He started practising meditation again. *You don't need to like these people*, he told himself over and over, *you just need to care what happens to them.*

He taught himself to sit there opposite the would-be's and vary his smiles and nods, crinkle his eyebrows and say 'Mmm' at the right bits. He kept his hands folded – priestly – and let the would-be's talk about whatever they needed to talk about. Some of them never mentioned writing at all. Others eventually revealed that they hadn't written a word since high school, but they were somehow convinced that they could if they tried. 'Because I've had such an interesting life and I've a lot to teach the world.'

'Because I'm retired now and I want to make some vacation money.'

'Because my doctor said it might help.'

One day the writer didn't say a word for thirty-five minutes while Maybelline Norris yammered on about how talented everybody said she was. If he'd been inventing a character for his novel, he couldn't have come up with such a combination of egotism and naked need. He looked at the girl's surprisingly bad teeth and wondered if she was bulimic. He would have liked to put his hand over her mouth, to hush and comfort her, but that was hardly possible with Mrs Norris sitting implacable, two feet behind her daughter.

Only in one session did he come close to nodding off, and it wasn't his fault. Mrs Pokowski was describing a self-hypnosis technique she'd learned 'for so as to unleash creativity', as she said in her mosquito-drone voice. She took him through it step by step – 'Now I'm falling down the hole, and I'm falling down deeper, and deeper, and now what do I see, I see another tunnel, so what do I do, I go down that one . . .'

The world began to melt; he had to writhe on his chair and bite the inside of his cheek to stay awake.

In the second week of November the writer turned sullen. He stopped practising meditation; he couldn't see the point in spending twenty minutes a day sitting very still on his couch while the entire lyric oeuvre of David Bowie raced through his head. He gave up on compassion.

He had cruel private names for most of the would-be's by now: as well as Stinking Steve there was Jawless Jennifer (whose face seemed to fall away below the nose), Mr Hypochondria, and Dottie-Date-Rape. He was just an ear to this pack of social rejects, an official representative of Literature who had to listen to their grievances and explain why they'd never been let into the club, why publishers invariably returned their fat single-spaced manuscripts with the floral designs on the cover page.

'I have to tell you, I just love this poem, I just think it says everything I've ever wanted to say in my life,' Meredith Lopez Jones told him, wet-eyed, her hand fondling the page.

I am so glad to have had this Opportunity to have Shared the story of Running Fox with you, wrote Herb Leland. *I take no credit for Running Fox, she germinated and Marinated in my head for many Moons then gave birth to herself in tune with the rhythms of her People's Spirituality. To have Helped bring her into this World makes me Proud.*

These people were philistines, pariahs, parasites. They haunted the writer's nights and stalked his days. When he tried going for a run along the riverbank to work off his tension, who should he meet but Herb Leland, who had the gall to lurch along behind him, rhapsodizing about the Crisp Fall Keatsian Air.

In fact, human beings in general repelled him these days. Marsha with her fat wrists; George W. Bush blustering at press conferences; even his old friends, who had taken to sending him irritating Internet jokes.

As for language – his former lover, his enigmatic deity – these days, it slunk through his office like a diseased cat. Language had a limp, a scab, a tumour, a death wish. Words on the page were a helpless leakage, a human stain.

In his tiny apartment, he opened the file called GREAT NOVEL and tinkered with the punctuation of a single sentence, then stared at the wall until his computer went into sleep mode to save energy. He sniffed the air. Parsnips? he wondered. Or cumin? Damp under the carpet?

He lay on the couch all evening watching the Home Shopping Network. They always seemed to be advertising some gadget that sealed things into plastic bags. Cubes of broth, apple pies, cashmere sweaters, silver spoons – just about everything, they said, would be cleaner and safer if stored in a vacuum pack.

He fell asleep on the couch and woke in the middle of the night with a crooked neck. He had been dreaming that he lured the would-be's, with their griefs and their odours and their terrible ambitions, into a giant plastic bag and sealed them all away.

The next morning he had a raging headache. He lay staring at the ceiling for some hours before he called Marsha to say, in an exaggeratedly gravelly voice, that he feared he was coming down with something, and could she reschedule all his appointments?

He moped around all week, dozing on the couch in the afternoons, staying close to home in case anybody saw him and reported he wasn't sick.

He went back into college on Monday, before Marsha could call and ask him for a doctor's note. But this time he was determined not to let the bastards grind him down.

He indulged in cruelty; it passed the time. He started reading the manuscripts again and marking them in red pen – a big circle round every mistake – not because he thought the would-be in question would really benefit, but simply as punishment. He made his marginalia deliberately intimidating. *Inexplicable POV slippages*, he would scribble, or *I suspect the irony of this double entendre is not intentional?*, or *See identical errors pp. 2,*

3, 9, 15, passim. Whereas in the early weeks he had used kind euphemisms like *A little overfamiliar?* he now wrote <u>CLICHÉ</u> in large red capitals.

He slouched in his office chair. 'Sharon, would you agree that the prevailing mood of this piece is self-pity?'

'Dr Partridge, you describe the mother's smile as *viscous.* Were you referring to a metaphorical oiliness about it, or failing to spell *vicious?*'

Dear Mr McCullen, he wrote on English department note-paper, *Thank you for your letter. I have read your manuscript, which appears to be largely based on* Gone with the Wind, *though lacking that novel's strengths. For your future reference, plagiarism has a better chance of going undetected when the source text is not one of the best-selling novels of the twentieth century.* Then his hand started to shake, so he tore the letter up.

Insomniac at four a.m., the writer fantasized about going one step further and speaking the plain truth. *No, Jonas,* he might say to the spotty boy, *this isn't a poem. These are pretentious words from an online thesaurus, typed out in no particular order.*

Maybelline, forget what your swim coach said. You have no talent. Zero. Zip!

Herb, we are not Soul-Friends, as you put it in your last note. You are suffering from a midlife homoerotic infatuation, and I only talk to you because I'm being paid.

People, give it up! he could bawl at them all. *Get over it! Try extreme sports, masturbation, anything. Stop violating the language I used to love.*

The worst thing the writer ever actually said was at the end of a long Friday. BJ came in with gold shades on, radiant. 'I did what you told me, man.'

'Really,' said the writer, trying to remember what he had told BJ.

'I made all those changes you asked for. And I'm gonna go for it.'

'For what?'

'The big time!' BJ delivered the line in rapper style, using his hands. 'You know how I was telling you John Grisham sold his first book out of his truck? Well, Wal-Mart's gonna let me set up a table.'

The writer's mind was foggy this morning. 'Is this about . . . self-publishing?'

'That's right, man.' BJ was only a little sheepish. 'I made a few calls, found a guy that'll do me five hundred copies for two grand. Charlene is gonna lend me most of it.'

The writer considered whether to tell BJ that to print five hundred copies of his so-called coming-of-age novel was a criminal waste of trees as well as his ex-girlfriend's money. That it would never get reviewed, stocked, or bought. Instead he dragged the dog-eared manuscript towards him and opened it at random. 'This sentence doesn't have a verb.'

The gilt shades looked back at him blankly.

'If you don't know what a verb is, BJ, why the fuck do you imagine you can write a novel?'

Tears skidded down BJ's face. The young man tried to speak; his Adam's apple jerked. He bent over as if he'd been stabbed. There were salt drops on the writer's desk, on the manuscript.

'I'm sorry,' the writer said, breathless, 'I'm so sorry—'

But BJ didn't seem to hear him. 'I just, you know,' he sobbed at last, 'I guess it was different for you 'cuz you're like a genius. I just think, I've spent so long on this thing, I just want it to be over and out there.' The breath rasped in his throat. 'If I could only see my name – I'd know I'd done something. On a book. Any kind of book of my own. My name on it. You know?'

The writer did know.

He flew home for the weekend and slept on a friend's futon. He wandered round town the way he always used to, and he felt sick, as if something were punctured in his stomach. The seats in his favourite café were all taken. In his local bookstore, the massed titles faced him down.

He sat on a park bench, bundled up against the December cold. It would be easy enough to tender his resignation on health grounds. Depression, he could call it, or a breakdown. He could send the rest of the money back, ask Marsha to box up his possessions and shred any papers in his office.

Three slim hardcovers proved nothing about him. There were hundreds of thousands of new books published every day. He thought about other ways of earning a living. He'd been quite good at selling fitness equipment, he seemed to remember. *WritOr Die,* he repeated in his head, *WritOr Die.* Was there any truth in that? Did he have a real gift, a sacred vocation? Maybe he was just as much of a self-deceiver as any of the would-be's. Maybe he'd be happier being a salesman.

The fact that he took the last flight back on Sunday night and was in his office at nine o'clock the next morning rather puzzled him afterwards. But he needed to get the job done.

That Monday was quiet. He surprised himself by writing a four-page scene for chapter four of his novel. Nothing that would change the course of literary history, but still, not bad: well-constructed, workmanlike, entirely readable.

A knock. It occurred to him not to answer. He wasn't visible through the smoky glass. How could anyone know he was there?

'Are you, like, the writer?' the girl asked when he opened the door.

'So they say,' he answered.

She stepped into the office. She held out a single sheet with flittered edges, ripped off from a refill pad.

'All writings have to be given in a week in advance,' he said automatically.

'Yeah,' the secretary said, 'but I just happened to be passing through this building, I never usually do. I only got this done last night; it's sort of a poem.'

He repressed a wince. He waved to indicate that she should sit down while he looked at it.

After he'd read the short lyric for the first time he turned towards the window, in his swivel chair, so he could be unobserved. He didn't want to have to worry about his face. He read it again, more slowly, then once more. Yes, his first impression hadn't deceived him. It wasn't just wishful thinking after all these awful months.

'So?' the girl asked, sounding a little bored.

He turned round, and gave a little shrug. 'It's . . . entirely beautiful.' He sounded hoarse.

She stared back at him for a second, then let out a hiccup of laughter. She was an ordinary, not-very-good-looking girl. 'Cool,' she said, and reached out to take her page back.

'No, but listen,' the writer told her, holding on to it. 'You have a rare talent.'

'Nice of you to say so.' The girl was strapping her bag across her shoulder blade.

'If you leave this copy with me—'

'Sorry, no can do,' she said, holding out her hand for it again; 'I send them to my boyfriend, he's in the Marines, though I don't know does he like them really, though he says he does.'

'But this poem must be published.'

'Get out,' she said, sheepish.

'I'm quite serious,' the writer told her. 'I know the editor of a marvellous little magazine . . .'

She shook her head. 'I wouldn't really be into that. I just like writing them.'

'You don't want to be published?' His voice was shrill.

'Not really. My friends would think it was kinda dumb. I mean, no offence,' she corrected herself.

He could feel his face contort. 'So why did you come here?'

'Gee, I'm sorry if I've wasted your time. I just thought, you know, as I was passing, I'd see what you had to say.'

'Well, I'm telling you, this poem is superb. So simple and so powerful. I don't know how you did it. I—' He made the great effort. 'I've never written anything that good in my life.'

She gave him an odd, pitying look. 'Hey, keep it, then. See ya,' she added, backing out the door.

Alone in his office, he read the poem twice more before realizing there was no name on the page. He called Marsha, but she didn't know who the girl was, either.

He kept the poem pinned to his corkboard. He read it once, at the end of every day, till the end of the year. It kept him dangling somewhere between hope and despair.

desire

team men

That was the kindest thing Saul could say about anyone, that he was a real team man. 'Jonathan,' he used to tell his son over their bacon, eggs, sausage, and beans, 'a striker's not put up front for personal glory. You'll only end up a star player if you keep your mind on playing for the good of the team. Them as tries to be first shall be last and vice versa.'

Jon just kept on eating his toast.

Saul King believed in fuel, first thing in the morning, when there was plenty of time ahead to burn it up. 'Breakfast like a legend, dine like a journeyman, and sup like a sub.' That made him cackle with laughter.

The boy was just sixteen and nearly six foot tall. Headers were his strong point. When the ball sailed down to him he could feel his neck tighten and every bit of force in his body surge towards the hard plate at the front of his skull. The crucial thing was to be ready for the ball; to meet all its force and slam it back into the sky. On good days Jon felt hard and shiny as a mirror. He knew that if the planet Mars came falling down, he could meet it head on and rocket it into the next galaxy.

But by now he had learned to pay no attention to his dad before a game. If Jon let the warnings get through to him, he couldn't swallow. If he didn't eat enough, he found himself knackered at halftime. If he flagged, he missed passes, and the goalmouth seemed ten miles away. If the team lost, his dad took it personally and harder than a coach should. Once when Jon fluffed a penalty kick, Saul hadn't spoken a word to him for a week.

'Nerves of steel,' the greying man said finally, as they sat at opposite ends of the table waiting for Mum to bring a fresh pot of tea.

Jon's fork clinked against his plate. 'What's that, Dad?'

'If a striker hasn't got nerves of steel when they're needed, he's no right to take a penalty kick at all.'

His son listened and learned. As if he had a choice.

The lads were already having a kickabout on the pitch when the Kings drove up. Saul got out; the car door steadied in his hand as he watched the lads over his shoulder. 'Well, well,' he said, 'who have we here?'

One unfamiliar coppery head, breaking away from the pack. 'Oh yeah, Shaq said he might bring someone from school,' Jon mentioned, hauling his kit bag out of the backseat.

'Now there's a pair of legs,' breathed Saul. He and his son stood a foot apart, watching the new boy run. He was runt-sized, but he moved as sleekly as cream.

'A winger?' hazarded Jon.

'We'll see,' said Saul, mysterious.

Davy turned out to be seventeen. Up close he didn't look so short; his limbs were narrow but pure muscle. The youngest of eight; one of those big rackety Irish families. His face went red as strawberries when he ran, but he never seemed to get out of breath; his laugh got a bit hoarser, that was all. He was a cunning bastard on the pitch. Beside him Jon felt lumbering and huge.

In the dressing room after that first practice Davy played his guitar as if it were electric. He sang along, confidently raucous.

Get knocked down

But I get up again . . .

'Best put a bit of meat on those bones,' observed Saul, and loaded Davy down with five bags of high-protein glucose supplement. It turned out Davy lived just down the road from the Kings, so Saul insisted on giving him a lift home.

After a fortnight Davy was pronounced a real team man. He was to be the new striker. Jon was switched to midfield. 'It's not a demotion,' his father repeated. 'This is a team, not a bloody corporation.'

Jon looked out the car window and thought about playing on a team where the coach wouldn't be his dad, wouldn't shove him from one position to another just to prove a point about not giving his son any special treatment. Jon visualized himself becoming a legend in some sport Saul King had never tried, could hardly spell, even – badminton, maybe, or curling, or luge.

The thing was, though, all he'd ever wanted to play was football.

Jon was over the worst of his sulks by the next training session. He had every reason to hate this Davy, but it didn't happen. The boy was a born striker, Jon had to admit; it would have been nonsense to put him anywhere else on the pitch. He wasn't a great header of the ball, but he was magic with his feet.

And midfield had its own satisfactions, Jon found. 'You lot are the big cog in the team's engine,' Saul told them solemnly. 'You slack off for a second, the game will fall apart.'

Pounding along with the ball at his feet, Jon saw Davy out of the corner of his eye. 'With ya!' Jon passed the ball sideways, and Davy took it without even looking. Only after he'd scored did he spin round to give Jon his grin.

'Your dad's a laugh. I mean,' Davy corrected himself in the shower, 'he's all right. He knows a lot.'

'Not half as much as he pretends,' said Jon, soaping his armpits.

'Is it true what Shaq says about him, that he got to the semi-final of the 1979 FA Cup?'

Jon nodded, sheepish.

Davy, under the stream of water, sprayed like a whale. 'Fuck. What did he play?'

'Keeper.' On impulse, Jon stepped closer to Davy's ear. 'Dad'd flay me if he knew I told you this. He's never forgiven himself.'

'What? What?' The boy's eyes were green as scales.

'He flapped at it. The winning goal.'

Davy sucked his breath in. It made a clean, musical note.

In October the days shortened. One foul wet afternoon Saul made them run fifteen laps of the field before they even started, and by the time he finally blew the whistle, they had mud to their waists and it was too dark to see the ball. Naz tripped over Jon's foot and landed on his elbow. 'You big ape,' moaned Naz; 'you lanky fucking ape-man.'

The other lads thought this was very funny.

'You can't let them get to you,' Davy said casually, afterwards, while they were warming down.

'Who?' said Jon, as if from a million miles away.

Davy shrugged. 'Any of them. Anyone who calls you names.'

Jon chewed his lip.

'I've got five big brothers,' Davy added, when he and Jon were sitting in the back of the car, counting their bruises. 'And my sisters are even worse. They've always taken the piss out of me. One of them called me the Little Stain till she got married.'

A grin loosened Jon's jaw. He stared out the window at his father, who was collecting the training cones.

'Just ignore the lads and remember what a good player you are.'

'Maybe I'm not,' said Jon, looking down into Davy's red hair.

'Maybe you're what?' Davy let out a yelp of laughter. 'Jon-boy, you're the best. You've got a perfect footballing brain, and you're a sweet crosser of the ball.'

Jon was glad of the twilight, then. Blood sang in his cheeks.

Davy came round every couple of days now. Mrs King often asked him to stop for dinner. 'That boy's not getting enough at home,' she observed darkly. But Jon thought Davy looked all right as he was.

Jon's little sister Michaela sat beside Davy at the table whenever she got the chance, even if she did call him Short-arse. She was only fifteen, but she looked old enough. As she was always reminding Jon, girls matured two years faster.

Davy ended up bringing Michaela to the local Hallowe'en Club Night and Jon brought her friend Tasmin. While the girls were queuing up for chips afterwards, Davy followed Jon into the loos. Afterwards, Jon could never be sure who'd started messing round; it just happened. It was sort of a joke and sort of a dare. In a white stall with a long crack in the wall they unzipped their jeans. They kept looking down; they didn't meet each other's eyes.

It was over in two minutes. It took longer to stop laughing.

When they got back to the girls, the chips were gone cold and Michaela wanted to know what was so funny. Jon couldn't think of anything, but Davy said it was just an old Diana joke.

Tasmin said in that case they could keep it to themselves because she didn't think it was very nice to muck around with the dead.

After Hallowe'en, some people said Davy was going out with Michaela. Jon didn't know what that meant exactly. He didn't think Davy and Michaela did stuff together, anyway. He didn't know what to think.

Saul King expressed no opinion on the matter. But he'd started laying into Davy at practice. 'Mind your back! Mind your house!' he bawled, hoarse. 'Keep them under pressure!'

Davy said nothing, just bounced around, grinning as usual.

'Where's your bleeding eyes?'

'Somebody's not the golden boy any more,' commented Peter to Naz under his breath.

Saul said he had errands to do in town, so Jon and Davy could walk home for once.

'Your dad's being a bit of a prick these days,' commented Davy as they turned the first corner.

'Don't call him that,' said Jon.

'But he is one.'

Jon shook his heavy head. 'Don't call him my dad, I mean.'

'Oh.'

The silence stretched between them. 'It's like the honey jar,' said Jon.

Davy glanced up. His lashes were like a cat's.

'I was about three, right, and I wanted a bit of honey from the jar, but he said no. He didn't put the jar away or anything – just said no and left it sitting there about six inches in front of me. So the minute he was out of the room I opened it up and stuck my spoon in, of course. And I swear he must have been waiting because he was in and had that spoon snatched out of my hand before it got near my face.'

'What's wrong with honey?' asked Davy, bewildered.

'Nothing.'

'I thought it was good for you.'

'It wasn't anything to do with the honey,' said Jon, dry-throated. 'He just wanted to win.'

Davy walked beside him, mulling it over.

They went the long way, through the park. When they passed a gigantic yew tree, Davy turned his head to Jon and grinned like a shark.

Without needing to say a word, they ducked and crawled underneath the tree. The dark branches hung down around them like curtains. Nobody could have seen what they were up to; a passerby wouldn't even have known they were there. Jon forgot to be embarrassed. He did a sliding tackle on Davy and toppled him onto the soft damp ground. 'Man on!' yelped Davy, pretending to be afraid. They weren't cold any more. They moved with sleek grace, this time. It was telepathic. It was perfect timing.

'For Christ's sake, stay onside,' Saul bawled at his team.

Davy's trainers blurred like Maradona's, Jon thought. The boy darted round the pitch confusing the defenders, playing to the imaginary crowd.

'Don't bother trying to impress us with the fancy footwork, Irish,' screamed Saul into the wintry wind, 'just try kicking the ball. This is footie, not bloody *Riverdance*.'

Afterwards in the showers, Jon watched the hard curve of Davy's shoulder. He wanted to touch it, but Naz was three feet away. He took a surreptitious glance at his friend's face, but it was shrouded in steam.

Saul never gave Jon and Davy a lift home from practice any more. He said the walk was good exercise and lord knew they could do with it.

'I don't know why, but your dad is out to shaft me,' said Davy, on the long walk home.

'No he's not,' said Jon weakly.

'Is so. He said he thought I might make less of a fool of myself in defence.'

'Defence?' repeated Jon, shrill. 'That's bollocks. Last Saturday's match, you scored our only goal.'

'You set it up for me. Saul said only a paraplegic could have missed it.'

Jon tried to remember the shot. He couldn't tell who'd done what. On a good day, he and Davy moved like one player, thought the same thing at the same split second.

'I don't suppose there's any chance he knows about us?'

Jon was so shocked he stopped walking. He had to put his hand on the nearest wall or he'd have fallen. The pebble dash was cold against his fingers. *Us,* he thought. There was an *us.* An *us* his dad might know about. 'No way,' he said at last, hoarsely.

Jon knew there were rules, even if they'd never spelled them out. He and Davy were sort of mates and sort of something else. They didn't waste time talking about it. In one way it was like football – the sweaty tussle of it, the heart-pounding thrill – and in another way, it was like a game played on Mars, with unwritten rules and a different gravity.

The afternoons were getting colder. On Bonfire Night they took the risk and did it in Jon's room. The door had no lock. They kept the stereo turned up very loud so there wouldn't be any suspicious silences. Outside the bangers went off at intervals like bombs. Jon's head pounded with noise and terror. It was the best time yet.

Afterwards, when they were slumped in opposite corners of the room, looking like two ordinary postmatch players, Jon turned down the music. Davy said, out of nowhere, 'I was thinking of telling the folks.'

'Telling them what?' asked Jon before thinking. Then he understood, and his stomach furled into a knot.

'You know. What I'm like.' Davy let out a mad chuckle.

'You're not . . .' His voice trailed off.

'I am, you know.' Davy still sounded as if he were talking about the weather. 'I've had my suspicions for years. I thought I'd give it a try with your sister, but *nada*, to be honest.'

Jon thought he was going to throw up. 'Would you tell them about us?'

'Only about me,' Davy corrected him. 'Name no names, and all that.'

'You never would.'

'I'll have to sometime, won't I?'

'Why?' asked Jon, choking.

'Because it's making me nervous,' explained Davy lightly, 'and I don't play well when I'm nervous. I know my family are going to freak out of their tiny minds whenever I tell them, so I might as well get it over with.'

He was brave, Jon thought. But he had to be stopped. 'Listen, you mad bastard,' said Jon fiercely, 'you can't tell anyone.'

Davy sat up and straightened his shoulders. He looked small, but not at all young; his face was an adult's. 'Is that meant to be an order? You sound like your dad,' he added, with a hint of mockery.

'He'll know,' whispered Jon. 'Your parents'll guess it's me. They'll tell my dad.'

'They won't. They'll be too busy beating the tar out of me.'

'My dad's going to find out.'

'How will he?' said Davy reasonably.

'He just will,' stuttered Jon. 'He'll kill me. He'll get me by the throat and never let go.'

'Bollocks,' said Davy, too lightly. 'We're not kids any more. The sky's not going to fall in on us. You're just shitting your shorts at the thought of anyone calling you a faggot, aren't you?'

'Don't say that.'

'Touchy, aren't you? It's only a word.'

'We're not, anyway,' he told Davy coldly. 'That's not what we are.'

The boy's mouth crinkled with amusement. 'Oh, so what are we then?'

'We're mates,' said Jon through a clenched throat.

One coppery eyebrow went up.

'Mates who mess around a bit.'

'Fag-got! Fag-got!' Davy sang the words quietly.

Jon's hand shot out to the stereo and turned it way up to drown him out.

Next door, Michaela started banging on the wall. '*Jonathan!*' she wailed.

He turned it down a little, but kept his hand on the knob. 'Get out,' he said.

Davy stared back at him blankly. Then he reached for his jacket and got up in one fluid movement. He looked like a scornful god. He looked like nothing could ever knock him down.

Jon avoided Davy all week. He walked home from the training sessions while Davy was still in the shower. In the back of his mind, he was preparing a contingency plan. *Deny everything. Laugh. Say the sick pervert made it all up.*

Nobody else seemed to notice the two friends weren't on speaking terms. Everyone was preoccupied with the big match on Saturday.

At night Jon gripped himself like a drowning man clinging to a spar.

Saturday came at last. The pitch was muddy and badly cut up before they even started. The other team were thugs, especially an enormous winger with a moustache. From the kickoff, Saul's team played worse than they'd ever done before. The left back crashed into his central defender, whose nose bled all down his shirt. Jon moved like he was shackled. Whenever he had to pass the ball to Davy, it fell short or went wide by a mile. It was as if there was a shield around the red-haired boy and nothing could get through. Davy was caught offside three times in the first half. Then, when Jon pitched up a loose ball on the edge of his own penalty area, one of the other team's forwards big-toed a fluke shot into the top right-hand corner.

'You're running round like blind men,' Saul told his team at halftime, with sorrow and contempt.

By the start of the second half, the rain was falling unremittingly. The fat winger stood on Peter's foot, and the ref never saw a thing. 'Look,' bawled Peter, trying to pull his shoe off to show the marks of the studs.

The other team found this hilarious. 'Wankers! Faggots!' crowed the fat boy.

Rage fired up Jon's thudding heart, stoked his muscles. He would have liked to take the winger by the throat and press his thumbs in till they met vertebrae. What was it Saul always used to tell him? *No son of mine gets himself sent off for temper.* Jon made himself turn and jog away. *No son of mine*, said the voice in his head.

Naz chipped the ball high over the defence. Jon was there first, poising himself under the flight of the ball. It was going to be a beautiful header. It might even turn the match around.

'Davy's,' barked Davy, jogging backwards towards Jon.

175

Jon kept his eyes glued to the falling ball. 'Jon's.'

'It's mine!' Davy repeated, at his elbow, crowding him.

'Fuck off!' He didn't look. He shouldered Davy away, harder than he meant to. Then all of a sudden Jon knew how it was going to go. He wasn't ready to meet the ball; he didn't believe he could do it. He lost his balance, and the ball came down on the side of his head and crushed him into the mud.

Jon had whiplash.

Saul came home from the next training session and said Davy was off the team.

'You cunt,' said Jon.

His father stared, slack-jawed. Michaela's fork froze halfway to her mouth. 'Jonathan!' appealed their mother.

Above his foam whiplash collar, Jon could feel his face burn. But he opened his mouth and it all spilled out. 'You're not a coach, you're a drill sergeant. You picked Davy to bully because you knew he's going to be a better player than you ever were. And now you've kicked him off the team just to prove you can. So much for team-fucking-spirit!'

'Jonathan.' His father's face was dark, unreadable. 'It was the lad who dropped out. He's quit the team and he's not coming back.'

One afternoon at the end of a fortnight, Davy came round. Jon was on his own in the living room, watching an old France '98 video of England versus Argentina. He thought Davy looked different: baggy-eyed, older somehow.

Davy stared at the television. 'Has Owen scored yet?'

'Ages ago. They're nearly at penalties.' Jon kept his eyes on the screen.

Davy dropped his bag by the sofa but didn't sit down, didn't take his jacket off. In silence they watched the agonizing shoot-out.

176

When it was over, Jon hit rewind. 'If Beckham hadn't got himself sent off, we'd have demolished them,' he remarked.

'In your dreams,' said Davy. They watched the flickering figures. After a long minute he added, 'I've been meaning to come round, actually, to say, you know, sorry and all that.'

'It's nothing much, just a bit of whiplash,' said Jon, deliberately obtuse. He put his hand to his neck, but his fingers were blocked by the foam collar.

'You'll get over it. No bother.'

'Yeah,' said Jon bleakly. 'So,' he added, not looking at Davy, 'did you talk to your parents?'

'Yeah.' The syllable was flat. 'Don't worry, your name didn't come up.'

'I didn't—'

'Forget it,' interrupted Davy softly. He was staring at the video as it rewound; a green square covered in little frenzied figures who ran backwards, fleeing from the ball.

That subject seemed closed. 'I hear you're not playing, these days,' said Jon.

'That's right,' said Davy, more briskly. 'Thought I should get down to the books for a while, before my A-Levels.'

Jon stared at him.

'I'm off to college next September, touch wood.' Davy rapped on the coffee table. 'I've already got an offer of a place in Law at Lancaster, but I'll need two Bs and an A.'

Law? Jon nodded, then winced as his neck twinged. So much he'd never known about Davy, never thought to ask. 'You could sign up again in the summer, though, after your exams, couldn't you?' he asked, as neutrally as he could.

There was a long second's pause before Davy shook his head. 'I don't think so, Jon-boy.'

So that was it, Jon registered. Not a proper ending. More

like a match called off because of a hailstorm or because the star player just walked off the pitch.

'I mean, I'll miss it, but when it comes down to it, it's only a game, eh? . . . Win or lose,' Davy added after a moment.

Jon couldn't speak. His eyes were wet, blinded.

Davy picked up his bag. Then he did something strange. He swung down and kissed Jon on the lips, for the first time, on his way out the door.

speaking in tongues

'Listen,' I said, my voice rasping, 'I want to take you home but Dublin's a hundred miles away.'

Lee looked down at her square hands. I couldn't believe she'd only spent seventeen years on this planet.

'Where're you staying?' I asked.

'Youth hostel.'

I mouthed a curse at the beer-stained carpet. 'I've no room booked in Galway and it's probably too late to get one. I was planning to drive back tonight. I have to be at the office by nine tomorrow.'

The last of the conference goers walked past just then, and one or two nodded at me; the sweat of the *céilí* was drying on their cheeks.

When I looked back, Lee was grinning like she'd just won the lottery. 'So is it comfortable in the back of your van then, Sylvia?'

I stared at her. It was not the first time I had been asked that question, but I had thought that the last time would be the last. She was exactly half my age, I reminded myself. She wasn't even an adult, legally. 'As backs of vans go, yes, very comfortable.'

*

The reason I got into that van was a poem.

I'd first heard Sylvia Dwyer on a CD of contemporary poetry in Irish. I'd borrowed it from the library to help me revise for the Leaving Cert that would get me out of convent school. Deirdre had just left me for a boy, so I was working hard.

Poem number five was called 'Dh a Theanga'. The woman's voice had peat and smoke in it, bacon and strong tea. I hadn't a notion what the poem was about; you needed to know how the words were spelt before you could look them up in the dictionary, and one silent consonant sounded pretty much like another to me. But I listened to the poem every night till I had to give the CD back to the library.

I asked my mother why the name sounded so familiar, and she said Sylvia must be the last of those Dwyers who'd taken over the Shanbally butchers thirty years before. I couldn't believe she was a local. I might even have sat next to her in Mass.

But it was Cork where I met her. I'd joined the Queer Soc in the first week, before I could lose my nerve, and by midterm I was running their chocolate-and-wine evenings. Sylvia Dwyer, down from Dublin for a weekend, was introduced all round by an ex of hers who taught in the French department. I was startled to learn that the poet was one of us – a 'colleen', as a friend of mine used to say. Her smooth bob and silver-grey suit were intimidating as hell. I couldn't think of a word to say. I poured her plonk from a box and put the bowl of chocolate-covered peanuts by her elbow.

After that I smiled at her in Mass once when I was home in Shanbally for the weekend. Sylvia nodded back, very minimally. Maybe she wasn't sure where she knew me from. Maybe she was praying. Maybe she was a bitch.

Of course I had heard of Lee Maloney in Shanbally. The whole town had heard of her, the year the girl appeared at Mass with a Sinéad O'Connor head shave. I listened in on a euphemistic conversation about her in the post office queue but contributed nothing to it. My reputation was a clean slate in Shanbally, and none of my poems had gendered pronouns.

When I was introduced to the girl in Cork she was barely civil. But her chin had a curve you needed to fit your hand to, and her hair looked seven days old.

On one of my rare weekends at home, who should I see on the way down from Communion but Lee Maloney, full of nods and smiles. Without turning my head I could sense my mother stiffen. In the car park afterwards she asked, 'How do you come to know that Maloney girl?'

I considered denying it, claiming it was a case of mistaken identity, then I said, 'I think she might have been at a reading I gave once.'

'She's a worry to her mother,' said mine.

It must have been after I saw Sylvia Dwyer's name on a flyer under the title DHÁ THEANGA/TWO TONGUES: A CONFERENCE ON BILIN-GUALISM IN IRELAND TODAY *that my subconscious developed a passionate nostalgia for the language my forebears got whipped for. So I skived off my Saturday lecture to get the bus to Galway. But only when I saw her walk into that lecture theatre in her long brown leather coat, with a new streak of white across her black fringe, did I realize why I'd sat four hours on a bus to get there.*

Some days I have more nerve than others. I flirted with Sylvia all that day, in the quarter hours between papers and forums and plenary sessions that meant equally little to me whether they were in Irish or English. I asked her questions and nodded before the answers had started. I told her about Deirdre, just so she wouldn't think I was a virgin. 'She left me for a boy with no earlobes,' I said carelessly.

'Been there,' said Sylvia.

Mostly, though, I kept my mouth shut and my head down and my

eyes shiny. I suspected I was being embarrassingly obvious, but a one-
day conference didn't leave enough time for subtlety.

Sylvia made me guess how old she was, and I said, 'Thirty?'
though I knew from the programme note that she was thirty-four. She
said if by any miracle she had saved enough money by the age of forty,
she was going to get plastic surgery on the bags under her eyes.

I played the cheeky young thing and the baby dyke and the strong
silent type who had drunk too much wine. And till halfway through the
evening I didn't think I was getting anywhere. What would a woman
like Sylvia Dwyer want with a blank page like me?

For a second in that Galway lecture hall I didn't recognize Lee
Maloney, because she was so out of context among the bearded
journalists and wool-skirted teachers. Then my memory
claimed her face. The girl was looking at me like the sun had
just risen, and then she stared at her feet, which was even more
of a giveaway. I stood up straighter and shifted my briefcase to
my other hand.

The conference, which I had expected to be about broad-
ening my education and licking up to small Irish publishers,
began to take on a momentum of its own. It was nothing I had
planned, nothing I could stop. I watched the side of Lee's jaw
right through a lecture called 'Scottish Loan-Words in Donegal
Fishing Communities'. She was so cute I felt sick.

What was most unsettling was that I couldn't tell who was
chatting up whom. It was a battle made up of feints and
retreats. As we sipped our coffee, for instance, I murmured
something faintly suggestive about hot liquids, then panicked
and changed the subject. As we crowded back into the hall, I
thought it was Lee's hand that guided my elbow for a few seconds, but she was staring forward so blankly I decided it must
have been somebody else.

Over dinner – a noisy affair in the cafeteria – Lee sat across the table from me and burnt her tongue on the apple crumble. I poured her a glass of water and didn't give her a chance to talk to anyone but me. At this point we were an island of English in a sea of Irish.

The conversation happened to turn (as it does) to relationships and how neither of us could see the point in casual sex, because not only was it unlikely to be much good but it fucked up friendships or broke hearts. Sleeping with someone you hardly knew, I heard myself pronouncing in my world-weariest voice, was like singing a song without knowing the words. I told her that when she was my age she would feel the same way, and she said, Oh, she did already.

My eyes dwelt on the apple crumble disappearing, spoon by spoon, between Lee's absentminded lips. I listened to the opinions spilling out of my mouth and wondered who I was kidding.

By the time it came to the poetry reading that was meant to bring the conference to a lyrical climax, I was too tired to waste time. I reached into my folder for the only way I know to say what I really mean.

Now, the word in Cork had been that Sylvia Dwyer was deep in the closet, which I'd thought was a bit pathetic but only to be expected. However.

At the end of her reading, after she'd done a few about nature and a few about politics and a few I couldn't follow, she rummaged round in her folder. 'This poem gave its name to this conference,' she said, 'but that's not why I've chosen it.' She read it through in Irish first; I let the familiar vowels caress my ears. Her voice was even better live than on the CD from the library. And then she turned slightly in her seat, and, after muttering, 'Hope it translates,' she read it straight at me.

your tongue and my tongue
have much to say to each other
there's a lot between them
there are pleasures yours has over mine
and mine over yours
we get on each other's nerves sometimes
and under each other's skin
but the best of it is when
your mouth opens to let my tongue in
it's then I come to know you
when I hear my tongue
blossom in your kiss
and your strange hard tongue
speaks between my lips

The reason I was going to go ahead and do what I'd bored all my friends with saying I'd never do again was that poem.

I was watching the girl as I read 'Dhá Theanga' straight to her, aiming over the weary heads of the crowd of conference goers. I didn't look at anyone else but Lee Maloney, not at a single one of the jealous poets or Gaelgóir purists or smirking gossips, in case I might lose my nerve. After the first line, when her eyes fell for a second, Lee looked right back at me. She was leaning her cheek on her hand. It was a smooth hand, blunt at the tips. I knew the poem off by heart, but tonight I had to look down for safety every few lines.

And then she glanced away, out the darkening window, and I suddenly doubted that I was getting anywhere. What would Lee Maloney, seventeen last May, want with a scribbled jotter like me?

*

I sat in that smoky hall with my face half hidden behind my hand, excitement and embarrassment spiralling up my spine. I reminded myself that Sylvia Dwyer must have written that poem years ago, for some other woman in some other town. Not counting how many other women she might have read it to. It was probably an old trick of hers.

But all this couldn't explain away the fact that it was me Sylvia was reading it to tonight in Galway. In front of all these people, not caring who saw or what they might think when they followed the line of her eyes. I dug my jaw into my palm for anchorage, and my eyes locked back onto Sylvia's. I decided that every poem was made new in the reading.

If this was going to happen, I thought, as I folded the papers away in my briefcase during the brief rainfall of applause, it was happening because we were not in Dublin surrounded by my friends and work life, nor in Cork cluttered up with Lee's, nor above all in Shanbally where she was born in the year I left for college. Neither of us knew anything at all about Galway.

If this was going to happen, I thought, many hours later as the cleaners urged Sylvia and me out of the hall, it was happening because of some moment that had pushed us over an invisible line. But which moment? It could have been when we were shivering on the floor waiting for the end-of-conference céilí band to start up, and Sylvia draped her leather coat round her shoulders and tucked me under it for a minute, the sheepskin lining soft against my cheek, the weight of her elbow on my shoulder. Or later when I was dancing like a berserker in my vest, and she drew the back of her hand down my arm and said, 'Aren't you the damp thing.' Or maybe the deciding moment was when the fan had stopped working and we stood at the bar waiting for drinks, my smoking hips armouring hers, and I blew behind her hot ear until the curtain of hair lifted up and I could see the dark of her neck.

*

Blame it on the heat. We swung so long in the *céilí* that the whole line went askew. Lee took off all her layers except one black vest that clung to her small breasts. We shared a glass of iced water and I offered Lee the last splash from my mouth, but she danced around me and laughed and wouldn't take it. Up on the balcony over the dance floor, I sat on the edge and leaned out to see the whirling scene. Lee fitted her hand around my thigh, weighing it down. 'You protecting me from falling?' I asked. My voice was meant to be sardonic, but it came out more like breathless.

'That's right,' she said.

Held in that position, my leg very soon began to tremble, but I willed it to stay still, hoping Lee would not feel the spasm, praying she would not move her hand away.

Blame it on the dancing. They must have got a late licence for the bar, or maybe Galway people always danced half the night. The music made our bones move in tandem and our legs shake. I tried to take the last bit of water from Sylvia's mouth, but I was so giddy I couldn't aim right and kept lurching against her collarbone and laughing at my own helplessness.

'Thought you were meant to be in the closet,' I shouted in her ear at one point, and Sylvia smiled with her eyes shut and said something I couldn't hear, and I said, 'What?' and she said, 'Not tonight.'

So at the end of the evening we had no place to go and it didn't matter. We had written our phone numbers on sodden beermats and exchanged them. We agreed that we'd go for a drive. When we got into her white van on the curb littered with weak-kneed céilí dancers, something came on the radio, an old song by Clannad or one of that crowd. Sylvia started up the engine and began to sing along with the chorus, her hoarse whisper catching every second or third word. She leaned over to fasten her seat belt and crooned a phrase into my ear. I didn't understand it — something about 'bóthar,' *or was it* 'máthar'? *— but it made my face go hot anyway.*

'Where are we heading?' *I said at last, as the hedges began to narrow to either side of the white van.*

Sylvia frowned into the darkness. 'Cashelagen, was that the name of it? Quiet spot, I seem to remember, beside a castle.'

After another ten minutes, during which we didn't meet a single other car, I realized that we were lost, completely tangled in the little roads leading into Connemara. And half of me didn't care. Half of me was quite content to bump along these lanes to the strains of late-night easy listening, watching Sylvia Dwyer's sculpted profile out the corner of my right eye. But the other half of me wanted to stretch my boot across and stamp on the brake, then climb over the gear stick to get at her.

Lee didn't comment on how quickly I was getting us lost. Cradle snatcher, I commented to myself, and not even a suave one at that. As we hovered at an unmarked fork, a man walked into the glare of the headlights. I stared at him to make sure he was real, then rolled down the window with a flurry of elbows. 'Cashelagen?' I asked. Lee had turned off the radio, so my voice sounded indecently loud. 'Could you tell us are we anywhere near Cashelagen?'

The man fingered his sideburns and stepped closer, beaming in past me at Lee. What in god's name was this fellow doing wandering round in the middle of the night anyway? He didn't even have our excuse. I was just starting to roll the window up again when 'Ah,' he said, 'ah, if it's Cashelagen you're wanting you'd have to go a fair few miles back through Ballyalla and then take the coast road.'

'Thanks,' I told him shortly, and revved up the engine. Lee would think I was the most hopeless incompetent she had ever got into a van for immoral purposes with. As soon as he had walked out of range of the headlights, I let off the hand brake and shot forward. I glanced over at Lee's bent head. The frightening thought occurred to me: *I could love this girl.*

The lines above Sylvia's eyebrow were beginning to swoop like gulls. If she was going to get cross, we might as well turn the radio back on and drive all night. I rehearsed the words in my head, then said them. 'Sure who needs a castle in the dark?'

Her grin was quick as a fish.

'Everywhere's quiet at this time of night,' I said rather squeakily. 'Here's quiet. We could stop here.'

'What, right here?'

Sylvia peered back at the road and suddenly wheeled round into the entrance to a field. We stopped with the bumper a foot away from a five-barred gate. When the headlights went off, the field stretched out dark in front of us, and there was a sprinkle of light that had to be Galway.

'What time did you say you had to be in Dublin?' I asked suddenly.

'Nine. Better start back round five in case I hit traffic,' said Sylvia. She bent over to rummage in the glove compartment. She pulled out a strapless watch, looked at it, brought it closer to her eyes, then let out a puff of laughter.

'What time's it now?'

'You don't want to know,' she told me.

I grabbed it. The hands said half past three. 'It can't be.'

We sat staring into the field. 'Nice stars,' I said, for something to say.

'Mmm,' she said.

I stared at the stars, joining the dots, till my eyes watered.

And then I heard Sylvia laughing in her throat as she turned side-

ways and leaned over my seat belt. I heard it hissing back into its socket as she kissed me on the mouth.

When I came back from taking a pee in the bushes, the driver's seat was empty. I panicked, and stared up and down the lane. Why would she have run off on foot? Then, with a deafening creak, the back doors of the van swung open.

Sylvia's bare shoulders showed over the blanket that covered her body. She hugged her knees. Her eyes were bright, and the small bags underneath were the most beautiful folds of skin I'd ever seen. I climbed in and kneeled on the sheepskin coat beside her, reaching up to snap off the little light. Her face opened wide in a yawn. The frightening thought occurred to me: I could love this woman.

'You could always get some sleep, you know,' I said, 'I wouldn't mind.' Then I thought that sounded churlish, but I didn't know how to unsay it.

'Oh, I know I could,' said Sylvia, her voice melodic with amusement. 'There's lots of things we could do with a whole hour and a half. We could sleep, we could share the joint in the glove compartment, we could drive to Clifden and watch the sun come up. Lots of things.'

I smiled. Then I realized she couldn't see my face in the dark.

'Get your clothes off,' she said.

I would have liked to leave the map-reading light on over our heads, letting me see and memorize every line of Lee's body, but it would have lit us up like a saintly apparition for any passing farmer to see. So the whole thing happened in a darkness much darker than it ever gets in a city.

There was a script, of course. No matter how spontaneous it may feel, there's always an unwritten script. Every one of these encounters has a script, even the very first time your hand undoes the button on somebody's shirt; none of us comes without expectations to this body business.

But lord, what fun it was. Lee was salt with sweat and fleshier than I'd imagined, behind all her layers of black cotton and wool. In thirty-four years I've found nothing to compare to that moment when the bare limbs slide together like a key into a lock. Or no, more like one of those electronic key cards they give you in big hotels, the open sesame ones marked with an invisible code, which the door must read and recognize before it agrees to open.

At one point Lee rolled under me and muttered, 'There's somewhere I want to go,' then went deep inside me. It hurt a little, just a little, and I must have flinched because she asked, 'Does that hurt?' and I said, 'No,' because I was glad of it. 'No,' I said again, because I didn't want her to go.

Sylvia's voice was rough like rocks grinding on each other. As she moved on top of me she whispered in my ear, things I couldn't make out, sounds just outside the range of hearing. I never wanted to interrupt the flow by saying, 'Sorry?' or 'What did you say?' Much as I wanted to hear and remember every word, every detail, at a certain point I just had to switch my mind off and get on with living it. But Sylvia's voice kept going in my ear, turning me on in the strangest way by whispering phrases that only she could hear.

I've always thought the biggest lie in the books is that women instinctively know what to do to each other because their bodies are the same. None of Sylvia's shapes were the same as mine, nor could I have guessed what she was like from how she seemed in her smart clothes. And we liked different things and took things in different order, showing each other by infinitesimal movings away and movings towards. She did some things to me that I knew I wanted, some I didn't think I'd much like and didn't, and several I was startled to find that I enjoyed much more than I would have imagined. I did some things Sylvia seemed calm about, and then something she must have really needed, because she started to let out her breath in a long gasp when I'd barely begun.

Near the end, Sylvia's long fingers moved down her body to ride alongside mine, not supplanting, just guiding. 'Go light,' she whispered in my ear. 'Lighter and lighter. Butterfly.' As she began to thrash at last, laughter spilled from her mouth.

'What? What are you laughing for?' I asked, afraid I'd done something wrong. Sylvia just whooped louder. Words leaked out of her throat, distorted by pleasure.

At one point I touched my lips to the skin under her eyes, first one and then the other. 'Your bags are gorgeous, you know. Promise you'll never let a surgeon at them?'

'No,' she said, starting to laugh again.

'No to which?'

'No promise.'

When Sylvia was touching me I didn't say a single one of the words that swam through my head. I don't know was I shy or just stubborn, wanting to make her guess what to do. The tantalization of waiting for those hands to decipher my body made the bliss build and build till when it came it threw me.

There was one moment I wouldn't swap anything for. It was in the lull beforehand, the few seconds when I stopped breathing. I looked at this stranger's face bent over me, twisted in exertion and tenderness, and I thought, Yes, you, whoever you are, if you're asking for it, I'll give it all up to you.

In the in-between times we panted and rested and stifled our laughter in the curve of each other's shoulders and debated when I'd noticed Lee and when she'd noticed me, and what we'd noticed and what we'd imagined on each occasion, the history of this particular desire. And during one of these in-between times we realized that the sun had come up, faint behind a yellow mist, and it was half five according to the strapless watch in the glove compartment.

I took hold of Lee, my arms binding her ribs and my head resting in the flat place between her breasts. The newly budded swollen look of them made my mouth water, but there was no time. I shut my mouth and my eyes and held Lee hard and there was no time left at all, so I let go and sat up. I could feel our nerves pulling apart like ivy off a wall.

The cows were beginning to moan in the field as we pulled our clothes on. My linen trousers were cold and smoky. We did none of the things parting lovers do if they have the time or the right. I didn't snatch at Lee's foot as she pulled her jeans on; she didn't sneak her head under my shirt as I pulled it over my face. The whole thing had to be over already.

It was not the easiest thing in the world to find my way back to Galway with Lee's hand tucked between my thighs. Through my trousers I could feel the cold of her fingers, and the hardness of her thumb, rubbing the linen. I caught her eye as we sped round a corner, and she grinned, suddenly very young. 'You're just using me to warm your hand up,' I accused.

'That's all it is,' said Lee.

I was still throbbing, so loud I thought the car was ringing with it. We were only two streets from the hostel now.

I wouldn't ask to see her again. I would just leave the matter open and drive away. Lee probably got offers all the time; she was far too young to be looking for anything heavy. I'd show her I was generous enough to accept that an hour and a half was all she had to give me.

I let her out just beside the hostel, which was already opening to release some backpacking Germans. I was going to get out of the car to give her a proper body-to-body hug, but while I was struggling with my seat belt, Lee knocked on the glass. I rolled down the window, put *Desert Hearts* out of my mind, and kissed her for what I had a hunch was likely to be the last time.

I stood shivering in the street outside the hostel and knocked on Sylvia's car window. I was high as a kite and dizzy with fatigue.

I wouldn't ask anything naff like when we were likely to see each other again. I would just wave as she drove away. Sylvia probably did this kind of thing all the time; she was far too famous to be wanting anything heavy. I'd show her that I was sophisticated enough not to fall for her all in one go, not to ask for anything but the hour and a half she had to give me.

When she rolled down the window, I smiled and leaned in. I shut my eyes and felt Sylvia's tongue against mine, saying something neither of us could hear. So brief, so slippery, nothing you could get a hold of.

the welcome

Women's Housing Coop Seeks Member. Low Rent, Central Manchester. Applicants Must Have Ability to Get On With People and Show Comittment To Cooperative Living. All Ethnic Backgrounds Particularly Welcome To Apply.

I tore stripes off Carola when I noticed that ad, taped up in the window of the newsagent's next door to our house. She said I could hardly complain if I'd missed the meeting where the wording of the ad was agreed on, but I should feel free to share my feelings with the policy group anyway. 'They're not feelings,' I said, 'they're facts.'

Dear Policy Group, I typed furiously.

Re: Recruitment Ad. I suggest we use a hyphen in Co-op, if we don't want the Welcome Co-operative to be confused with a chicken coop. Some other problems with this ad: 'Seeks Member' sounds like we don't have any members yet. Do you mean 'Seeks New Member'? – and, besides, it sounds rather like a giant dildo. Also, I'm just curious, why should the applicants HAVE 'Ability To Get On With People' (and is People a euphemism for Women, by the way, given that this is a women-only co-op?), but only SHOW

*'Commitment To Co-operative Living' (*commitment *being spelled with two m's and one t, not vice versa, by the way, in case anyone cares)? Or are you suggesting that an applicant might claim to HAVE such a commitment but needs to be forced to SHOW it, e.g. through housework? And if so, why not say so?*

The way I see it, there's not a lot of point having policies on Equal Opportunities and Accessibility and Class and Race Issues if we're going to keep on writing our ads in politically correct gobbledygook that would put off anyone who's not doing a PhD. And speaking of Race Issues, what on earth does it mean to say that ALL ethnic backgrounds (members of all ethnic groups, I think you mean) are 'Particularly Welcome To Apply'? Who's not-so-particularly-welcome, then? Or do you mean white people don't count as an ethnic group? I can't believe one five-line ad can give such an impression of confusion, illiteracy, and pomposity all at once. Why can't we just say what we mean?

My hands were shaking, so I left it at that and printed out the page. *Yours, Luce,* I'd added at the bottom, as if it weren't obvious who'd written the letter from vocabulary alone. As Di was always telling me, 'It's like you've got the *Oxford English Dictionary* hidden up your arse.' She had a point; some days I sounded more like eighty than eighteen. I suppose I'd read too many books to be normal.

It was only when I was sealing the letter into the envelope that I remembered: in my absence, at the last co-op meeting, they'd decided to rotate me from the maintenance crew to the policy group, because, as I'd been pointing out for ages, my syntax was a lot better than my plumbing. I was meant to replace Nuala, who was moving back to Cork, and if Rachel made up her mind to go off for three months to that organic farm in Cornwall, it occurred to me now, there'd be no one left in the policy group but myself and Di, and I'd end up handing her my letter like some mad silent protestor. Or if Di happened to be away that evening, on one of those Buddhist retreats her boyfriend ran, it would be just me having a one-person meeting, and I'd have to read my own letter aloud and make snide comments about it.

Arghhhh. The joys of communal living. After two years in the Welcome Co-op, I could hardly remember living any other way.

I ripped the envelope open and went downstairs. In the kitchen I pinned my letter up on the corkboard over the oven – the only place you could be sure everyone would see it. I went back down for a prawn cracker five minutes later and found Di reading it as she stirred her miso. 'The ad was appalling,' I said defensively.

'Yeah. Carola wrote it after the rest of us had gone down the pub. You know you use the word "mean" four times in the last paragraph?' she asked, grinning.

I ripped the thing down and stuffed it into the recycling bin.

'Temper, temper,' she said, tucking away a pale curl that had come out of her bun.

I licked my prawn cracker. 'What's wrong with me these days, Di?'

'You know what's wrong with you.'

'Apart from that.' I shifted uncomfortably against the wooden counter.

'There is no apart from that, Luce. You've been a virgin too long.'

My head was hammering; I rubbed the stiff muscles at the back of my neck. 'Why does every conversation in this house have to come back to the same-old same-old?'

'Well Jesus, child, take a look at yourself.'

I glanced down as if I'd got food on my shirt.

'You came out at fifteen, but you haven't done a thing about it yet. For years now you've seen every kind of woman pass through these doors, and you haven't let one of them lay a hand on you. No wonder you've got a headache!'

I was out the door and halfway up the garden by then. Di was fabulous, but I could do without another of her rants about regular orgasms being crucial to health. Nurses were all like that.

The June sun was slipping behind the crab apple tree. My courgettes were beginning to flower, a wonderful pale orange. I picked a couple of insects off them. When I'd moved into the Welcome, the week after my sixteenth birthday – the date chosen to ensure my mother would have had no legal way of dragging me back home, if she'd tried, not that she did – anyway, at first I found the constant company unbearable. I'd been used to spending all my after-school time locked in my bedroom with a book, living in the world of the Brontës or Jung or Isabel Allende; just about any world would do so long as it wasn't the one my mother lived in. And now all at once I was supposed to become part of some bizarre nine-woman feminist family. The housing co-op was what I'd chosen but it freaked me out all the same. In the early weeks, digging the garden was the only thing that kept me halfway sane. The vegetable plot had been strictly organic ever since I'd taken it over, but sometimes I got the impression that most of my sweat went into providing a feast for the crawlies.

Di was sort of right. I was a pedant, a twitching spinster, dried up before my time, and I'd only just finished secondary school! Sixty-seven fortnightly co-op meetings (I'd counted them up, recently) had frayed me to a thread: all those good intentions, all that mind-numbingly imprecise jargon. These days even typos in the *Guardian* made me itch. When I was old, I knew I wouldn't wear purple, like in the poem; instead I'd limp around under cover of darkness, correcting the punctuation on billboards with a spray can. Rachel said I should become a proofreader and make a mint, instead of starting political studies at the university this October and probably ending up politically somewhere to the right of Baroness Thatcher. On my eighteenth birthday, when Di gave me a T-shirt that read DOES ANAL RETENTIVE HAVE A HYPHEN?, I was too busy considering the question to get the joke.

It wasn't that I didn't like the idea of sex, by the way. I was just picky. And somehow, the more free-floating fornication that went on in the Welcome – the louder the shrieks from Carola's attic room, the more often I walked into the living room and found anonymous bodies pillowing the sofa – the less I felt like attempting it. Besides, there was never enough privacy. At my birthday party I got as far as kissing a German acupuncturist, and by breakfast the next morning my housemates had given me: (*a*) a pack of latex gloves (Di), (*b*) much conflicting advice about sexual positions (Rachel, Maura, Iona, and the two Londoners whose names I was always getting wrong way around), and (*c*) a paperback called *Safe Space: Coping with Issues around Intimacy* (Carola, of course). The acupuncturist left me a message, but I never rang back. Collectively my housemates had managed to put me right off.

So Nuala went back to Cork, and that's how it all began. The Welcome's rent was so low, it was never hard to fill a place. We interviewed seven women, one endless hot Saturday at the end of June. I was the one who volunteered to tell JJ she was the lucky winner.

'I wasn't sure was it all right to ring at nearly midnight—,' I told her, down the phone.

'Yeah, no problem. That's . . . excellent.' Her voice was as deep as Tracy Chapman's, and hoarse with excitement.

'Well, we're all really glad,' I added, somehow not wanting the call to be over so soon.

I could hear JJ let out a long breath of relief. 'I never thought I'd hear from you people again, actually. I made such a cock-up of the interview.'

'Not at all!' I said, laughing too loudly.

'But I hardly said a word.'

'Well, we figured you were just shy, you know. All the others were brash young things who got on our nerves.'

Di, passing through with a tray of margaritas for her hospital friends who were partying on the balcony, raised one eyebrow.

It was kind of a lie; we hadn't been at all unanimous. Carola had voted for a ghastly woman from Leeds who claimed to be very vulnerable after a series of relationships with emotionally abusive men and wanted to know did we do co-counselling after house meetings? But in the end I played the race card, like the hypocrite I was; I told Carola that if we were serious about Particularly Welcoming and all that – if we wanted to improve the co-op's representation of women of colour from none in nine to one in nine – then we had to pick JJ.

Not that her being black had anything to do with it, for me. I wanted JJ because her fingers were long and broad and made me feel slightly shaky.

The day she was to move in, I came downstairs to find the living room transformed. There was a Mexican blanket slung over the back of the pink couch, an African head scarf wrapped around the lampshade, and my framed print of Gertrude Stein appeared to have metamorphosed into a dog-eared poster of a woman carrying a stack of bricks on her head that said OXFAM IN INDIA: EMPOWERMENT THROUGH EDUCATION.

Rachel, Di, and Iona claimed to know nothing about the

changes. Carola said she was only acting on the advice of a book called *Anti-Racism for Housing Co-ops.* She was trying to make the atmosphere more inclusive, less Anglo-Saxon.

'Gertrude Stein was an American Jew!' I protested.

'She lived on inherited wealth,' said Carola, spooning up her porridge.

'So?'

'So I just don't think we should cover our walls with images of women of privilege; it sends out the wrong signals.'

'Gertrude Stein only covered about three square feet of the wall!'

Carola rolled her pale blue eyes. 'You're being petty, Luce. I wonder why you've got so much invested in the status quo?'

'Because the status quo was a pretty stylish living room. And you know what signals this room is sending out now, Carola? Embarrassingly obvious, geographically muddled, white guilt signals!'

She pointed out that we all had feelings around these issues.

'Feelings about,' I corrected her, 'not around, *about,*' and it all went downhill from there, especially when I pulled down the Oxfam poster and a corner tore off. Di had to intervene, and it took hours of 'feelings around' before we reached a grudging compromise: yes to the Mexican blanket, no to the lampshade wrap, and OK to a laminated poster of dolphins that none of us liked.

I'd been planning to do some weeding that afternoon because my eyes were sore from reading Dostoevsky in a Victorian edition with tiny print, but I was afraid I wouldn't hear the front door. I pottered around in my room instead, and when I heard the bell I ran downstairs to help JJ carry up her stuff. But she didn't have much in the way of stuff, it turned out: two backpacks, a duvet, and a rat.

I backed away from the cage.

'Ah, yeah, his name's Victor,' she said nervously, clearing her throat. 'I forgot to mention him at the interview.'

'Oh, I'm sure everyone'll love him,' I told her, grabbing the cage by its handle and frantically thinking, *Hamster, it's more or less a hamster.* I managed to carry the cage all the way upstairs without looking inside.

I was going to offer to help JJ unpack, but somehow I lost my nerve. There was something private about the way she dropped her bags in the corner beside Victor's cage and stood looking out the window. 'This room gets the sun in the late afternoons,' I told her; 'I lived here, my first year in the co-op,' but she just nodded and smiled a little, without looking back at me.

That night we had a communal dinner in JJ's honour, even though when the nine of us sat down together there was barely elbow room to use a fork. I talked too much, ate too much of Melissa's sushi and Kay's gooseberry fool, and felt rather ill. JJ seemed to listen attentively to the conversation – which covered global warming, how to eat a lychee, the government's treachery, what we wanted done with our bodies when we died, and (the inevitable topic) female ejaculation – but she said even less than she had at her interview, though I wouldn't have thought that was possible. I wondered whether we sounded peculiar to her, or ranty, or Anglo-Saxon.

Iona carried in the tray of coffee, chai, peppermint tea, and soy shake. 'So tell us, JJ,' said Carola with a sympathetic smile, 'is it going to make you feel at all uncomfortable, d'you think, being the only woman of colour in the co-op?'

Di rolled her eyes at me, but it was too awful to be funny. I stared out the window at my tomato plants, mortified.

But JJ just shrugged and sipped her coffee.

Carola wouldn't let it rest, of course. 'How old would you say you were, like, when you first became aware of systemic racism?'

'Carola!' Di and I groaned in unison.

This time JJ let out a little grunt that could have been the beginning of a laugh. Then she muttered something that sounded like 'Bodies are an accident'.

If I hadn't been sitting right beside her, I mightn't have caught that at all. Startled, I looked down at myself. A short, skinny, pale, post-adolescent Anglo-Saxon body; a random conglomeration of genes.

Afterwards JJ volunteered to wash up, so I said she and I would do it and everybody else was to get out of the kitchen. Some went to bed, and some went out to smoke dope by the bonfire, and I got to stand beside JJ, watching how gently she handled the plates. I took them dripping from her big hands, one by one, and wiped them dry.

Her hundreds of skinny plaits gleamed; I wondered how she kept them like that. Under her army surplus shirt her shoulders were wider than anyone's I knew. She had all she needed to be a total butch and didn't seem to realize it.

'So how did you pick the name?' she asked at last, jerking me out of my daze.

'What, Luce? Well, I was christened Lucy, but I've always—'

'No,' she interrupted softly, 'the co-op's name, the Welcome.'

'Oh,' I said, with an embarrassed laugh.

'Is it, like, meant to sound like everyone's welcome?'

'No, actually, it's named after some defunct co-op down in London, on Welcome Street,' I told her. 'When they folded they passed the leftover money to a group in Manchester that was just starting up. Before my time.'

'So are you really only eighteen?'

I almost blushed as I nodded.

JJ had to be in her twenties, but she didn't specify. In fact she hadn't volunteered any information about herself yet, it occurred to me now.

The whole time I'd lived in the Welcome – with all the guff that got talked about acceptance and non-judgmentalism – I'd never met anyone half as accepting as JJ. Her tolerance even crossed the species barrier; it didn't seem to have occurred to her, for instance, that a rat wasn't a suitable pet. (And Victor did turn out to be a total charmer.) Like a visitor from Mars, JJ displayed no fixed opinions about race, class, or any other label. Though she'd chosen to live in a women-only housing co-op, I never heard her make a single generalization about men (unlike, say, Iona, whose favourite joke that summer was 'What's the best way to make a man come?' – 'Who the fuck cares!').

When various of our housemates talked as if all the world was queer, JJ didn't join in, but she didn't make any objection, either. She listened with her head bent, wearing what Di called her 'wary Bambi' look. At JJ's interview, I remembered, it was Rachel who'd come out with the usual uncomfortable spiel about 'This co-op has members of a variety of sexualities,' and instead of giving either of the two usual responses – 'Oh, but I have a boyfriend' or 'Fab!' – JJ had just nodded, eyes elsewhere, as if she were being told how the washing machine worked.

Shy people annoyed Di; she thought it was too much hard work, digging conversation out of them, and the results were rarely worth it.

'But is she or isn't she, though?' I begged Di.

'How should I know, Luce?'

'Didn't they teach you how to assess people at nursing school?'

Di laughed and flicked her hair back from her soup bowl. She blew on her spoon before she answered me. 'Only their health. All I can tell you is the woman seems in good shape, apart from a bit of acne and a few stone she could afford to lose.'

I felt mildly offended by that – JJ being the perfect shape, in my book – but I stuck to the point. 'Yeah, but is she a dyke?'

Di twinkled at me. 'What do you care, Miss Celibate?'

Not that I thought I had much of a chance, whatever kind of sexuality the woman had, but I needed to know anyway. Just to have some information on JJ. Just to find out whether it was worth letting her into my dreams.

One evening when I came in after the news, JJ told me, 'The government are cutting housing benefit,' and before I could stop myself, I said, 'The government *is*.'

Her thick black eyebrows contracted.

'Sorry. It's just—'

'Yeah?'

'It's a collective noun,' I muttered, mortified. 'It takes the singular. But it doesn't matter.' I suddenly heard myself: what an unbearably tedious teenager!

But JJ's bright teeth widened into a grin. 'You like to classify things, don't you, Luce?' she said. 'Everything in its little box.'

'I suppose so.' I thought about how good my name sounded in her husky voice.

'Do you classify people, too?'

'Sometimes,' I said, trying to sound cheeky, now, rather than obnoxious. 'Like, you, for instance, I'd say . . .' I was bluffing; I tried to think of something she'd like to hear. 'I'd say you're someone who's at peace with yourself, I suppose,' I told her. 'Because you only speak when you've something to say. Unlike someone like me, who rabbits on and on and on all the time.' I shut my mouth, then, and covered it with my hand.

The light was behind JJ; I couldn't read her eyes. 'That's how you'd describe me, is it, Luce? At peace with myself?'

'Yeah,' I said doubtfully.

She put her throat back and roared. Her deep laughter filled the room.

'What's the joke?' asked Rachel, sticking her head in the door, but I just shrugged.

Well, at least JJ found me funny, I told myself. It was better than nothing.

I still hadn't gathered a single clue about her sexual orientation. Some mornings, I woke with the clenched face that told me I'd been grinding my teeth again. To me, the fact that I was a dyke had been clear as glass by my thirteenth birthday, but then, precision was my thing. Maybe JJ was one, too, and didn't know it yet, would never know it till my kiss woke her. Or maybe she was one of those 'labels are for clothes' people, who couldn't bear to be categorized. She dressed like a truck driver, but so did half the straight girls nowadays. With anyone else I would have pumped her friends for information, but JJ didn't seem to have any friends in Manchester. She worked long shifts at the Pizza Palace, and she never brought anyone home.

We got on best, I found, when we just talked about day-to-day matters like the colour of the sky. No big questions, no heavy issues. The sweetest times that summer were when she came out to help me with the vegetables. After a long July day we'd each take a hose and water one side of the garden, not speaking till we met at the end by the crab apple tree. Sometimes she brought Victor's cage down from her room for an airing. If Iona – who called him *that rodent* – wasn't in the garden, JJ would let him out for a run; once I even fed him a crumb from my hand.

We got talking once about why I wanted to do politics at

college in the autumn. 'I just think it'll be interesting to find out how things work,' I said.

'What things?'

'Big things,' I said, trying to sound dry and witty. 'Countries, information systems, the global economy, that sort of thing. What goes on, and why.'

JJ shook her head as if marvelling and bent down to rip up some bindweed. I waited to hear what she thought; you couldn't rush her. 'I dunno,' she said at last, 'I find it hard enough to understand what's going on inside me.'

I waited, as I trained the hose on the tomato patch, but she didn't say another word.

Some days that summer I had this peculiar sense of waiting, from when I first rolled out of my single bed till long after midnight when I switched off my light; my stomach was tight with it. But nothing momentous ever happened. JJ never told me what I was waiting to hear – whatever that was.

She lavished care on Victor the rat, stroking his coat and scratching behind his ears with a methodical tenderness that softened me like candle wax. But she never touched another human being, that I could see. She wouldn't take or give massages; instead of goodbye hugs, she nodded at people. It was just how JJ was. I knew I shouldn't take it personally, but of course I did.

Iona didn't like her one bit, I could tell. Iona specialized in having enough information to take the piss out of anyone; pinned to her bedroom wall was a sprawling multicoloured diagram of who'd shagged who on the Manchester women's scene since 1990. One evening a few of us were in the living room, and JJ was stroking Victor all the way down his spine with one finger, very slowly and firmly. Iona walked in and said, 'I get it! You don't fancy humans at all, just rats.'

JJ threw Iona one unreadable look, scooped Victor back into his cage, and disappeared up the stairs.

The room was silent. 'Aren't you ever going to give up?' I asked, without looking up from my book.

'Oh, she's probably just another repressed virgin,' Iona threw in my direction.

But it didn't even have to be questions about sex that made JJ bolt, I discovered. She was prickly about the slightest things. For instance, one Sunday morning, most of us were lying around in the garden, half naked. JJ was wrapped up in her huge white flannel dressing gown, as usual. Rachel, bored of the newspapers, started teasing me about waxing my moustache off.

'What are you talking about?'

'I saw your little box of wax strips in the bathroom, Luce. Trying to get all respectable before you start college, are you?'

JJ lurched out of her deck chair so fast she knocked it over. She stomped off into the house, her dressing gown enveloping her like a ghostly monk. We all stared at each other.

'Which particular sore point was that?' snapped Rachel.

I shrugged uncertainly. 'Maybe the wax is hers.'

'Who cares if it is?' Iona butted in. 'I've got pubes down to my knees, for god's sake!'

Di spoke from behind her magazine. 'Hands up who didn't need to know that.'

Di, Kay, and I put our hands in the air. Maura let out a yelp of laughter.

'Well, one reason I moved in here,' growled Iona, 'was to get away from that crap about what should and shouldn't be talked about. Nothing's unmentionable!'

'Yeah, well you can mention what you like as long as you leave JJ alone.' That came out more loudly than I meant it to.

I kept my eyes on the article on permaculture I was skimming. In the silence I could almost hear the others exchange amused glances. Nothing was ever private in the Welcome.

It troubled me that JJ would be so embarrassed about something petty like having a slight, faint moustache. Hadn't anybody ever told her what a handsome face she had? Now I came to think about it, she couldn't bear praise. '*Seriously* cute,' I'd let myself say once when she'd come in wearing a new pair of combat trousers – that was all, two words – and she'd glanced down as if she'd never seen herself before and froze up. Could it be that she didn't like her body – the solid, glorious bulk that I let myself think of only last thing at night, in the dark?

Di was doing the pressure points in my neck one night during the news; she said I felt like old rope.

'Sleek and flexible?'

'No, all hard with salt and knotted round itself.'

I stared glumly at the TV pictures.

'Jesus, Luce,' asked Di out of nowhere, 'why her?'

My head whipped round.

Di pushed it back into place gently. 'And don't say "who?" You're so obvious. Whenever JJ's in the room you sit with your limbs sort of *parted* at her.'

My face scalded. 'No I don't.'

'Even Kay's noticed, and Kay wouldn't register the fall of a nuclear bomb.'

I hid my face in my hand.

'Of all people to fall for!' said Di crossly.

'What's wrong with her?' I asked.

'JJ's an untouchable, honey.'

I flinched at the word.

'You know it's true. That rat is the only one let into her bed.

208

You'll never get anywhere with her in a million years. Don't take it personally; nobody could get past that force field.'

'I think she cares about me,' I said, very low. 'When I had bad cramps, last month,' I added in what I knew was a pathetic voice, 'she left a tulip outside my door.'

'Of course she cares about you,' said Di pityingly. 'Leave it at that.'

But she didn't know how it was. JJ and I stayed up late sometimes; after the others had all gone to bed, we raided the fruit bowl and watched any old rubbish that was on television. Once, in the middle of a rerun of *Some Like It Hot,* my hand was lying on the couch about half an inch from hers, but no matter what I told myself, I couldn't bring myself to close the gap. JJ stared at the flickering screen, quite unaware.

I couldn't sleep, too many nights like that one, wondering what it would be like. Just the back of her hand against mine, that's all I imagined. I had a feeling it would be hot enough to burn.

August came in hot and cloudy. The tomatoes hung fat but green in the humid garden. Di and I were peeling carrots one morning. She was looking baggy-eyed after a bad shift in the emergency room. 'Your problem is, Luce,' she began out of nowhere, 'you're too picky. You'll never find everything you're looking for in one woman.'

'What if I already have?' I muttered, mutinous.

She let out a heavy sigh to show what she thought of that.

I knew I shouldn't push it, but I couldn't stop. 'What if JJ's my ideal woman?'

'Your ideal fantasy, you mean. Listen, next time try picking someone who's willing to sleep with you. Call me old-fashioned, but it's a big plus!'

Irritated, I gave my finger a bad scrape on the peeler.

'You should have copped off with someone your first week in this house,' said Di.

'With whom, exactly?' I asked, sucking the blood off my knuckle.

'I don't know,' she said, 'someone old and wise and relaxed who wouldn't have put you through any of this angst. Someone like me,' she added, lopping off a carrot top.

I stared at her through my sweaty fringe. 'You're not serious,' I told her.

'Well, no,' said Di with one of her dirty laughs. There was a pause. 'But I might have been, two years ago,' she added lightly, 'when you were all fresh and tempting.'

'It's a bit bloody late to tell me now!' My voice was shrill with confusion.

'Oh, chop your carrots, child.'

We worked on. I thought about Di and about her current boyfriend, Theo, quite a witty guy who remembered to put the seat down and, judging by the retreats he ran, which involved sitting cross-legged on a mat for six hours a day and Understanding the Pain, he seemed to have more staying power than her others. 'Besides,' I said at last, getting my thoughts in order, 'you're straight.'

She laughed again and did her *Star Trek* voice. '*Classification Error Alert!*'

I was sad then, and Di could tell.

'Don't worry about it, Luce,' she said gently, shovelling the chopped carrots into the pot. 'In the long run, you know, if two people matter to each other, it doesn't make much difference whether they've ever actually done the business or not.'

She meant her and me, but in the weeks that followed I tried applying her words to me and JJ. I repeated them to myself

210

whenever JJ left the room. If it was love, it should be enough on its own.

On the August bank holiday the weather was so sticky I felt like my skin was crawling. It was too unpleasant to work in the garden, even. JJ was at the Pizza Palace all day; I just hoped they were paying her time and a half. I sat in the shady living room and did a cryptic crossword with 108 clues. Whenever any of the others wandered by they offered to help, but they only gave stupid answers.

At ten that evening, Carola came downstairs to watch some grim documentary about child abuse. I kept on struggling with the crossword. JJ walked in at half ten, limp, with her uniform still on. I offered her cold mint tea from my herb patch; she grinned and said she'd love some, after her shower. I decided it was going to be a good night after all.

It still would have been, if Iona hadn't been such a maladjusted bollocks. She and her latest, Lynn, were sitting round on the balcony drinking beer. They came downstairs just as JJ was emerging from the bathroom, swaddled in her white dressing gown as usual. She looked cool and serene now; there were tiny flecks of water caught in her dreadlocks. She stood back against the wall to let Iona and Lynn go by; that was the kind of person she was, gentlemanly.

But Iona caught her by the lapel of her dressing gown and said, 'Hey, Lynn, have you met JJ? She's the house prude!'

JJ didn't smile. She just kept a tight hold of the neck of her thick robe.

Lynn was giggling, and Iona wouldn't leave it at that. She wasn't even drunk, she was just showing off. 'Jesus, woman,' she said in JJ's face, 'how hot does it have to get before you'll show a little flesh?' She put on a parodic games-mistress voice: 'We're all gells here, y'know!' As she spoke she hauled on the dressing gown, and it fell open, and the next thing I knew Iona was on the floor, clutching her face.

JJ, knotted into her robe again, had backed against the door.

'She hit me,' howled Iona. 'The bitch hit me in the eye!'

The next hour was the most awful I'd known in the Welcome. Rachel left her curry on high in the kitchen and ran in with the naturopathic first aid kit. After dabbing Iona's eyelid with arnica, she wanted to take her off to a hospital to have it checked out, 'in case the co-op's legally liable,' but Di told her not to be such a fuckwit. Every time one of the housemates came down to ask what all the noise was about, this time of night, the story had to be told all over again, in its various competing versions. JJ just sat on the edge of the couch with her face hidden in her hands, except when she was muttering, 'Sorry, I overreacted, I'm so sorry,' over and over again.

But Carola was the worst. It was as if, for the five years she'd been attending co-op meetings and volunteering to go off to weekend workshops, she'd been in training for this. She got the Policy Book out of the kitchen drawer and read out clause 13 about 'unreasonable and unacceptable behaviour'.

'*Behaviour* means longer than half a second,' I spat at her.

'Violence is unacceptable no matter how long it lasts,' she said smoothly.

Kay burst into tears and said she'd come to this co-op to escape male aggression (which was the first any of us had heard of it). 'I thought I'd be safe with women,' she snuffled.

'You are safe,' said Di coldly. 'Nothing's happened to you. You were upstairs watering your plants till ten minutes ago.'

'And besides,' I said incoherently, 'what about Iona's aggression? She started it. She tried to rip JJ's dressing gown off.'

'I did not,' growled Iona from behind the bag of frozen peas Lynn was holding to her face.

'You did so. You're the most aggressive person I've ever met, male or female,' I bawled at her.

At which point Di tried to calm us all down. 'OK, OK,' she said, 'let's agree that Iona . . . violated JJ's bodily integrity' – I could see her mouth twitch with laughter at the phrase – 'and that JJ . . .'

'Made a totally inappropriate response.' Carola was icy.

'Oh come on.' I was pleading with her now. 'Who's to say what's an appropriate response? These things happen. You can't make rules for everything.'

But I was wrong, apparently. Carola had the Policy Book open to another page, and she was reading aloud. 'Step one, a formal letter of caution will be sent to Member B to instruct her to cease the offending behaviour—'

'She has ceased!' I looked over at JJ, who was bent over on the couch as if she had cramps.

'Or not to repeat it.'

There was a long pause. I drew breath. Well, who cared about a formal letter anyway? It would all blow over. We'd be laughing at this by next weekend.

'We don't know that she won't repeat the behaviour,' said Kay, quavering.

JJ stood up, then. Her hands hung heavy by her sides. 'That's right,' she said hoarsely. 'You all don't know the first thing about anything.'

The silence was broken by Carola, reading from the Policy Book again. 'In the case of an act of violence, the co-op may proceed directly to step three, eviction.'

Everyone stared at her. None of us had noticed the smell, till then, or the smoke fingering its way along the corridor. Only when the alarm began to squeal did we come to our senses.

In the kitchen the cork notice-board over Rachel's curry pot had gone up in flames. Di threw a bowl of water at it, putting out the fire and soaking Kay's pyjamas. The smell was hideous. Phone messages, recycling schedules, minutes of meetings, a postcard from an ex-housemate in Java, and a pop-up card I'd got for my eighteenth birthday were all black and curled as feathers.

The eviction clause was never put to the test. JJ gave her notice the next day.

I was so full of rage I couldn't uncurl my fingers. 'You could have stayed,' I told her in her bedroom, not bothering to keep my voice down. 'Why do the petty bureaucrats always have to win? It's Iona we should have kicked out, or Carola. All you did was defend yourself for half a second. Why is physical violence so much worse than the emotional kind, anyway?'

JJ said nothing, just carried on stowing away her rolled-up socks in the bottom of her backpack.

'My father hit my mother once,' I told her, 'and you know what?'

That made her look up.

'She deserved it. The things my mother used to say, I should have hit her myself.' Now the tears were snaking down my face.

'Ah, Luce,' said JJ. 'Don't cry.'

I sobbed like a child.

'I'd like to have stayed,' she told me. 'But I just don't feel welcome any more.'

'You are! Welcome to me, anyway,' I choked, ungrammatically.

JJ came over to hug me then. I didn't quite believe she was going to do it. She hunched, a little, as if her back was hurting her. She took me by the shoulders and warily laid her heavy head on my neck. I could feel her hot breath. She smelt of jasmine.

A mad idea came to me then. 'Well, I'll move out, too,' I said brightly. 'We can find a flat to share.'

I could see her answer in her face, even before she shook her head.

My ribs felt cold and leaden. 'Where are you going, though? You don't have anywhere else to go. Listen, why don't I ring round some of the letting agencies for you? I've nearly a thousand pounds in my account. You can have it.'

Her head kept gently swinging from side to side, saying no to everything. 'I'll be OK,' she whispered.

And then I saw in the back of her dark eyes that she did have somewhere to go, she just wasn't telling me. So I took a step backwards and put my hands by my sides.

The taxi took her away. 'Keep in touch,' I shouted – a meaningless phrase, because JJ and I had never touched in our lives except for about five seconds, just before she left.

I didn't stay long at the Welcome myself, as it happened. Once I started college in the autumn, it seemed to make more sense to live in a student residence so I wouldn't have to trek across town.

The letter didn't reach me for months, because by then Di was off in Tibet and the others at the Welcome claimed to have mislaid my new address. I finally read it the day after Christmas, sitting on a park bench in the college grounds.

If I say hi, this is John, you won't know who I mean, will you? I used to think if anybody found me out, it would be you, Luce. Sometimes you used to look at me so intensely, like there was something on the tip of your tongue, I thought maybe you knew. But I was probably just kidding myself so I'd feel less guilty about bullshitting you all.

They said the hormones would be hard. But what I've found much worse is not quite belonging anywhere and having to lie all the time. Not that I ever had to actually claim to be a woman, because none of you ever asked.

And I am one, you know. Inside. Not where people usually mean by inside, but farther inside than that. I've known since I was four years old. I'm not John any more, except on my birth certificate; I don't think I ever really was. I've been JJ for a long time now. That's why it wasn't exactly a lie, what I let you all think. To have said 'Hi, my name is John' would have been the biggest lie.

But the body I've got is mostly wrong, still, and the doctors won't give me the operation because they say I'm not serious enough about wanting it. According to their classifications, I should wear makeup and tights and get a boyfriend. I have to keep telling them that's not the kind of woman I am. I spent too many years pretending already, to want to start all over again.

I did like living in the co-op, more than I showed, probably. Most days I was able to forget about the whole man/woman business and just be one of the girls. I'm sorry I cocked it all up in the end (no pun intended).

I just wanted to tell you something, Luce, that's why I'm writing. I just wanted to say (here goes), if I had the right body – if I had any kind of body I was wanting to show or share, or if I could feel much of anything these days – then it would be you I'd want to do it with. You'd be welcome. That's all. I just thought I'd tell you that, because what the hell.

It all happened years ago. I wouldn't believe how many years, except for the date on the letter, which I keep folded up small in a sandalwood box with a couple of other important things, like my grandfather's pipe and an iris from the bouquet Di chucked me at her and Theo's wedding.

These days I have a very normal happy life, in a two-dykes-and-their-dogs-and-their-mortgage kind of way. I'm not quite so picky any more, and I don't let myself correct people's grammar, at least out loud. Last I heard, the Welcome was still going, though I don't know anyone who lives there. I wonder are the potatoes still sprouting down the back of the garden, the ones I watered with JJ? I thought I saw her at Pride one year – or the back of her neck, anyway – but I might have been imagining it.

In case this sounds like some kind of doomed first-love story, I should admit that I was grateful there was no return address on that letter. I was young, that summer – younger than I knew, it occurs to me now. JJ must have known that I wouldn't have been able to write back; that I'd have had no idea what to say.

Her letter has gone all shiny at the folds. I don't read it for nostalgia; I prefer not to read it at all. It brings back that bruised, shivery feeling of being in love and making one mistake after another, of waking up to find myself in the wrong story. I keep the letter in my box for anytime I catch myself thinking I know the first thing about anything.

death

the dormition of
the virgin

Fiorenze (Florence), Stazione Rifredi, Monday, Day 1. Caffe Latte.

George had a brown leather notebook to record his impressions so that he could tell his friends at college exactly what Italy was like, rather than blabbing on vaguely. The caffe latte was much weaker than in the college café in Loughborough, but subtler, more authentic. He was killing half an hour in Stazione Rifredi, which had turned out not to be the main Florence station; because it had said FIORENZE on the sign, he'd leapt off the train like a twat, so now he had to wait for a local train to take him south to Stazione di Santa Maria Novella, which was the real one. He thought the Italians should label things more clearly.

They eat and drink standing up at the counter, very odd – meant to be laid-back Mediterranean people?

People kept leaving the door of the buffet open and the February air skated in. But the guidebook said you really had to come off-season if you wanted to see the art without peering over stinky hordes.

As soon as he got to Florence proper, George went into Santa Maria Novella, the first church on his list.

Said to be finest Gothic church in Tuscany. Stripy b/w facade, not at all like Gothic at home.

The wheels of his suitcase squeaked embarrassingly on the church's flagstones. It was hard to see in the chapels, but he'd brought his small torch, as the guidebook had suggested. He leaned against the wall and pencilled in some notes.

Lots of martyrdoms (St Lawrence on his griddle, St Catherine? with breasts on plate, St Sebastian stuck with arrows) and a raising of Drusiana, who she?

George had picked out the Hotel Annunziata because the guidebook said it was cheap, five minutes from Ponte Vecchio, and had lashings of atmosphere. It was three floors up over a posh wineshop. The Signora who ran the place could have been anything between sixty and ninety; despite his Linguaphone course, he couldn't understand a word she said, and he thought she must be speaking some kind of heavy Tuscan dialect. She uncurled a hand at the frescoes in the lounge, then led him down a skinny corridor to indicate the toilet and the shower. The Signora took George's passport away to her own apartment for a few minutes, leaving him standing round gazing at the frescoes, and then she came back with a police form for him to sign. He wondered whether all tourists had to do that or just young guys, potential troublemakers.

Unpacking in his bare square room, it occurred to George that he might be the only person staying there. He hadn't heard any voices, but maybe the others would come in later. This place was like something from another century – the pensione from *A Room with a View.*

No view but what can expect for €49 a night? What's that in sterling? – must check. Hallway's got stucco putti, I think probably real. For lunch had pasta in gritty squid ink (not good), outside because there was a bit of sun but pretty cold.

George had been planning this trip ever since he was seven and saw a film about the Medicis. He was doing social studies at Loughborough but was thinking of changing to art history. His Florence itinerary was only provisional; he knew he probably wouldn't get to all these churches and museums, but he meant to try, because for all he knew he'd never be here again. (His aunt had always wanted to go to Bali, but now she had emphysema.) If he started to flag, he could always have an espresso.

George knew the statues outside Orsanmichele were nearly all copies, but he had decided that looking at the full-size copies in their original setting was actually more authentic than looking at the originals (brought inside to escape the acid rain) in the museum, and besides, the museum was shut on Mondays.

The guidebook says most tourists rush right past Orsanmichele wh. is prob. single most important series of early Renaissance statues. I know I'm one too (a tourist) but they repel me (tourists, not statues). E.g. trying to soak up ancient atmosphere in this little piazza Santa something-or-other but scooters keep roaring by and there's two girls at the next table with Liverpool accents.

The guidebook said the closed museum also had an excellent *Transition of the Virgin.*

There's just as much art about Mary as about JC, really, they're like his 'n' her deities. What was she transitioning from, I wonder? Sounds like a sex change.

George just wanted to know, so that the art would make sense; he wasn't into any of that stuff personally. He'd stopped going to church when he was thirteen, and his parents hadn't seemed bothered.

In the Baptistery he craned up at the ancient mosaics. There was Jesus, twenty feet high, with under him all the sarcophagi opening and the dead crawling out, the ones on the left being escorted away to heaven by huge trumpeting angels.

and the poor buggers on the right being grabbed by devils like some-
thing out of Star Trek, *leathery bat wings, and enormous Satan*
munching them two at a time!

The Baptistery doors were those famous ones Ghiberti had
won the competition for in 1401, and George stood with his
arms folded and tried to examine the panels closely, but tourists
kept pushing past him to get in and out.

In a tiny *osteria* he ordered *pasta e fagioli,* thinking it was pasta
with beans, but it turned out to be a bean soup with a few bits
of pasta in it, and he was still hungry afterwards. He read his
guidebook in bed and thought of asking the Signora for
another pillow. There was a bell beside the door to her private
apartment, but he didn't want to hassle her; she was probably
down on her arthritic knees saying the rosary or something
(though, actually, her radio was on). His phrase book didn't
have *pillow* in it; he would have to mime the concept, or bring
along the one pillow he had and point to it, and then she might
think he was allergic to it. Never mind, he could sit cross-
legged and lean back against the wall.

Tuesday, Day 2. I know it sounds pretentious, but this isn't a hol-
iday — it's a pilgrimage.

George stood flinching under the shower, fiddling to try to find
something between scalding and icy. His hair was still wet as he
hurried past the Duomo. He felt like Michelangelo, on his way to
choose a block of perfect translucent Carrara marble by the dawn
light. Passing a tour party who were emitting the usual clicking
and whirring sounds as they squinted up at Brunelleschi's orange
dome, George was gratified that he'd decided to leave his camera
in his room in Loughborough. This way he would really see things
and really remember.

Standing in Piazza della Signoria beside gigantic statues, e.g.
Donatello's Judith cutting off the head of Holofernes, noticed I was

standing on a purple circle which turned out to be a disc of porphyry to mark where Savonarola (the hellfire-spouting, bonfire of the vanities priest) got burnt alive on 23 May 1498. Fuck!

Every inch of Florence meant something; there were no blank bits. It was slightly exhausting.

At the Uffizi he saw a Greek statue which had once been known as *The Knife Grinder,* but scholars had now established that it was a Scythian preparing his blade in order to flay Marsyas. There was another statue of a man hanging upside down and laughing, only he wasn't laughing, he was howling, and that was Marsyas again. *Gladiator* was nothing to this, George thought queasily. But he definitely preferred art in which something was happening: a fight or a miracle or a death or something. He was already bored with all those pictures of the Madonna tickling the Bambino under his chin.

When he's got his crown of thorns on it's called Ecce Homo, then the Deposition is when his friends lift him down off the cross (NB you never see them taking the nails out with pliers, maybe it would look too undignified). A Lamentation can also be called Dead Christ or Pietà (he's not always on Mary's lap, sometimes just propped up by angels, looking sick or hungover rather than actually dead, hard to tell).

Back at the Annunziata, his bed had not been made; maybe that was the difference between a pensione and a hotel? Anyway, he liked the privacy; he wouldn't fancy the Signora shuffling round pawing through his stuff. She seemed to keep the radio on all the time; it was a bit sad. George stared at the picture over his bed, the one that looked like two wrestlers going in for a clinch. After he'd taken it down and cleaned the glass on the bedspread, it turned out to be a Visitation of Mary and Elizabeth; they were touching each other's pregnant stomachs. He was starting to recognize all the scenes, now; it was like a code, and he was cracking it.

Wednesday, Day 3. Never never go on holiday with only one pair of shoes if they're suede. Pissing down all day and I'm soaked to the ankles, my feet feel like dead fish.

George sat in a cafeteria eating a calzone out of a napkin. He was tempted to go back to the counter and complain that it was cold in the middle, but he'd left his phrase book in his room. He flicked through his notes, trying to figure out whether the Virgin Mary had died or not. In several churches he'd seen paintings called *The Death of the Virgin,* where she was lying there like a normal dying person with grieving relatives (including Jesus holding a baby – maybe his childhood self?). There were other pictures called the 'Transition' or 'Assumption,' which showed Mary floating up to Heaven, looking pretty alive. As far as George could tell, Jesus 'ascended' (actively) whereas Mary 'was assumed', but what was the difference, apart from grammar? Could you say God assumed her? No, that sounded like he took her for granted. Maybe JC flew up by his own will, whereas Mary was sort of sucked up as if by aliens?

George hadn't time to obsess over these arcane details; he was two-thirds of a day behind on his itinerary. Reckless, he crossed off all the Baroque churches – the Renaissance was more than enough to be going on with – and squelched off to Santa Spirito, which bore a huge, crass sign proclaiming that its restoration was being funded by Gucci. The Church of the Ognissanti meant the 'Church of All the Saints'; that was a good way to hedge your bets, George thought a little cynically. He saw a postcard of a painting that used to be there but was now in Berlin: a Giotto from 1310 called *The Dormition of the Virgin.*

Now what the hell's a dormition? Abstract word for sleep? Mary looks comatose in the picture (and about eight feet long), people are standing beside her bed, one guy is hugging her, but you can't tell if her eyes are open.

All the saints died, and so did Jesus (even if he rose again), so if Mary hadn't actually died, that would make her the only human being ever who had avoided it. Not that any of this stuff was actually true, George had to remind himself.

Some gravestones say 'fell asleep' meaning died, but it's a stupid phrase, I bet they're totally different feelings. Unless you happen to die in your sleep, which a lot of people claim they'd like, but I think it's cowardly, I'd rather be hit by a lorry and look it in the face. The thing is, whatever's happening, to be totally AWARE and AWAKE.

He was starting to shake with cold; he'd have to go back for dry socks. Passing a bookshop, he had a brain wave. In the English section he found a dictionary of religious terms and looked up *dormition*. He turned away so the girl at the counter wouldn't see him taking notes and scribbled in his leather journal.

Turns out Mary died in the ordinary way, then three days later Archangel Michael brought her soul back down to reunite it with her body, Jesus and everybody was clapping, then she got assumed into heaven again!

It was very satisfying to sort out the full story.

At the Annunziata, George was suddenly knackered and let himself get under the sheets. He wished the Signora would turn her radio off the odd time; all that Western stuff wrecked the atmosphere. Well, of course, Italy was the West, but they could still do better than Eminem.

When he woke up after an hour, he wanted to borrow an iron, so he looked it up in his phrase book and knocked on the Signora's door, but she didn't answer; maybe she'd gone out in the rain. George decided to wear his crumpled jacket for dinner; who'd be looking at him, anyway?

227

Thursday, Day 4. My last day, arghhhhh!

George almost ran from church to church that morning, ticking them off on his list. He had to fend off dozens of leather-jacket salesmen to get into San Lorenzo. Donatello's late-period pulpit was the grimmest George had seen, even the *Ascension* panel, with a wrecked-looking Jesus trying to float off into the sky, but sinking back down.

So many of these guys seemed to start out all idealistic but got burnt out. Suppose life in Cinquecento would do that – plagues, revolutions, etc. Whereas now everything's easy and comfortable, no mysteries left, life comes prepackaged by Disney or the Gap, we just drift along and nothing ever really happens compared with back then.

In a café, flicking through his highlights of the Uffizi book, he came across a little panel by Fra Filippo Lippi called *Predella of the Barbadori: Announcement of the Death of the Virgin*. He didn't know how he could have missed it when he'd done the Uffizi; maybe because it was so small.

It looks like an Annunciation at first, because she's standing up (not old or anything), and the angel's handing her something like a magic wand, or a tall gold candle. Wow. Imagine if we all got told when we were about to snuff it – like an e-mail, on the day, telling you to pack your bags.

Speaking of which, time to go. George headed reluctantly back to the Hotel Annunziata via a cash machine.

When he'd zipped up his case, he went to the door of the Signora's apartment and knocked a few times, quite loudly. Her radio was playing 'Nights in White Satin'; she had to be a bit deaf, he thought, though she hadn't seemed it on Monday. '*Bon giorno?*' he called a few times, then, almost shouting, 'Signora?' She knew he'd be checking out this afternoon, didn't she?

George was beginning to panic about missing his train. He tried the door handle and walked down the narrow hall.

'Signora?' There was an armchair with an ancient-looking radio playing beside it, and an empty espresso cup. He felt it, in case she'd just popped out, but it was cold. He wanted to turn the music down – something old of Sheryl Crow's – but he didn't dare. He got out his wad of cash and counted it, €196; that way he could wave it at her if she appeared, so she'd see why he'd barged in on her.

No one in the tiny kitchen. George's armpits were damp. If you were running a pensione or whatever, you just couldn't behave that way, even if it was off-season. It would serve the old bag right if he walked off without paying. Then it occurred to him to leave the money beside the radio with a note, but he'd packed his pen away with his journal. He put his head into the bedroom to see was there any sign of a ballpoint. It was very dim in there, with the curtains shut, but when George's eyes got used to it, he saw her on the bed.

He dropped some of the money on the floor, and when he bent down to pick it up he thought he might keel over. The Signora could have been asleep; she could have taken a pill or something. But it didn't look like sleep, the way she was lying quite straight on top of the bedspread with her shoes turned up. And he couldn't be sure in the bad light but he thought her eyes were open; he saw some kind of glimmer that had to be an eye. He ran back out to the room with the frescoes and sat on his case to catch his breath. He put the money back in his pocket; one of the notes had stuck to his hand and he had to peel it off.

George knew he should probably go back to check. He hadn't smelled anything, but it was pretty cold in her room. It could have been days she'd been lying there.

In the end, he crept back into the apartment, just as far as the phone. He had to turn the radio off. He rang 999, but of course that was the British number; what a moron! There wasn't a phone book that he could see, so he had to go back out to his room to find the guidebook. The Italian emergency number turned out to be 113, not very memorable at all, he thought. George didn't make much sense on the phone; all he could say was *'Signora vecchio morte!'*, which was partly French, but the woman on the other end spoke some English and in the end she managed to get the address from him.

After he'd opened all the doors upstairs and downstairs in the lobby, too – he dreaded that he mightn't hear the bell – George waited in the hall with the stucco, and he tried to pass the time by figuring out what all the little *putti* in the frescos were doing. He felt sick. If he never saw another picture again as long as he lived it would be soon enough for him.

When the ambulance guys walked in, George jumped up and started crying, more out of embarrassment than anything else. They didn't seem bothered by this; after all, he told himself, continental men cried more anyway. There were policemen, too, but not swaggering and fierce, as George had been imagining. He realized that he'd been afraid they'd suspect him of killing the Signora for her heirlooms (the frescoes? the stucco? it was absurd). But it hardly counted as an interrogation; they only took down his name and address from his passport and asked him in English when he had last seen the Signora. 'About twenty minutes ago,' he said stupidly, and then realized they meant *alive*. 'Monday,' he told them, 'and since then there's only been the radio.' Then he thought they might ask him, *Did you not wonder, boy, did you not think it was strange that an old lady would play her radio all day and all night for three days?*

As soon as the draped stretcher had been carried out, George was told that he could go.

At the train station he queued up at the ticket office to

explain, but the girl behind the counter seemed bored; she said, 'Next train to Paris, 16:22,' and he gathered that his old ticket would still work. They were very casual about these things here. Of course he didn't have a couchette on the next train, so he had to sit up all night.

It got cold. About three in the morning, George realized that what was digging into his leg was his pensione money. He took it out and felt like a criminal. It occurred to him to post it back from London, marked *For the heirs and assigns of the Signora of Hotel Annunziata, Florence.* But what would be the point of that? They were about to inherit a prime bit of Florentine property even though they clearly never gave enough of a shit about their grandmother (or whatever she was) to come round and see her, once in a while. She could have been eaten by dogs, if she'd had dogs!

George wondered why he was getting so angry. For all he knew, the Signora didn't have any heirs and assigns. He'd been the last person to see her, and for three days, all he'd done was wish she'd turn the bloody music off.

He put the money back in his pocket. He took out his notebook.

Left Florence, night train.

He couldn't think what else to put. He thought he should probably get some sleep, and he put his head back against the cracked leather of his seat and shut his eyes, but he didn't feel sleepy, not at all.

enchantment

Pitre and Bunch knew each other from the old time. They were Louisiana crawfishermen, at least as long as the crawfish were biting. These days, what with global warming and so forth, the cages were mostly empty, and it was hardly worth the trouble of heading out to Mudd Swamp every morning.

The two men were having a smoke at the Bourdreaux Landing one May evening, and discussing whether there was any such thing as a coloured Cajun, which is what Bunch claimed to be. Pitre mentioned, not for the first time, that what flowed in his own veins was one hundred per cent French wine. 'Every ancestor I ever have was a full-blood Acadian. Cast out of Nova Scotia back in 1755 at the point of a British gun.'

'Maybe so,' said Bunch, grinning, 'but you were born in the state of Texas.'

'About one inch over the border,' growled Pitre. He was twenty years older than Bunch, and his reddened scalp was grizzled like a mouldy loaf.

'Well, whatever, you know, I'm a live-and-let-live sort of Cajun, my friend,' said Bunch, sucking the last from his Marlboro. 'I was born and reared in these swamps, but I'm willing to call you brother.'

'Brother!' snorted Pitre. 'You're a black Creole with a few Sonniers for cousins; that's not the same thing at all.'

Just then a candy-apple red Jeep came down the dirt road. Four old ladies spilled out and started taking photographs of the boats. Pitre asked them in French if they wanted to buy some crawfish, then mumbled it again in English; he hauled a cage out of his boat and held it up, with a few red creatures waving inside. The ladies just lengthened their zoom lenses for close-ups.

'Are you fishermen?' one of them asked excitedly, and Bunch said, 'No, ma'am. We're federal agents.' They peered at his dark, serious face and twittered even more, and one of them asked if she could have her picture taken with him, and afterwards she tipped him ten dollars.

'I don't think the Bureau's gonna approve, *cher,*' commented Pitre as the tourists drove off waving through their shiny windows.

'I'll put it in the Poor Box on Sunday,' said the younger man.

Pitre let out a sort of honk through his nose, got back in his boat, and said something about checking that alligator bait he'd left hanging off a tree.

'You marinade the chicken good?'

'It stinks worse than your wife,' Pitre assured him, and drove off, the snarl of his engine ripping the blue lake like paper.

When the older man got to the other side of the cypress swamp, the shadows were lengthening. His gator bait dangled, untouched except by the hovering flies. Pitre cut the rope down and hung it from another tree at the south edge of the basin, where he'd seen a big fellow the year before, thirteen feet if he was an inch. Pitre wondered how much gators were going for an inch, these days. You could sell the dried jaws to tourists, too. Tourists would buy turds if you labelled them A LITTLE BIT OF BON TEMPS FROM CAJUN COUNTRY.

It was cool, there under the trees, with the duckweed thick as guacamole, making the water look like ground you could stretch out on. All the other guys had gone home; Mudd Swamp was his own. Pitre leaned back against an empty craw-fish cage and rested his eyes. The air was live with small sounds: a bullfrog, the tock-tock of a woodpecker, the whirr of wings.

He thought it had only been a minute or two, but when he opened his eyes they were crusted at the corners, and the evening was as dark as a snakeskin around him. He was some-what ashamed of dozing off like that, like an infant or an old man. He couldn't read his watch by the faint light of the clouded moon. He supposed he was hungry, though he couldn't feel it; his appetite had shrunk with the years. Maybe he could fancy some fried oysters. The outboard motor started up with a cough, and Pitre manoeuvred his way through the flooded forest. He veered right by the big cypress with the wood-duck box nailed onto it, then picked up some speed.

The stump reared up beneath his boat like a monster. Pitre flew free. The water swallowed him with a cool, silken gulp; it filled his eyes, his ears, plugged his nostrils, and got under his tongue. Pitre couldn't figure which way was up. He reared, shook the duckweed off his face, retched for breath. The water was no higher than his waist. You could drown in a couple of inches. He tried to take a step, but one of his legs wasn't work-ing, damn the thing.

He told himself to stop splashing around. Gators were drawn to dogs, or to anything that moved like a dog. Pitre was shud-dering with cold now; it sounded like he was sobbing. He turned his face up to the mottled sky. *Que Dieu me sauve.* A tag from a prayer his grandmother used to say. *Que Dieu me sauve.*

The moon came out like the striking of a match. Vast and pearly, it slipped through the branches of a willow tree and lit up the whole swamp. Pitre looked round and saw exactly where he was. His boat was only the length of a man behind him, not even overturned. He crawled over, got himself in after a couple of tries. There was a water hyacinth caught in the bootlaces of his smashed leg. He heard himself muttering, *Merci merci merci*. The motor started on the first try.

Before Pitre was off his crutches he'd started putting up signs. The ones nailed to electricity poles along the Interstate said simply SWAMP TOURS EXIT NOW. Along the levee road they went into more detail: EXPLORE THE WONDERS OF MUDD SWAMP 2 + ½ MILES FARTHER, or PITRE'S WILDLIFE TOURS TWICE DAILY NEXT LEFT.

Bunch rode the older man pretty hard for it. 'What makes you think anybody want to get in your beat-up skiff and go round a little swamp no one's ever heard of? When they could be cruising in comfort in Atchafalaya Basin or Lake Martin?'

'If you build the signs, they will come.' Pitre pursed his chapped lips and banged in another nail.

Bunch snorted. 'And what's that marker you've hung up on the big willow that says "Site of Miracle"?'

'You may mock,' said Pitre, fixing Bunch with his small eyes, 'but I know what I know.'

'What do you know, *mon vieux*?'

'I know I was saved.'

'Here we go.' Nearly dying was a funny thing; Bunch had seen it take one of his aunts the same way: she kept her rosary knotted round her fingers like some voodoo charm.

'And now,' said Pitre, wiping his forehead, 'I've been called by the Spirit of the Lord to turn away from killing.'

'Killing? Who've you been killing?' asked Bunch, pretending to be impressed.

'Crawfish, I mean.'

The younger man let out a whoop of delight.

'I've been called to lead tours of the wonders of creation,' said Pitre, thrusting a blurred photocopied leaflet into Bunch's hands.

Bunch read it over smothered chicken at his uncle's Cracklin' Café in Eunice. It made him snigger. Old Pitre couldn't spell, for one thing. '*I will tell you and show you also, a great variety of mammals, fish, and foul.*'

As he drove back to the Bourdreaux Landing that afternoon to check his cages, he noticed that FRENCH SPOKEN had been added in fresh paint to all the signs.

By the beginning of June there was a little queue of tourists at the landing, most mornings. They shaded their eyes and gawked at the glittering blue sky, the lushly bearded trees. They were from Belgium and Mississippi, Seattle and Quebec, all over the map. They giggled and flicked dragonflies out of each other's hair.

'Hey, Pitre,' Bunch called, as he drove up in his truck one day.

The other man walked over, counting twenties.

'I've got to hand it to you, my friend, you've drummed up more trade than I ever thought you could. You or the Spirit of the Lord!'

Pitre nodded guardedly.

'How many tours a day you and your heavenly buddy doing now?'

'If you're going to mock—'

Religion was one of those points folks couldn't bear to be pricked on, but how could Bunch resist? He put his hand on his heart. '*Mon vieux*, you've known me since I was a child. You probably got liquored at my christening! Don't you know mocking's my nature? It's him upstairs that made me that way,' he added, straight-faced.

'Or the other guy,' said Pitre, turning on his heel.

'So how many tours?' Bunch called after him.

'Four. Maybe five.'

Bunch whistled sweetly. 'Five tours a day at two hours long? What say I give you a hand, before these tourists wear you out, your time of life?'

But age was another of those sensitive points. 'I'll manage,' growled Pitre, and walked back to his boat.

In the middle of the night Bunch had a bright idea. He picked up a five-dollar box of pecan pralines in Grand Coteau, scattered them over tissue paper in his wife's old sewing basket, and sold them to the Mudd Swamp Tour queue at two dollars a pop. When he turned up the following day with a tray of alligator jerky, a party was staggering off Pitre's boat, their eyes bright with wonder. 'It's so green out there,' said one of them, and her friend said, 'I've never been anywhere so green.'

Bunch had sold a fistful of jerky by the time Pitre came over, his burnt-brick arms tightly crossed. 'Get away from my clientele.'

'Your what?' laughed Bunch.

'You heard me. Parasite!' Pitre cleared his throat wetly. The next boat party, filing past, were all agog. 'I'm trying to do the Spirit's work here, like I've been called to—'

'You've been called, all right, old man. Called to make a fast buck!'

Pitre turned his back and jumped in the boat, surprisingly lithe. It bobbed in the water, and the tourists squealed a little.

By the time he got them out under the cypresses, he'd recovered his temper. The sun was a dazzling strobe, and the sky was ice blue. Iridescent dragonflies skimmed the water, clustered in a mating frenzy. 'Lookit there, folks,' Pitre said quietly, pointing through the trees at a great white egret on a log, its body one slim brushstroke.

'Is that a swan?' shrieked one little girl. At the sound, the bird lifted off, its huge snowy wings pulling it into the sky.

Pitre's visitors knew nothing about the wonders of creation. He considered it the least he could do to teach them the names of things. He showed them anhinga and glossy ibis; 'Go to the state prison, you'll find twenty guys serving time for shooting ibis, that's the tastiest meat,' he said sorrowfully. He pointed out water hyacinths in purple bloom, a turtle craning its neck on a stump, and a baby nutria wiping its face with its paws.

'So where's the alligators?' asked a New Yorker with a huge camera round his neck.

'Well, as I told you at the start of the tour, I can't guarantee one,' said Pitre. 'They mostly look like logs. Yesterday's tour we saw three, but it's colder today; they don't come up much till it's sixty degrees or thereabouts.'

'There!' yelped a small boy, pointing at a log.

Just then Bunch roared by in his boat, which was ten years newer than Pitre's, with a fancy air-cooled outboard on the back. Cutting the motor, he floated within ten feet of the tour. 'Morning, all.'

'Crawfish biting?' asked Pitre, cold.

'Some,' said Bunch with his gleaming smile. 'You folks seen that big-fella gator over there by the houseboat?'

It sounded like bullshit to Pitre, but of course his party clamoured to be taken over there right away, where the nice young man had said. Pitre spent fifteen minutes edging the boat round the shoreline, peering at dead wood and doing slow hand claps to attract any gators in the vicinity. 'I'm sorry, folks, I try my best for you, but there's no guarantees in this life,' he said at last. 'We gotta learn to be grateful, you know?'

But the tourists were not grateful, especially when he admitted that no Louisiana alligators had ever been known to kill a human being. They were not content with blue herons and water snakes, or a fifteen-hundred-year-old cypress, and even when he rounded up the tour by taking them to the SITE OF MIRACLE sign and narrating his rescue from drowning by the God-sent appearance of the full moon, they were unimpressed. When they had driven off in their various SUVs, Pitre saw that there was only seventy cents in his tip jar.

Monday was wet and chilly, but on Tuesday the sun came up strongly again. Pitre sat by his boat all morning, squinting into the distance. His throat was dry. At noon a group drove up in a Dodge Caravan.

'Over here,' he called to them hoarsely, 'Pitre's Tours, that's me.'

'No, I think we're booked on the other one,' a lady told him brightly.

He was about to tell her that there was no other one, when a motor started up behind him with a flamboyant roar and he turned and saw Bunch, wearing a fresh white T-shirt that said BUNCH'S ENCHANTED SWAMP TOURS, CHIEF GUIDE VIRGIL BUNCH.

'This way, ladies, gentlemen!' cried Bunch.

Pitre just stared.

'What's enchanted about this swamp?' asked a fat man, looking up from his guidebook.

'Wait and see.'

Once his party was on board, Bunch roared out into the middle of the lake as fast as the motor could go, then headed into the flooded woods and ducked in between the stumps. He bumped into a floating log to make the boat jump and the tourists yelp. Then he cut the engine and said, 'My friends, welcome to paradise! This just happens to be the only Enchanted Swamp in all of Louisiana.'

He had paid the older man's techniques the compliment of extensive study and had decided that the whole experience needed a little bit of personality and pizzazz. Bunch began the tour by claiming ancestry from every culture that made up the tasty gumbo of present-day Acadiana: the Cajuns; the Creoles, black and white; the *gens de couleur libre,* as well as slaves; even the Chitimacha Indians, 'who took what they needed and left the balance at peace, you know?' He assured his party that the twenty-foot, flat-bottomed aluminum skiff they were sitting in had been personally designed by him to reach the parts of the swamp where other boats just couldn't go.

'Has this boat a name?' asked one Frenchwoman.

'Sure does,' Bunch improvised; 'it's called the *Zydeco.*'

Another of his tricks was to present everything in the best light. Instead of telling his tour party that blue herons were very common in this part of the river system, he instructed them to keep an eye out for any flash of blue in the trees, because they just might be lucky enough to spot the rare blue heron, who brought ten years' good luck to anyone who glimpsed him. Finally, catching sight of the head and shoulders of a little gator basking on some driftwood, Bunch made his eyes bulge with amazement and told the tourists that this fellow must be fifteen feet long.

'No!'

'No way!'

'Mr Bunch? Virgil? Did you say fifteen?'

'They're just like icebergs, that way,' he hissed, paddling the boat near enough for them to take photographs. 'For every inch you see, there's a foot underneath the water. Not too close!' he told one little girl. Rolling up his jeans, he showed

240

them an old scar on his shin from one time he'd had too much rum and fallen over someone's guitar case: 'Gator bite.'

One lady took a picture of his scar.

'The only sure way to keep them from attacking,' said Bunch, taking out a squashy paper bag, 'is to give them some snacks.' And he started lobbing lumps of rancid chicken at the alligator, who snapped at one or two before sinking beneath the surface.

On the way back, he gave his happy party the rundown on good ole Cajun humour and *joie de vivre*, not to mention *laissez les bons temps rouler* on the bayou, winding up with a dirty joke about a priest. Finally, he produced his tip jar, which had an alligator jaw glued on top, and they crowed with delight and stuffed their notes through its wicked teeth.

That night Bunch was eating steak and listening to the Breaux Bridge Playboys at Mulate's when Pitre walked in. The older man took one look at him across a crowd of Canadian college kids, then turned and walked back out the door. So that's how it was now, Bunch thought. He wasn't hungry any more; he pushed away his plate.

The summer turned hot, and there was more than enough business to keep both men busy. Old Pitre didn't alter his methods. He turned up at nine every morning and sat there in the sun waiting for custom, pretending his former friend was invisible. The sun cooked him to red leather; you could nearly hear him sizzle. That was the downside of being a hundred per cent pure white Acadian, Bunch thought wryly, but a crack like that wasn't so funny unless you could say it out loud. Ah, to hell, this was none of Bunch's doing; blame the Spirit of the Lord.

He himself had bought a cheap cell phone so tourists could book their tours with him direct. He got his sixteen-year-old daughter to make him a Web site with ten pages of photographs

241

of alligators, and linked it to every listing on Louisiana tourism. *'See local indigenous wildlife in its natural ecohabitat which makes it a photographer's dream. Fishing also available.'* Bunch's real stroke of brilliance was finding a medium-sized gator with a stubby tail and feeding it meat scraps daily, until it would come when he called. After a few weeks he scrawled *'Performance of Live Cajun Music Included'* on his leaflets, threw a small accordion into his bag, and upped the fare from twenty dollars to twenty-five.

Whenever he felt his spiel was getting a little flat, he'd spice it up with a tall tale about a six-foot catfish or a ghost. He took great pleasure in transforming Pitre's near-death experience into a tale he called the Swamp Man. 'My grandpère used to say the Swamp Man was a crawfisherman, stayed out too late one night, crashed his boat into a tree in the dark and drowned in no more than two feet of water. What's he look like? Well, kind of decayed, you know – holes for his eyes, and dripping weeds all over him . . .'

Pitre overheard that story, one day, as he was drifting along with his own tour. He listened in, but didn't look in Bunch's direction. As their boats floated past each other, the tourists waved in solidarity. Pitre pulled down a tangled clump of grey Spanish moss and explained in his hoarse monotone that this was an airborne plant that did no harm to the trees it hung from.

He kept on telling it how it was. He didn't think the Spirit wanted him soft-soaping things. He broke it to his tourists that the trees in Mudd Swamp were slowly dying because the government's levee kept the water at an artificially high level all year round. Yes, the birds were pretty, but their waste was poisoning the trees from the top down. And a nutria was no relation to a beaver; it was more of a rat.

What bugged him the most, as the first summer of his new

saved life wore on, was that his customers were always asking him where the restroom was – as if an open skiff or a knot of trees could be hiding such a thing. He wrote at the top of his leaflets, *NO RESTROOM FACILITIES*, but the tourists didn't seem to take it literally. One of them, when Pitre had explained the situation at the landing, said to her husband, 'Let's go, hon. I've never been anywhere that didn't have a restroom.'

One July afternoon, after the dust of the departing cars had settled, Bunch walked over to Pitre. 'I was thinking of renting a Port-o-Let,' he remarked, as if resuming an interrupted conversation.

Pitre slowly shifted his gaze from the cypress forest to the man in front of him.

'But they cost a bit, you know, because the company has to drive all the way out here to empty it. What say we go halves?'

'What say nothing,' said Pitre through his teeth.

'Oh well, *cher*, if you're going to be like that,' said the younger man with a shrug. 'Though I don't think your heavenly friend would like your attitude . . .'

Pitre's face never flickered, but the remark had got under his skin. He headed out to the swamp that evening, on his own, to see if it was any cooler than the land. When he got to the Site of Miracle, he cut the engine. He squinted up at the willow tree, but it looked much the same as all the others: a swollen base, tapering to a skinny top. He tried to feel again what it was that had touched him that moonlit night when he'd come within an inch of drowning. A sensation of being marked out, prodded awake, as distinct as a fingertip in the small of the back. He'd been so sure about his new calling at first, but now it seemed as if he'd mistaken some small but crucial marker a while back and gone astray.

A few days later there was a Port-o-Let standing in the shade of a live oak by Bourdreaux Landing. It looked like a grey plastic alien craft. Pitre pretended not to notice. At noon, he was emptying his boat of one group and filling it up with another when a girl ran over. 'Uh, I wanted to use the restroom?'

'No restroom,' said Pitre automatically.

'I tried the one over there, but it's, like, locked! It says, "For use of Bunch's Enchanted Swamp Tours only."'

Pitre's teeth clamped together, and his bad molar started to throb. 'That's a mistake,' he muttered. 'Very sorry, ladies and gentlemen. You'll just have to wait.'

'I can't wait two hours,' wailed the girl.

'That's the trouble with you kids nowadays,' Pitre told her. 'Nobody's got any self-control of themselves.'

Her family drove back to the hotel, and he didn't get any tips that day, either.

In August it was hitting a hundred by ten in the morning.

Bunch bought a cap with a visor to keep the glare out of his eyes. He took to claiming that his name was authentically Acadian. 'Sure is, ma'am. Used to be Bonche, you know, back in Canada, but when the British kicked us out at gunpoint back in 1755, my ancestors had to change to Bunch to avoid persecution.'

The young man varied his tall tales to keep himself from getting stale. He always took his tours past a duck blind in the middle of the lake, but sometimes he said it was a man-made nesting sanctuary for orphaned cormorants, and other times he called it a shelter for canoeists caught out on the lake in a lightning storm. Once – just to see if he could get away with it – he claimed it was a Dream Hut for young Chitimacha boys undergoing spiritual initiation.

'The Swamp Man? That's a terrible story,' he said towards the end of all his tours, lowering his voice as if he was almost afraid to tell it. 'This crawfisherman, back in old-time days, it was a long hard season, and he was desperate to know where the fish were biting, so he did voodoo. You know voodoo?'

Fervent nods all round.

'I bought a how-to book on it in New Orleans,' confided one old lady.

Bunch darkened his tone. 'So this guy, he conjured up this spirit, and he didn't know it, but it was the devil. This guy struck a bargain that his crawfish cages would always be full, you know? So now the devil had a hold of his soul. And the very first time the guy went out fishing, it was in the evening, getting dark, and he bent down to pull up his first cage, and it was so full, it was so heavy that it pulled him right down into the water.'

The tourists looked into the oily sheen, shuddering.

'Did he drown?' asked a small girl.

Bunch nodded. 'Only he never really died. The flesh rotted off his bones, that's all. And if you ever come out here in the evening, just when it's getting dark, well, all I'll say is, don't put your hand into the water, because the Swamp Man might grab hold of it and pull you in!'

Two women moaned theatrically. They weren't really afraid, Bunch knew; in this day and age it was hard to really scare anybody.

As trade fell off a little in the worst of the heat, he couldn't have done without his cell phone. It meant he could sit around in the shade at the Lobster Shack, drinking homemade root beer, till he got a call to say there was a group wanting a tour. Whereas old Pitre squatted in the dust at Bourdreaux Landing every day like some kind of scarlet lunatic, under a limp banner that said PITRE'S HOLY SPIRIT TOURS ANYTIME.

One morning Pitre turned up at Mudd Swamp at eight; he'd

had a pain in his jaw all night that had kept him from sleeping. His stomach wasn't right, either. He sat down in his usual spot and tried to pray. The problem was that he'd never got the knack of it in his childhood. And now he was a man of the Spirit, he still didn't know quite what to say, once he'd got beyond *Oh Lord, here I am, like you told me.*

By noon not a soul had turned up. Pitre's tongue was stuck to the roof of his mouth. He'd forgotten to bring any water. His jaw was hurting bad now; he blamed his molar. His boat floated motionless beside the landing, not ten feet from the other man's, which had a duck decoy glued on the prow and a freshly painted name: *Zydeco.* Pitre narrowed his eyes at the dirt track that led down from the road. There was no shade; the sun bored into his head through his eyelids, his ear holes, his cracked lips. In the long grass he saw a sledgehammer and recognized it as his own; he must have left it there after banging in a sign. He lurched to his feet at last, feeling the old break in his leg. His body was just a collection of bad memories. But there was something he could do, anyway.

He picked up the sledgehammer and staggered under the weight of it. He cradled it against his shoulder like an old friend. At the landing, he climbed down into the *Zydeco;* the skiff skittered under his feet. His heart was sounding strangely. He hoisted the hammer over his head and brought it down with all he had.

Pitre was lying in the bottom of the boat. He couldn't tell if he'd managed to hole it. The light was behaving like water. He seemed to have stopped breathing. He couldn't tell whether something had gone wrong with the whole world or whether it was just him; he felt like he was under some kind of dreadful enchantment.

*

At the hospital the nurse was a big black lady from Lafayette; she got pissy with him when he tried to pull the oxygen tube out of his nose. Kept saying, did he know he could have died?

'So could we all,' said Pitre balefully. A phrase floated back to him, and he pointed one unsteady finger at her: 'You know not the day nor the hour.'

They let him out on the third morning, just to shut him up, according to the nurse. 'You take it easy now,' she growled, 'because nobody gets three chances.'

When he got back to the Landing, Bunch was sitting on the side of the *Zydeco*. The boat seemed unmarked, Pitre noticed with a slight pang, and the sledgehammer was nowhere to be seen.

He was obliged to speak. 'Understand you called me an ambulance on that cell phone of yours.'

'That's right,' said Bunch, as if they were chatting about the weather.

Pitre stared past him, at the cypresses, their heavy greenery. 'I received a message,' he said, jerking his chin upwards.

'Another one?'

He ignored that. 'We don't want another Cain and Abel situation. In a spirit of brotherhood,' said Pitre, then paused to clear his throat, 'I propose that we unite our tour companies.'

Not a smirk from Bunch.

'No use both doing six trips a day when we could each do three.'

'Whatever the Spirit says, my friend,' said Bunch, letting his teeth show when he grinned.

baggage

Niniane Molloy had never been anywhere like the Los Angeles Neverland. They sold melatonin for jet lag and chromium picolinate for sugar cravings. There was chocolate-free chocolate and honey-pickled ginseng. In the next aisle, two huge young men debated whether powdered pearl would help them achieve definition. There were trays labelled JUICE-YOUR-OWN WHEATGRASS; Niniane stroked the tender stalks with one finger, then moved away in case she would be seen and made to pay. Sacks of one hundred per cent unbromated flour weighed down a shelf. She had never known that flour was bromated before. She wondered what harm she'd been done by thirty-four years of bromate. Or was it bromide? Or brome?

Arthur used to drink echinacea, even though their mother called it one of his fancy American habits. It made him retch, but he swore he never got colds.

Now Niniane was studying the little rolls of homeopathic tablets. One was for travel sickness and general nausea, another for sleeplessness and irritability. She hadn't slept since the night before last. Or was it only yesterday? It tired her to keep adding eight to everything. If it was blazing sun outside the Neverland Health Store in La-La Land, then it must be pub-closing time

248

back in Ireland. EXHAUSTION DUE TO FEAR, said the next label. Niniane thought maybe what she needed was Fear Due to Exhaustion. Did the tablets know the difference?

In the end she didn't buy anything. She couldn't find a remedy for partial deafness due to having the dregs of the cold to end all colds and flying halfway round the world anyway, because it was a free ticket from a supermarket competition, no changes, no refunds. And anyway, she couldn't bring herself to stand at the Neverland's counter, holding up the queue while she peered at dimes and nickels like a visitor from another planet.

It was hard to cross the road in this town, she found; cars saw only each other.

Back at the Hollywood Hills Hotel, Niniane sat in the single chair, its metal tubing impressed on her thighs. She thought of Doris Day's motto for decor – 'Better to please the fanny than the eye' – and it almost made her smile. The room was bare as a stage set. A woollen jumper, glasses, purse, a three-pack of knickers she'd bought at the airport when she realized her bag wasn't going to come down the carousel no matter how long she waited; they'd turned out to be thongs. And a broken-spined copy of Marcel Proust's *Remembrance of Things Past*, volume one. It wasn't being read that had worn the book out, but being carried. Niniane had found it in Arthur's room at home in Limerick, years ago, after he left for good, on the shelf in between *How to Get a Green Card* and *Complete Poems of Walt Whitman*. She always took it on holiday in the hopes of getting into it. Not that this was a holiday, exactly.

She took the creased card out of her pocket again. '*LA Self-Storage*', it said; '*The No-Fuss Solution*'. Below the address, what had to be a room number, scribbled in red: *2011*. Someone had stuck the key to the back of the card; the tape was brittle with dust. She'd found it at Christmas in the ashtray in the drawer, the ashtray Arthur wasn't supposed to have had in his room, because as their mother always said, no child of hers would be stupid enough to smoke. Niniane had kept it in her purse for months now. What did it mean that her brother had left the key in the ashtray? That it didn't open anything any more, didn't matter at all? Or that it just wasn't worth coming home to Ireland for?

Later. Later would do.

Niniane lay diagonally across the brown and orange coverlet. The slatted blinds made a bright shadow on the wall. She considered taking her tights off, but she had no socks with her, and her heels would be sure to blister as soon as she went out for a walk. She lifted her head off the bed for a moment to contemplate her black nylon legs. Her tights were all that were holding her together; if she peeled them off, the skin might come, too.

It didn't seem to her that she had slept, only that the next time she looked at the wall it was the colour of ashes, and the clock said ten to midnight.

There was a phone beside the bed, but she couldn't hear a dial tone. Had her ears stopped up completely? She sniffed and yawned like a goldfish on dry land. 'Hello,' she said into the mouthpiece. At least she could hear herself. Then she noticed the sign on the table: EXTRA CHARGE TO PLUG IN PHONE.

Niniane went around the corner to the Five and Diner and rang the airline. It always slightly embarrassed her to give her name. Arthur used to call her Ninny. Her mother had got them both out of some trashy novel about Merlin. Doris Day always hated her name, too; she had her friends call her Clara, or Susie, or Eunice, or even Do-Do. In America you didn't have to stay what you were. You could change your name or your nose or just get in your Chevy and drive away.

The airline told her that her bag might have gone to Cincinnati.

Niniane's mouth still tasted of sour orange juice from the plane. She sank into the bulging plastic of a corner booth and ordered the All-Day Pancake Special. She picked out new words from the conversation in the next booth: *brewskis*, she heard, and *high colonic*, and *that's bitchin'*.

She sat up in bed reading Proust with watering eyes till half past two, while a moth charred itself against the bulb. Then she switched on the Weather Channel with the sound turned down and fell asleep watching a tornado inch its way up the East Coast. In her dream Niniane had the strangest sense that Arthur was nearby, maybe in the shower or parking his yellow convertible on the street below her window.

How long had it been, she wondered when she woke up. Five years this summer since her brother's last trip home, she was sure of that. He'd told them he was living in Dallas, but was very vague about his job, something to do with sales. And when was that slightly peculiar phone call from San Diego, the time he didn't sound happy enough to be drunk?

One Christmas, early on, she remembered, her mother had been loud in complaint. 'Nothing but a card!' The postmark was from LA, no address on the back of the envelope. Dark inked words inside, scattered like seeds across the printed message. *Happy Christmas folks, hope you're all well* – was that it? Or *Take care of yourselves, love A.*? If Niniane had known it was going to be the last message, she'd have read it more carefully.

A year later, there was no card, and her mother said the American postal system was known for its deficiencies. But Niniane suspected Arthur had forgotten. Men without wives were notoriously bad at keeping in touch.

The following year, no card, no comment.

A friend from the office, waiting by the photocopier, asked after that handsome big brother of Niniane's she'd gone to a college ball with. 'My god, how long has it been?' And then, brutally, 'Don't you miss him?'

Niniane had felt an immense weariness and walked away.

On the rare occasions Arthur came up in conversation at home these days he was like a figure in a children's book, frozen in time. When neighbours asked, her mother always said that her son was on the West Coast and doing very well. But after tea one New Year's Eve, alone with her father in the kitchen, Niniane had finally asked it, that question without a verb: 'Any word from Arthur?'

Her father had said nothing, just kept drying his hands on the dishcloth. The dishwasher was pumping and he was slightly deaf these days. She liked to tell herself that he hadn't heard what she said.

There were some people splashing round in the motel pool already. As soon as Niniane was dressed she walked out to the railing and squinted down. She didn't have anything to swim in, and besides, the pool looked so small, it would be like float-ing in a petri dish. These toffee-coloured girls and boys with their candy-floss hair would flinch from her pale Irish body.

The man at the desk asked where her car was; she really should have rented a car. 'I can't drive,' she told him, smiling placatingly. It was obviously a sentence he'd never heard before.

Back home in Limerick, Arthur had been the one who was always borrowing the Fiat to drive to godknowswhere and leaving the seat pushed too far back. Niniane was the one who had stayed in with their parents and made tea and toast in the intervals of *The Late Late Show.* If there were only two of you, things got divided up that way.

She walked out into the shiny street. The morning sun was

252

strange on her skin. She considered buying a clean T-shirt from a stall, but they all had palm trees on them, or Elvis. She'd never known heat like this, so thick you could slice it, so heavy the streets seemed to waver. But she looked up at the glassy sky and for a moment caught that feeling. Songs with the word *California* in them wandered through her mind. If ever a place was the polar opposite of Limerick, this was it. Once you got here, how could you ever go home? Which reminded her of the key, back in the hotel in the ashtray. But it could wait a few hours more. She had come here for herself, really, for a break from ordinary life. She could be a tourist like anybody else.

Only Niniane didn't look like anybody else, as she sat at the very back of the Stars' Homes tour bus. Her skirt was three feet longer than anyone else's, hot on the back of her knees. Her jumper was knotted round her hips. Her black vest revealed tufts of hair at her armpits, which was just about as unacceptable as leprosy in this town; she kept her elbows clamped by her sides. She sang grimly in her head: *Take me back to the Black Hills, the Black Hills of DA-KO-TA.*

As the bus wormed its way up a steep avenue, she was pressed back in her seat. She'd stopped listening to the commentary a while back, after Boris Karloff and Marlene Dietrich. Most of these mansions looked the same, anyway: lush trees protruding over twenty feet of security fence. She tried to imagine Arthur behind one of these shaded windows, sipping wheatgrass juice.

Niniane tried to follow the little red stars on the map, but they danced before her eyes like chicken pox. It was too hot to sit still.

The speaker behind her head crackled. 'That was Vincent Minnelli's and now look to your left, you'll see coming up at 713 North Crescent Drive, the lovely home of Miss Doris Day.'

She pressed her cheek to the glass, but there was a eucalyptus tree in the way. The prickling air was closing in around her. She couldn't bear this any longer. She lurched to the front of the bus.

'Take your seat, ma'am,' the driver said. 'No standing while the bus is in motion.'

'Would you stop the bus, please?'

'We gotta respect the privacy of the stars.'

'Let me off, I can't breathe,' she bawled. She had never shouted at a stranger before.

As the bus drew away from the curb, leaving her standing on the shoulder, Niniane felt almost wonderful. The grass under her feet was unnaturally plump. The sun went behind a cloud for a moment and the air seemed a little cooler. There wasn't another human being in sight; only high walls and hedges, and the soft whirr of sprinklers, and the bark of a pedigree dog. Maybe Arthur was a gardener. Any minute now he would stroll along the path with a sack of clippings in each hand.

She walked back as far as No. 713. It looked like all the others. The light bounced off the sidewalk like a chorus line. Maybe Doris would come out in a minute, wearing yellow, with that toothy smile. Niniane had a look at the plush lawn and sang in a whisper: '*Please, please, don't eat the daisies.*' Then, all at once, she was so tired she had to sit down on the curb. Her face cream was melting into her eyes; she seemed to be wearing false lips made of paper.

When she looked up, a police officer was getting out of his car. On his hip was a huge gun, the only one she'd ever seen in real life. Niniane stood up so fast that everything went black before her eyes.

'I was walking,' she said in answer to his questions. 'Just walking, and I got tired.'

He put away his notebook and opened the car door for her.

'I wasn't going to hassle her or anything,' she repeated as she fastened the seat belt.

The police officer asked who she meant.

'Doris Day.'

'Miss Day hasn't lived in that house since 1975, ma'am.'

He drove her all the way back to the Hollywood Hills Hotel. There was one moment, when they paused at a red light, when she thought of asking how long a person, a family member, would have to be gone before he could be reported as missing. But then the lights changed.

She apologized for putting the officer to the trouble and asked him to let her off anywhere, she could walk, but he told her this was not a walking kind of city.

Such an odd word for it, *missing,* she thought as she sat on the thin hotel mattress. Maybe Arthur wasn't missing them at all; maybe he was incommunicado. Now there was a grand phrase. Maybe her brother was alive and well in his condo, just around the corner from the Hollywood Hills Hotel, and living such a wonderful new life that he couldn't be bothered to write home about it. Selfish bastard.

A shriek, outside in the street. The window was dusty above the air conditioner; she pressed her face to it. On the street two young men on Rollerblades were greeting each other with loud cries. The black guy had short white hair. They kissed on both cheeks, then slid off in opposite directions.

That wasn't it, was it? Not enough of a reason to never come home. Niniane had always known Arthur wasn't the marrying kind, even though it had taken her nearly thirty-five years to put words on it. She had tried to bring it up once, but he'd changed the subject, which was fair enough. And their parents must have known, too, in their way. Nothing was said, but they never nagged him with questions about girlfriends.

Maybe Arthur had somebody over here. Maybe that was enough for him. *A chosen family* – that was the phrase, she'd read it in a magazine. But he was kidding himself because you couldn't unchoose your old family. You couldn't just walk away, not when they'd never done anything to deserve it.

Niniane had always thought her brother liked her. But how little he knew of her any more. He'd been away for her breakup with Mark, and her promotion, and that time she had the ovarian cyst and for a month thought she was dying. Whereas, to give them their due, her parents had always been there. Sunday after Sunday. Always on the same sofa in the same front room in the same terraced house on the same street in Limerick, the same sofa both she and Arthur had clung to when they were learning to walk. Her father getting balder and more taciturn, her mother rather more irritable since her hip operation, but both still there, in their places. And so was Niniane. Her own job, her own flat, but a daughter still, a daughter till the end.

She put her few possessions in her bag and went outside to hail a taxi.

The worst pictures always came when she was only half awake, or stuck in traffic. Arthur in prison, crouched in the corner of a cell. Arthur shooting up in an alley, his hairless arms pockmarked with holes. Arthur hawking himself on a street corner, bony with disease. What was it, his mystery? What was so bad that he couldn't lift the phone?

It occurred to her for the first time that he was dead. Doris Day's only brother died of epilepsy when she was thirty-three. These things happened. Was that relief Niniane felt, that curious surge in her throat? It couldn't be. She felt sick with shame. She pressed her face against the sweaty glass of the cab window.

Light-headed, she walked through the white corridors of LA Self-Storage. Fluorescent strips crackled overhead. The only sound was the pant of the air-conditioning. She thought if she turned a corner and bumped into a stranger she might scream. But who else would come here on a Sunday evening? She whispered the chorus of 'Hotel California' to give herself courage. This place was like a prison for misbehaving furniture.

She came to 2011 at last; it looked like all the other doors. The key was in her hand. What could furniture tell her? Arthur always had good taste, but there wouldn't be some vault of treasures. There wouldn't be a film of the missing years.

For a moment, as she slid the key into the door, she hoped it wouldn't open.

Niniane felt for the light switch and flicked it on. The locker was about ten by ten by ten feet of nothing. She stepped in, as if to search the bare corners. Nothing at all. She shut the door behind her back and for a moment feared she'd locked herself in. She was more alone than she'd ever been. There weren't even gaps in the dust to hint at whatever Arthur had once kept here; not even the marks of his size-thirteen feet from the day he must have taken it all away.

Niniane let herself slide down the door till she was sitting on her heels. She began to cry, slow and grudging, like loosening a tooth. The hard walls multiplied her breath. In between sobs she kept listening for footsteps.

At the pay phone, various options ran through her head as the receiver played 'Greensleeves' in her ear, but each seemed more improbable than the last. If she missed this flight home, she had no way of paying for another. If she went to the police, they would look embarrassed for her and tell her to come back with some evidence that a crime had been committed. No known associates. No last address.

'But I'm his sister, I swear,' she told the voice at the other end of the phone. 'You must still have his address, because he's paying for one of your storage lockers, he must be, or else you'd have changed the lock, wouldn't you?'

The voice sounded computer-generated.

'Will you at least take my address in Ireland?' she butted in. 'Just in case. I don't know, in case he ever stops paying or something. I'm his sister,' she repeated, like a bad actress from a soap. 'He'd want me to know where he was.'

Which was a lie, she thought, as she jammed the phone onto the hook. She had no idea what Arthur wanted. Most likely she would never find out if the empty locker meant that he was dead, with his bank account slowly draining, or that he was living high on a hill with all his chairs and lamps around him, rich enough not to mind paying for an empty locker, too careless to remember where he had left the key.

'The airport, now, please,' she repeated to the taximan, who was barely visible behind the smoked glass. Niniane lay back against the sticky leather and let the traffic draw her into its slipstream. LIVE NUDE GIRLS, said a neon sign, NOW HIRING. Now there would be a quick way to change her life.

The sky was full of planes, crisscrossing like fireflies. In the far distance she caught a glimpse of the famous white letters lit up on the hill. If she hadn't known they said *Hollywood* she would have had no idea: *No Food*, she would have read, maybe, or *Hullaballoo*, or *Home Now*.

At the airport, Niniane was told that her bag had just arrived from Pittsburgh. She stood in line to pick it up, then queued again to check it in for Shannon. In Duty Free, she bought her parents a $19.95 gilt Oscar that had a hopeful, dazed expression. She would bring it over next Sunday. It would give them something to talk about so they wouldn't have to talk about

Arthur. She would see it on the mantelpiece every Sunday for the rest of her parents' lives, and someday she would have to decide whether to give it to Oxfam with the rest of their stuff or take it home and put it on her own mantelpiece.

She had a window seat. All night she stared out at darkness or read Proust. When the sun came up over Shannon, hurting her eyes, she had finally got as far as the bit about the madeleine.

The American pilot announced that they would be landing momentarily. Niniane's head shot up out of her doze; for a second, she misunderstood his use of the word and believed him, thought the plane was only going to dip down like a bird onto the runway, gather strength for a moment, then wing away to somewhere else entirely.

When she emerged from Customs there were people waiting with cardboard signs held against their chests like X-rays. None of them had her name on. Trunks and totes spilled along the conveyor belt, climbing over each other at corners. She edged into the crowd, watching the procession of bags. A sign over the conveyor belt said in red letters, ALL BAGGAGE LOOKS THE SAME. BE SURE YOU HAVE YOUR OWN.

necessary noise

May blew smoke out of the car window.

Her younger sister made an irritated sound between her teeth.

'I'm blowing it away from you,' May told her.

'It comes right back in,' said Martie. She leaned her elbows on the steering wheel and looked through the darkness between the streetlamps. 'You told him to be at the corner of Fourth and Leroy at two, yeah?'

May inhaled, ignoring the question.

'Fifteen's way too young to go to clubs,' observed Martie, tucking her hair behind one ear.

'I don't know,' said May thoughtfully. 'You're not even eighteen yet and you're totally middle-aged.'

That was an old insult. Martie rolled her eyes. 'Yeah, well Laz is so immature. Dad shouldn't let him start clubbing yet, that's all I'm saying. When I heard Laz asking him, on the phone, I said let me talk to Dad, but he hung up.'

May flicked the remains of her cigarette into the gutter. Somewhere close by a siren yowled.

Martie was peering up at a dented sign. 'It says "No Stopping," but I can't tell if it applies when it's two a.m. Do you think we'll get towed?'

'Not as long as we're sitting in the car,' said her elder sister, deadpan.

'If the traffic cops come by, I could always drive round the block.'

May yawned.

'I guess Dad was feeling guilty about being away for Laz's birthday, so that's why he said he could go clubbing,' said Martie.

'Yeah, well the man's always feeling guilty about something.'

Martie gave her big sister a wary look. 'It's not easy,' she began, 'it can't be easy for Dad, holding everything together.'

'Does he?' asked May.

'Well, we all do. I mean, he may not do the cooking and laundry and stuff, but he's still in charge. And it's hard when he's got to be on the road so much—'

'Oh, right, yeah, choking down all those Texas sirloins, I weep for him.'

'He's not in Texas,' said Martie, 'he's in New Mexico.'

May got out another cigarette, contemplated it, then shoved it back in the box.

'Are you still thinking of giving up the day after your twenty-first?' asked Martie.

'Not if you remind me about it even one more time.' May combed her long pale hair with both hands.

Silence fell, at least in the old Pontiac. Outside the streets droned and screamed in their nighttime way.

'Actually, I don't think Laz gives a shit that Dad's away for his birthday,' remarked May at last. 'I wouldn't have, when I was his age. Normal fifteen-year-olds don't want to celebrate with their parents, or go on synchronized swimming courses or whatever it was you did for your fifteenth.'

'Life Saving,' Martie told her coldly.

'The boy wants to go to some under-eighteens hiphop juice-bar thing where they won't even sell him a Bud, that doesn't seem like a problem to me, except that he better get his ass in gear,' said May, slapping the side of the car, 'because I've got a party to go to.'

'I said you should have called a cab.'

'I'm broke till payday. Besides, Dad only lets you use the car when he's away so long as you give me and Laz rides.'

'You could use it yourself if you'd take some lessons,' Martie pointed out.

'There's no point learning to drive in New York,' said May witheringly. 'Besides, next year I'll be off to Amsterdam and it's all bikes there.'

'Motorbikes?'

'No, just bicycles.'

Martie's eyebrows went up. 'What are you going to do in Amsterdam?'

'I don't know. Hang out. It's just a fabulous city.'

'You've never been,' Martie pointed out.

'I've heard a lot about it.'

Martie tapped a tune on the steering wheel. 'It'll be weird if you go.'

'Not if. When.'

'When, then.'

May yawned. 'You're always complaining I never clean up round the apartment.'

'Yeah, but when you're gone, there'll still be Laz, and his mess will probably expand to fill the place.'

'Oh, admit it,' said May, 'you love playing Martyr Mommie.'

Martie gave her elder sister a bruised look. Then she scanned the street again, on both sides, as if their brother might be lurking in the shadows. 'This thing you're going to tonight,' she said, 'is it a dyke party?'

Her sister sighed. 'It's just a party. With some dykes at it. I hope.'

'Is Telisse going?'

'I don't know. She's not really doing the dyke thing any more, anyway.'

'Oh.'

'Why,' her sister teased her, 'did you like Telisse?'

'No, I just thought you did,' said Martie stiffly. She checked her watch in the yellow streetlight. 'Come on, Laz,' she muttered. 'I bet he's doing this deliberately. Testing our limits.'

'God, you're so parental,' May hooted. 'No wonder Laz hates you.'

'He does not.'

'He so does! He's always telling you to get off his case. "Get her off my fuckin' case, May!" he says to me.' May's imitation of her brother's voice was gruff with testosterone.

'He doesn't mean he hates me,' said Martie. 'He doesn't actually hate any of us.'

May groaned and shifted in her seat, leaned her head back, and shut her eyes. 'G'night, Ma Walton . . .'

The minutes lengthened. Martie stared into the rearview mirror. A truck went by slowly, picking up garbage bags. 'We could call Laz on your cell phone,' she said, 'except he probably wouldn't hear it over the music. Maybe I should go in and look for him,' she added under her breath. 'Or no, I can't leave the car, in case it needs to be moved. Maybe you should go.'

Her sister gave no sign of hearing that.

'There he is.' Martie threw open the door in relief. 'Laz!'

The boy was stumbling a little, head down.

'Come *on,*' she cried. 'We've been waiting. May's got a party to get to.'

'What do you know, the boy is wasted,' said May in amusement, turning her head as Laz struggled to fold his long legs into the backseat.

'He couldn't be,' Martie told her, 'it was a juice bar.'

May giggled. 'Now there's a first. *Teens Gain Access to Alcoholic Beverage!*'

'Okay, okay,' said Martie, starting the car with a rumble. 'Laz, are you in? Your seat belt.' She waited.

'Can we just drive?' asked May.

'Anyone who doesn't wear a seat belt is a human missile,' Martie quoted. 'If I had to slam on the brakes suddenly, he could snap your neck.'

'Oh Jesus, I'll snap yours in a minute if you don't get going. Laz!' snapped May, turning to face her brother. 'Get your belt on now.'

He grinned at her, his eyes drowned in his dark hair. His fingers fumbled with the catch of the seat belt.

The car moved off at last. 'Good night, was it?' May asked over her shoulder at the next traffic light.

The only answer was the sound of retching.

'For god's sake,' wailed Martie, taking a sharp right. 'Not on the seat covers!'

But the noises got worse.

'That's really vile,' said May, breathing through her mouth as she rolled down her window as far as it would go.

'Are you all right now?' Martie asked her brother, peering in the mirror. 'Do you want a Kleenex?' But he had slid down, out of sight. She wormed one hand into the back of the car, grabbed his knee. 'Sit up, Laz.'

'Leave him alone for a minute, why can't you?'

'May, he could choke on his own vomit.'

'You're being hysterical.'

Martie twisted round again. 'I said sit up now!'

'OK, pull over,' said May, for once sounding like the eldest.

'But—'

'You're going to crash. Stop the car.'

Martie bit her lip and braked beside a fire hydrant.

May got out and slammed her own door. She opened the one behind and bent in. 'Laz?'

No answer.

She pulled him upright, wiped his mouth with his own sleeve. 'He stinks.' After a long minute, she said, in a different voice, 'I think he may be on something.'

'On something?'

'Laz? Wake up! Did you take something?'

'Like what? Like what?' repeated the younger sister, her hands gripping the steering wheel.

'Oh, Martie, I don't even know the names for what kids are taking these days. Laz!' May shouted, trying to lift his left eyelid.

The boy moaned something.

Martie let go of the wheel and started scrabbling in her sister's bag. 'Where's your phone, May? I'm going to call 911.'

May climbed over her brother's legs and wrenched the passenger door shut. 'Are you kidding? Do you know how long they take to respond? We'll be faster driving to Emergency.'

'Which? Where?'

'I don't know, try St Jude's.'

'You'll have to navigate for me,' stammered Martie.

'I'm busy holding Laz's head out of this pool of vomit,' said May, shrill. 'Just go down Fourth; there'll be signs on Thirtieth. Move it!'

Martie drove above the speed limit for the first time in her life. Laz didn't make a sound. May gripped him hard.

'You should be talking to him,' Martie told her, at a red light. 'Keep him awake.'

'I don't think he is awake.'

'Is he asleep? He could be asleep.'

'He's out of it; he's unconscious,' snapped her sister.

'Is his windpipe open? Check his pulse.'

'I can't tell.' May was gripping her brother's limp wrist. 'There's a pulse but I think it's mine.'

The light was still red. 'Let me.' Martie burst open her seat belt, squeezed one knee through the gap between the seats. 'Laz?' she shouted, pressing her fingers against the side of her brother's damp throat.

'Shouldn't you—'

'Shut up. I'm listening.'

Silence in the car, except for a little wheeze in Martie's breathing. She put her ear against her brother's mouth, as if she was asking for a kiss. Then the car behind sounded its horn, and Martie jerked back so fast she hit her head on the roof. 'He's not—'

'What? What?'

More horns blared. 'Green,' roared May, blinking at the lights, and Martie slammed the car into drive.

'I think it fucked him up when Mom went off,' said May. The sisters were sitting on the end of a row of orange seats in the Emergency waiting area, their legs crossed in opposite directions. 'They say the younger you are when something like that happens, the more it messes up your head.'

'That's garbage,' said Martie unsteadily, examining her cuticles. 'Laz was too young; he wasn't even three. He doesn't

266

remember Mom being at home; he doesn't know what she looked like apart from photos.'

'He must remember her being missing,' May pointed out. 'You do.'

'That's different. I was five.' Elbows on her knees, Martie stared up at the wall, where a sign said UNNECESSARY NOISE PROHIBITED.

'That first couple of years, when all Dad fed us was out of cans—'

'She had postpartum depression that never got diagnosed,' Martie put in. 'That's what Dad says.'

After a second, May shrugged.

'What does that mean?' Martie imitated the shrug.

'Well yeah, that's what Dad *would* say,' said May. 'He'd have to say something. He couldn't just tell us, "Hey kids, your mom took off for no reason."' May pulled out her cigarettes. 'I mean, we could all have something *undiagnosed,*' she added scornfully.

Martie pointed at the NO SMOKING sign.

'I know. I know. I'm just seeing how many I've got left. What's taking them so long? You'd think at least they could tell us what's going on,' barked May in the direction of the reception desk.

Her younger sister watched her.

'At the hotel, did they say where Dad was?'

Martie shook her head. 'Just that he wasn't back yet. They'll give him our message as soon as he comes in.'

'He's probably boinking some Texan hooker.'

'He's in New Mexico,' said Martie furiously, 'and you can just shut up. You don't know why Mom left any more than any of us – you were only eight,' she added after a second. 'I think it makes sense that she was depressed.'

267

'Well sure, it must have been pretty depressing pretending to be our mom if all the time she was longing to take off and never see us again.'

'I hate it when you talk like that,' said Martie through her teeth.

No answer.

'You think you're so savvy about the ways of the whole, like, world, when really you're just bitter and twisted.'

May raised her eyes to heaven.

The woman behind the reception desk called out a name, and Martie jumped to her feet. Then she sat down again. 'I thought she said Laurence. Laurence Coleman.'

'No, it was something else.'

'I forgot to get milk,' said Martie irrelevantly. 'Unless you did?'

May shook her head.

'Laz didn't eat any dinner. I kept some couscous for him to microwave, but he didn't want it; he said it looked gross.' Martie put her face in her hands.

'Take it easy,' said her sister.

'They say if there's nothing lining the stomach . . .'

'He probably got some fries on the way to the club. I bet he had a burger and fries,' said May.

Martie spoke through her fingers. 'What could he have taken?'

'Nothing expensive,' said May. 'He's always broke.'

'I just wish we knew, you know, why he did it.'

'Oh, don't start the whole eighth-grade lecture on self-esteem and peer pressure,' snapped May. 'Look, everyone takes something sometime in their life.'

'You just say that because you did. Do,' added Martie, her cheeks red. 'It just better not have been you who gave it to him.'

'For Christ's sake!' barked May. A woman with a child asleep on her stomach stared at them, and May brought her voice down. 'I would never. I don't do anything scary and if I did I wouldn't give it to my moronic kid brother.'

'You can't know what's scary,' said Martie miserably. 'People can die after half an ecstasy tablet.'

May let out a scornful puff of breath. 'They said he was fitting. Having fits, in the cubicle. E doesn't give you fits.'

Her sister sat hunched over. 'You know when she asked us about our insurance provider?'

'Yeah. Thank god Dad's got family coverage in this job, at least.'

'No, but I think she was calling them, the insurance people. She picked up the phone. Why would she call them right away?'

May shrugged.

Martie nibbled the edge of her thumb. 'Do you think maybe they won't cover something . . . self-inflicted?'

'It's not like he jumped off the Brooklyn Bridge,' said May.

'But if he took it—'

'Shut up! We don't know what he took or what he thought it was. Get off his case!'

There was a long silence. 'I care about Laz as much as you do,' said Martie. 'Probably more.'

'Fine,' said May, her voice tired.

Martie got up and walked off. She dawdled by the vending machines, and came back with something called Glucozip.

A girl had come into the waiting area, arm in arm with her mother. The girl had a deformed face, something red and terrible bulging between her huge lips. Martie looked away at once.

May whispered, 'I didn't think that was possible.'

'Don't stare,' said Martie, mortified.

'She's put a pool ball in her mouth! I tried it once, but no way.'

Martie looked over her shoulder. So that's what it was. 'You tried to do that?' she repeated, turning on her elder sister. 'Why would you do that?'

'I was thirteen or so; I don't know. It was a dare.'

'That's not a reason!'

Her sister shrugged.

Martie sneaked another look at the girl with the ball in her mouth. The mother was scolding loudly. 'Where's your so-called friends now, then?' The girl twisted her head, made a small moan in her throat.

Martie turned away again and offered her sister some Glucozip. 'You should, even if you don't feel thirsty,' she urged her. 'We're probably dehydrated. Unless we're in shock, in which case they say you shouldn't drink anything, in case they have to operate.'

May stared at her sister.

'Are your extremities cold?' Martie persisted.

'What do you know?' said May, harsh.

The younger sister looked away, took another drink. Her throat moved violently as she swallowed.

'One crappy First Aid for Beginners course, and suddenly you're an expert?'

Martie took a breath, paused, then spoke after all. 'I know more than you.'

'Like what? Like what do you know?'

She spoke rapidly. 'For instance, if someone's got no pulse and he's not breathing, he's dead. Technically.'

'He fucking isn't!'

'Technically he is. That's the definition of death,' Martie told her sister shakily. 'It's not brain death but it's technically death, until they get the heart started again.'

'It's you who's brain-dead,' growled May.

'I just—'

'I don't want to hear it!'

Silence. Martie, eyes shining, read the back of her can.

'They've probably infibrillated him,' May told her, 'and now they're just letting him rest.'

'I think you mean defibrillate.'

'I don't think so,' snapped May. 'And also, they've got chemicals they can use. There was that scene in *Pulp Fiction,* when Uma Thurman snorts heroin by mistake, and they stick an adrenaline needle in her heart.'

'I can't stand that kind of movie,' said Martie. 'They're totally unreal.'

'No, they're too real,' her sister told her, 'that's what you can't stand.' She let out a long breath. 'When are they going to tell us something?' she said, leaping to her feet. 'I mean, Jesus!'

'Could you keep your voice down?' whispered Martie. 'Everybody's staring.'

'So?' roared May. 'I mean, what the fuck does that mean?' – throwing out her arm at the sign that said UNNECESSARY NOISE PROHIBITED. 'What the hell is unnecessary noise? If I make a noise, it's because I need to.'

'You don't need to shout.'

'Yes I do!'

Martie seized her elder sister by the hand and pulled her back into her seat. May went limp. Her head hung down. The people who had been watching looked away again.

'Do you think,' Martie asked May half an hour later, 'I know this probably sounds really stupid, but do you think it's any use, do you think it's any help to people, if you're there?'

'Where?' asked May, eyes vacant, taking a sip of Glucozip.

'Near them. Thinking about them.'

'Like, faith healing?'

Martie's mouth twisted. 'Not necessarily. I just mean, is it doing Laz any good that we're here?'

'I think maybe we're irrelevant,' said May, without bitterness. 'He never liked either of us that much in the first place.'

'You don't have to like your family,' said Martie uncertainly.

'Just as well,' said May under her breath. 'Just as well.'

'Laurence Coleman? Laurence Coleman?'

They both registered the words at last and jerked in their seats. 'He's not here,' said Martie confusedly to the man in the white coat, whose small badge said DR P.J. HASSID. 'They took him in there,' pointing vaguely.

'If you would come this way—'

They both scurried after Dr Hassid. May plucked at the doctor's sleeve. 'Is he alive?' she asked, and burst into tears.

Martie stared at her elder sister, who had tears dripping from her chin. One of them landed on the scuffed floor of the corridor.

'Just about,' said Dr Hassid, not stopping. There were dark bags under his eyes.

Laz, lying in a cubicle, didn't look alive. He was stretched out on his back like a specimen of an alien, with tubes up his nose, machines barricading. May wailed. Martie took hold of her elbow.

'Laurence will get through this,' said Dr Hassid, fiddling with a valve.

'Laz,' May sobbed the word. 'He's called Laz.'

'It doesn't matter,' said Martie.

But Dr Hassid was amending the clipboard that hung at the end of the bed. 'L-A-S?'

'Zee,' gulped May.

'L–A–Z, very good. It's better to use the familiar name. Laz?' the doctor said, louder, bending over the boy. 'Will you wake up now?'

One eyelid quivered. Then both. The boy blinked at his sisters.

acknowledgments

'Touchy Subjects' was first published as a self-contained chapter in *Ladies' Night at Finbar's Hotel,* devised and edited by Dermot Bolger (Dublin: New Island, and London: Macmillan; San Diego and New York: Harcourt, 1999).

'Expecting' was broadcast on BBC Radio 4 in 1996, and first published in *You Magazine/Mail On Sunday,* 8 October 2000.

'Oops' was first published in a shorter form in *Sunday Express* (Summer 2000).

'Do They Know It's Christmas?' is adapted from a short radio play, part of my *Humans and Other Animals* series (2003), produced by Tanya Nash for BBC Radio 4.

'The Cost of Things' was first published in *The Diva Book of Short Stories,* edited by Helen Sandler (London: Diva Books, 2000), and then adapted into a short radio play as part of my *Humans and Other Animals* series (2003), produced by Tanya Nash for BBC Radio 4.

'Pluck' was first published in *The Dublin Review* (Autumn 2002); before publication, I adapted it into a ten-minute film of the same name, directed by Neasa Hardiman and produced by Vanessa Finlow (Language, 2001).

'Good Deed' was first published in *Rush Hour,* edited by Michael Cart (Volume 1, 2004).

'The Sanctuary of Hands' was first published in *Telling Moments,* edited by Lynda Hall (Madison: The University of Wisconsin Press, 2003).

'Team Men' was first published in *One Hot Second: Stories of Desire,* edited by Cathy Young (New York: Knopf, 2002).

'Speaking in Tongues' was first published in *The Mammoth Book of Lesbian Erotica,* edited by Rose Collis (London: Constable/Robinson; New York: Carroll & Graf, 2000).

'The Welcome' was first published in *Love and Sex: Ten Stories of Truth,* edited by Michael Cart (New York: Simon & Schuster, 2001).

'Enchantment' was first published in *Magic,* edited by Sarah Brown and Gil McNeil (London: Bloomsbury, 2002).

'Necessary Noise' was first published in *Necessary Noise,* edited by Michael Cart (New York: Joanna Cotler Books, 2003).

I'd like to record my gratitude to Sinéad McBrearty for providing all the soccer knowledge for 'Team Men', to Dermot Bolger for editing 'Touchy Subjects', to Tanya Nash for her work on the radio version of 'Do They Know It's Christmas?' and to Vanessa Finlow and Neasa Hardiman for their work on the film version of 'Pluck'.

For inspiring these stories, on the other hand, I want to thank Maria Walsh for 'Speaking in Tongues'; Helen Stanton for 'Oops'; Sharon Switzer and Claire Sykes for taking me on the trip to LA that lies behind 'Baggage'; Helen Donoghue for the one in Belgium that led to 'The Sanctuary of Hands' (and also Catherine Dhavernas for her conference on The Hand which was the story's occasion); Denis Donoghue for proposing I take a fresh look at Martha, Mary, and Lazarus in 'Necessary Noise'; all my former housemates at Paradise Housing Co-operative in Cambridge for 'The Welcome'; Wen Adams and Nairne Holtz for 'Do They Know It's Christmas?'; and Emma our late great cat for 'The Cost of Things'.

Also by Emma Donoghue

The Woman Who Gave Birth to Rabbits

'And, who can tell what's true and what's not true in these
times, Mary, why then might not this rabbit story be
as true as anything else?'

Resurrecting buried scandals, audacious hoaxes and private
tragedies, Emma Donoghue has written a sequence of short
stories about peculiar moments in the history of the British Isles.
Here artists mix with poisoners; countesses rub shoulders with
cross-dressers, vicar and revolutionaries. Fiery Irish poteen
seduces a young English captain into a hasty marriage; a young
woman fights a lonely battle against cruelty to animals; the
Second Coming is proclaimed in Scotland; a miniature girl
becomes a tiny skeleton in a London museum.
This is a book of real treasures.

Slammerkin

Slammerkin: a loose dress, a loose woman

'Inspired by fragments of a story from the newspapers of the day, Slammerkin tells the story of Mary Saunders, an 18th-century girl who falls, for love of a ribbon, into prostitution and ultimate disaster . . . A compelling novel, her best to date' *Financial Times*

'As we follow her from whorehouse to the Magdalen Hospital for reformed prostitutes to a quiet country town, Mary (ambitious, refusing to conform, bitterly resenting anyone with the finery that symbolises a better life) is a memorable and unexpectedly touching character' *Sunday Times*

'Utterly gripping' *The Times*

**You can order other Virago titles through our website: *www.virago.co.uk*
or by using the order form below**